WELCOME TO ONCE UPON A SPACE-TIME!
TO ACTIVATE THE HOLOGRAM GUIDE
FUNCTION, SAY "BEGIN SPACE-TIME." IF THE
HOLOGRAPHIC GUIDANCE DOES NOT START
AUTOMATICALLY, SAY "BEGIN SPACE-TIME!"
IN A LOUD, CLEAR VOICE.

IF YOUR HOLOGRAPHIC GUIDANCE HAS STILL
NOT ENGAGED, OR IF YOU ARE READING
THIS STORY PRIOR TO THE YEAR 2557,
PLEASE FOLLOW THE ANALOG OPERATING
INSTRUCTIONS FOUND BELOW.

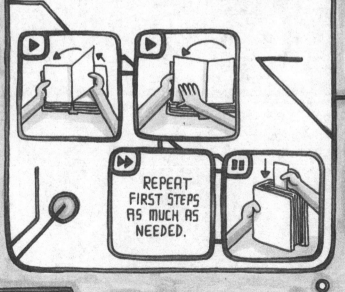

REPEAT FIRST STEPS AS MUCH AS NEEDED.

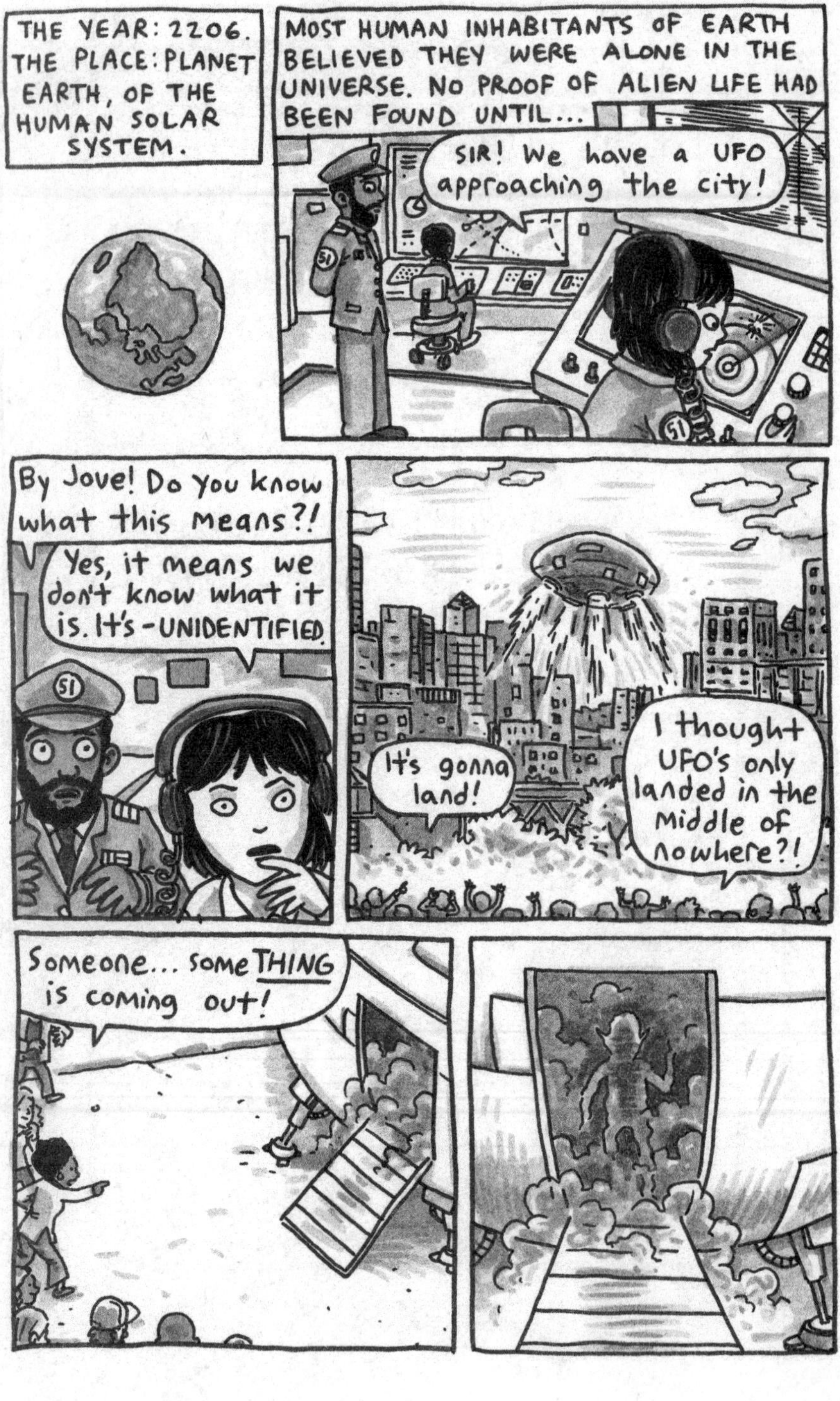
THE YEAR: 2206. THE PLACE: PLANET EARTH, OF THE HUMAN SOLAR SYSTEM.
MOST HUMAN INHABITANTS OF EARTH BELIEVED THEY WERE ALONE IN THE UNIVERSE. NO PROOF OF ALIEN LIFE HAD BEEN FOUND UNTIL...
SIR! We have a UFO approaching the city!
By Jove! Do you know what this means?!
Yes, it means we don't know what it is. It's -UNIDENTIFIED.
It's gonna land!
I thought UFO's only landed in the middle of nowhere?!
Someone... someTHING is coming out!

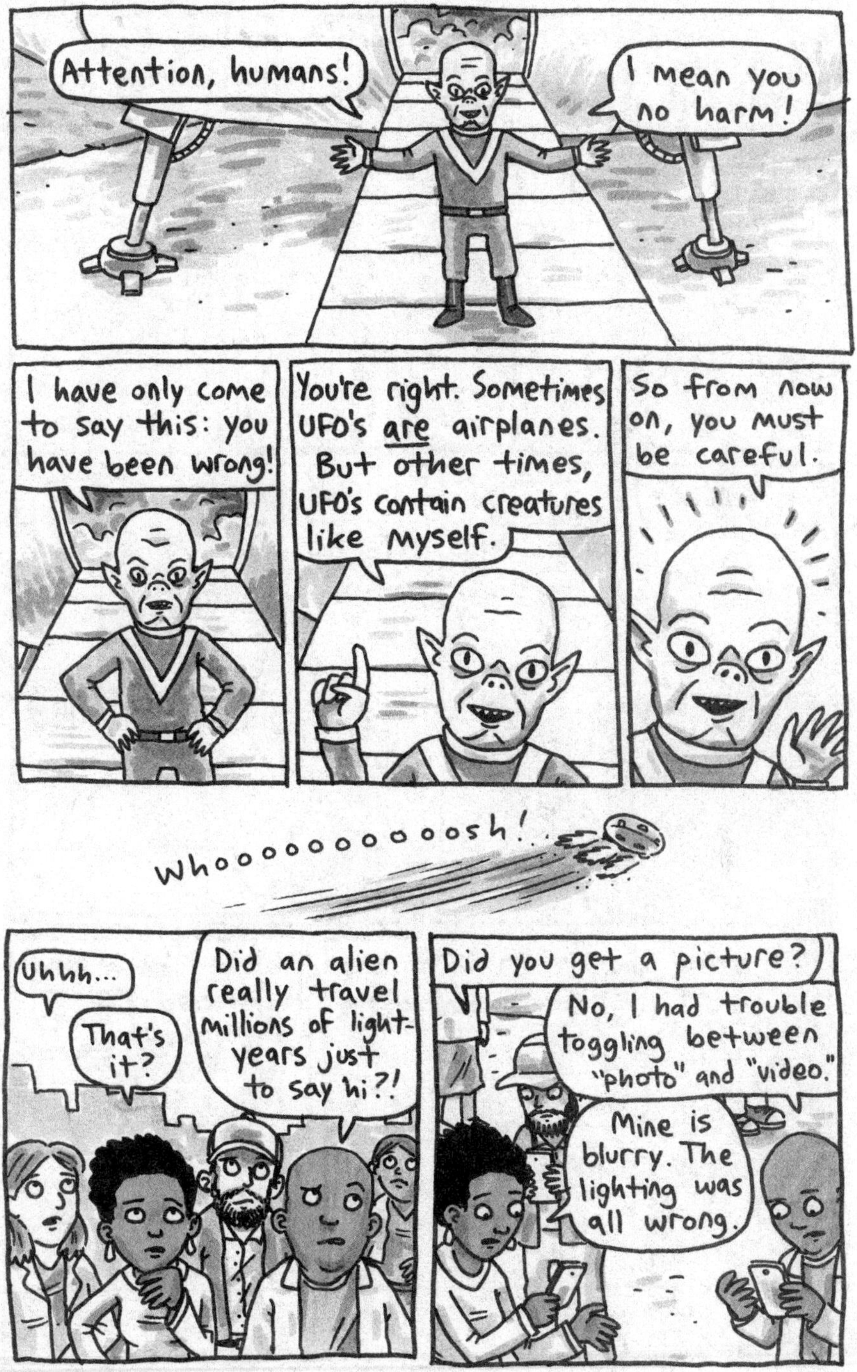
Attention, humans!
I mean you no harm!
I have only come to say this: you have been wrong!
You're right. Sometimes UFO's are airplanes. But other times, UFO's contain creatures like myself.
So from now on, you must be careful.
Whoooooooooooosh!
Uhhh...
That's it?
Did an alien really travel millions of light-years just to say hi?!
Did you get a picture?
No, I had trouble toggling between "photo" and "video."
Mine is blurry. The lighting was all wrong.

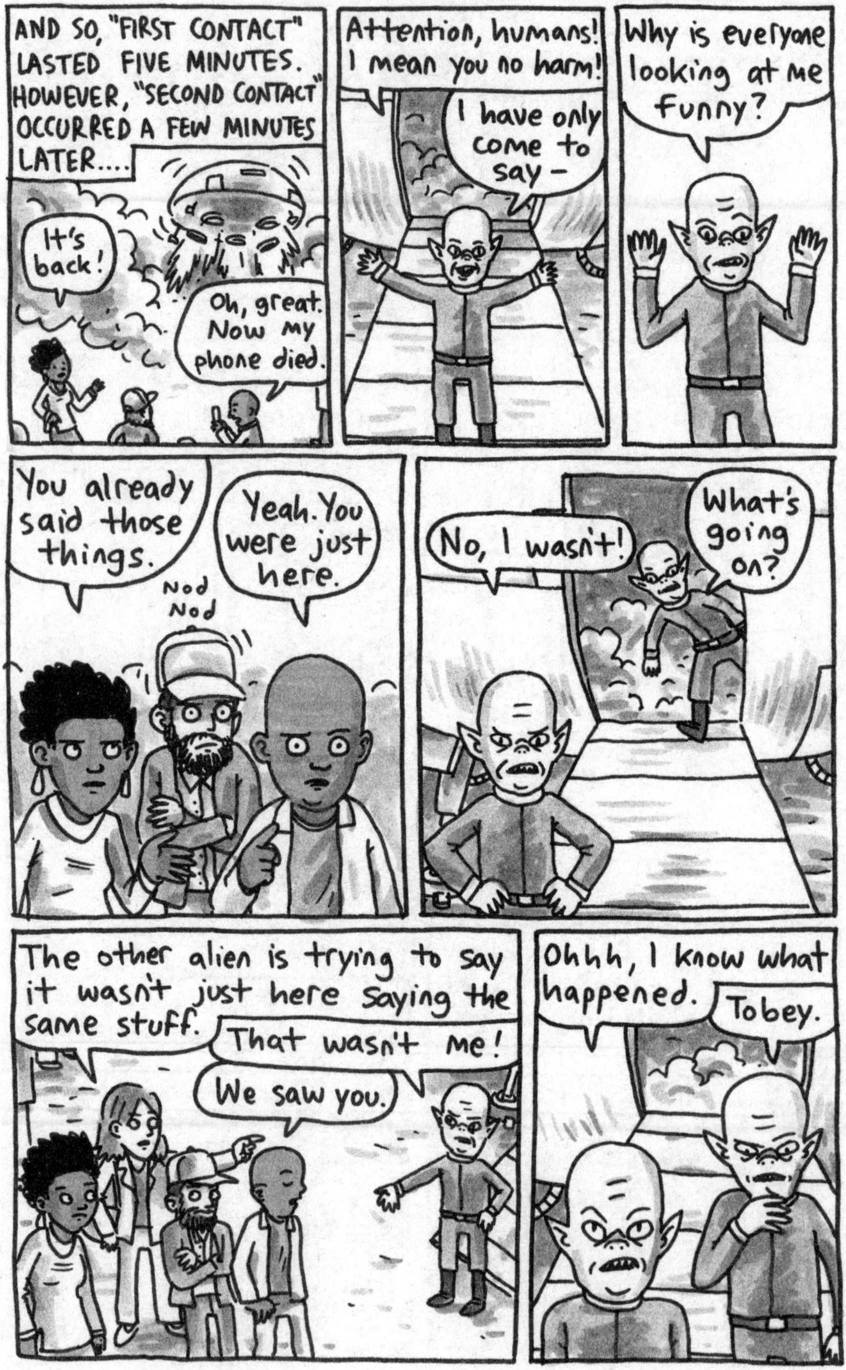
AND SO, "FIRST CONTACT" LASTED FIVE MINUTES. HOWEVER, "SECOND CONTACT" OCCURRED A FEW MINUTES LATER....
It's back!
Oh, great. Now my phone died.
Attention, humans! I mean you no harm!
I have only come to say –
Why is everyone looking at me funny?
You already said those things.
Nod Nod
Yeah. You were just here.
No, I wasn't!
What's going on?
The other alien is trying to say it wasn't just here saying the same stuff.
That wasn't me!
We saw you.
Ohhh, I know what happened.
Tobey.

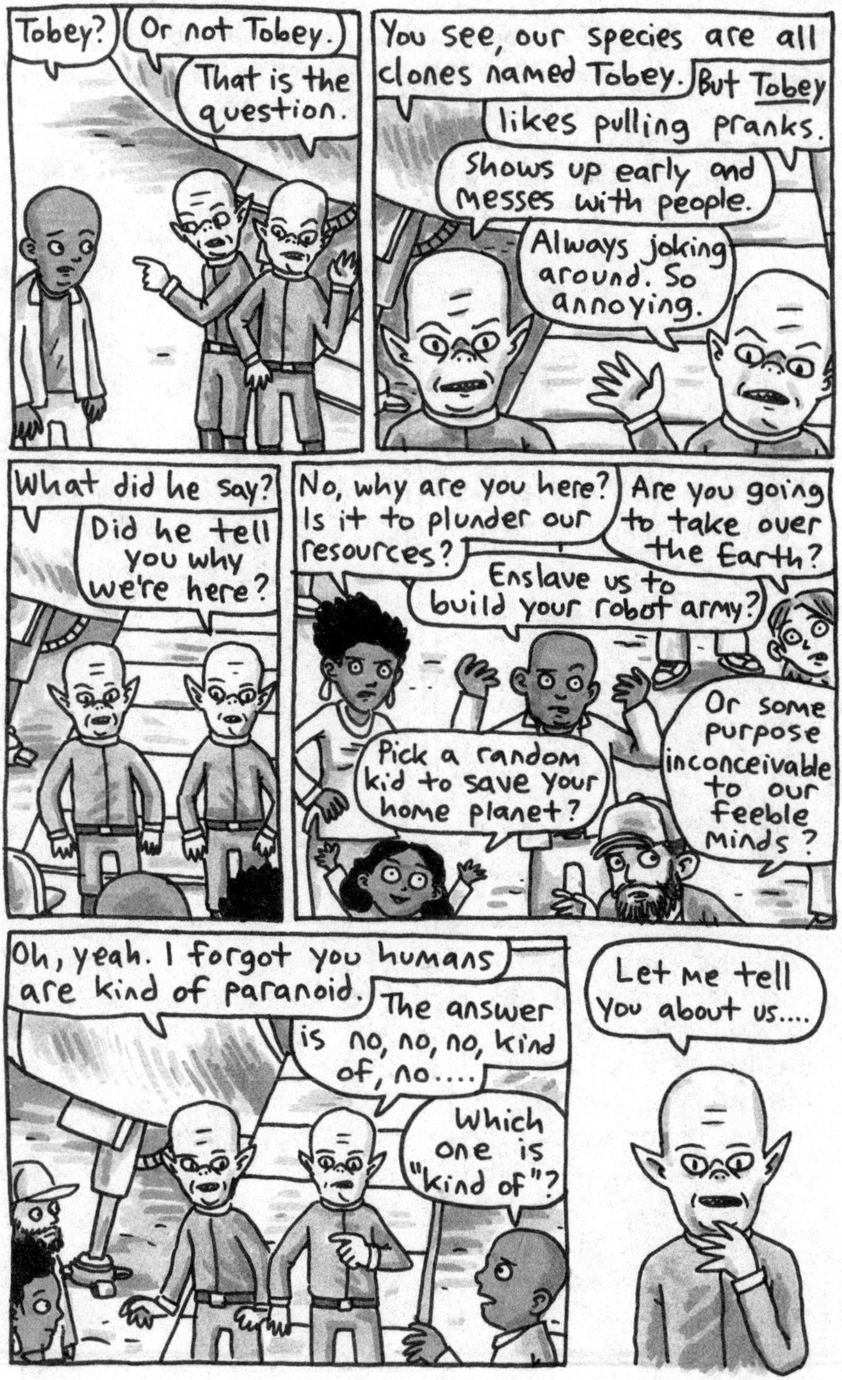
Tobey?
Or not Tobey.
That is the question.
You see, our species are all clones named Tobey.
But Tobey likes pulling pranks.
Shows up early and messes with people.
Always joking around. So annoying.
What did he say?
Did he tell you why we're here?
No, why are you here? Is it to plunder our resources?
Are you going to take over the Earth?
Enslave us to build your robot army?
Pick a random kid to save your home planet?
Or some purpose inconceivable to our feeble minds?
Oh, yeah. I forgot you humans are kind of paranoid.
The answer is no, no, no, kind of, no....
Which one is "kind of"?
Let me tell you about us....

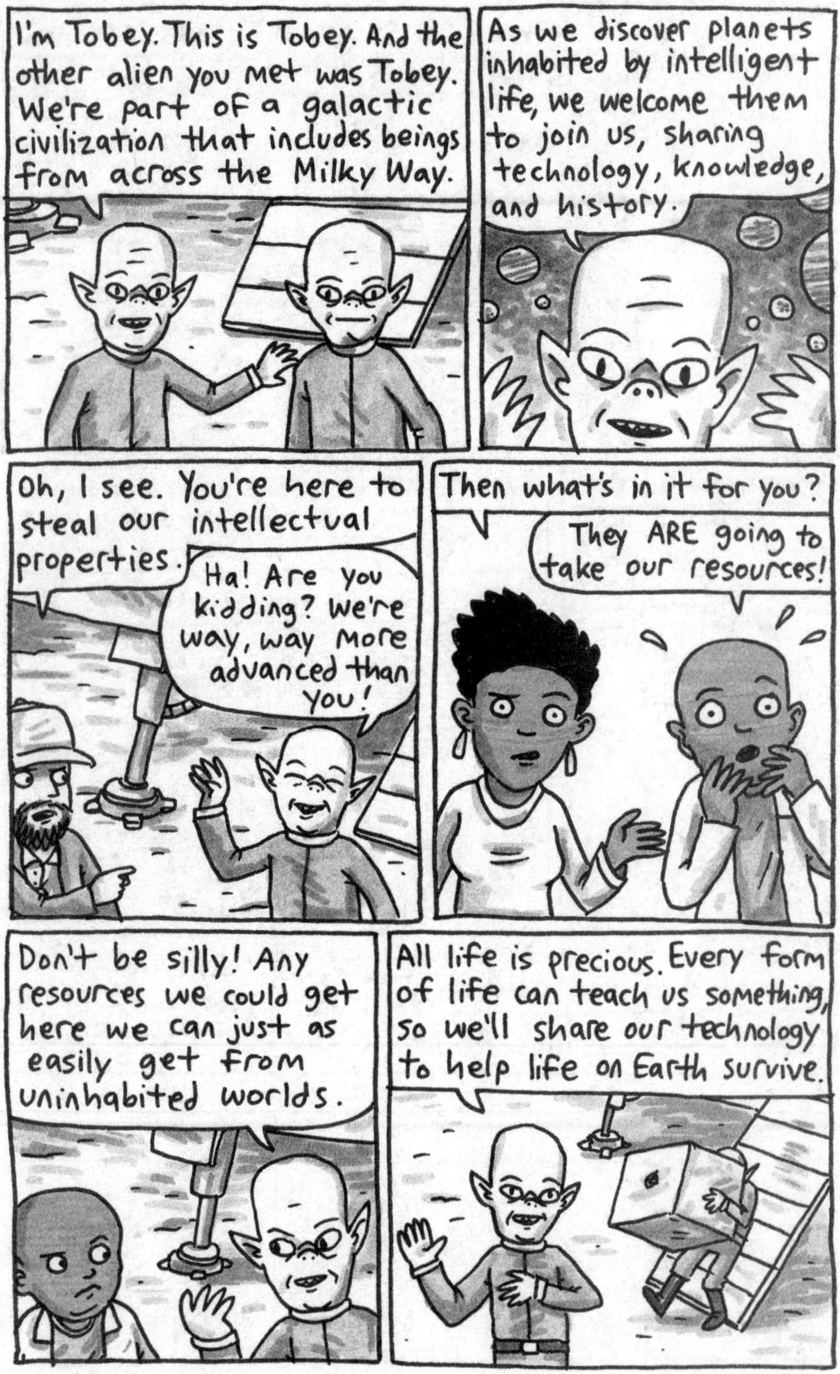
I'm Tobey. This is Tobey. And the other alien you met was Tobey. We're part of a galactic civilization that includes beings from across the Milky Way.
As we discover planets inhabited by intelligent life, we welcome them to join us, sharing technology, knowledge, and history.
Oh, I see. You're here to steal our intellectual properties.
Ha! Are you kidding? We're way, way more advanced than you!
Then what's in it for you?
They ARE going to take our resources!
Don't be silly! Any resources we could get here we can just as easily get from uninhabited worlds.
All life is precious. Every form of life can teach us something, so we'll share our technology to help life on Earth survive.

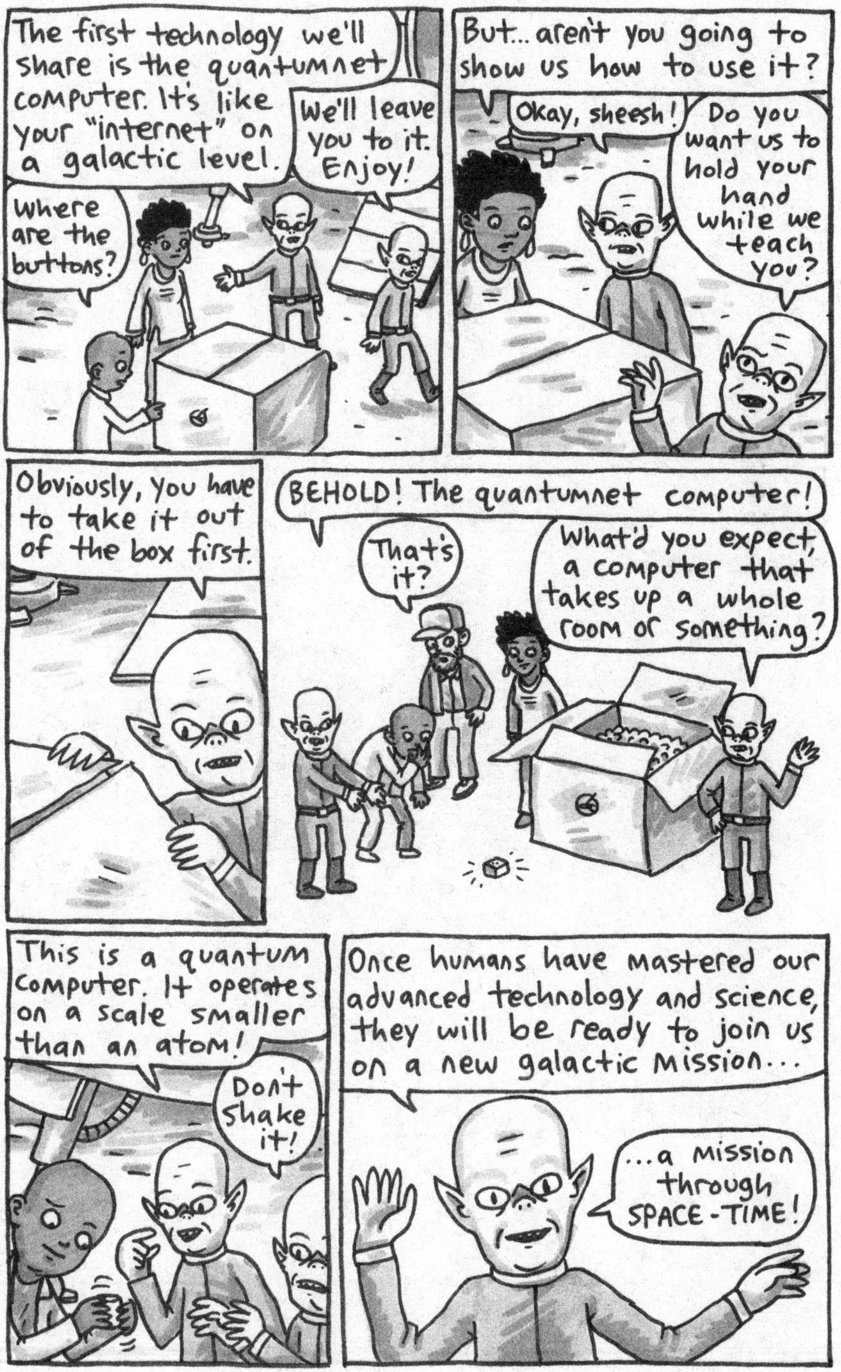
The first technology we'll share is the quantumnet computer. It's like your "internet" on a galactic level.
We'll leave you to it. Enjoy!
Where are the buttons?
But... aren't you going to show us how to use it?
Okay, sheesh!
Do you want us to hold your hand while we teach you?
Obviously, you have to take it out of the box first.
BEHOLD! The quantumnet computer!
That's it?
What'd you expect, a computer that takes up a whole room or something?
This is a quantum computer. It operates on a scale smaller than an atom!
Don't shake it!
Once humans have mastered our advanced technology and science, they will be ready to join us on a new galactic mission...
...a mission through SPACE-TIME!

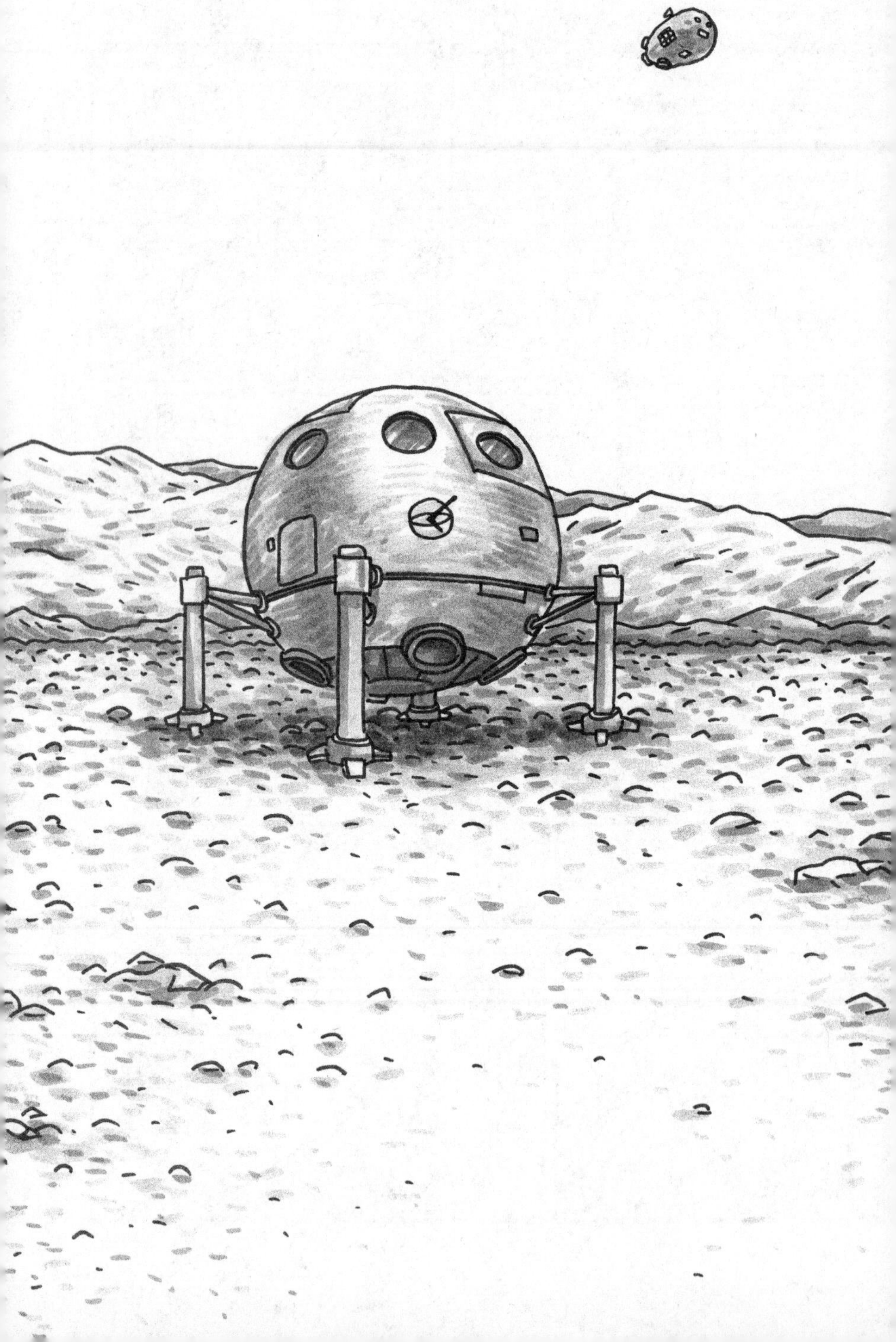

ONCE UPON A SPACE-TIME!

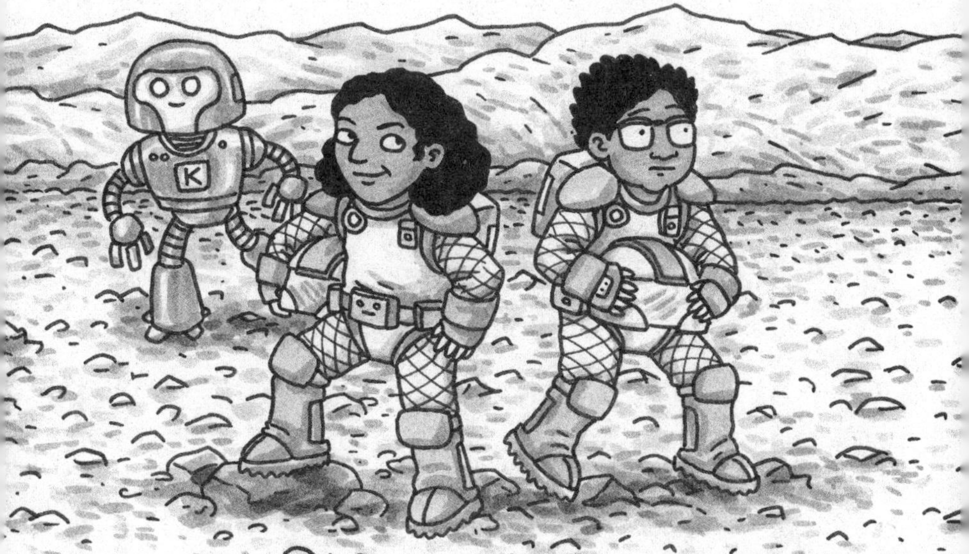
K

JEFFREY BROWN

A YEARLING BOOK

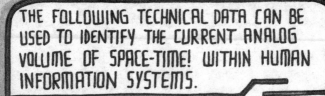

THE FOLLOWING TECHNICAL DATA CAN BE USED TO IDENTIFY THE CURRENT ANALOG VOLUME OF SPACE-TIME! WITHIN HUMAN INFORMATION SYSTEMS.

Copyright © 2020 by Jeffrey Brown

All rights reserved. Published in the United States by Yearling, an imprint of Random House Children's Books, a division of Penguin Random House LLC, New York. Originally published in hardcover in the United States by Crown Books for Young Readers, an imprint of Random House Children's Books, a division of Penguin Random House LLC, New York, in 2020.

Yearling and the jumping horse design are registered trademarks of Penguin Random House LLC.

RH Graphic with the book design is a trademark of Penguin Random House LLC.

Visit us on the Web! rhcbooks.com

Educators and librarians, for a variety of teaching tools, visit us at RHTeachersLibrarians.com

The Library of Congress has cataloged the hardcover edition of the work as follows:
Names: Brown, Jeffrey, author, illustrator.
Title: Once upon a space-time! / Jeffrey Brown.
Description: First edition. | New York: Crown Books for Young Readers, (2022) | Series: Space-time! | Audience: Ages 8–12 | Audience: Grades 4–6 | Summary: Jide and Petra are just two normal kids until they are selected to leave Earth and join their new alien classmates on an intergalactic research mission to Mars.
Identifiers: LCCN 2021053922 | ISBN 978-0-553-53435-1 (hardcover) | ISBN 978-0-553-53436-8 (library binding) | ISBN 978-0-553-53437-5 (ebook) | ISBN 978-0-553-53438-2 (trade paperback)
Subjects: CYAC: Graphic novels. | Space flight—Fiction. | Schools—Fiction. | Human-alien encounters—Fiction. | LCGFT: Action and adventure comics. | Science fiction comics. | Graphic novels.
Classification: LCC PZ7.7.B78 On 2022 | DDC 741.5/973—dc23

Printed in the United States of America
10 9 8 7 6 5 4 3 2 1
First Yearling Edition 2022

NOT QUITE THE RIGHT STUFF

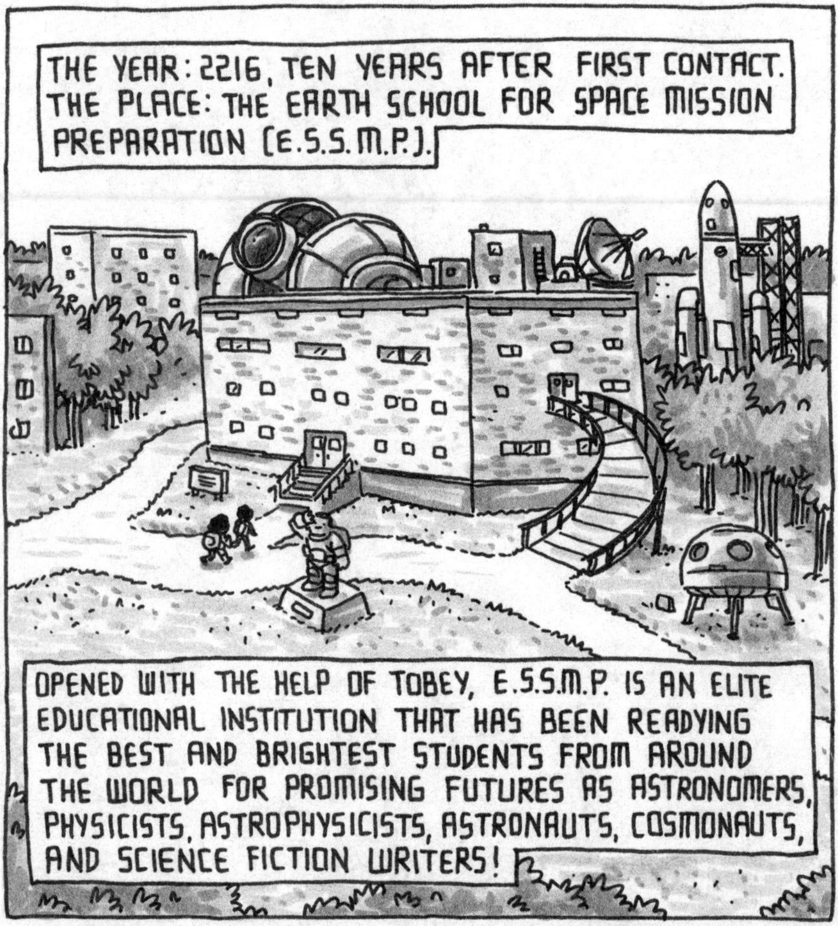
THE YEAR: 2216, TEN YEARS AFTER FIRST CONTACT. THE PLACE: THE EARTH SCHOOL FOR SPACE MISSION PREPARATION (E.S.S.M.P.).
OPENED WITH THE HELP OF TOBEY, E.S.S.M.P. IS AN ELITE EDUCATIONAL INSTITUTION THAT HAS BEEN READYING THE BEST AND BRIGHTEST STUDENTS FROM AROUND THE WORLD FOR PROMISING FUTURES AS ASTRONOMERS, PHYSICISTS, ASTROPHYSICISTS, ASTRONAUTS, COSMONAUTS, AND SCIENCE FICTION WRITERS!

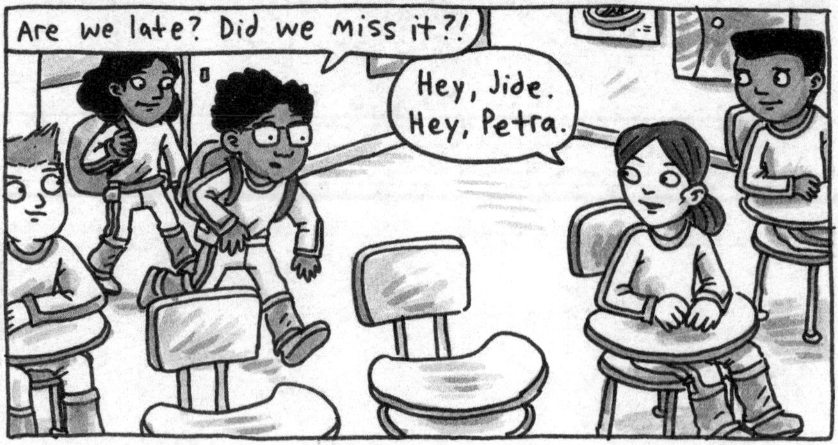
Are we late? Did we miss it?!
Hey, Jide. Hey, Petra.

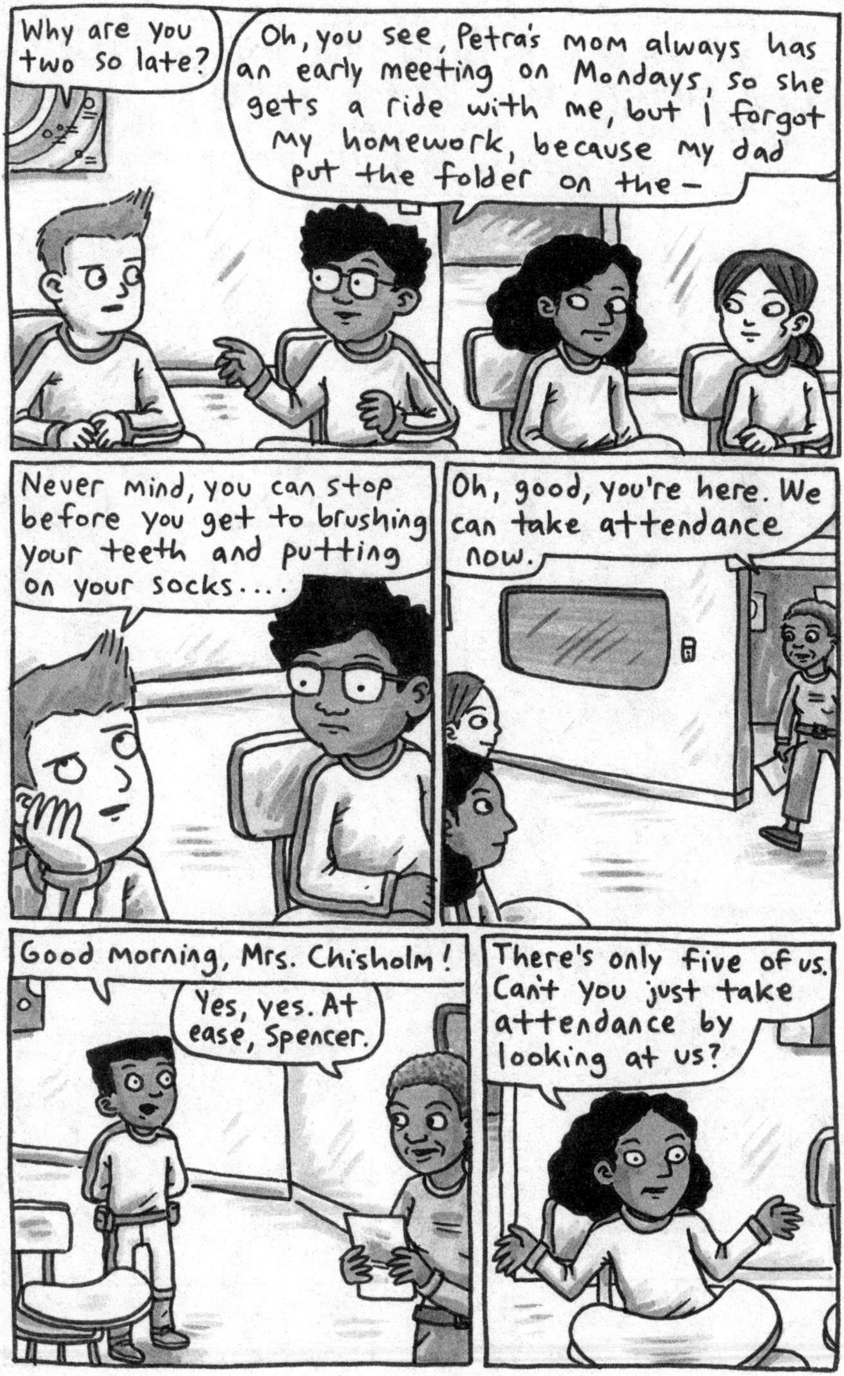
Why are you two so late?
Oh, you see, Petra's mom always has an early meeting on Mondays, so she gets a ride with me, but I forgot my homework, because my dad put the folder on the-
Never mind, you can stop before you get to brushing your teeth and putting on your socks....
Oh, good, you're here. We can take attendance now.
Good morning, Mrs. Chisholm!
Yes, yes. At ease, Spencer.
There's only five of us. Can't you just take attendance by looking at us?

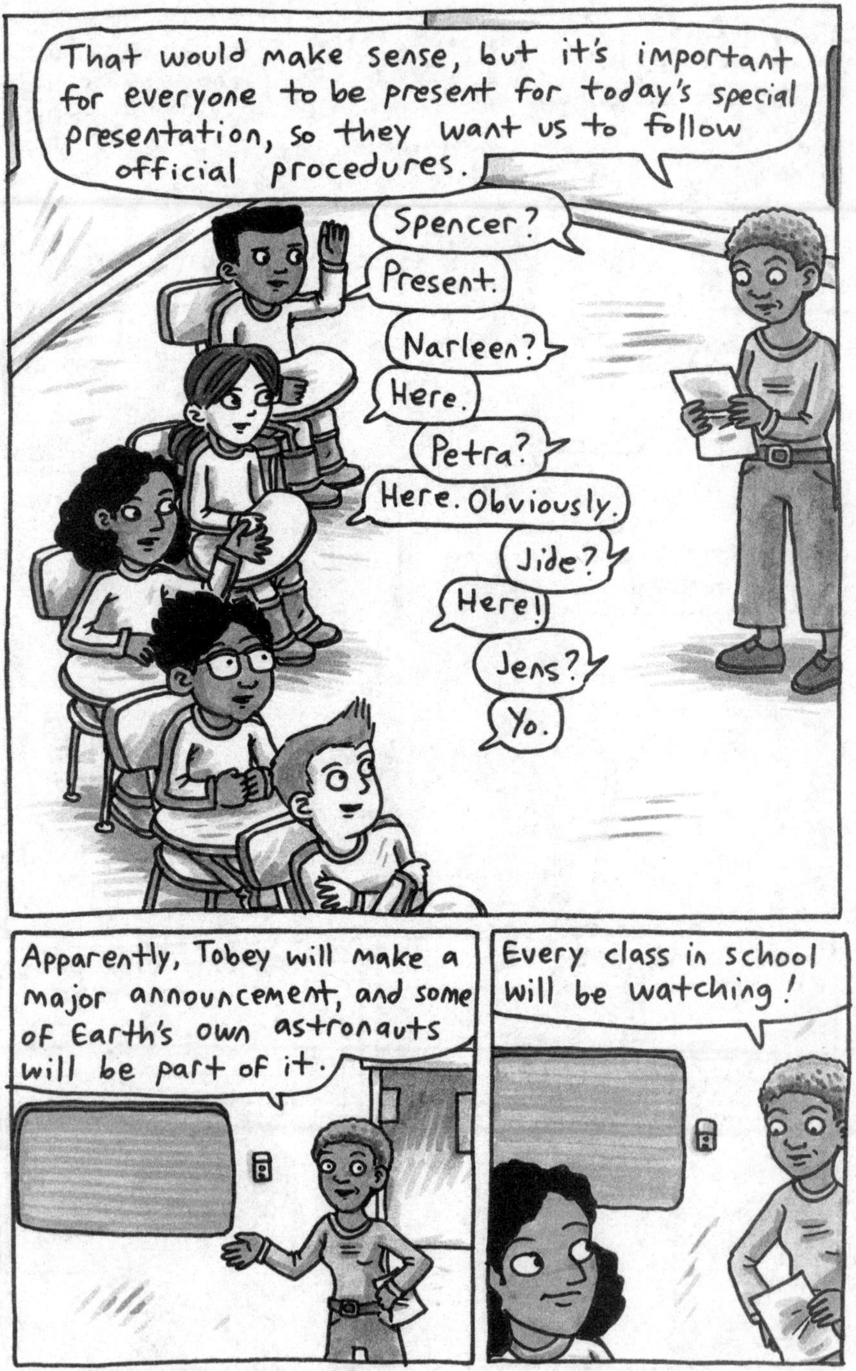
That would make sense, but it's important for everyone to be present for today's special presentation, so they want us to follow official procedures.
Spencer?
Present.
Narleen?
Here.
Petra?
Here. Obviously.
Jide?
Here!
Jens?
Yo.
Apparently, Tobey will make a major announcement, and some of Earth's own astronauts will be part of it.
Every class in school will be watching!

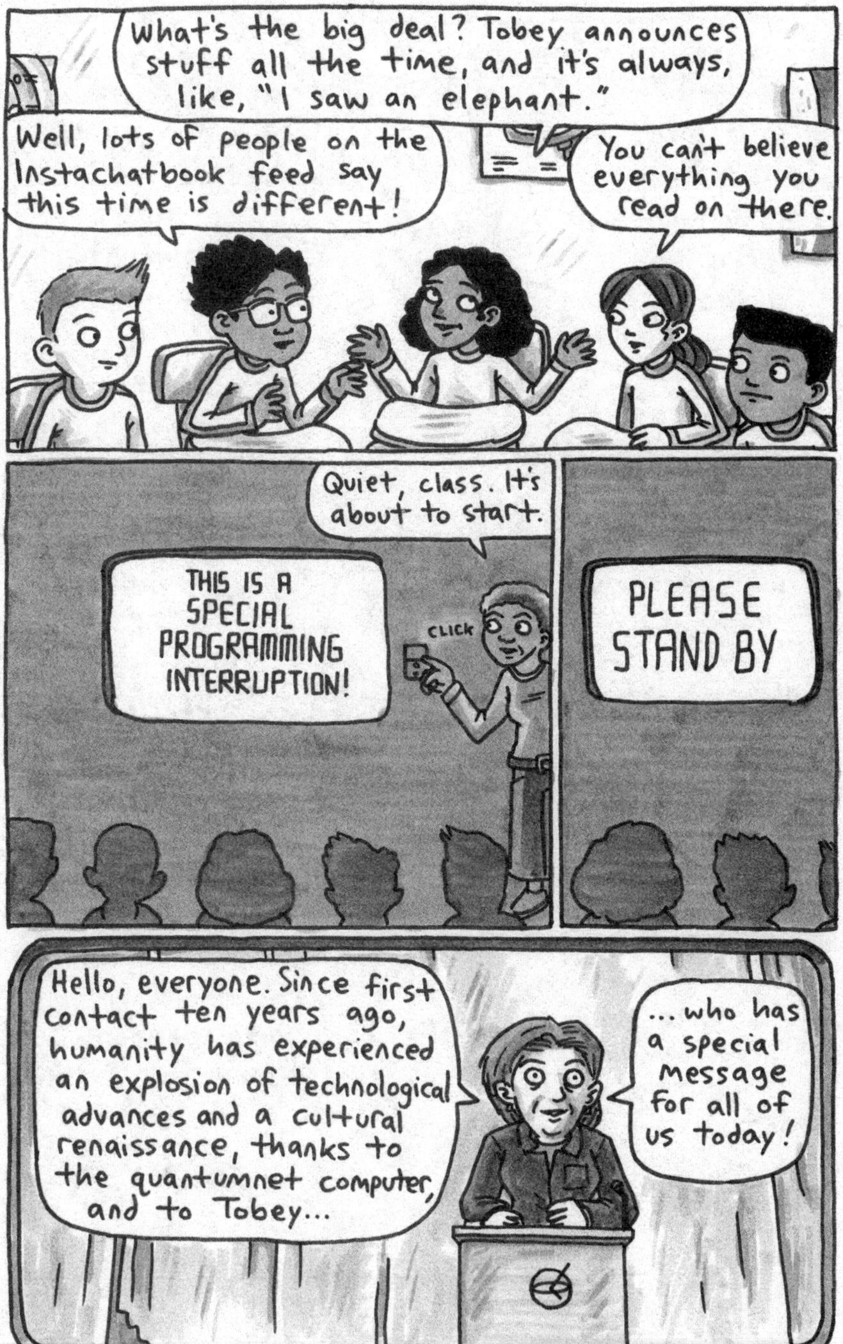
What's the big deal? Tobey announces stuff all the time, and it's always, like, "I saw an elephant."
Well, lots of people on the Instachatbook feed say this time is different!
You can't believe everything you read on there.
Quiet, class. It's about to start.
THIS IS A SPECIAL PROGRAMMING INTERRUPTION!
CLICK
PLEASE STAND BY
Hello, everyone. Since first contact ten years ago, humanity has experienced an explosion of technological advances and a cultural renaissance, thanks to the quantumnet computer, and to Tobey...
...who has a special message for all of us today!

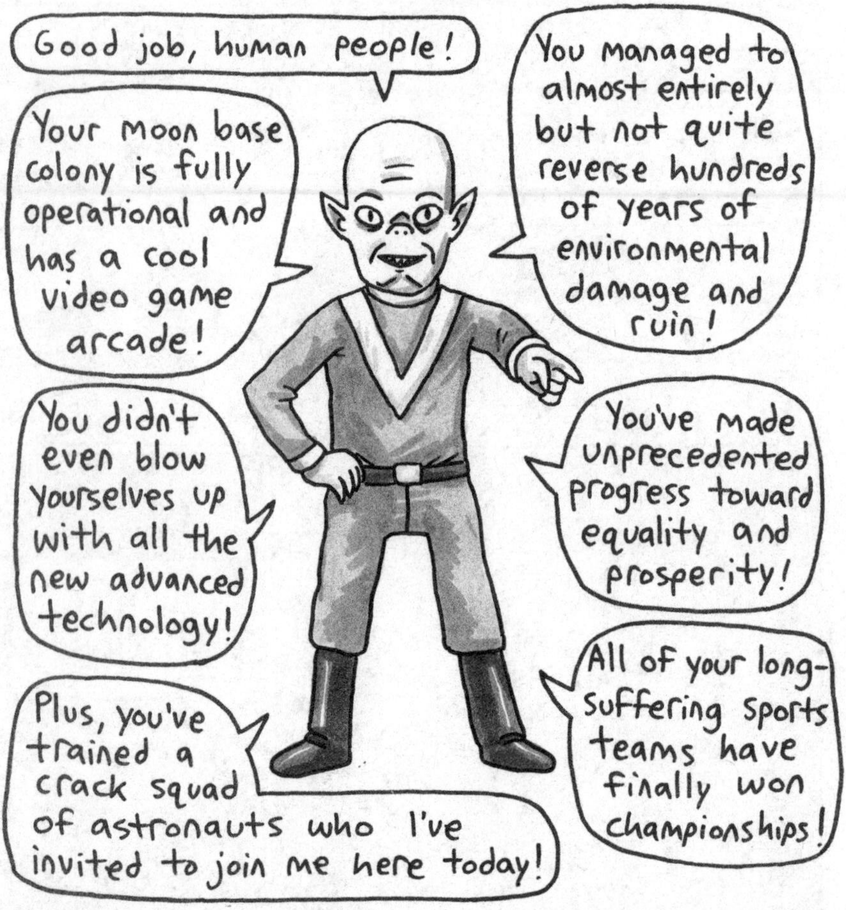
Good job, human people!
Your moon base colony is fully operational and has a cool video game arcade!
You managed to almost entirely but not quite reverse hundreds of years of environmental damage and ruin!
You didn't even blow yourselves up with all the new advanced technology!
You've made unprecedented progress toward equality and prosperity!
Plus, you've trained a crack squad of astronauts who I've invited to join me here today!
All of your long-suffering sports teams have finally won championships!

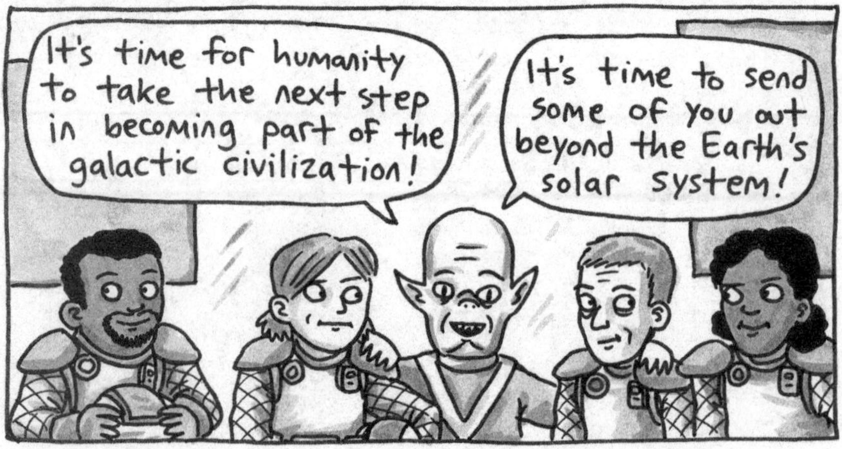
It's time for humanity to take the next step in becoming part of the galactic civilization!
It's time to send some of you out beyond the Earth's solar system!

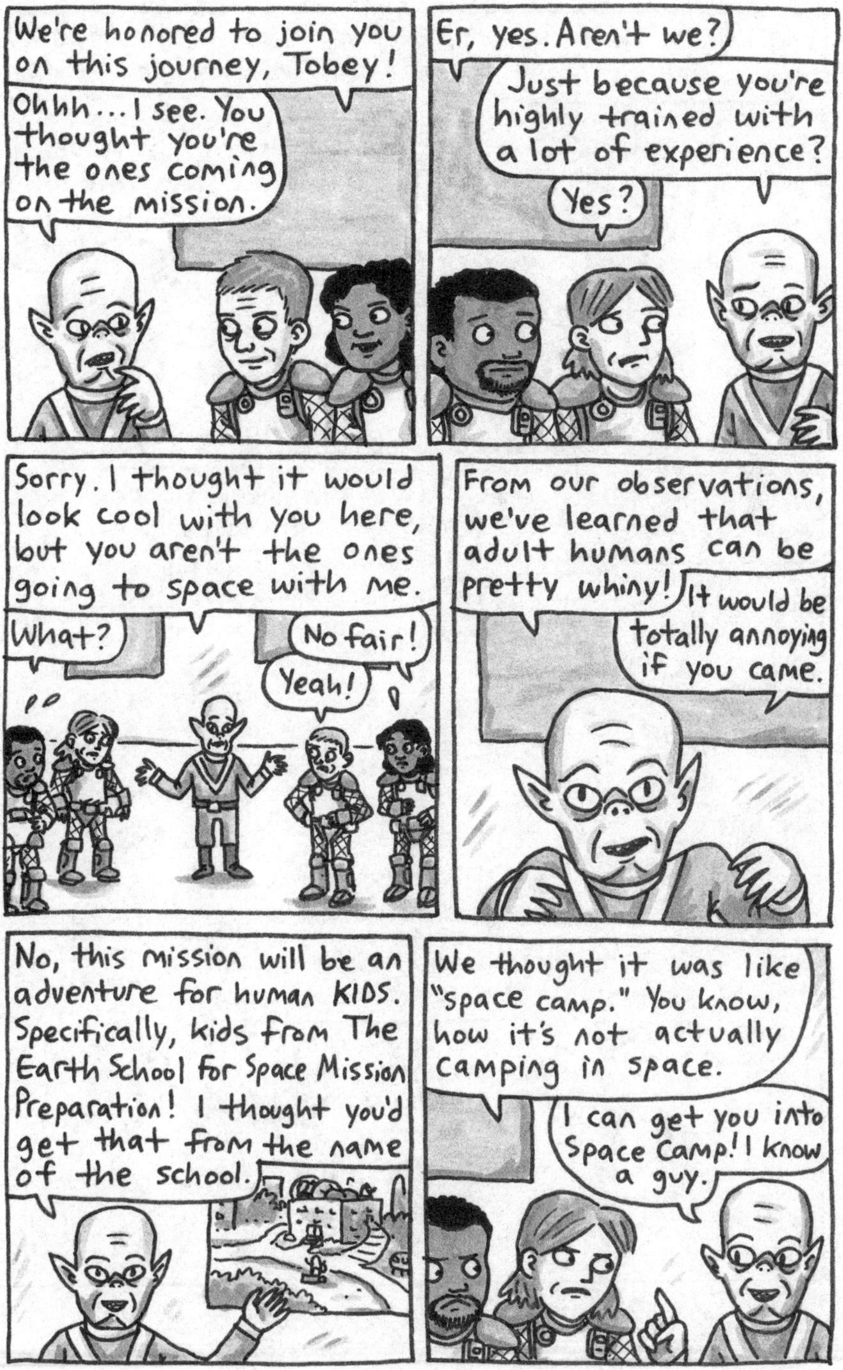
We're honored to join you on this journey, Tobey!
Ohhh... I see. You thought you're the ones coming on the mission.
Er, yes. Aren't we?
Just because you're highly trained with a lot of experience?
Yes?
Sorry. I thought it would look cool with you here, but you aren't the ones going to space with me.
What?
No fair!
Yeah!
From our observations, we've learned that adult humans can be pretty whiny!
It would be totally annoying if you came.
No, this mission will be an adventure for human KIDS. Specifically, kids from The Earth School for Space Mission Preparation! I thought you'd get that from the name of the school.
We thought it was like "space camp." You know, how it's not actually camping in space.
I can get you into Space Camp! I know a guy.

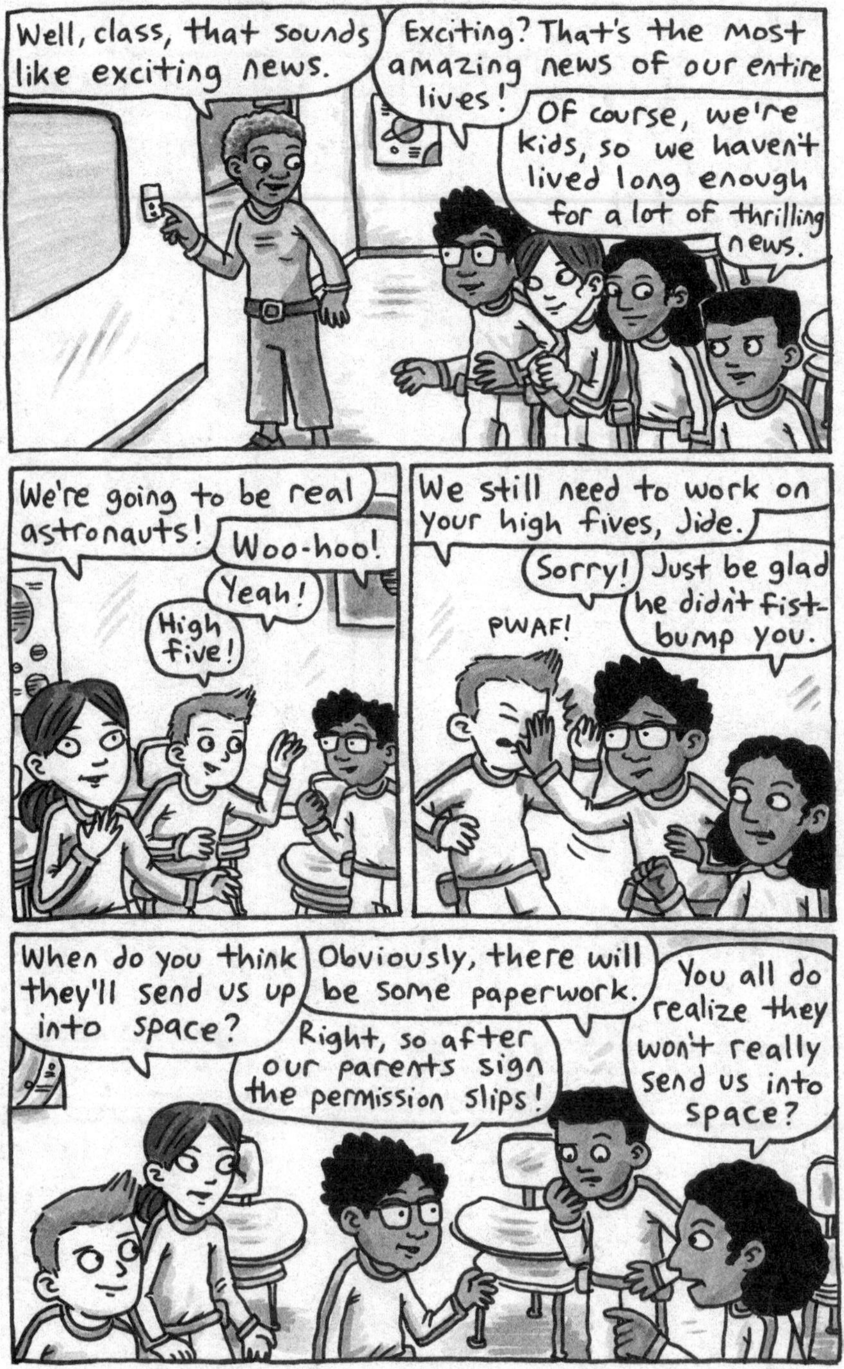
Well, class, that sounds like exciting news.
Exciting? That's the most amazing news of our entire lives!
Of course, we're kids, so we haven't lived long enough for a lot of thrilling news.
We're going to be real astronauts!
Woo-hoo!
Yeah!
High five!
We still need to work on your high fives, Jide.
Sorry!
PWAF!
Just be glad he didn't fist-bump you.
When do you think they'll send us up into space?
Obviously, there will be some paperwork.
Right, so after our parents sign the permission slips!
You all do realize they won't really send us into space?

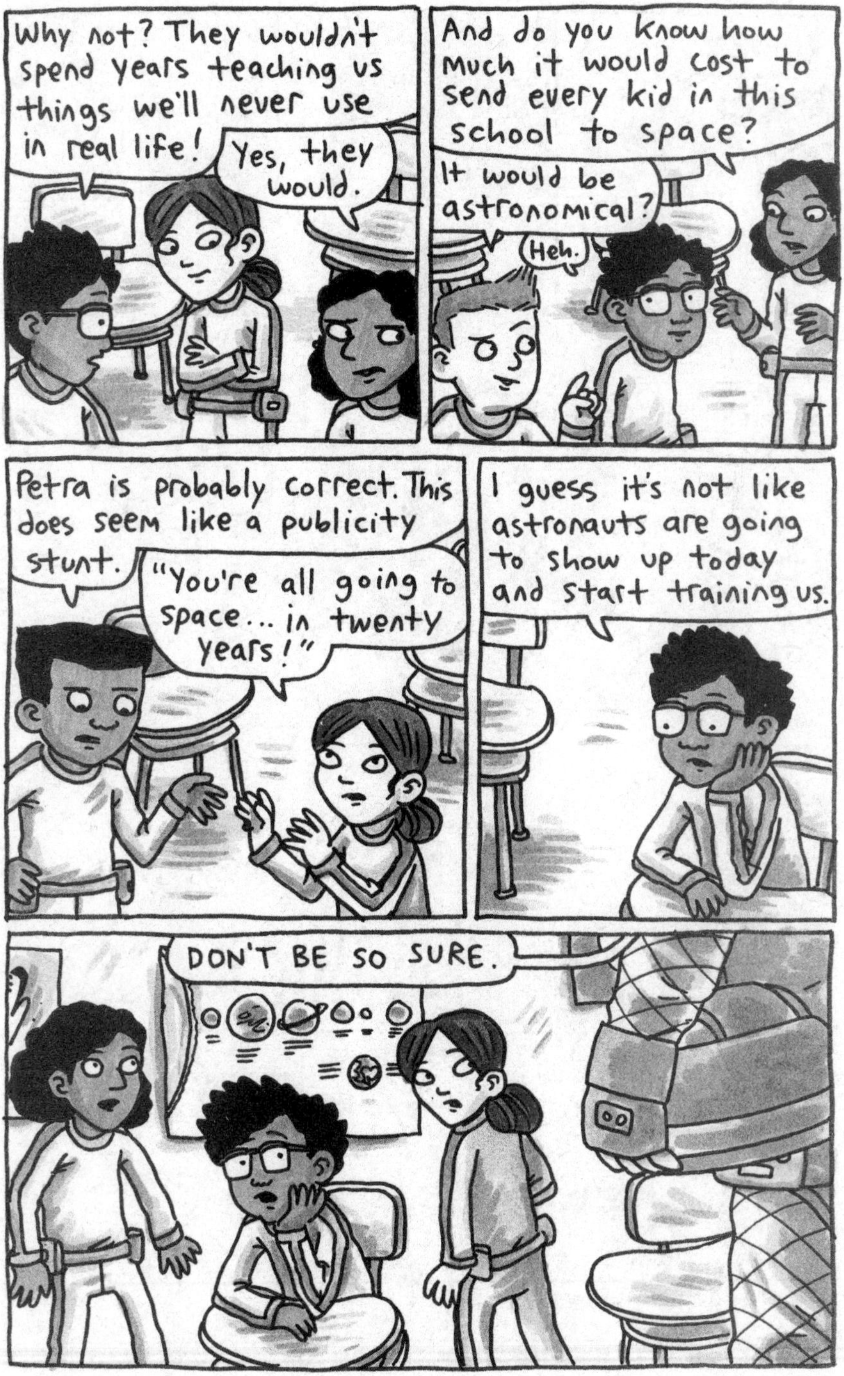
Why not? They wouldn't spend years teaching us things we'll never use in real life!
Yes, they would.
And do you know how much it would cost to send every kid in this school to space?
It would be astronomical?
Heh.
Petra is probably correct. This does seem like a publicity stunt.
"You're all going to space... in twenty years!"
I guess it's not like astronauts are going to show up today and start training us.
DON'T BE SO SURE.

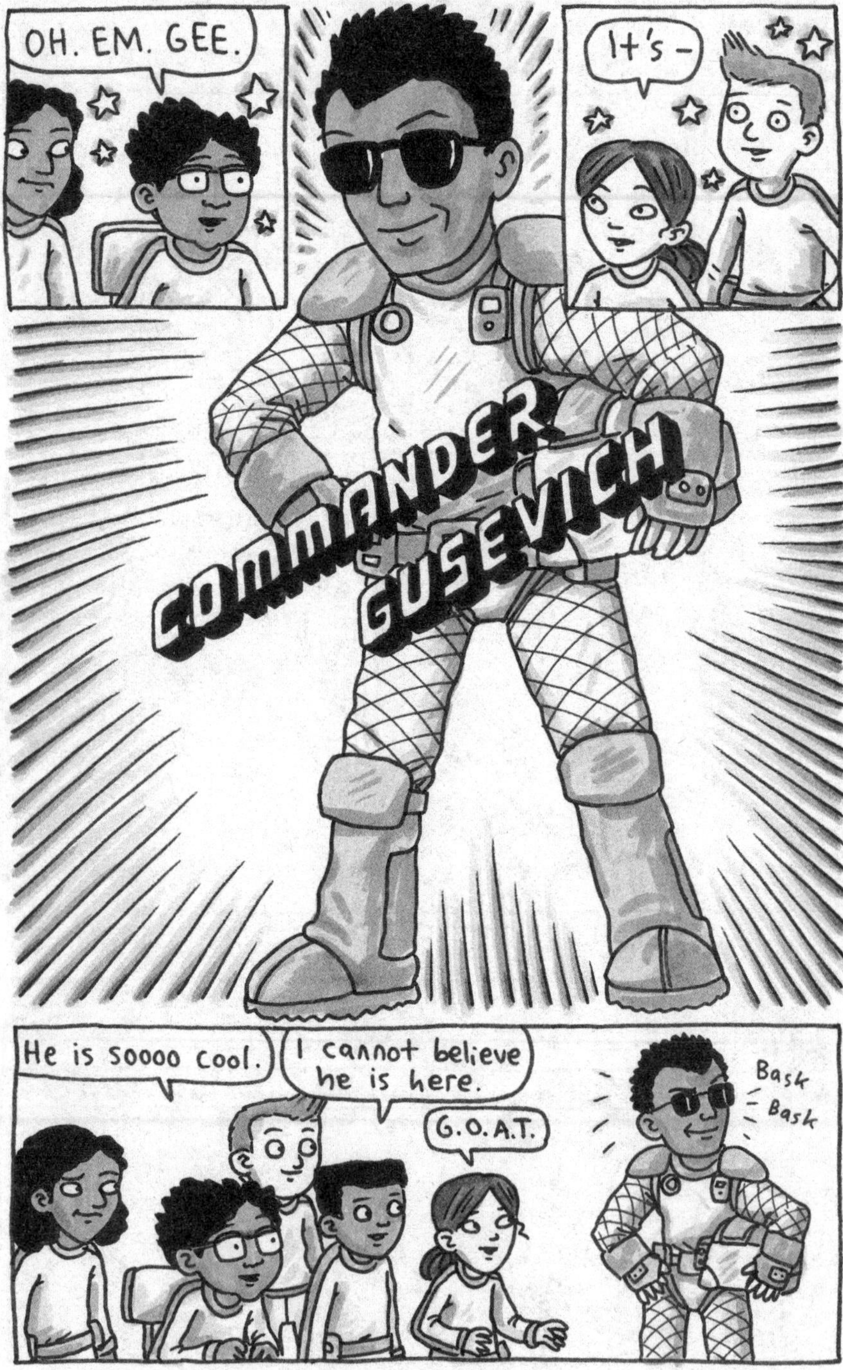
OH. EM. GEE.
It's –
COMMANDER GUSEVICH
He is soooo cool.
I cannot believe he is here.
G.O.A.T.
Bask
Bask

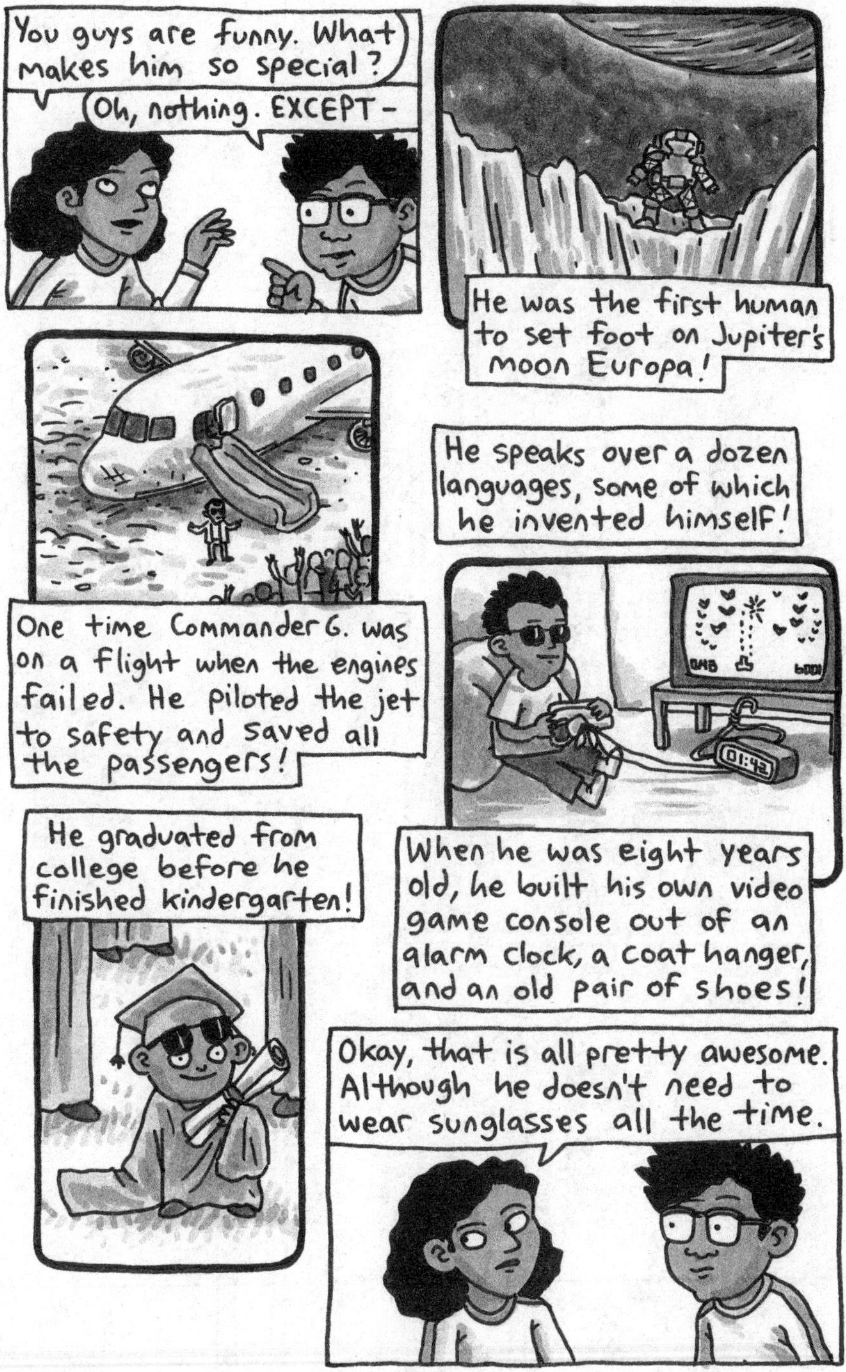
You guys are funny. What makes him so special?
Oh, nothing. EXCEPT-
He was the first human to set foot on Jupiter's moon Europa!
One time Commander G. was on a flight when the engines failed. He piloted the jet to safety and saved all the passengers!
He speaks over a dozen languages, some of which he invented himself!
When he was eight years old, he built his own video game console out of an alarm clock, a coat hanger, and an old pair of shoes!
01:42
He graduated from college before he finished kindergarten!
Okay, that is all pretty awesome. Although he doesn't need to wear sunglasses all the time.

That's a good perspective, Petra. Famous people are just like us. They put their socks on one at a time.

Not Commander G.!

Yeah! He throws his socks in the air and then double karate kicks his feet into them!

Yeah!

Are you going to teach us how to do that?

No, I can't teach you that.

Because it's too dangerous?

No, because that's a myth! It's physically impossible to do. Didn't you listen to the announcement?

You would just kick your socks away!

We'll be teaching you what you need to know to go to space.

We?

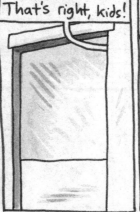

That's right, kids!

Commander G. has an awesome co-teacher!

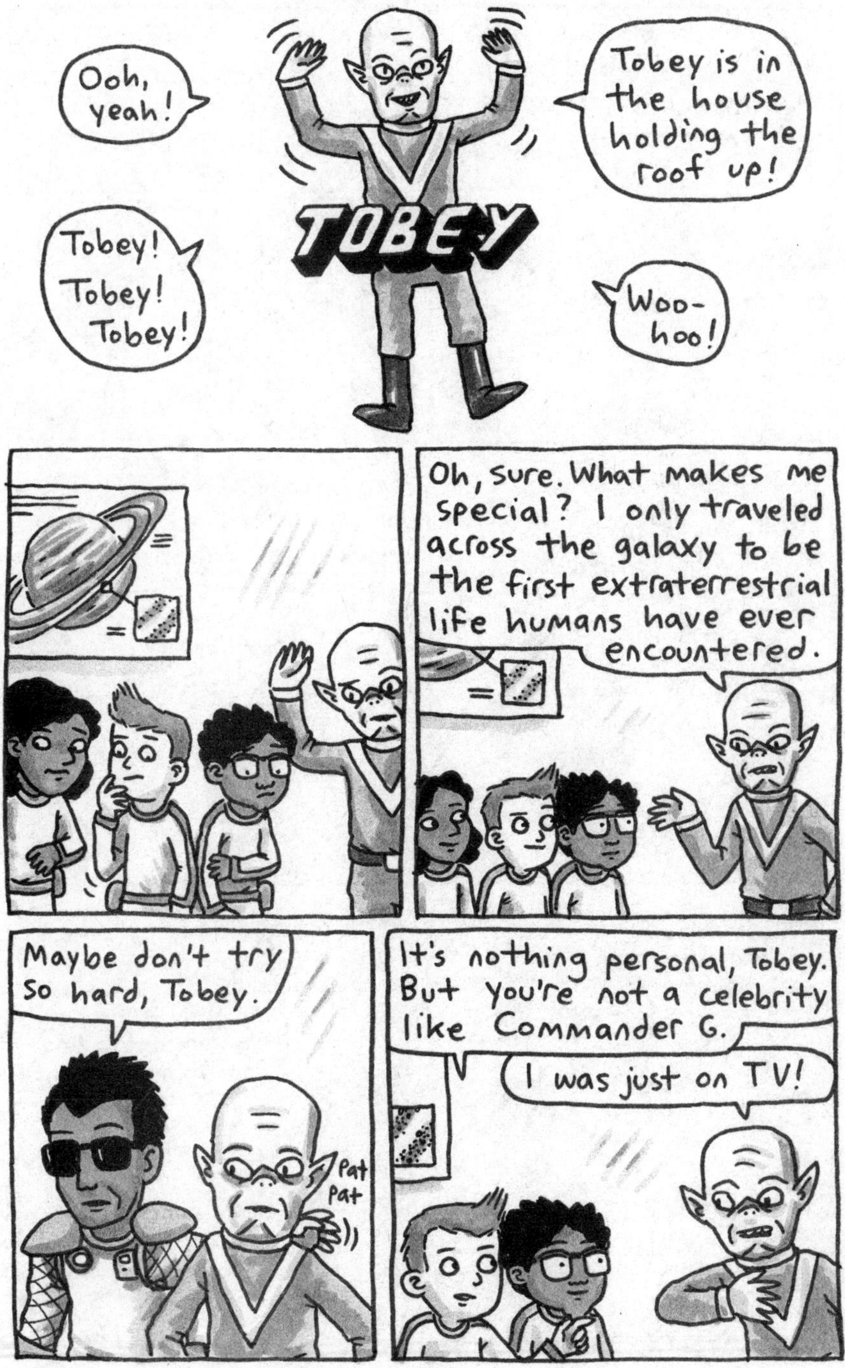
Ooh, yeah!
TOBEY
Tobey is in the house holding the roof up!
Tobey! Tobey! Tobey!
Woo-hoo!
Oh, sure. What makes me special? I only traveled across the galaxy to be the first extraterrestrial life humans have ever encountered.
Maybe don't try so hard, Tobey.
Pat pat
It's nothing personal, Tobey. But you're not a celebrity like Commander G.
I was just on TV!

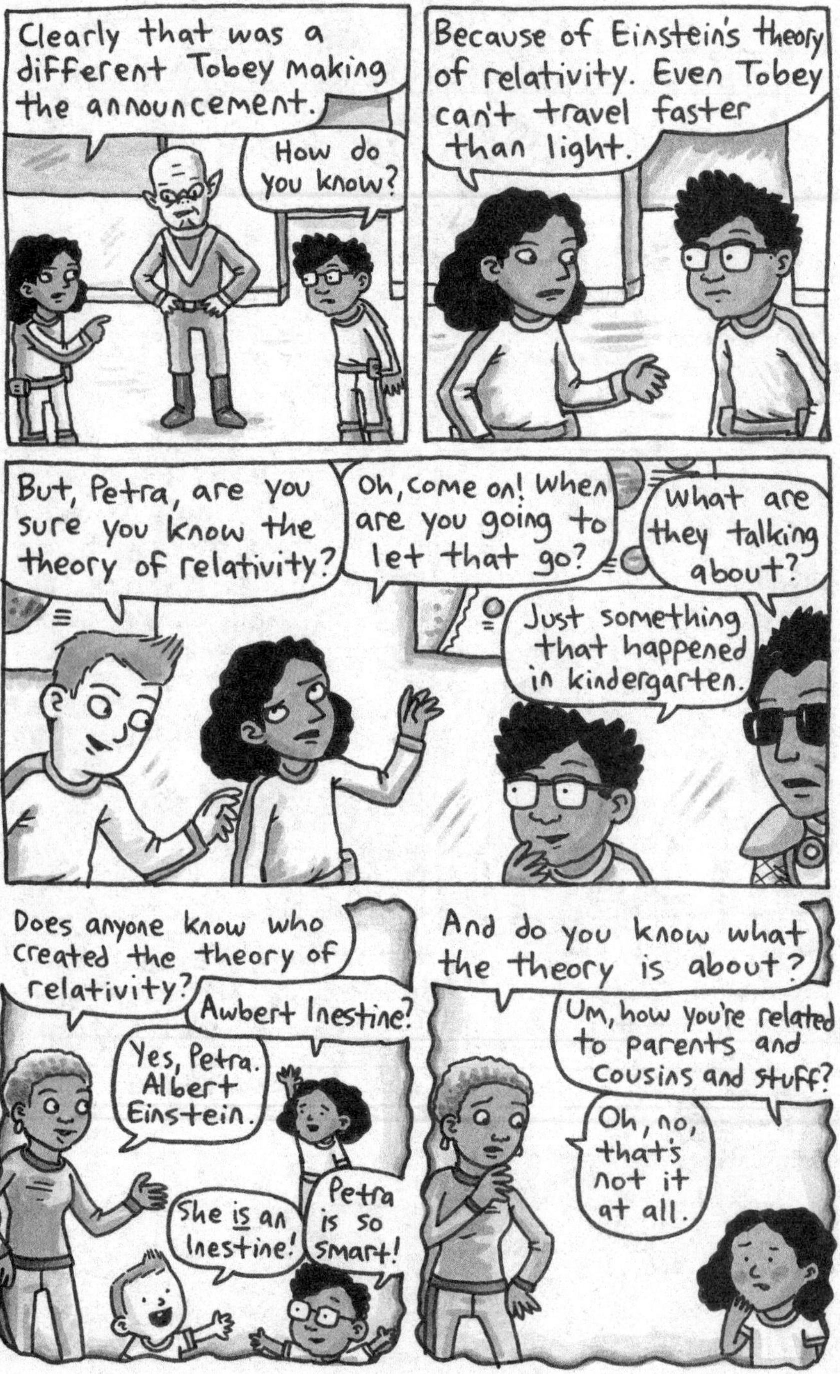
Clearly that was a different Tobey making the announcement.
How do you know?
Because of Einstein's theory of relativity. Even Tobey can't travel faster than light.
But, Petra, are you sure you know the theory of relativity?
Oh, come on! When are you going to let that go?
What are they talking about?
Just something that happened in kindergarten.
Does anyone know who created the theory of relativity?
Awbert Inestine?
Yes, Petra. Albert Einstein.
She is an Inestine!
Petra is so smart!
And do you know what the theory is about?
Um, how you're related to parents and cousins and stuff?
Oh, no, that's not it at all.

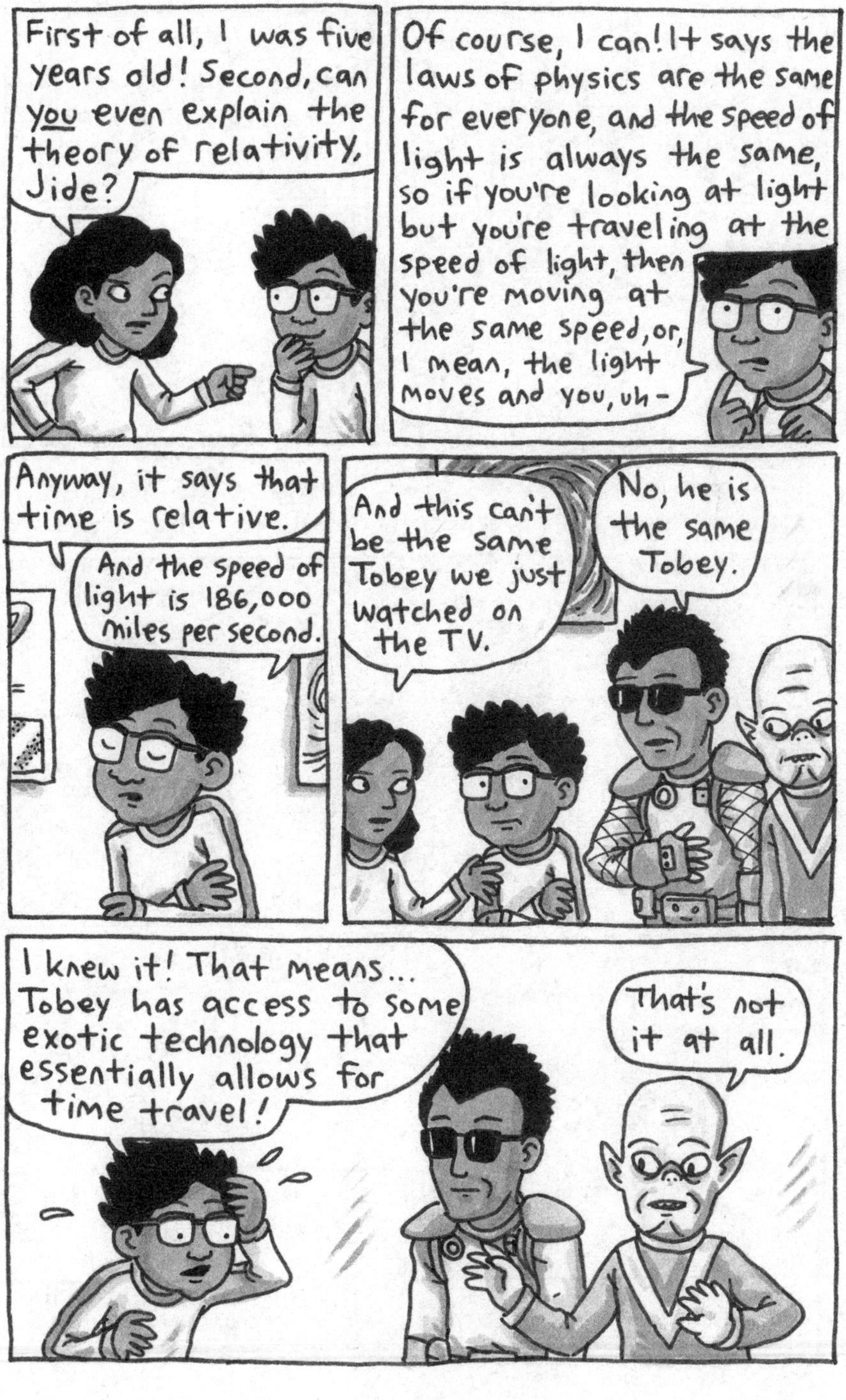
First of all, I was five years old! Second, can you even explain the theory of relativity, Jide?
Of course, I can! It says the laws of physics are the same for everyone, and the speed of light is always the same, so if you're looking at light but you're traveling at the speed of light, then you're moving at the same speed, or, I mean, the light moves and you, uh-
Anyway, it says that time is relative.
And the speed of light is 186,000 miles per second.
And this can't be the same Tobey we just watched on the TV.
No, he is the same Tobey.
I knew it! That means... Tobey has access to some exotic technology that essentially allows for time travel!
That's not it at all.

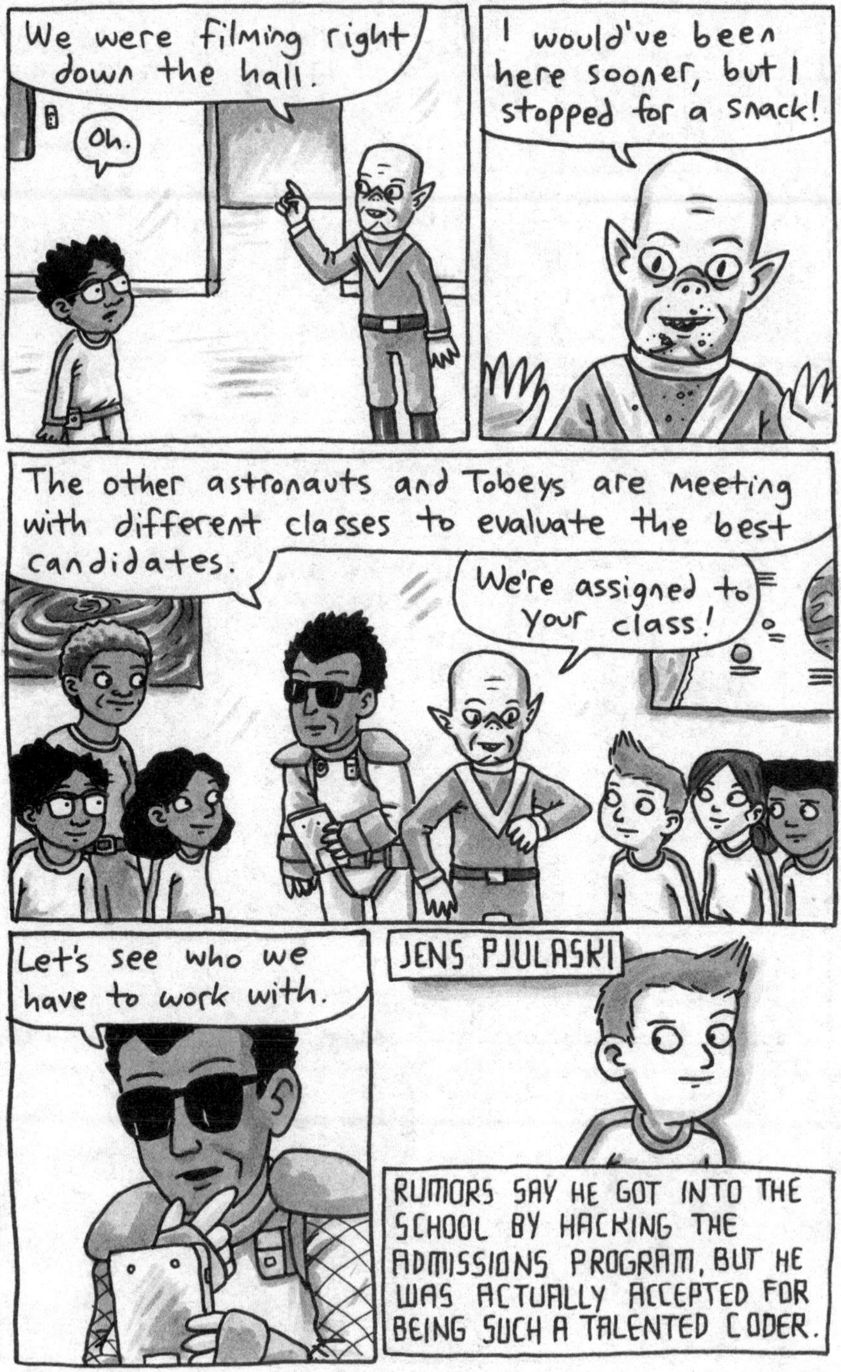

We were filming right down the hall.
Oh.
I would've been here sooner, but I stopped for a snack!
The other astronauts and Tobeys are meeting with different classes to evaluate the best candidates.
We're assigned to your class!
Let's see who we have to work with.
JENS PJULASKI
RUMORS SAY HE GOT INTO THE SCHOOL BY HACKING THE ADMISSIONS PROGRAM, BUT HE WAS ACTUALLY ACCEPTED FOR BEING SUCH A TALENTED CODER.

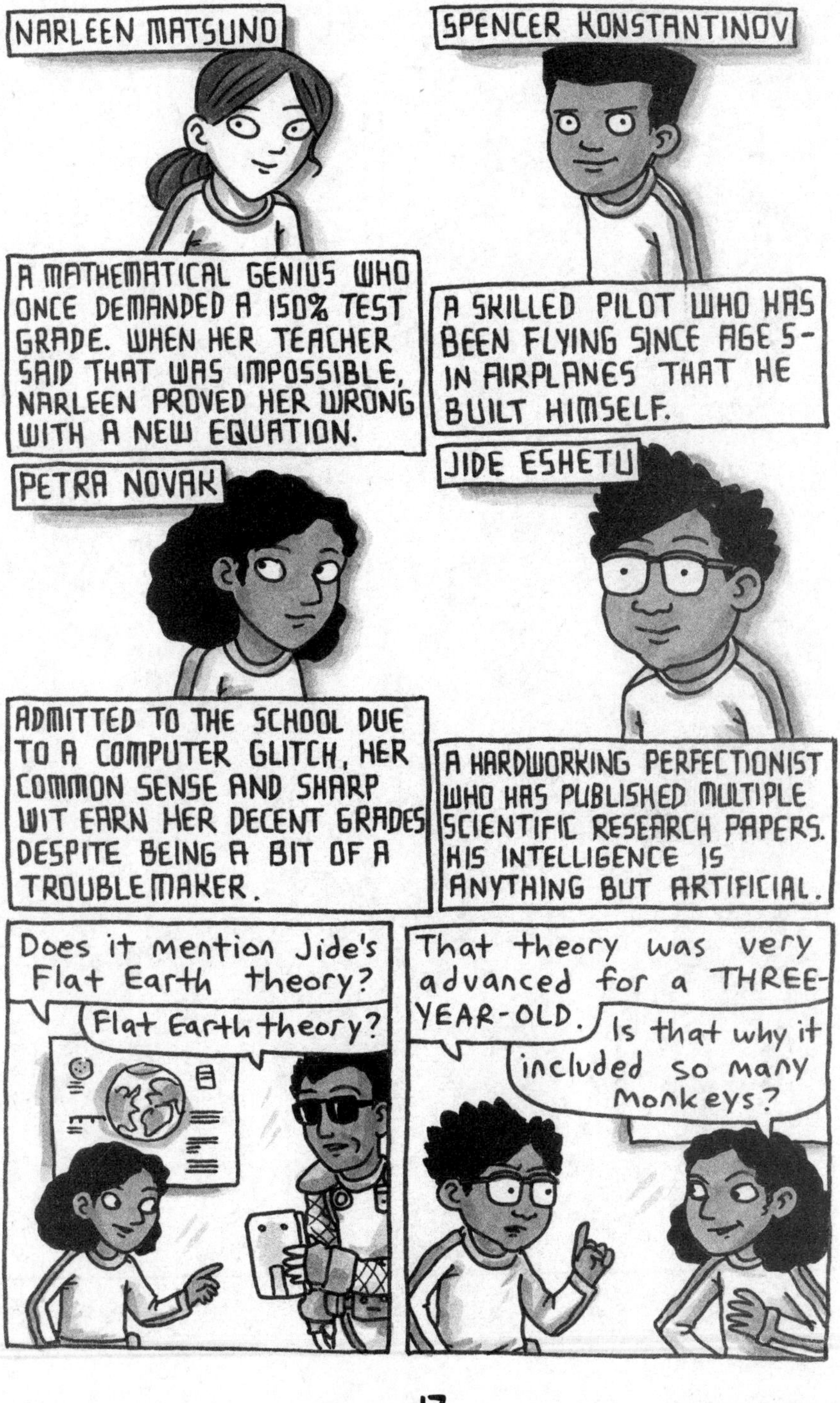
NARLEEN MATSUNO
A MATHEMATICAL GENIUS WHO ONCE DEMANDED A 150% TEST GRADE. WHEN HER TEACHER SAID THAT WAS IMPOSSIBLE, NARLEEN PROVED HER WRONG WITH A NEW EQUATION.
SPENCER KONSTANTINOV
A SKILLED PILOT WHO HAS BEEN FLYING SINCE AGE 5 - IN AIRPLANES THAT HE BUILT HIMSELF.
PETRA NOVAK
ADMITTED TO THE SCHOOL DUE TO A COMPUTER GLITCH, HER COMMON SENSE AND SHARP WIT EARN HER DECENT GRADES DESPITE BEING A BIT OF A TROUBLEMAKER.
JIDE ESHETU
A HARDWORKING PERFECTIONIST WHO HAS PUBLISHED MULTIPLE SCIENTIFIC RESEARCH PAPERS. HIS INTELLIGENCE IS ANYTHING BUT ARTIFICIAL.
Does it mention Jide's Flat Earth theory?
Flat Earth theory?
That theory was very advanced for a THREE-YEAR-OLD.
Is that why it included so many Monkeys?

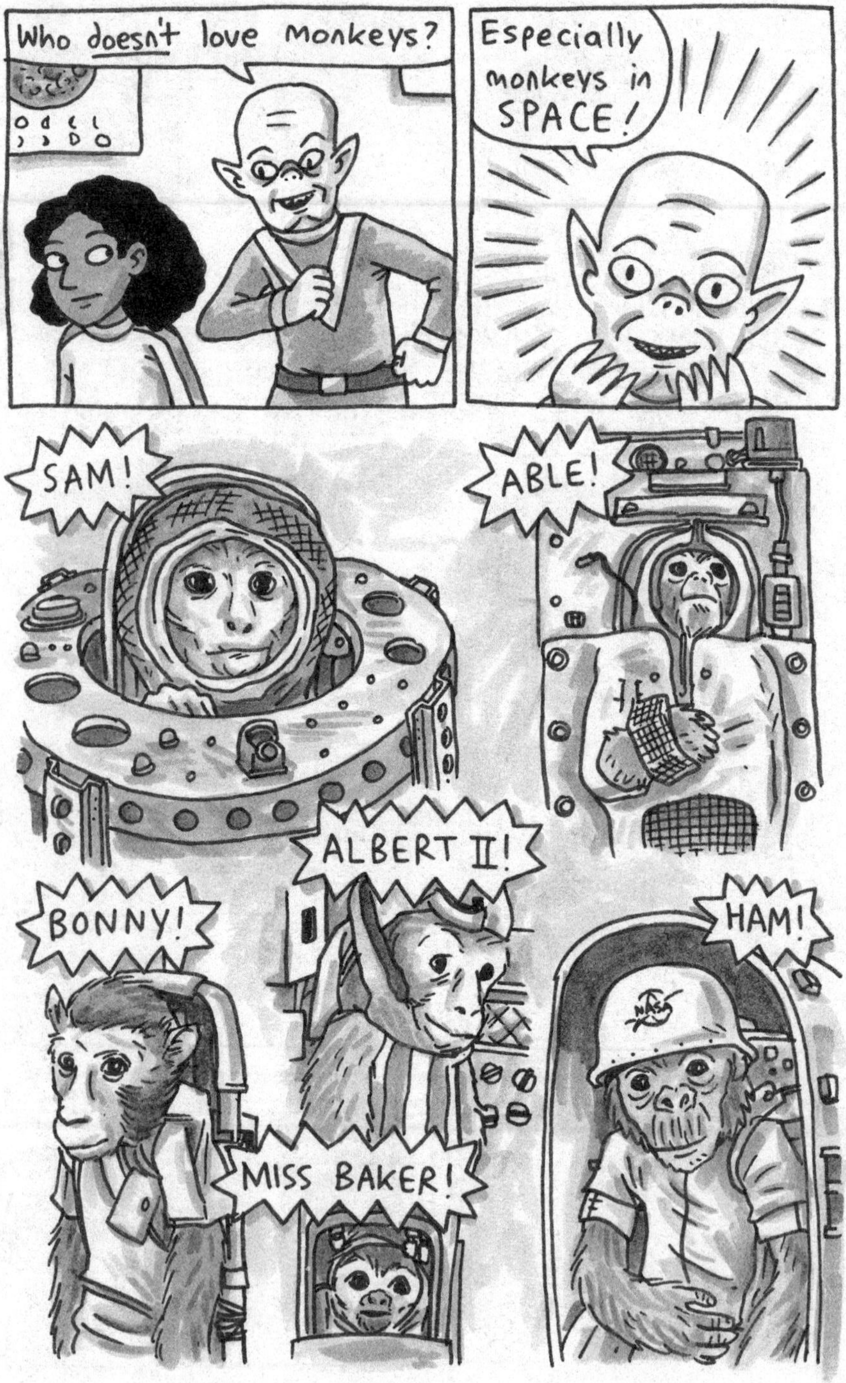
Who doesn't love monkeys?
Especially monkeys in SPACE!
SAM!
ABLE!
ALBERT II!
BONNY!
HAM!
MISS BAKER!

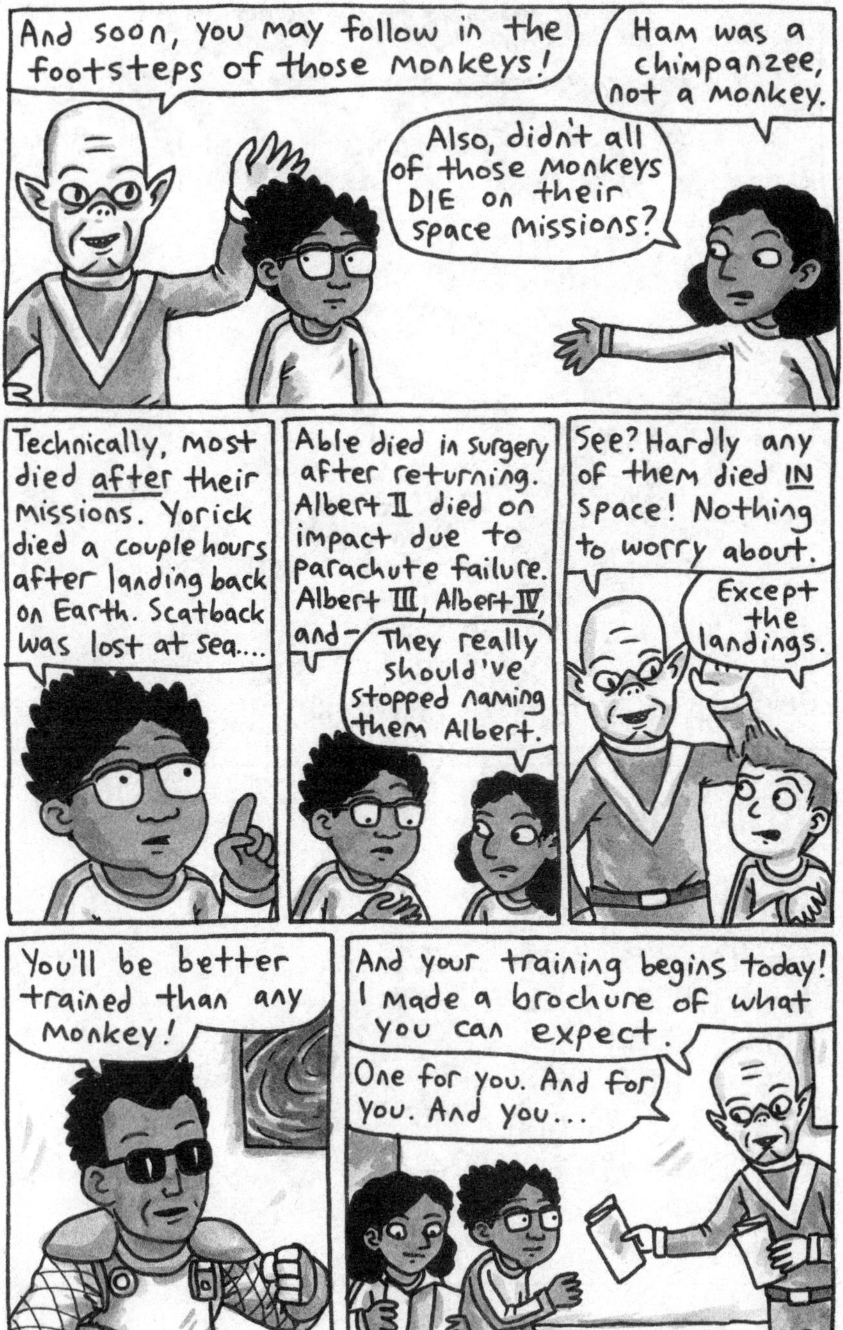
And soon, you may follow in the footsteps of those monkeys!
Ham was a chimpanzee, not a monkey.
Also, didn't all of those monkeys DIE on their space missions?
Technically, most died after their missions. Yorick died a couple hours after landing back on Earth. Scatback was lost at sea....
Able died in surgery after returning. Albert II died on impact due to parachute failure. Albert III, Albert IV, and–
They really should've stopped naming them Albert.
See? Hardly any of them died IN space! Nothing to worry about.
Except the landings.
You'll be better trained than any monkey!
And your training begins today! I made a brochure of what you can expect.
One for you. And for you. And you...

PREPARE TO BE
TESTED!

THE VOMINATOR!

WE STRAP YOU INTO A CHAIR RIGHT AFTER LUNCH AND SPIN YOU AROUND TO SEE HOW LONG YOU CAN GO BEFORE THROWING UP!

MANUAL DEXTERITY CHALLENGE!

YOU MUST UNSCREW THE TINY COVER OF A CONTROL PANEL WHILE WEARING HUGE GLOVES AND SOMEONE IS YELLING AT YOU TO HURRY, "OR WE'RE ALL GOING TO DIE!"

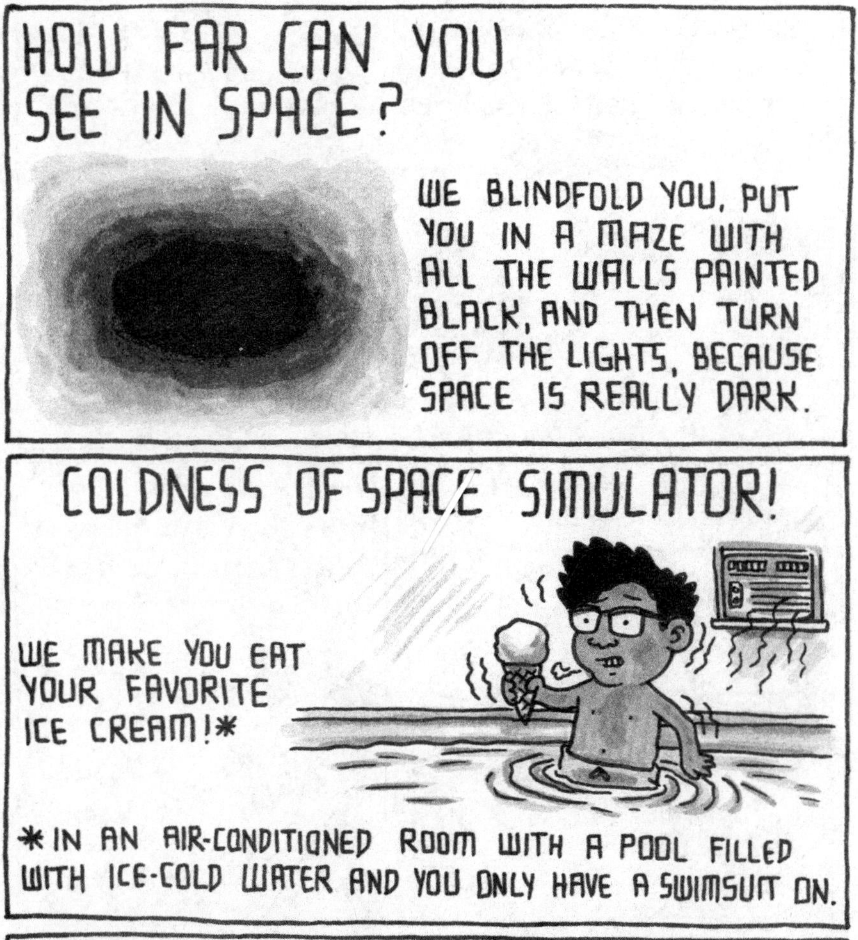
HOW FAR CAN YOU SEE IN SPACE?
WE BLINDFOLD YOU, PUT YOU IN A MAZE WITH ALL THE WALLS PAINTED BLACK, AND THEN TURN OFF THE LIGHTS, BECAUSE SPACE IS REALLY DARK.
COLDNESS OF SPACE SIMULATOR!
WE MAKE YOU EAT YOUR FAVORITE ICE CREAM!*
*IN AN AIR-CONDITIONED ROOM WITH A POOL FILLED WITH ICE-COLD WATER AND YOU ONLY HAVE A SWIMSUIT ON.
ULTIMATE PATIENCE EVALUATOR!
WAIT TIME
2 HOURS
MUCH OF SPACE TRAVEL CAN BE SIMULATED ON ROLLER COASTERS AND OTHER RIDES, SO WE TAKE YOU TO THE WORLD'S BEST, MOST FUN, MOST EXCITING THEME PARK—ON THE BUSIEST DAY WITH THE LONGEST LINES. AND EVERY TIME YOU GET NEAR THE FRONT OF A LINE, YOU HAVE TO GO GET INTO A DIFFERENT LINE.

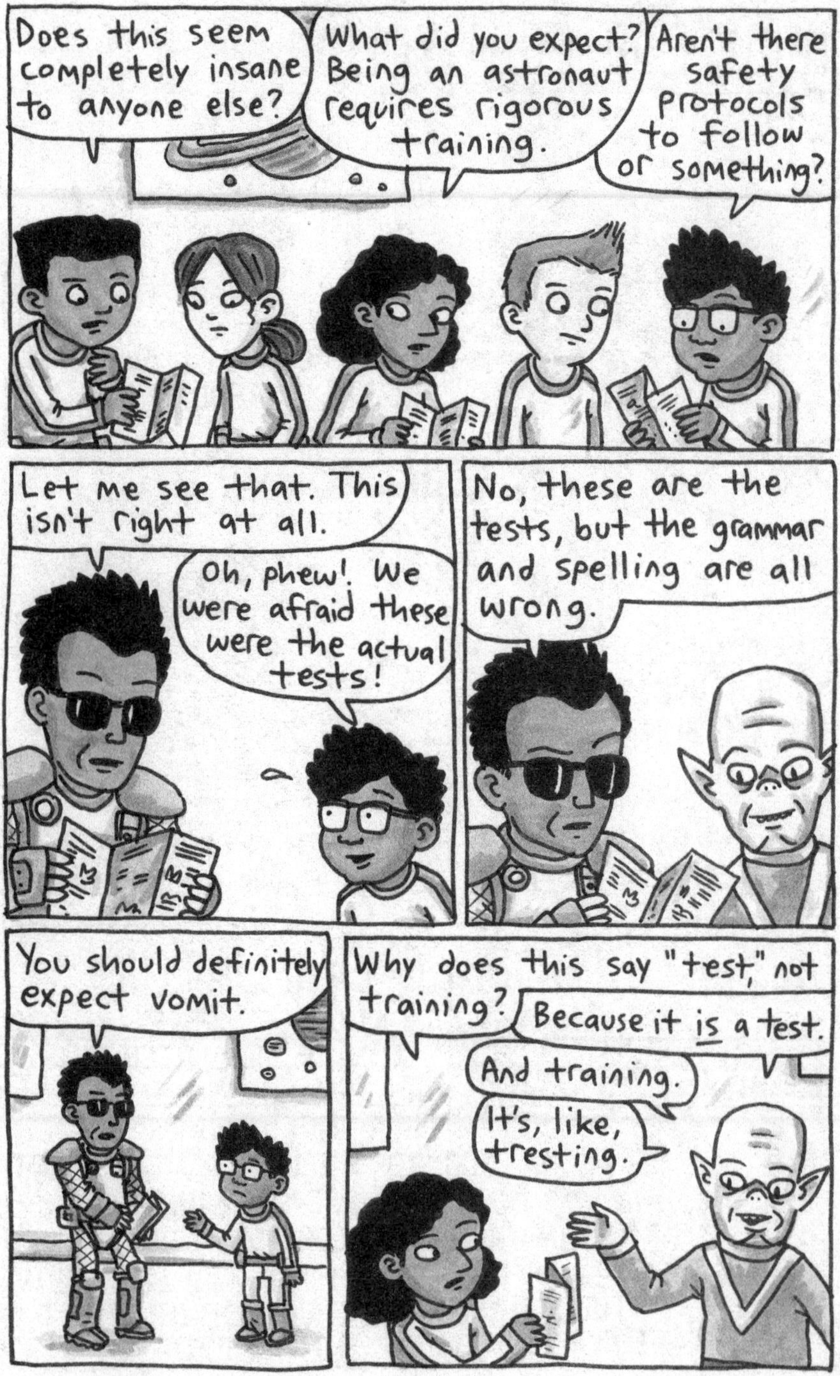
Does this seem completely insane to anyone else?
What did you expect? Being an astronaut requires rigorous training.
Aren't there safety protocols to follow or something?
Let me see that. This isn't right at all.
Oh, phew! We were afraid these were the actual tests!
No, these are the tests, but the grammar and spelling are all wrong.
You should definitely expect vomit.
Why does this say "test," not training?
Because it is a test.
And training.
It's, like, tresting.

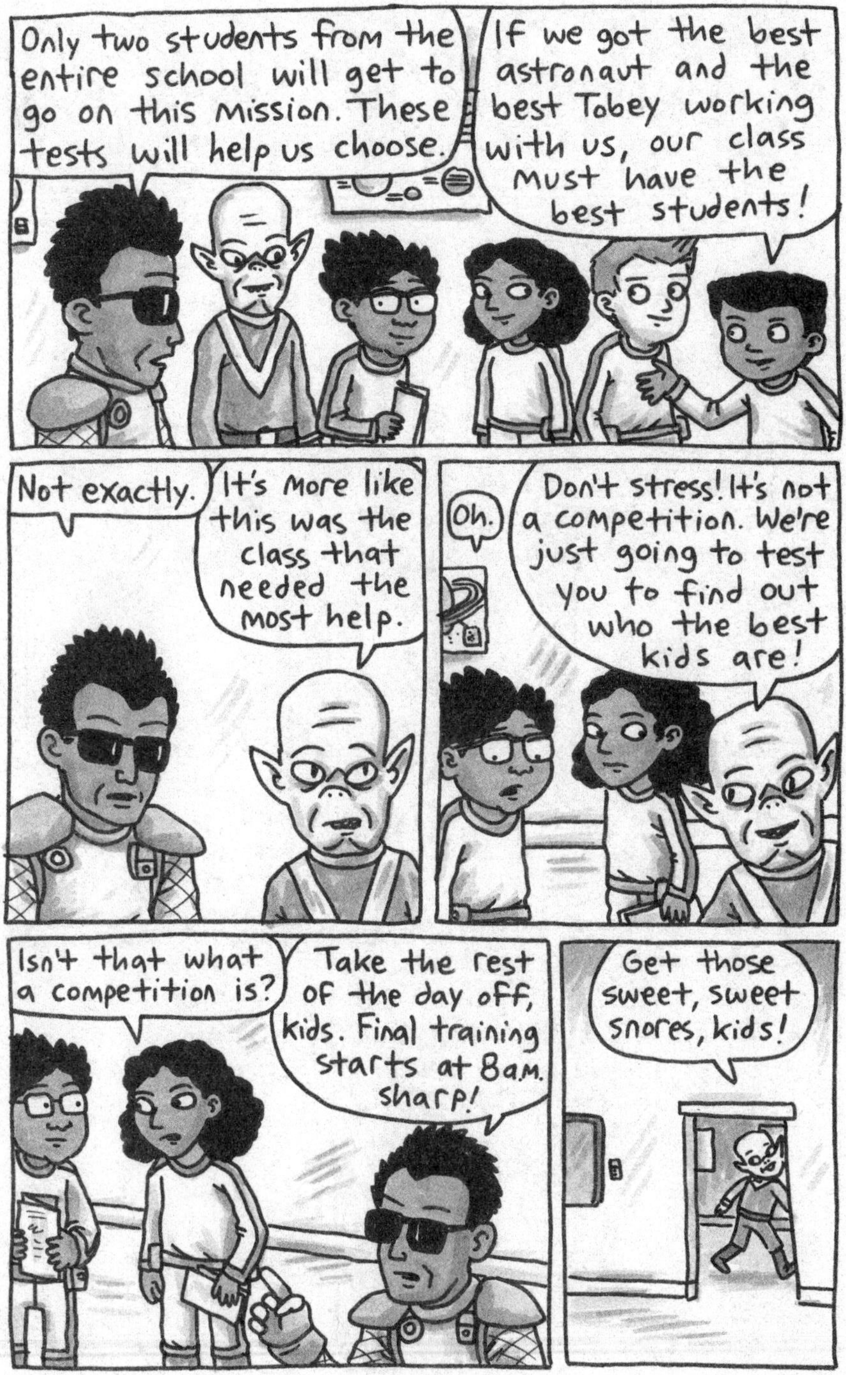
Only two students from the entire school will get to go on this mission. These tests will help us choose.
If we got the best astronaut and the best Tobey working with us, our class must have the best students!
Not exactly.
It's more like this was the class that needed the most help.
Oh.
Don't stress! It's not a competition. We're just going to test you to find out who the best kids are!
Isn't that what a competition is?
Take the rest of the day off, kids. Final training starts at 8 A.M. sharp!
Get those sweet, sweet snores, kids!

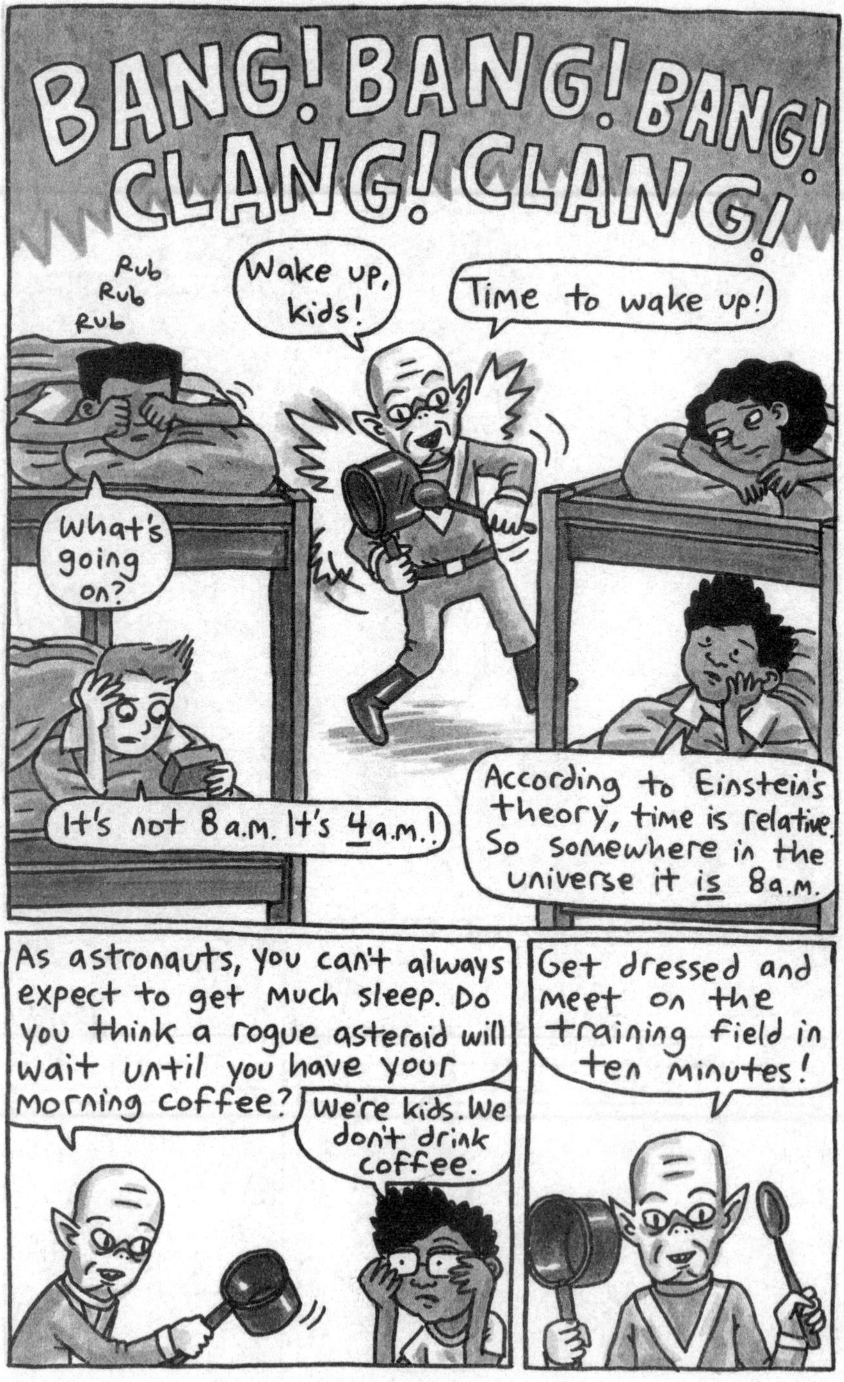
BANG! BANG! BANG!
CLANG! CLANG!
Rub Rub Rub
Wake up, kids!
Time to wake up!
What's going on?
It's not 8 a.m. It's 4 a.m.!
According to Einstein's theory, time is relative. So somewhere in the universe it is 8 a.m.
As astronauts, you can't always expect to get much sleep. Do you think a rogue asteroid will wait until you have your morning coffee?
We're kids. We don't drink coffee.
Get dressed and meet on the training field in ten minutes!

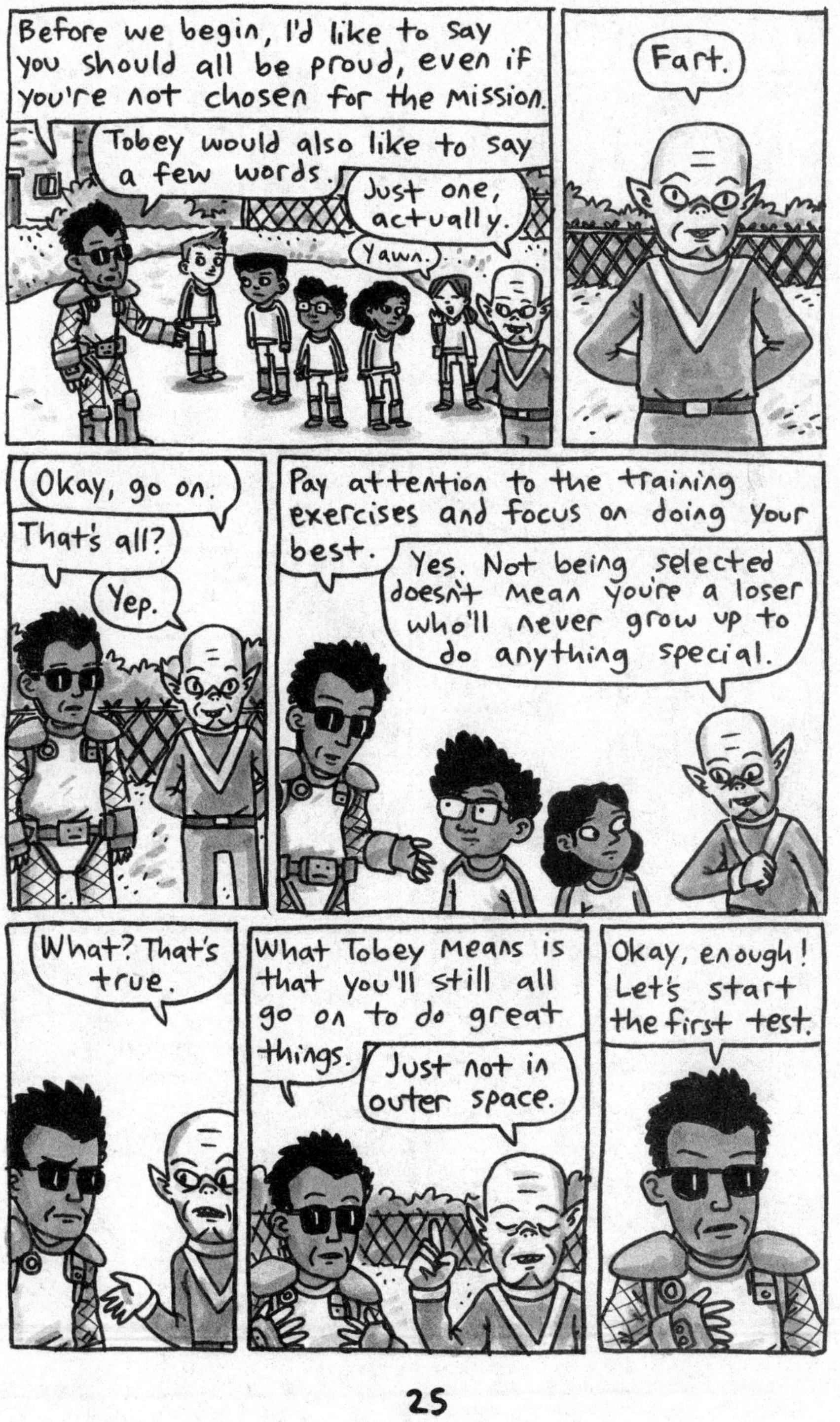
Before we begin, I'd like to say you should all be proud, even if you're not chosen for the mission.
Tobey would also like to say a few words.
Just one, actually.
Yawn.
Fart.
Okay, go on.
That's all?
Yep.
Pay attention to the training exercises and focus on doing your best.
Yes. Not being selected doesn't mean you're a loser who'll never grow up to do anything special.
What? That's true.
What Tobey means is that you'll still all go on to do great things.
Just not in outer space.
Okay, enough! Let's start the first test.

TEST #1: WHAT'S IN THE BOX? YOU ARE!

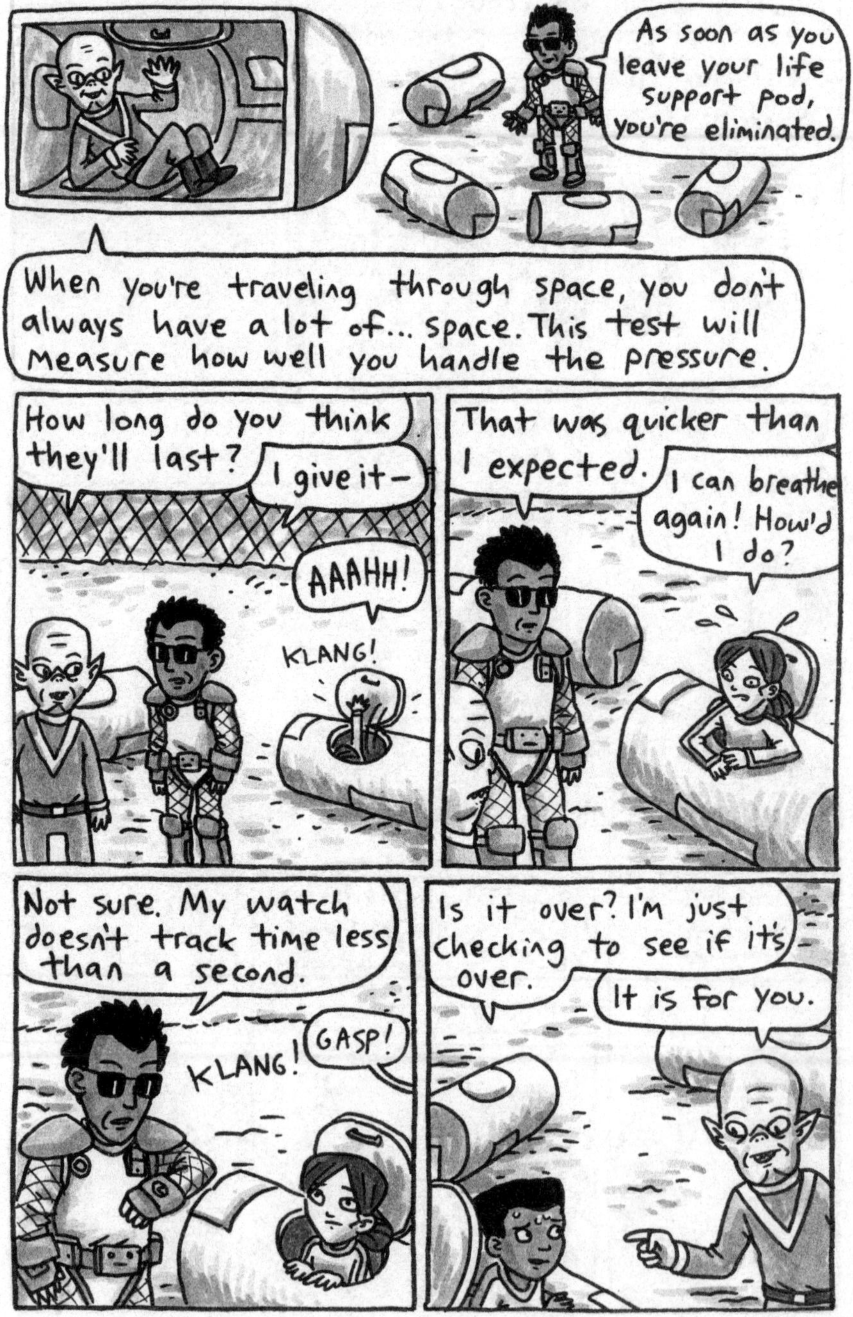
As soon as you leave your life support pod, you're eliminated.
When you're traveling through space, you don't always have a lot of... space. This test will measure how well you handle the pressure.
How long do you think they'll last?
I give it—
AAAHH!
KLANG!
That was quicker than I expected.
I can breathe again! How'd I do?
Not sure. My watch doesn't track time less than a second.
KLANG!
GASP!
Is it over? I'm just checking to see if it's over.
It is for you.

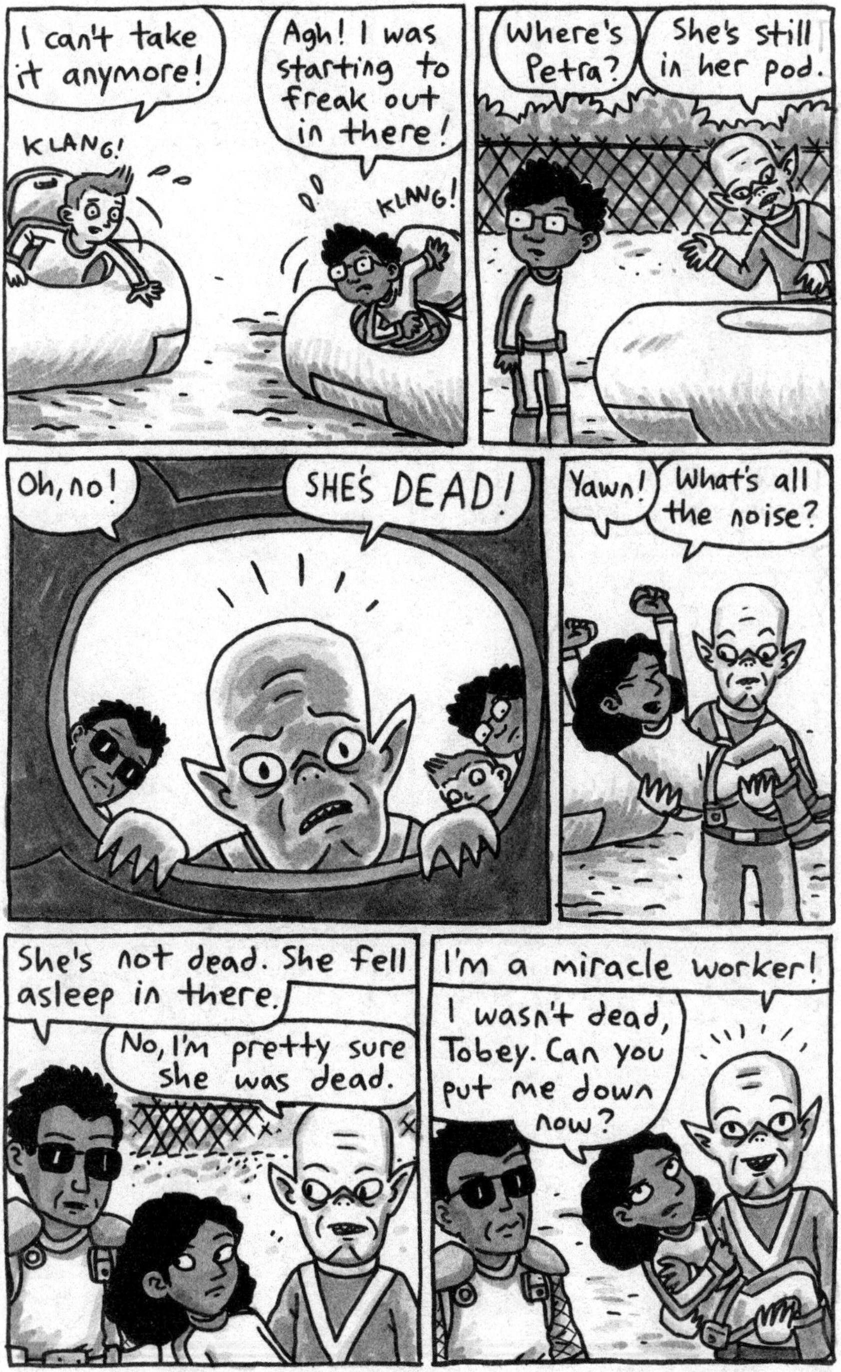
I can't take it anymore!
KLANG!
Agh! I was starting to freak out in there!
KLANG!
Where's Petra?
She's still in her pod.
Oh, no!
SHE'S DEAD!
Yawn!
What's all the noise?
She's not dead. She fell asleep in there.
No, I'm pretty sure she was dead.
I'm a miracle worker!
I wasn't dead, Tobey. Can you put me down now?

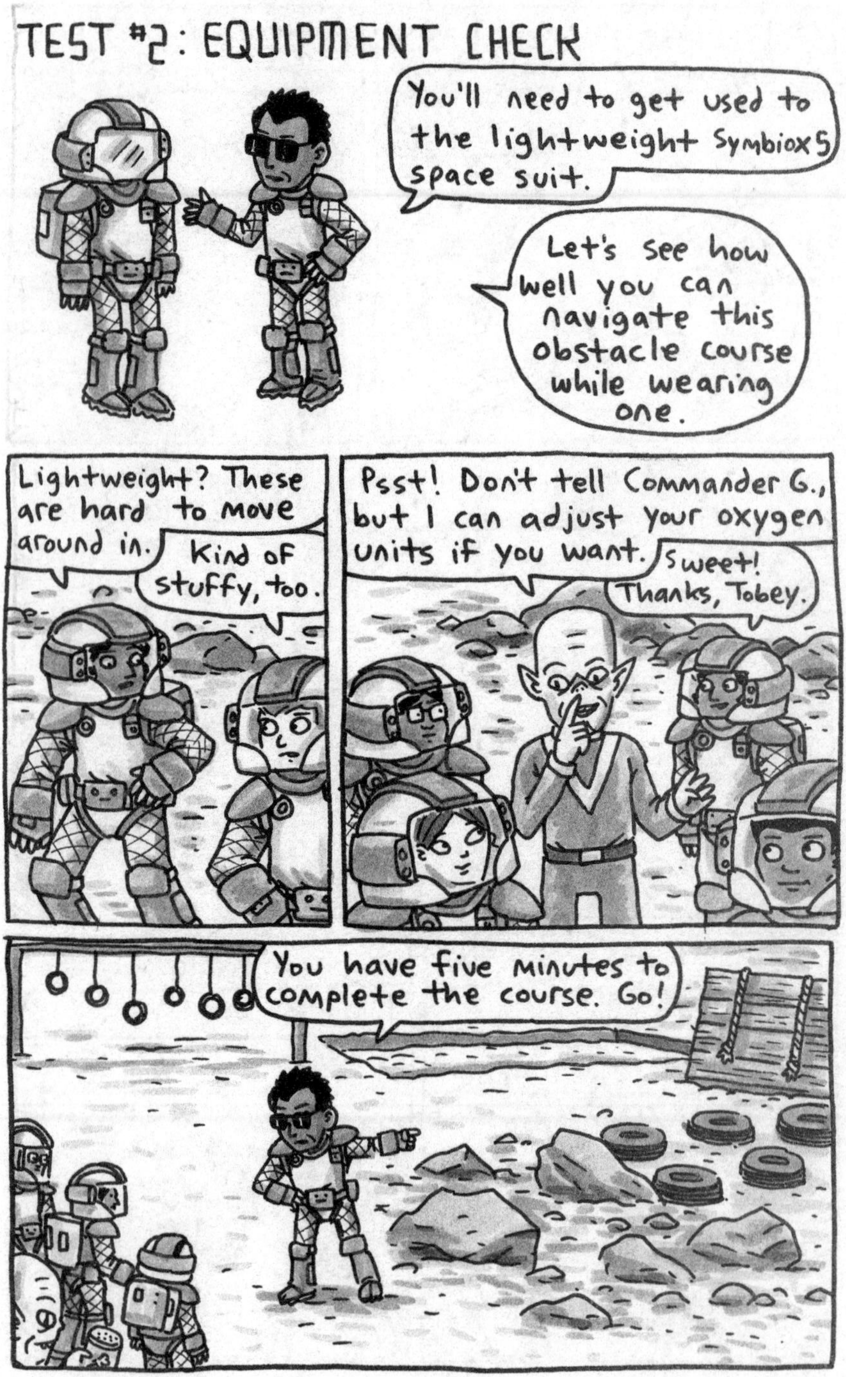
TEST #2: EQUIPMENT CHECK
You'll need to get used to the lightweight Symbiox 5 space suit.
Let's see how well you can navigate this obstacle course while wearing one.
Lightweight? These are hard to move around in.
Kind of stuffy, too.
Psst! Don't tell Commander G., but I can adjust your oxygen units if you want.
Sweet! Thanks, Tobey.
You have five minutes to complete the course. Go!

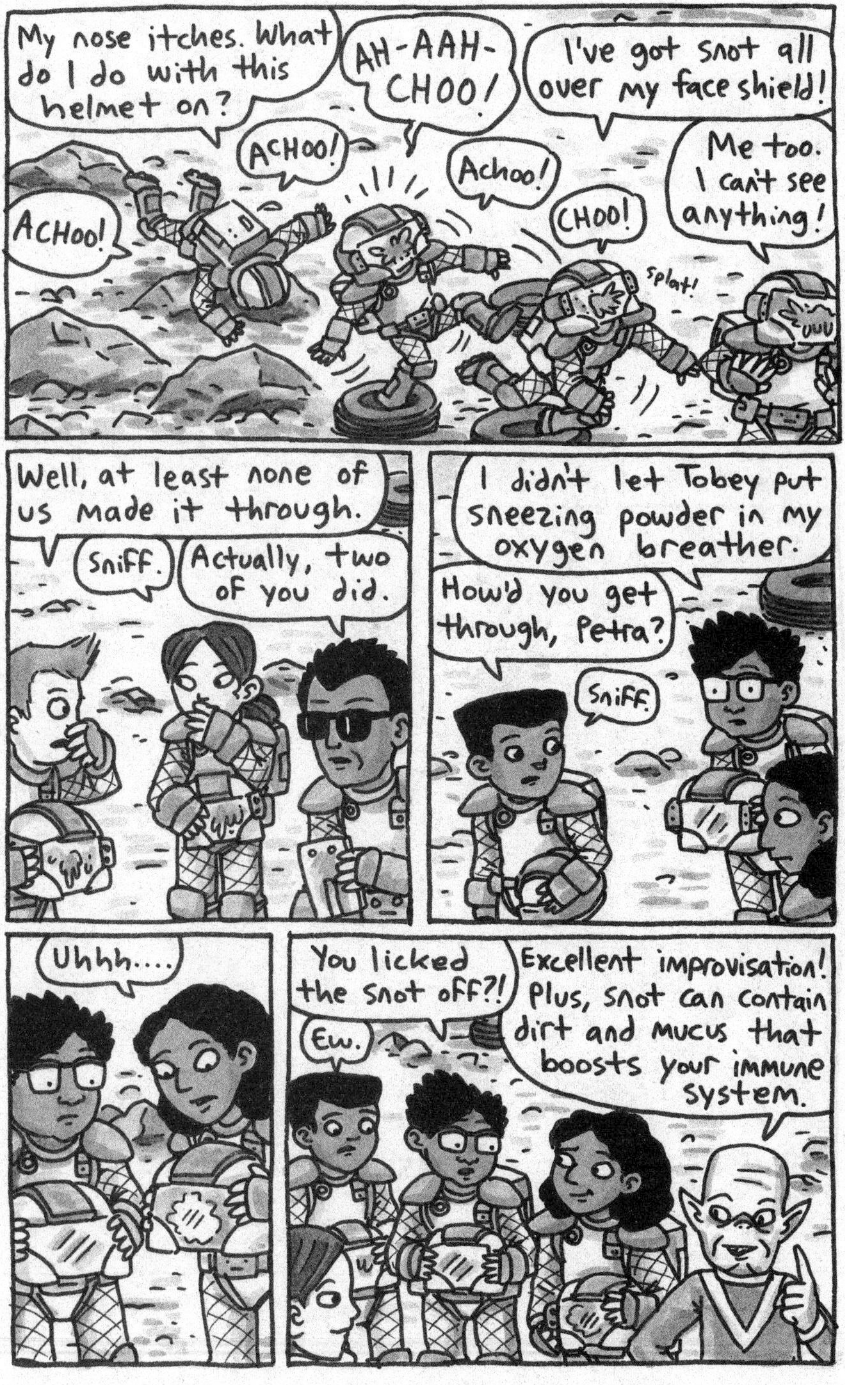
My nose itches. What do I do with this helmet on?
AH-AAH-CHOO!
I've got snot all over my face shield!
ACHOO!
ACHOO!
Achoo!
CHOO!
Me too. I can't see anything!
splat!
Well, at least none of us made it through.
Sniff.
Actually, two of you did.
I didn't let Tobey put sneezing powder in my oxygen breather.
How'd you get through, Petra?
Sniff.
Uhhh....
You licked the snot off?!
Ew.
Excellent improvisation! Plus, snot can contain dirt and mucus that boosts your immune system.

TEST #3: UNDER WHERE? UNDER WATER!

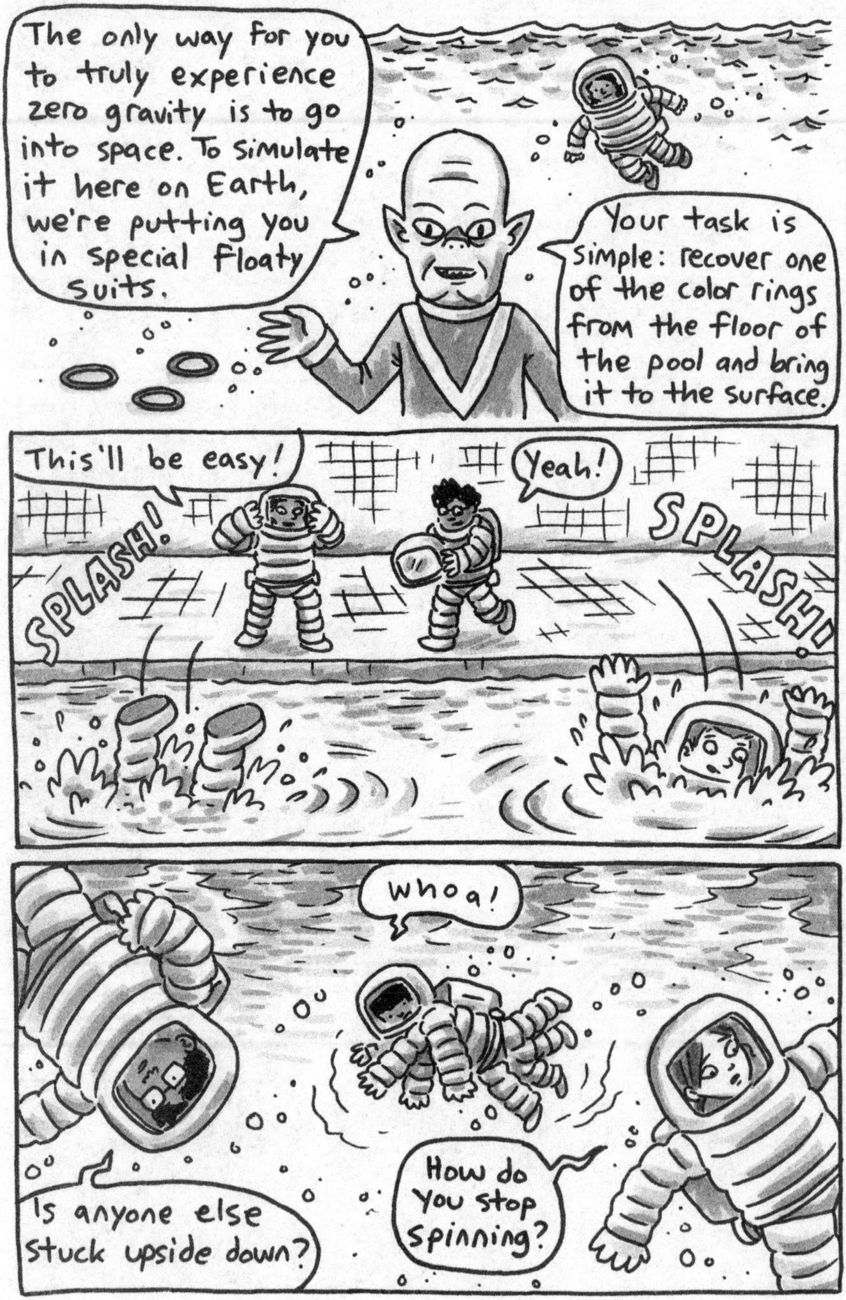
The only way for you to truly experience zero gravity is to go into space. To simulate it here on Earth, we're putting you in special floaty suits.
Your task is simple: recover one of the color rings from the floor of the pool and bring it to the surface.
This'll be easy!
Yeah!
SPLASH!
SPLASH!
Whoa!
Is anyone else stuck upside down?
How do you stop spinning?

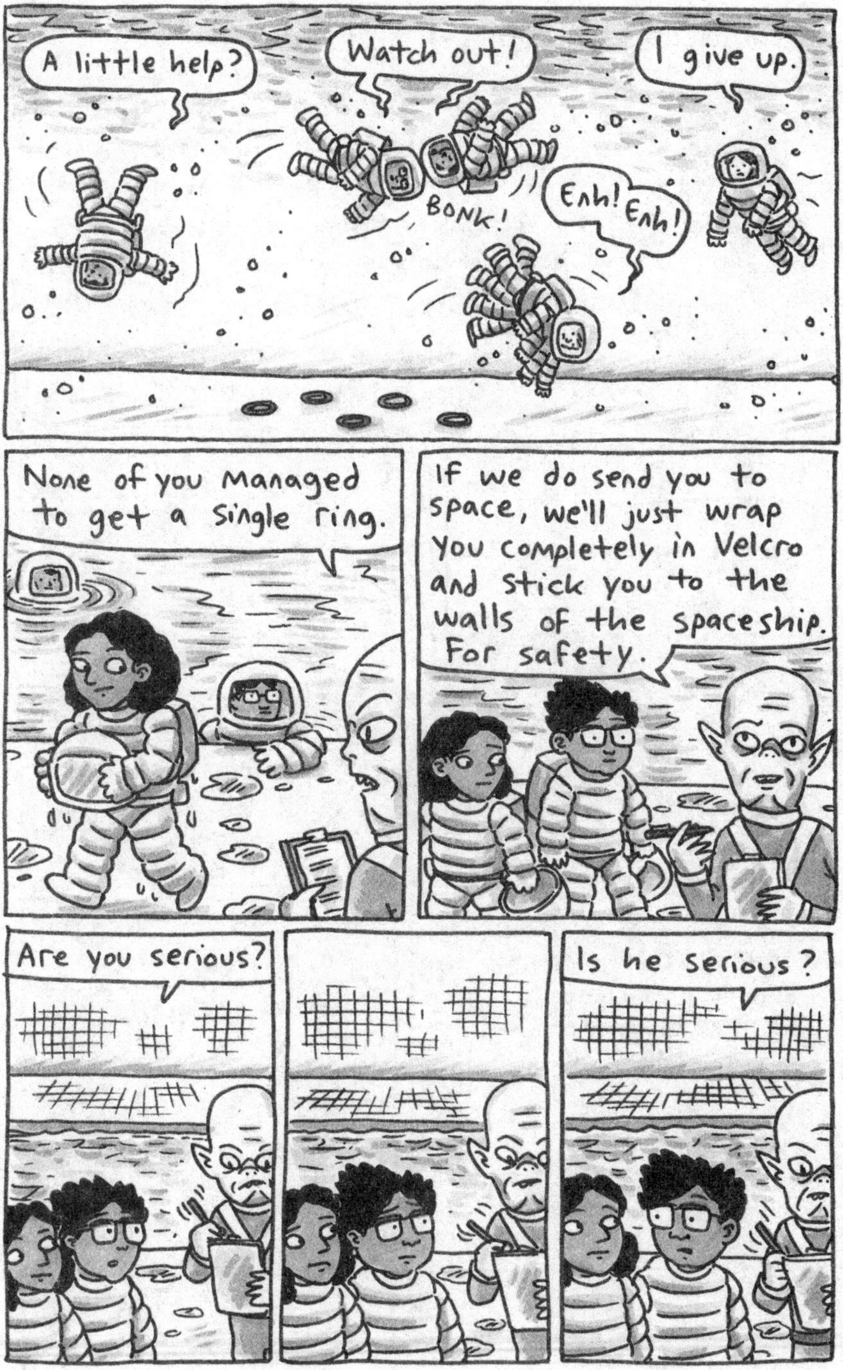
A little help?
Watch out!
I give up.
BONK!
Enh! Enh!
None of you managed to get a single ring.
If we do send you to space, we'll just wrap you completely in Velcro and stick you to the walls of the spaceship. For safety.
Are you serious?
Is he serious?

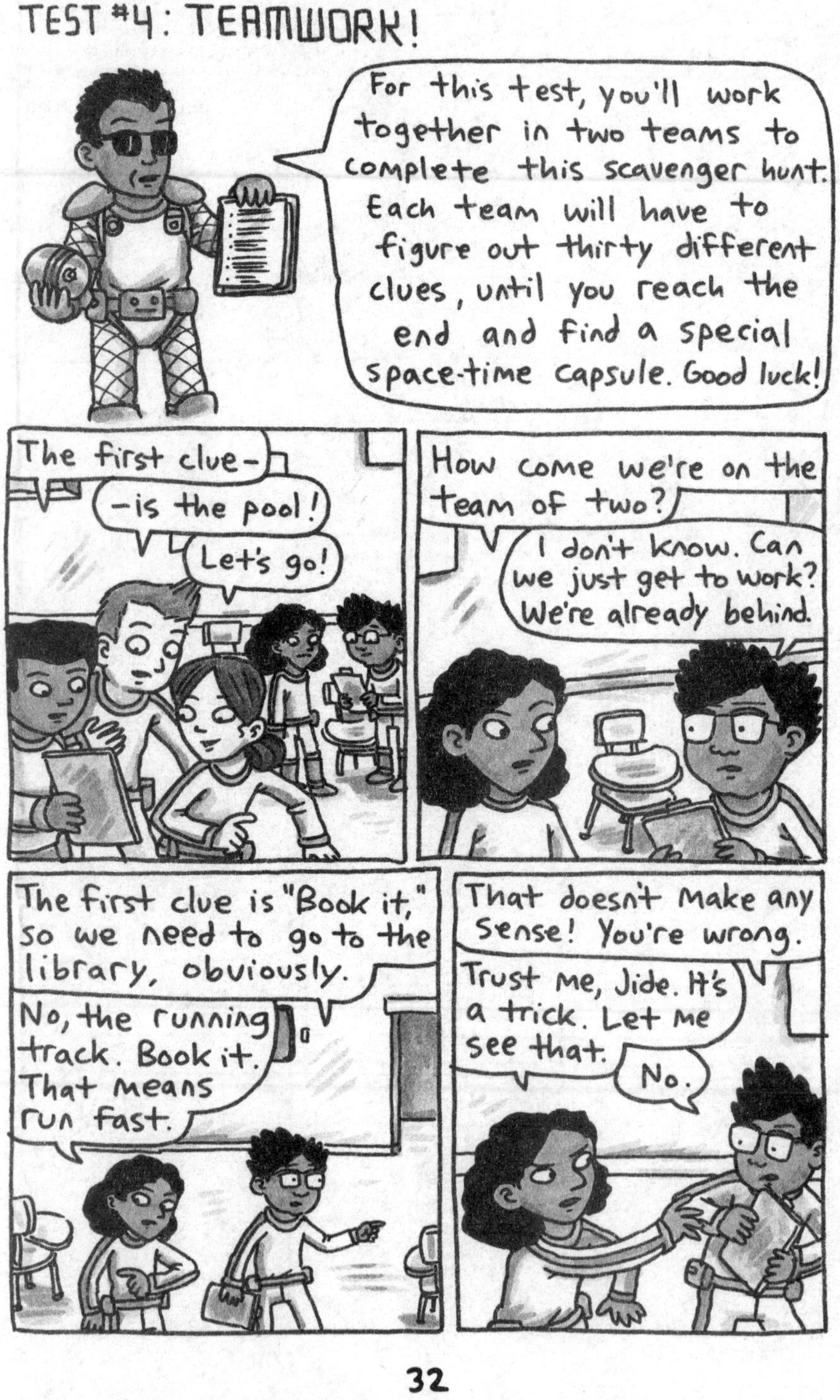
TEST #4: TEAMWORK!
For this test, you'll work together in two teams to complete this scavenger hunt. Each team will have to figure out thirty different clues, until you reach the end and find a special space-time capsule. Good luck!
The first clue-
-is the pool!
Let's go!
How come we're on the team of two?
I don't know. Can we just get to work? We're already behind.
The first clue is "Book it," so we need to go to the library, obviously.
No, the running track. Book it. That means run fast.
That doesn't make any sense! You're wrong.
Trust me, Jide. It's a trick. Let me see that.
No.

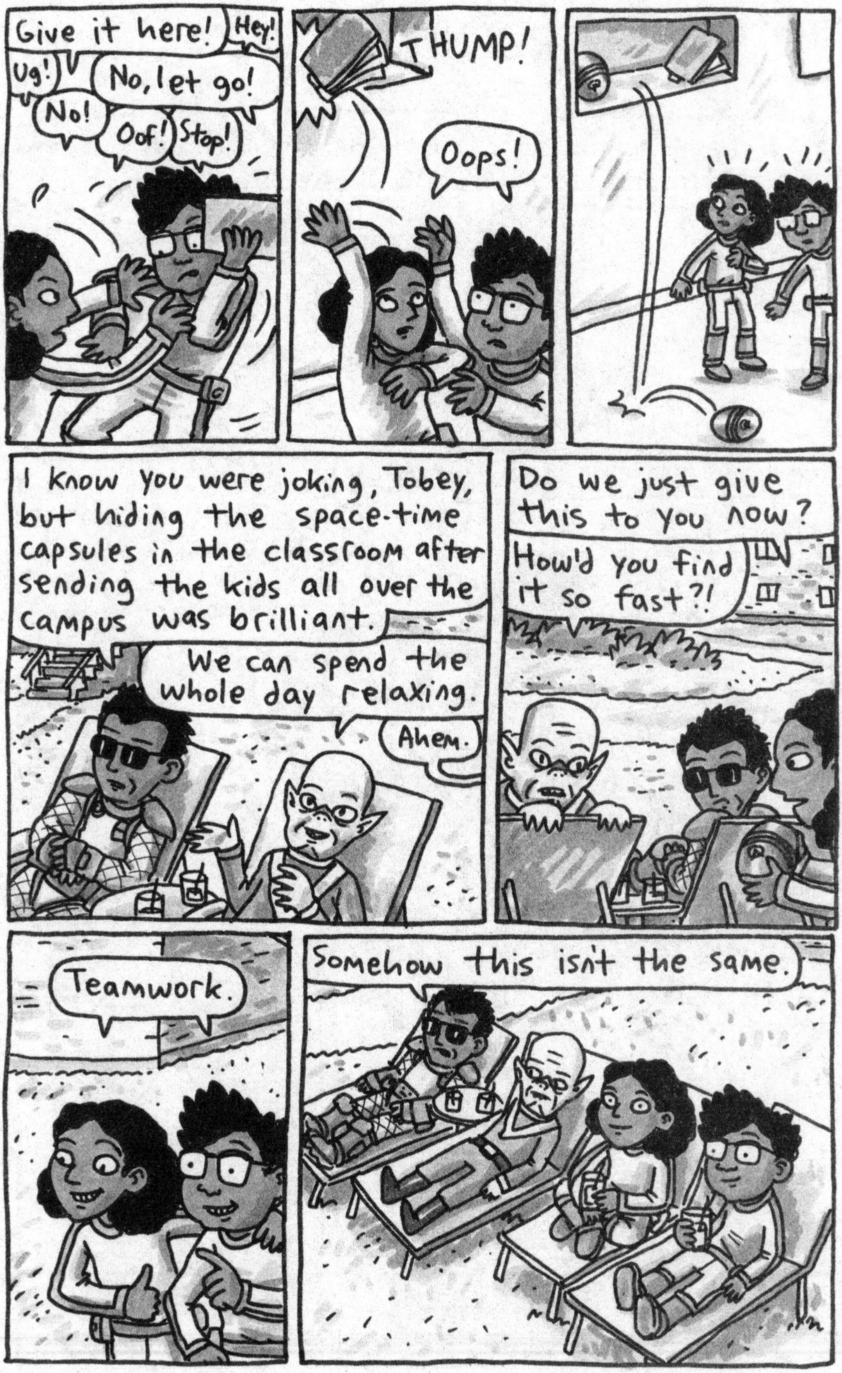
Give it here!
Hey!
Ug!
No, let go!
No!
Oof!
Stop!
THUMP!
Oops!
I know you were joking, Tobey, but hiding the space-time capsules in the classroom after sending the kids all over the campus was brilliant.
We can spend the whole day relaxing.
Ahem.
Do we just give this to you now?
How'd you find it so fast?!
Teamwork.
Somehow this isn't the same.

TEST #5: ASTROPHYSICS!

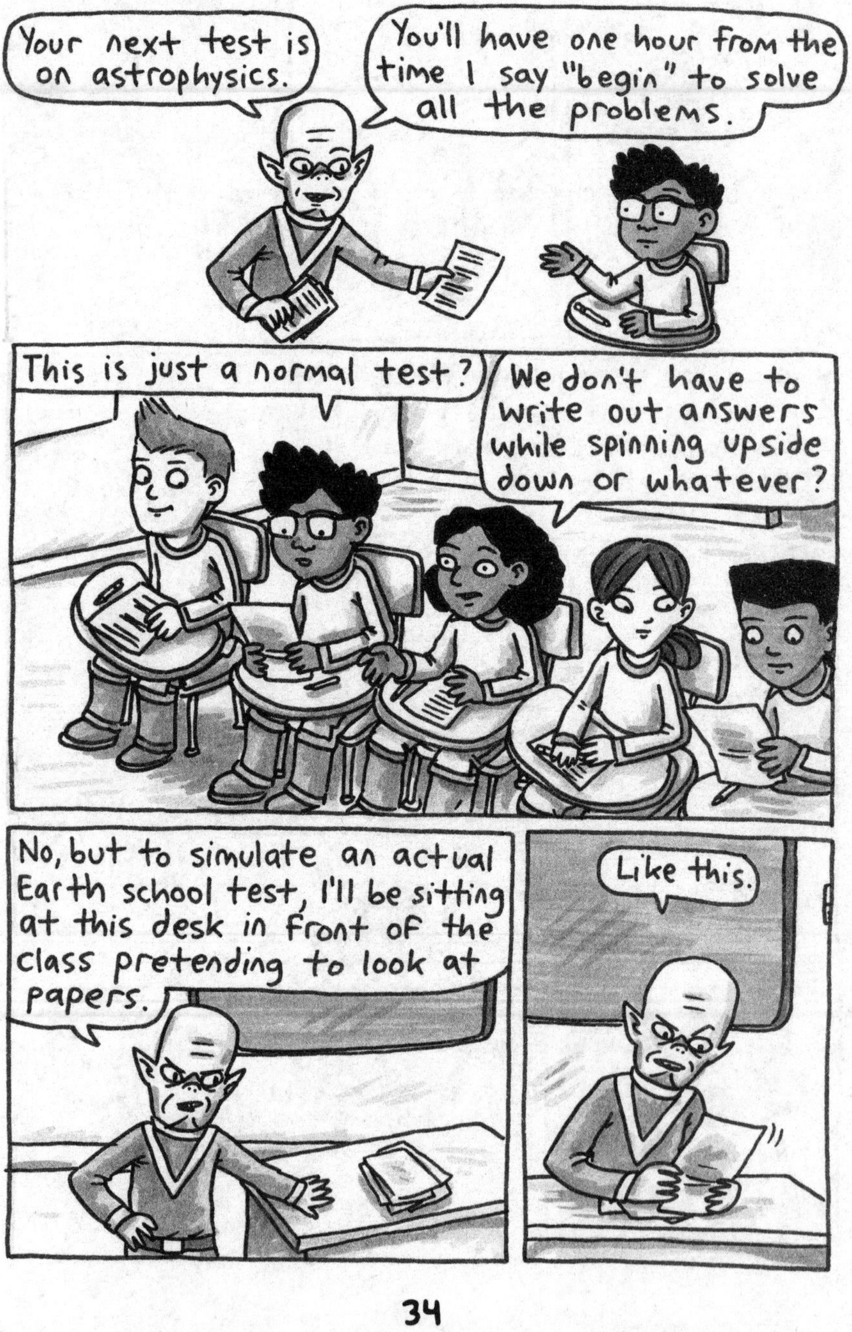
Your next test is on astrophysics.
You'll have one hour from the time I say "begin" to solve all the problems.
This is just a normal test?
We don't have to write out answers while spinning upside down or whatever?
No, but to simulate an actual Earth school test, I'll be sitting at this desk in front of the class pretending to look at papers.
Like this.

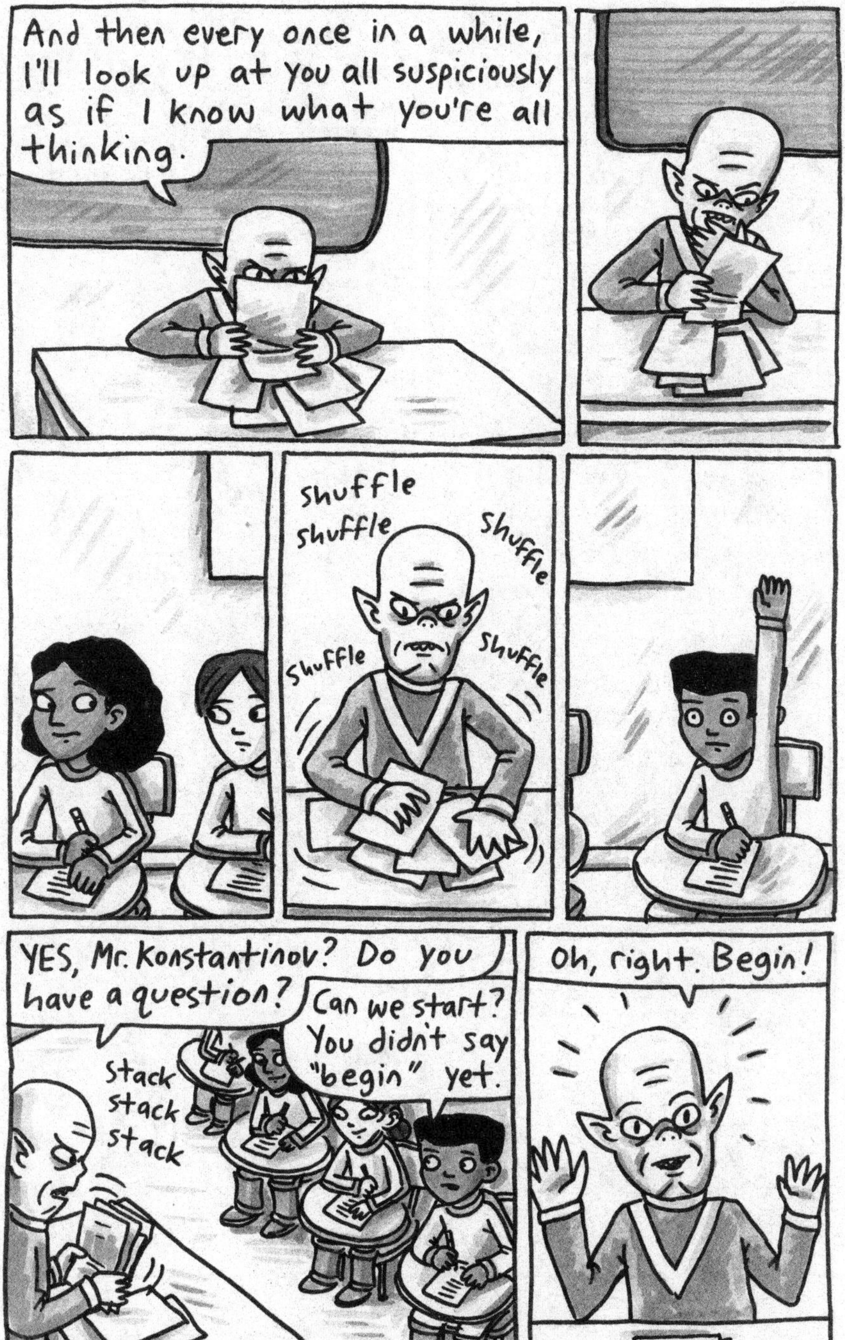
And then every once in a while, I'll look up at you all suspiciously as if I know what you're all thinking.
shuffle
shuffle
Shuffle
Shuffle
Shuffle
YES, Mr. Konstantinov? Do you have a question?
Stack
stack
stack
Can we start? You didn't say "begin" yet.
Oh, right. Begin!

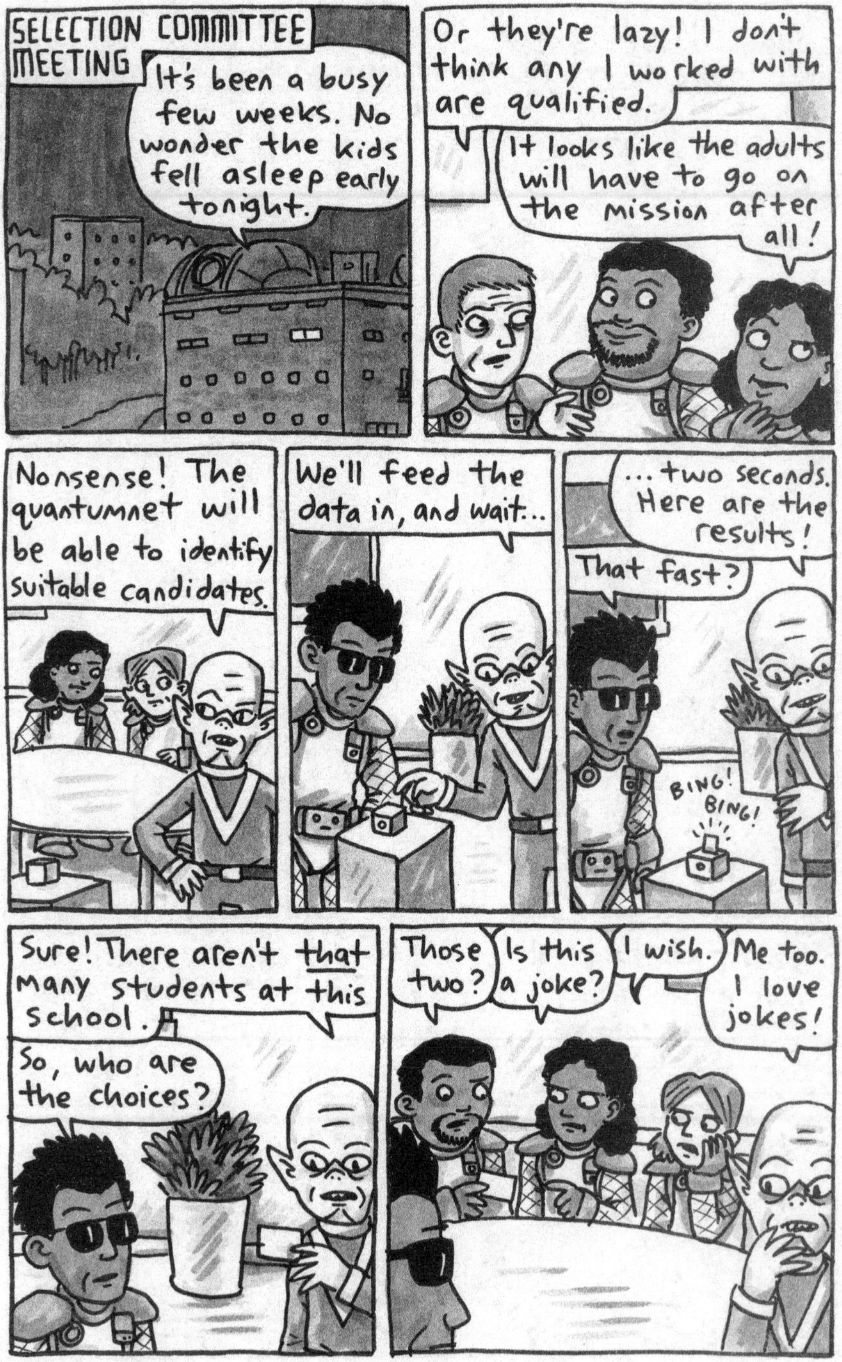
SELECTION COMMITTEE MEETING
It's been a busy few weeks. No wonder the kids fell asleep early tonight.
Or they're lazy! I don't think any I worked with are qualified.
It looks like the adults will have to go on the mission after all!
Nonsense! The quantumnet will be able to identify suitable candidates.
We'll feed the data in, and wait...
...two seconds. Here are the results!
That fast?
BING! BING!
Sure! There aren't that many students at this school.
So, who are the choices?
Those two?
Is this a joke?
I wish.
Me too. I love jokes!

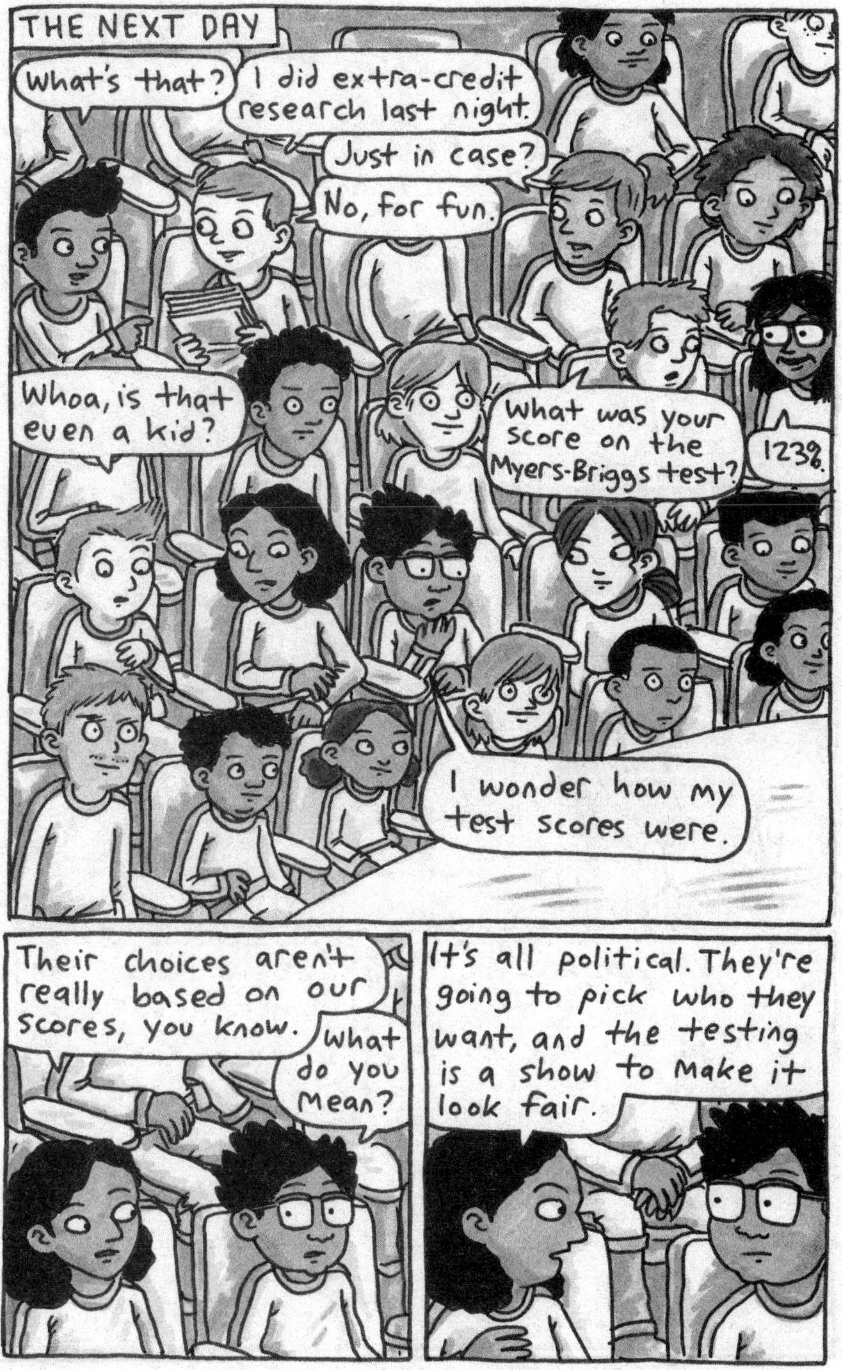
THE NEXT DAY
What's that?
I did extra-credit research last night.
Just in case?
No, for fun.
Whoa, is that even a kid?
What was your score on the Myers-Briggs test?
123%.
I wonder how my test scores were.
Their choices aren't really based on our scores, you know.
What do you mean?
It's all political. They're going to pick who they want, and the testing is a show to make it look fair.

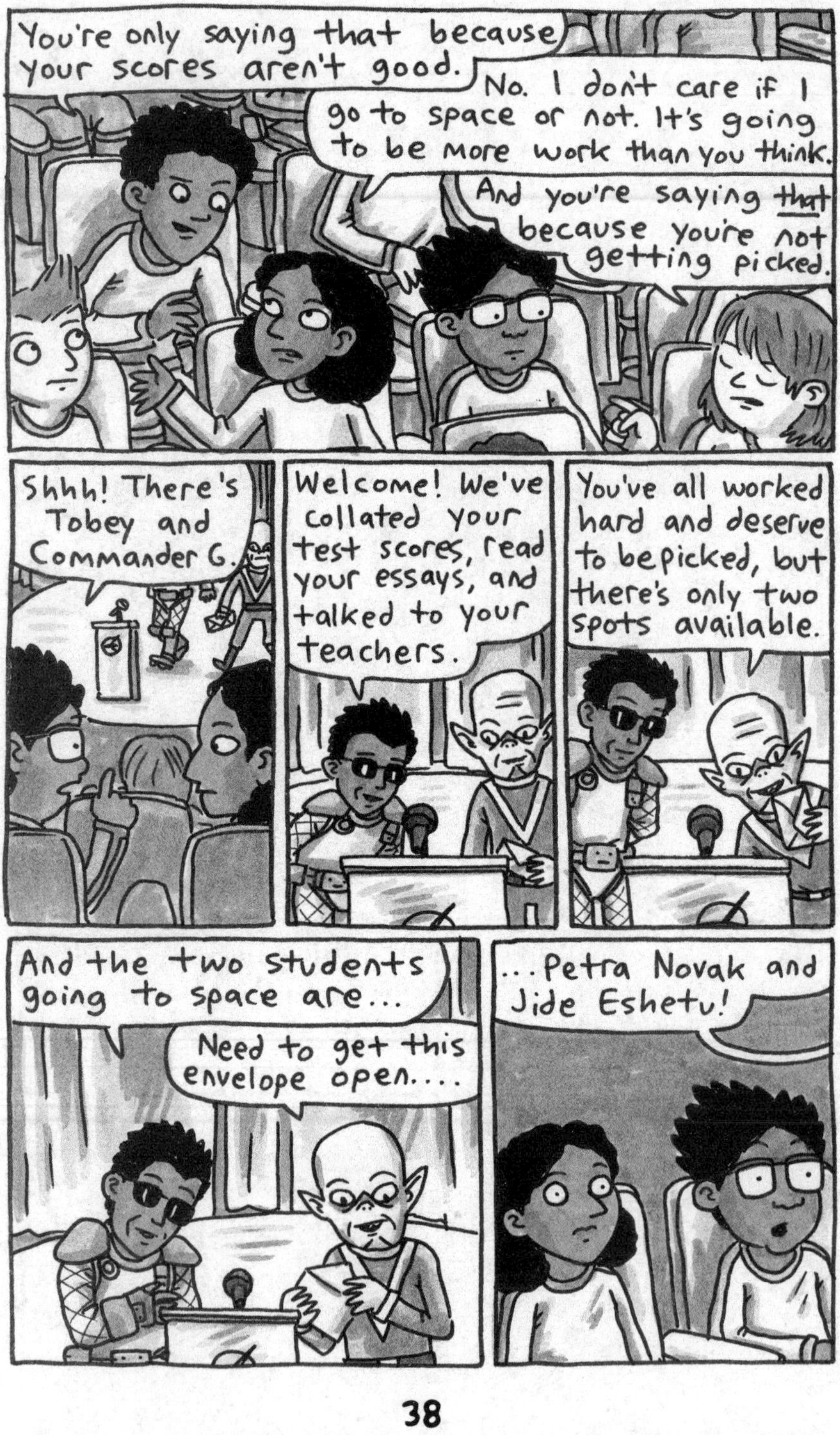
You're only saying that because your scores aren't good.
No. I don't care if I go to space or not. It's going to be more work than you think.
And you're saying that because you're not getting picked.
Shhh! There's Tobey and Commander G.
Welcome! We've collated your test scores, read your essays, and talked to your teachers.
You've all worked hard and deserve to be picked, but there's only two spots available.
And the two students going to space are...
Need to get this envelope open....
...Petra Novak and Jide Eshetu!

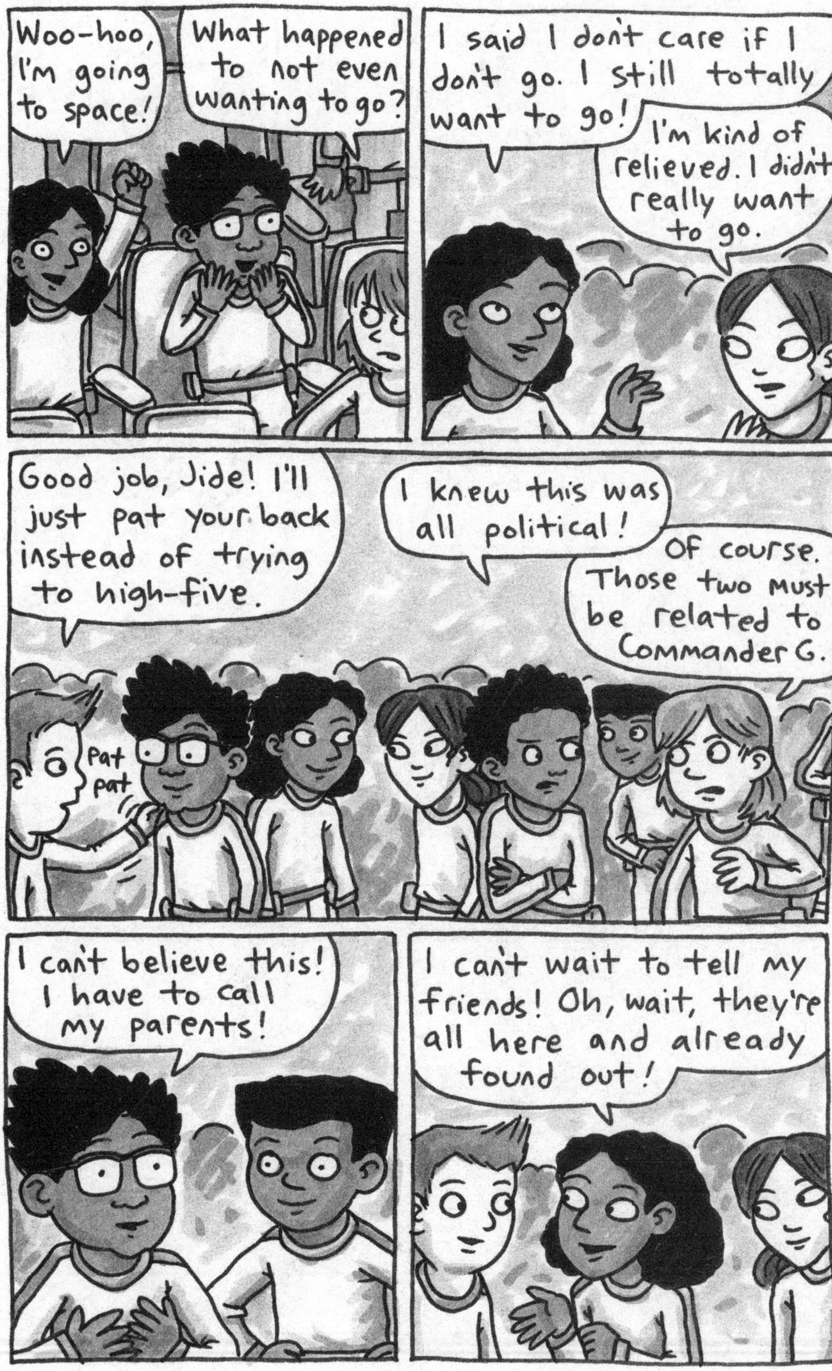
Woo-hoo, I'm going to space!
What happened to not even wanting to go?
I said I don't care if I don't go. I still totally want to go!
I'm kind of relieved. I didn't really want to go.
Good job, Jide! I'll just pat your back instead of trying to high-five.
Pat pat
I knew this was all political!
Of course. Those two must be related to Commander G.
I can't believe this! I have to call my parents!
I can't wait to tell my friends! Oh, wait, they're all here and already found out!

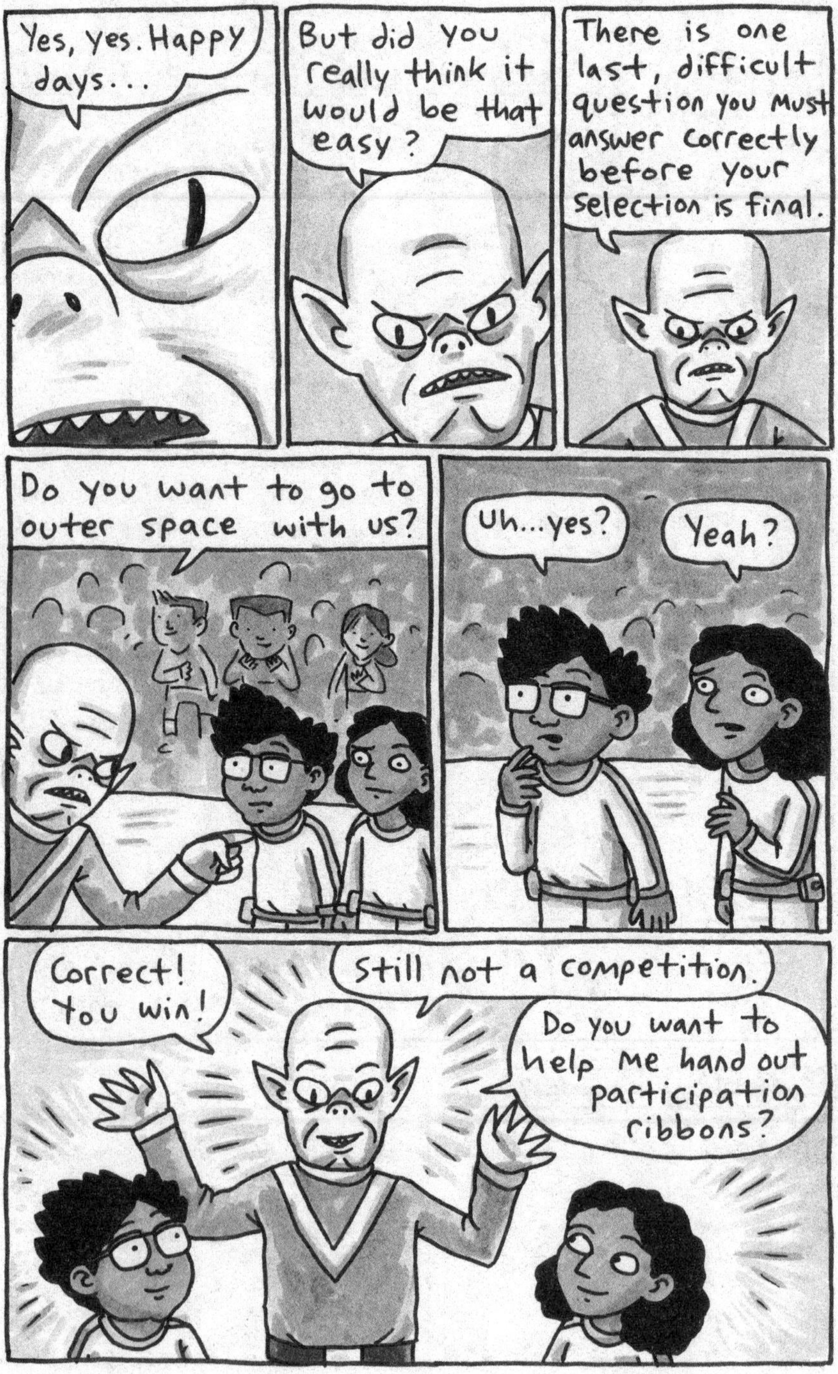
Yes, yes. Happy days...
But did you really think it would be that easy?
There is one last, difficult question you must answer correctly before your selection is final.
Do you want to go to outer space with us?
Uh...yes?
Yeah?
Correct! You win!
Still not a competition.
Do you want to help me hand out participation ribbons?

MARS, OUR DESTINATION!

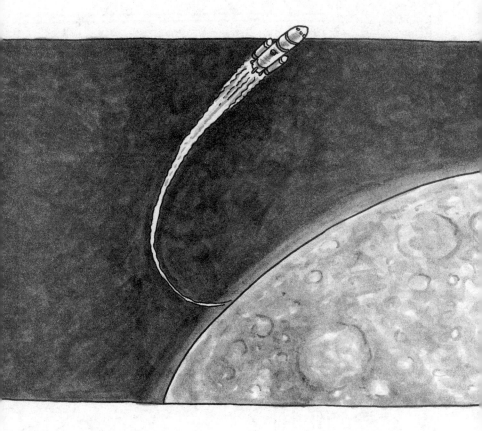

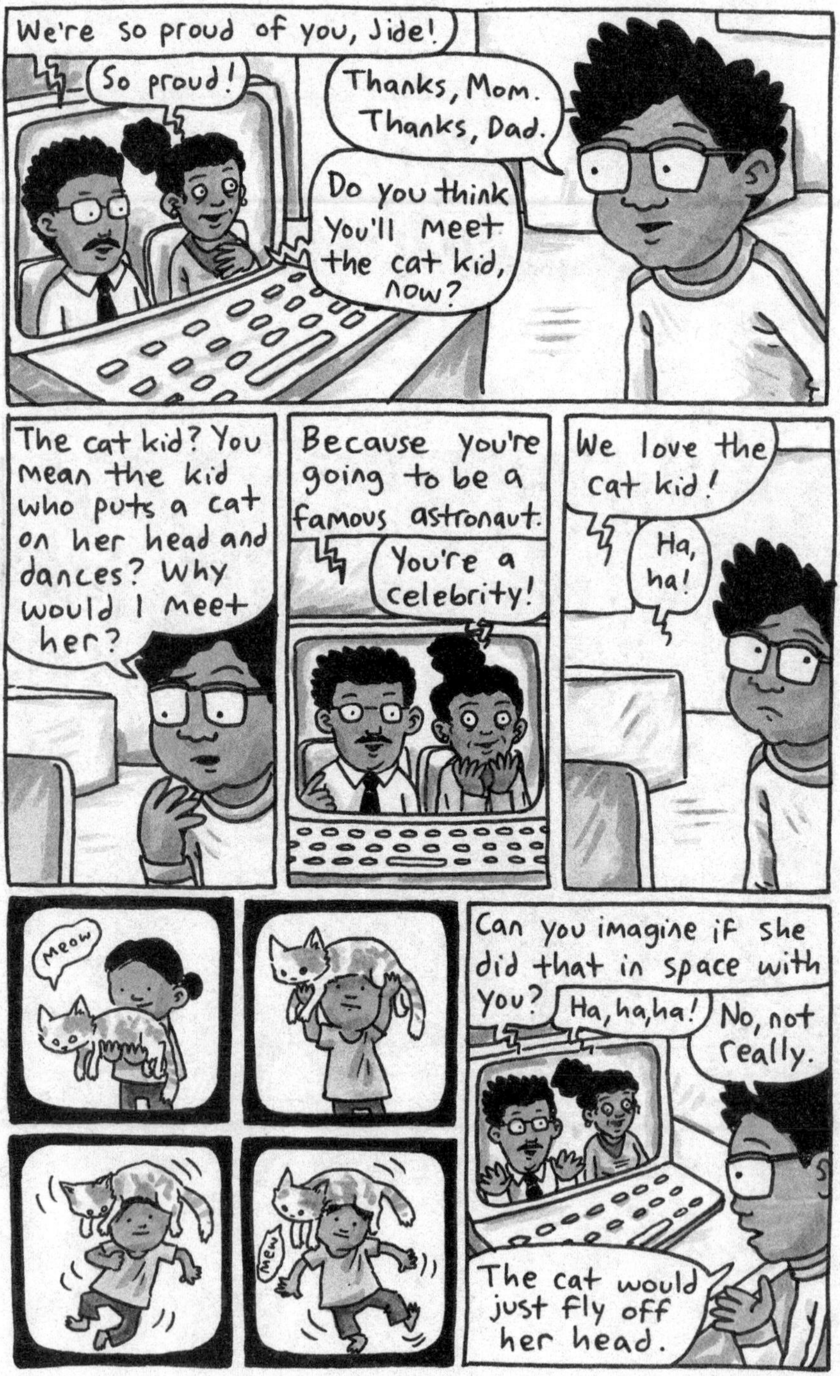
We're so proud of you, Jide!
So proud!
Thanks, Mom. Thanks, Dad.
Do you think you'll meet the cat kid, now?
The cat kid? You mean the kid who puts a cat on her head and dances? Why would I meet her?
Because you're going to be a famous astronaut.
You're a celebrity!
We love the cat kid!
Ha, ha!
MEOW
MEW
Can you imagine if she did that in space with you?
Ha, ha, ha!
No, not really.
The cat would just fly off her head.

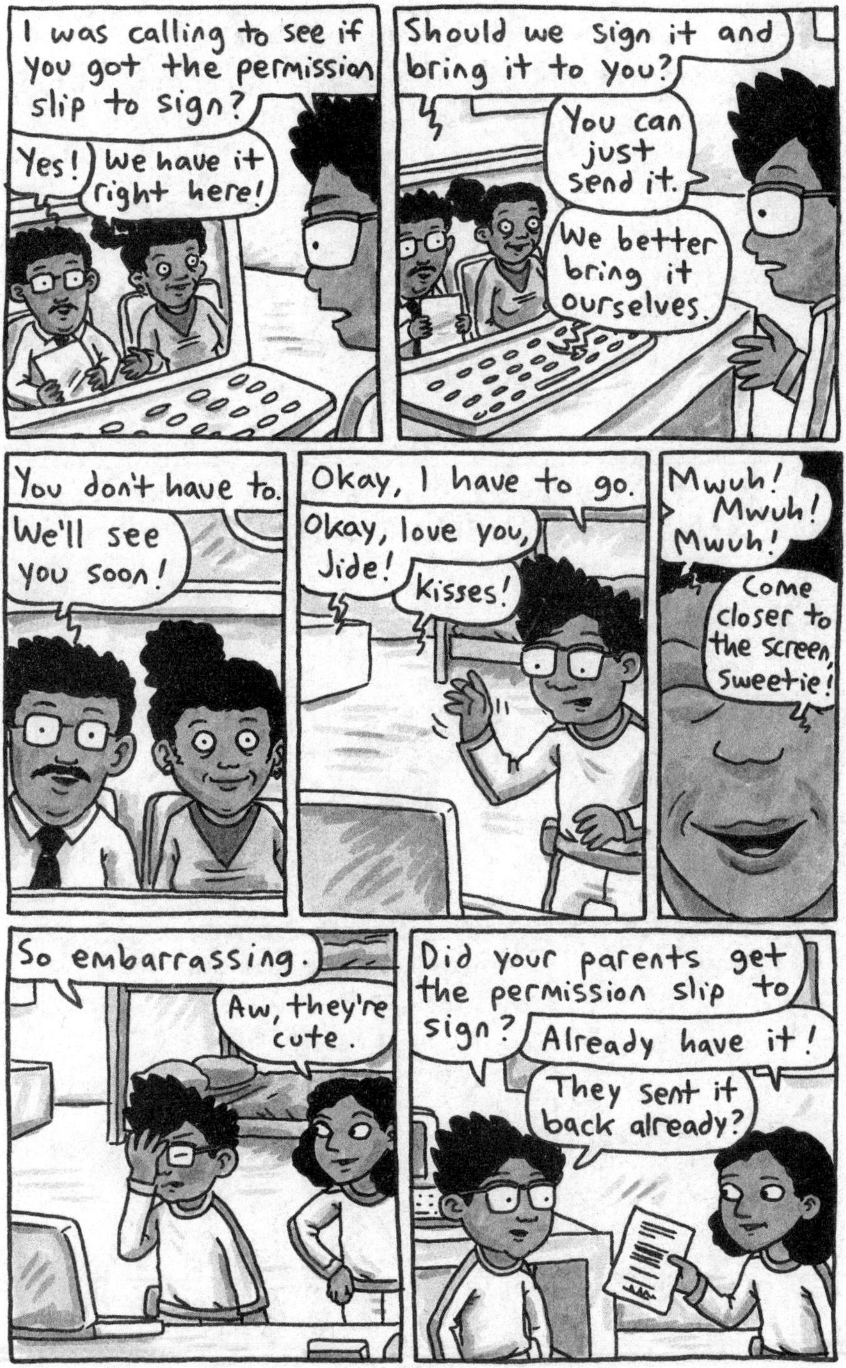
I was calling to see if you got the permission slip to sign?
Yes!
We have it right here!
Should we sign it and bring it to you?
You can just send it.
We better bring it ourselves.
You don't have to.
We'll see you soon!
Okay, I have to go.
Okay, love you, Jide!
Kisses!
Mwuh! Mwuh! Mwuh!
Come closer to the screen, sweetie!
So embarrassing.
Aw, they're cute.
Did your parents get the permission slip to sign?
Already have it!
They sent it back already?

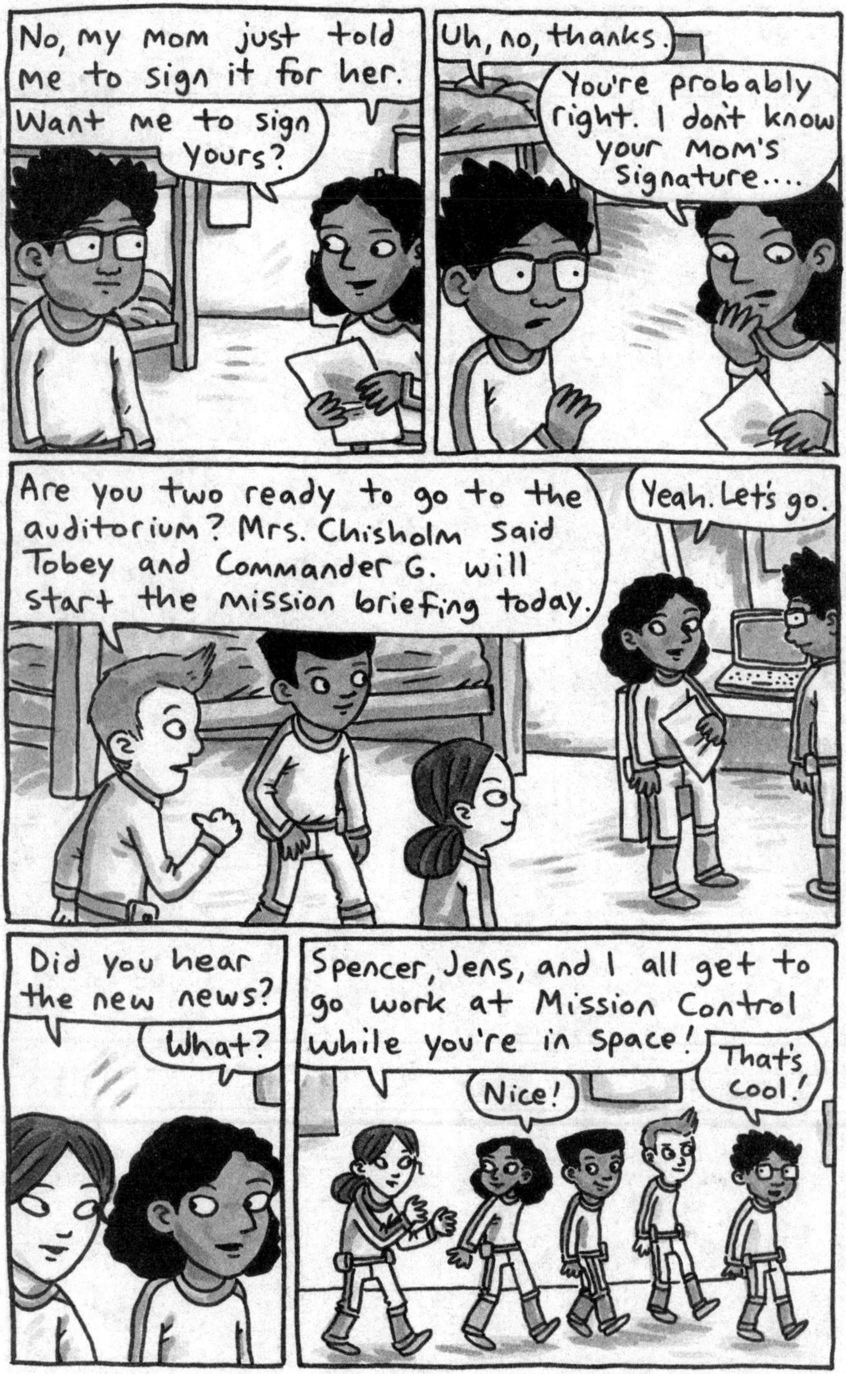
No, my mom just told me to sign it for her.
Want me to sign yours?
Uh, no, thanks.
You're probably right. I don't know your MOM'S signature....
Are you two ready to go to the auditorium? Mrs. Chisholm said Tobey and Commander G. will start the mission briefing today.
Yeah. Let's go.
Did you hear the new news?
What?
Spencer, Jens, and I all get to go work at Mission Control while you're in space!
Nice!
That's cool!

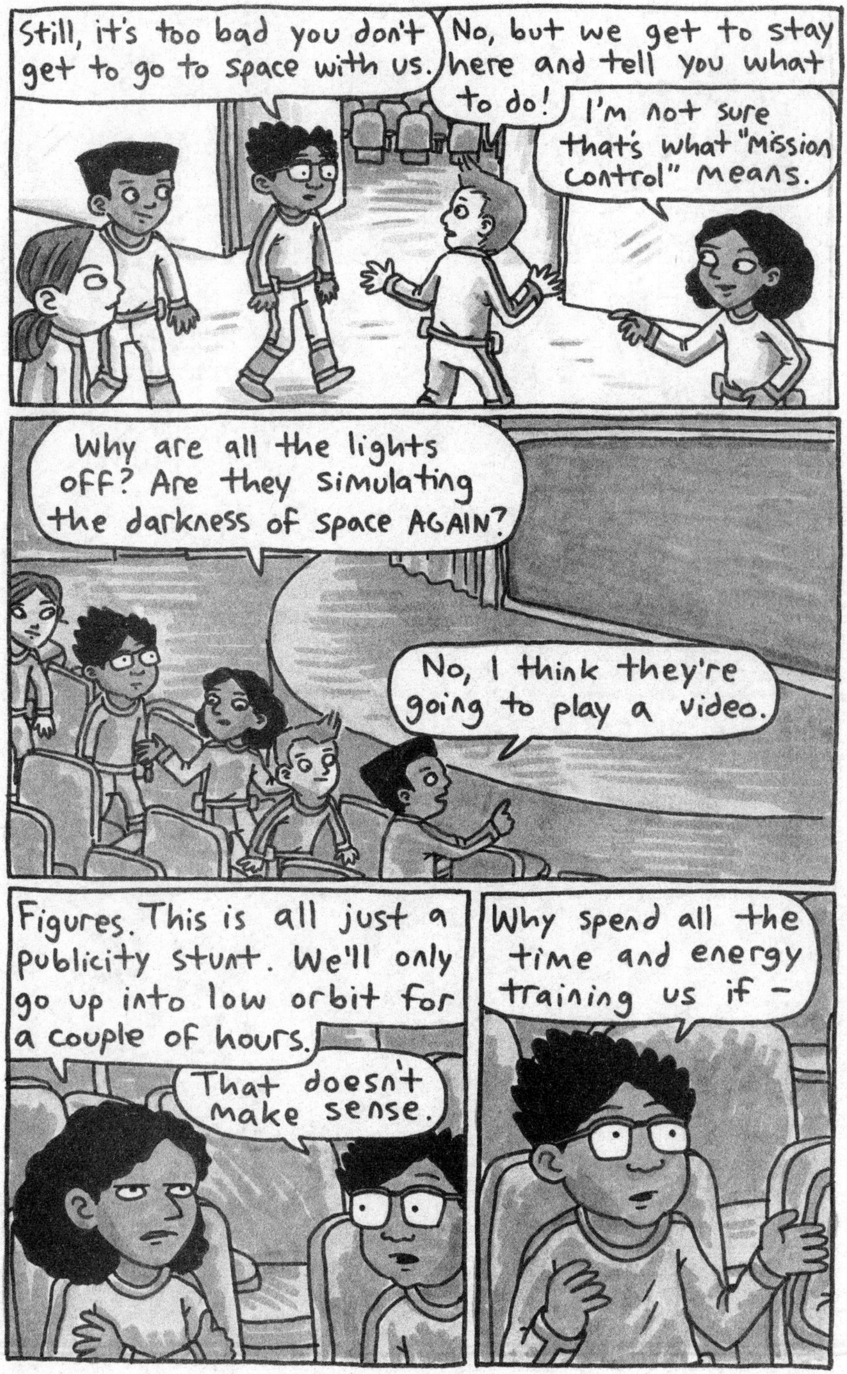
Still, it's too bad you don't get to go to space with us.
No, but we get to stay here and tell you what to do!
I'm not sure that's what "Mission control" means.
Why are all the lights off? Are they simulating the darkness of space AGAIN?
No, I think they're going to play a video.
Figures. This is all just a publicity stunt. We'll only go up into low orbit for a couple of hours.
That doesn't make sense.
Why spend all the time and energy training us if –

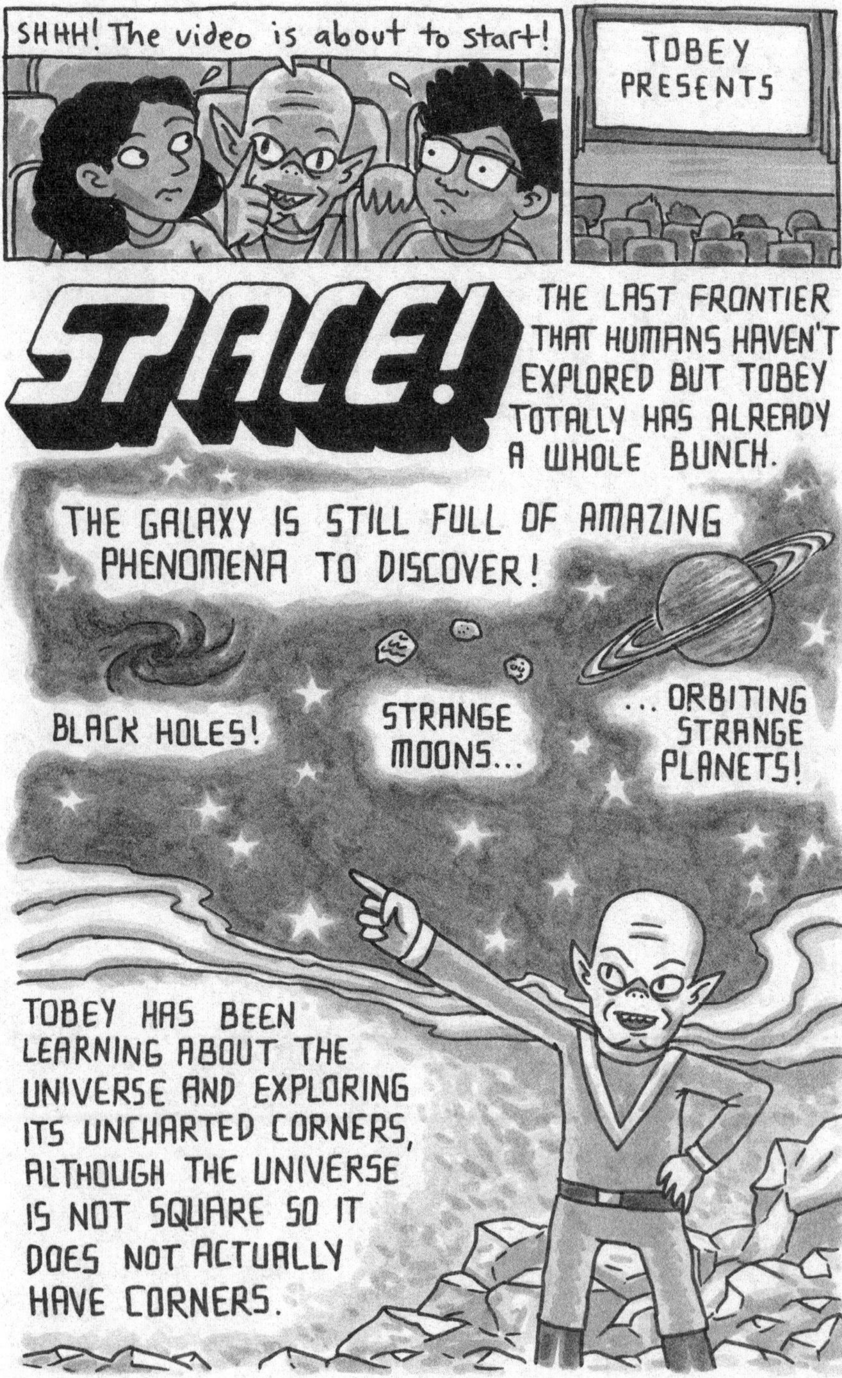
SHHH! The video is about to start!
TOBEY PRESENTS
SPACE!
THE LAST FRONTIER THAT HUMANS HAVEN'T EXPLORED BUT TOBEY TOTALLY HAS ALREADY A WHOLE BUNCH.
THE GALAXY IS STILL FULL OF AMAZING PHENOMENA TO DISCOVER!
BLACK HOLES!
STRANGE MOONS...
...ORBITING STRANGE PLANETS!
TOBEY HAS BEEN LEARNING ABOUT THE UNIVERSE AND EXPLORING ITS UNCHARTED CORNERS, ALTHOUGH THE UNIVERSE IS NOT SQUARE SO IT DOES NOT ACTUALLY HAVE CORNERS.

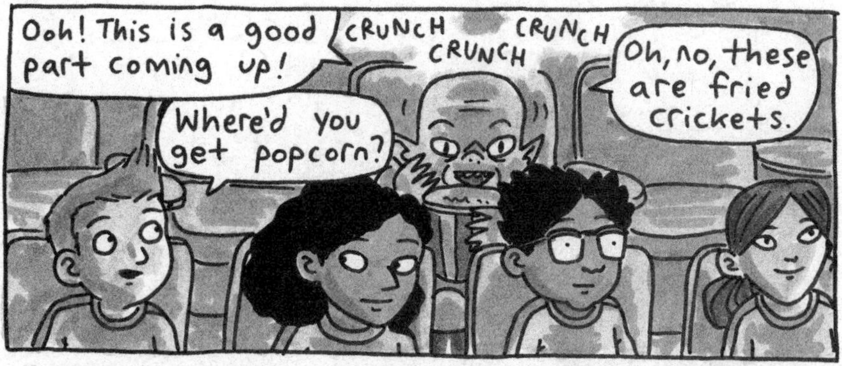
Ooh! This is a good part coming up!
Where'd you get popcorn?
CRUNCH CRUNCH CRUNCH
Oh, no, these are fried crickets.

ALONG THE WAY, HE HAS MET MANY OTHER CULTURES AND LIFE-FORMS, AND HAS MADE IT HIS GOAL TO SHARE HIS LOVE OF ADVENTURE!

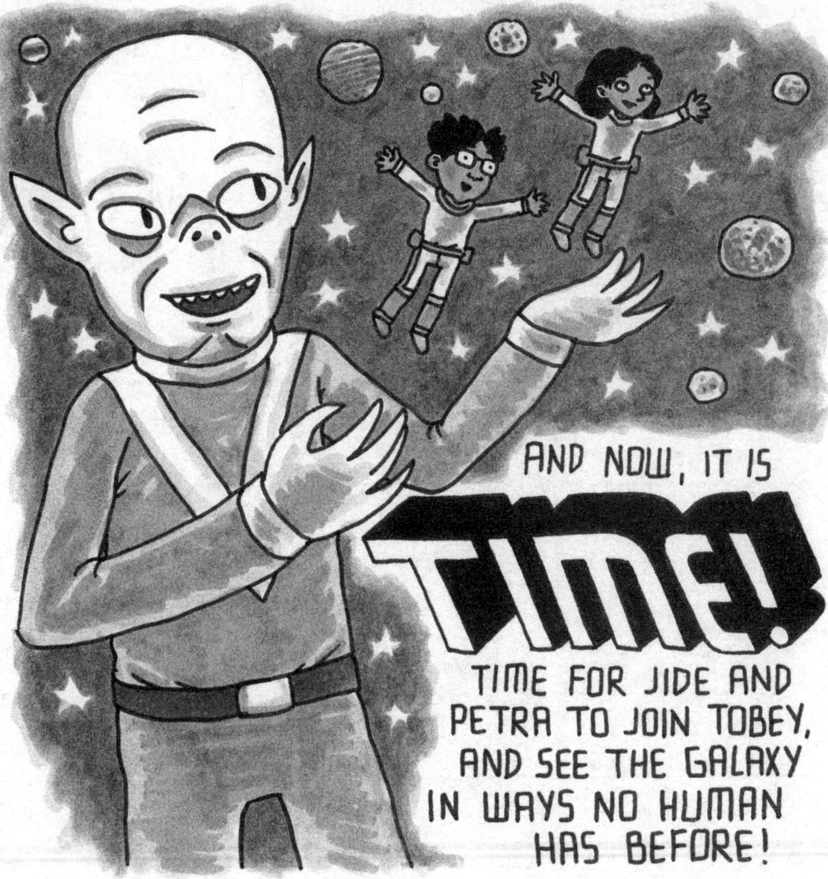
AND NOW, IT IS
TIME!
TIME FOR JIDE AND PETRA TO JOIN TOBEY, AND SEE THE GALAXY IN WAYS NO HUMAN HAS BEFORE!

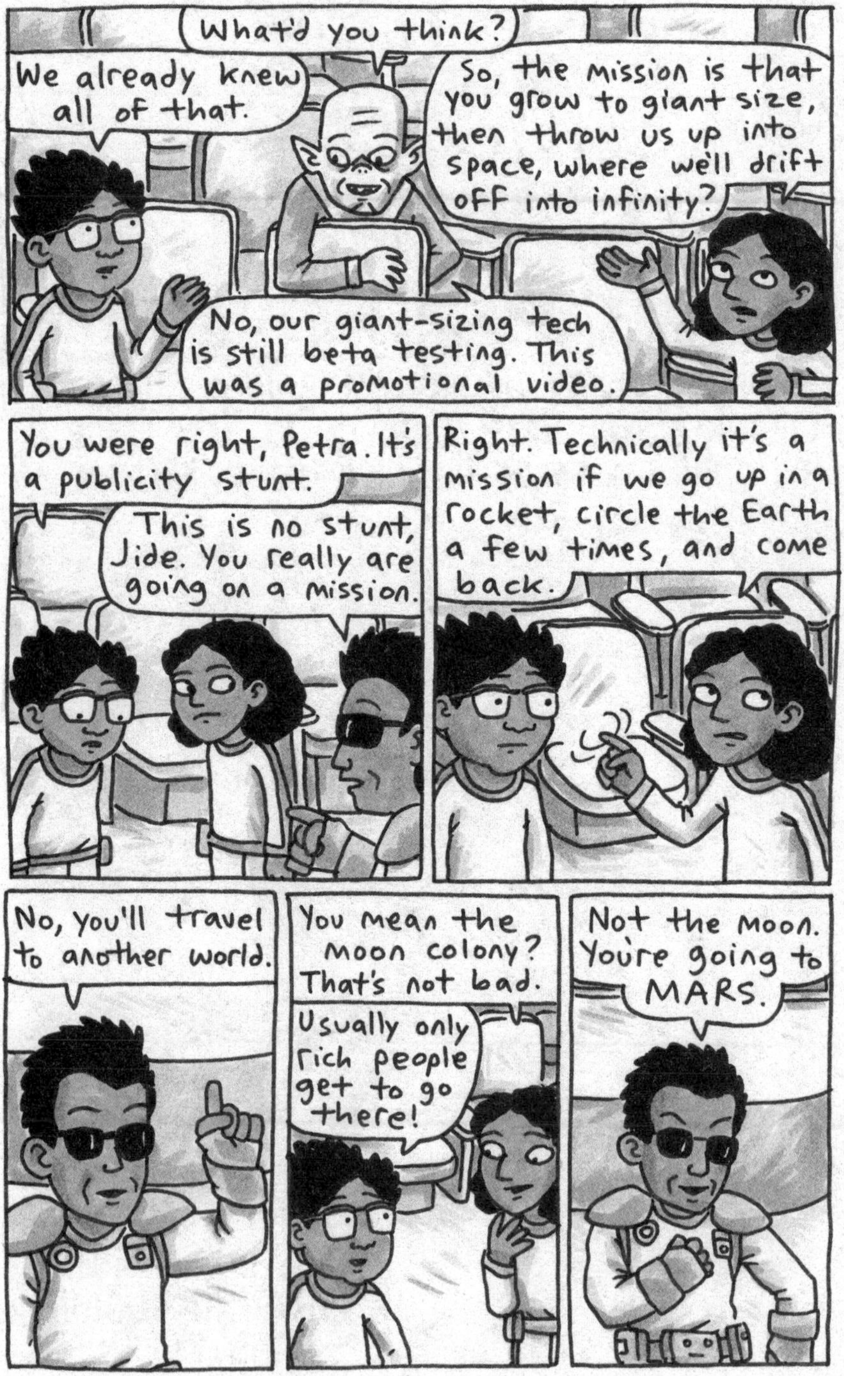
What'd you think?
We already knew all of that.
So, the mission is that you grow to giant size, then throw us up into space, where we'll drift off into infinity?
No, our giant-sizing tech is still beta testing. This was a promotional video.
You were right, Petra. It's a publicity stunt.
This is no stunt, Jide. You really are going on a mission.
Right. Technically it's a mission if we go up in a rocket, circle the Earth a few times, and come back.
No, you'll travel to another world.
You mean the moon colony? That's not bad.
Usually only rich people get to go there!
Not the moon. You're going to MARS.

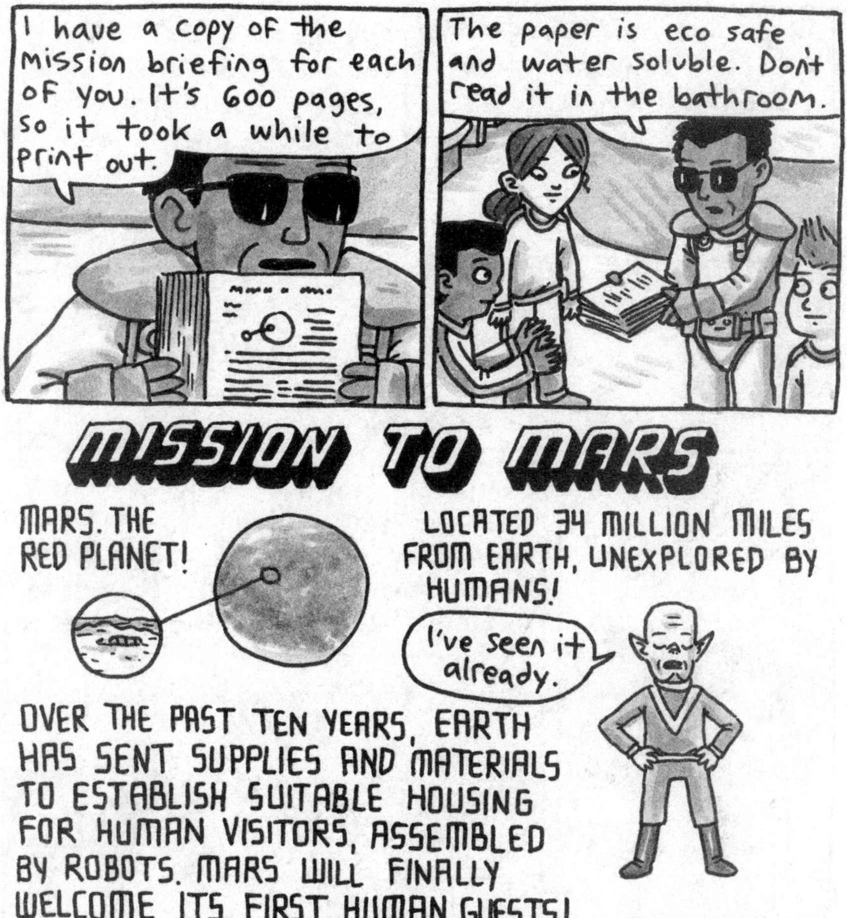
I have a copy of the mission briefing for each of you. It's 600 pages, so it took a while to print out.
The paper is eco safe and water soluble. Don't read it in the bathroom.
MISSION TO MARS
MARS. THE RED PLANET!
LOCATED 34 MILLION MILES FROM EARTH, UNEXPLORED BY HUMANS!
I've seen it already.
OVER THE PAST TEN YEARS, EARTH HAS SENT SUPPLIES AND MATERIALS TO ESTABLISH SUITABLE HOUSING FOR HUMAN VISITORS, ASSEMBLED BY ROBOTS. MARS WILL FINALLY WELCOME ITS FIRST HUMAN GUESTS!
If there's a base set up, why aren't humans on Mars already?
Because it's too expensive. It's not rocket science.
Actually, it is rocket science.

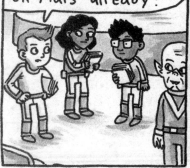

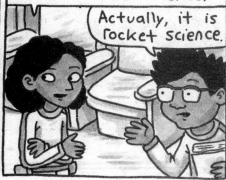

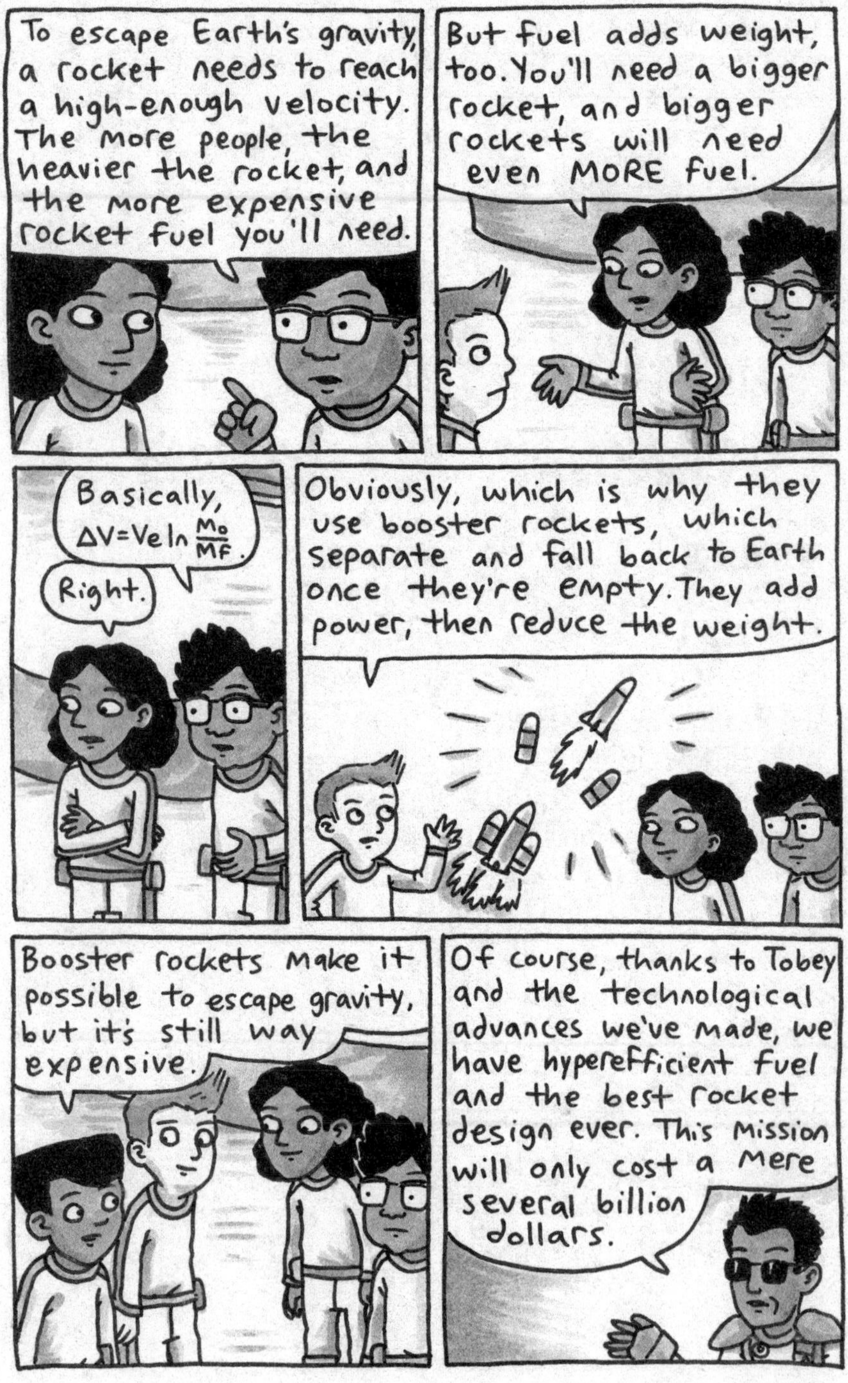
To escape Earth's gravity, a rocket needs to reach a high-enough velocity. The more people, the heavier the rocket, and the more expensive rocket fuel you'll need.
But fuel adds weight, too. You'll need a bigger rocket, and bigger rockets will need even MORE fuel.
Basically, $\Delta V = Ve \ln \frac{Mo}{MF}$.
Right.
Obviously, which is why they use booster rockets, which separate and fall back to Earth once they're empty. They add power, then reduce the weight.
Booster rockets make it possible to escape gravity, but it's still way expensive.
Of course, thanks to Tobey and the technological advances we've made, we have hyperefficient fuel and the best rocket design ever. This mission will only cost a mere several billion dollars.

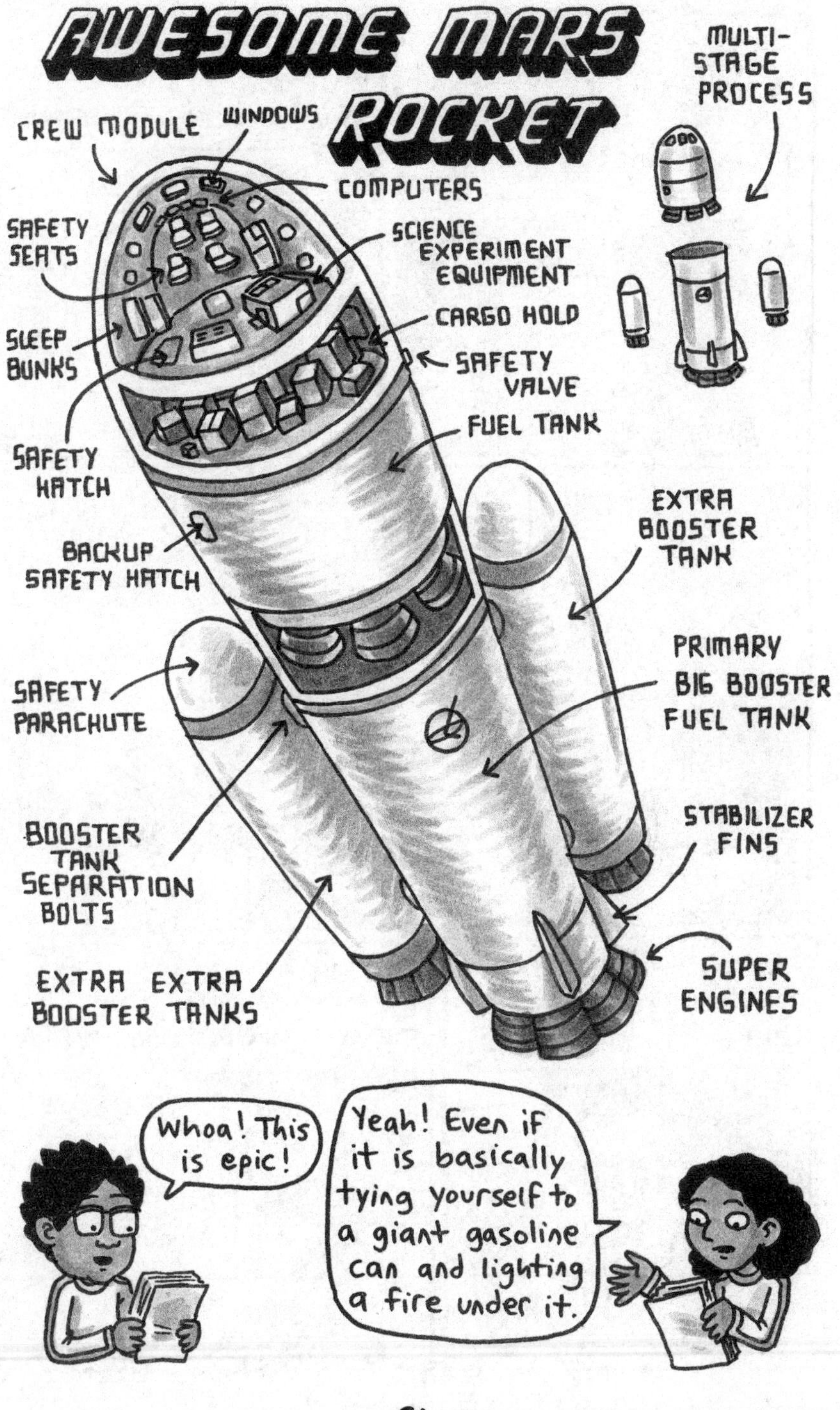
AWESOME MARS ROCKET
MULTI-STAGE PROCESS
CREW MODULE
WINDOWS
COMPUTERS
SAFETY SEATS
SCIENCE EXPERIMENT EQUIPMENT
CARGO HOLD
SLEEP BUNKS
SAFETY VALVE
FUEL TANK
SAFETY HATCH
BACKUP SAFETY HATCH
EXTRA BOOSTER TANK
PRIMARY BIG BOOSTER FUEL TANK
SAFETY PARACHUTE
STABILIZER FINS
BOOSTER TANK SEPARATION BOLTS
SUPER ENGINES
EXTRA EXTRA BOOSTER TANKS
Whoa! This is epic!
Yeah! Even if it is basically tying yourself to a giant gasoline can and lighting a fire under it.

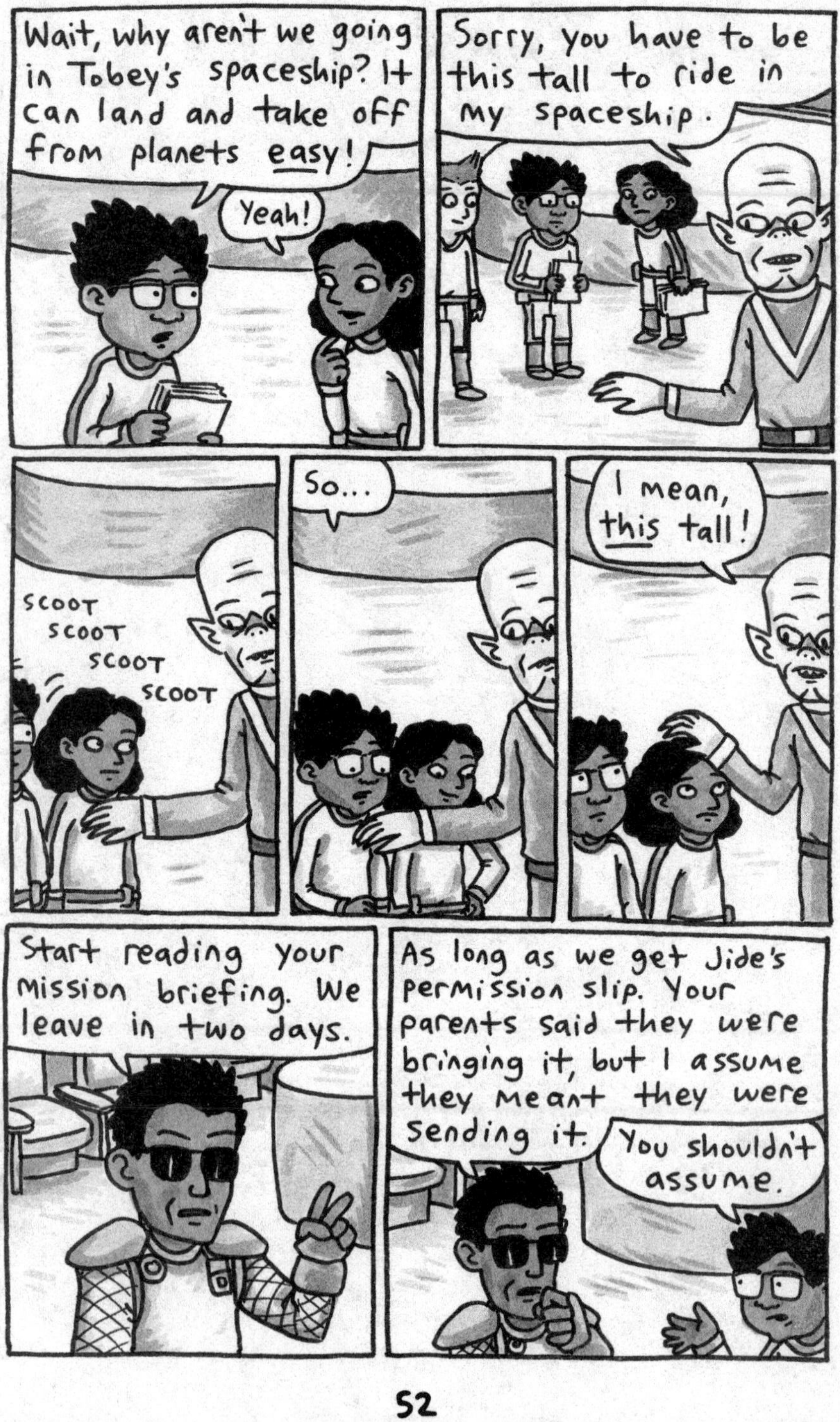
Wait, why aren't we going in Tobey's spaceship? It can land and take off from planets easy!
Yeah!
Sorry, you have to be this tall to ride in my spaceship.
SCOOT
SCOOT
SCOOT
SCOOT
So...
I mean, this tall!
Start reading your mission briefing. We leave in two days.
As long as we get Jide's permission slip. Your parents said they were bringing it, but I assume they meant they were sending it.
You shouldn't assume.

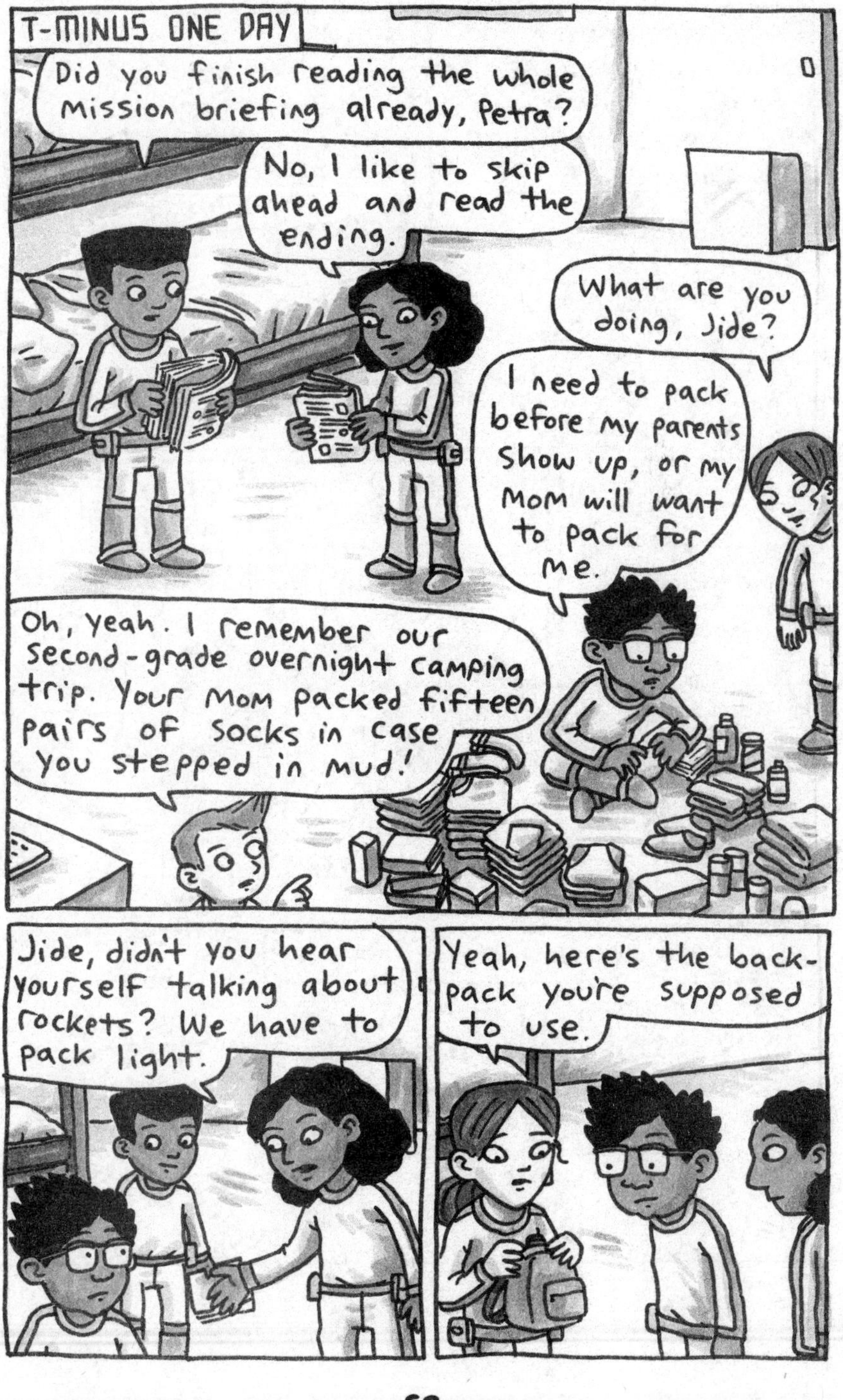
T-MINUS ONE DAY
Did you finish reading the whole mission briefing already, Petra?
No, I like to skip ahead and read the ending.
What are you doing, Jide?
I need to pack before my parents show up, or my mom will want to pack for me.
Oh, yeah. I remember our second-grade overnight camping trip. Your mom packed fifteen pairs of socks in case you stepped in mud!
Jide, didn't you hear yourself talking about rockets? We have to pack light.
Yeah, here's the back-pack you're supposed to use.

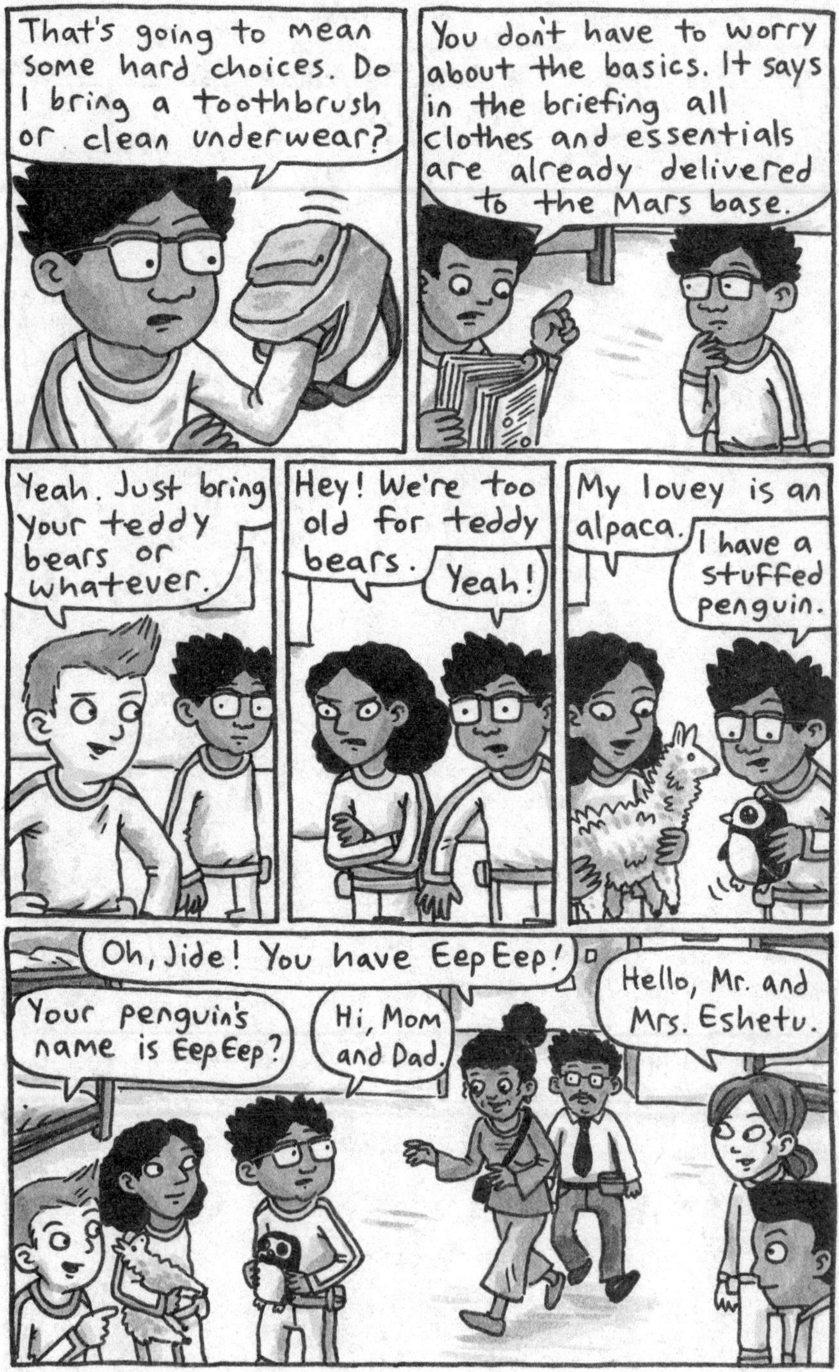
That's going to mean some hard choices. Do I bring a toothbrush or clean underwear?
You don't have to worry about the basics. It says in the briefing all clothes and essentials are already delivered to the Mars base.
Yeah. Just bring your teddy bears or whatever.
Hey! We're too old for teddy bears.
Yeah!
My lovey is an alpaca.
I have a stuffed penguin.
Oh, Jide! You have Eep Eep!
Your penguin's name is Eep Eep?
Hi, Mom and Dad.
Hello, Mr. and Mrs. Eshetu.

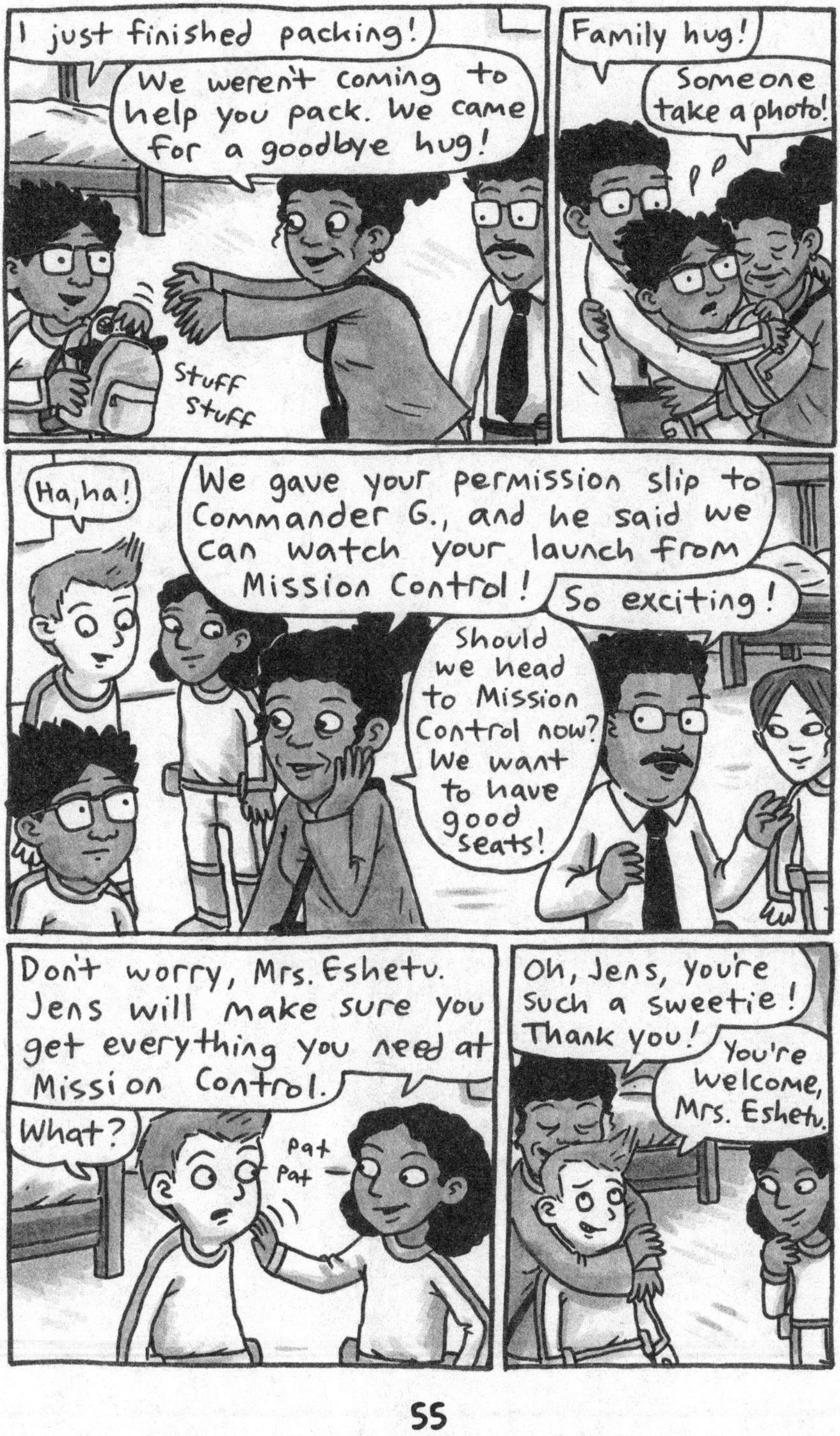

I just finished packing!
We weren't coming to help you pack. We came for a goodbye hug!
Stuff stuff
Family hug!
Someone take a photo!
Ha, ha!
We gave your permission slip to Commander G., and he said we can watch your launch from Mission Control!
So exciting!
Should we head to Mission Control now? We want to have good seats!
Don't worry, Mrs. Eshetu. Jens will make sure you get everything you need at Mission Control.
What?
Pat pat
Oh, Jens, you're such a sweetie! Thank you!
You're welcome, Mrs. Eshetu.

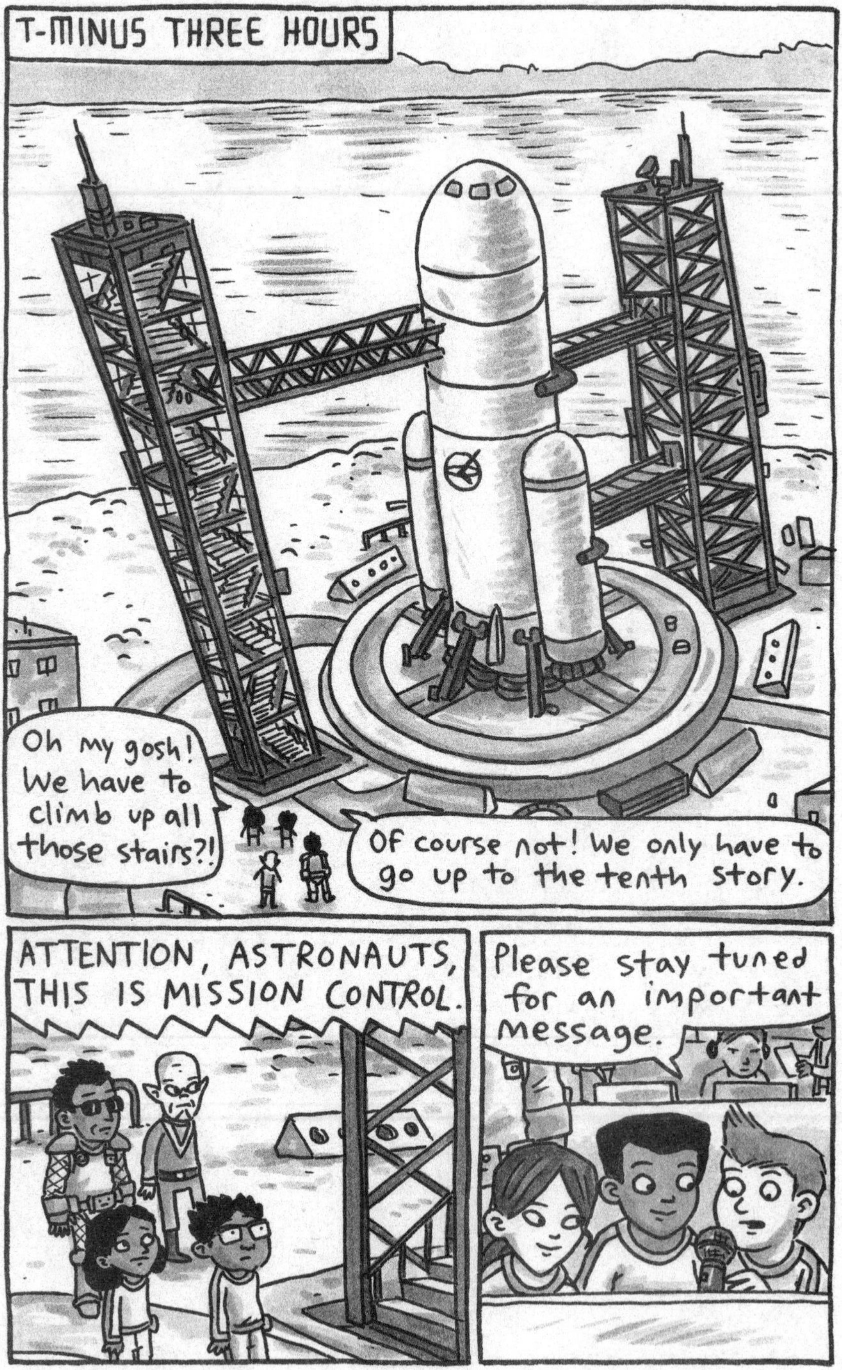
T-MINUS THREE HOURS
Oh my gosh! We have to climb up all those stairs?!
Of course not! We only have to go up to the tenth story.
ATTENTION, ASTRONAUTS, THIS IS MISSION CONTROL.
Please stay tuned for an important message.

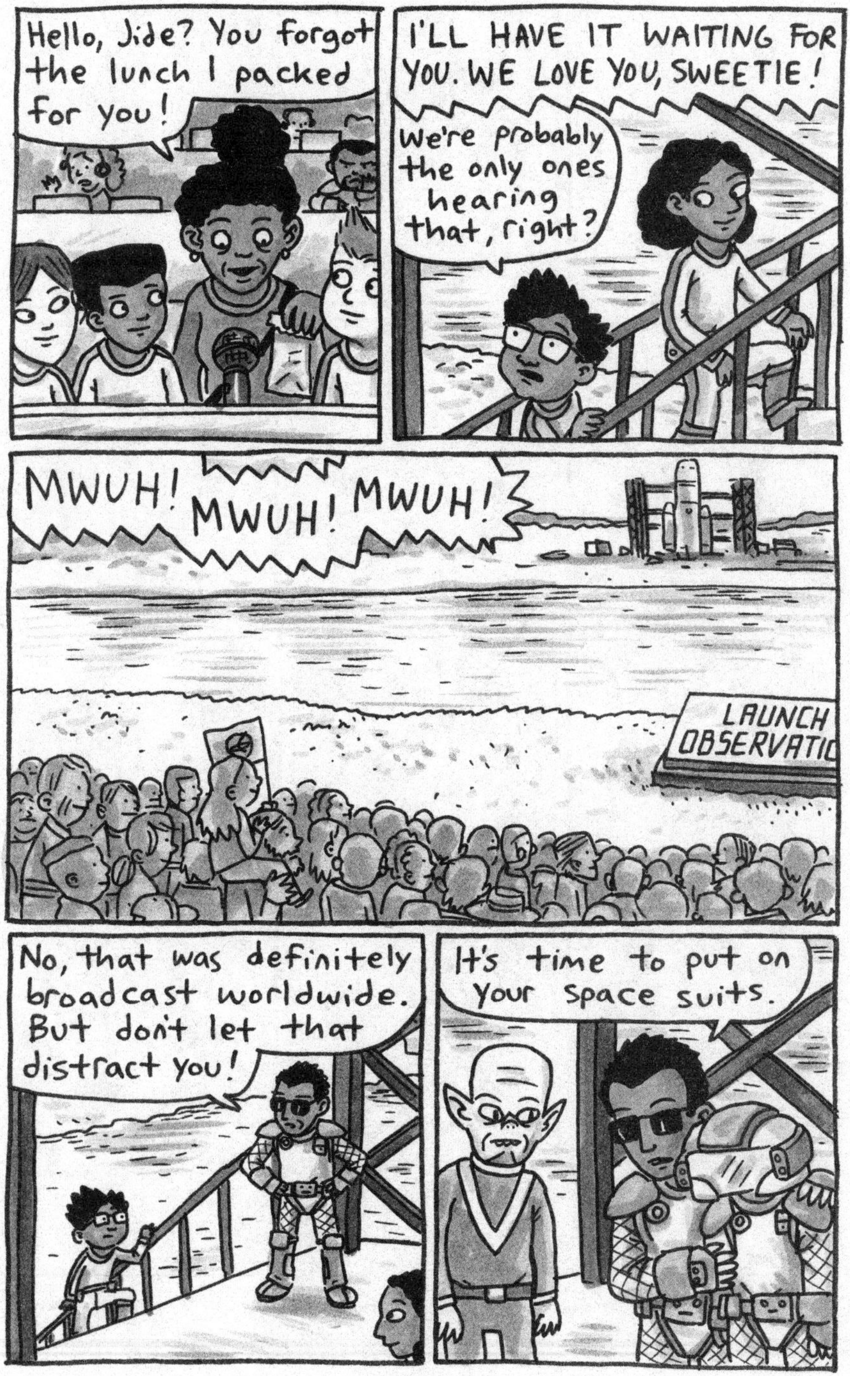
Hello, Jide? You forgot the lunch I packed for you!
I'LL HAVE IT WAITING FOR YOU. WE LOVE YOU, SWEETIE!
We're probably the only ones hearing that, right?
MWUH! MWUH! MWUH!
LAUNCH OBSERVATIC
No, that was definitely broadcast worldwide. But don't let that distract you!
It's time to put on your space suits.

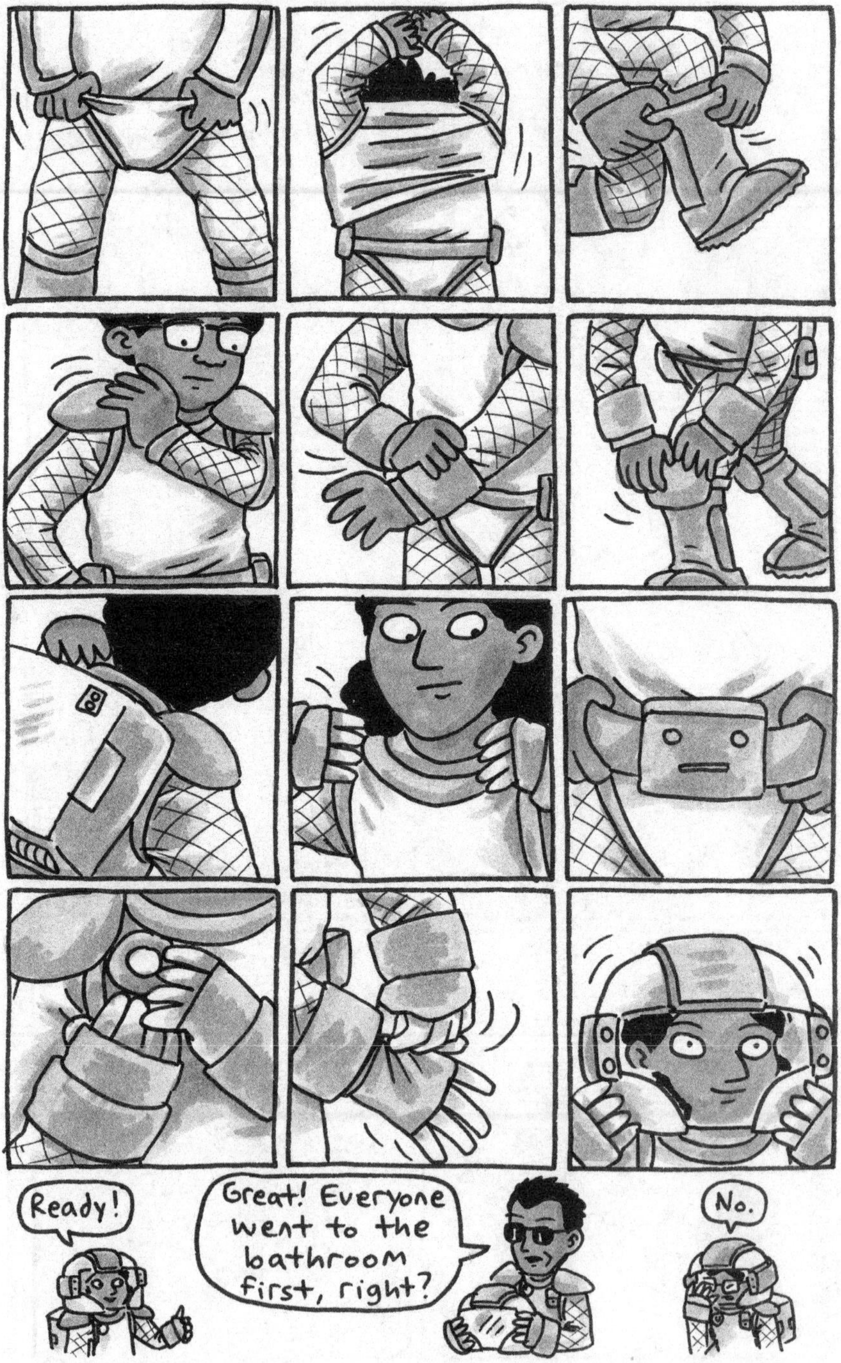

Ready!
Great! Everyone went to the bathroom first, right?
No.

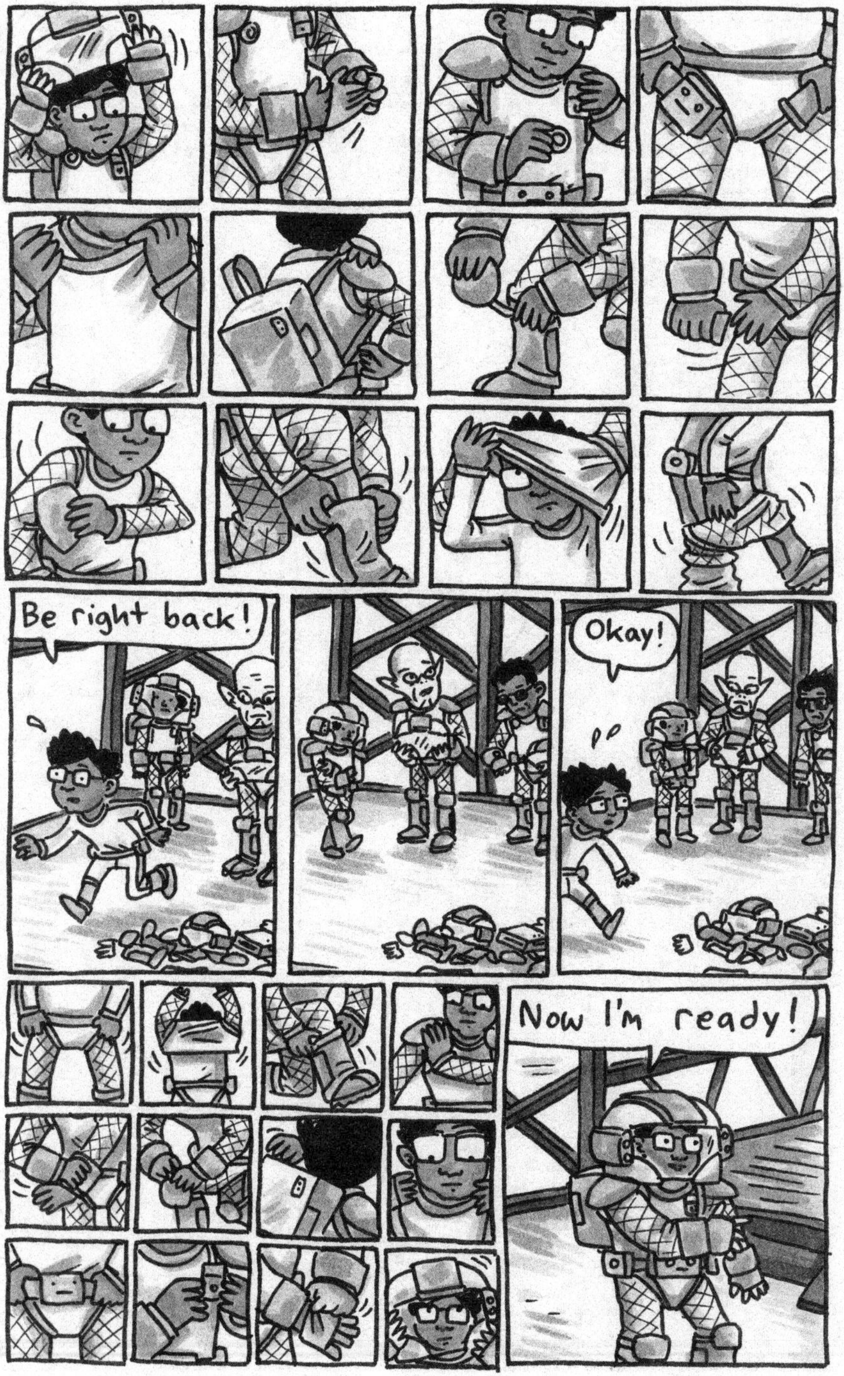
Be right back!
Okay!
Now I'm ready!

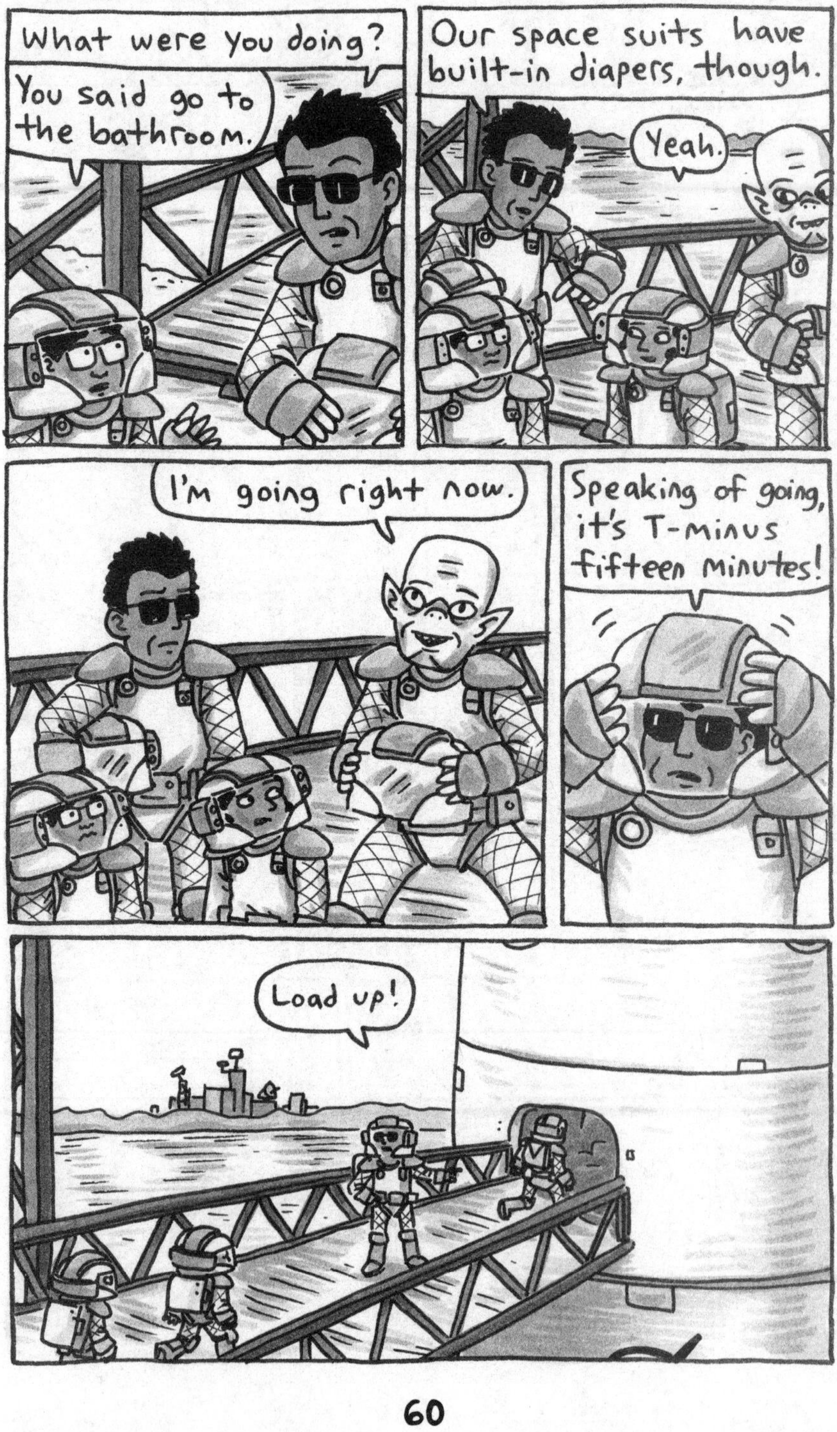
What were you doing?
You said go to the bathroom.
Our space suits have built-in diapers, though.
Yeah.
I'm going right now.
Speaking of going, it's T-minus fifteen minutes!
Load up!

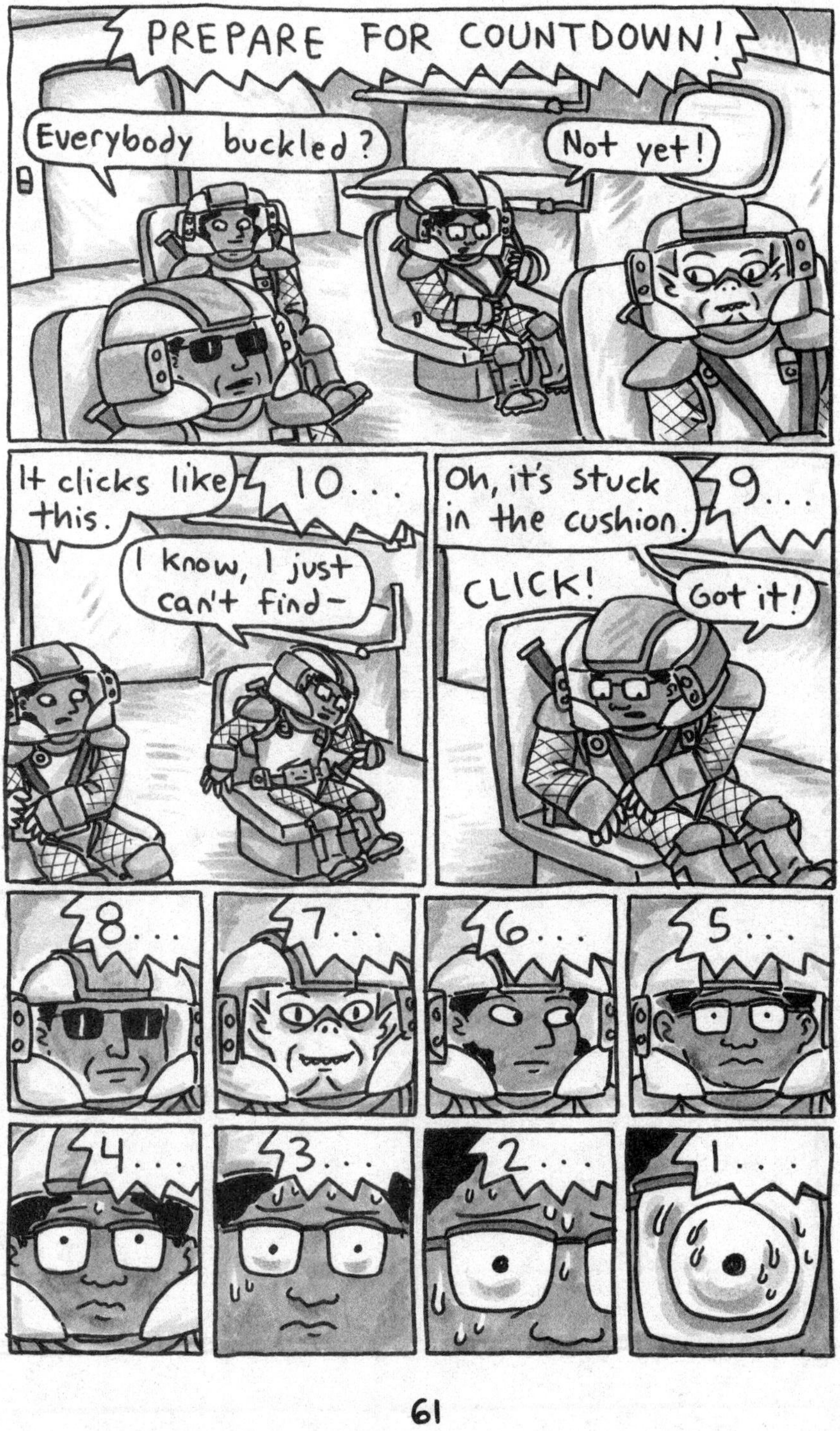
PREPARE FOR COUNTDOWN!
Everybody buckled?
Not yet!
It clicks like this.
10...
I know, I just can't find-
Oh, it's stuck in the cushion.
9...
CLICK!
Got it!
8...
7...
6...
5...
4...
3...
2...
1...

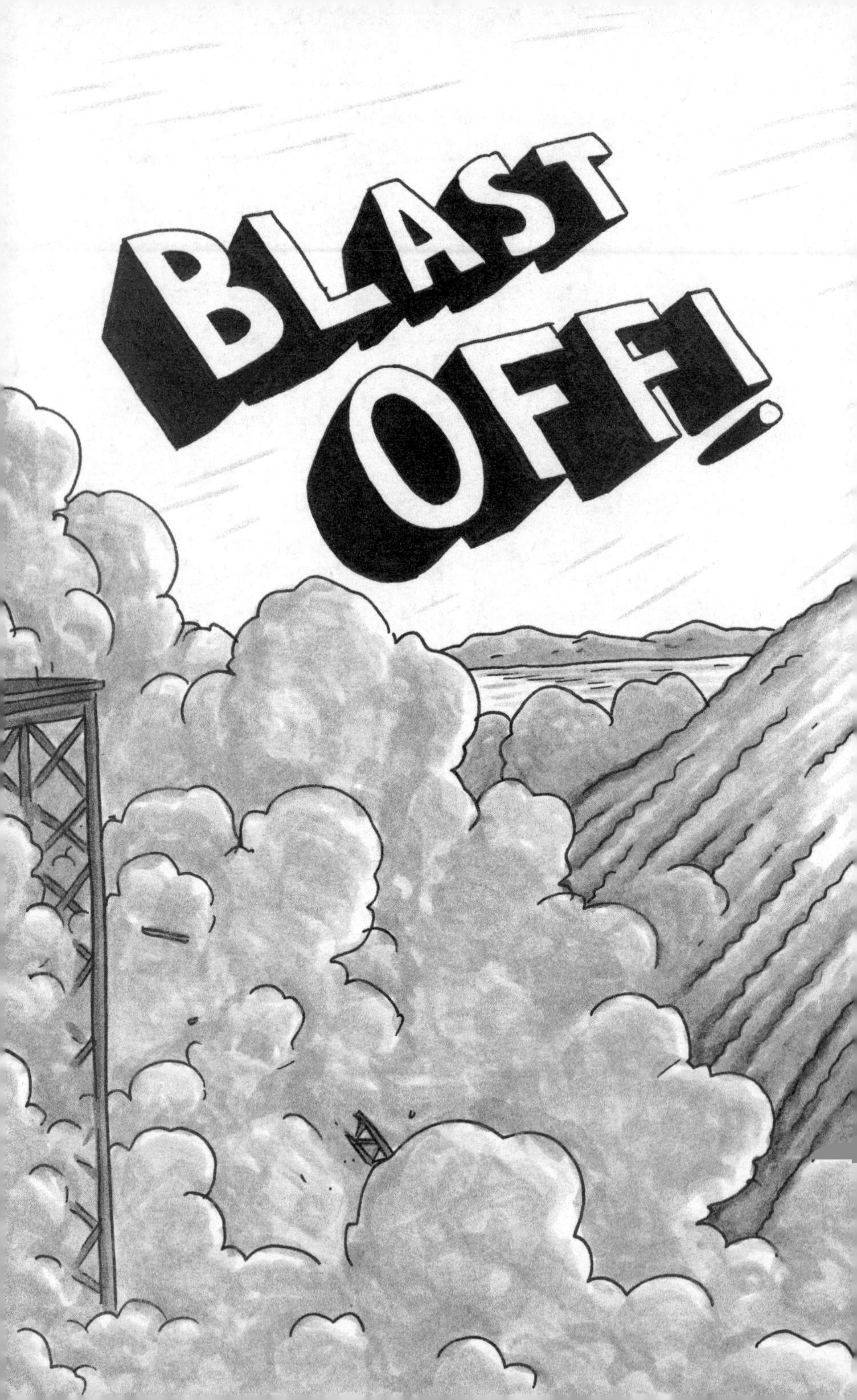
BLAST OFF!

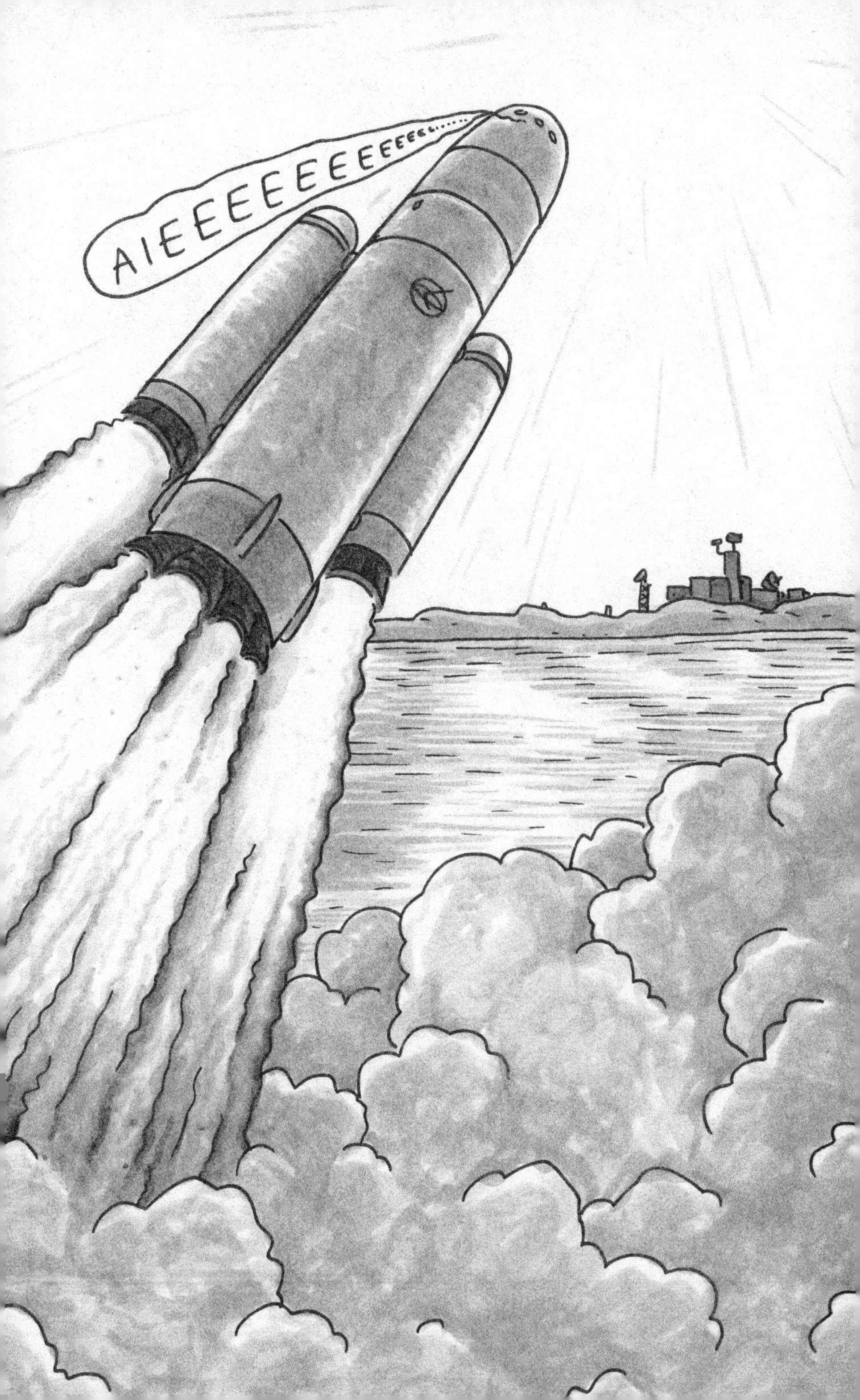
AIEEEEEEEEEEeeee.....

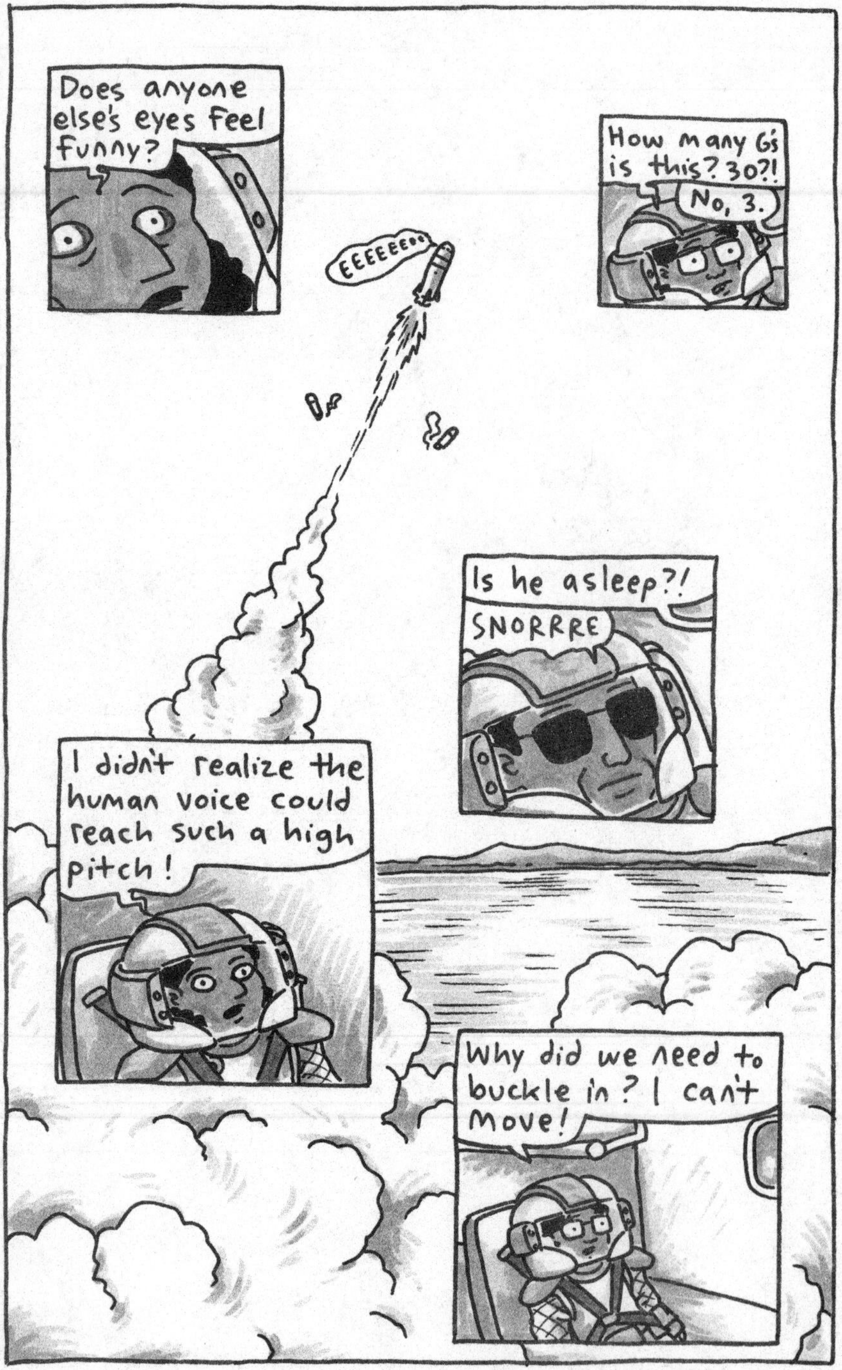
Does anyone else's eyes feel funny?
How many G's is this? 30?!
No, 3.
EEEEEEE...
Is he asleep?!
SNORRRE
I didn't realize the human voice could reach such a high pitch!
Why did we need to buckle in? I can't move!

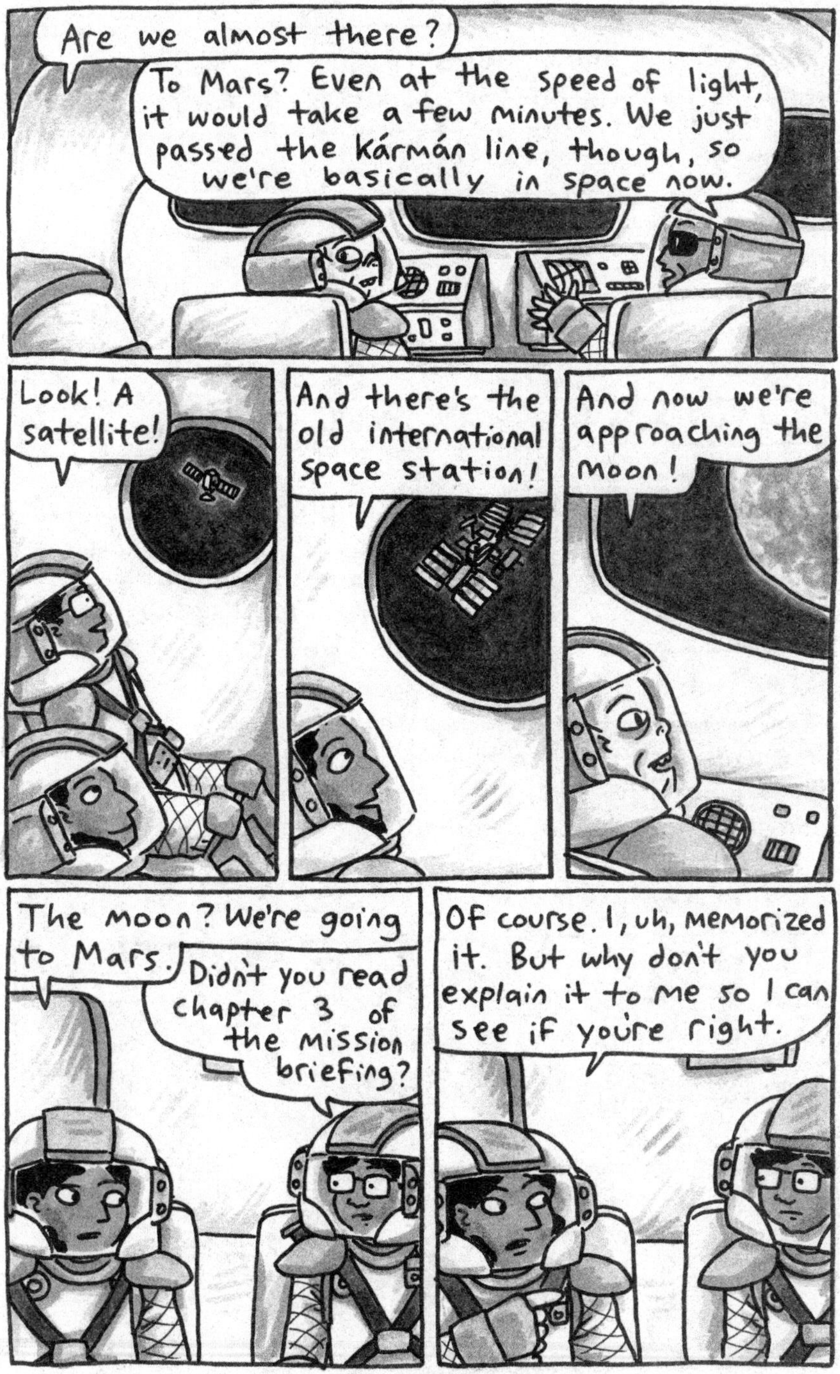
Are we almost there?
To Mars? Even at the speed of light, it would take a few minutes. We just passed the Kármán line, though, so we're basically in space now.
Look! A satellite!
And there's the old international space station!
And now we're approaching the moon!
The moon? We're going to Mars.
Didn't you read chapter 3 of the mission briefing?
Of course. I, uh, memorized it. But why don't you explain it to me so I can see if you're right.

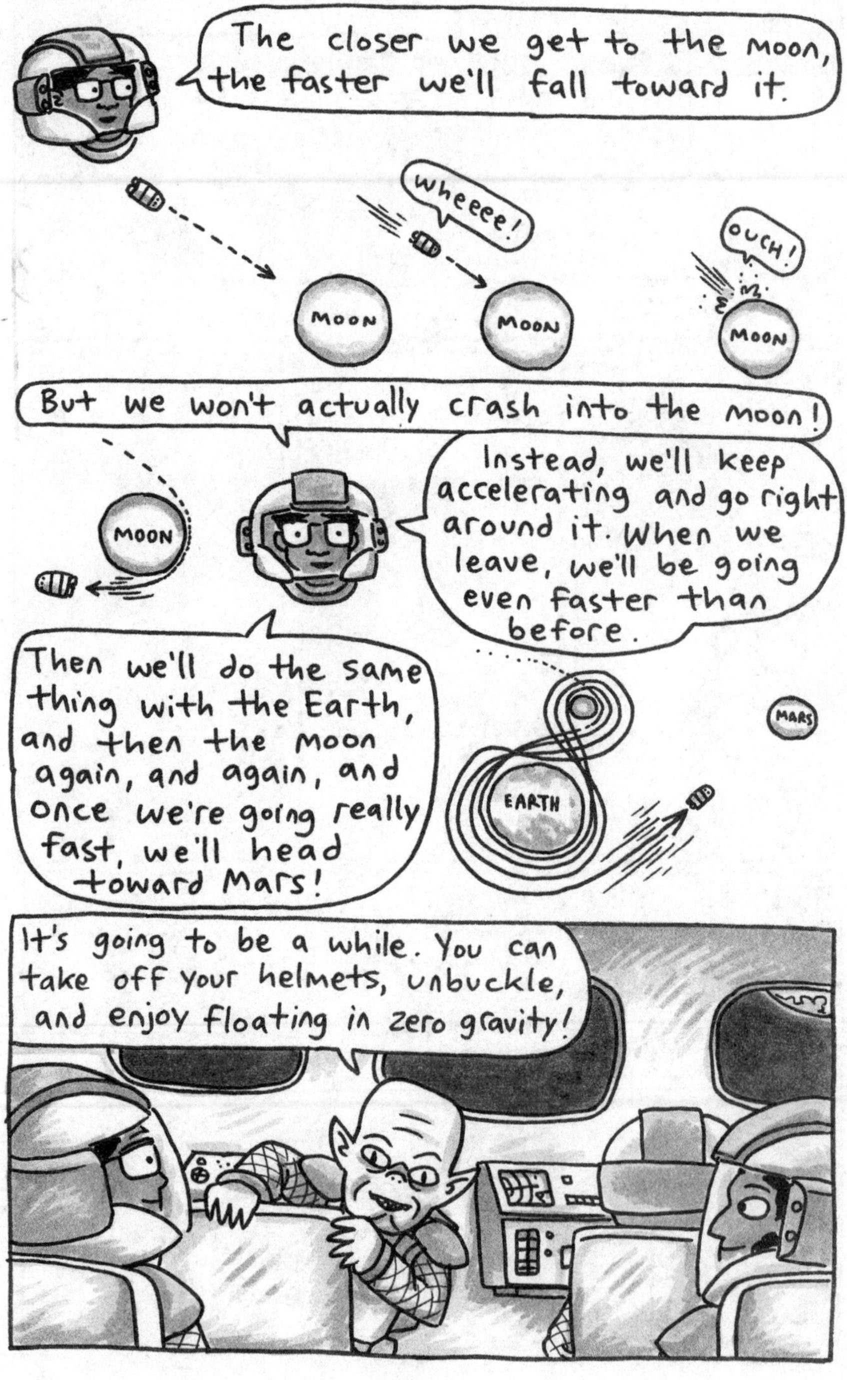
The closer we get to the moon, the faster we'll fall toward it.
Wheeee!
OUCH!
MOON
MOON
MOON
But we won't actually crash into the moon!
Instead, we'll keep accelerating and go right around it. When we leave, we'll be going even faster than before.
MOON
Then we'll do the same thing with the Earth, and then the moon again, and again, and once we're going really fast, we'll head toward Mars!
EARTH
MARS
It's going to be a while. You can take off your helmets, unbuckle, and enjoy floating in zero gravity!

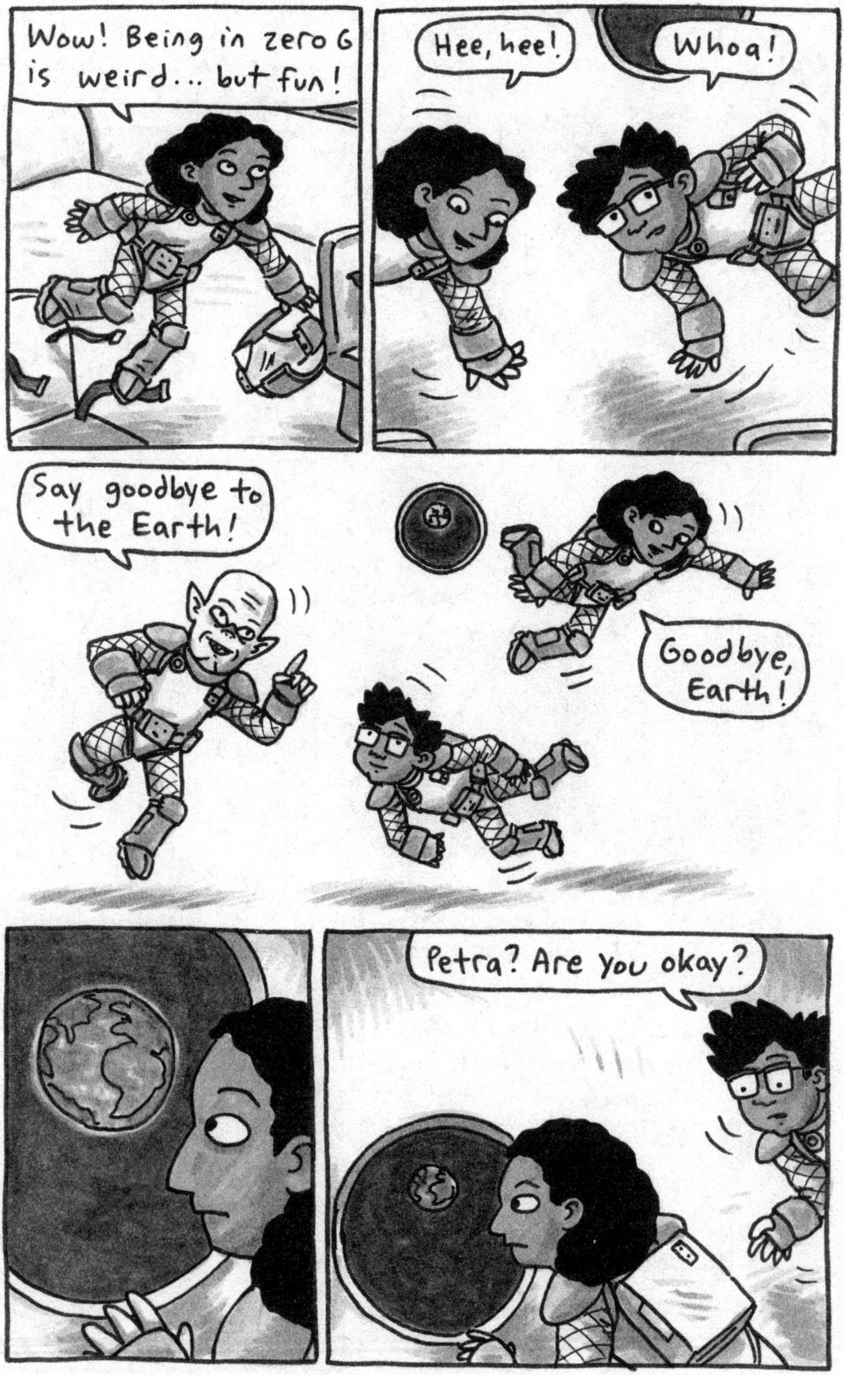
Wow! Being in zero G is weird... but fun!
Hee, hee!
Whoa!
Say goodbye to the Earth!
Goodbye, Earth!
Petra? Are you okay?

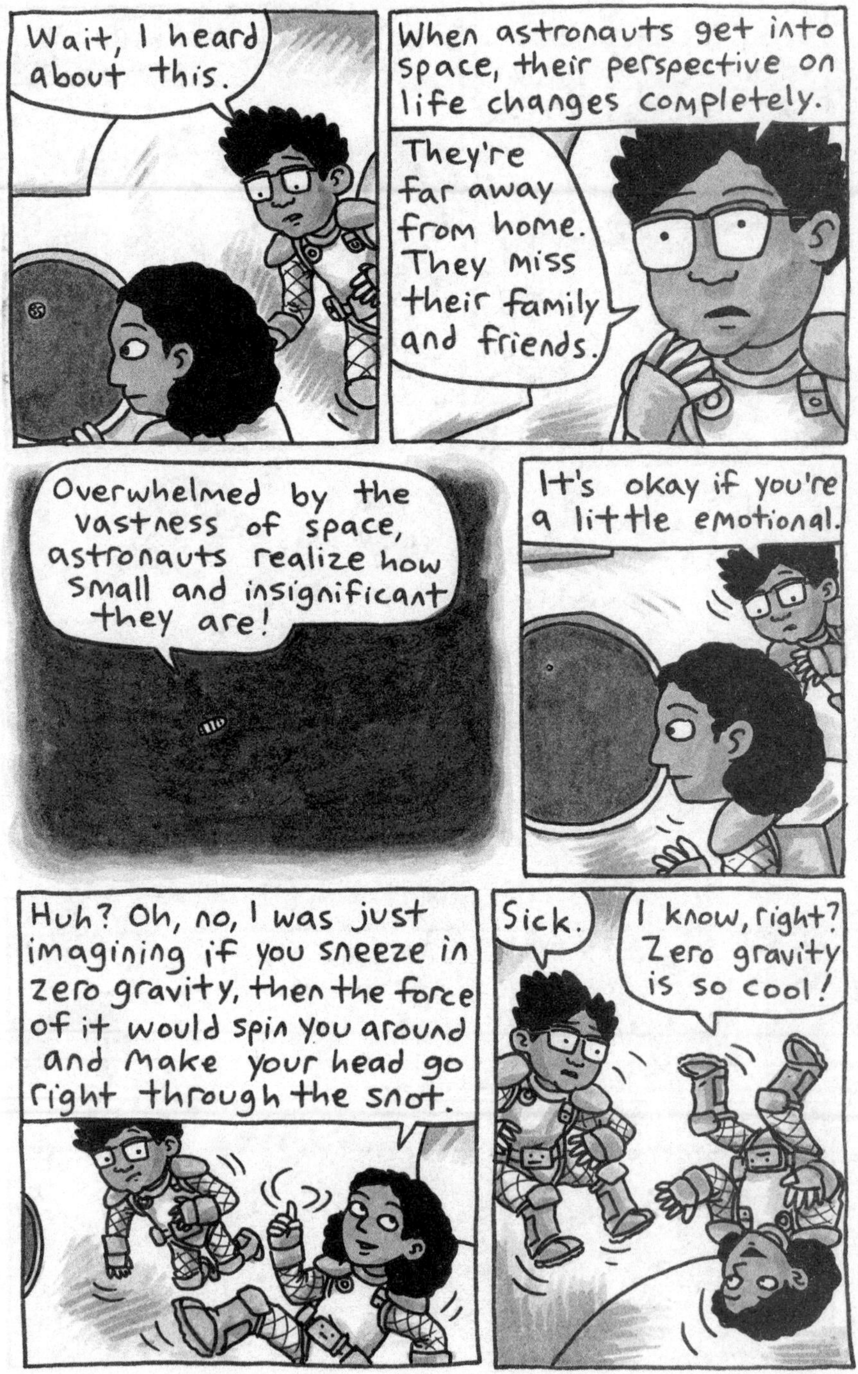
Wait, I heard about this.
When astronauts get into space, their perspective on life changes completely.
They're far away from home. They miss their family and friends.
Overwhelmed by the vastness of space, astronauts realize how small and insignificant they are!
It's okay if you're a little emotional.
Huh? Oh, no, I was just imagining if you sneeze in zero gravity, then the force of it would spin you around and make your head go right through the snot.
Sick.
I know, right? Zero gravity is so cool!

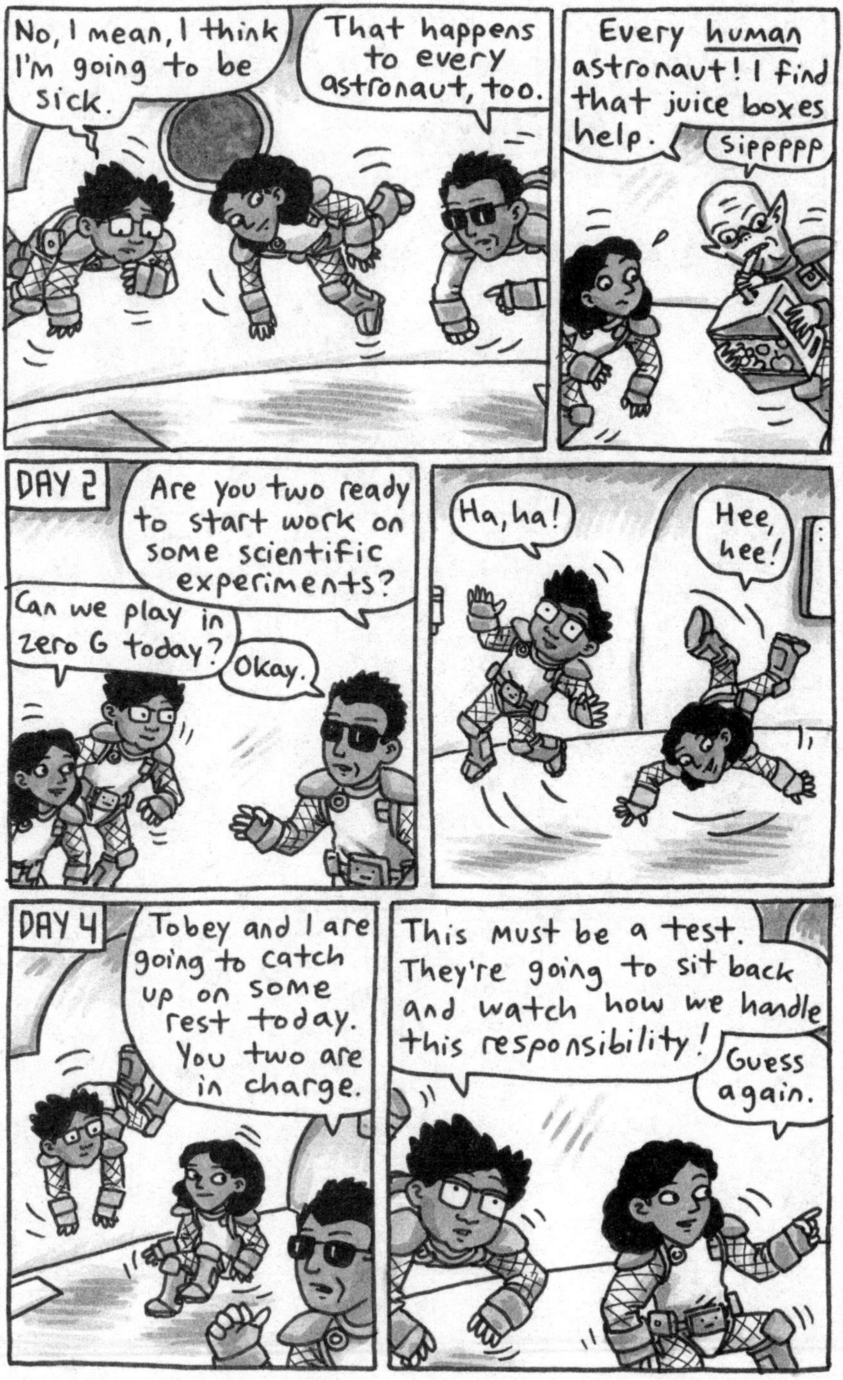
No, I mean, I think I'm going to be sick.
That happens to every astronaut, too.
Every human astronaut! I find that juice boxes help.
SIPPPPP
DAY 2
Are you two ready to start work on some scientific experiments?
Can we play in zero G today?
Okay.
Ha, ha!
Hee, hee!
DAY 4
Tobey and I are going to catch up on some rest today. You two are in charge.
This must be a test. They're going to sit back and watch how we handle this responsibility!
Guess again.

They're already asleep?

Yep.

ZZZZZZ

You're going to draw mustaches on them while they're asleep?

Definitely. Tobey loves jokes.

Didn't you hear Commander G.? We're in charge.

Not really. Everything is on auto or run by the computer.

We can look at our status, make sure everything - OH, NO!

What?

We launched off course by an entire Planck length!

A Planck length? That's only, like, .0000000000 0000000000 00000000 000016 meters. That's 10,000,000 times smaller than an atom. What's the big deal?

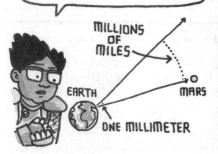

If we're off even one millimeter at launch, we'll end up millions of miles off course!

MILLIONS OF MILES

EARTH

MARS

ONE MILLIMETER

We won't just miss Mars. We're headed off to drift hopelessly lost in deep space!

BEEP.

70

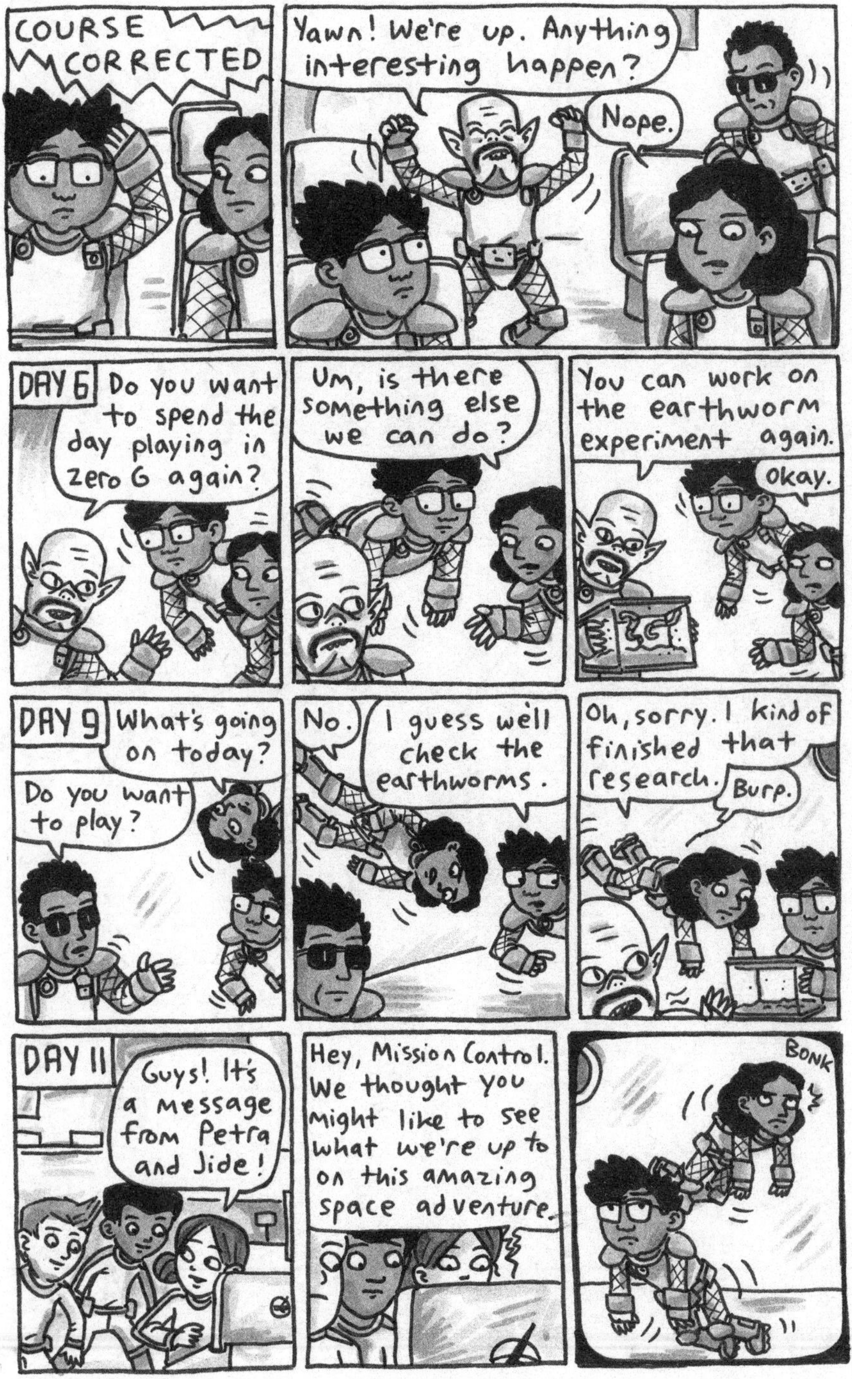
COURSE CORRECTED
Yawn! We're up. Anything interesting happen?
Nope.
DAY 6
Do you want to spend the day playing in zero G again?
Um, is there something else we can do?
You can work on the earthworm experiment again.
Okay.
DAY 9
What's going on today?
Do you want to play?
No.
I guess we'll check the earthworms.
Oh, sorry. I kind of finished that research.
Burp.
DAY 11
Guys! It's a message from Petra and Jide!
Hey, Mission Control. We thought you might like to see what we're up to on this amazing space adventure.
BONK

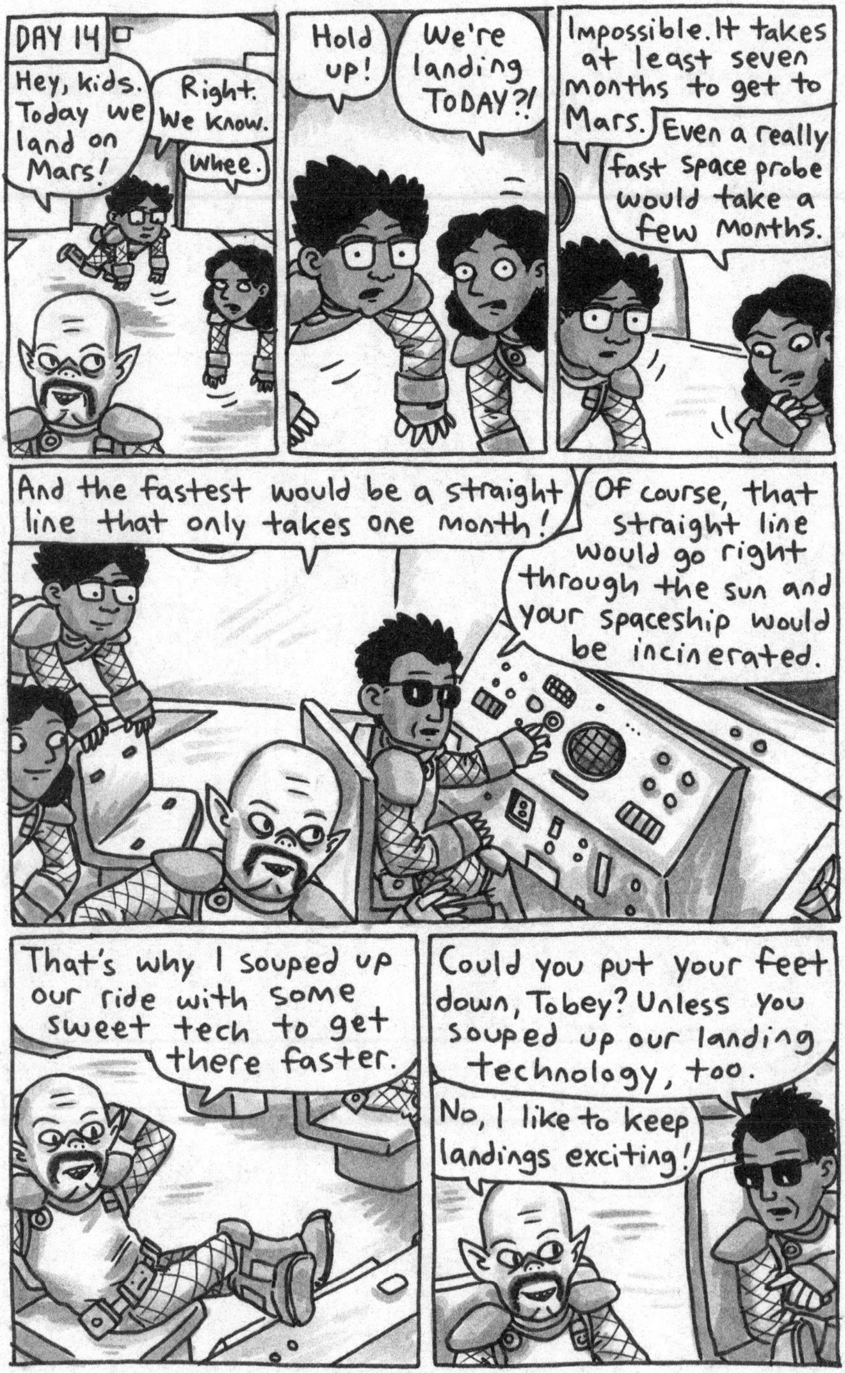
DAY 14
Hey, kids. Today we land on Mars!
Right. We know.
Whee.
Hold up!
We're landing TODAY?!
Impossible. It takes at least seven months to get to Mars.
Even a really fast space probe would take a few months.
And the fastest would be a straight line that only takes one month!
Of course, that straight line would go right through the sun and your spaceship would be incinerated.
That's why I souped up our ride with some sweet tech to get there faster.
Could you put your feet down, Tobey? Unless you souped up our landing technology, too.
No, I like to keep landings exciting!

I prefer the most boring landing imaginable.

That's why we meticulously planned the safest landing possible.

Our spaceship has been circling Mars, slowing down due to the atmosphere, but protected by our heat shield.

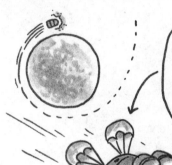

As we approach for final descent, tiny parachutes will deploy, slowing us more. But not so suddenly that we smack into the windshield.

Next, our retro-thrusters will fire.

Then our crash cushions will self-inflate, which will allow us to bounce to a stop at our prepared arrival zone.

Buckle up again, everyone!

Let us know if you need help, Jide.

73

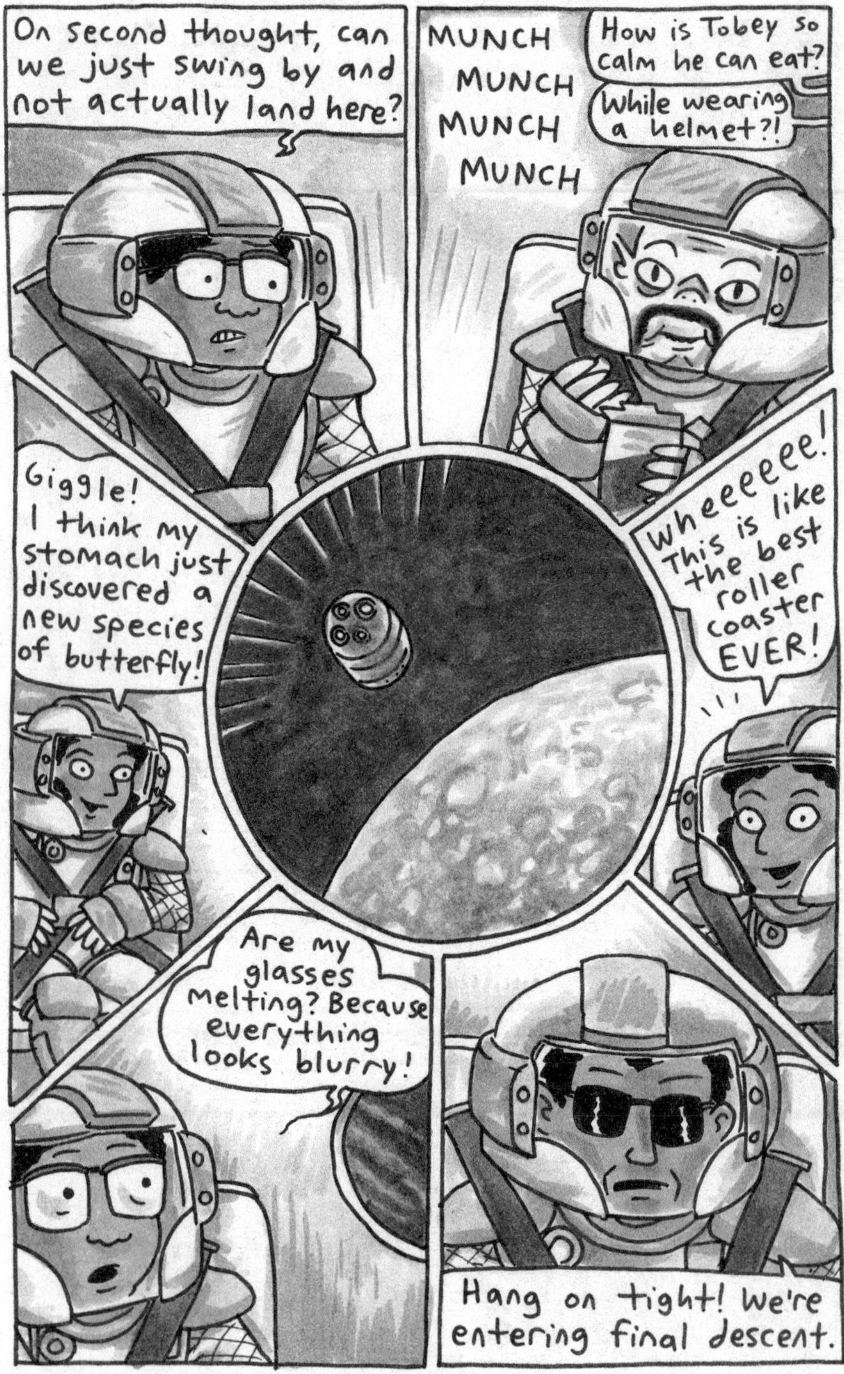
On second thought, can we just swing by and not actually land here?
MUNCH MUNCH MUNCH MUNCH
How is Tobey so calm he can eat?
While wearing a helmet?!
Giggle! I think my stomach just discovered a new species of butterfly!
Wheeeeeee! This is like the best roller coaster EVER!
Are my glasses melting? Because everything looks blurry!
Hang on tight! We're entering final descent.

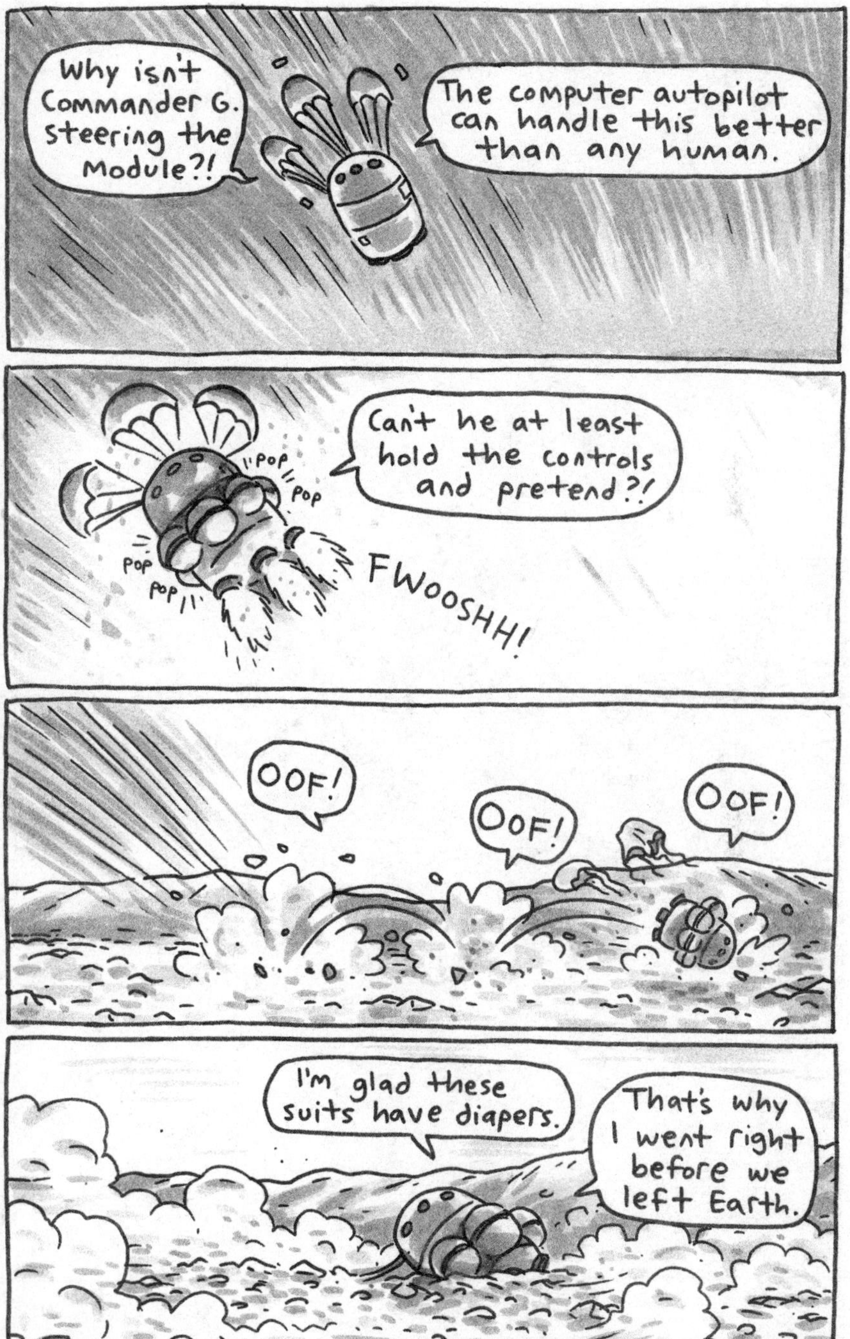
Why isn't Commander G. steering the Module?!
The computer autopilot can handle this better than any human.
Can't he at least hold the controls and pretend?!
POP
POP
POP
POP
FWOOSHH!
OOF!
OOF!
OOF!
I'm glad these suits have diapers.
That's why I went right before we left Earth.

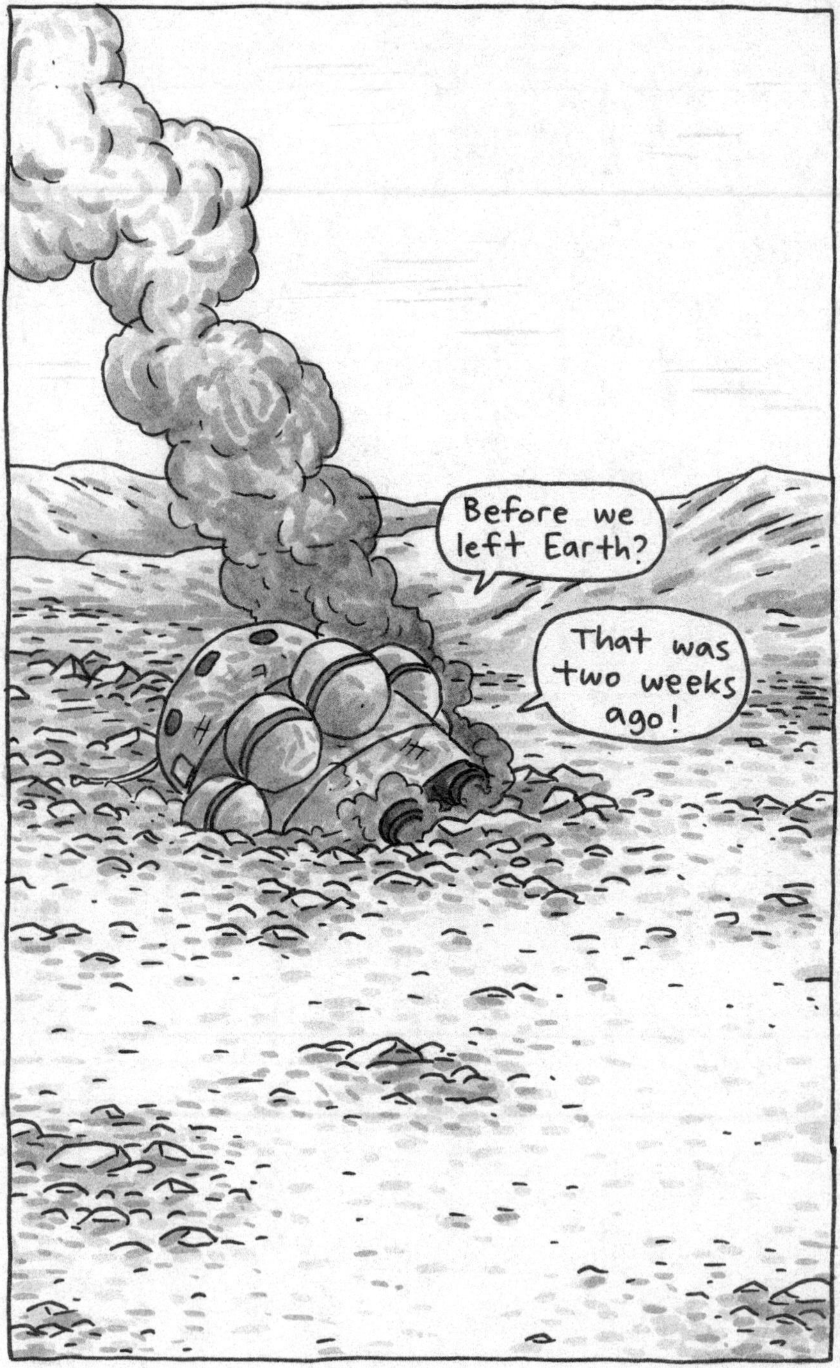
Before we left Earth?
That was two weeks ago!

RED CARPET ON THE RED PLANET

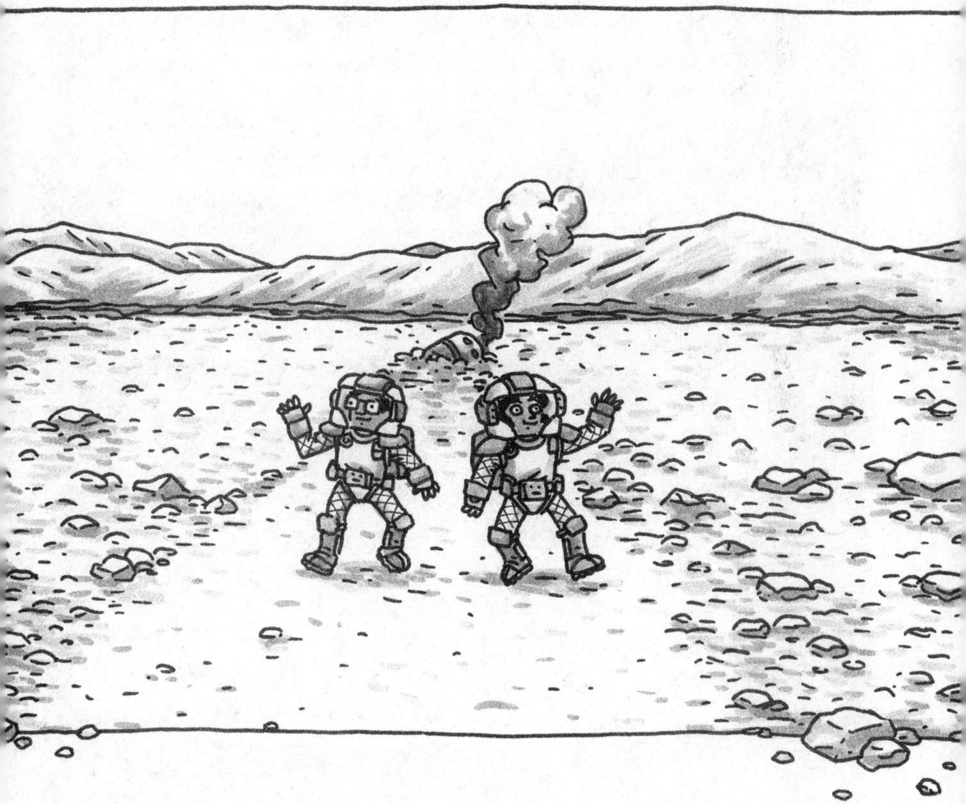

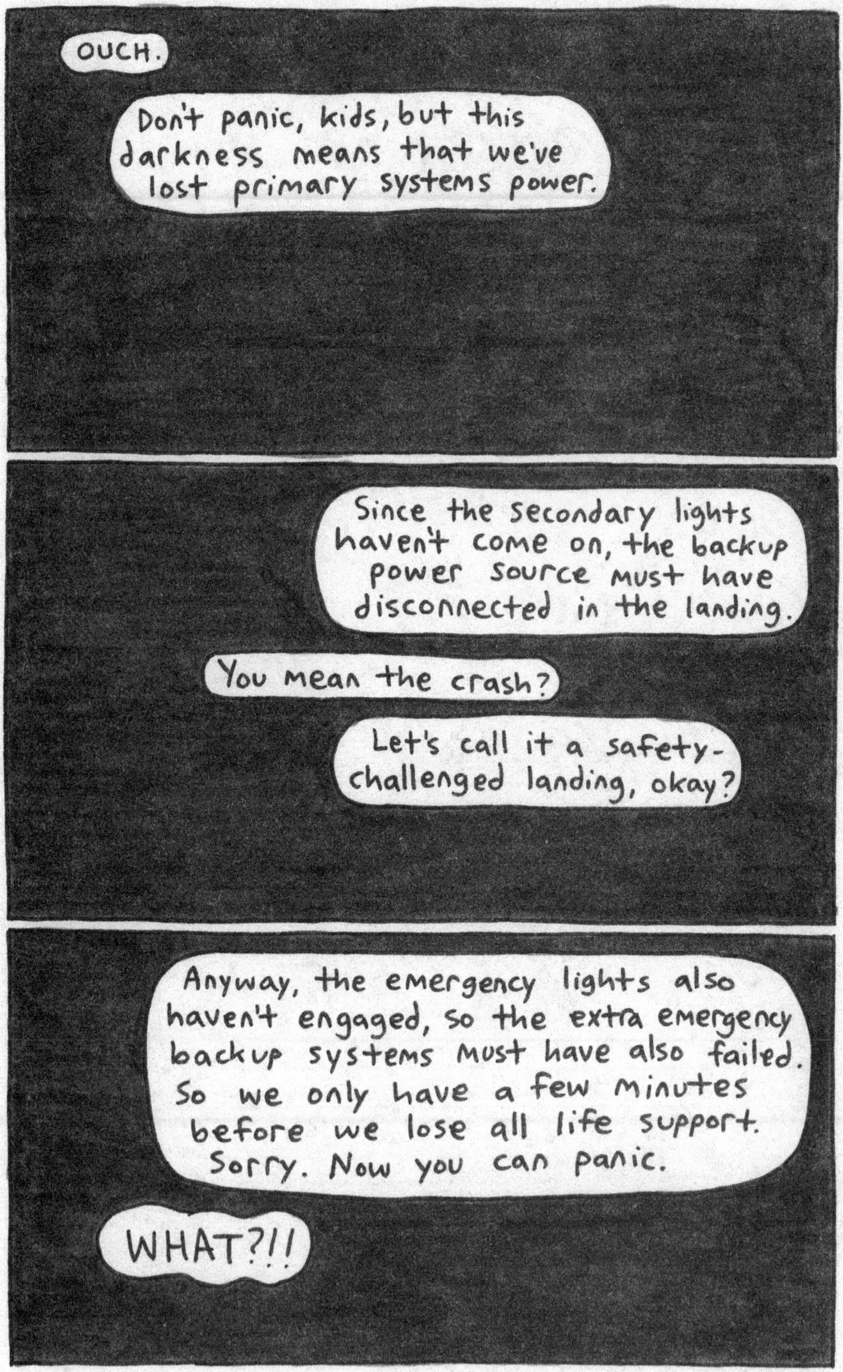
OUCH.
Don't panic, kids, but this darkness means that we've lost primary systems power.
Since the secondary lights haven't come on, the backup power source must have disconnected in the landing.
You mean the crash?
Let's call it a safety-challenged landing, okay?
Anyway, the emergency lights also haven't engaged, so the extra emergency backup systems must have also failed. So we only have a few minutes before we lose all life support. Sorry. Now you can panic.
WHAT?!!

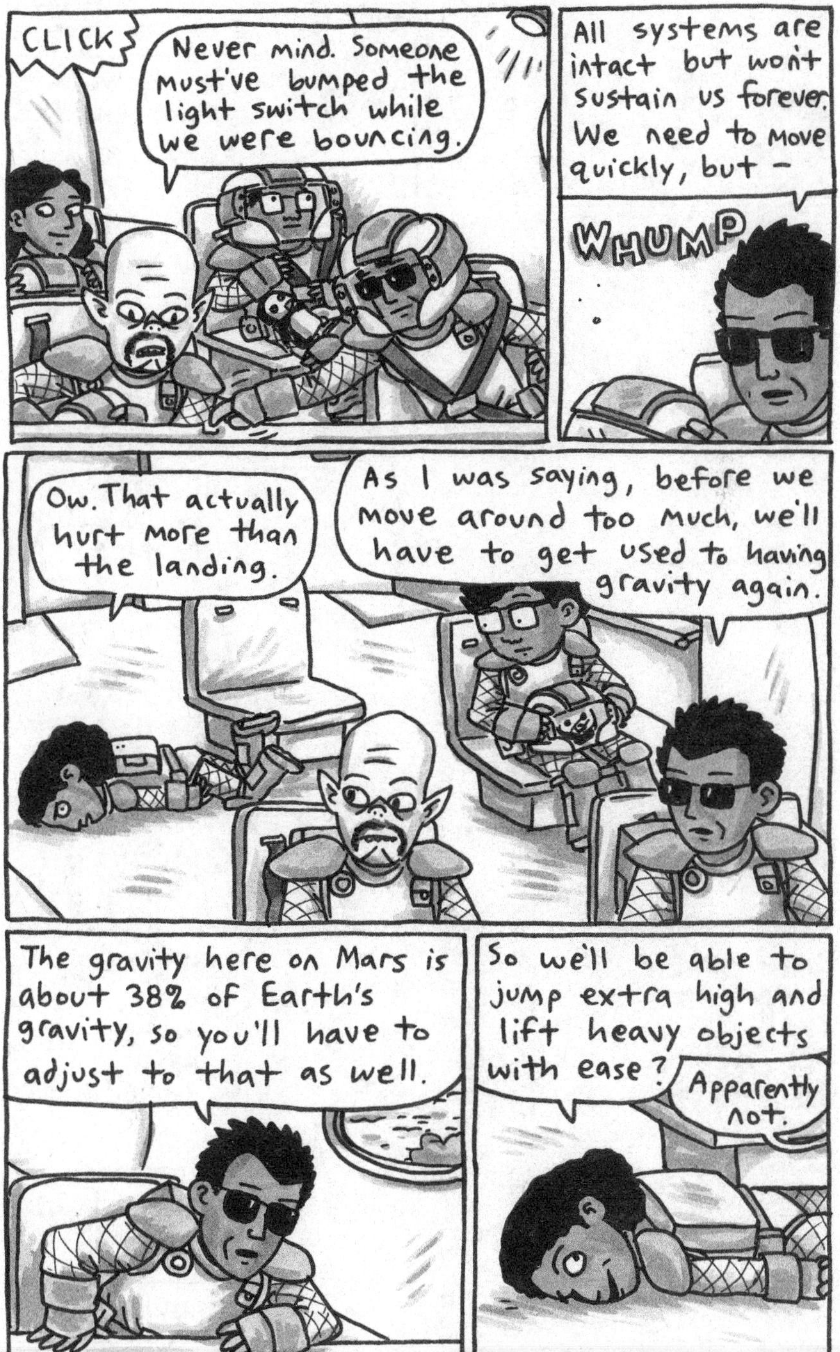
CLICK
Never mind. Someone must've bumped the light switch while we were bouncing.
All systems are intact but won't sustain us forever. We need to move quickly, but –
WHUMP
Ow. That actually hurt more than the landing.
As I was saying, before we move around too much, we'll have to get used to having gravity again.
The gravity here on Mars is about 38% of Earth's gravity, so you'll have to adjust to that as well.
So we'll be able to jump extra high and lift heavy objects with ease?
Apparently not.

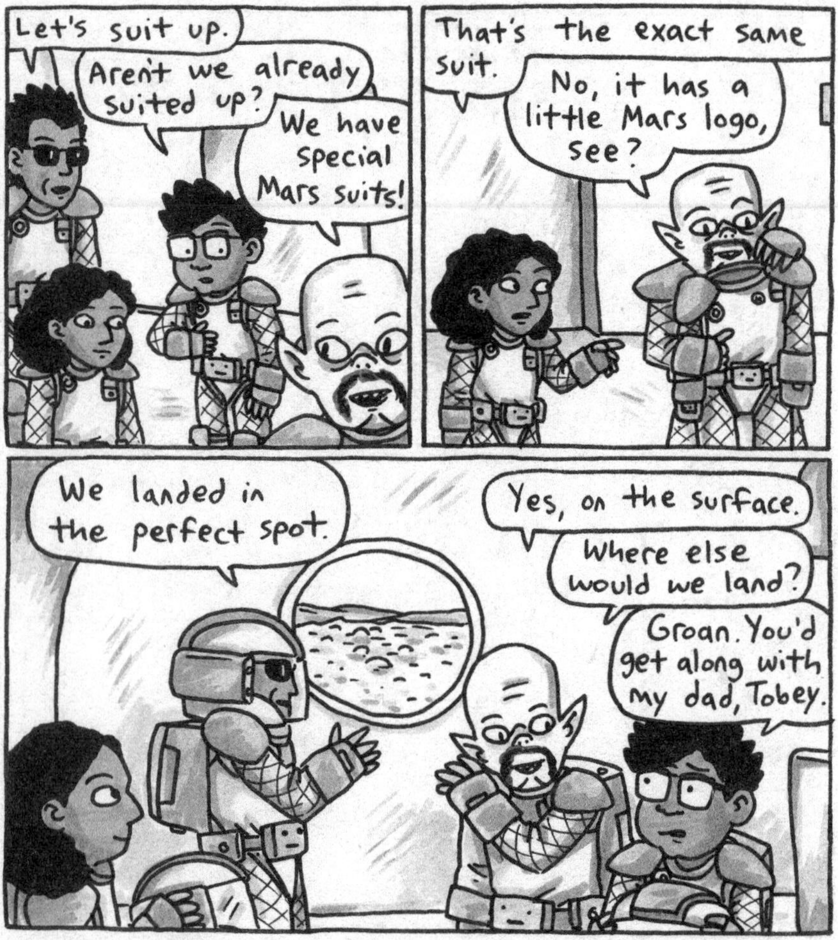
Let's suit up.
Aren't we already suited up?
We have special Mars suits!
That's the exact same suit.
No, it has a little Mars logo, see?
We landed in the perfect spot.
Yes, on the surface.
Where else would we land?
Groan. You'd get along with my dad, Tobey.

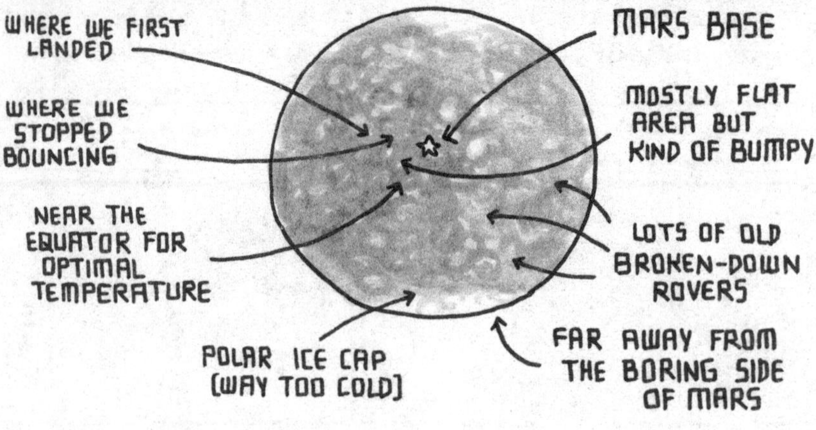
WHERE WE FIRST LANDED
MARS BASE
WHERE WE STOPPED BOUNCING
MOSTLY FLAT AREA BUT KIND OF BUMPY
NEAR THE EQUATOR FOR OPTIMAL TEMPERATURE
LOTS OF OLD BROKEN-DOWN ROVERS
POLAR ICE CAP (WAY TOO COLD)
FAR AWAY FROM THE BORING SIDE OF MARS

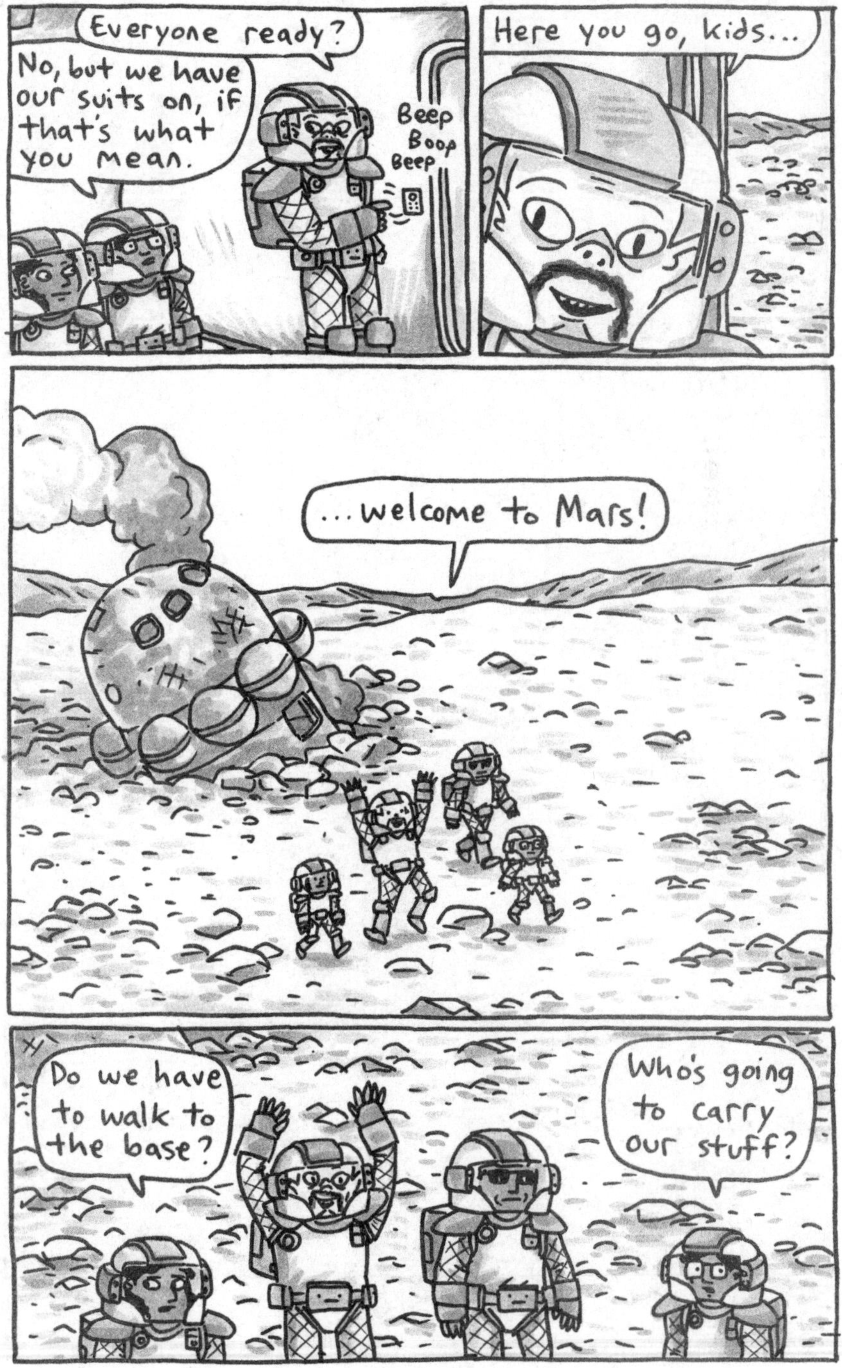
Everyone ready?
No, but we have our suits on, if that's what you mean.
Beep Boop Beep
Here you go, kids...
...welcome to Mars!
Do we have to walk to the base?
Who's going to carry our stuff?

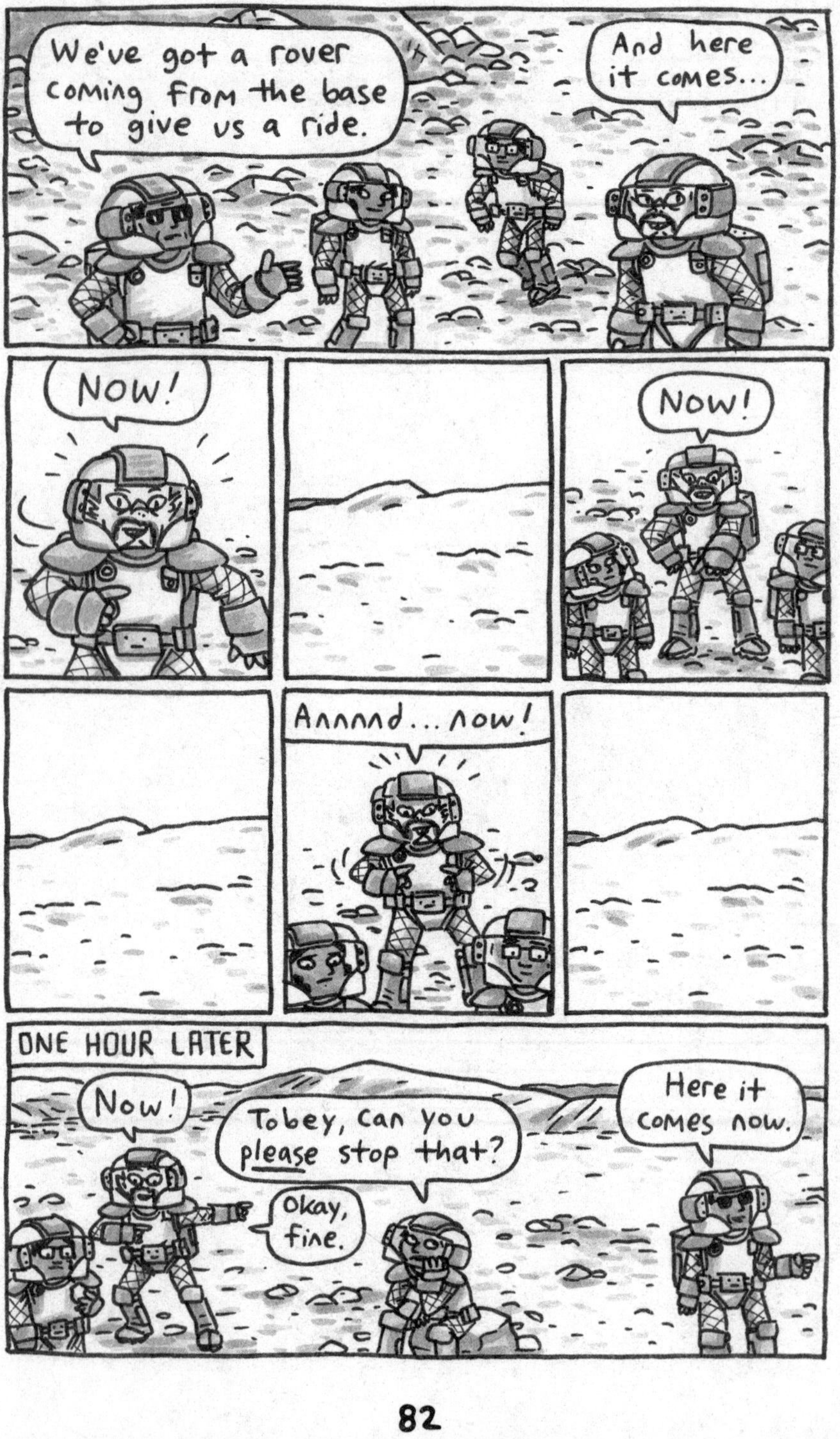
We've got a rover coming from the base to give us a ride.
And here it comes...
NOW!
NOW!
Annnnd... now!
ONE HOUR LATER
Now!
Tobey, can you please stop that?
Okay, fine.
Here it comes now.

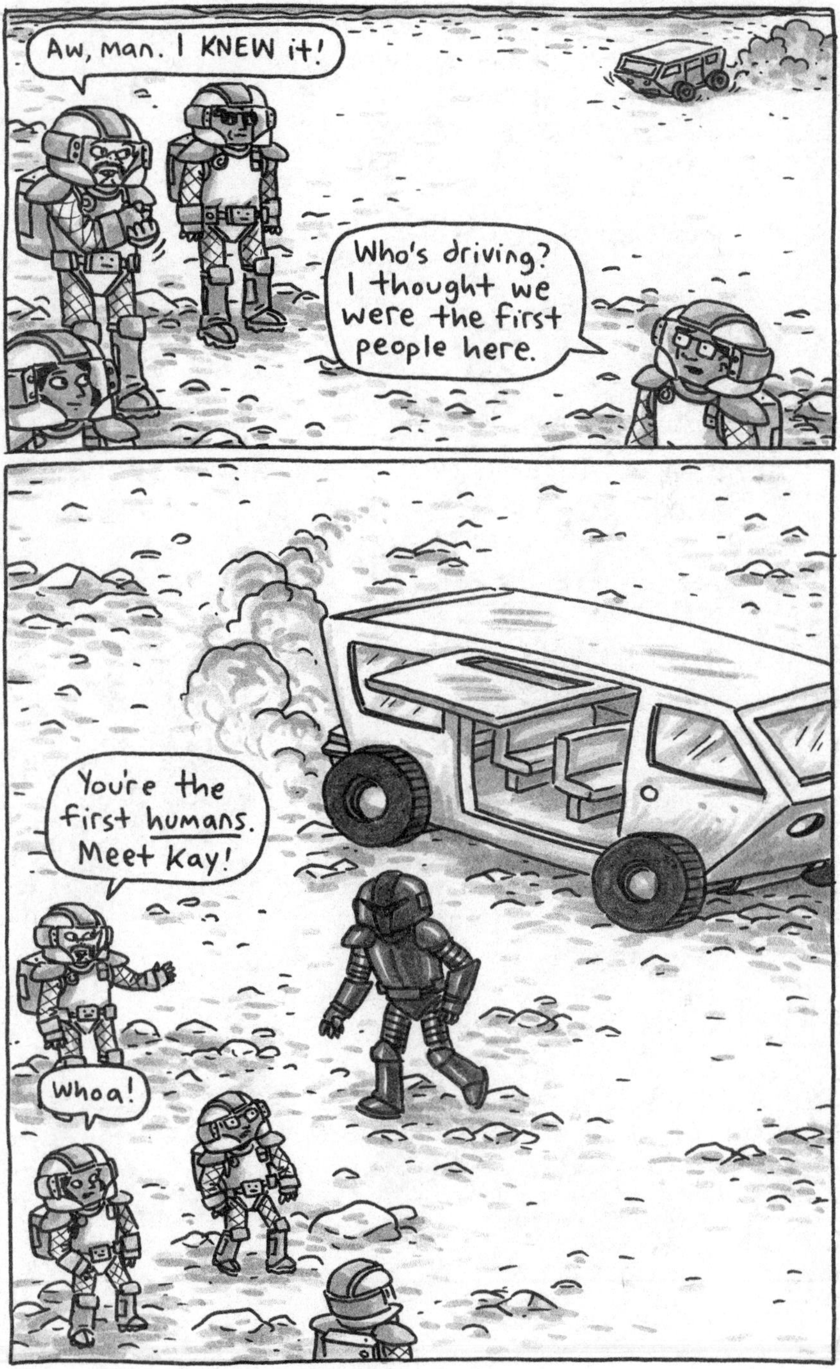
Aw, man. I KNEW it!
Who's driving? I thought we were the first people here.
You're the first humans. Meet Kay!
Whoa!

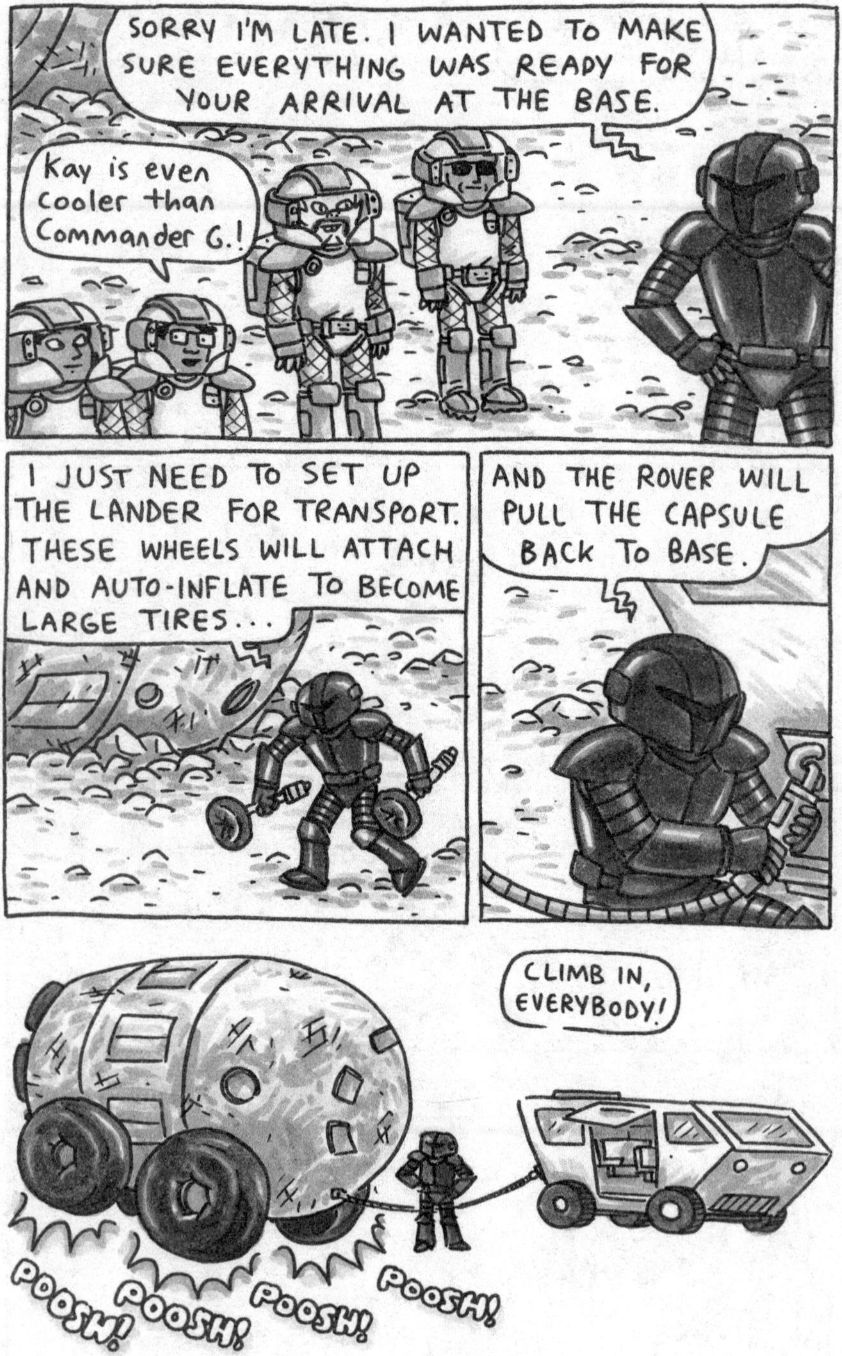
SORRY I'M LATE. I WANTED TO MAKE SURE EVERYTHING WAS READY FOR YOUR ARRIVAL AT THE BASE.
Kay is even cooler than Commander G.!
I JUST NEED TO SET UP THE LANDER FOR TRANSPORT. THESE WHEELS WILL ATTACH AND AUTO-INFLATE TO BECOME LARGE TIRES...
AND THE ROVER WILL PULL THE CAPSULE BACK TO BASE.
CLIMB IN, EVERYBODY!
POOSH!
POOSH!
POOSH!
POOSH!

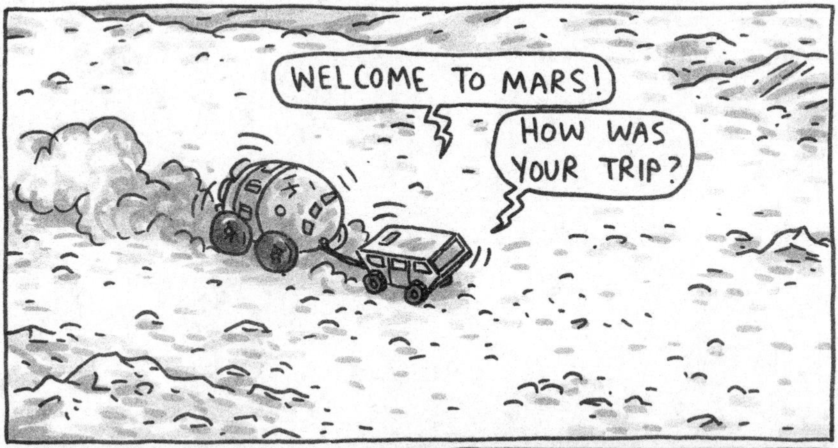
WELCOME TO MARS!
HOW WAS YOUR TRIP?

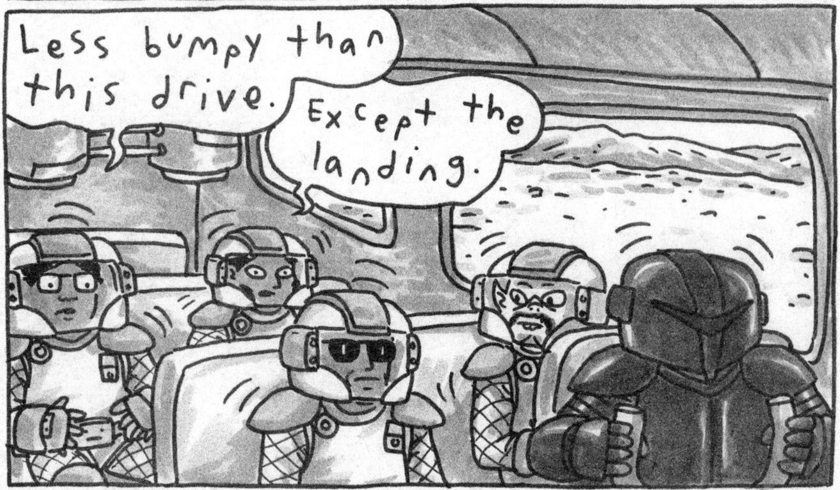
Less bumpy than this drive.
Except the landing.

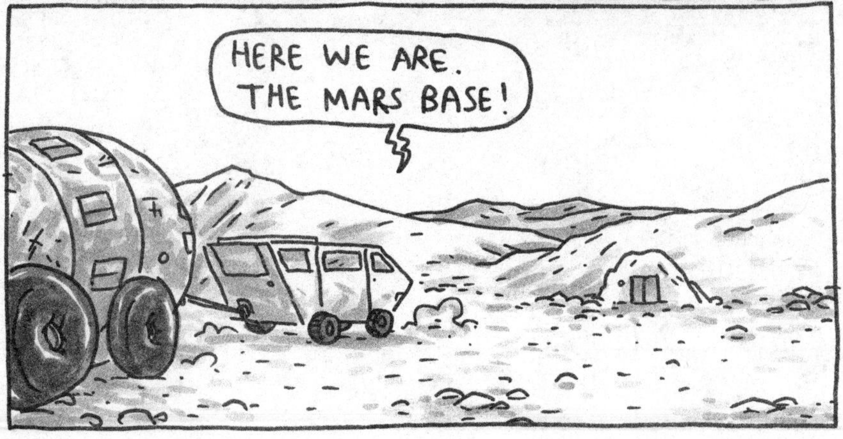
HERE WE ARE. THE MARS BASE!

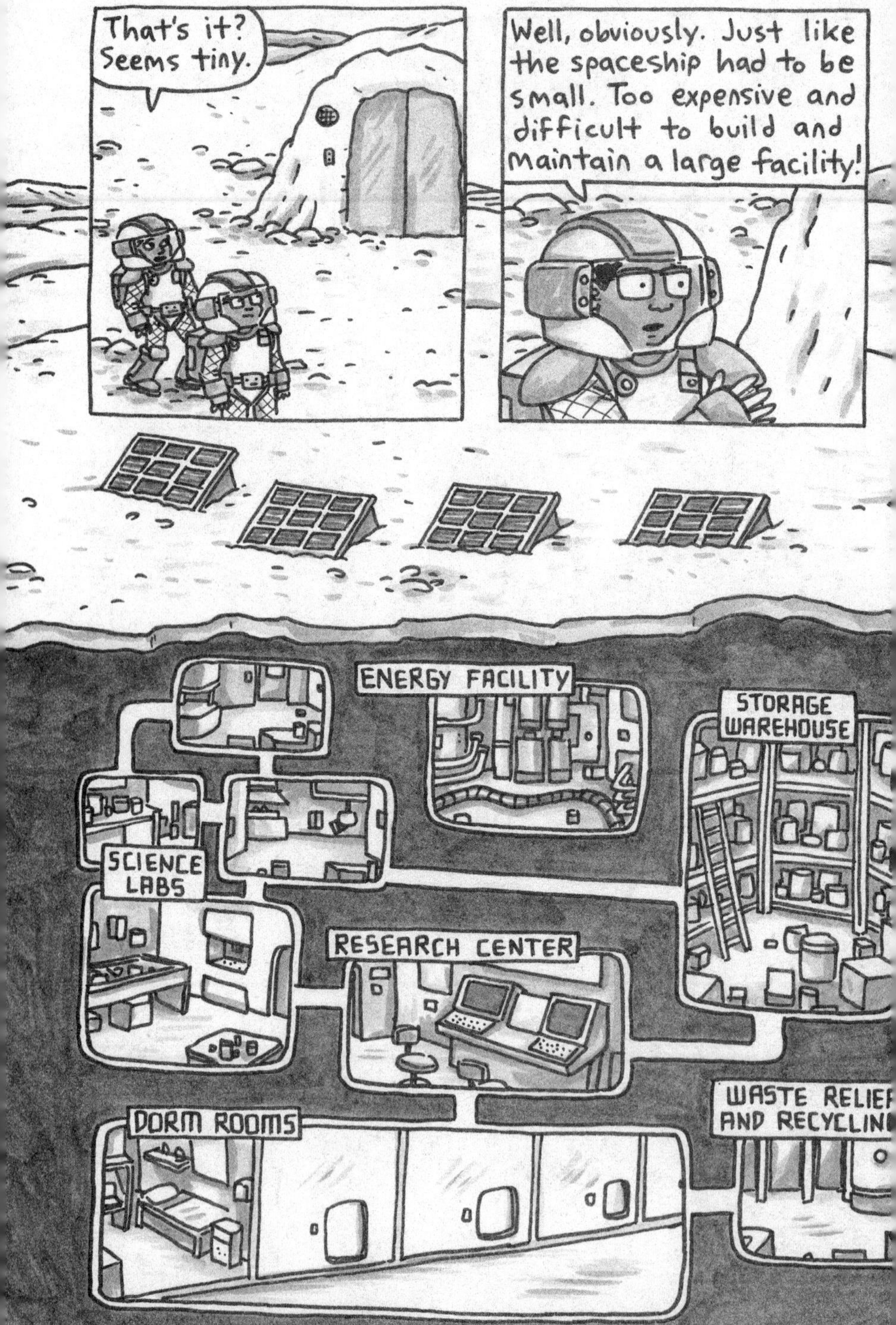
That's it? Seems tiny.
Well, obviously. Just like the spaceship had to be small. Too expensive and difficult to build and maintain a large facility!
ENERGY FACILITY
STORAGE WAREHOUSE
SCIENCE LABS
RESEARCH CENTER
DORM ROOMS

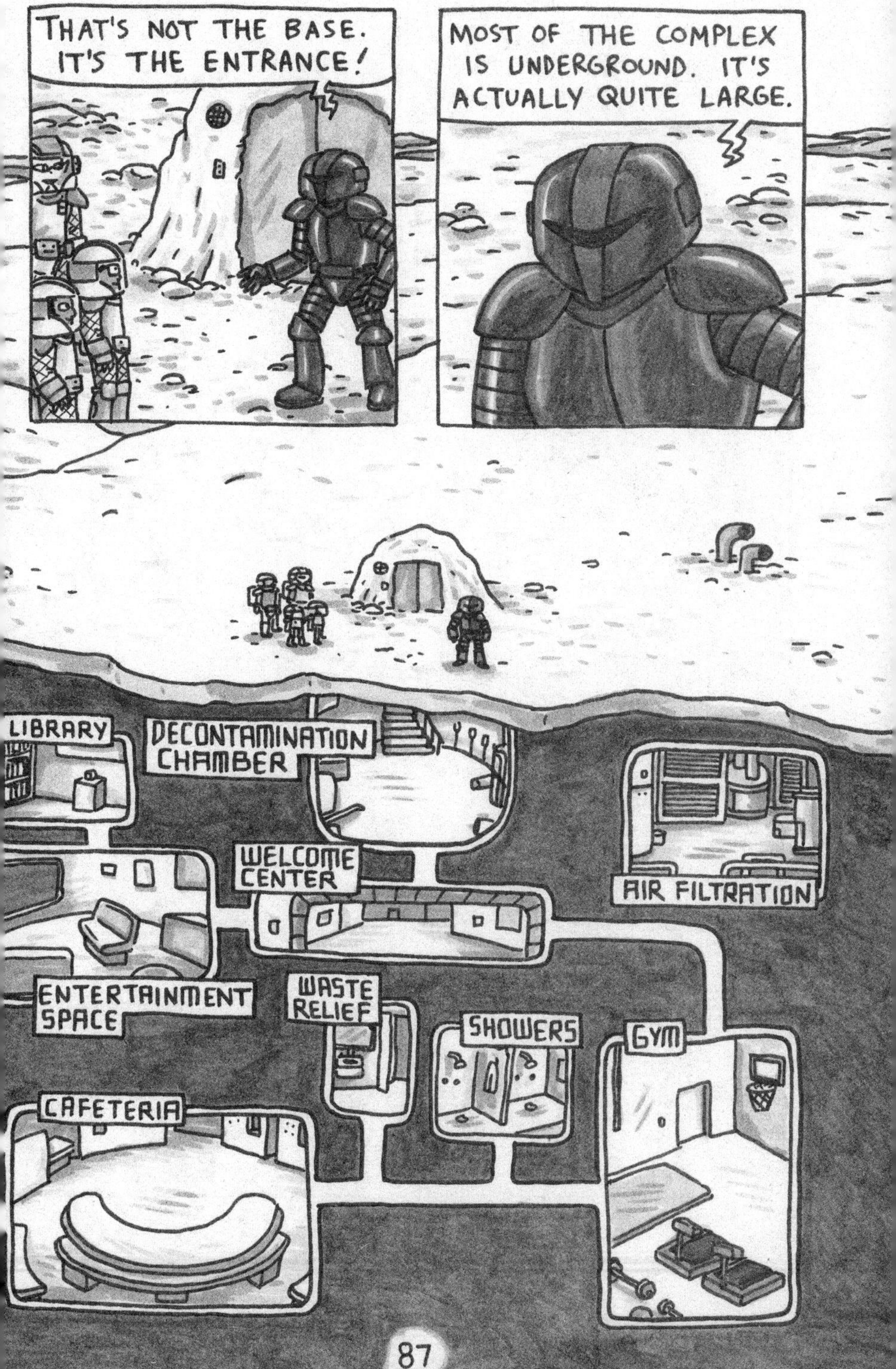
THAT'S NOT THE BASE. IT'S THE ENTRANCE!
MOST OF THE COMPLEX IS UNDERGROUND. IT'S ACTUALLY QUITE LARGE.
LIBRARY
DECONTAMINATION CHAMBER
AIR FILTRATION
WELCOME CENTER
ENTERTAINMENT SPACE
WASTE RELIEF
SHOWERS
GYM
CAFETERIA

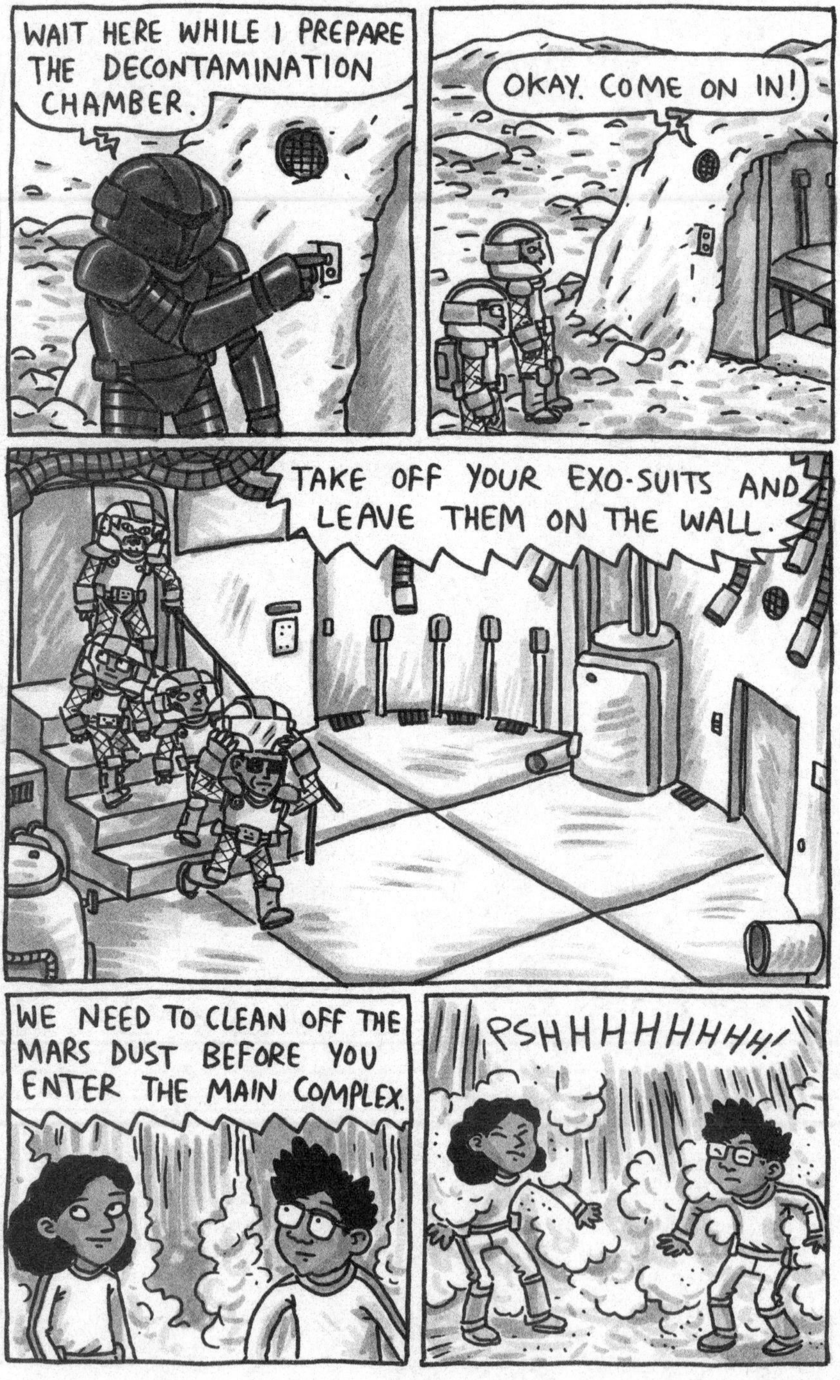
WAIT HERE WHILE I PREPARE THE DECONTAMINATION CHAMBER.
OKAY. COME ON IN!
TAKE OFF YOUR EXO-SUITS AND LEAVE THEM ON THE WALL.
WE NEED TO CLEAN OFF THE MARS DUST BEFORE YOU ENTER THE MAIN COMPLEX.
PSHHHHHHHH!

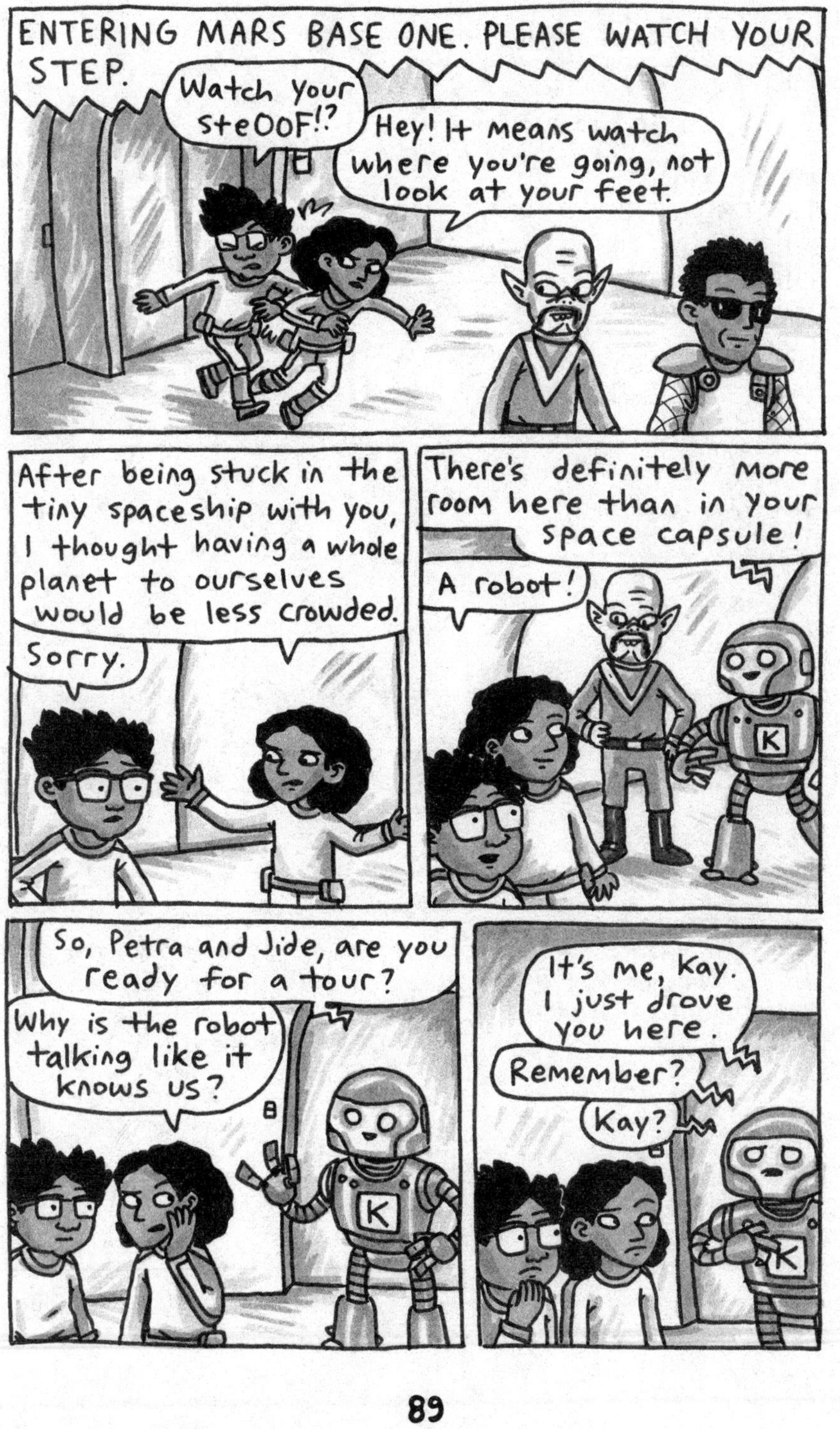
ENTERING MARS BASE ONE. PLEASE WATCH YOUR STEP.
Watch your steOOF!?
Hey! It means watch where you're going, not look at your feet.
After being stuck in the tiny spaceship with you, I thought having a whole planet to ourselves would be less crowded.
Sorry.
There's definitely more room here than in your space capsule!
A robot!
So, Petra and Jide, are you ready for a tour?
Why is the robot talking like it knows us?
It's me, Kay. I just drove you here.
Remember?
Kay?

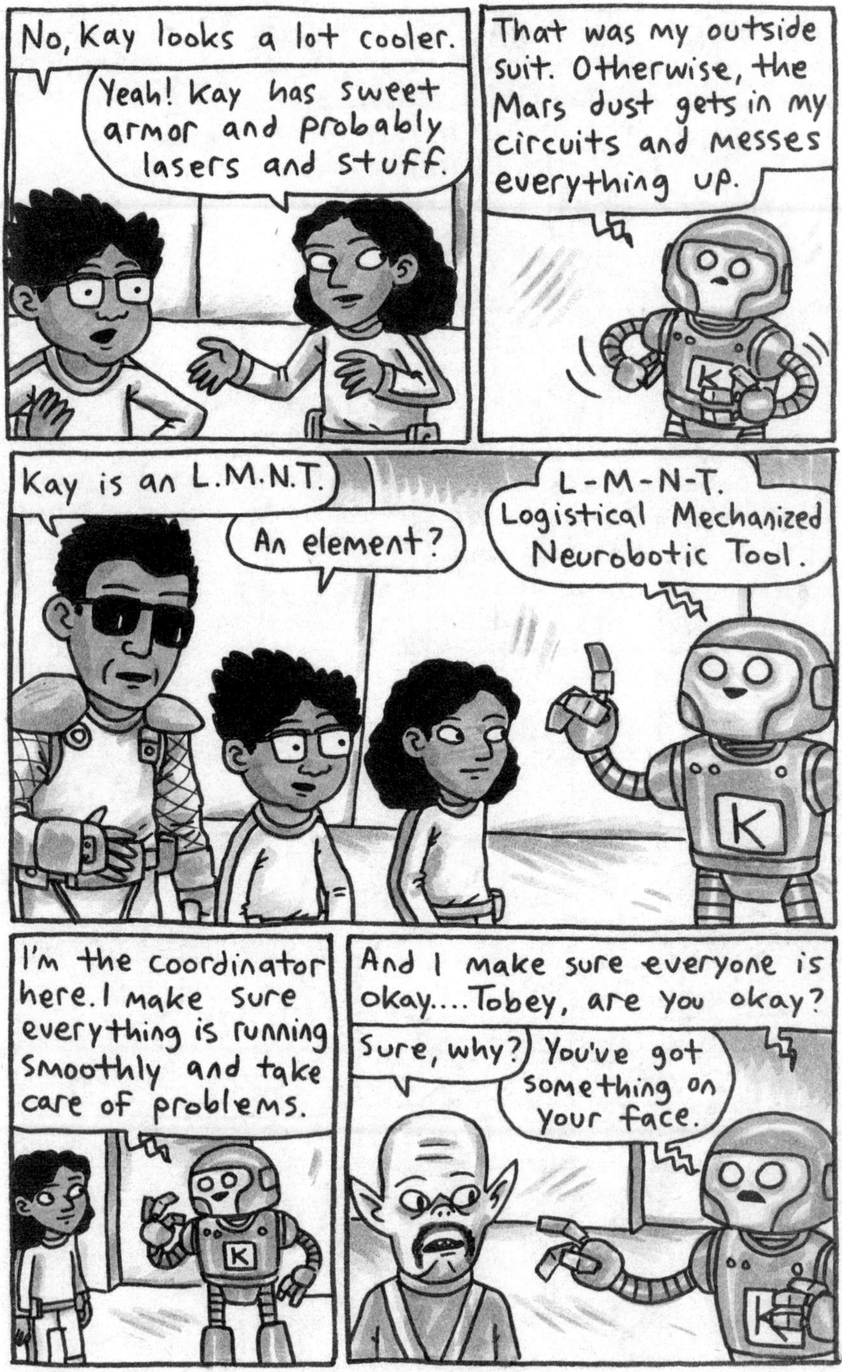
No, Kay looks a lot cooler.
Yeah! Kay has sweet armor and probably lasers and stuff.
That was my outside suit. Otherwise, the Mars dust gets in my circuits and messes everything up.
K
Kay is an L.M.N.T.
An element?
L-M-N-T. Logistical Mechanized Neurobotic Tool.
K
I'm the coordinator here. I make sure everything is running smoothly and take care of problems.
K
And I make sure everyone is okay.... Tobey, are you okay?
Sure, why?
You've got something on your face.

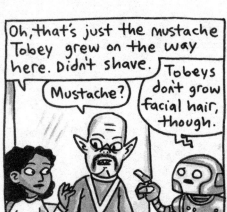

Oh, that's just the mustache Tobey grew on the way here. Didn't shave.

Mustache?

Tobeys don't grow facial hair, though.

Let me look at myself on the back of your shiny head, kay.

WHAT?! Do you know what this means?

Someone drew a mustache on me. Someone... PRANKED ME!!

I assumed you drew it yourself.

This means WAR.

PRANK war.

Uh-oh.

As soon as I find out who it was.

Well, I know who it wasn't.

Who?

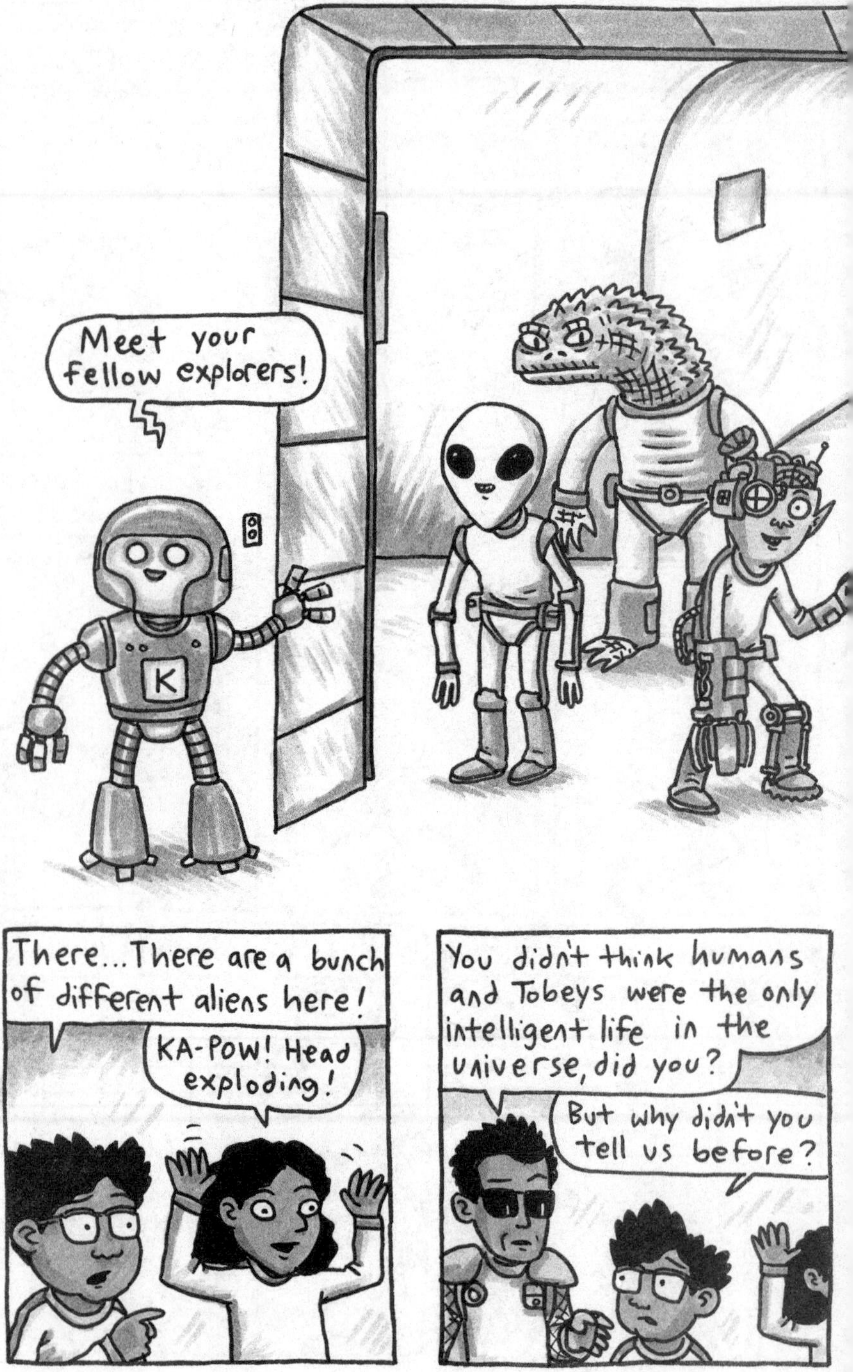
Meet your fellow explorers!
There...There are a bunch of different aliens here!
KA-POW! Head exploding!
You didn't think humans and Tobeys were the only intelligent life in the universe, did you?
But why didn't you tell us before?

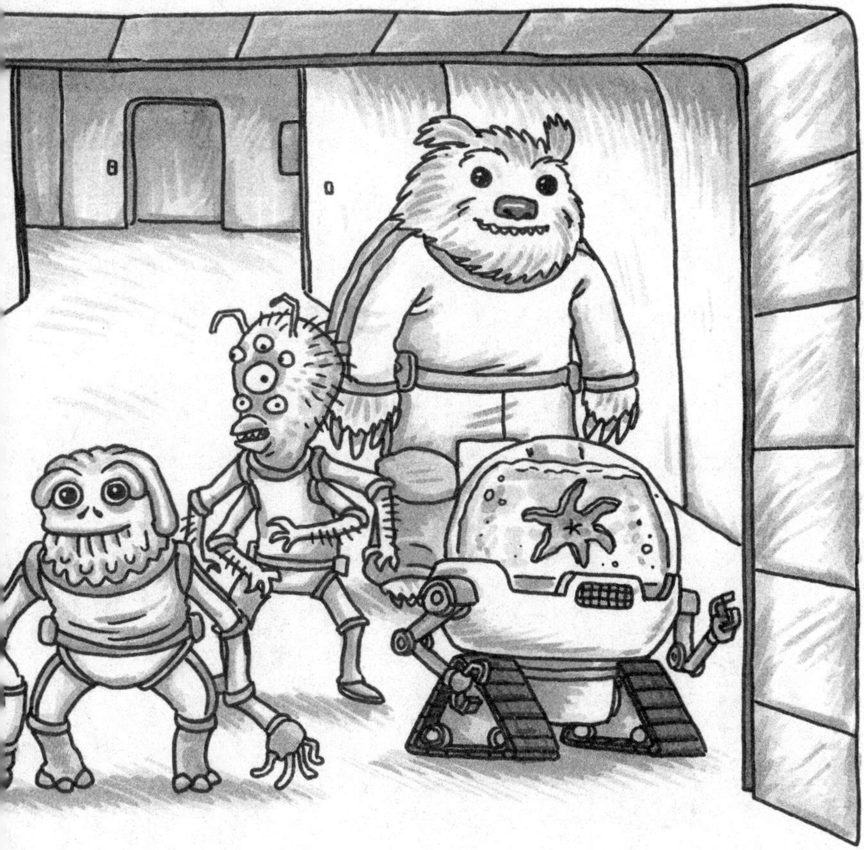

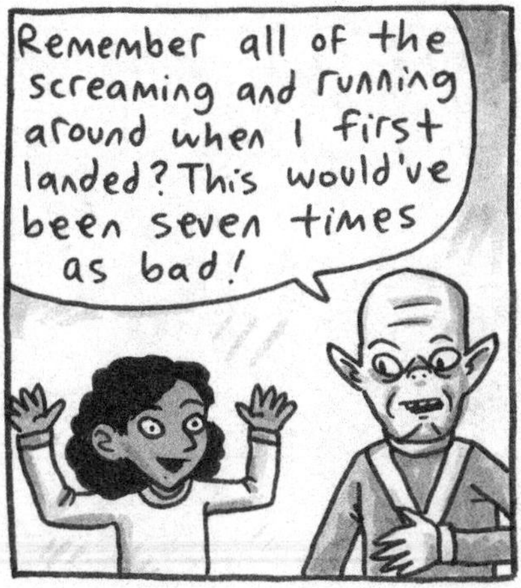
Remember all of the screaming and running around when I first landed? This would've been seven times as bad!

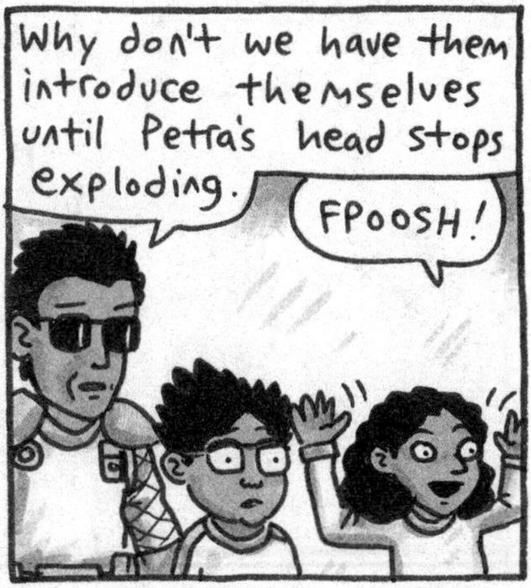
Why don't we have them introduce themselves until Petra's head stops exploding.
FPOOSH!

I am Sheila.

Please do not get too close.

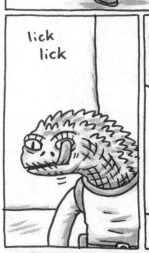

lick
lick

I do not want bits of Petra's exploding head to get on me.

That was a joke.

Sheila has a dry sense of humor. You'll get used to it.

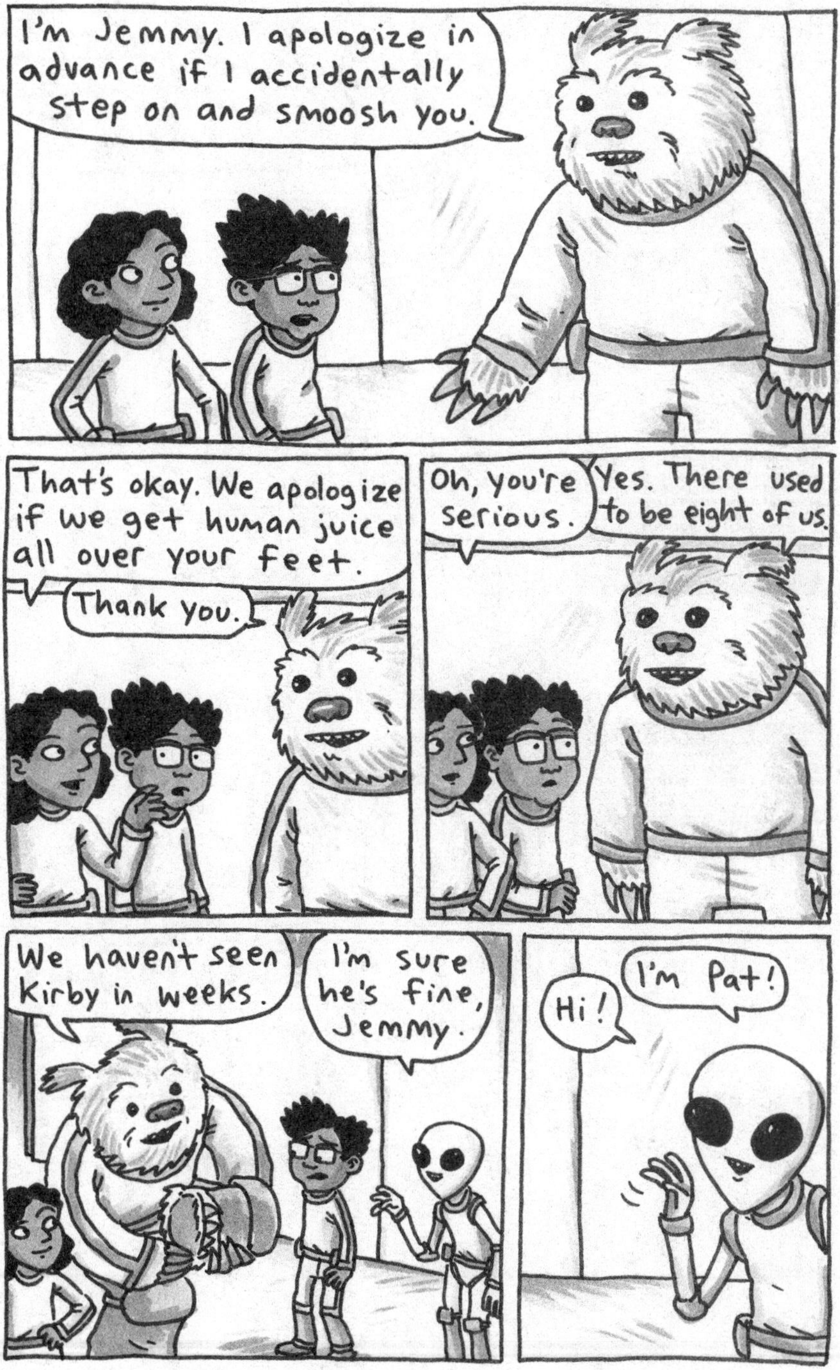
I'm Jemmy. I apologize in advance if I accidentally step on and smoosh you.
That's okay. We apologize if we get human juice all over your feet.
Thank you.
Oh, you're serious.
Yes. There used to be eight of us.
We haven't seen Kirby in weeks.
I'm sure he's fine, Jemmy.
Hi!
I'm Pat!

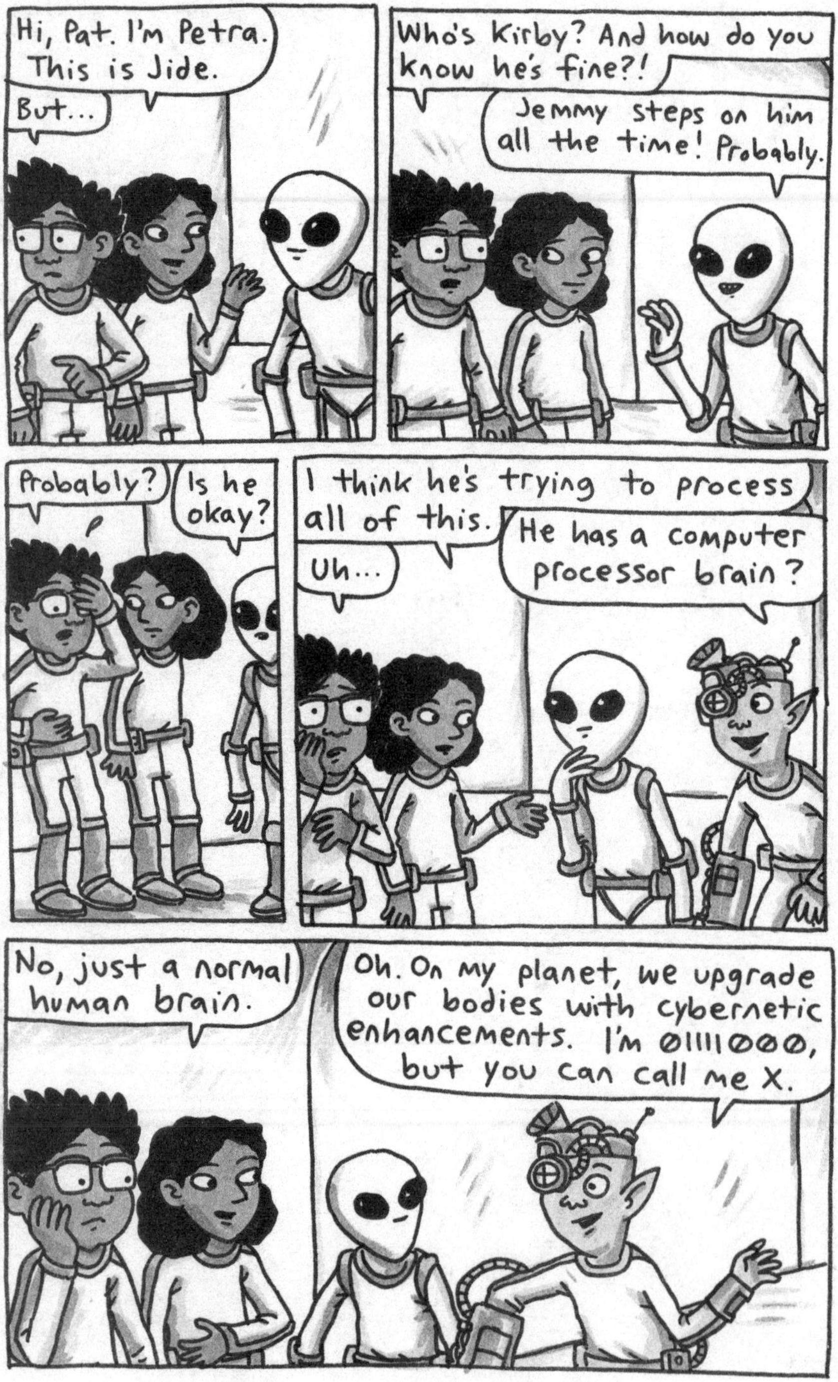

Hi, Pat. I'm Petra. This is Jide.
But...
Who's Kirby? And how do you know he's fine?!
Jemmy steps on him all the time! Probably.
Probably?
Is he okay?
I think he's trying to process all of this.
Uh...
He has a computer processor brain?
No, just a normal human brain.
Oh. On my planet, we upgrade our bodies with cybernetic enhancements. I'm 0111000, but you can call me X.

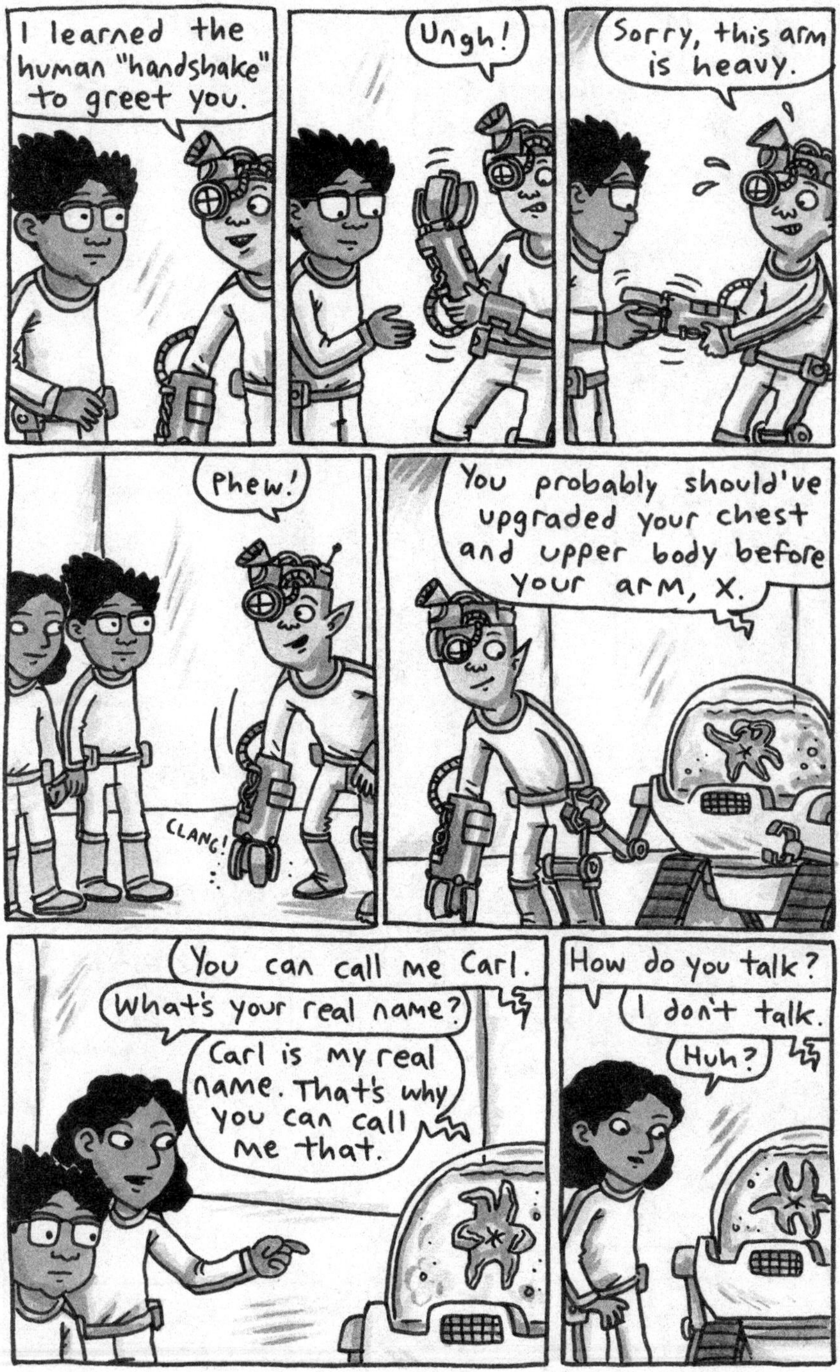
I learned the human "handshake" to greet you.
Ungh!
Sorry, this arm is heavy.
Phew!
CLANG!
You probably should've upgraded your chest and upper body before your arm, X.
You can call me Carl.
What's your real name?
Carl is my real name. That's why you can call me that.
How do you talk?
I don't talk.
Huh?

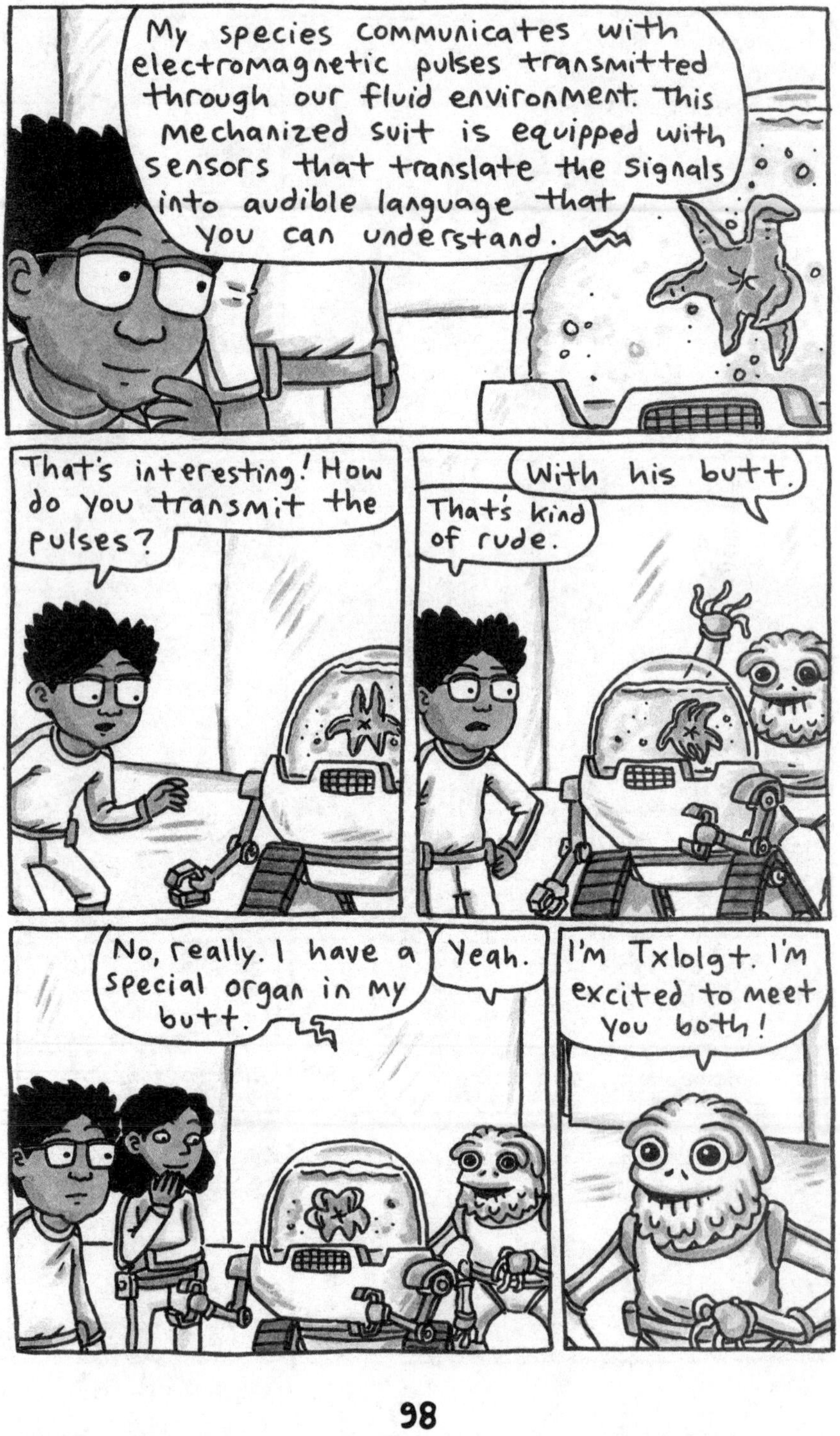
My species communicates with electromagnetic pulses transmitted through our fluid environment. This mechanized suit is equipped with sensors that translate the signals into audible language that you can understand.
That's interesting! How do you transmit the pulses?
With his butt.
That's kind of rude.
No, really. I have a special organ in my butt.
Yeah.
I'm Txlolgt. I'm excited to meet you both!

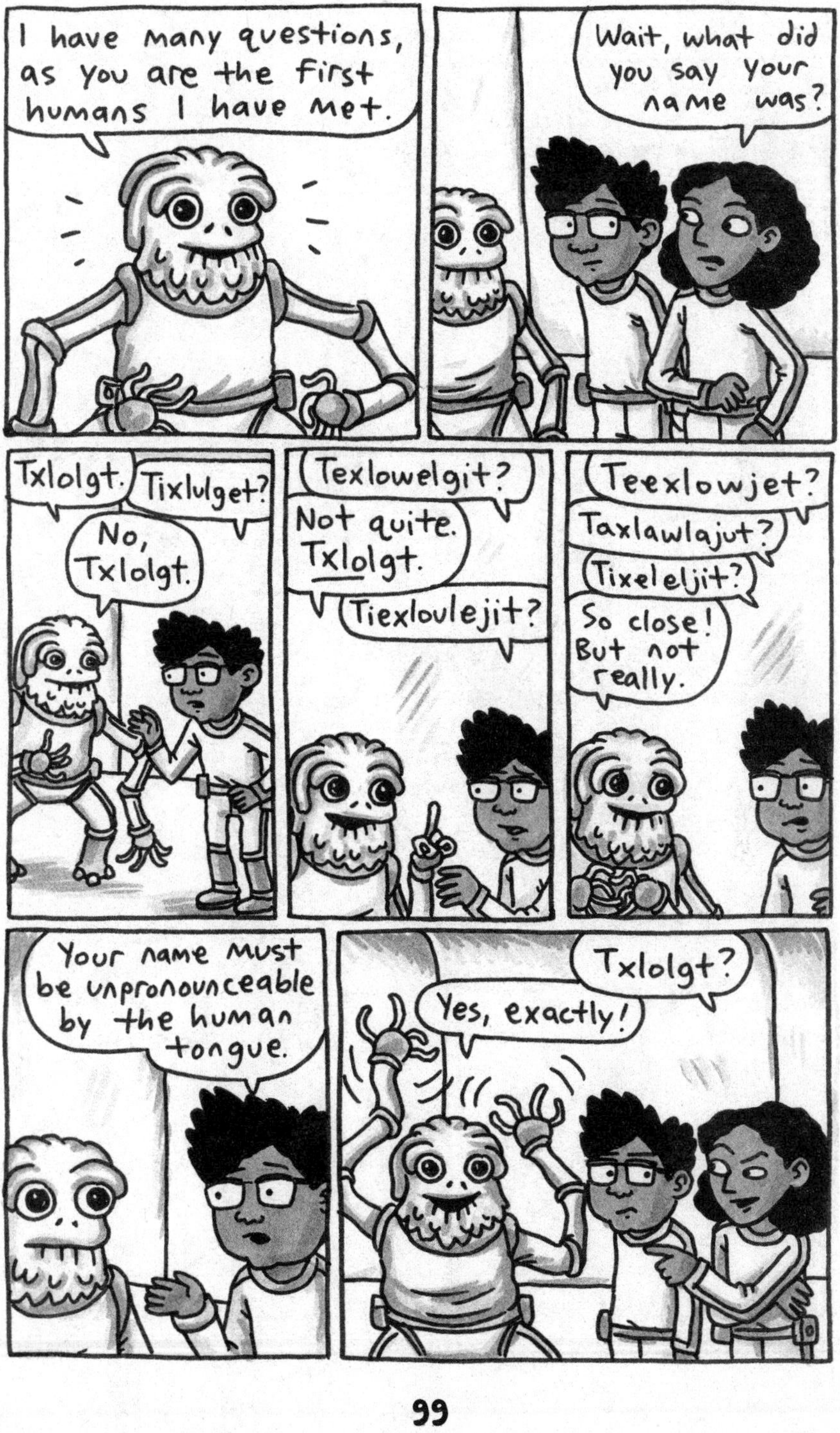
I have many questions, as you are the first humans I have met.
Wait, what did you say your name was?
Txlolgt.
Tixlulget?
No, Txlolgt.
Texlowelgit?
Not quite. Txlolgt.
Tiexloulejit?
Teexlowjet?
Taxlawlajut?
Tixeleljit?
So close! But not really.
Your name must be unpronounceable by the human tongue.
Txlolgt?
Yes, exactly!

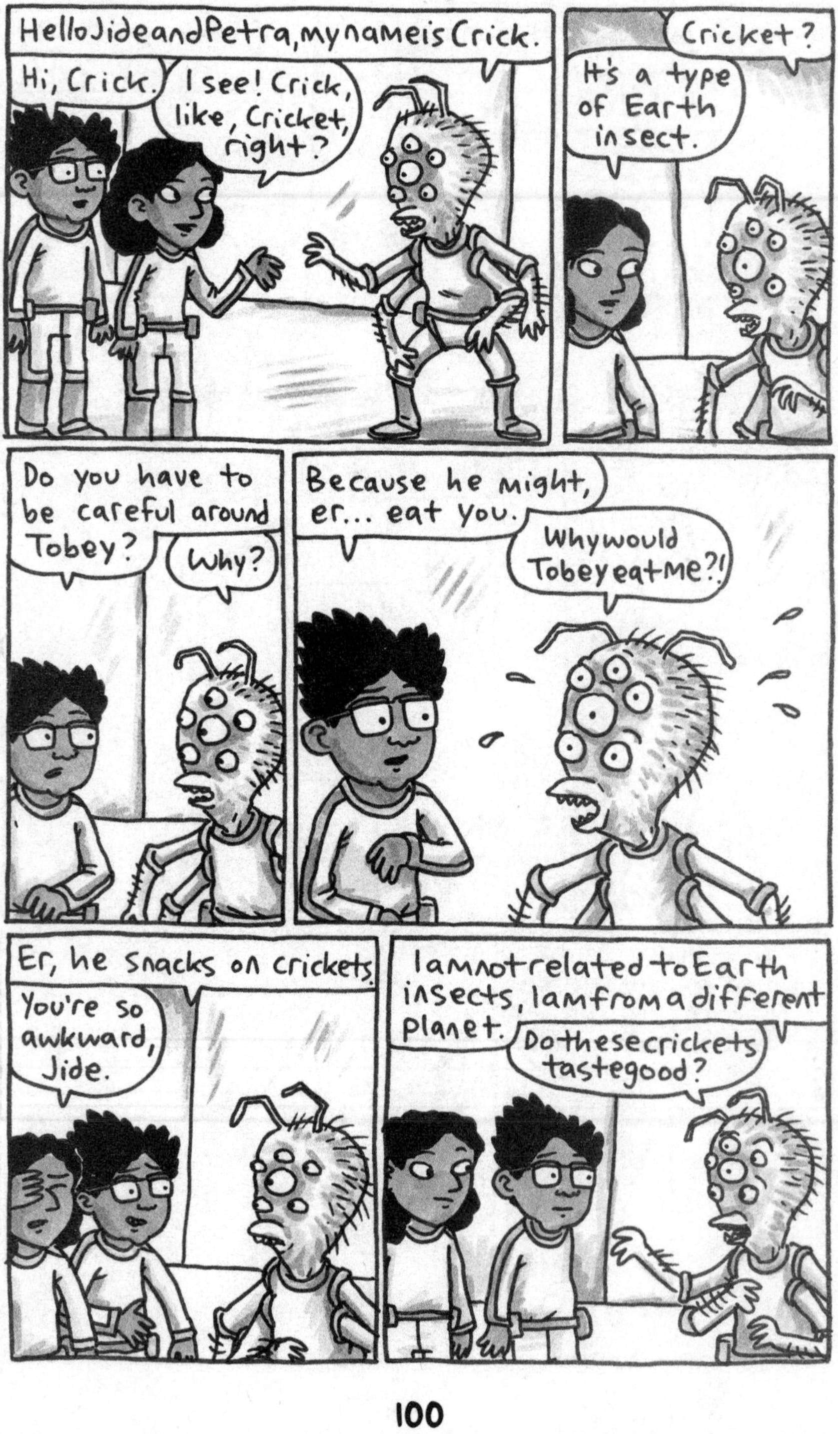
HelloJideandPetra,mynameisCrick.
Hi, Crick.
I see! Crick, like, Cricket, right?
Cricket?
It's a type of Earth insect.
Do you have to be careful around Tobey?
Why?
Because he might, er... eat you.
Whywould TobeyeatMe?!
Er, he snacks on crickets.
You're so awkward, Jide.
Iamnotrelated toEarth insects, Iamfroma different planet.
Dothesecrickets tastegood?

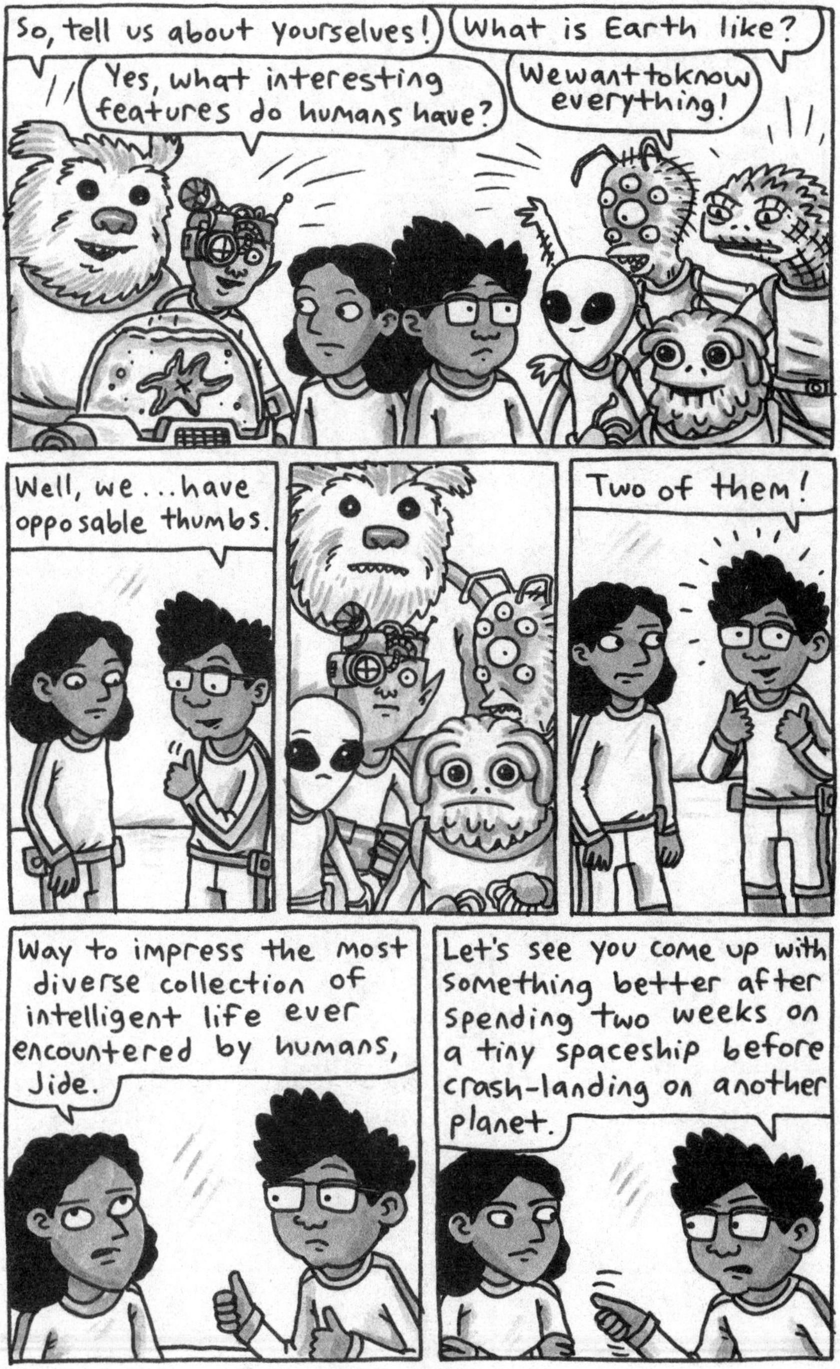
So, tell us about yourselves!
Yes, what interesting features do humans have?
What is Earth like?
We want to know everything!
Well, we...have opposable thumbs.
Two of them!
Way to impress the most diverse collection of intelligent life ever encountered by humans, Jide.
Let's see you come up with something better after spending two weeks on a tiny spaceship before crash-landing on another planet.

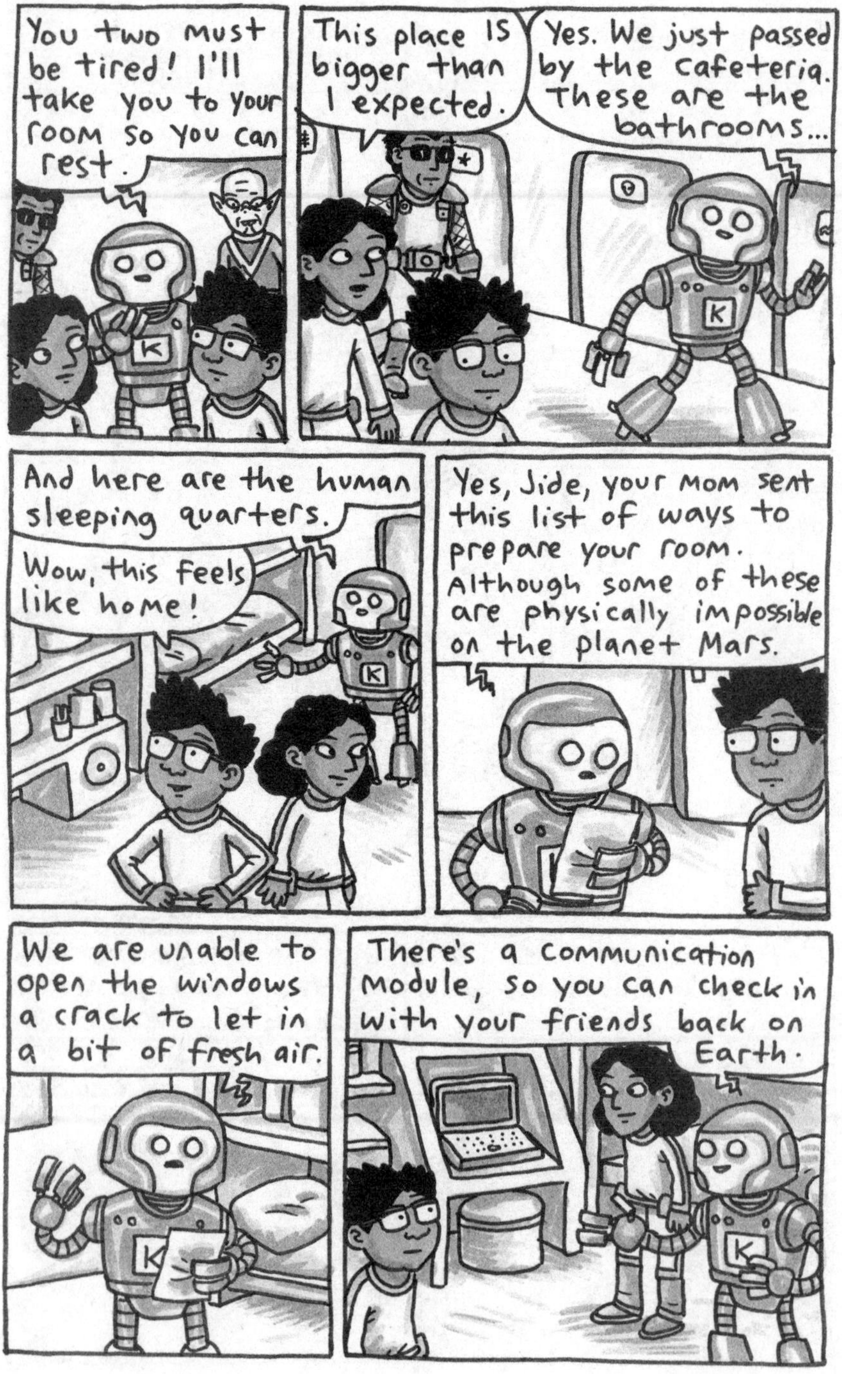
You two must be tired! I'll take you to your room so you can rest.
This place IS bigger than I expected.
Yes. We just passed by the cafeteria. These are the bathrooms...
And here are the human sleeping quarters.
Wow, this feels like home!
Yes, Jide, your mom sent this list of ways to prepare your room. Although some of these are physically impossible on the planet Mars.
We are unable to open the windows a crack to let in a bit of fresh air.
There's a communication module, so you can check in with your friends back on Earth.

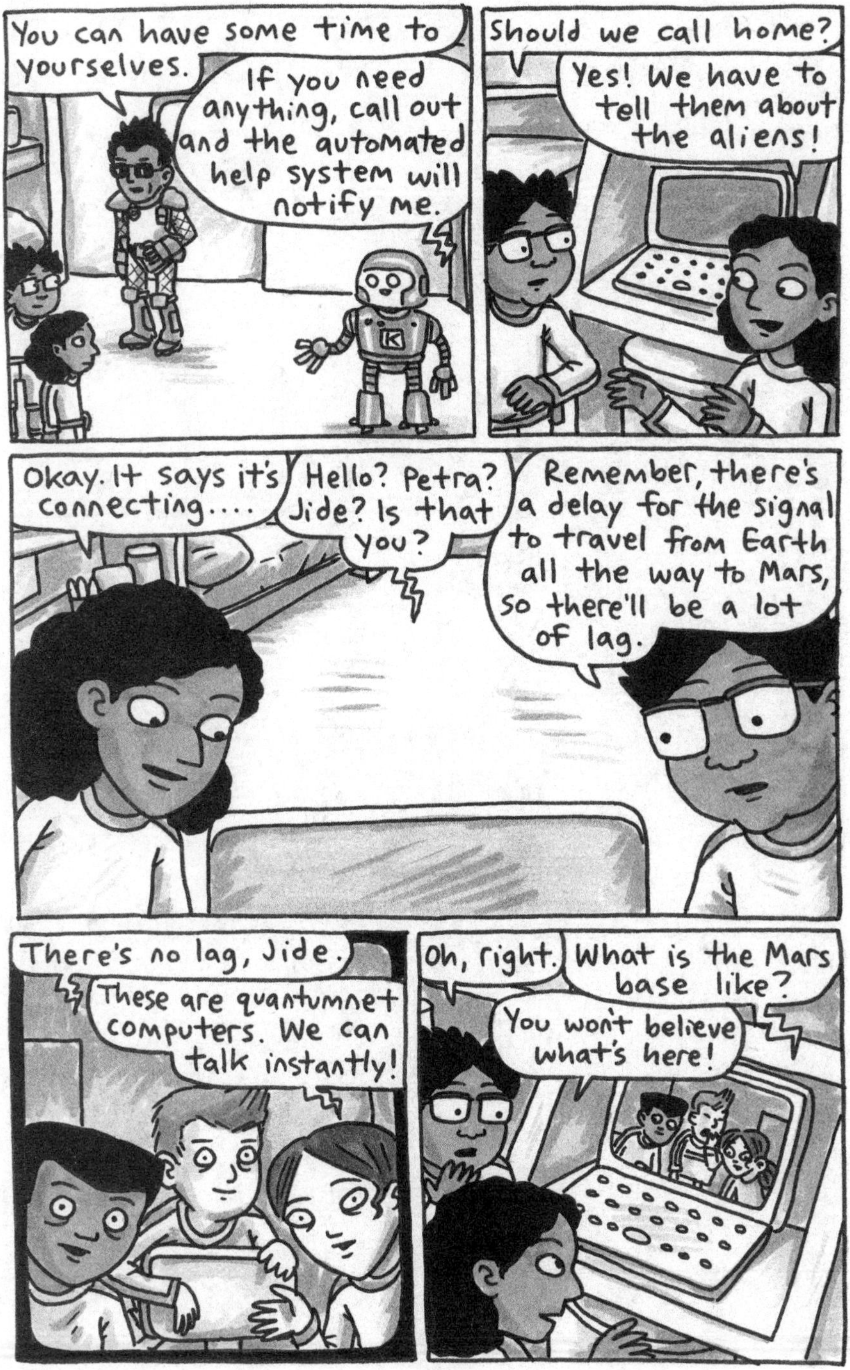
You can have some time to yourselves.
If you need anything, call out and the automated help system will notify me.
Should we call home?
Yes! We have to tell them about the aliens!
Okay. It says it's connecting....
Hello? Petra? Jide? Is that you?
Remember, there's a delay for the signal to travel from Earth all the way to Mars, so there'll be a lot of lag.
There's no lag, Jide.
These are quantumnet computers. We can talk instantly!
Oh, right.
What is the Mars base like?
You won't believe what's here!

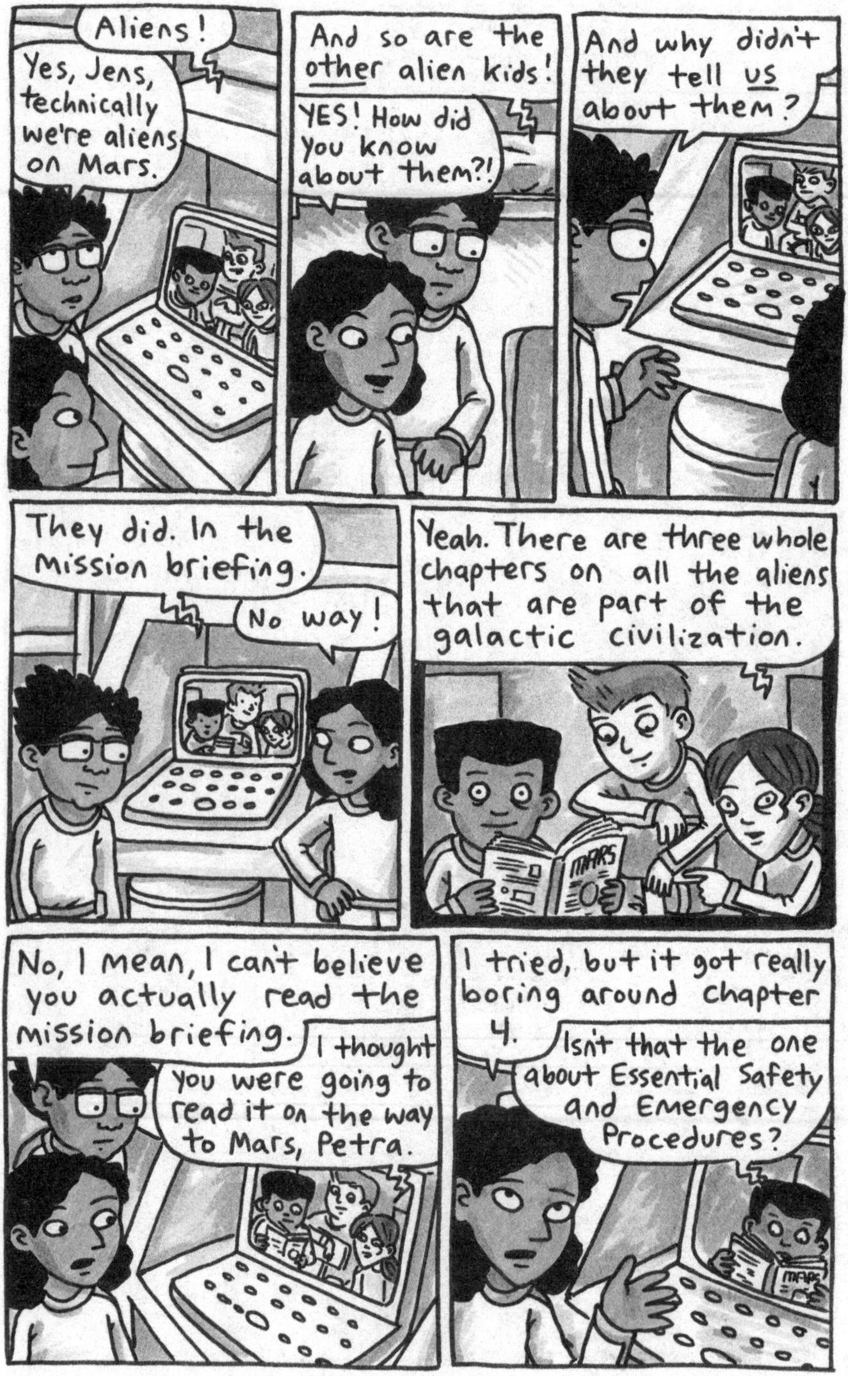
Aliens!
Yes, Jens, technically we're aliens on Mars.
And so are the other alien kids!
YES! How did you know about them?!
And why didn't they tell us about them?
They did. In the mission briefing.
No way!
Yeah. There are three whole chapters on all the aliens that are part of the galactic civilization.
MARS
No, I mean, I can't believe you actually read the mission briefing.
I thought you were going to read it on the way to Mars, Petra.
I tried, but it got really boring around chapter 4.
Isn't that the one about Essential Safety and Emergency Procedures?
MARS

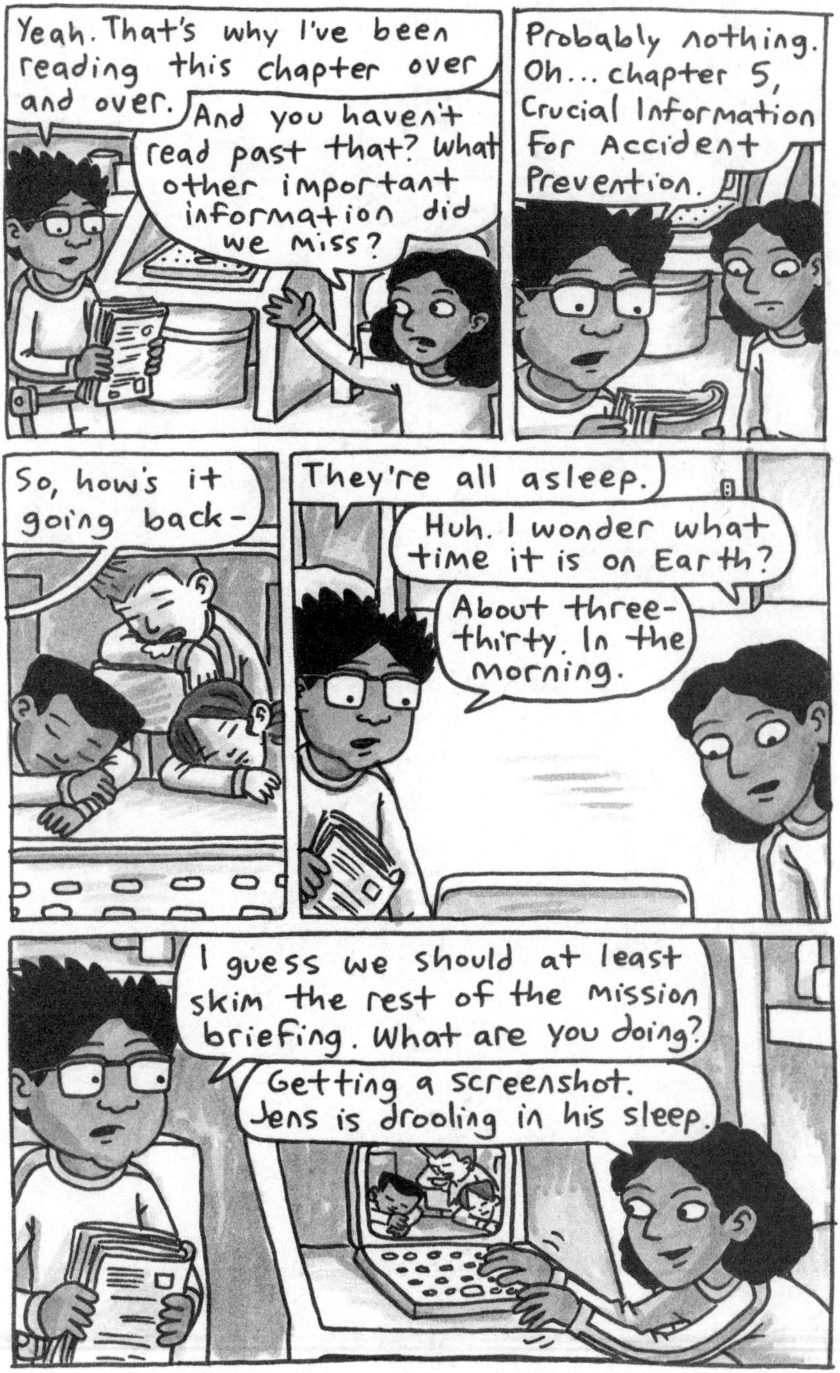
Yeah. That's why I've been reading this chapter over and over.
And you haven't read past that? What other important information did we miss?
Probably nothing. Oh... chapter 5, Crucial Information For Accident Prevention.
So, how's it going back-
They're all asleep.
Huh. I wonder what time it is on Earth?
About three-thirty. In the morning.
I guess we should at least skim the rest of the mission briefing. What are you doing?
Getting a screenshot. Jens is drooling in his sleep.

There's a whole section on activities we'll do.

Activities? Like, craft projects?

Is "Solar Panel Maintenance and Repair" considered a craft project?

No. What else is there?

MARTIAN GARDENING

TRY TO GROW A VARIETY OF EDIBLE PLANTS IN MARTIAN SOIL AND MAKE DELICIOUS* MEALS WITH THEM.

*ADULT AND KID OPINIONS OF DELICIOUS MAY DIFFER.

MOBILE HABITAT CONSTRUCTION

DESIGN AND BUILD PORTABLE SHELTERS THAT CAN ENDURE THE EXTREME CONDITIONS OF BARREN PLANETS.

SYSTEMS RESOURCE ANALYSIS

OPERATE STATISTICAL SOFTWARE TO MANAGE RESOURCE ALLOCATION UTILIZING DATA RELAY METHODS WITHIN THE SCOPE OF DISTRIBUTION THEORY MECHANICS AND RELATED EFFICIENCY TOOLS FOR THE PURPOSE OF INCREASED MISSION SUCCESS PROBABILITY.

Beep
Beep
Beep
Beep
Beep
Beep

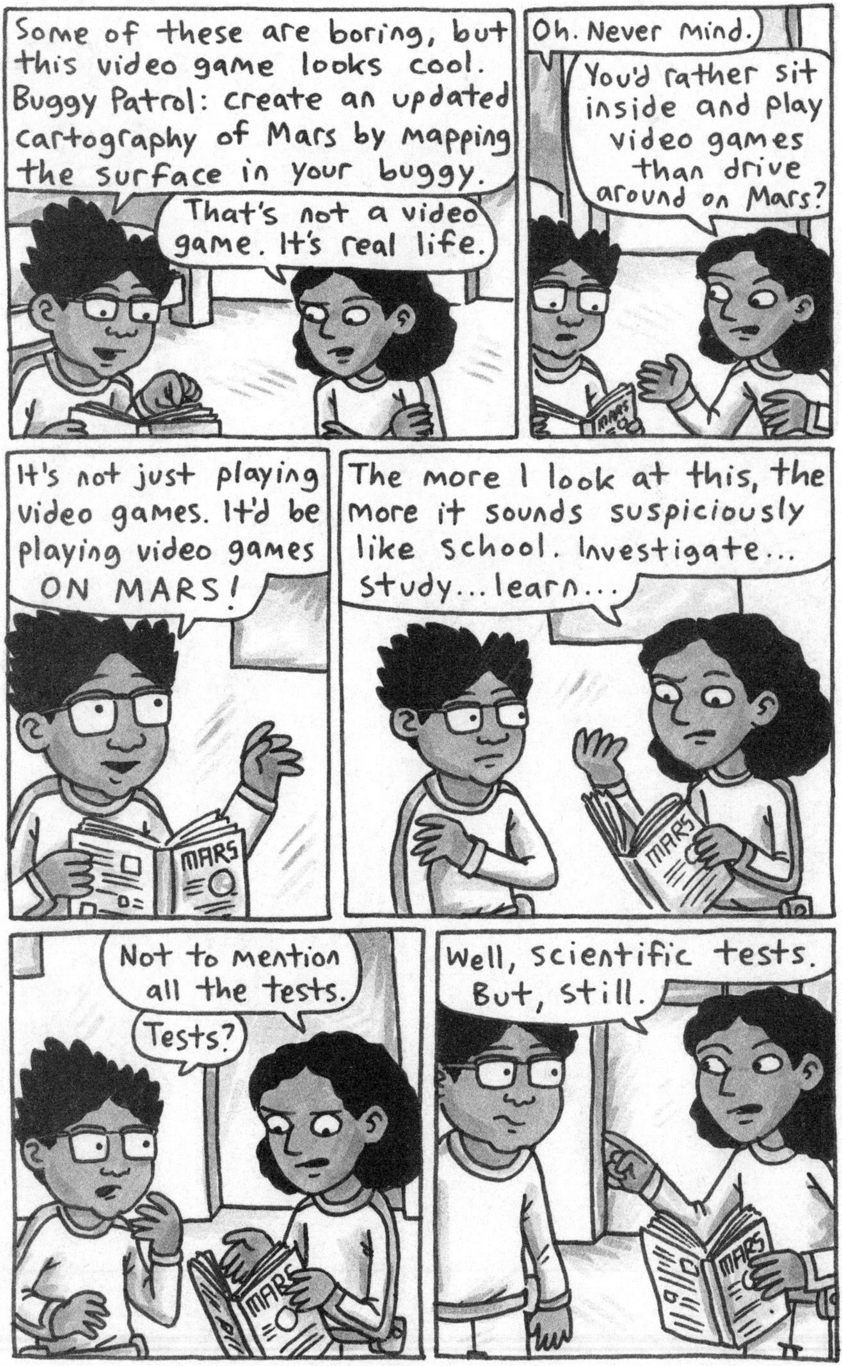
Some of these are boring, but this video game looks cool. Buggy Patrol: create an updated cartography of Mars by mapping the surface in your buggy.
That's not a video game. It's real life.
Oh. Never mind.
You'd rather sit inside and play video games than drive around on Mars?
MARS
It's not just playing video games. It'd be playing video games ON MARS!
MARS
The more I look at this, the more it sounds suspiciously like school. Investigate... study... learn...
MARS
Not to mention all the tests.
Tests?
MARS
Well, scientific tests. But, still.
MARS

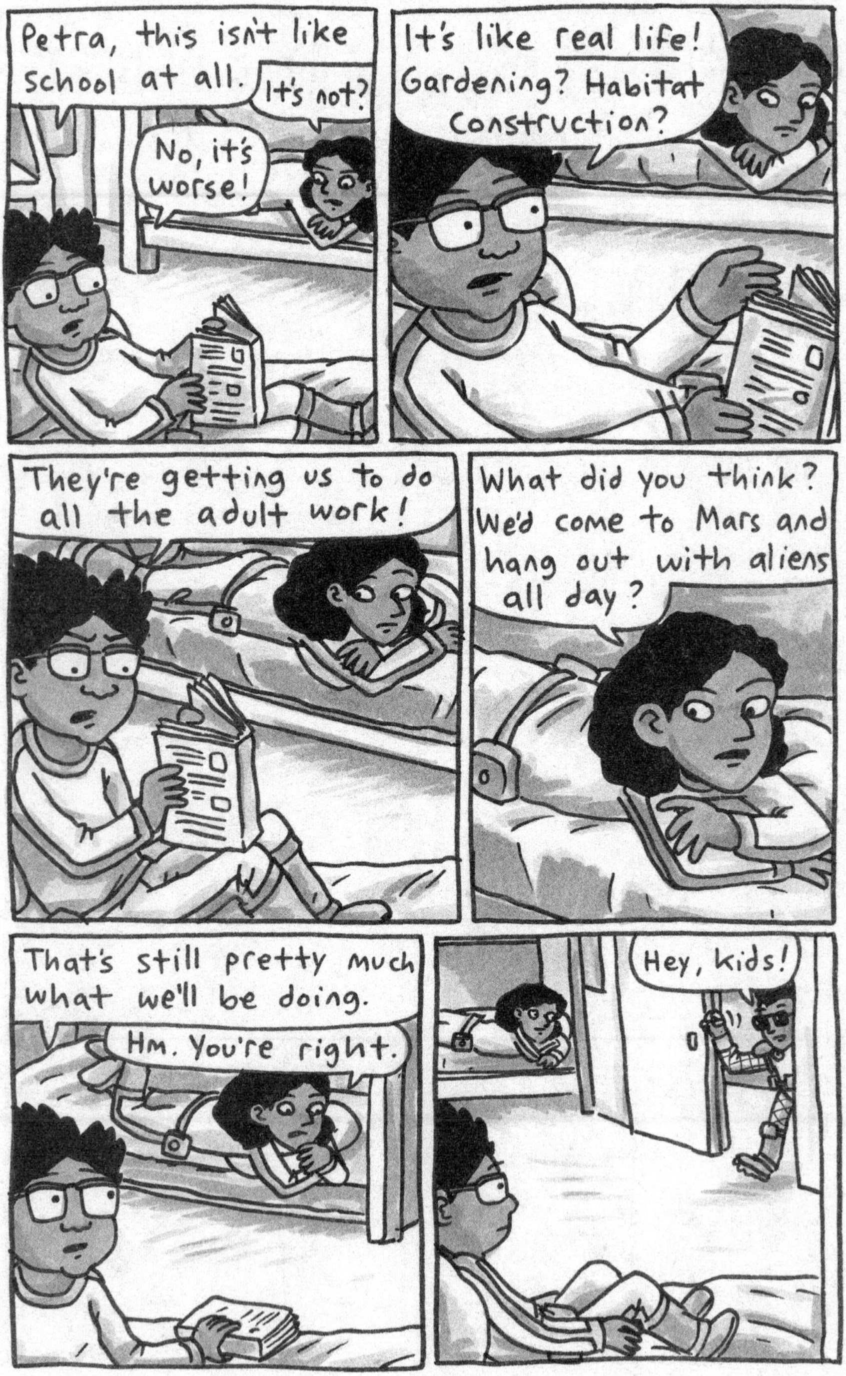
Petra, this isn't like school at all.
It's not?
No, it's worse!
It's like real life! Gardening? Habitat Construction?
They're getting us to do all the adult work!
What did you think? We'd come to Mars and hang out with aliens all day?
That's still pretty much what we'll be doing.
Hm. You're right.
Hey, kids!

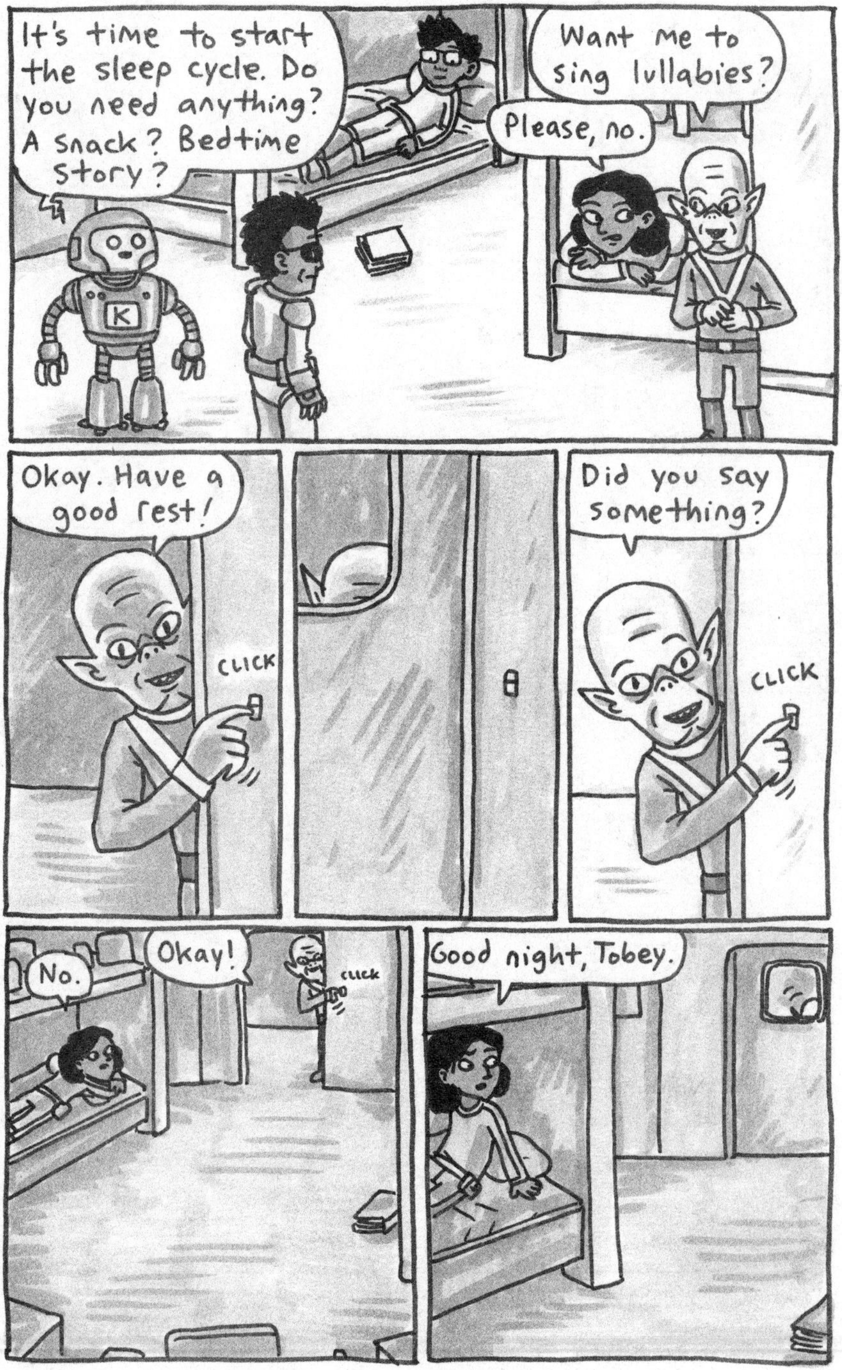
It's time to start the sleep cycle. Do you need anything? A snack? Bedtime story?
Want me to sing lullabies?
Please, no.
Okay. Have a good rest!
CLICK
Did you say something?
CLICK
No.
Okay!
CLICK
Good night, Tobey.

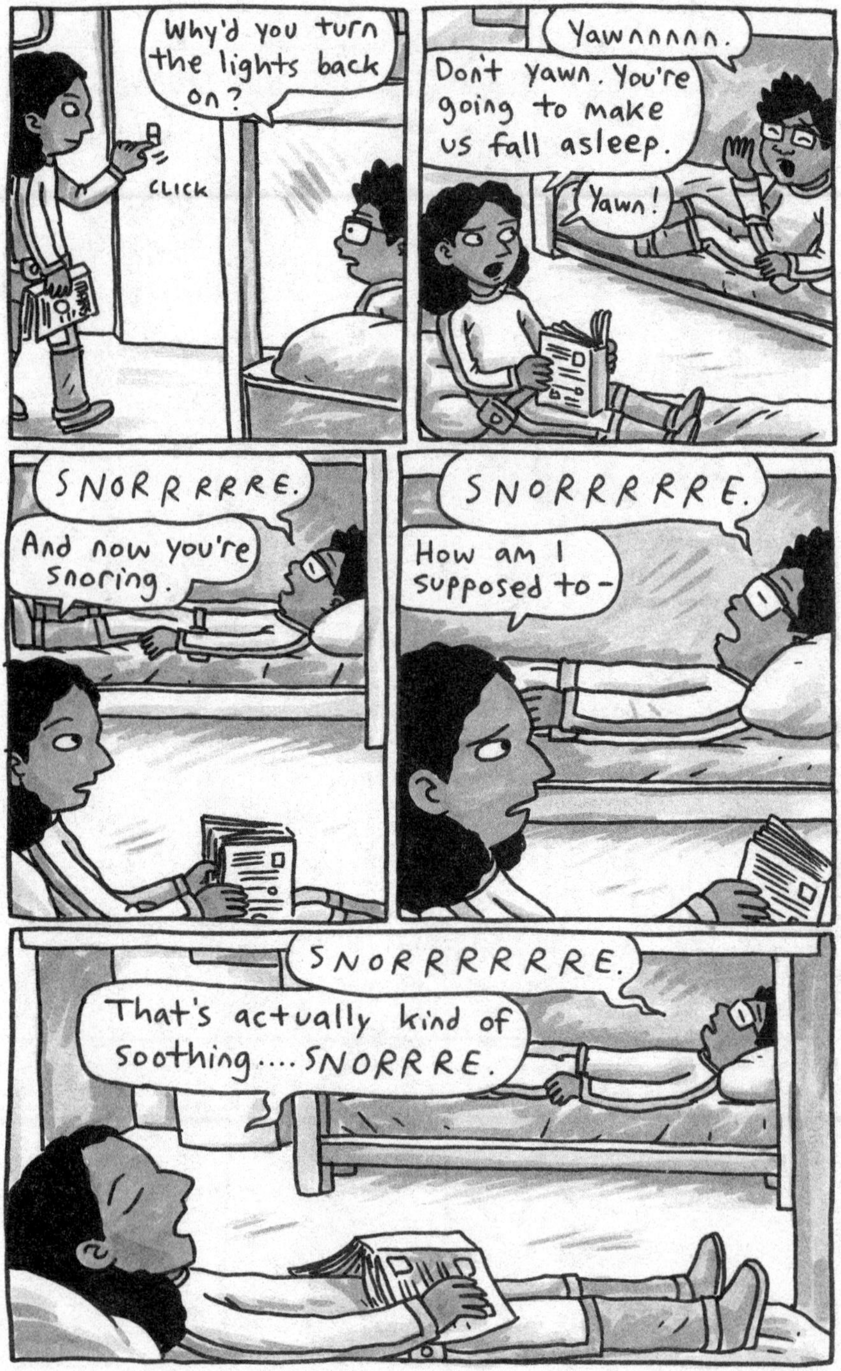
Why'd you turn the lights back on?
CLICK
Yawnnnnn.
Don't yawn. You're going to make us fall asleep.
Yawn!
SNORRRRRE.
And now you're snoring.
SNORRRRRRE.
How am I supposed to-
SNORRRRRRRE.
That's actually kind of soothing.... SNORRRE.

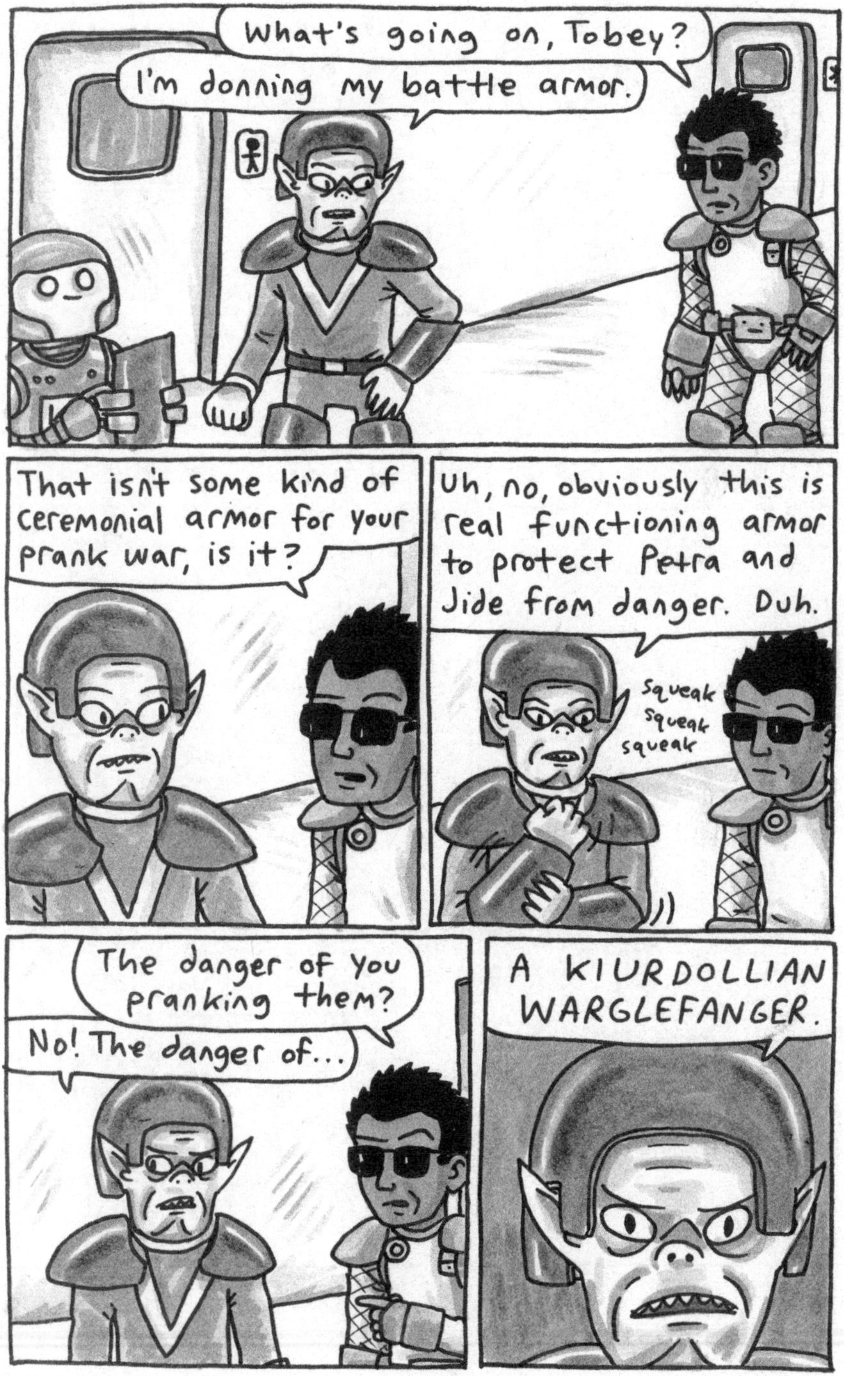
What's going on, Tobey?
I'm donning my battle armor.
That isn't some kind of ceremonial armor for your prank war, is it?
Uh, no, obviously this is real functioning armor to protect Petra and Jide from danger. Duh.
squeak squeak squeak
The danger of you pranking them?
No! The danger of...
A KIURDOLLIAN WARGLEFANGER.

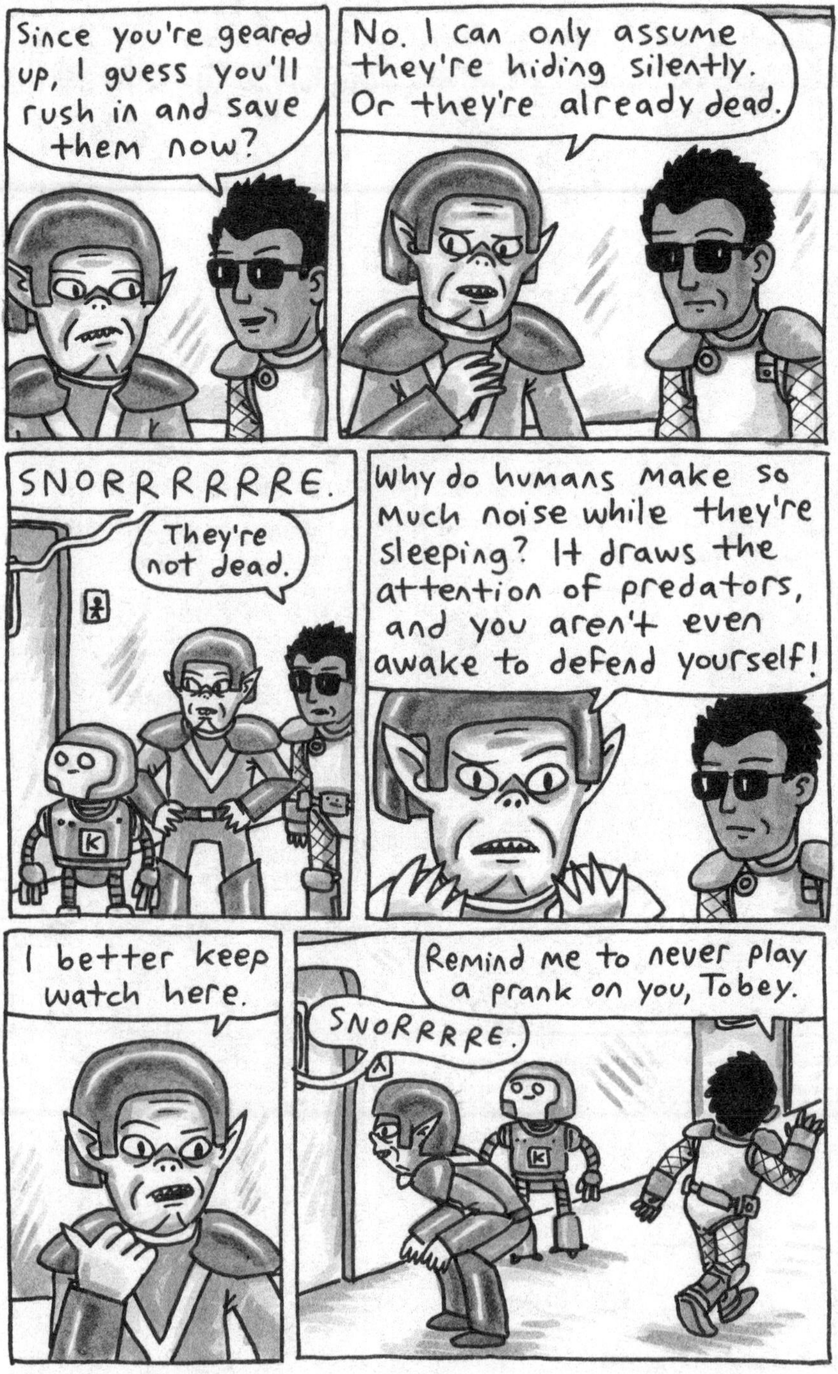
Since you're geared up, I guess you'll rush in and save them now?
No. I can only assume they're hiding silently. Or they're already dead.
SNORRRRRRE.
They're not dead.
Why do humans make so much noise while they're sleeping? It draws the attention of predators, and you aren't even awake to defend yourself!
I better keep watch here.
Remind me to never play a prank on you, Tobey.
SNORRRRE.

LIFE ON MARS

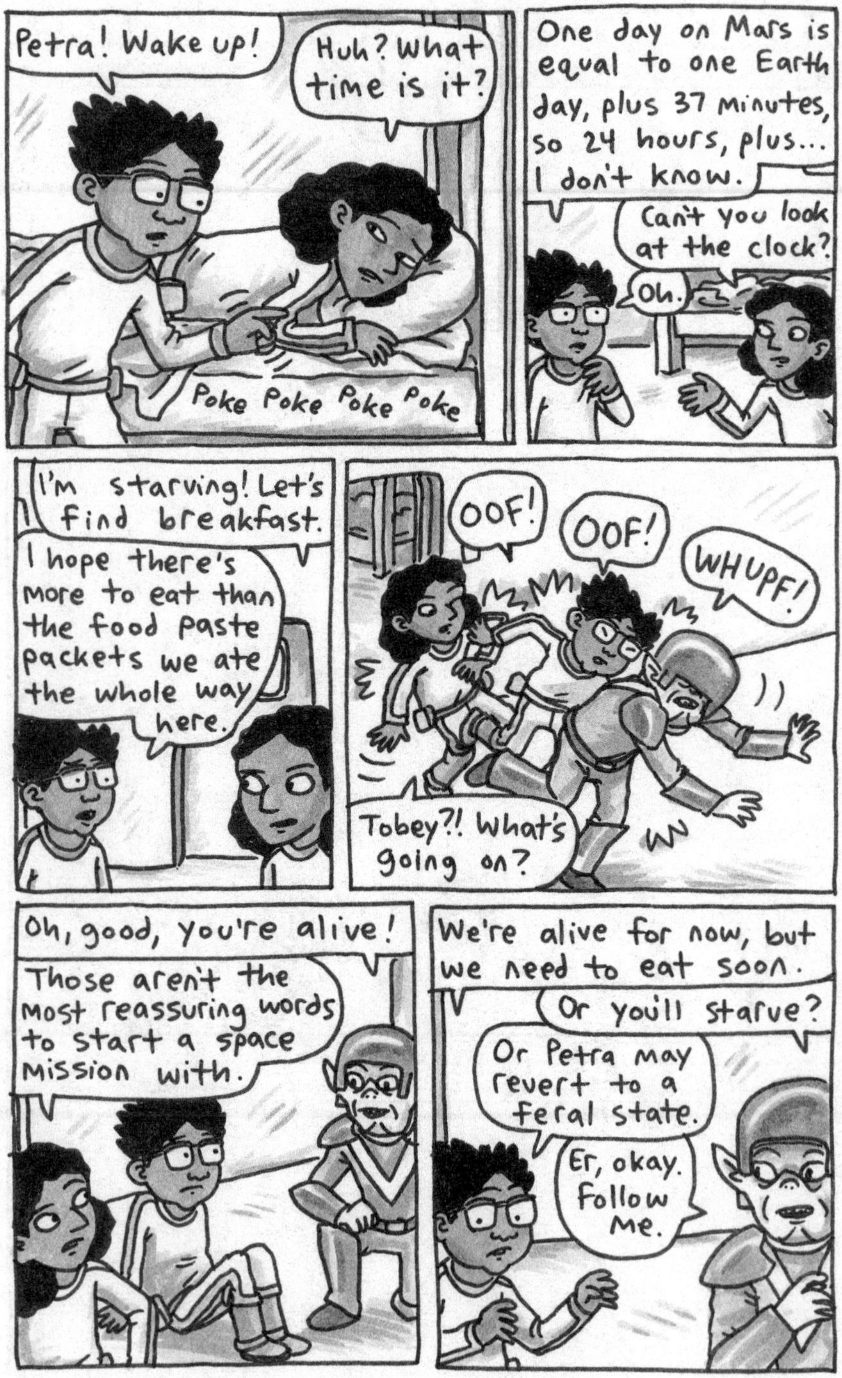
Petra! Wake up!
Huh? What time is it?
Poke Poke Poke Poke
One day on Mars is equal to one Earth day, plus 37 minutes, so 24 hours, plus... I don't know.
Can't you look at the clock?
Oh.
I'm starving! Let's find breakfast.
I hope there's more to eat than the food paste packets we ate the whole way here.
OOF!
OOF!
WHUPF!
Tobey?! What's going on?
Oh, good, you're alive!
Those aren't the most reassuring words to start a space mission with.
We're alive for now, but we need to eat soon.
Or you'll starve?
Or Petra may revert to a feral state.
Er, okay. Follow me.

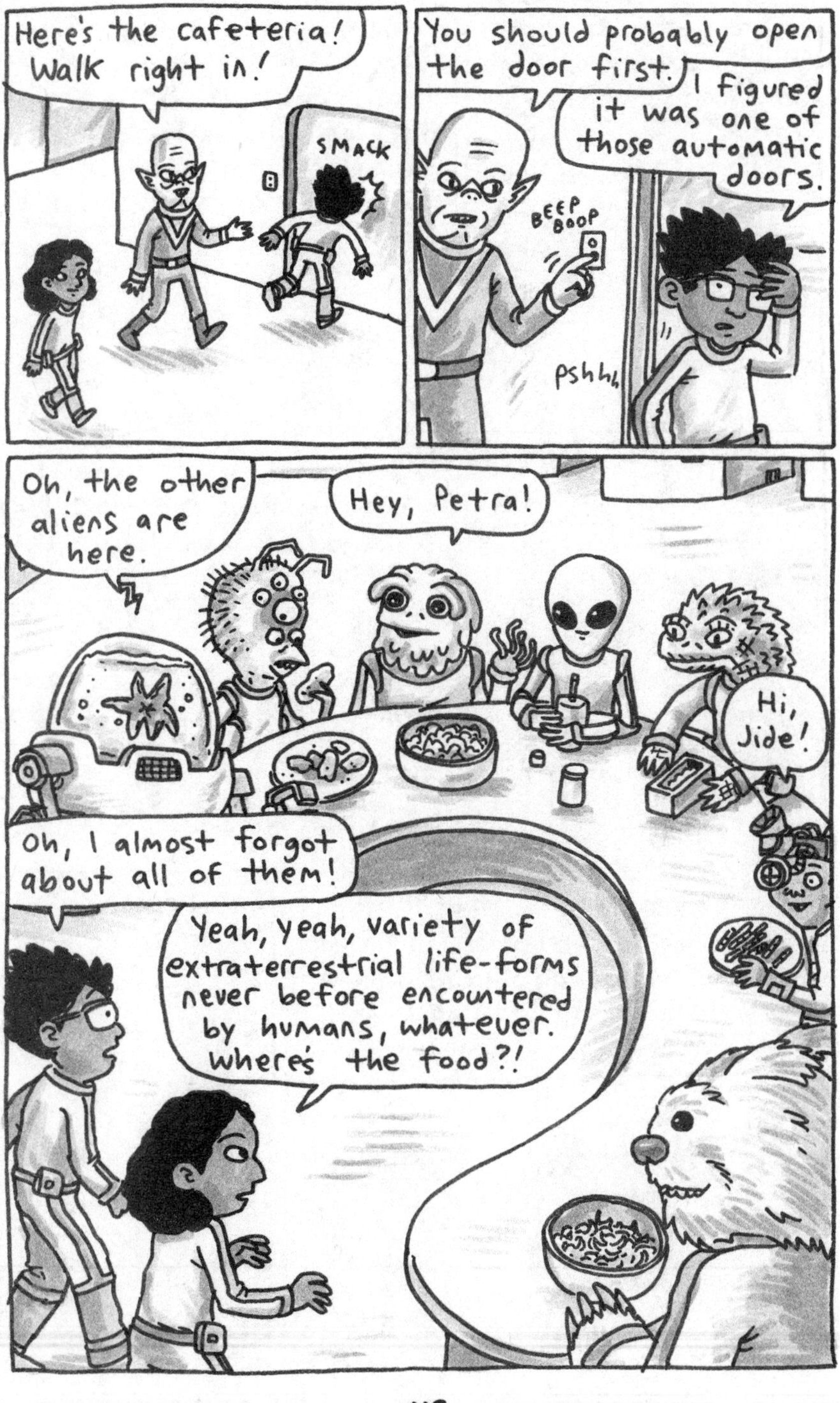
Here's the cafeteria! Walk right in!
SMACK
You should probably open the door first.
I figured it was one of those automatic doors.
BEEP BOOP
pshhh
Oh, the other aliens are here.
Hey, Petra!
Hi, Jide!
Oh, I almost forgot about all of them!
Yeah, yeah, variety of extraterrestrial life-forms never before encountered by humans, whatever. Where's the food?!

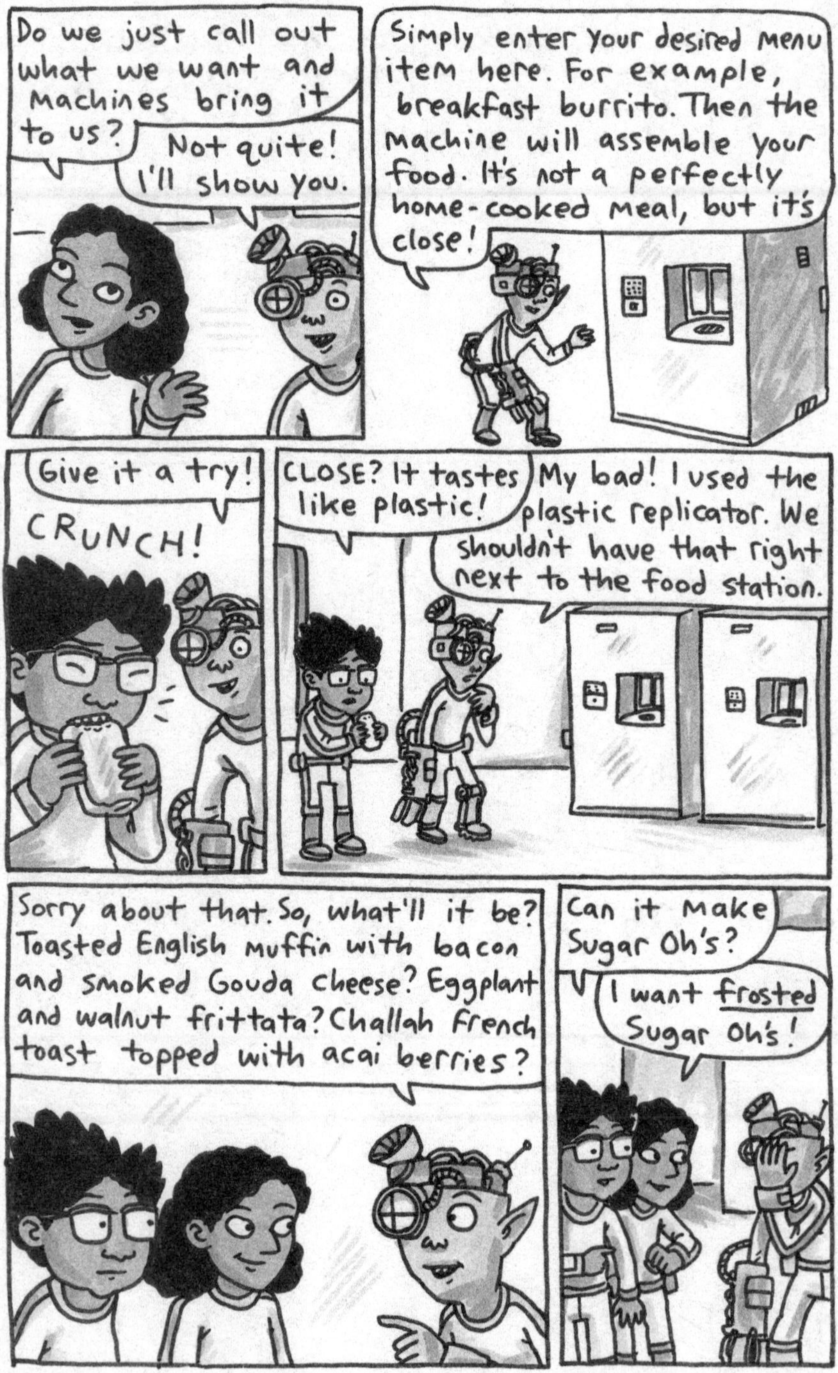
Do we just call out what we want and machines bring it to us?
Not quite! I'll show you.
Simply enter your desired menu item here. For example, breakfast burrito. Then the machine will assemble your food. It's not a perfectly home-cooked meal, but it's close!
Give it a try!
CRUNCH!
CLOSE? It tastes like plastic!
My bad! I used the plastic replicator. We shouldn't have that right next to the food station.
Sorry about that. So, what'll it be? Toasted English muffin with bacon and smoked Gouda cheese? Eggplant and walnut frittata? Challah French toast topped with acai berries?
Can it make Sugar Oh's?
I want frosted Sugar Oh's!

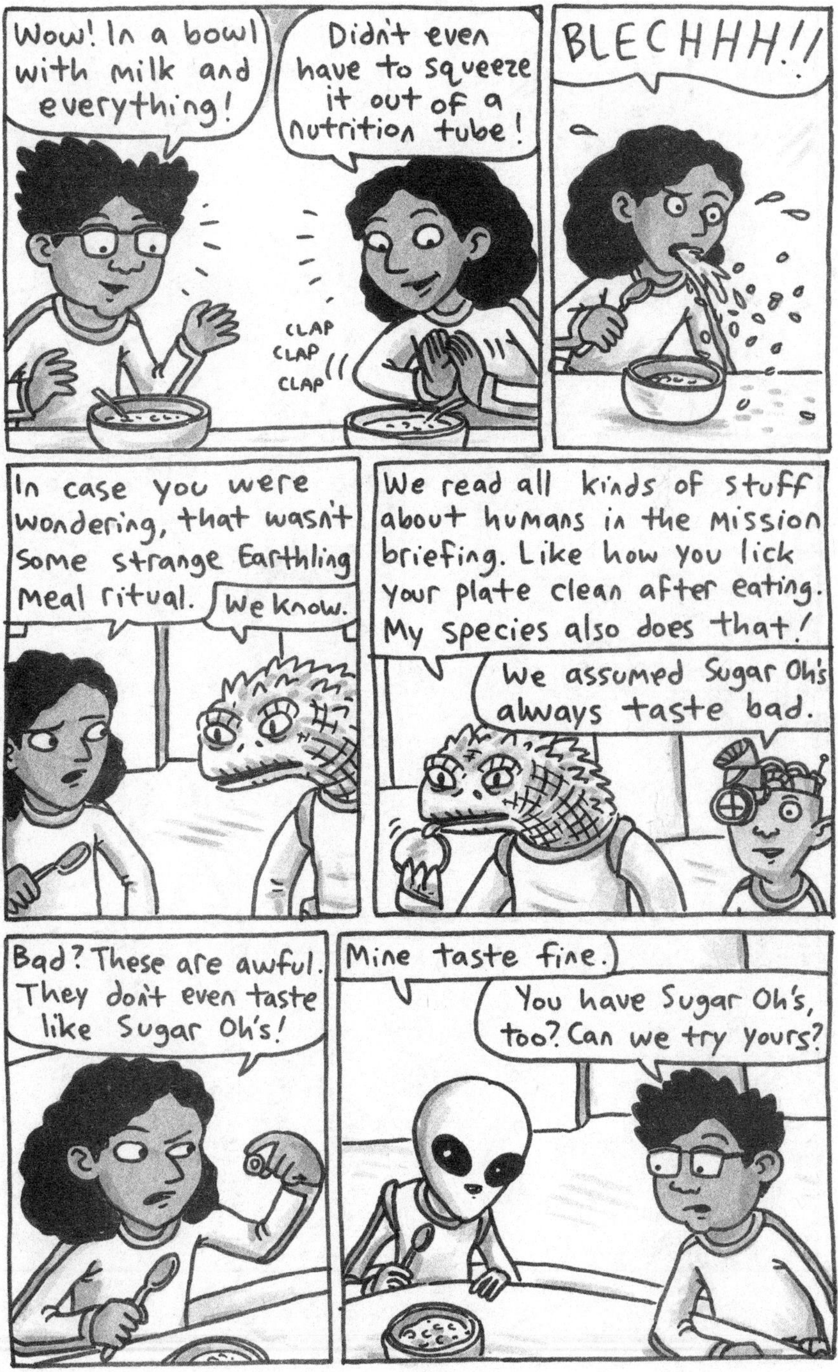
Wow! In a bowl with milk and everything!
Didn't even have to squeeze it out of a nutrition tube!
CLAP
CLAP
CLAP
BLECHHH!!
In case you were wondering, that wasn't some strange Earthling meal ritual.
We know.
We read all kinds of stuff about humans in the mission briefing. Like how you lick your plate clean after eating. My species also does that!
We assumed Sugar Oh's always taste bad.
Bad? These are awful. They don't even taste like Sugar Oh's!
Mine taste fine.
You have Sugar Oh's, too? Can we try yours?

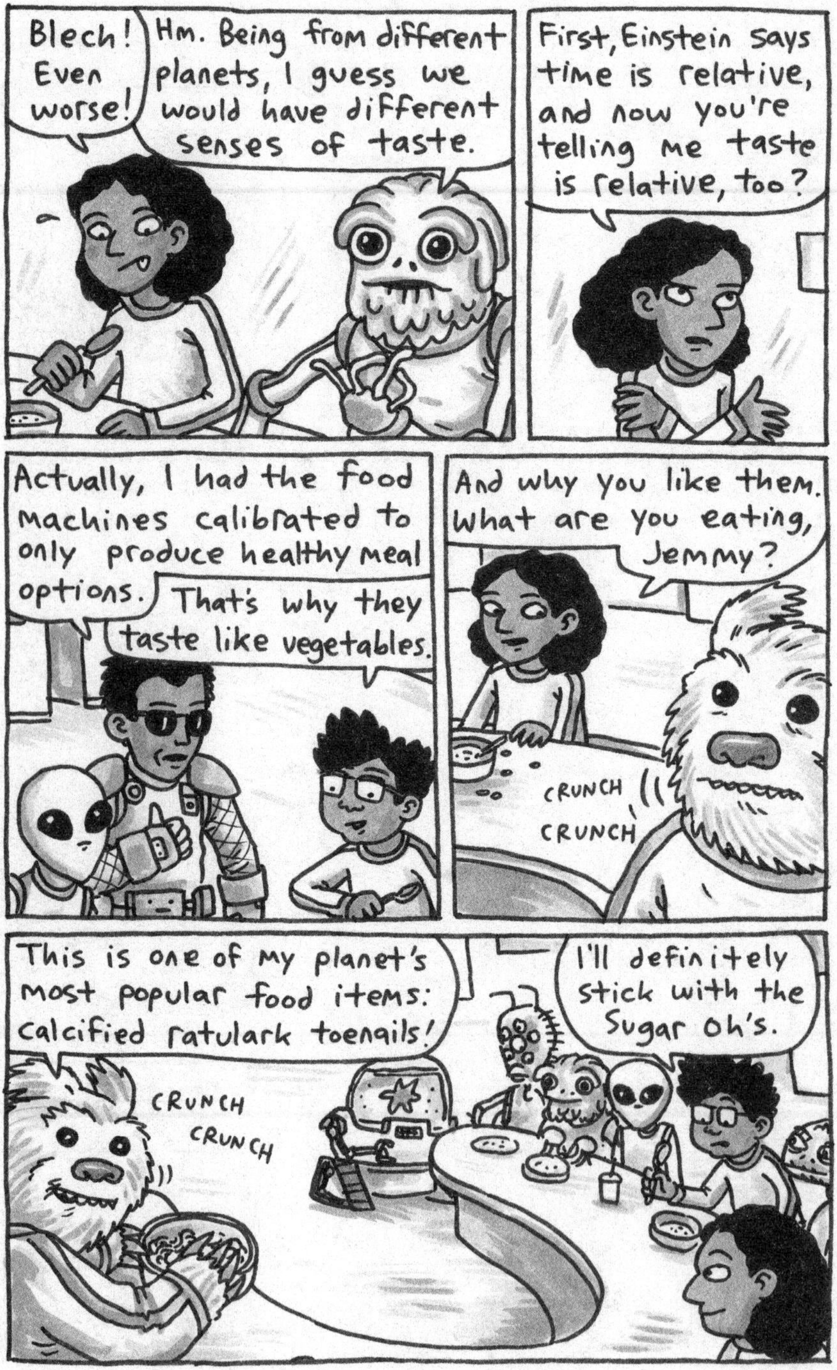
Blech! Even worse!
Hm. Being from different planets, I guess we would have different senses of taste.
First, Einstein says time is relative, and now you're telling me taste is relative, too?
Actually, I had the food machines calibrated to only produce healthy meal options.
That's why they taste like vegetables.
And why you like them. What are you eating, Jemmy?
CRUNCH
CRUNCH
This is one of my planet's most popular food items: calcified ratulark toenails!
CRUNCH
CRUNCH
I'll definitely stick with the Sugar Oh's.

MARS MISSION DESIGNATION: BIOMECHATRONICS

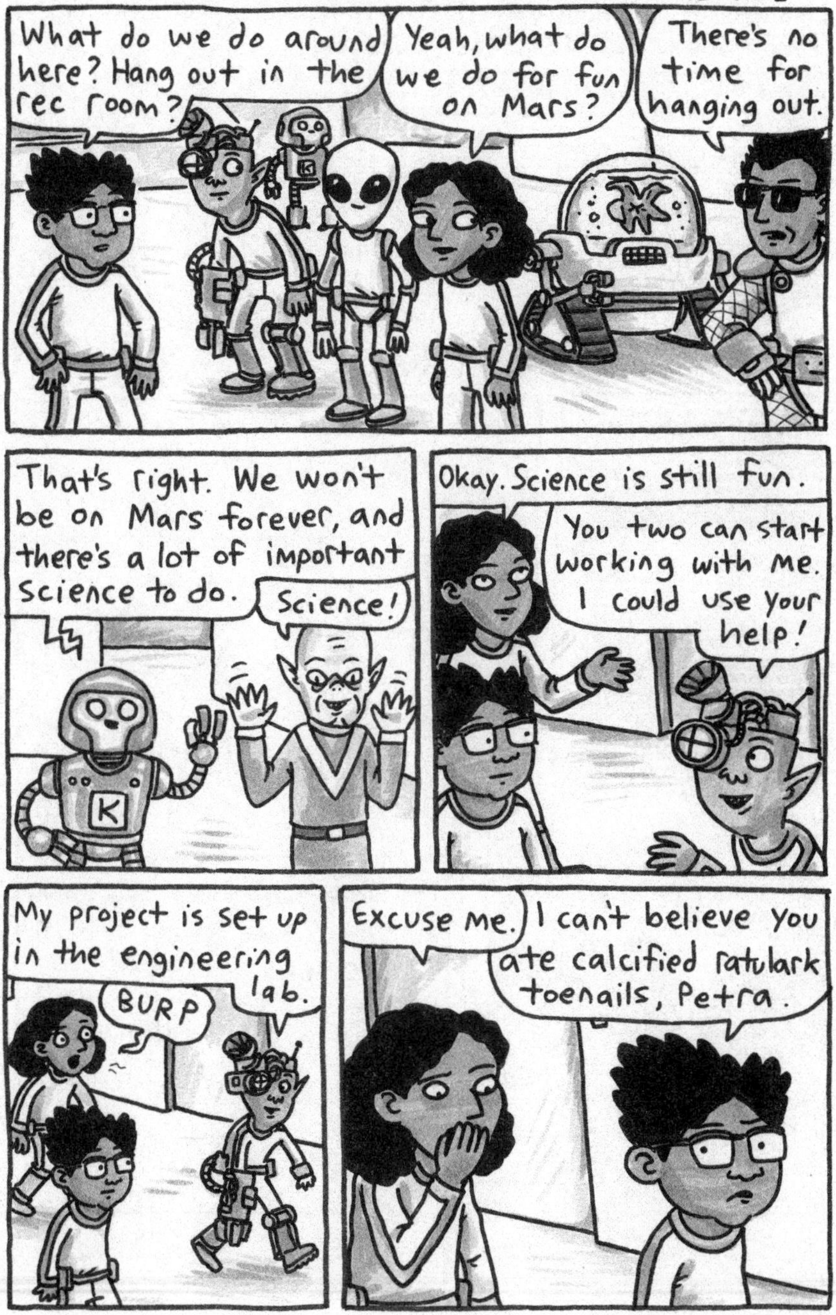

What do we do around here? Hang out in the rec room?
Yeah, what do we do for fun on Mars?
There's no time for hanging out.
That's right. We won't be on Mars forever, and there's a lot of important science to do.
Science!
Okay. Science is still fun.
You two can start working with me. I could use your help!
My project is set up in the engineering lab.
BURP
Excuse me.
I can't believe you ate calcified ratulark toenails, Petra.

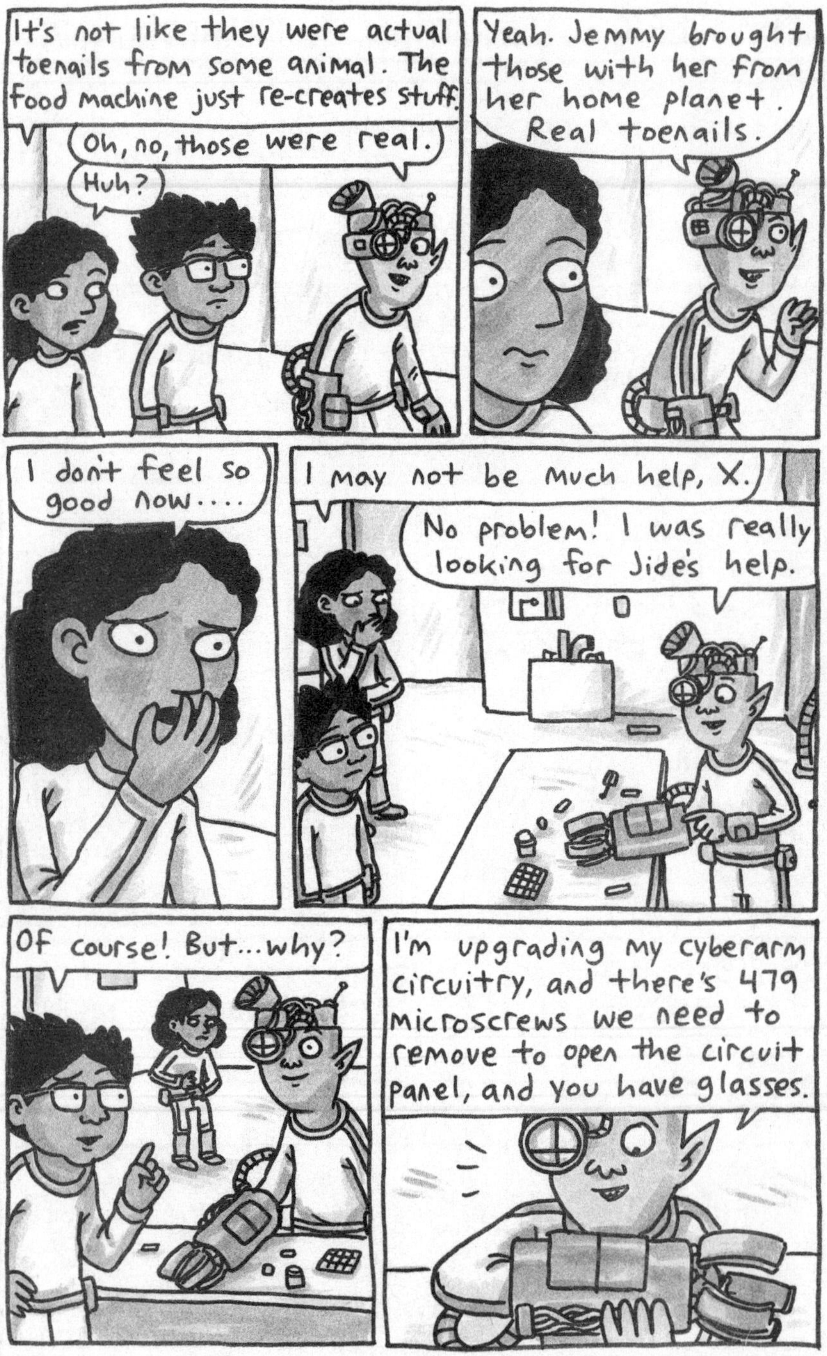
It's not like they were actual toenails from some animal. The food machine just re-creates stuff.
Oh, no, those were real.
Huh?
Yeah. Jemmy brought those with her from her home planet. Real toenails.
I don't feel so good now....
I may not be much help, X.
No problem! I was really looking for Jide's help.
Of course! But...why?
I'm upgrading my cyberarm circuitry, and there's 479 microscrews we need to remove to open the circuit panel, and you have glasses.

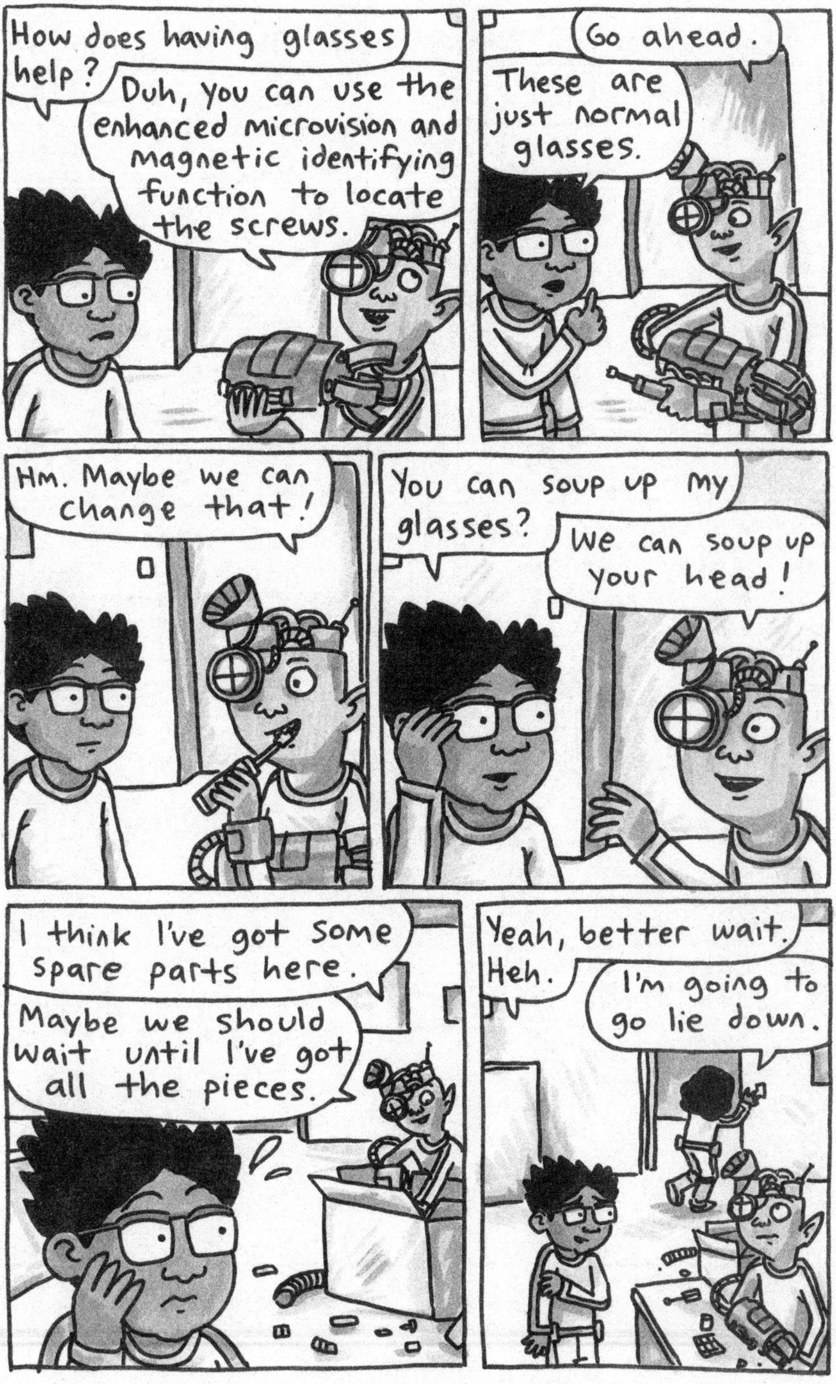
How does having glasses help?
Duh, you can use the enhanced microvision and magnetic identifying function to locate the screws.
Go ahead.
These are just normal glasses.
Hm. Maybe we can change that!
You can soup up my glasses?
We can soup up your head!
I think I've got some spare parts here.
Maybe we should wait until I've got all the pieces.
Yeah, better wait. Heh.
I'm going to go lie down.

MARS MISSION DESIGNATION: MARTIAN CARTOGRAPHY

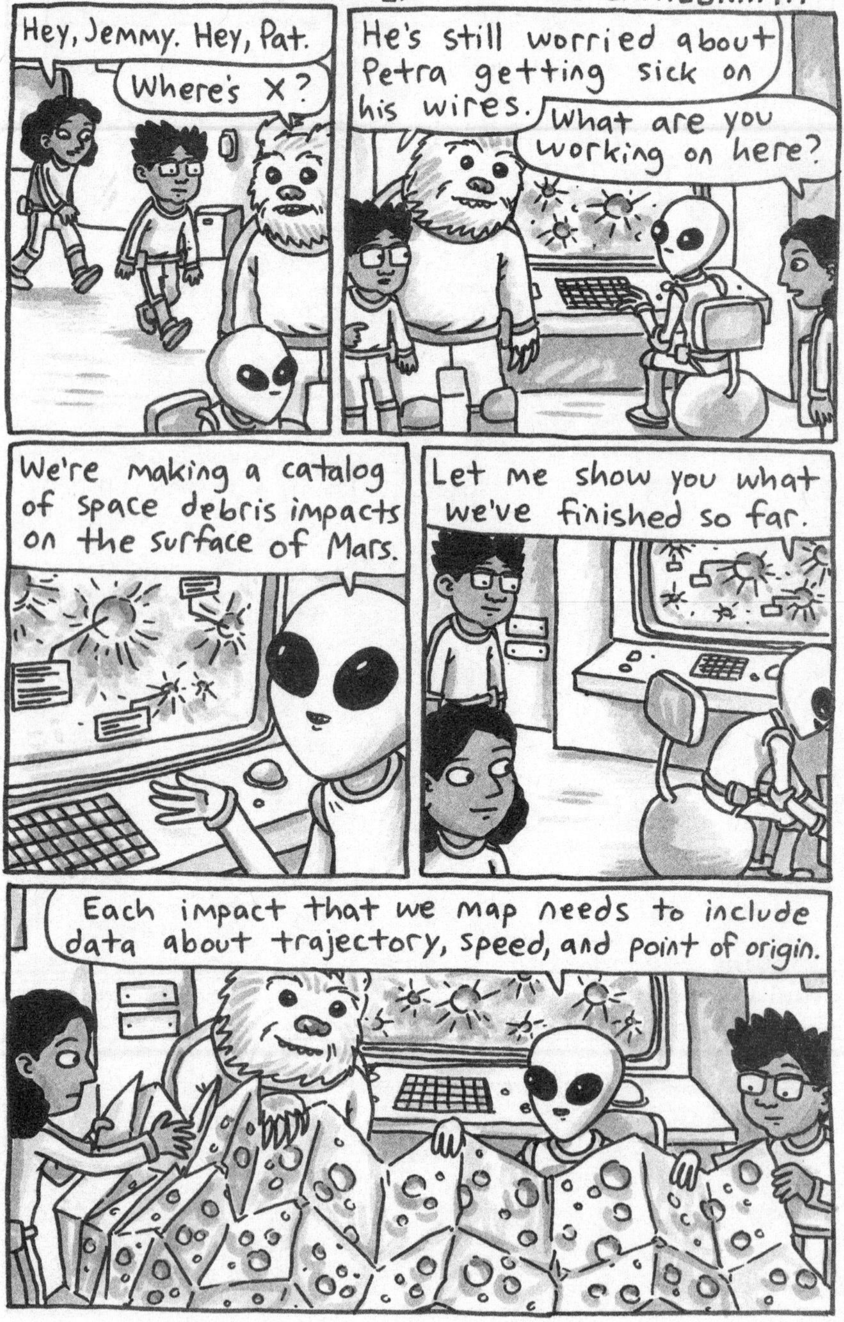
Hey, Jemmy. Hey, Pat.
Where's X?
He's still worried about Petra getting sick on his wires.
What are you working on here?
We're making a catalog of space debris impacts on the surface of Mars.
Let me show you what we've finished so far.
Each impact that we map needs to include data about trajectory, speed, and point of origin.

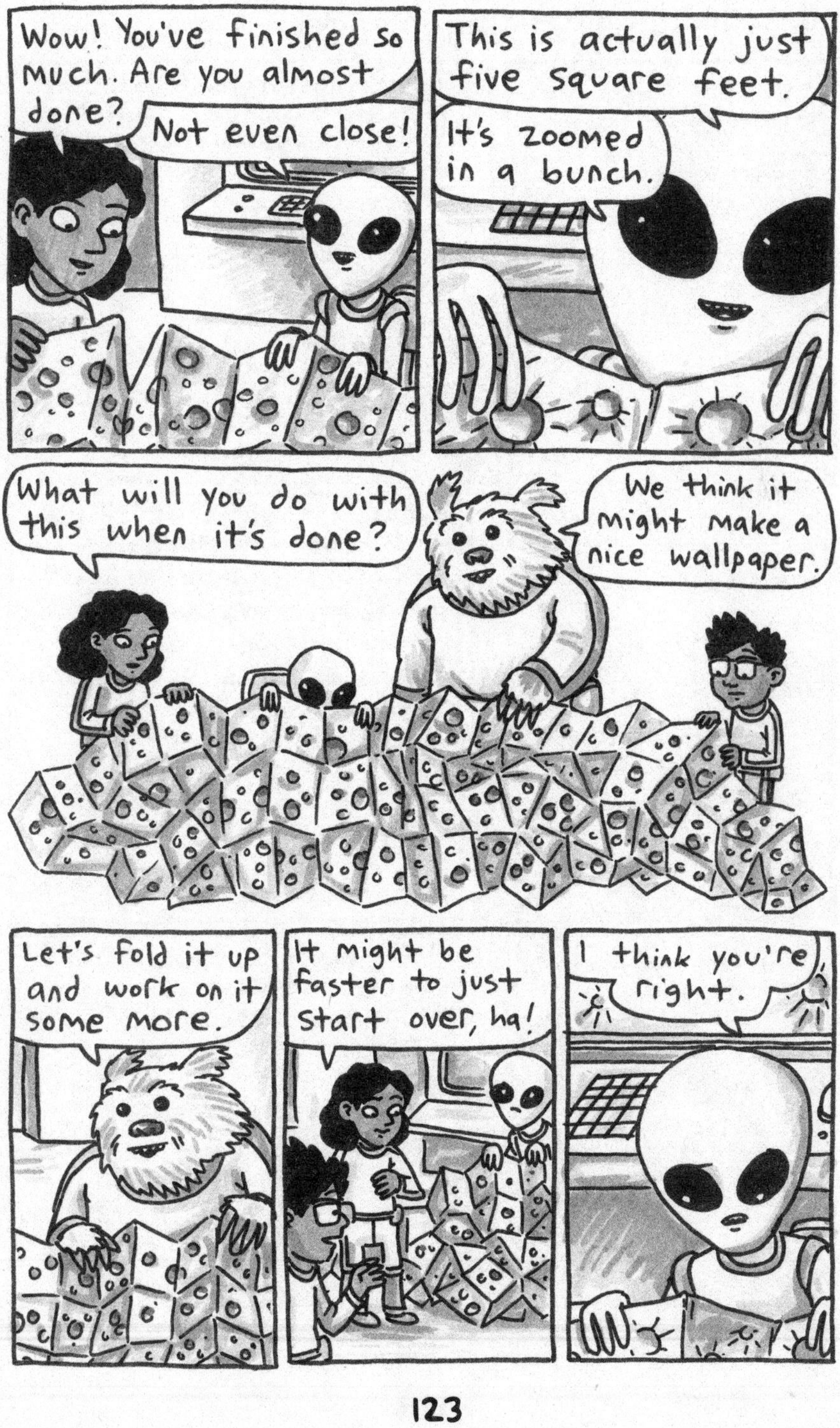
Wow! You've finished so much. Are you almost done?
Not even close!
This is actually just five square feet.
It's zoomed in a bunch.
What will you do with this when it's done?
We think it might make a nice wallpaper.
Let's fold it up and work on it some more.
It might be faster to just start over, ha!
I think you're right.

MARS MISSION DESIGNATION: OPTIMAL ROUTE PLANNING

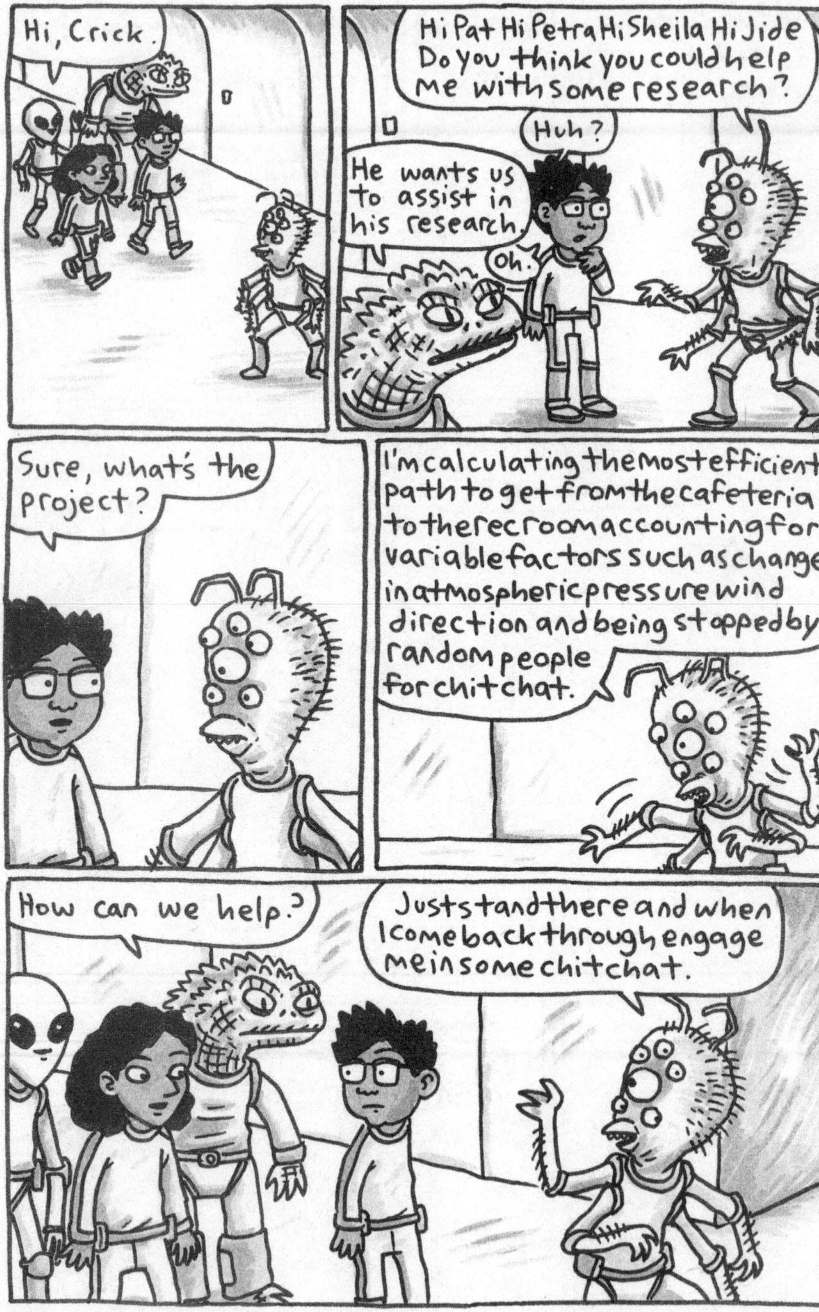
Hi, Crick.
Hi Pat Hi Petra Hi Sheila Hi Jide Do you think you could help me with some research?
Huh?
He wants us to assist in his research.
Oh.
Sure, what's the project?
I'm calculating the most efficient path to get from the cafeteria to the rec room accounting for variable factors such as change in atmospheric pressure wind direction and being stopped by random people for chitchat.
How can we help?
Just stand there and when I come back through engage me in some chitchat.

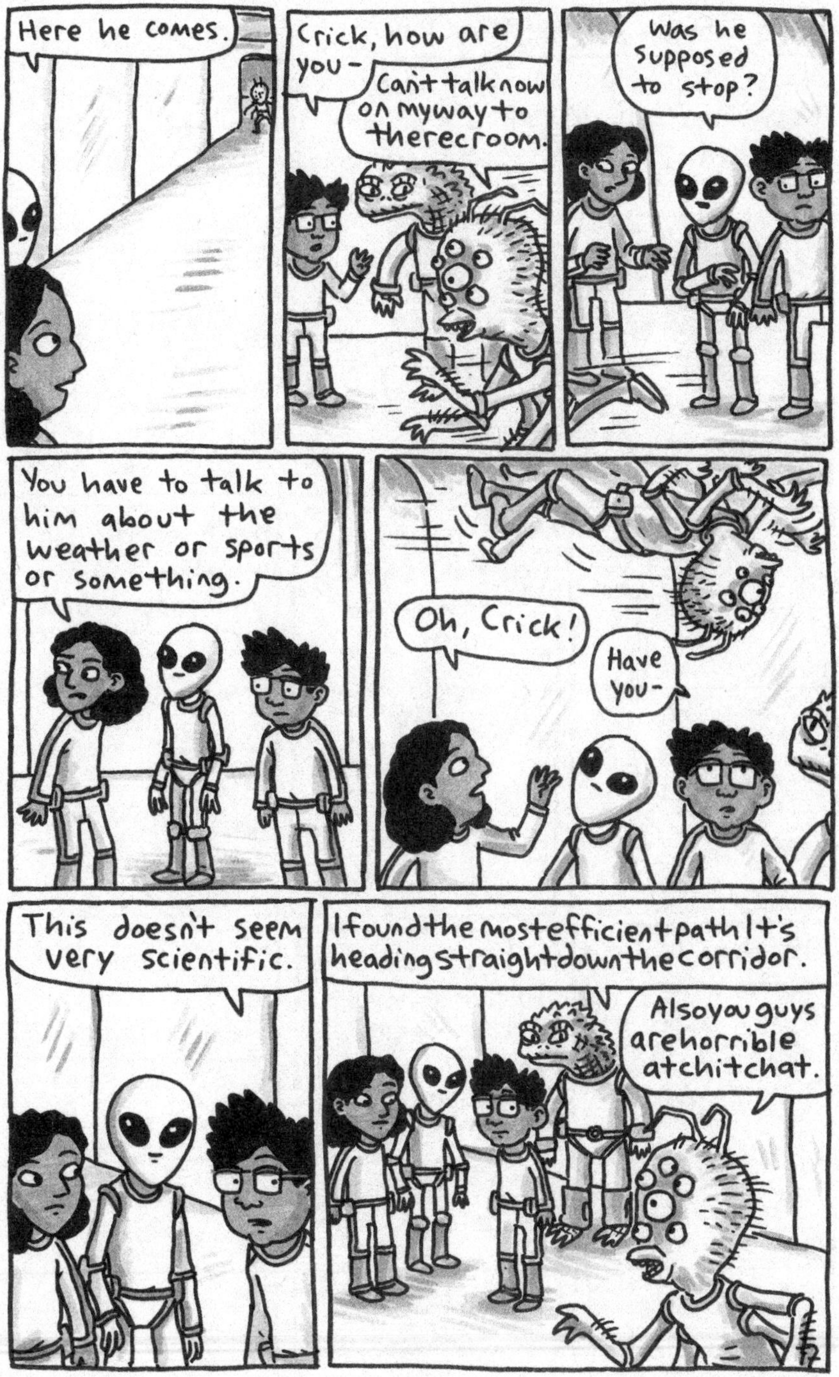
Here he comes.
Crick, how are you-
Can't talk now on my way to the rec room.
Was he supposed to stop?
You have to talk to him about the weather or sports or something.
Oh, Crick!
Have you-
This doesn't seem very scientific.
I found the most efficient path. It's heading straight down the corridor.
Also you guys are horrible at chitchat.

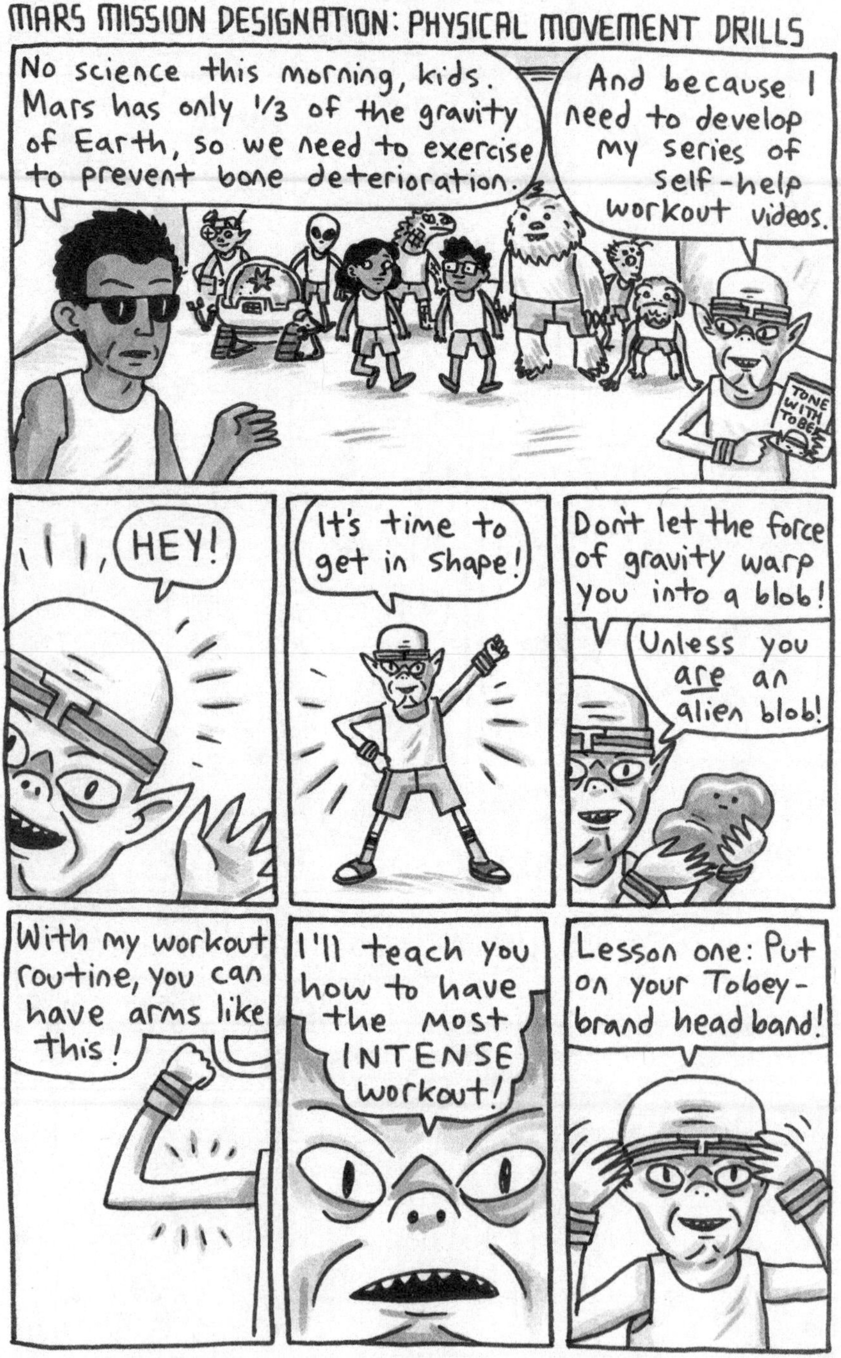
MARS MISSION DESIGNATION: PHYSICAL MOVEMENT DRILLS
No science this morning, kids. Mars has only 1/3 of the gravity of Earth, so we need to exercise to prevent bone deterioration.
And because I need to develop my series of self-help workout videos.
TONE WITH TOBEY
HEY!
It's time to get in shape!
Don't let the force of gravity warp you into a blob!
Unless you are an alien blob!
With my workout routine, you can have arms like this!
I'll teach you how to have the most INTENSE workout!
Lesson one: Put on your Tobey-brand head band!

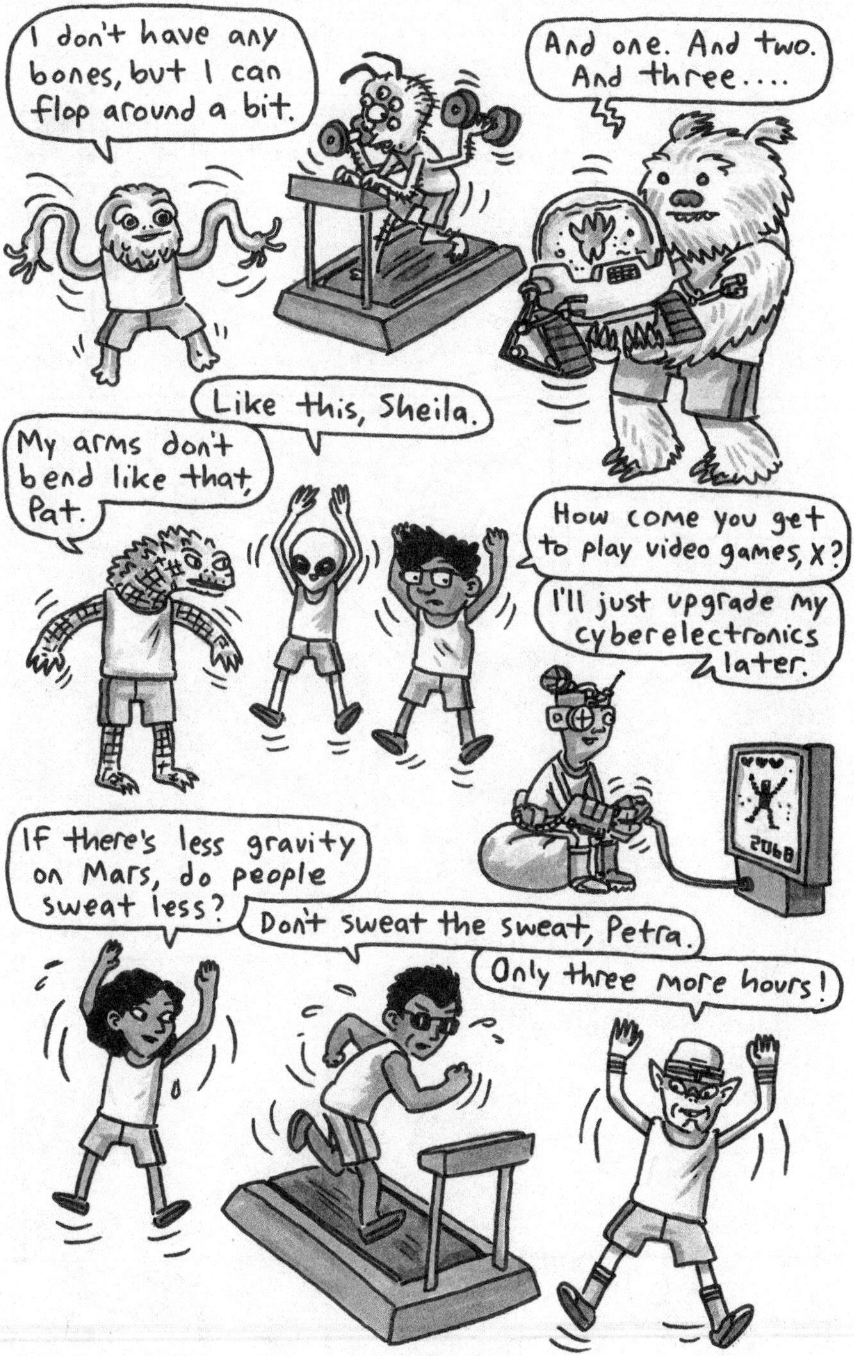
I don't have any bones, but I can flop around a bit.
And one. And two. And three....
Like this, Sheila.
My arms don't bend like that, Pat.
How come you get to play video games, X?
I'll just upgrade my cyberelectronics later.
2068
If there's less gravity on Mars, do people sweat less?
Don't sweat the sweat, Petra.
Only three more hours!

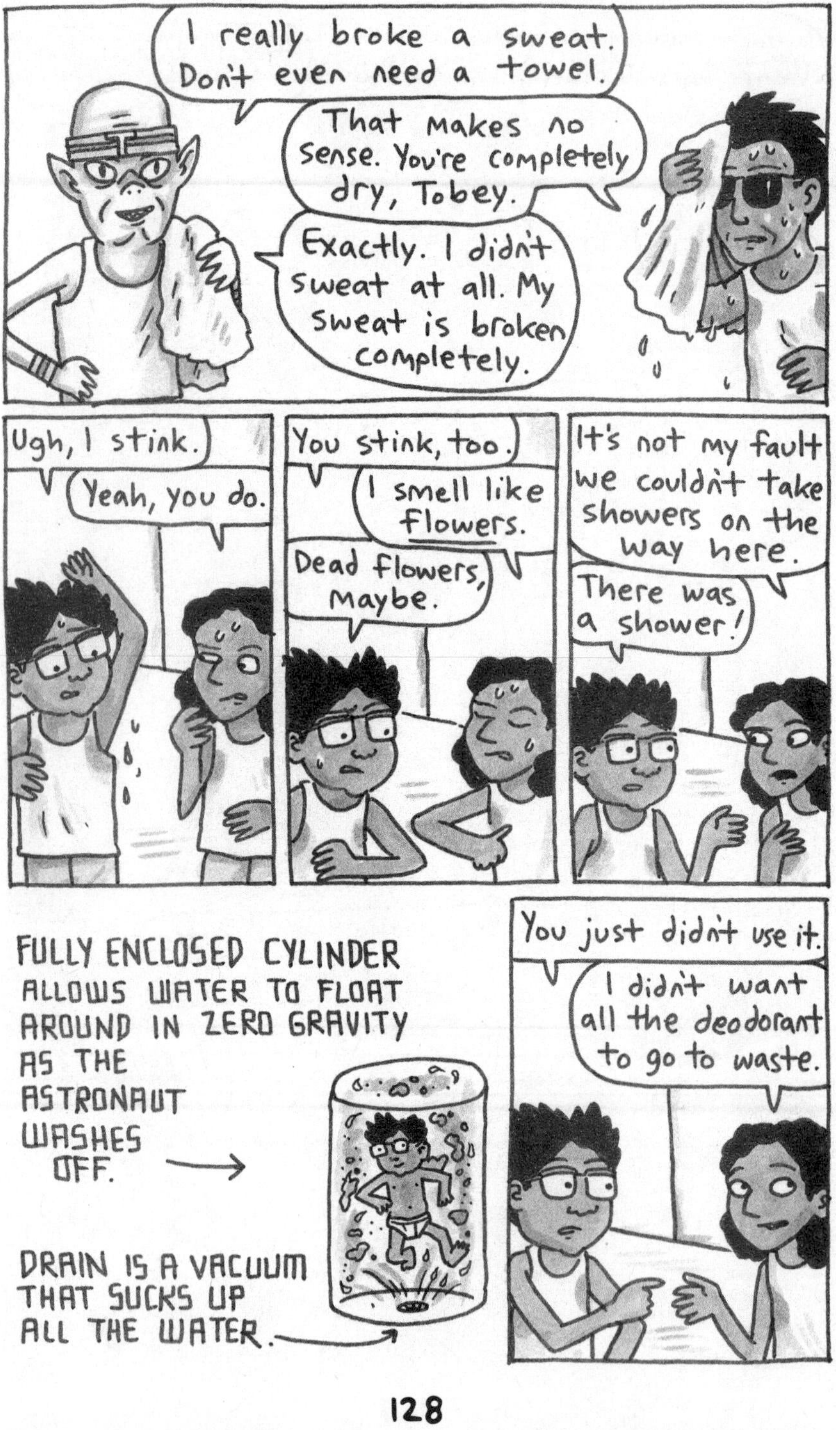
I really broke a sweat. Don't even need a towel.
That makes no sense. You're completely dry, Tobey.
Exactly. I didn't sweat at all. My sweat is broken completely.
Ugh, I stink.
Yeah, you do.
You stink, too.
I smell like flowers.
Dead flowers, maybe.
It's not my fault we couldn't take showers on the way here.
There was a shower!
FULLY ENCLOSED CYLINDER ALLOWS WATER TO FLOAT AROUND IN ZERO GRAVITY AS THE ASTRONAUT WASHES OFF.
DRAIN IS A VACUUM THAT SUCKS UP ALL THE WATER.
You just didn't use it.
I didn't want all the deodorant to go to waste.

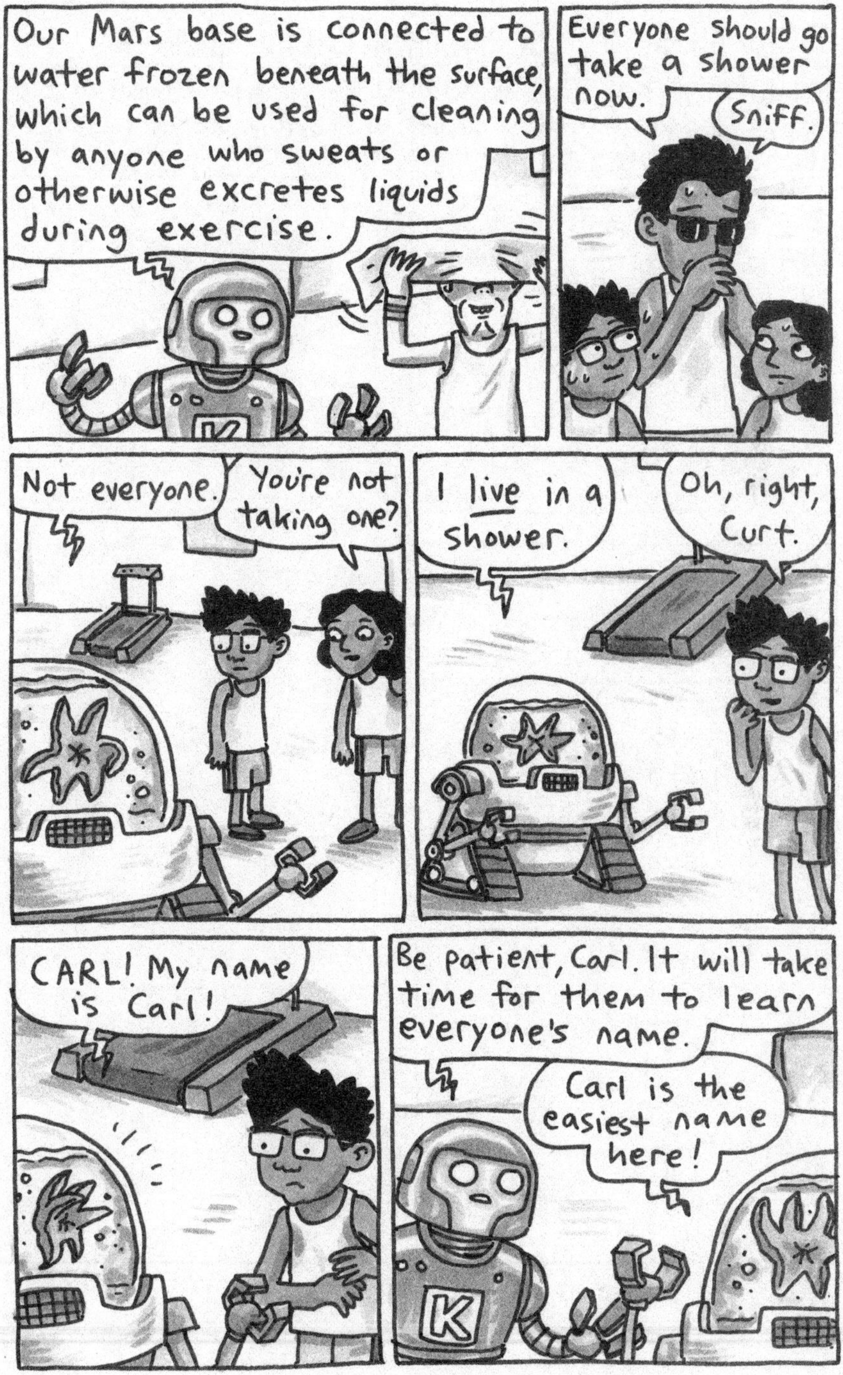
Our Mars base is connected to water frozen beneath the surface, which can be used for cleaning by anyone who sweats or otherwise excretes liquids during exercise.
Everyone should go take a shower now.
Sniff.
Not everyone.
You're not taking one?
I live in a shower.
Oh, right, Curt.
CARL! My name is Carl!
Be patient, Carl. It will take time for them to learn everyone's name.
Carl is the easiest name here!

MARS MISSION DESIGNATION: CHEMICAL REACTIONS

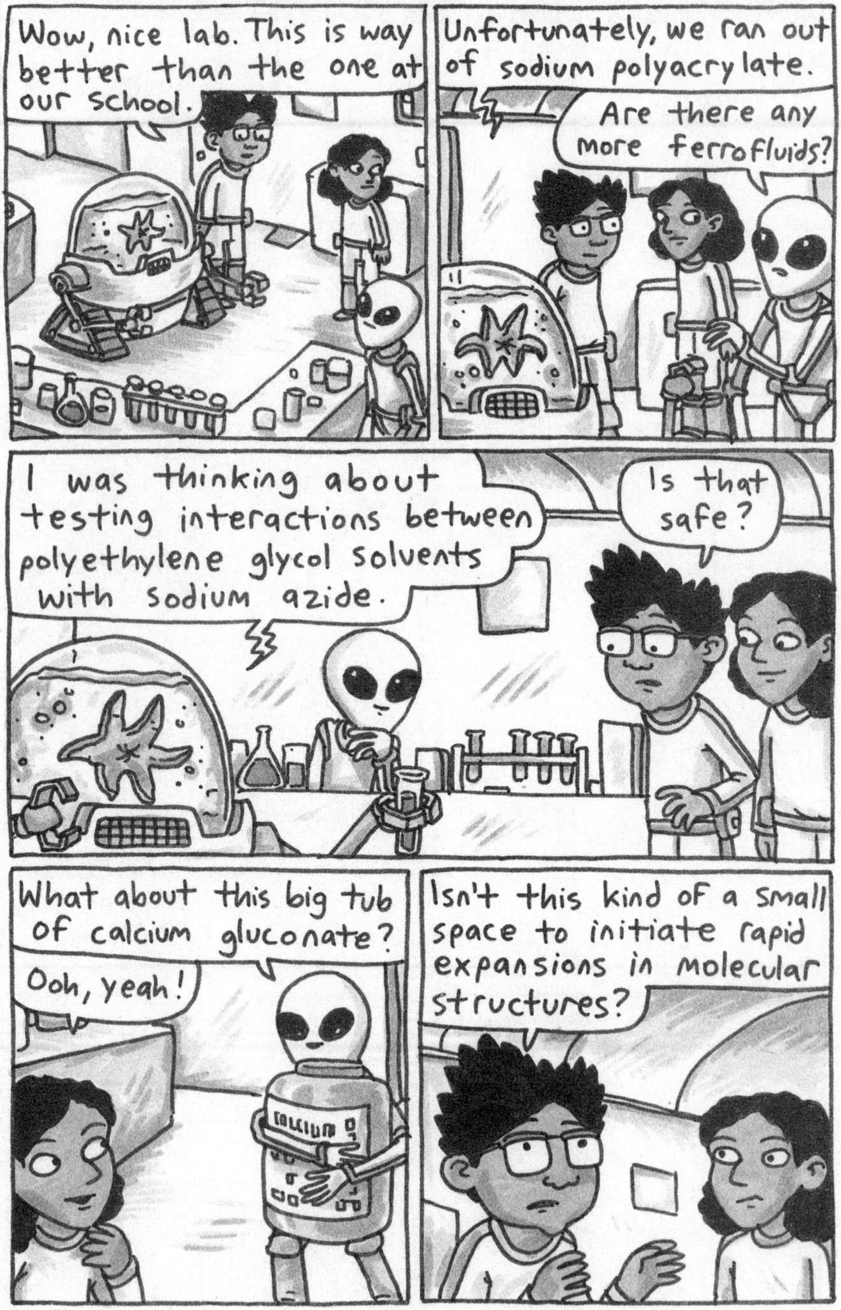
Wow, nice lab. This is way better than the one at our school.
Unfortunately, we ran out of sodium polyacrylate.
Are there any more ferrofluids?
I was thinking about testing interactions between polyethylene glycol solvents with sodium azide.
Is that safe?
What about this big tub of calcium gluconate?
Ooh, yeah!
Isn't this kind of a small space to initiate rapid expansions in molecular structures?

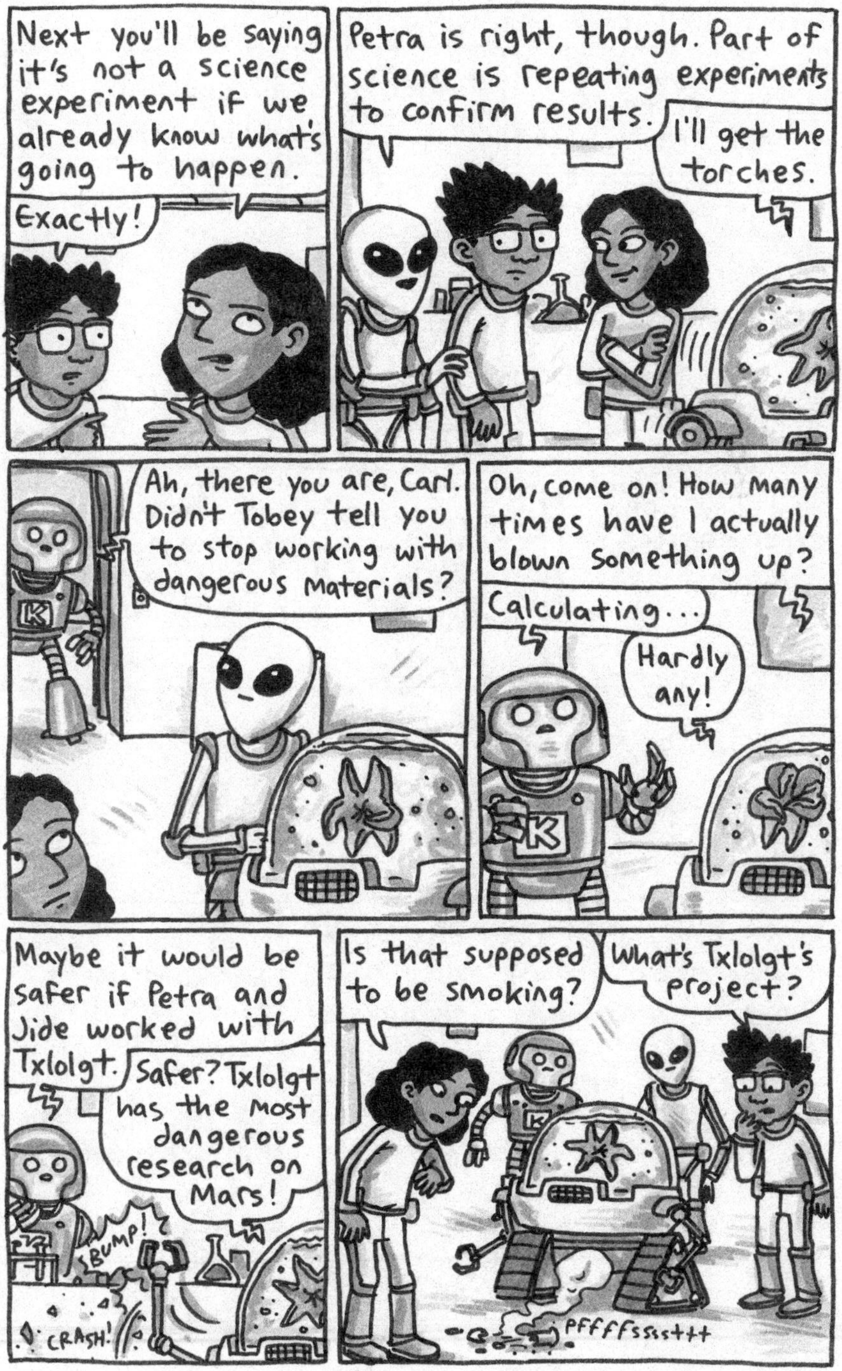
Next you'll be saying it's not a science experiment if we already know what's going to happen.
Exactly!
Petra is right, though. Part of science is repeating experiments to confirm results.
I'll get the torches.
Ah, there you are, Carl. Didn't Tobey tell you to stop working with dangerous materials?
Oh, come on! How many times have I actually blown something up?
Calculating...
Hardly any!
Maybe it would be safer if Petra and Jide worked with Txlolgt.
Safer? Txlolgt has the most dangerous research on Mars!
BUMP!
CRASH!
Is that supposed to be smoking?
What's Txlolgt's project?
PFFFFSSSSTTT

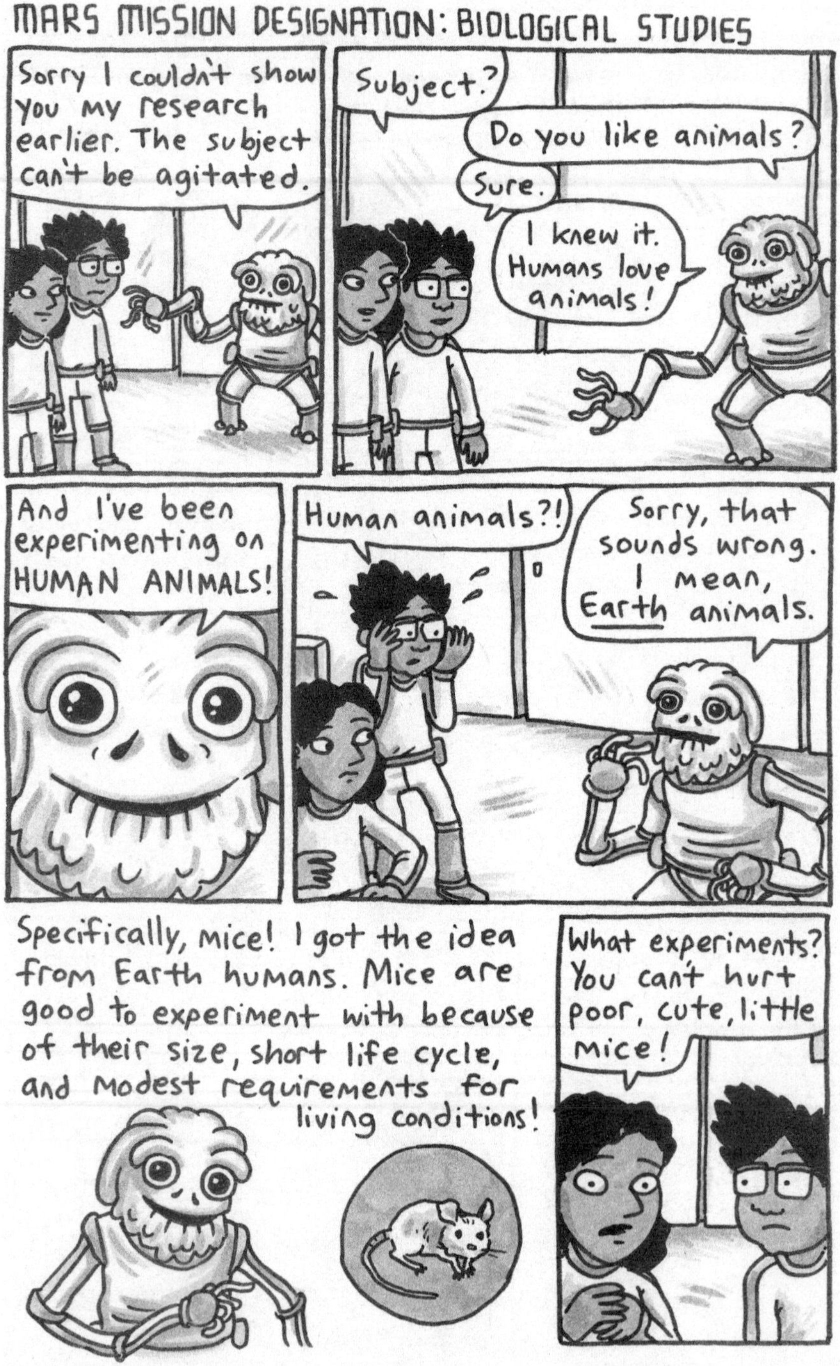
MARS MISSION DESIGNATION: BIOLOGICAL STUDIES
Sorry I couldn't show you my research earlier. The subject can't be agitated.
Subject?
Do you like animals?
Sure.
I knew it. Humans love animals!
And I've been experimenting on HUMAN ANIMALS!
Human animals?!
Sorry, that sounds wrong. I mean, Earth animals.
Specifically, mice! I got the idea from Earth humans. Mice are good to experiment with because of their size, short life cycle, and modest requirements for living conditions!
What experiments? You can't hurt poor, cute, little mice!

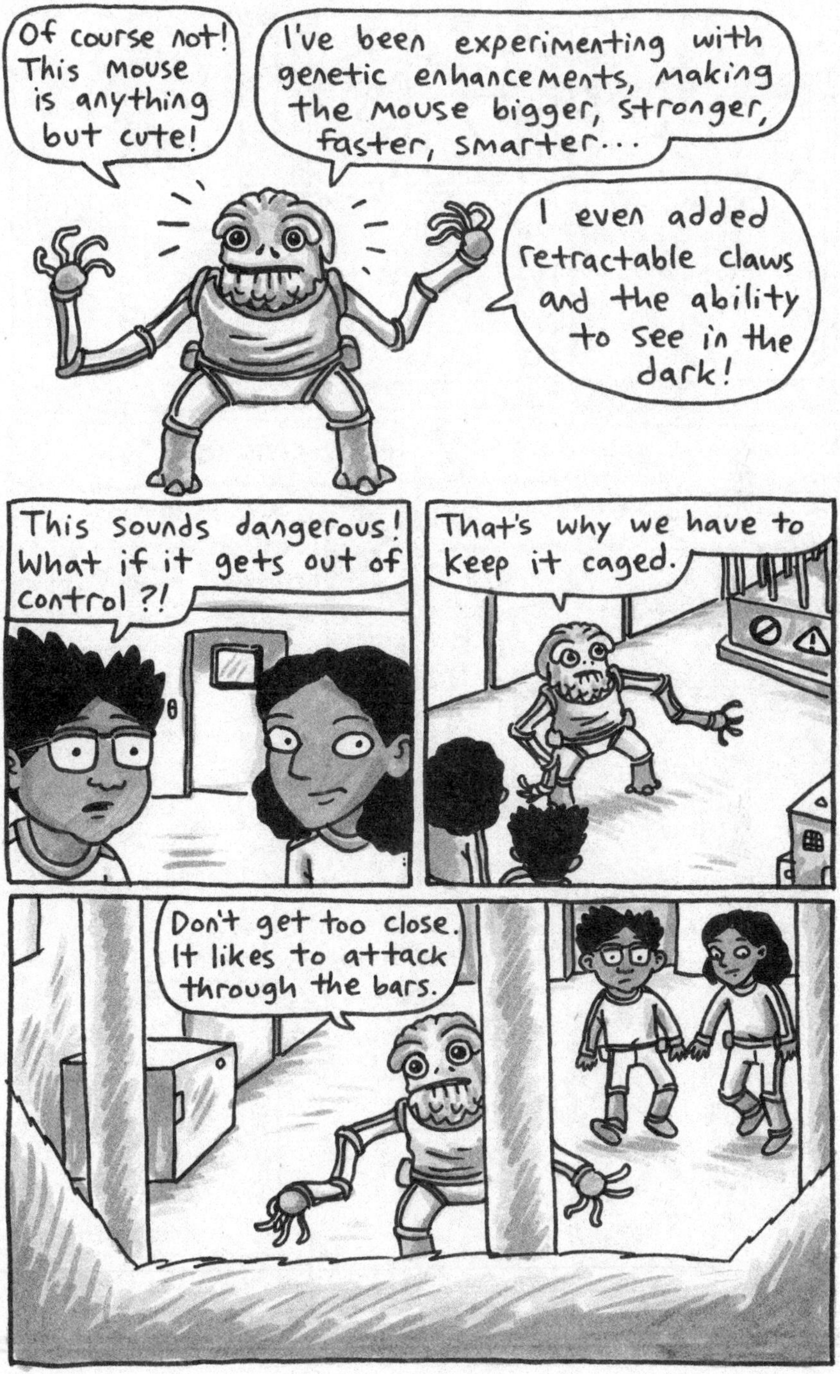
Of course not! This mouse is anything but cute!
I've been experimenting with genetic enhancements, making the mouse bigger, stronger, faster, smarter...
I even added retractable claws and the ability to see in the dark!
This sounds dangerous! What if it gets out of control?!
That's why we have to keep it caged.
Don't get too close. It likes to attack through the bars.

Meow.

FLOP!

Purrrrrrrrr.

What are you doing?! Watch out!

It's a cat!

Giggle.

No, its name is Squeak.

We mean it's a cat, a different animal from Earth. Not a mouse.

It's definitely a mouse. See, here's the genetic code of mice....

Then I altered the sequences, adjusted some characteristics using recombinant nucleic acids, and created—

A cat. You made a cat.

Meow!

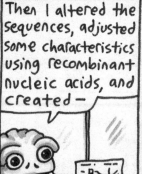

MARS MISSION DESIGNATION: PRODUCE PRODUCTION

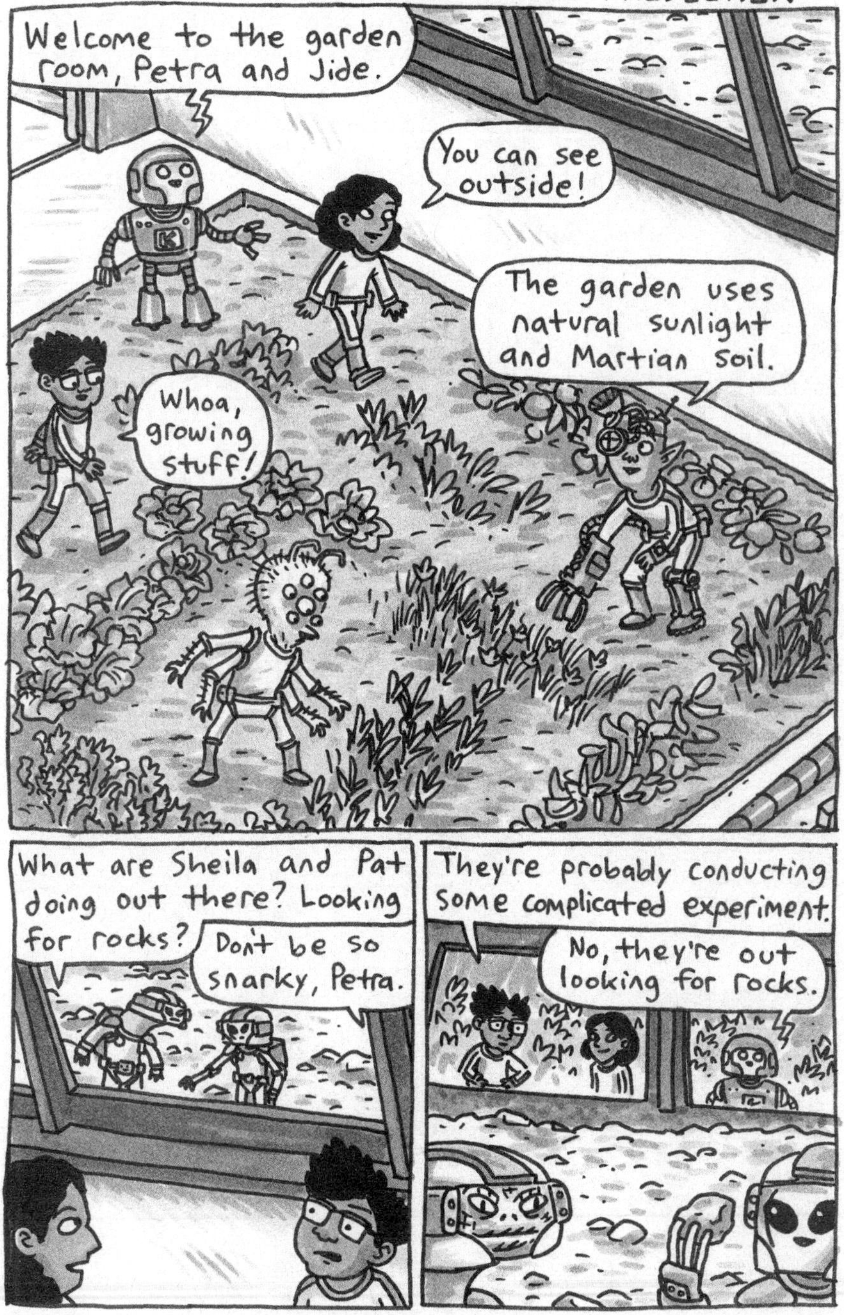
Welcome to the garden room, Petra and Jide.
You can see outside!
The garden uses natural sunlight and Martian soil.
Whoa, growing stuff!
What are Sheila and Pat doing out there? Looking for rocks?
Don't be so snarky, Petra.
They're probably conducting some complicated experiment.
No, they're out looking for rocks.

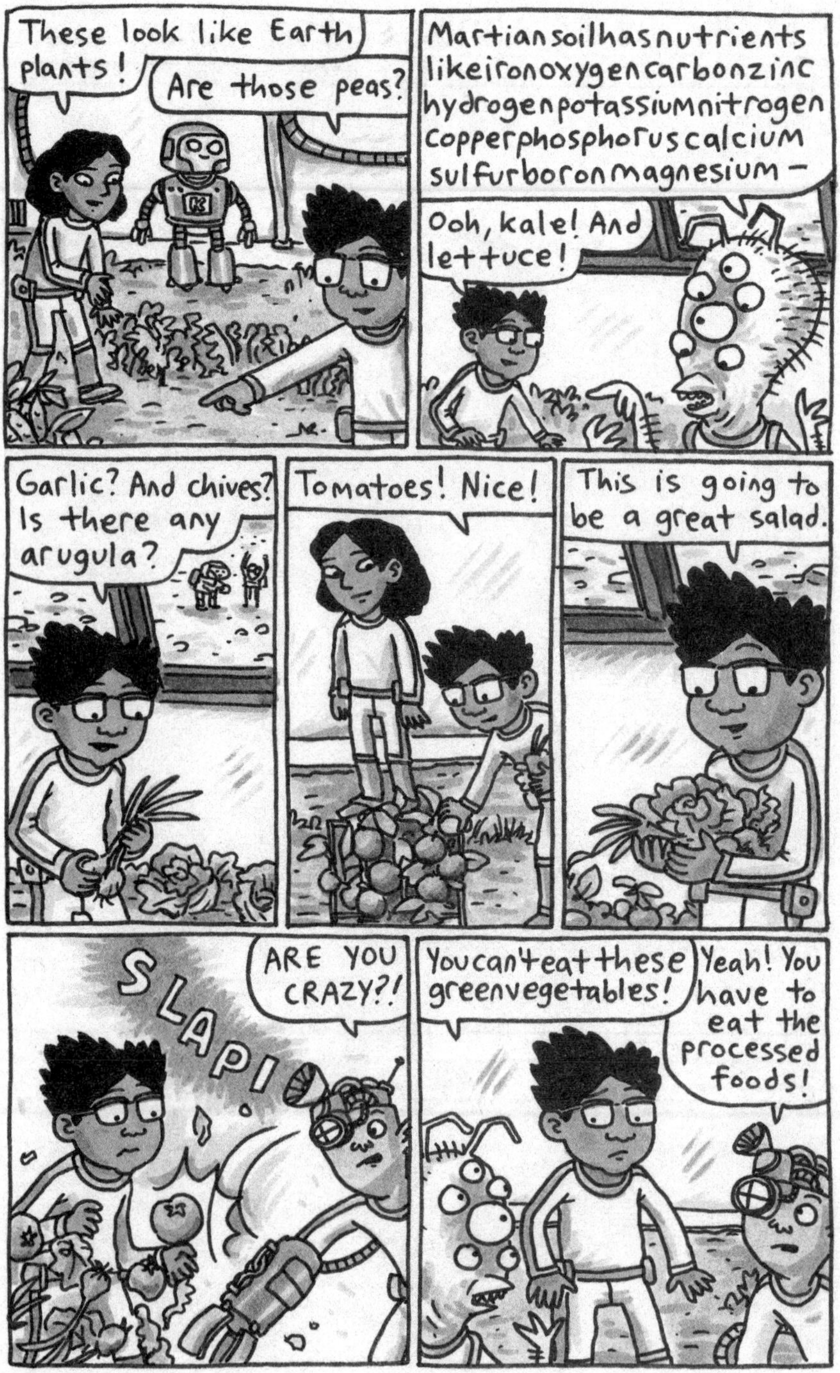
These look like Earth plants!
Are those peas?
Martiansoilhasnutrients likeironoxygencarbonzinc hydrogenpotassiumnitrogen copperphosphoruscalcium sulfurboronmagnesium –
Ooh, kale! And lettuce!
Garlic? And chives? Is there any arugula?
Tomatoes! Nice!
This is going to be a great salad.
SLAP!
ARE YOU CRAZY?!
Youcan'teatthese greenvegetables!
Yeah! You have to eat the processed foods!

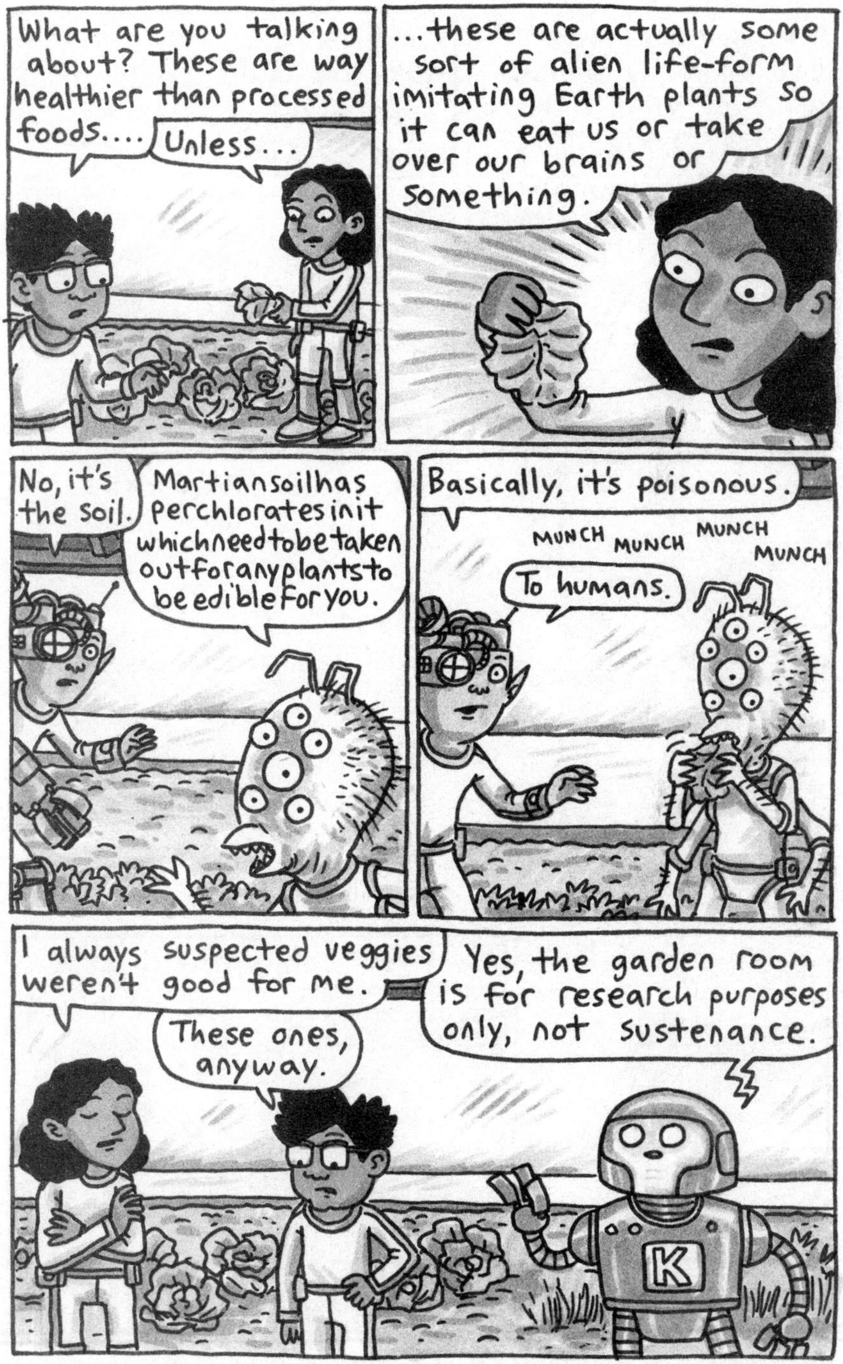
What are you talking about? These are way healthier than processed foods....
Unless...
...these are actually some sort of alien life-form imitating Earth plants so it can eat us or take over our brains or something.
No, it's the soil.
Martiansoilhas perchloratesinit whichneedtobetaken outforanyplantsto be edibleforyou.
Basically, it's poisonous.
MUNCH MUNCH MUNCH MUNCH
To humans.
I always suspected veggies weren't good for me.
These ones, anyway.
Yes, the garden room is for research purposes only, not sustenance.
K

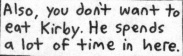

Also, you don't want to eat Kirby. He spends a lot of time in here.

Kirby? The imaginary alien Jemmy stepped on?

Kirby is real! He's just microscopically small. He's pretty tough. Jemmy worries too much.

What kind of alien is he?

He's actually an Earthling!

What?!

He's a tardigrade that came to Mars on one of your rovers years ago.

Tobey found him and made Kirby the first astronaut resident at the Mars base!

Oh. What does Kirby do, then?

Mostlyfeedsonplantcells.

He's too small to do much else.

138

MARS MISSION DESIGNATION: MATHEMATICAL INNOVATIONS

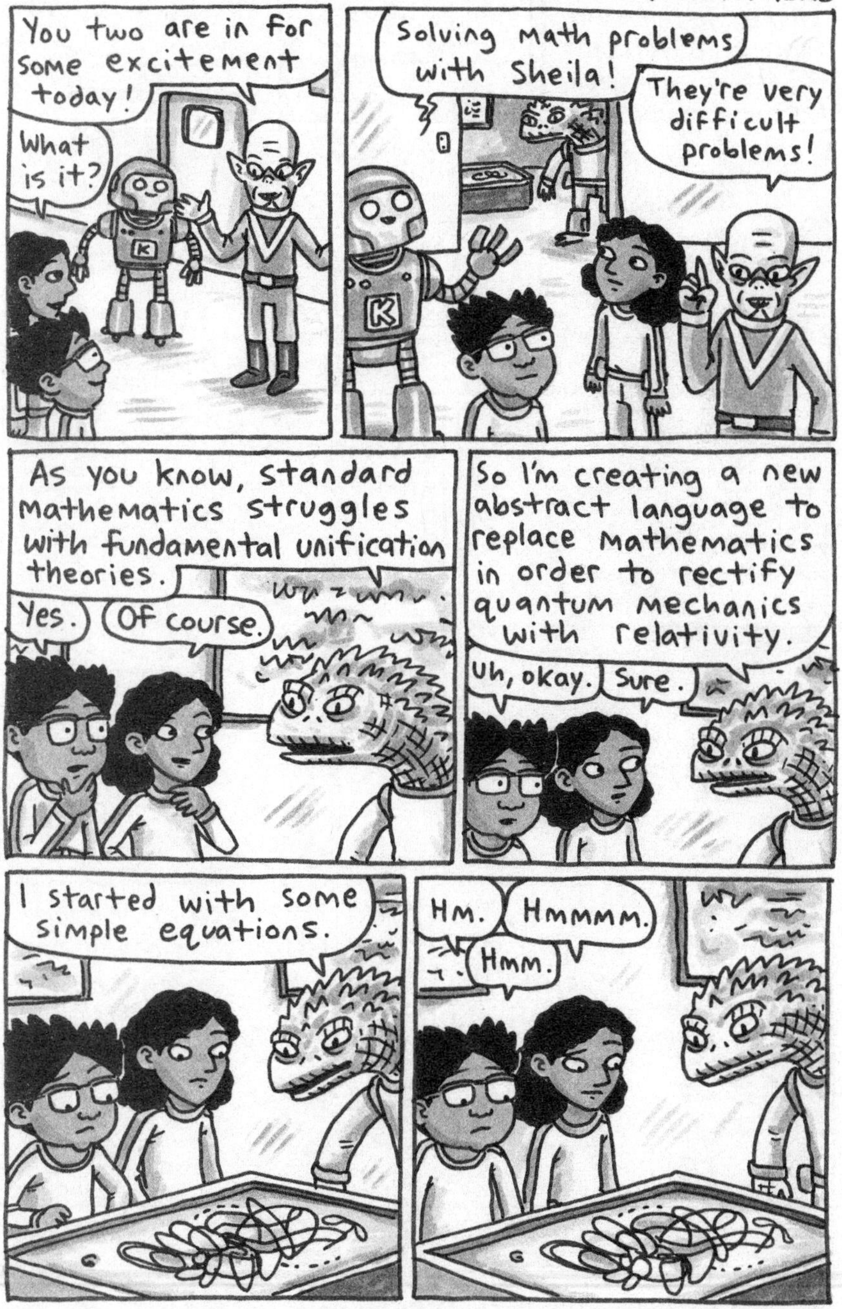
You two are in for some excitement today!
What is it?
Solving math problems with Sheila!
They're very difficult problems!
As you know, standard mathematics struggles with fundamental unification theories.
Yes.
Of course.
So I'm creating a new abstract language to replace mathematics in order to rectify quantum mechanics with relativity.
Uh, okay.
Sure.
I started with some simple equations.
Hm.
Hmmmm.
Hmm.

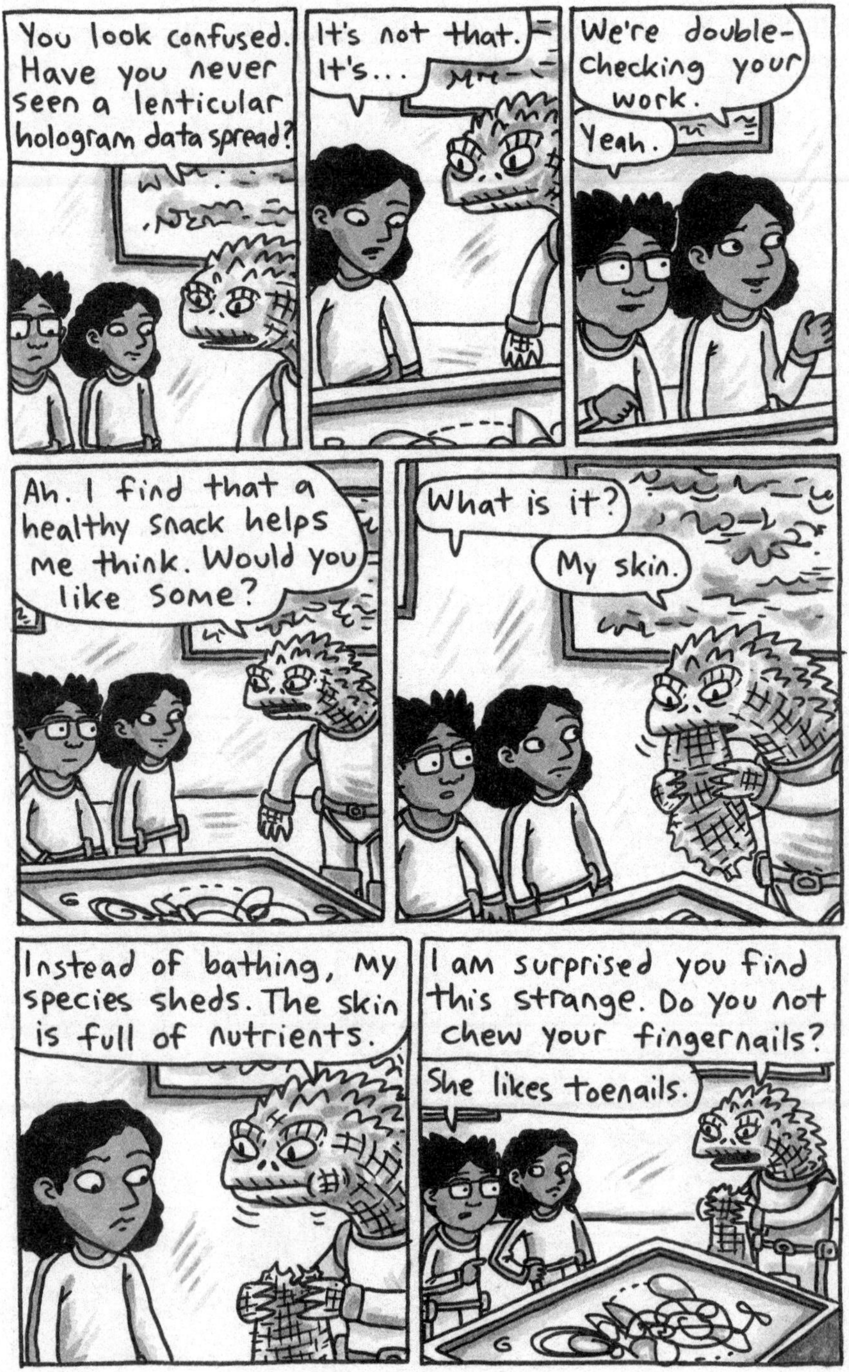
You look confused. Have you never seen a lenticular hologram data spread?
It's not that. It's...
We're double-checking your work.
Yeah.
Ah. I find that a healthy snack helps me think. Would you like some?
What is it?
My skin.
Instead of bathing, my species sheds. The skin is full of nutrients.
I am surprised you find this strange. Do you not chew your fingernails?
She likes toenails.

MARS MISSION DESIGNATION: GEOLOGICAL SURVEY

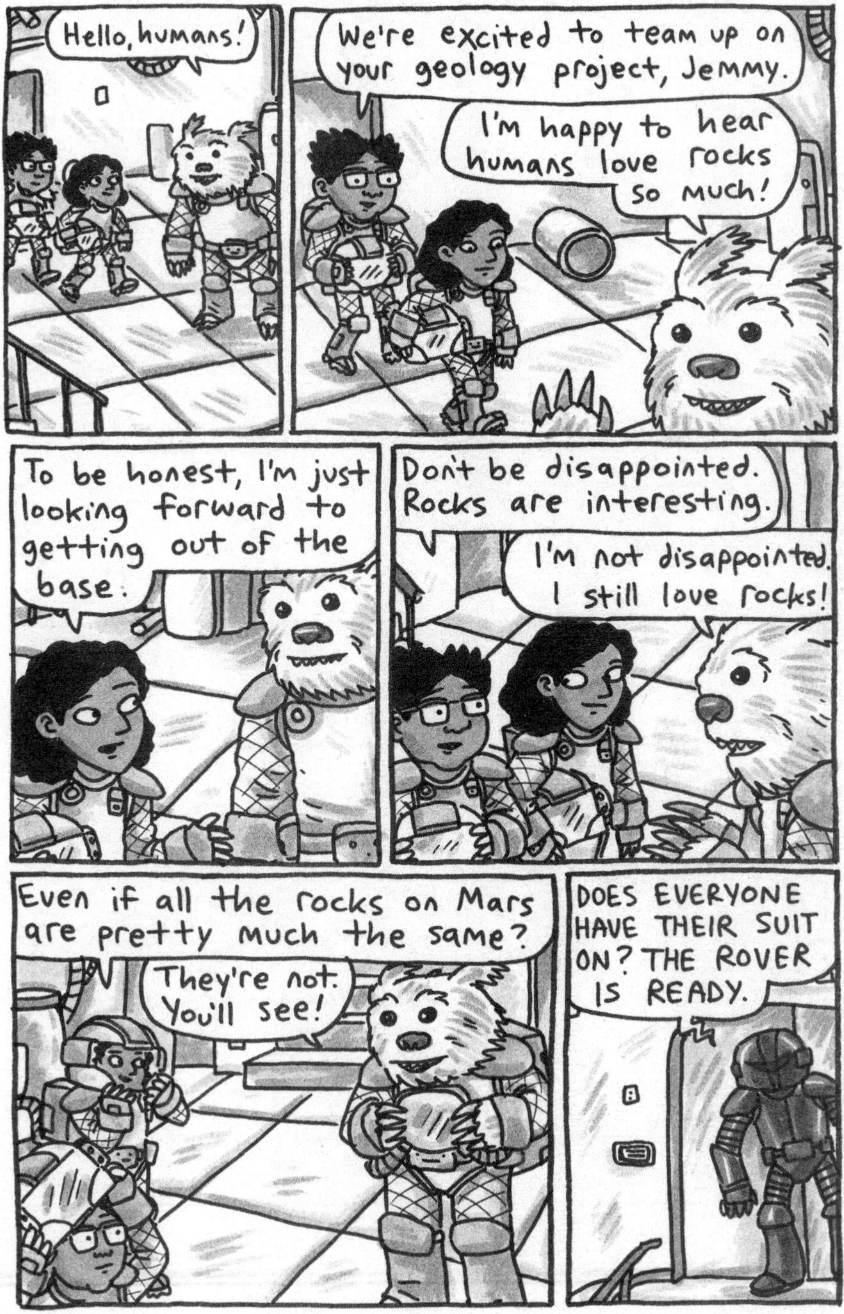
Hello, humans!
We're excited to team up on your geology project, Jemmy.
I'm happy to hear humans love rocks so much!
To be honest, I'm just looking forward to getting out of the base.
Don't be disappointed. Rocks are interesting.
I'm not disappointed. I still love rocks!
Even if all the rocks on Mars are pretty much the same?
They're not. You'll see!
DOES EVERYONE HAVE THEIR SUIT ON? THE ROVER IS READY.

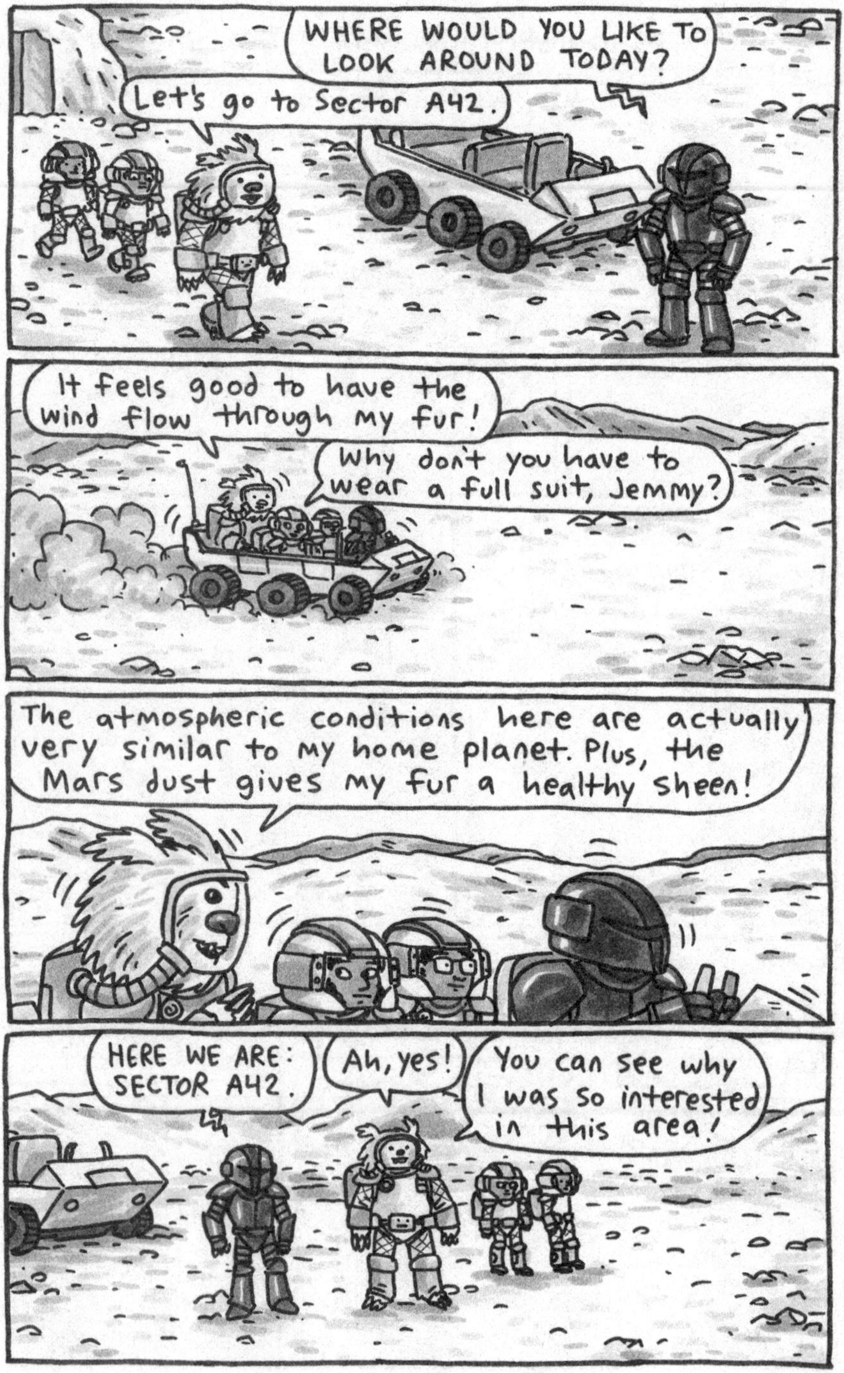
WHERE WOULD YOU LIKE TO LOOK AROUND TODAY?
Let's go to Sector A42.
It feels good to have the wind flow through my fur!
Why don't you have to wear a full suit, Jemmy?
The atmospheric conditions here are actually very similar to my home planet. Plus, the Mars dust gives my fur a healthy sheen!
HERE WE ARE: SECTOR A42.
Ah, yes!
You can see why I was so interested in this area!

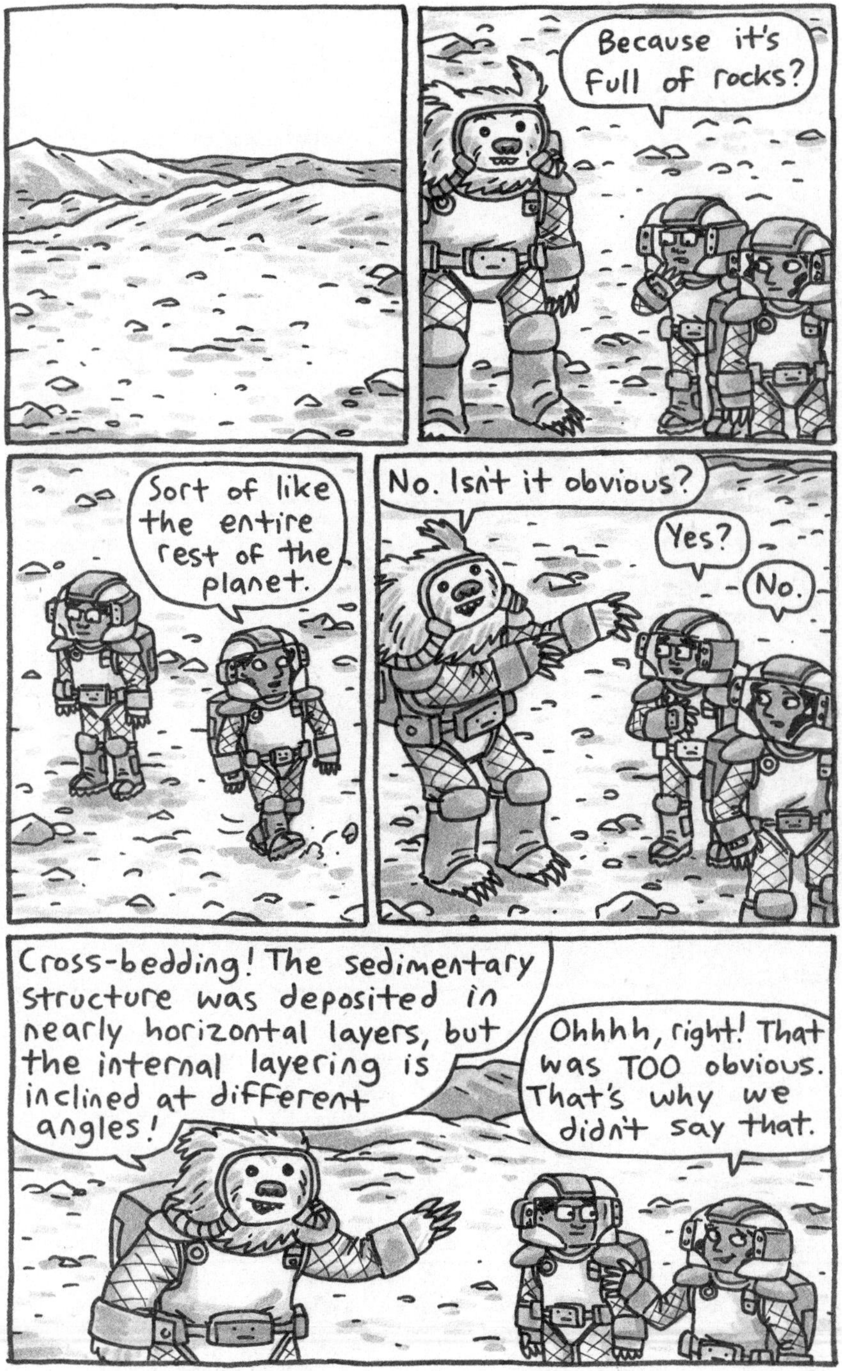
Because it's full of rocks?
Sort of like the entire rest of the planet.
No. Isn't it obvious?
Yes?
No.
Cross-bedding! The sedimentary structure was deposited in nearly horizontal layers, but the internal layering is inclined at different angles!
Ohhhh, right! That was TOO obvious. That's why we didn't say that.

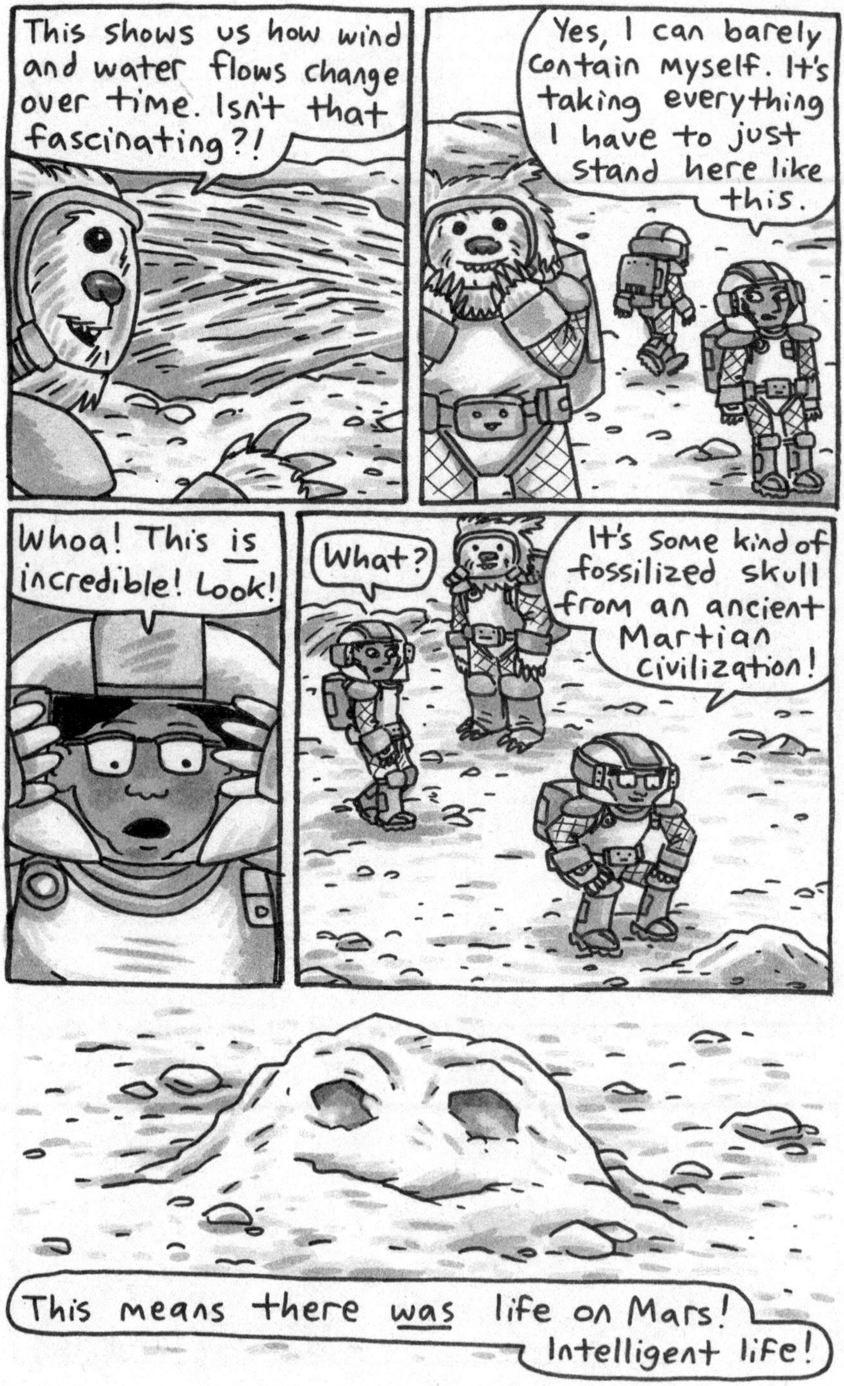
This shows us how wind and water flows change over time. Isn't that fascinating?!
Yes, I can barely contain myself. It's taking everything I have to just stand here like this.
Whoa! This is incredible! Look!
What?
It's some kind of fossilized skull from an ancient Martian civilization!
This means there was life on Mars! Intelligent life!

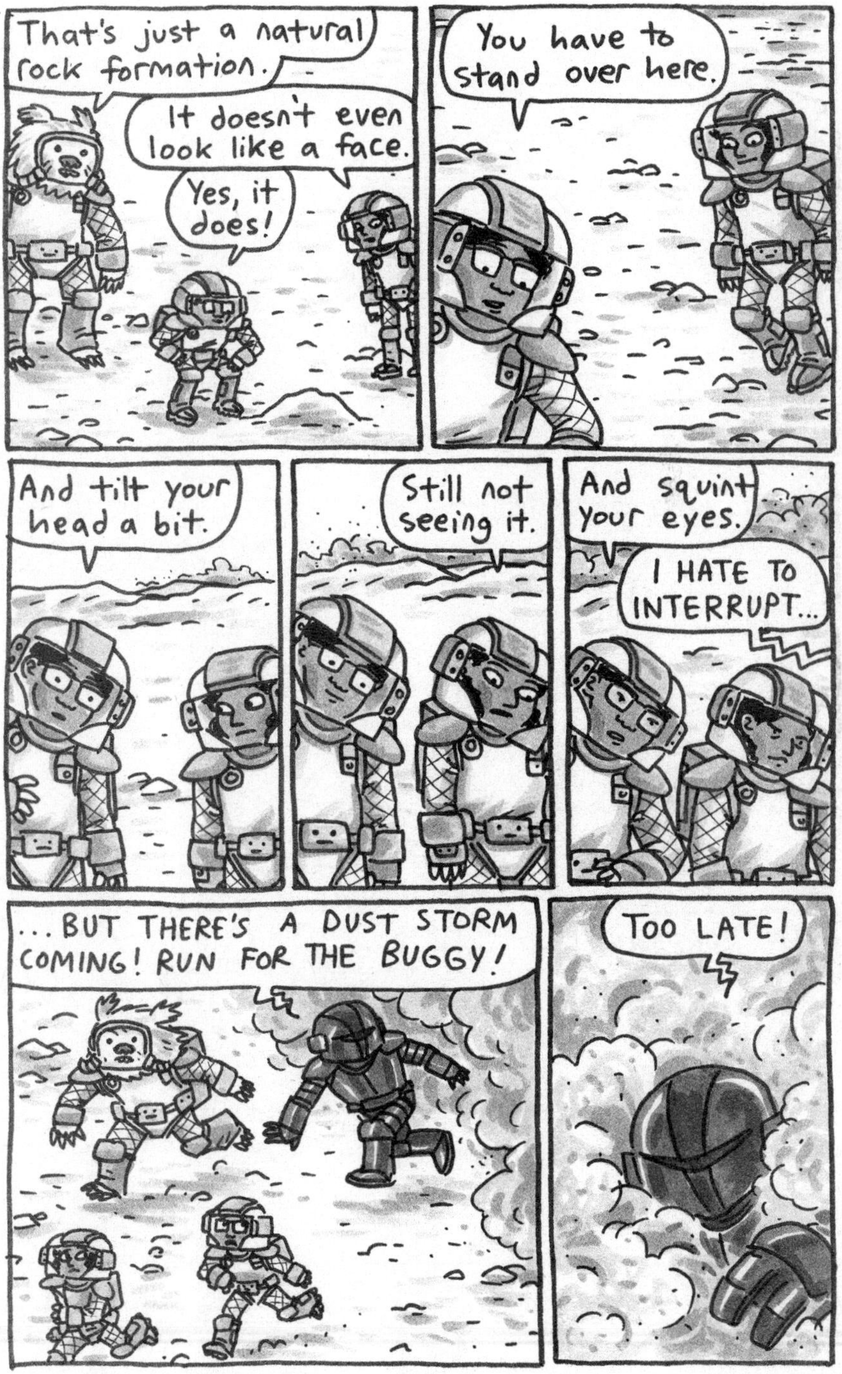
That's just a natural rock formation.
It doesn't even look like a face.
Yes, it does!
You have to stand over here.
And tilt your head a bit.
Still not seeing it.
And squint your eyes.
I HATE TO INTERRUPT...
...BUT THERE'S A DUST STORM COMING! RUN FOR THE BUGGY!
TOO LATE!

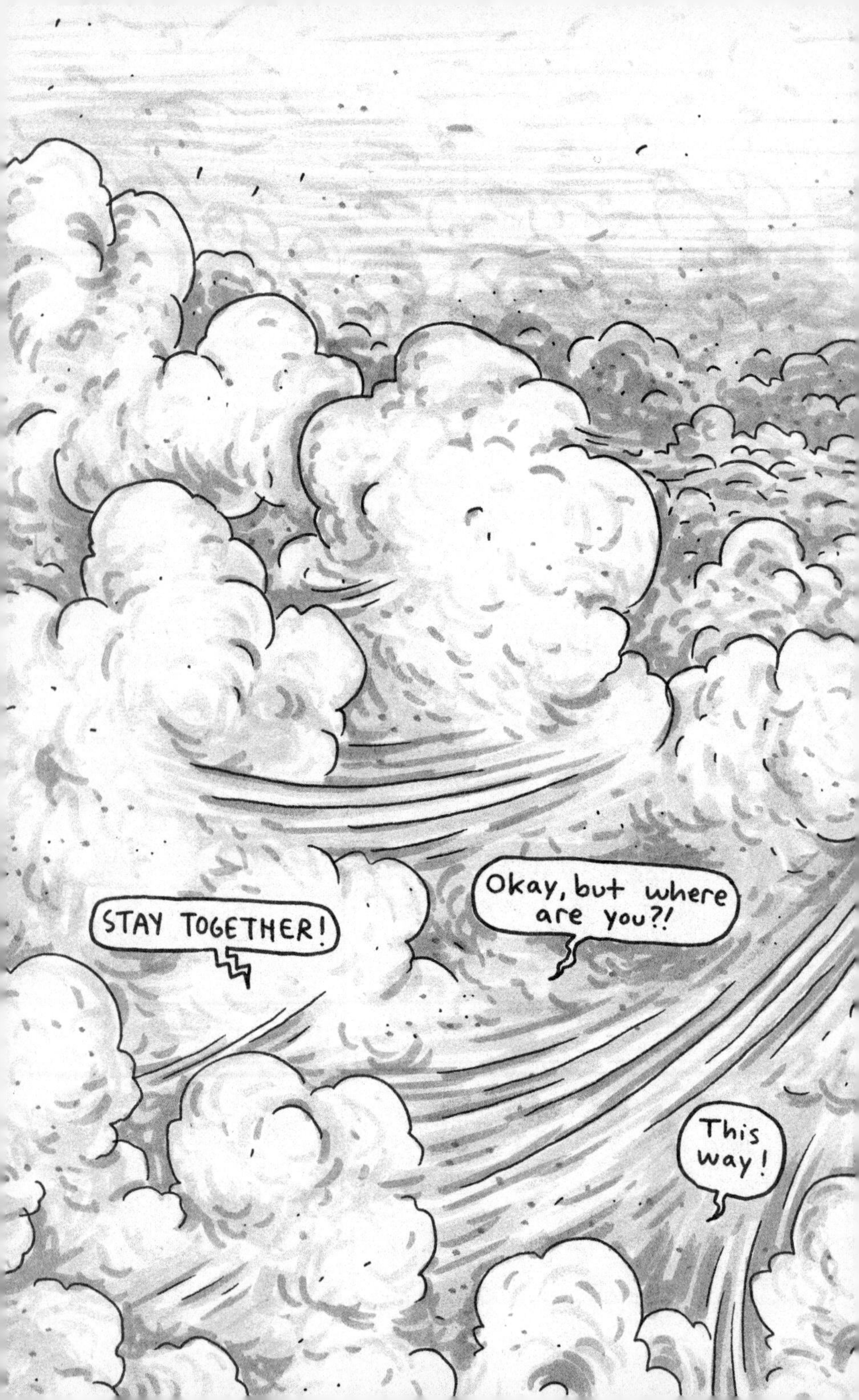
STAY TOGETHER!
Okay, but where are you?!
This way!

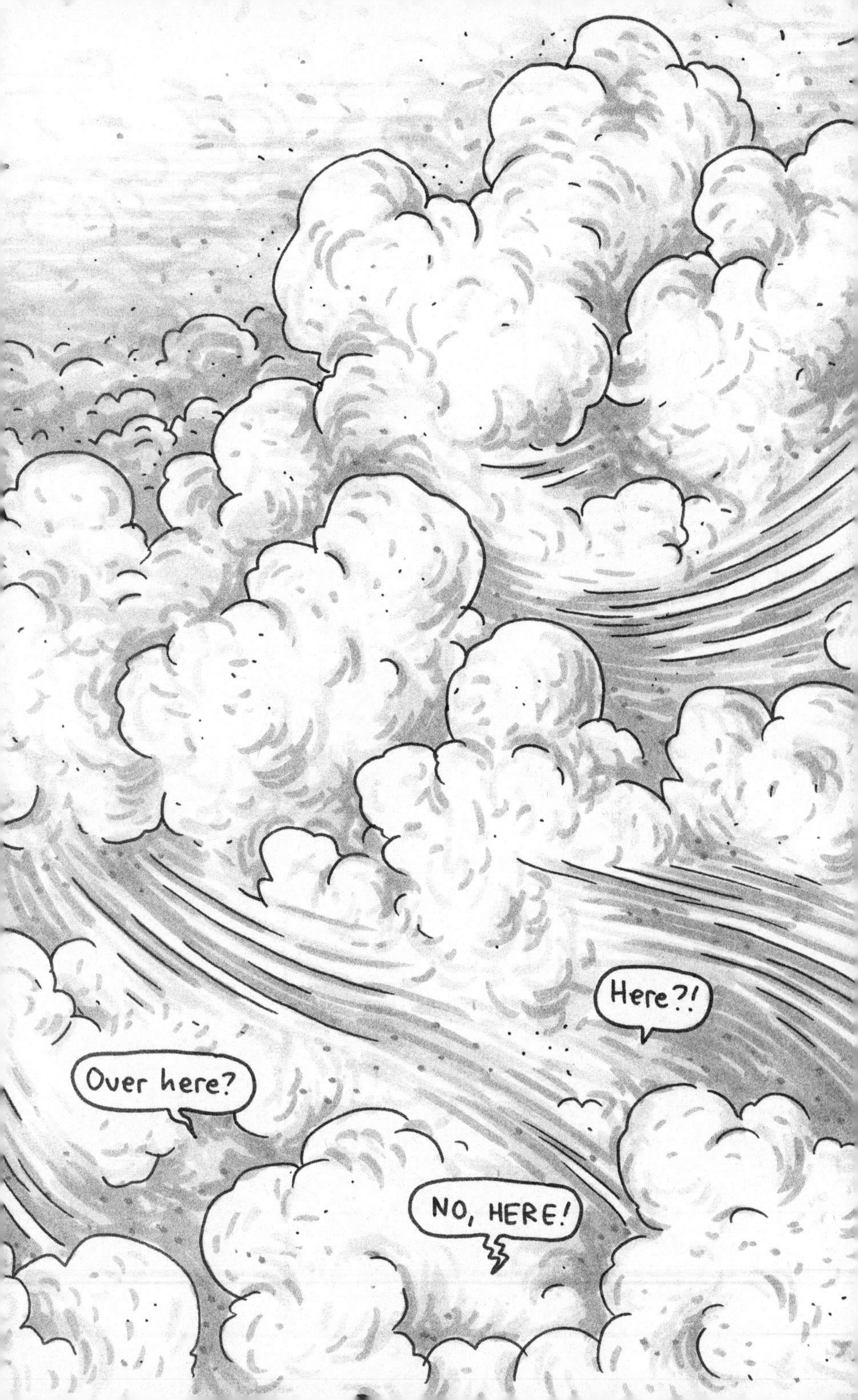
Here?!
Over here?
NO, HERE!

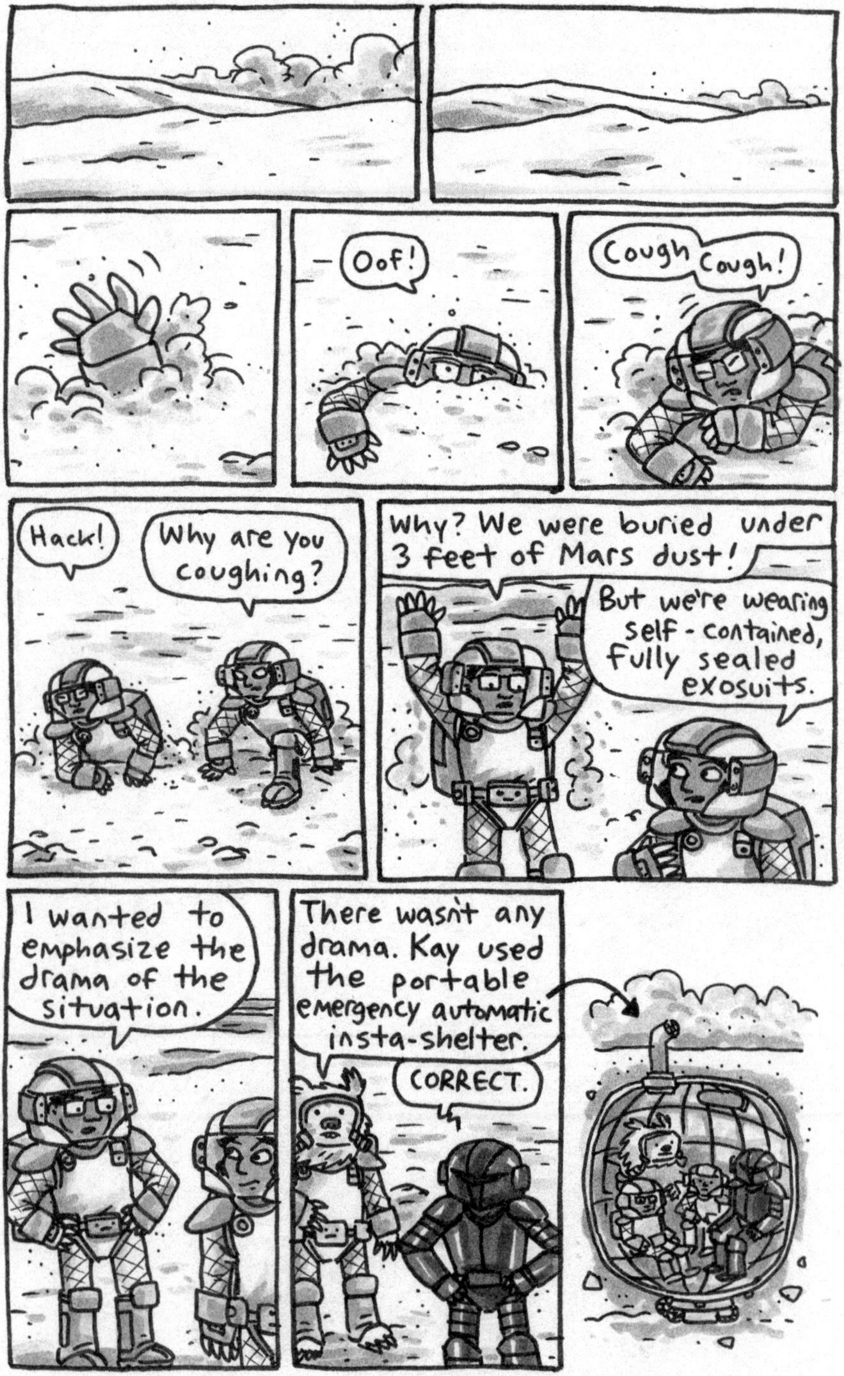
Oof!
Cough Cough!
Hack!
Why are you coughing?
Why? We were buried under 3 feet of Mars dust!
But we're wearing self-contained, fully sealed exosuits.
I wanted to emphasize the drama of the situation.
There wasn't any drama. Kay used the portable emergency automatic insta-shelter.
CORRECT.

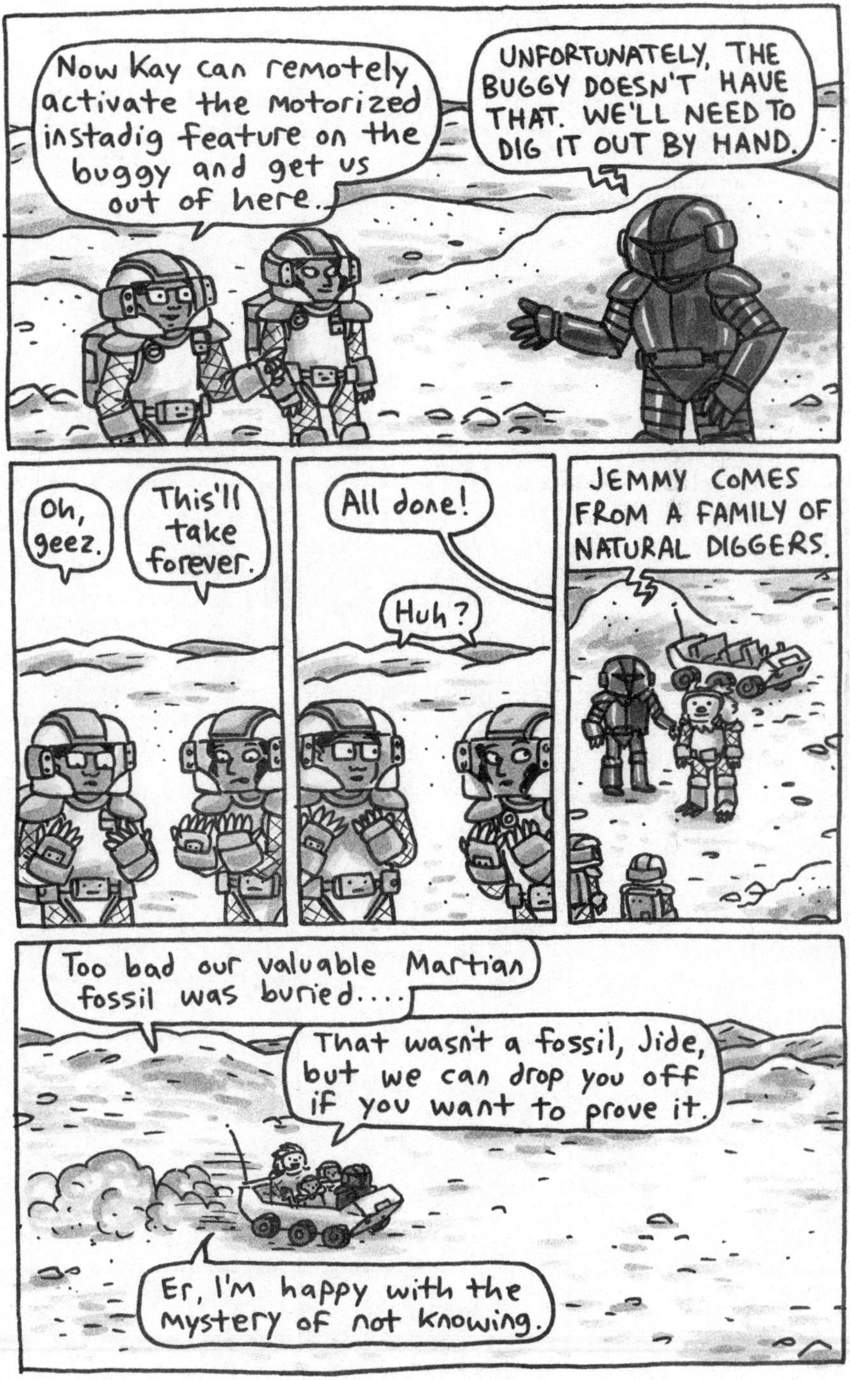
Now Kay can remotely activate the motorized instadig feature on the buggy and get us out of here...
UNFORTUNATELY, THE BUGGY DOESN'T HAVE THAT. WE'LL NEED TO DIG IT OUT BY HAND.
Oh, geez.
This'll take forever.
All done!
Huh?
JEMMY COMES FROM A FAMILY OF NATURAL DIGGERS.
Too bad our valuable Martian fossil was buried....
That wasn't a fossil, Jide, but we can drop you off if you want to prove it.
Er, I'm happy with the mystery of not knowing.

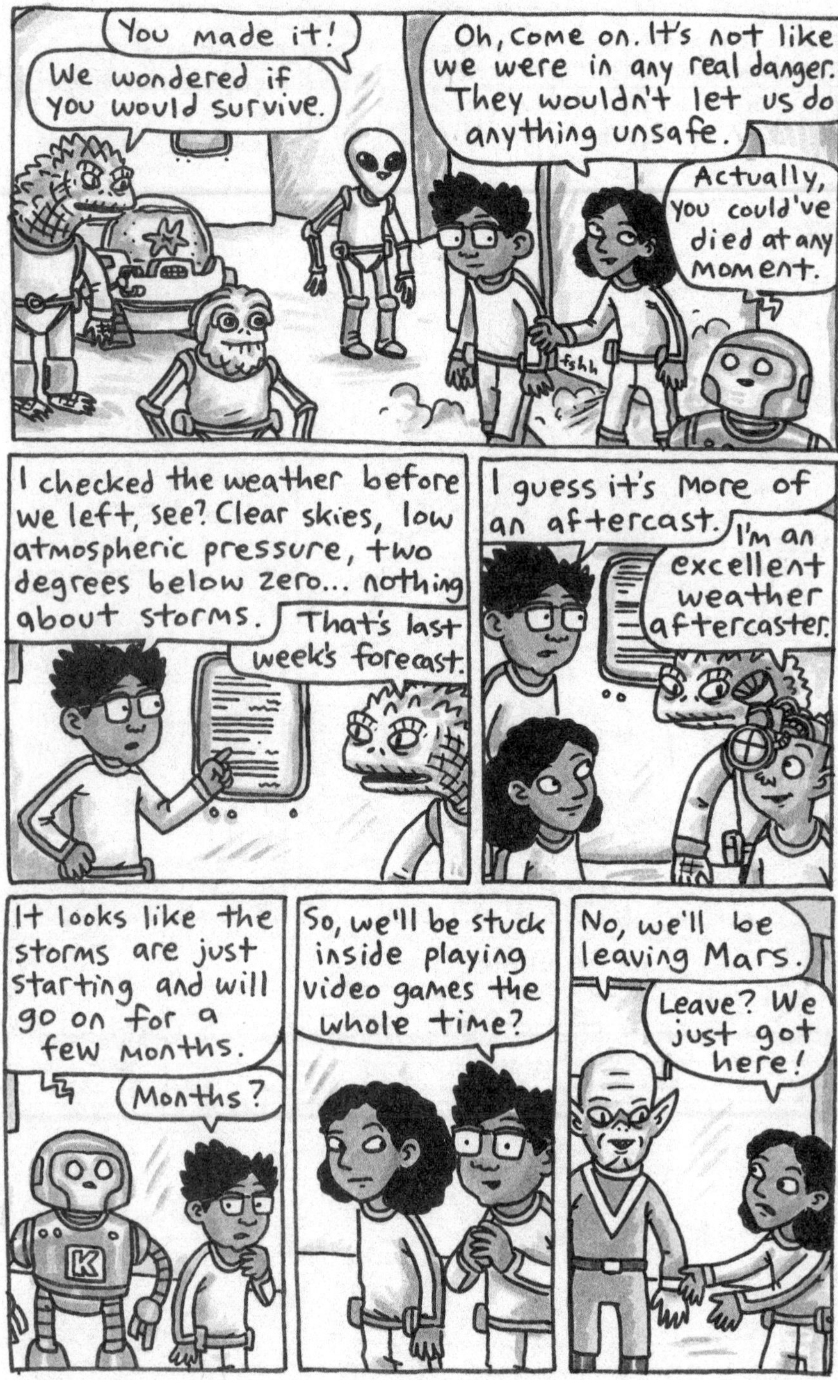
You made it!
We wondered if you would survive.
Oh, come on. It's not like we were in any real danger. They wouldn't let us do anything unsafe.
Actually, you could've died at any moment.
fshh
I checked the weather before we left, see? Clear skies, low atmospheric pressure, two degrees below zero... nothing about storms.
That's last week's forecast.
I guess it's more of an aftercast.
I'm an excellent weather aftercaster.
It looks like the storms are just starting and will go on for a few months.
Months?
So, we'll be stuck inside playing video games the whole time?
No, we'll be leaving Mars.
Leave? We just got here!

A little storm activity could be a great opportunity for some extreme research.

Not little. Planet-wide! Nowhere will be safe.

We can weather minor weather, but whether you're inside or out, these storms will be a problem.

Dust covers our solar panels and buries our equipment.

Plus everything looks all red. BORING.

So we have to go back to Earth?

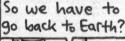

We're not going to Earth.

Yeah, Petra. Space travel is massively expensive. They'll probably need to turn us into nutrient paste for these guys.

No one is making me into nutrient paste!

Where'd she get a fork?

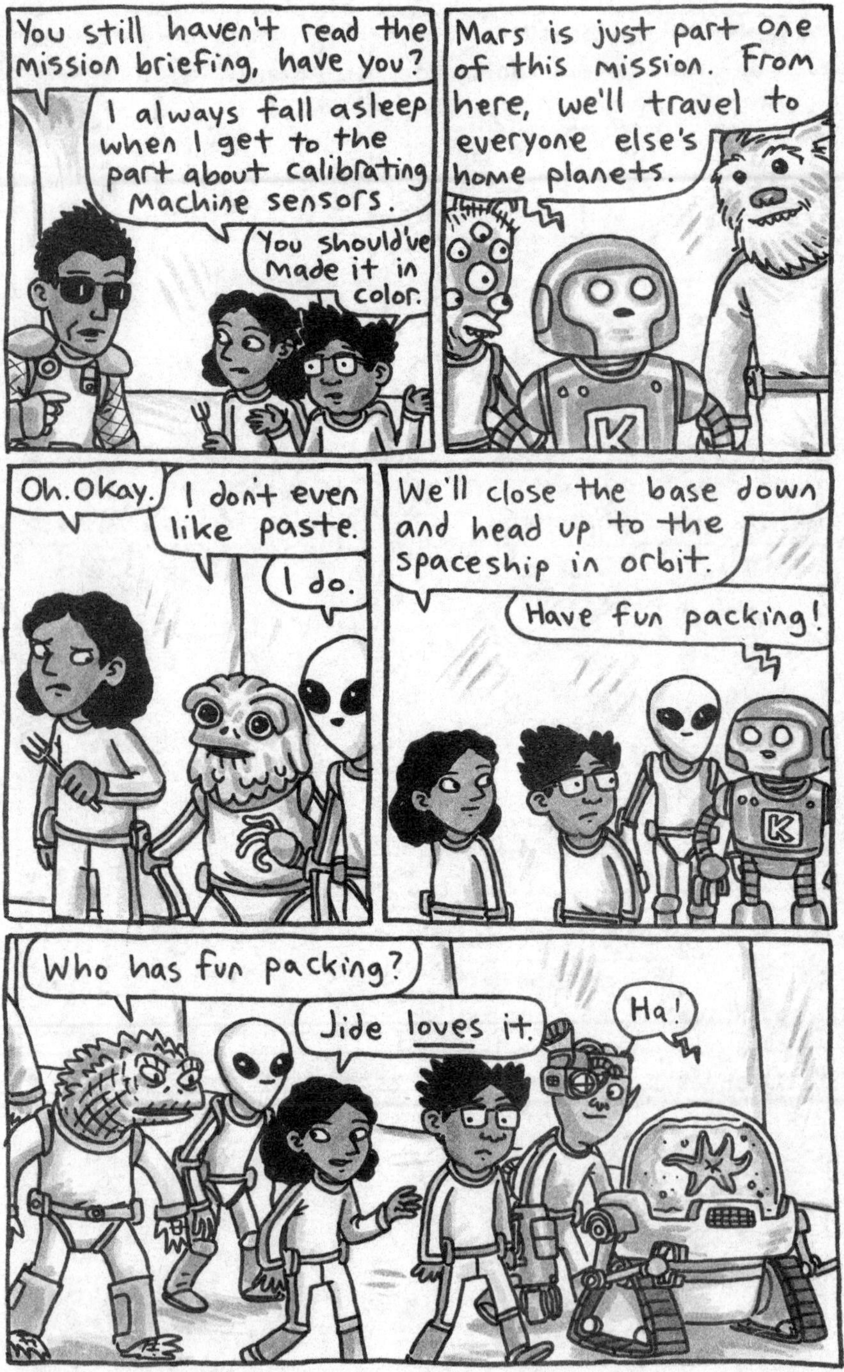
You still haven't read the mission briefing, have you?
I always fall asleep when I get to the part about calibrating machine sensors.
You should've made it in color.
Mars is just part one of this mission. From here, we'll travel to everyone else's home planets.
Oh. Okay.
I don't even like paste.
I do.
We'll close the base down and head up to the spaceship in orbit.
Have fun packing!
Who has fun packing?
Jide loves it.
Ha!

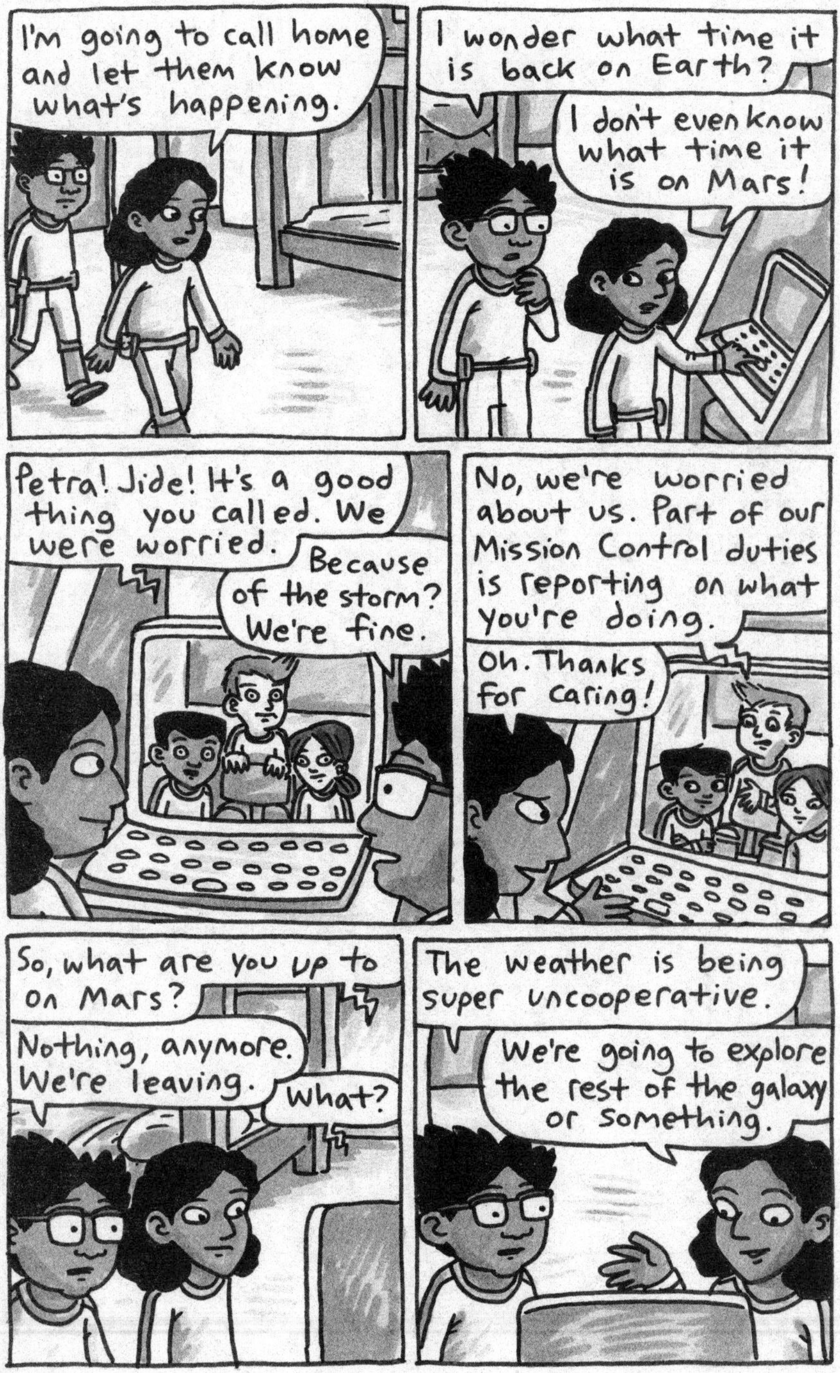
I'm going to call home and let them know what's happening.
I wonder what time it is back on Earth?
I don't even know what time it is on Mars!
Petra! Jide! It's a good thing you called. We were worried.
Because of the storm? We're fine.
No, we're worried about us. Part of our Mission Control duties is reporting on what you're doing.
Oh. Thanks for caring!
So, what are you up to on Mars?
Nothing, anymore. We're leaving.
What?
The weather is being super uncooperative.
We're going to explore the rest of the galaxy or something.

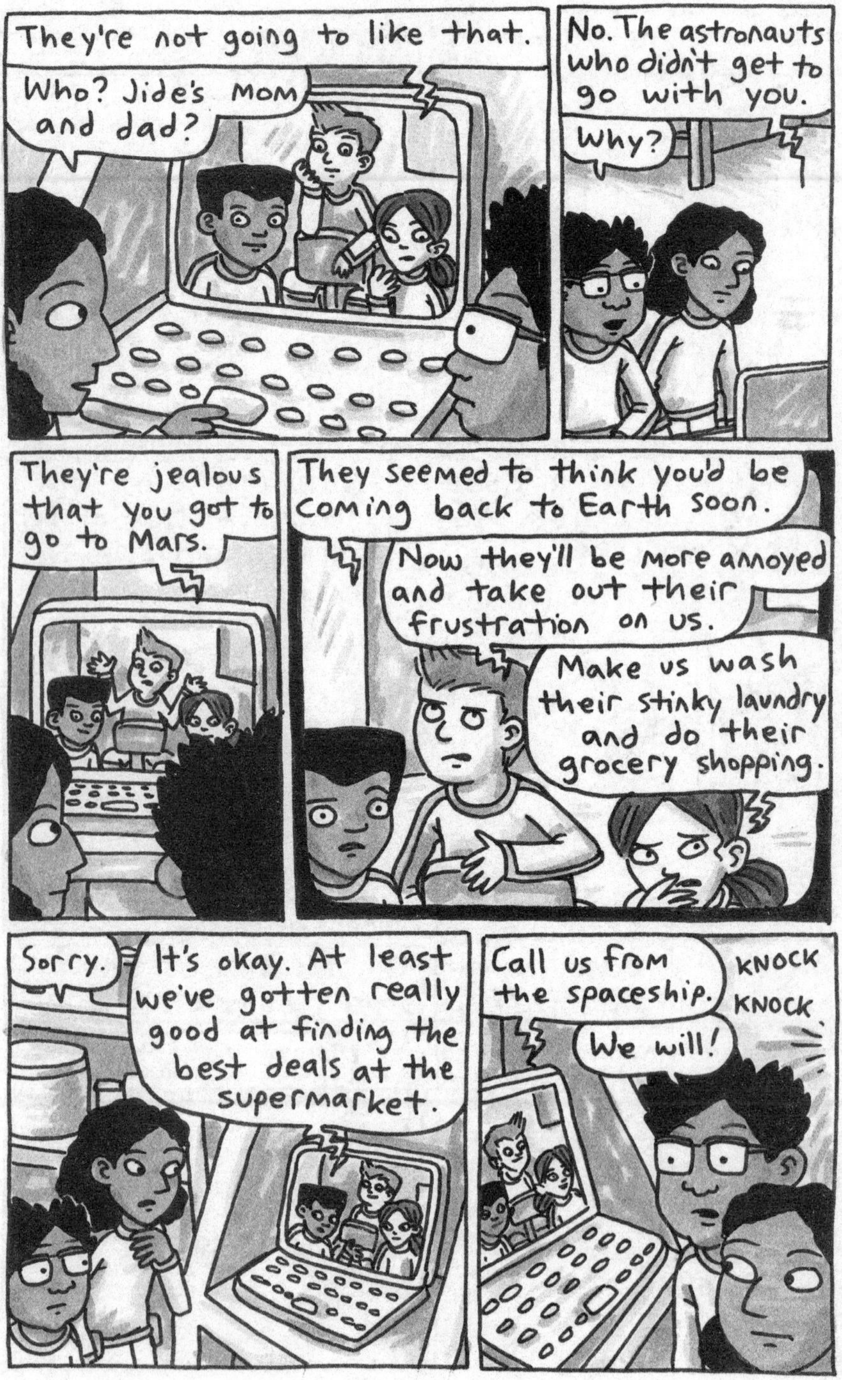
They're not going to like that.
Who? Jide's mom and dad?
No. The astronauts who didn't get to go with you.
Why?
They're jealous that you got to go to Mars.
They seemed to think you'd be coming back to Earth soon.
Now they'll be more annoyed and take out their frustration on us.
Make us wash their stinky laundry and do their grocery shopping.
Sorry.
It's okay. At least we've gotten really good at finding the best deals at the supermarket.
Call us from the spaceship.
KNOCK KNOCK
We will!

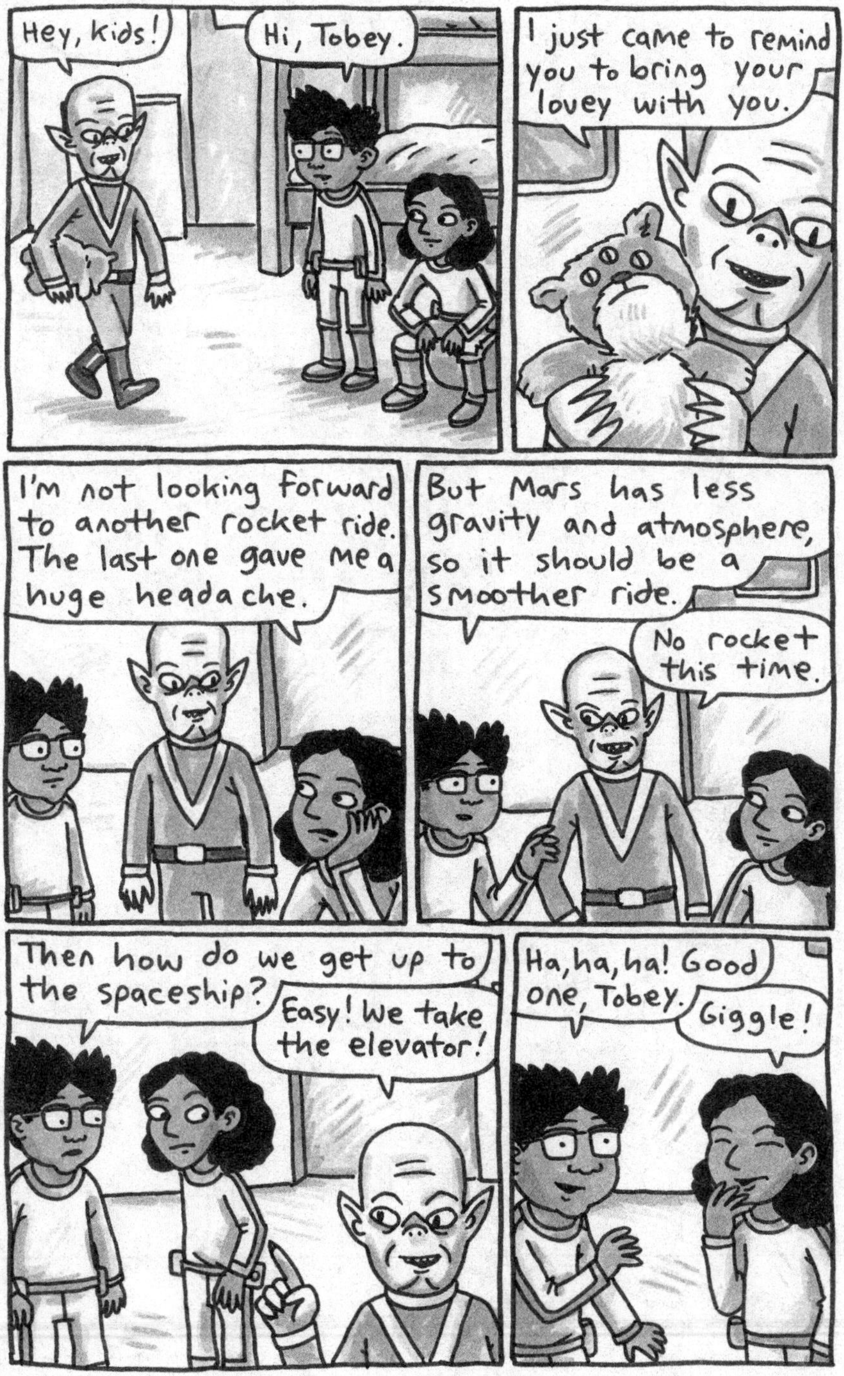
Hey, kids!
Hi, Tobey.
I just came to remind you to bring your lovey with you.
I'm not looking forward to another rocket ride. The last one gave me a huge headache.
But Mars has less gravity and atmosphere, so it should be a smoother ride.
No rocket this time.
Then how do we get up to the spaceship?
Easy! We take the elevator!
Ha, ha, ha! Good one, Tobey.
Giggle!

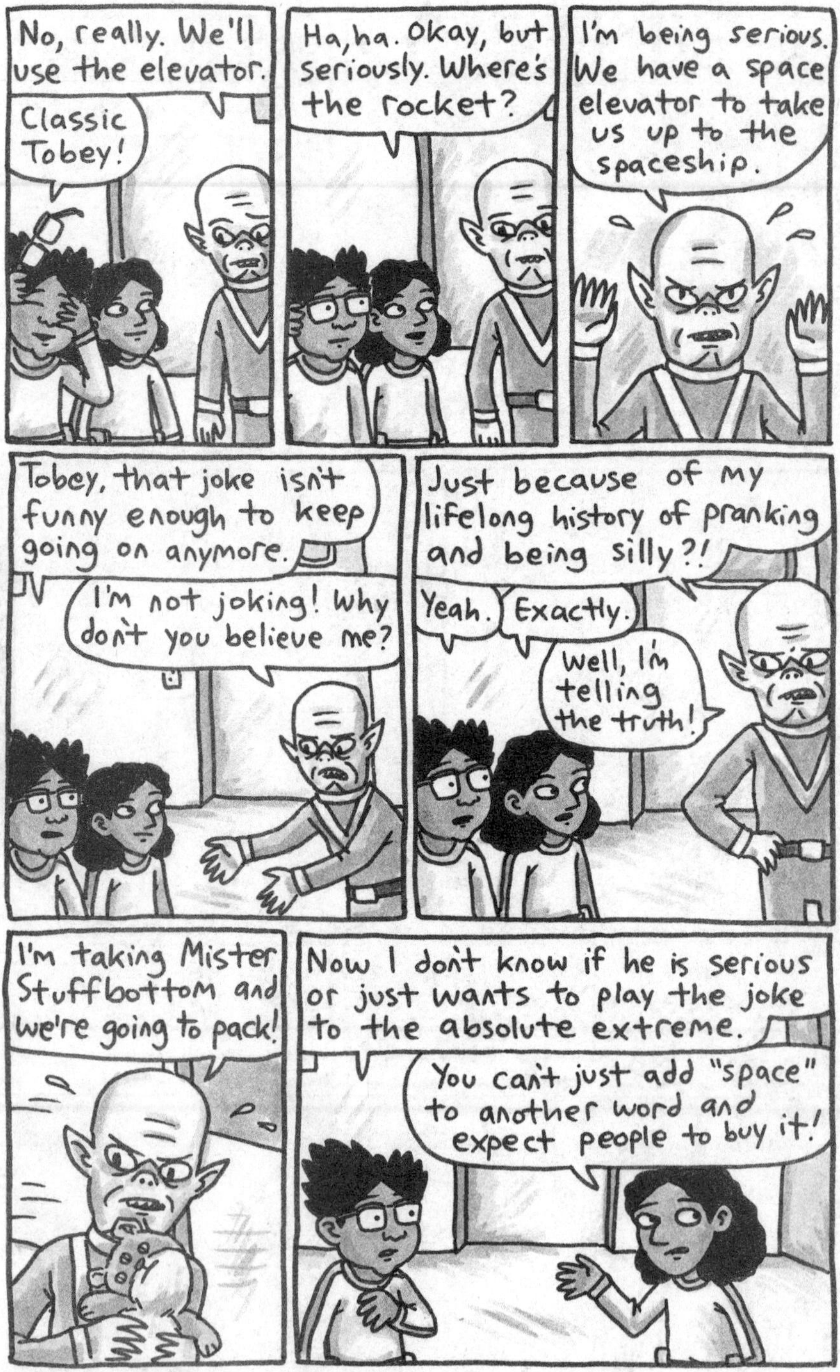
No, really. We'll use the elevator.
Classic Tobey!
Ha, ha. Okay, but seriously. Where's the rocket?
I'm being serious. We have a space elevator to take us up to the spaceship.
Tobey, that joke isn't funny enough to keep going on anymore.
I'm not joking! Why don't you believe me?
Just because of my lifelong history of pranking and being silly?!
Yeah.
Exactly.
Well, I'm telling the truth!
I'm taking Mister Stuffbottom and we're going to pack!
Now I don't know if he is serious or just wants to play the joke to the absolute extreme.
You can't just add "space" to another word and expect people to buy it!

SPUDNIK

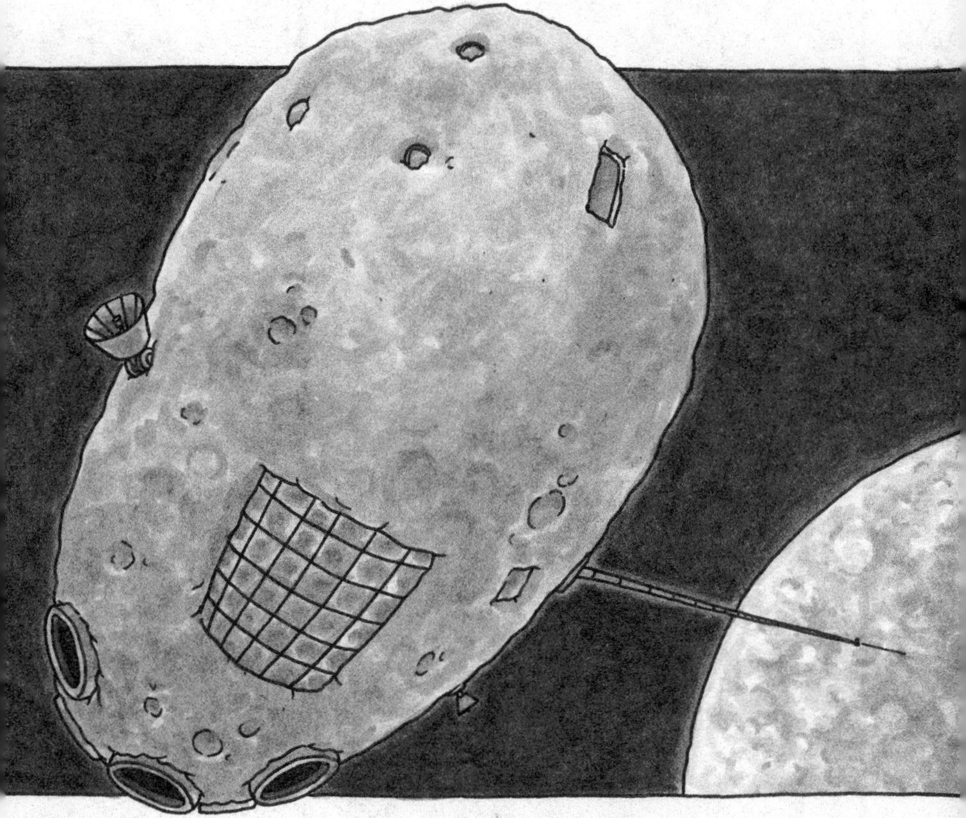

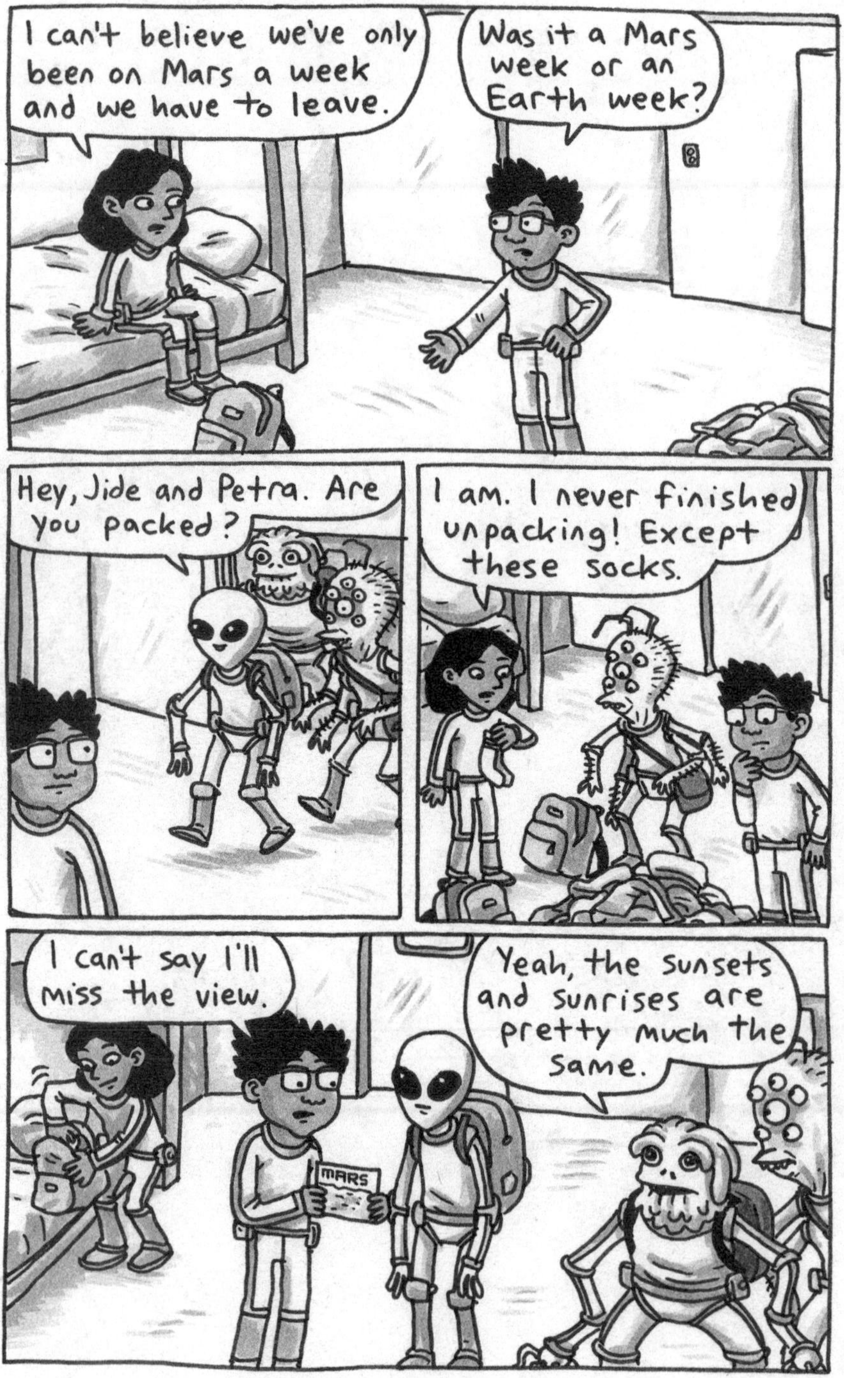
I can't believe we've only been on Mars a week and we have to leave.
Was it a Mars week or an Earth week?
Hey, Jide and Petra. Are you packed?
I am. I never finished unpacking! Except these socks.
I can't say I'll miss the view.
MARS
Yeah, the sunsets and sunrises are pretty much the same.

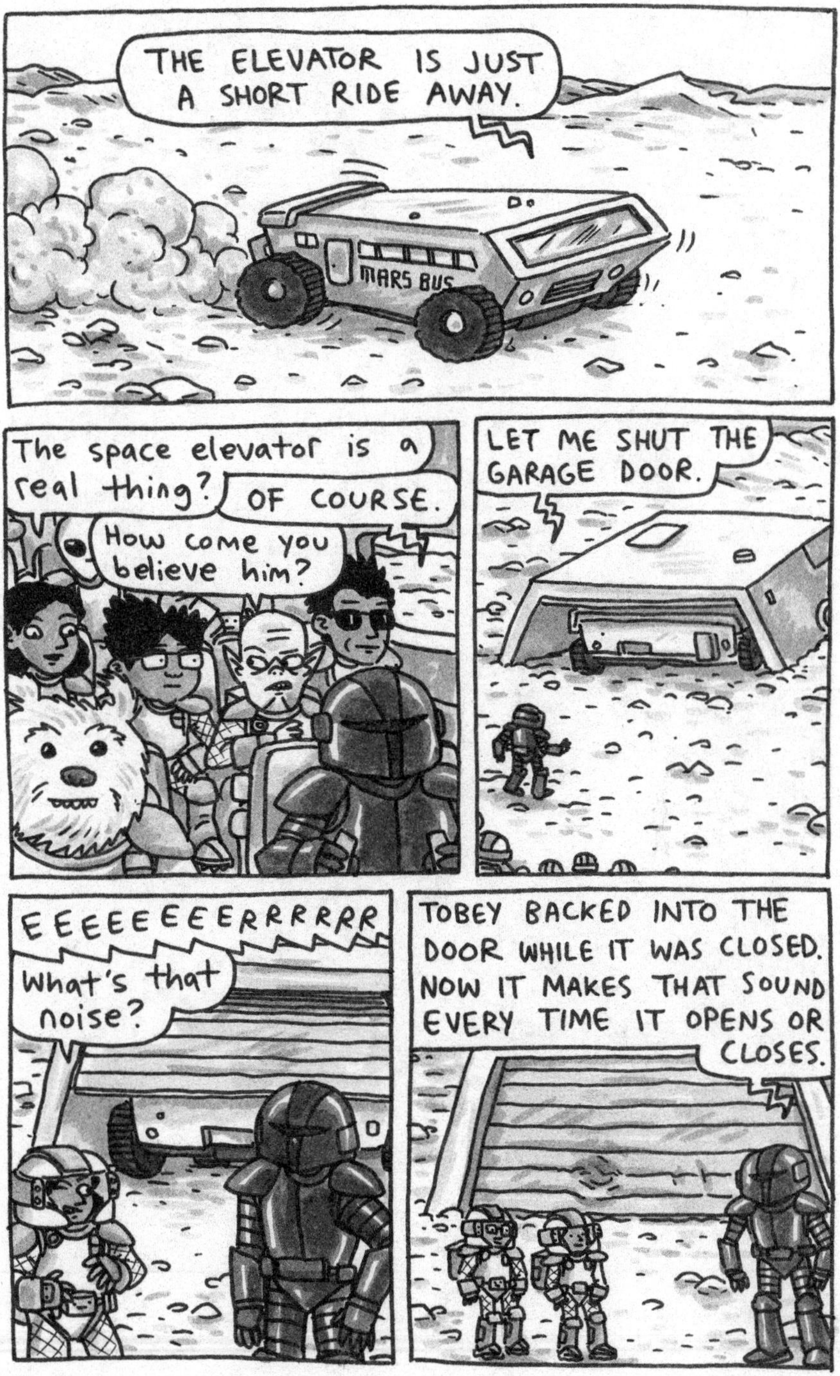
THE ELEVATOR IS JUST A SHORT RIDE AWAY.
MARS BUS
The space elevator is a real thing?
OF COURSE.
How come you believe him?
LET ME SHUT THE GARAGE DOOR.
EEEEEEEERRRRRR
What's that noise?
TOBEY BACKED INTO THE DOOR WHILE IT WAS CLOSED. NOW IT MAKES THAT SOUND EVERY TIME IT OPENS OR CLOSES.

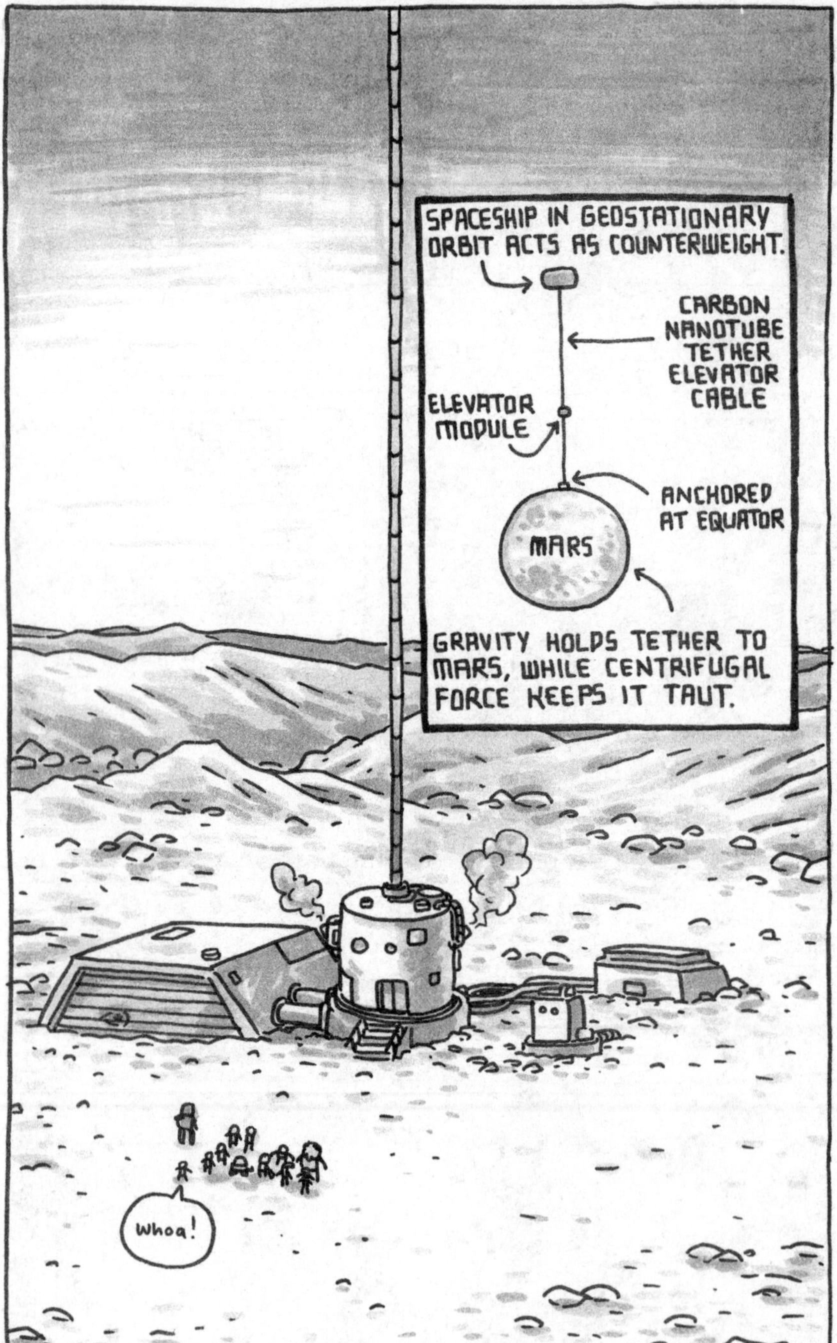
SPACESHIP IN GEOSTATIONARY ORBIT ACTS AS COUNTERWEIGHT.
CARBON NANOTUBE TETHER ELEVATOR CABLE
ELEVATOR MODULE
ANCHORED AT EQUATOR
MARS
GRAVITY HOLDS TETHER TO MARS, WHILE CENTRIFUGAL FORCE KEEPS IT TAUT.
Whoa!

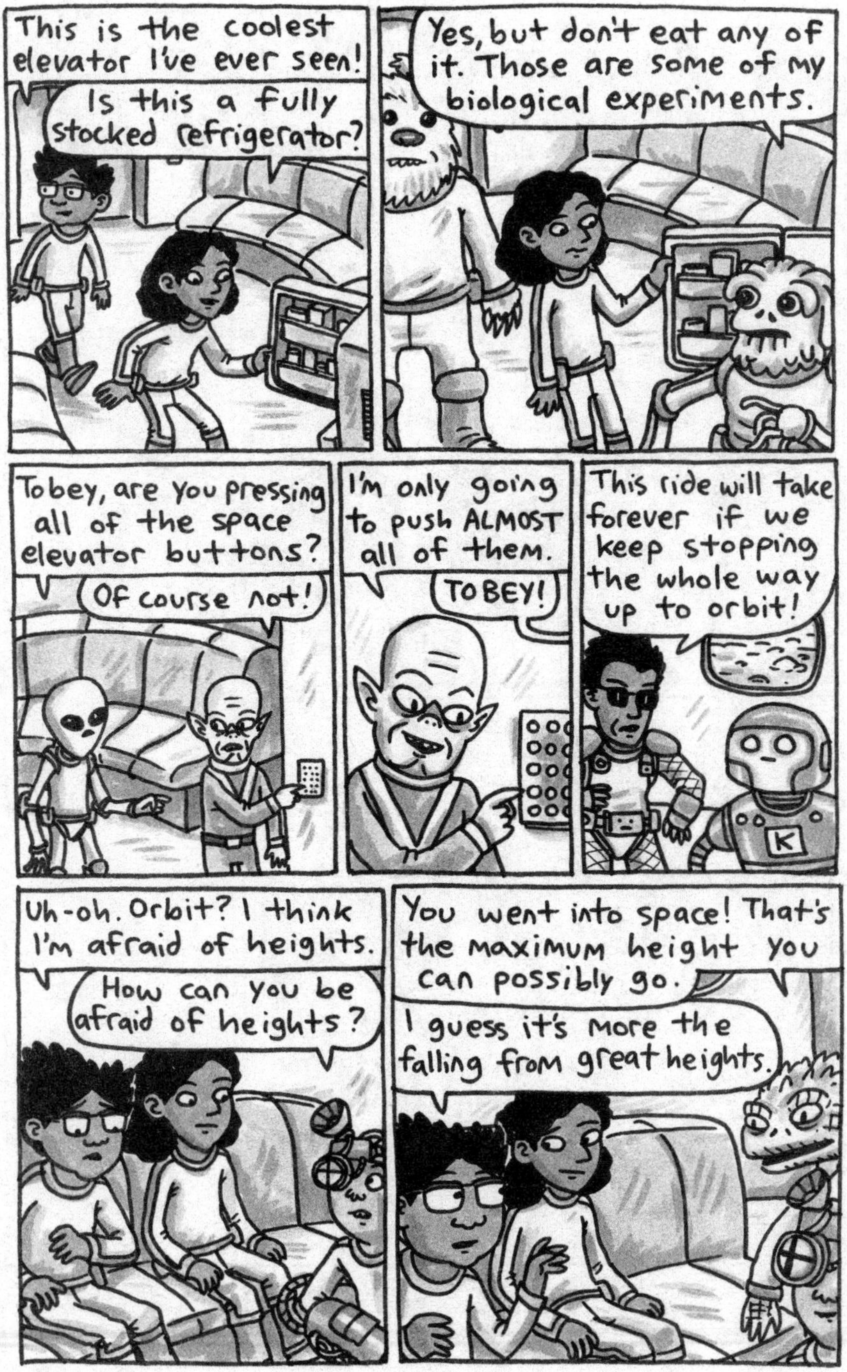
This is the coolest elevator I've ever seen!
Is this a fully stocked refrigerator?
Yes, but don't eat any of it. Those are some of my biological experiments.
Tobey, are you pressing all of the space elevator buttons?
Of course not!
I'm only going to push ALMOST all of them.
TOBEY!
This ride will take forever if we keep stopping the whole way up to orbit!
K
Uh-oh. Orbit? I think I'm afraid of heights.
How can you be afraid of heights?
You went into space! That's the maximum height you can possibly go.
I guess it's more the falling from great heights.

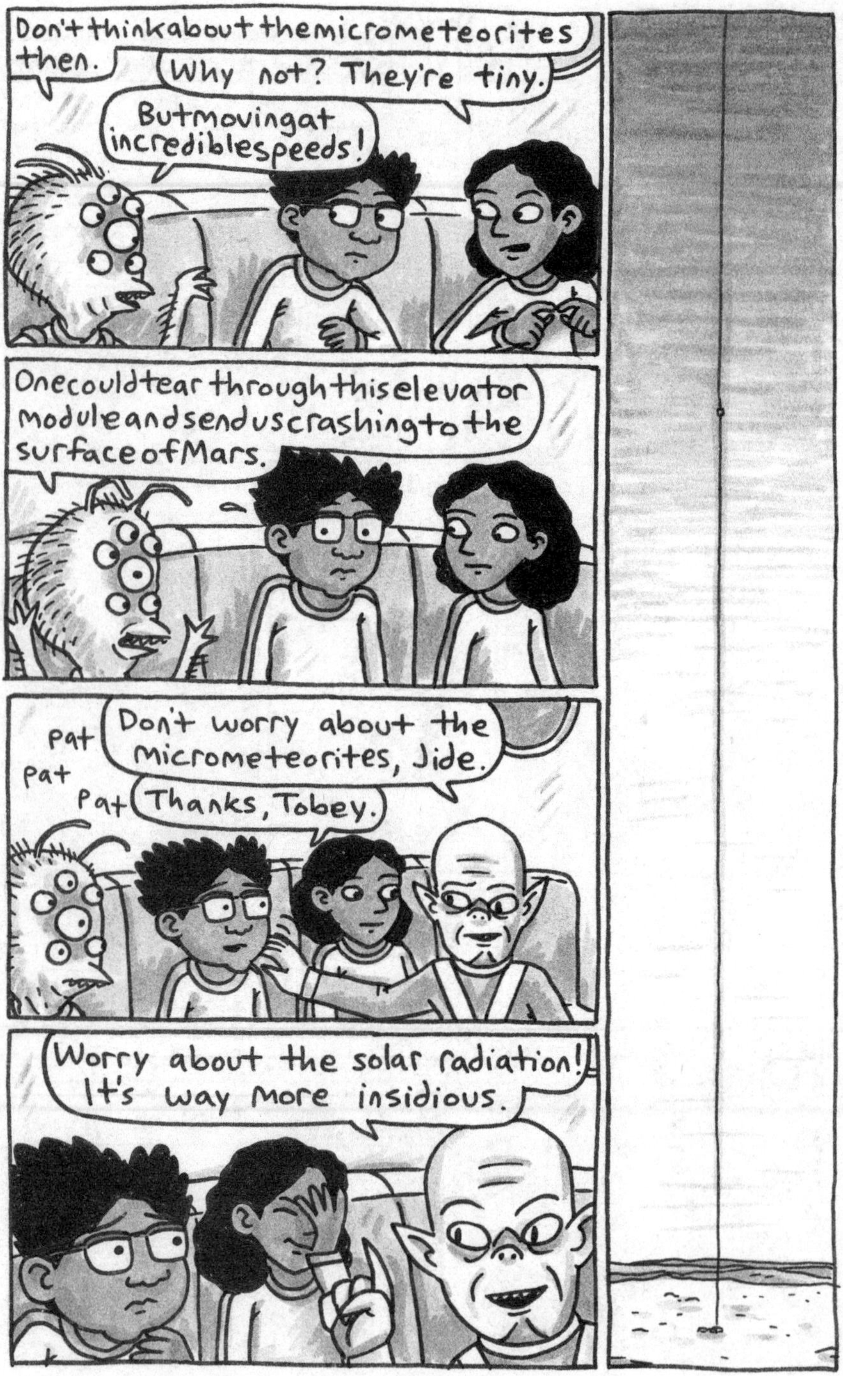
Don't think about the micrometeorites then.
Why not? They're tiny.
But moving at incredible speeds!
One could tear through this elevator module and send us crashing to the surface of Mars.
pat
pat
pat
Don't worry about the micrometeorites, Jide.
Thanks, Tobey.
Worry about the solar radiation! It's way more insidious.

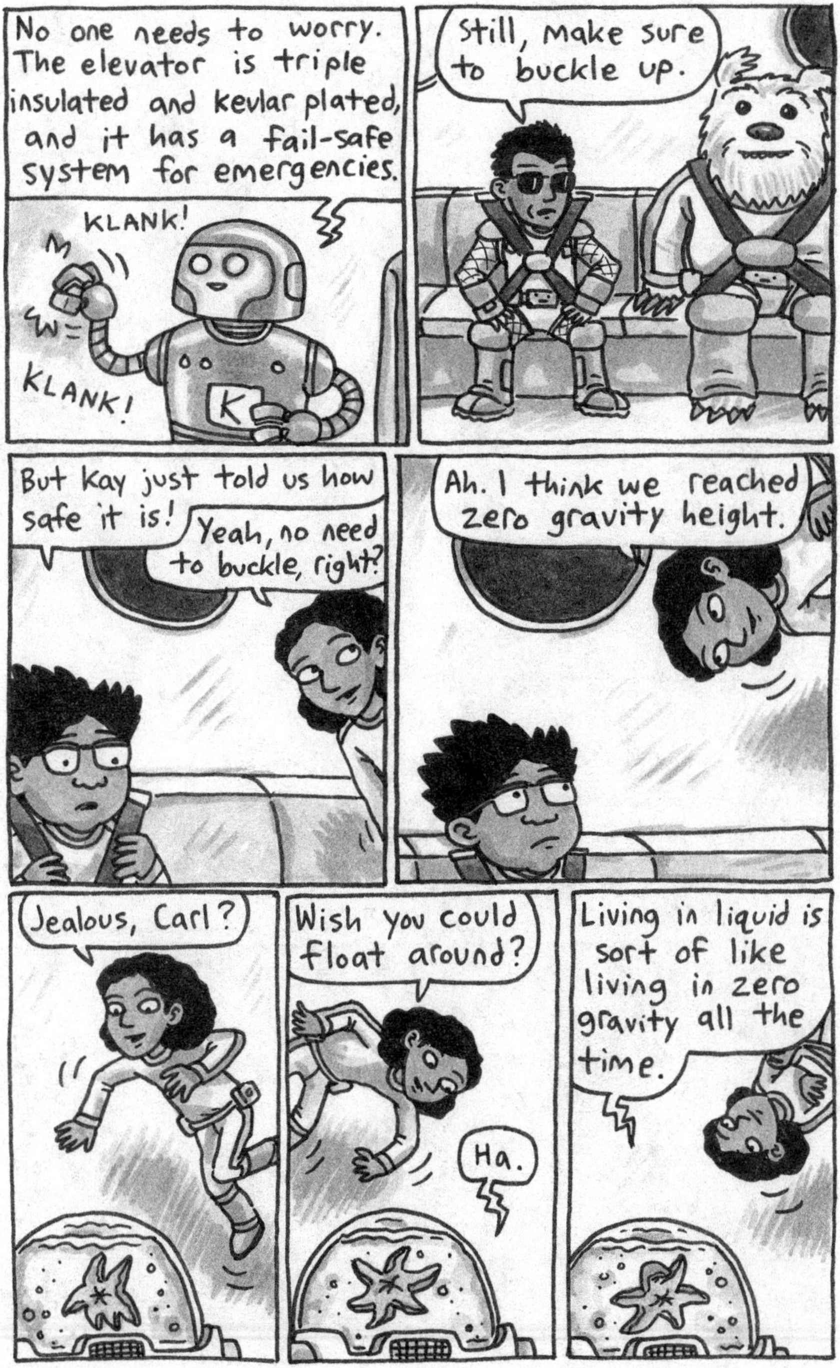
No one needs to worry. The elevator is triple insulated and kevlar plated, and it has a fail-safe system for emergencies.
KLANK!
KLANK!
K
Still, make sure to buckle up.
But Kay just told us how safe it is!
Yeah, no need to buckle, right?
Ah. I think we reached zero gravity height.
Jealous, Carl?
Wish you could float around?
Ha.
Living in liquid is sort of like living in zero gravity all the time.

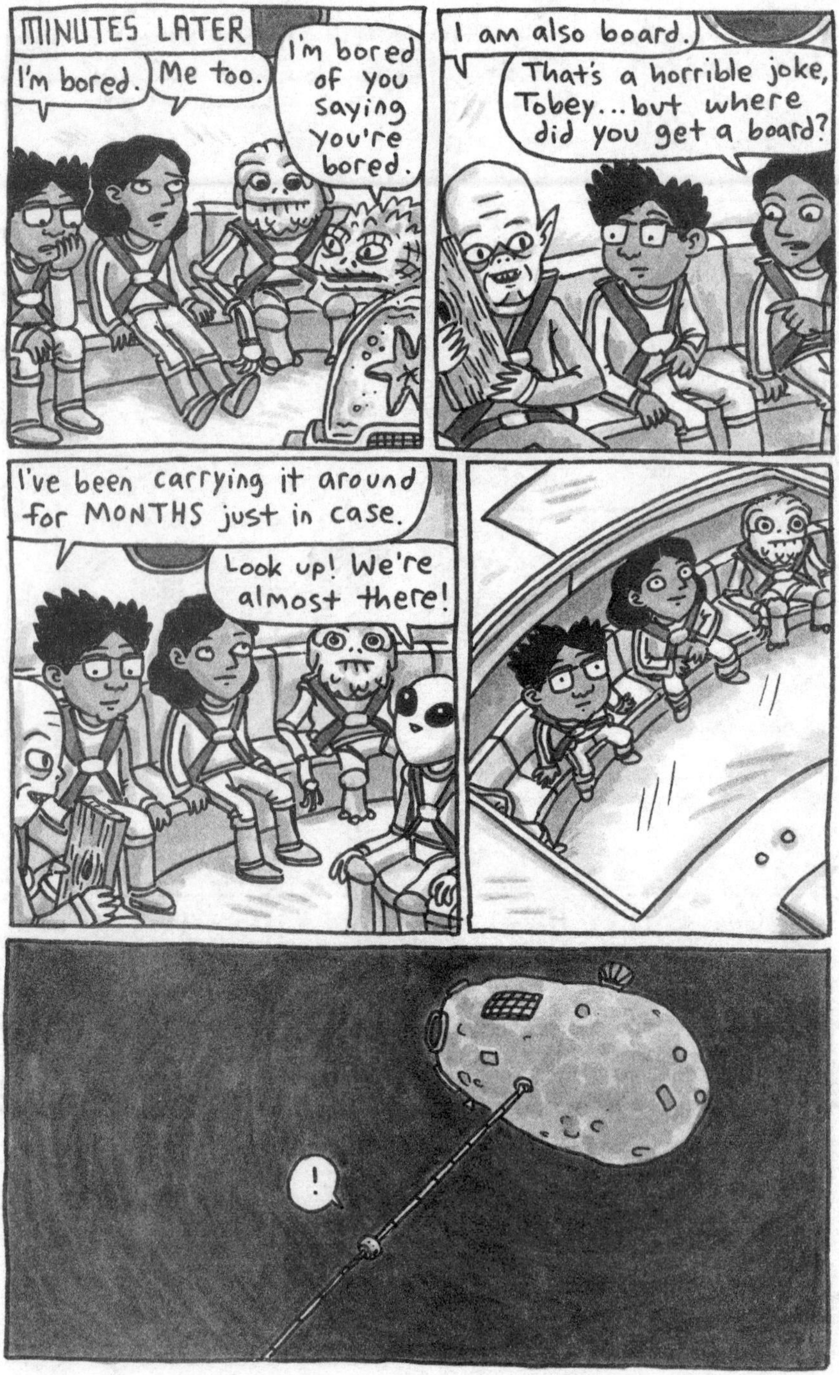
MINUTES LATER
I'm bored.
Me too.
I'm bored of you saying you're bored.
I am also board.
That's a horrible joke, Tobey... but where did you get a board?
I've been carrying it around for MONTHS just in case.
Look up! We're almost there!
!

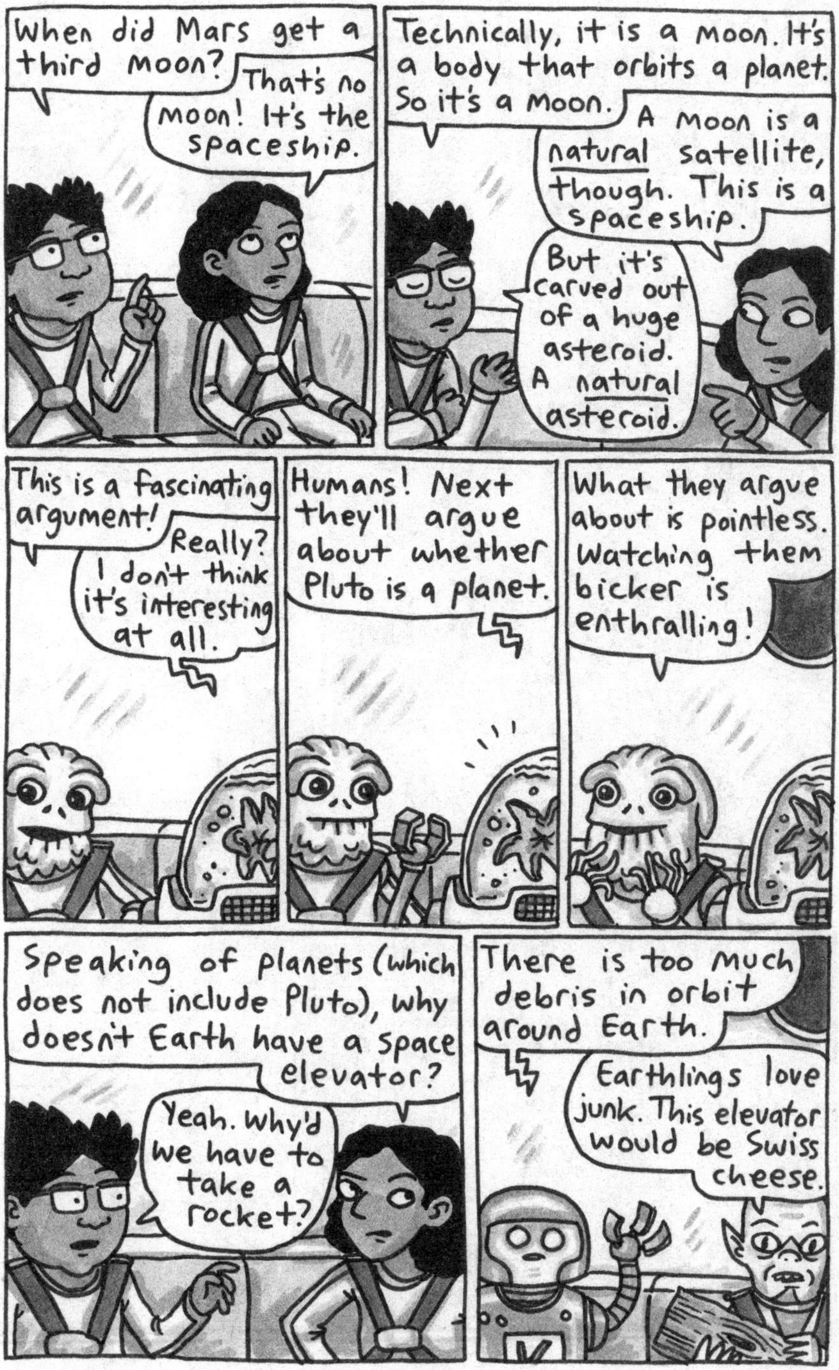
When did Mars get a third moon?
That's no moon! It's the spaceship.
Technically, it is a moon. It's a body that orbits a planet. So it's a moon.
A moon is a natural satellite, though. This is a spaceship.
But it's carved out of a huge asteroid. A natural asteroid.
This is a fascinating argument!
Really? I don't think it's interesting at all.
Humans! Next they'll argue about whether Pluto is a planet.
What they argue about is pointless. Watching them bicker is enthralling!
Speaking of planets (which does not include Pluto), why doesn't Earth have a space elevator?
Yeah. Why'd we have to take a rocket?
There is too much debris in orbit around Earth.
Earthlings love junk. This elevator would be Swiss cheese.

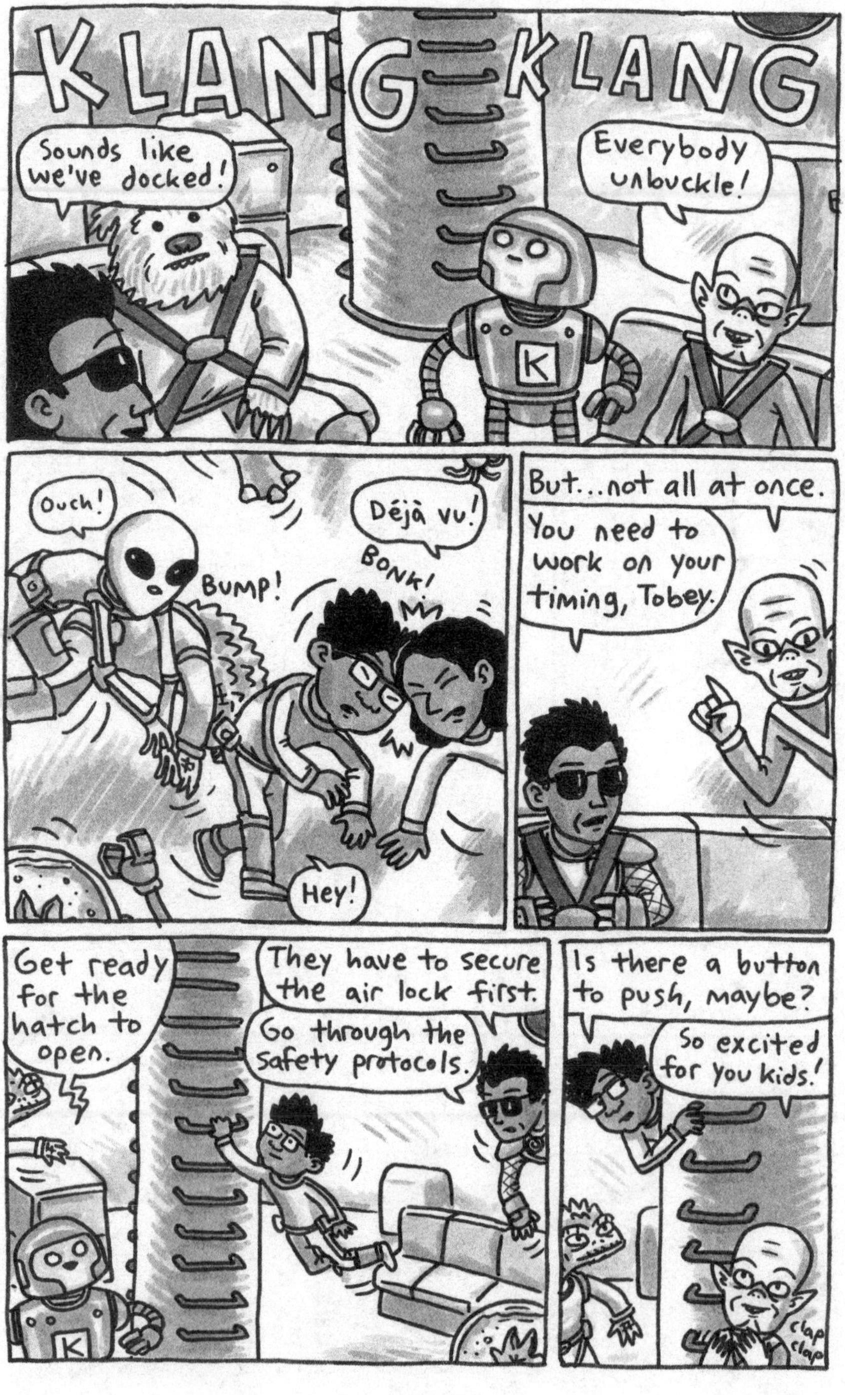
KLANG KLANG
Sounds like we've docked!
Everybody unbuckle!
Ouch!
Déjà vu!
BUMP!
BONK!
Hey!
But...not all at once.
You need to work on your timing, Tobey.
Get ready for the hatch to open.
They have to secure the air lock first.
Go through the safety protocols.
Is there a button to push, maybe?
So excited for you kids!
clap clap

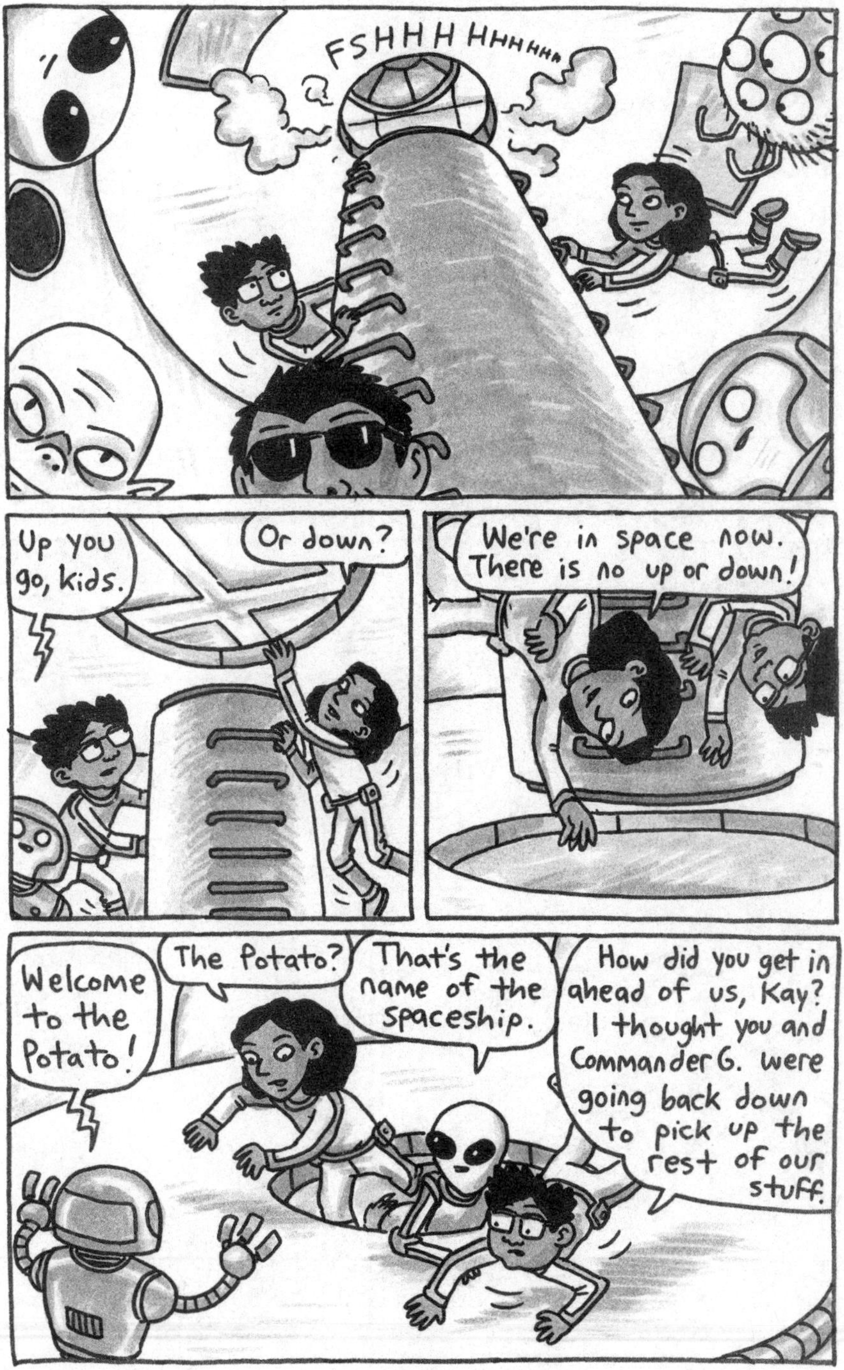
FSHHHHHHHHH
?
Up you go, kids.
Or down?
We're in space now. There is no up or down!
Welcome to the Potato!
The Potato?
That's the name of the spaceship.
How did you get in ahead of us, Kay? I thought you and Commander G. were going back down to pick up the rest of our stuff.

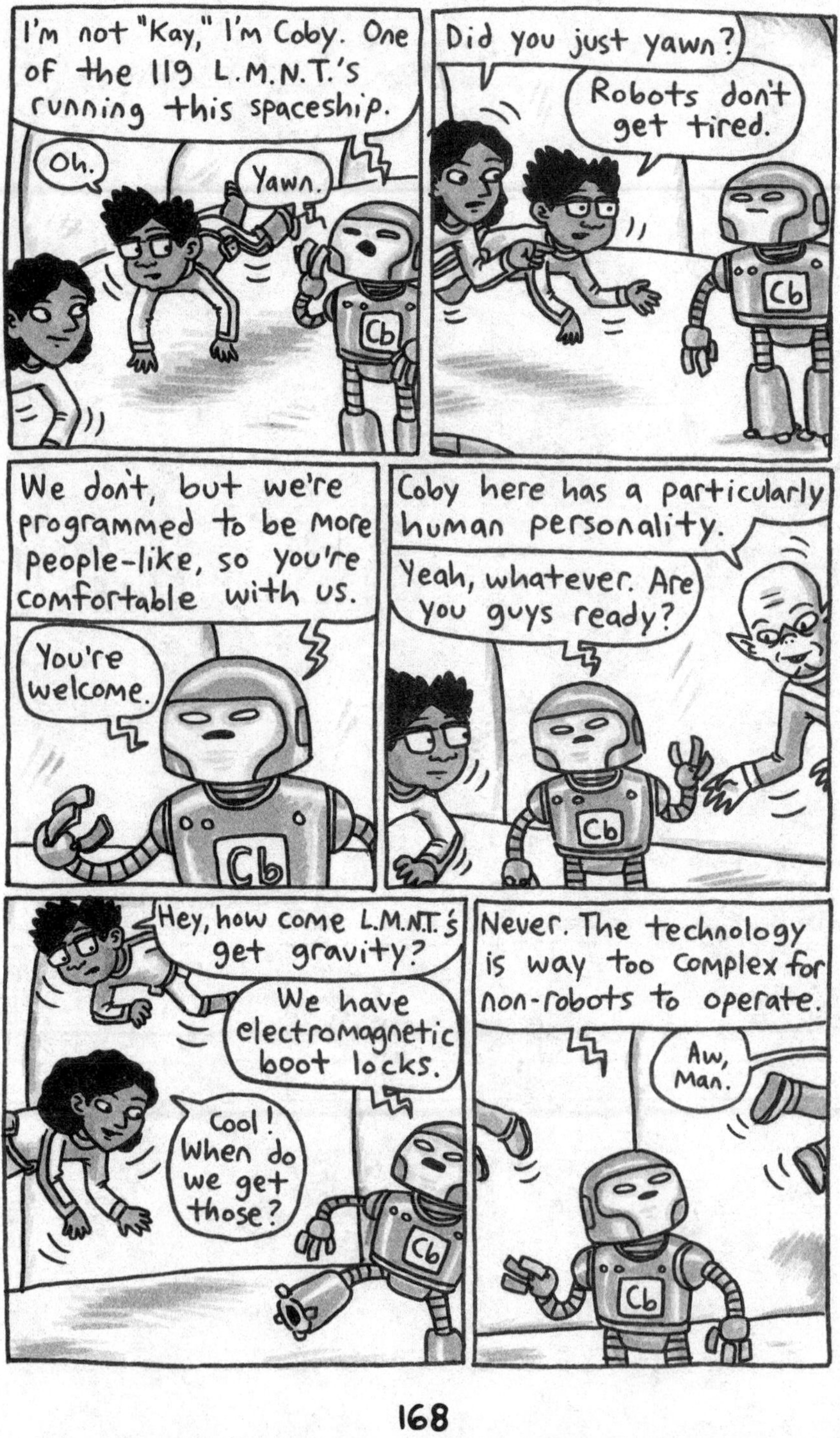

I'm not "Kay," I'm Coby. One of the 119 L.M.N.T.'s running this spaceship.
Oh.
Yawn.
Did you just yawn?
Robots don't get tired.
We don't, but we're programmed to be more people-like, so you're comfortable with us.
You're welcome.
Coby here has a particularly human personality.
Yeah, whatever. Are you guys ready?
Hey, how come L.M.N.T.'s get gravity?
We have electromagnetic boot locks.
Cool! When do we get those?
Never. The technology is way too complex for non-robots to operate.
Aw, Man.

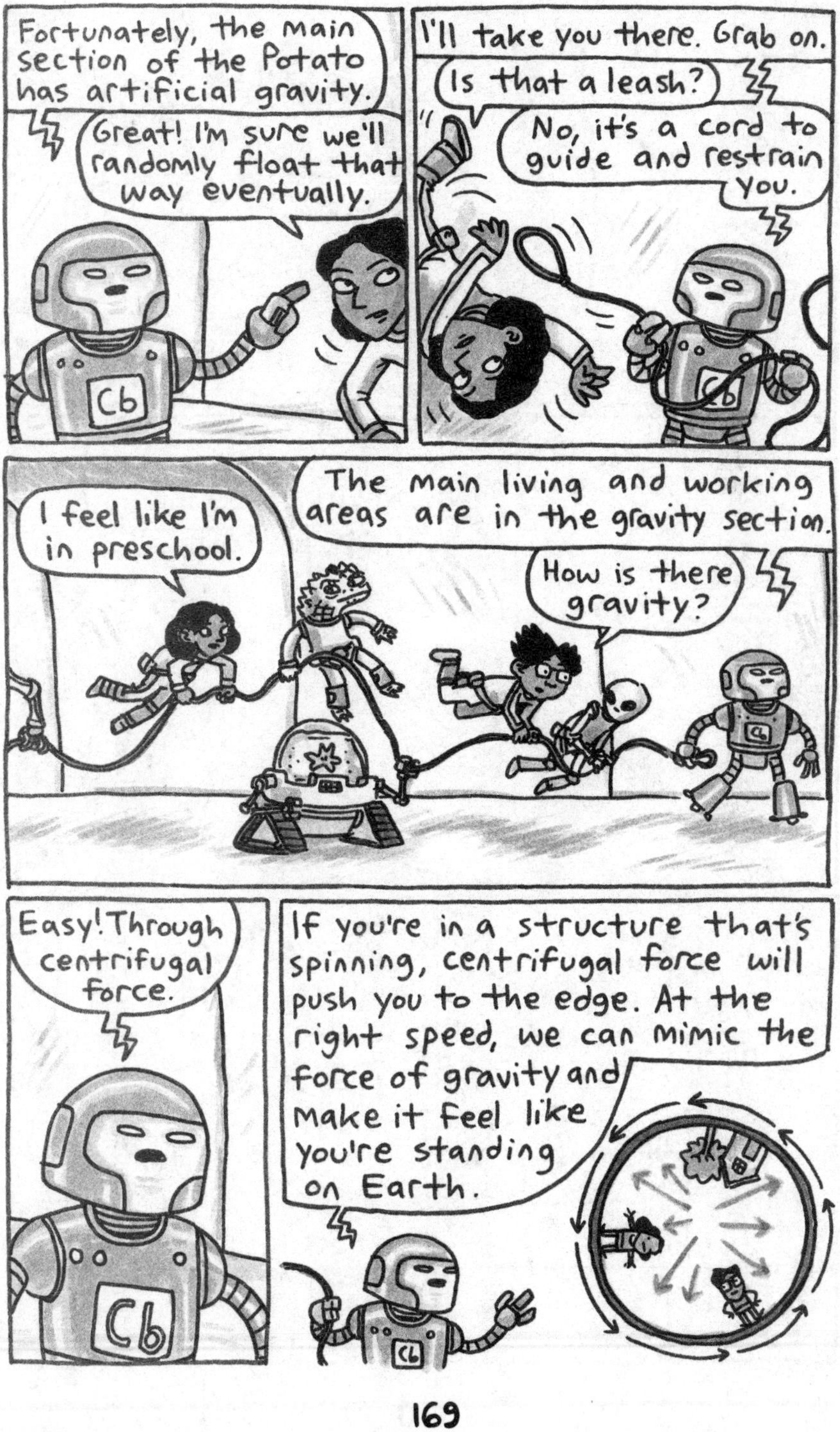
Fortunately, the main section of the Potato has artificial gravity.
Great! I'm sure we'll randomly float that way eventually.
I'll take you there. Grab on.
Is that a leash?
No, it's a cord to guide and restrain you.
I feel like I'm in preschool.
The main living and working areas are in the gravity section.
How is there gravity?
Easy! Through centrifugal force.
If you're in a structure that's spinning, centrifugal force will push you to the edge. At the right speed, we can mimic the force of gravity and make it feel like you're standing on Earth.

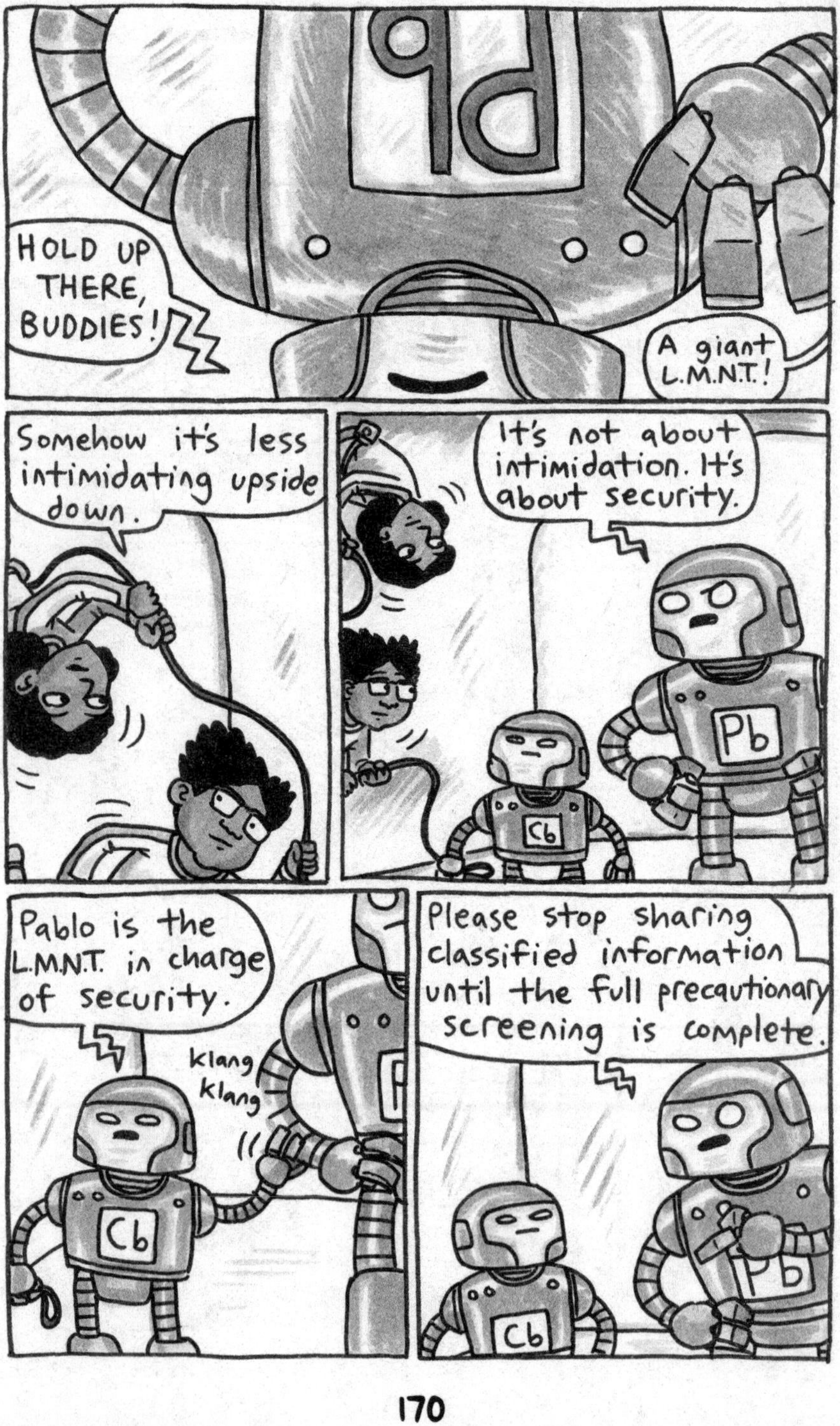
HOLD UP THERE, BUDDIES!
A giant L.M.N.T.!
Somehow it's less intimidating upside down.
It's not about intimidation. It's about security.
Pb
Cb
Pablo is the L.M.N.T. in charge of security.
klang klang
Please stop sharing classified information until the full precautionary screening is complete.

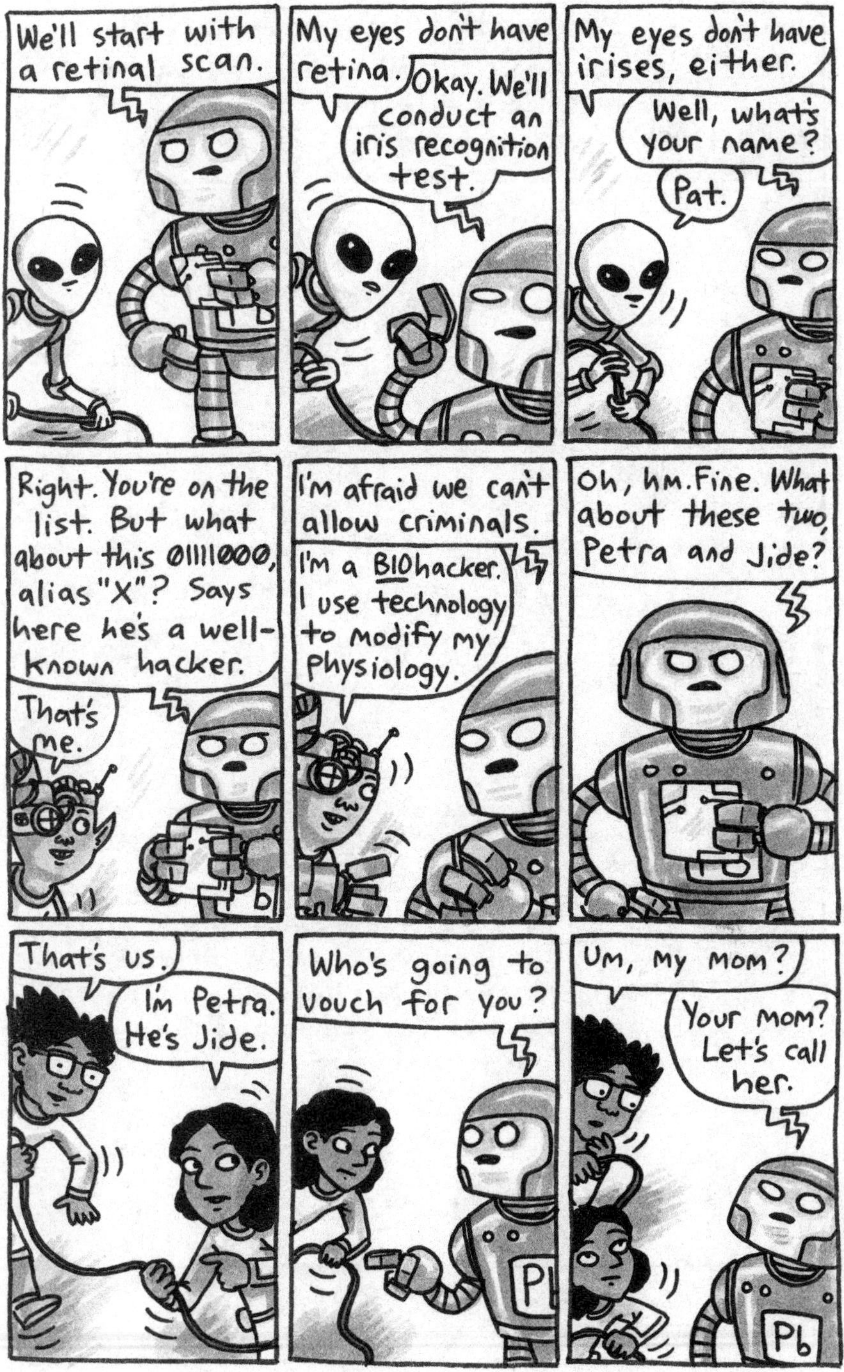
We'll start with a retinal scan.
My eyes don't have retina.
Okay. We'll conduct an iris recognition test.
My eyes don't have irises, either.
Well, what's your name?
Pat.
Right. You're on the list. But what about this 01111000, alias "X"? Says here he's a well-known hacker.
That's me.
I'm afraid we can't allow criminals.
I'm a BIOhacker. I use technology to modify my physiology.
Oh, hm. Fine. What about these two, Petra and Jide?
That's us.
I'm Petra. He's Jide.
Who's going to vouch for you?
Um, my mom?
Your mom? Let's call her.
Pb
Pb

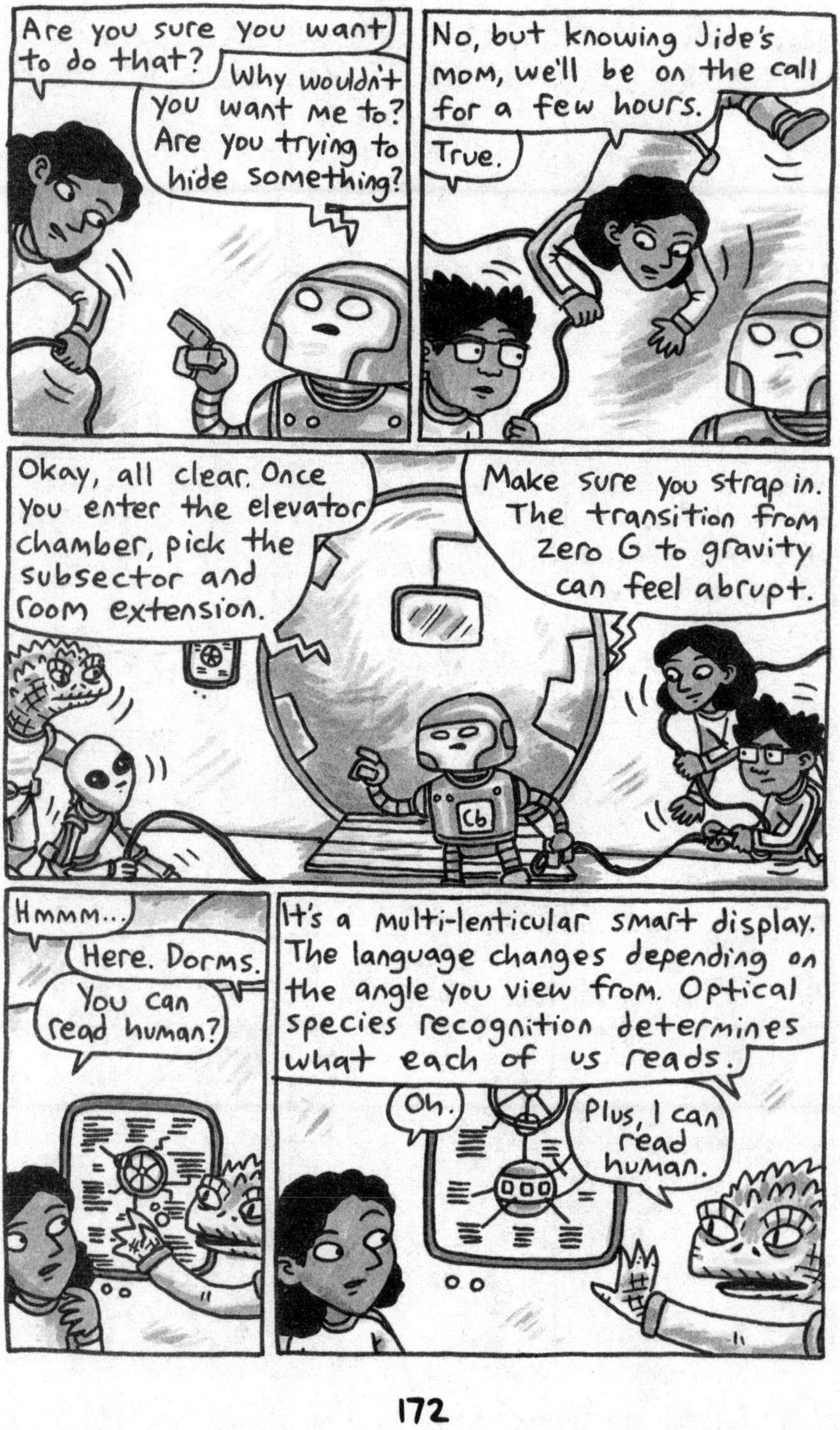
Are you sure you want to do that?
Why wouldn't you want me to? Are you trying to hide something?
No, but knowing Jide's mom, we'll be on the call for a few hours.
True.
Okay, all clear. Once you enter the elevator chamber, pick the subsector and room extension.
Make sure you strap in. The transition from zero G to gravity can feel abrupt.
Cb
Hmmm...
Here. Dorms.
You can read human?
It's a multi-lenticular smart display. The language changes depending on the angle you view from. Optical species recognition determines what each of us reads.
Oh.
Plus, I can read human.

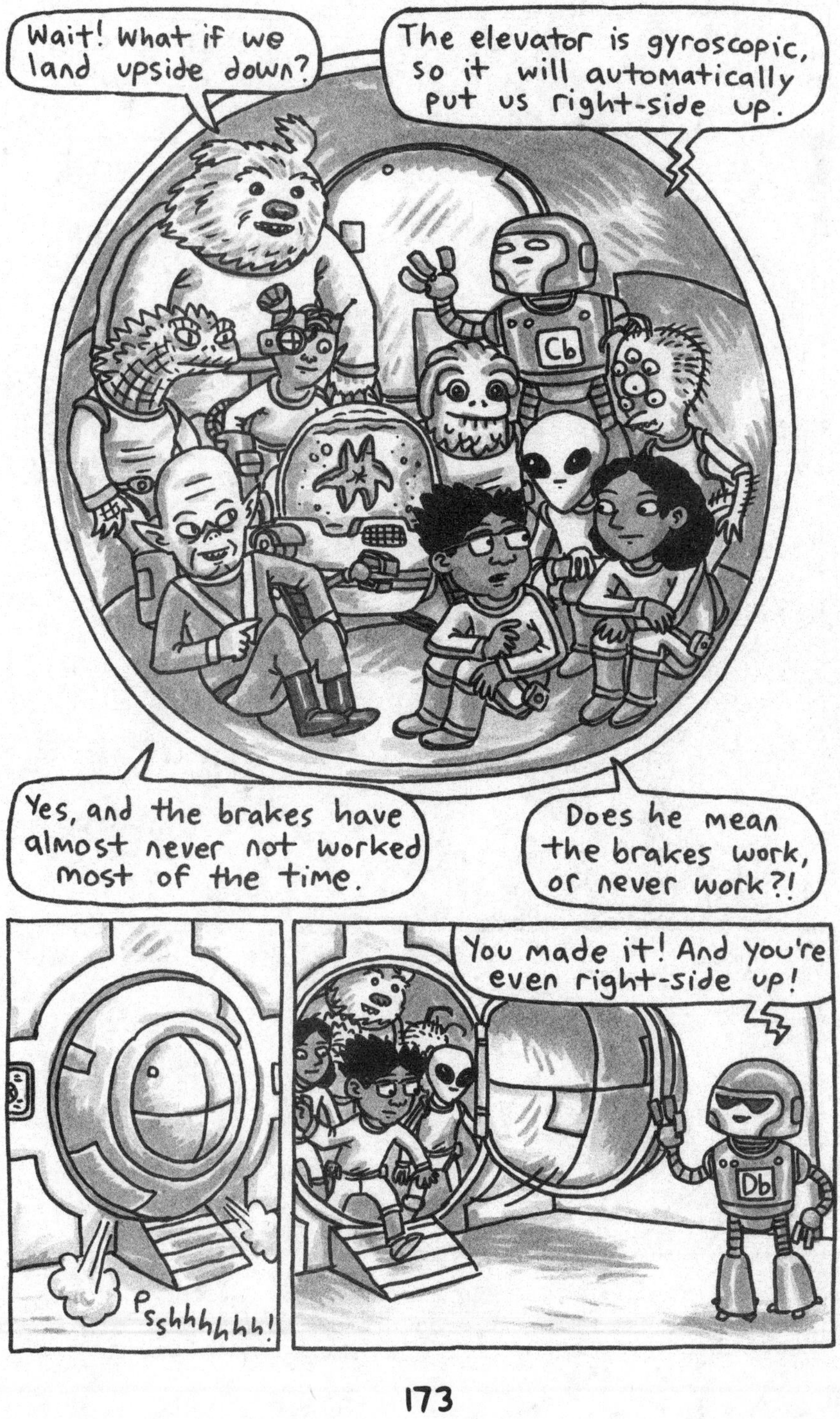
Wait! What if we land upside down?
The elevator is gyroscopic, so it will automatically put us right-side up.
Yes, and the brakes have almost never not worked most of the time.
Does he mean the brakes work, or never work?!
Psshhhhhh!
You made it! And you're even right-side up!
Cb
Db

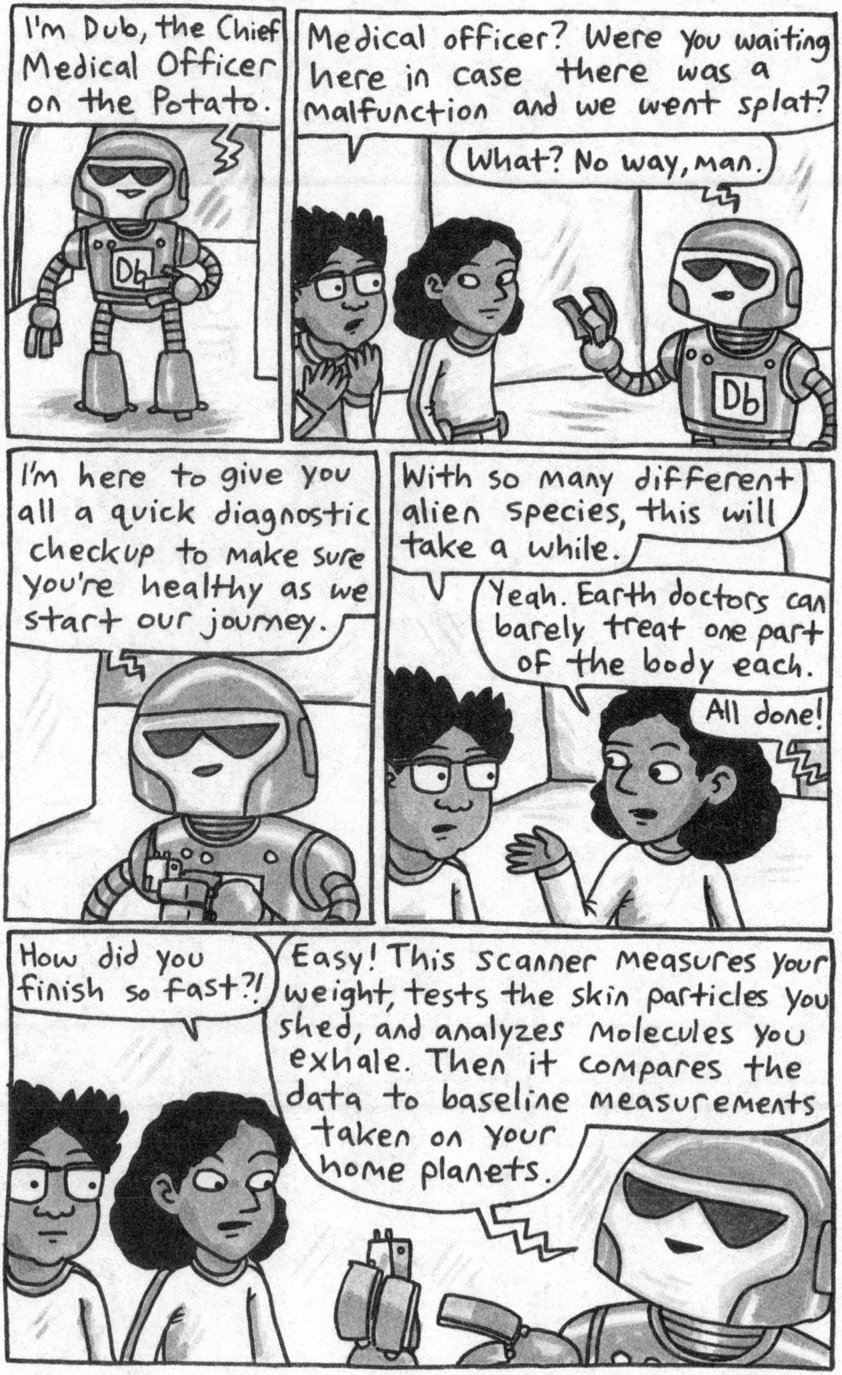
I'm Dub, the Chief Medical Officer on the Potato.
Db
Medical officer? Were you waiting here in case there was a malfunction and we went splat?
What? No way, man.
Db
I'm here to give you all a quick diagnostic checkup to make sure you're healthy as we start our journey.
With so many different alien species, this will take a while.
Yeah. Earth doctors can barely treat one part of the body each.
All done!
How did you finish so fast?!
Easy! This scanner measures your weight, tests the skin particles you shed, and analyzes molecules you exhale. Then it compares the data to baseline measurements taken on your home planets.

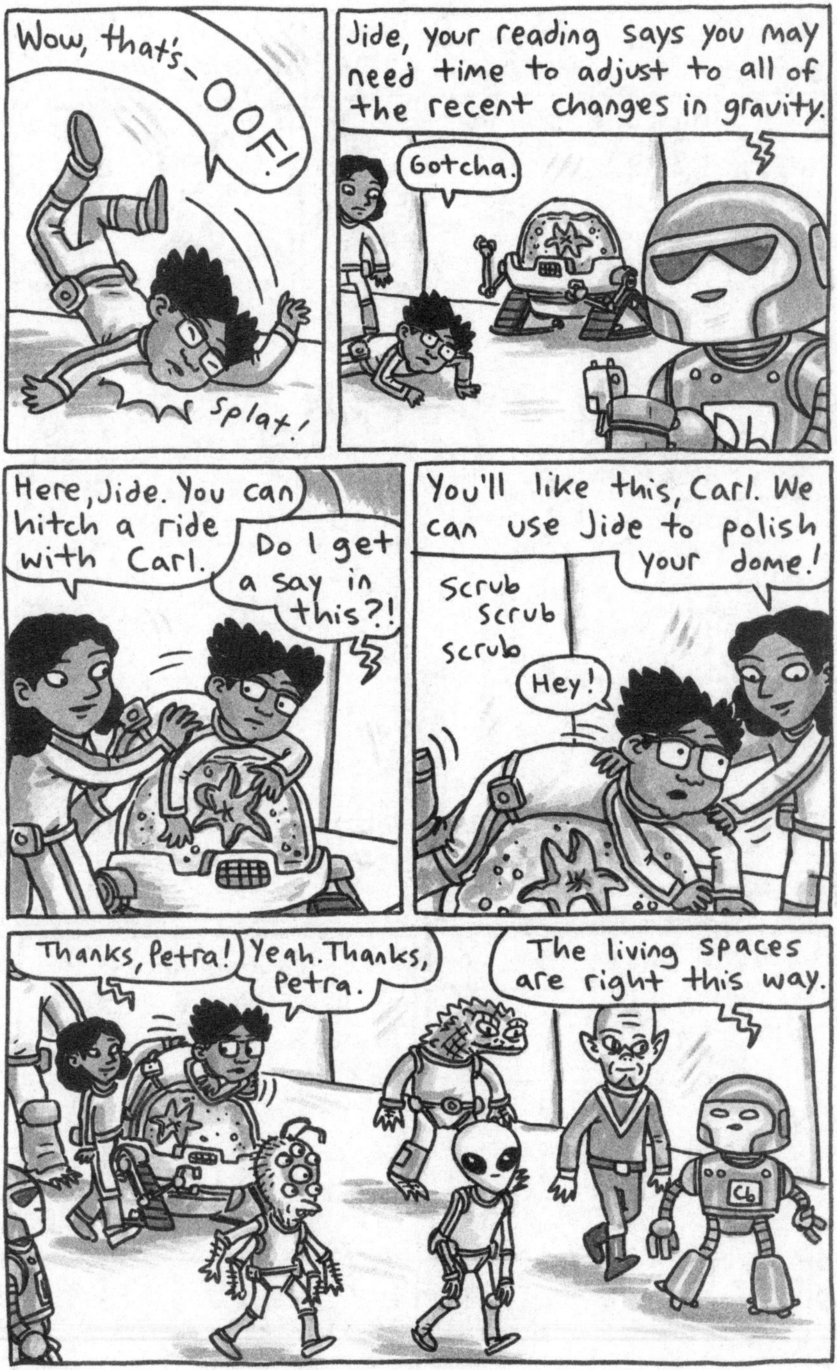
Wow, that's—OOF!
Splat!
Jide, your reading says you may need time to adjust to all of the recent changes in gravity.
Gotcha.
Here, Jide. You can hitch a ride with Carl.
Do I get a say in this?!
You'll like this, Carl. We can use Jide to polish your dome!
Scrub
scrub
scrub
Hey!
Thanks, Petra!
Yeah. Thanks, Petra.
The living spaces are right this way.
Cb

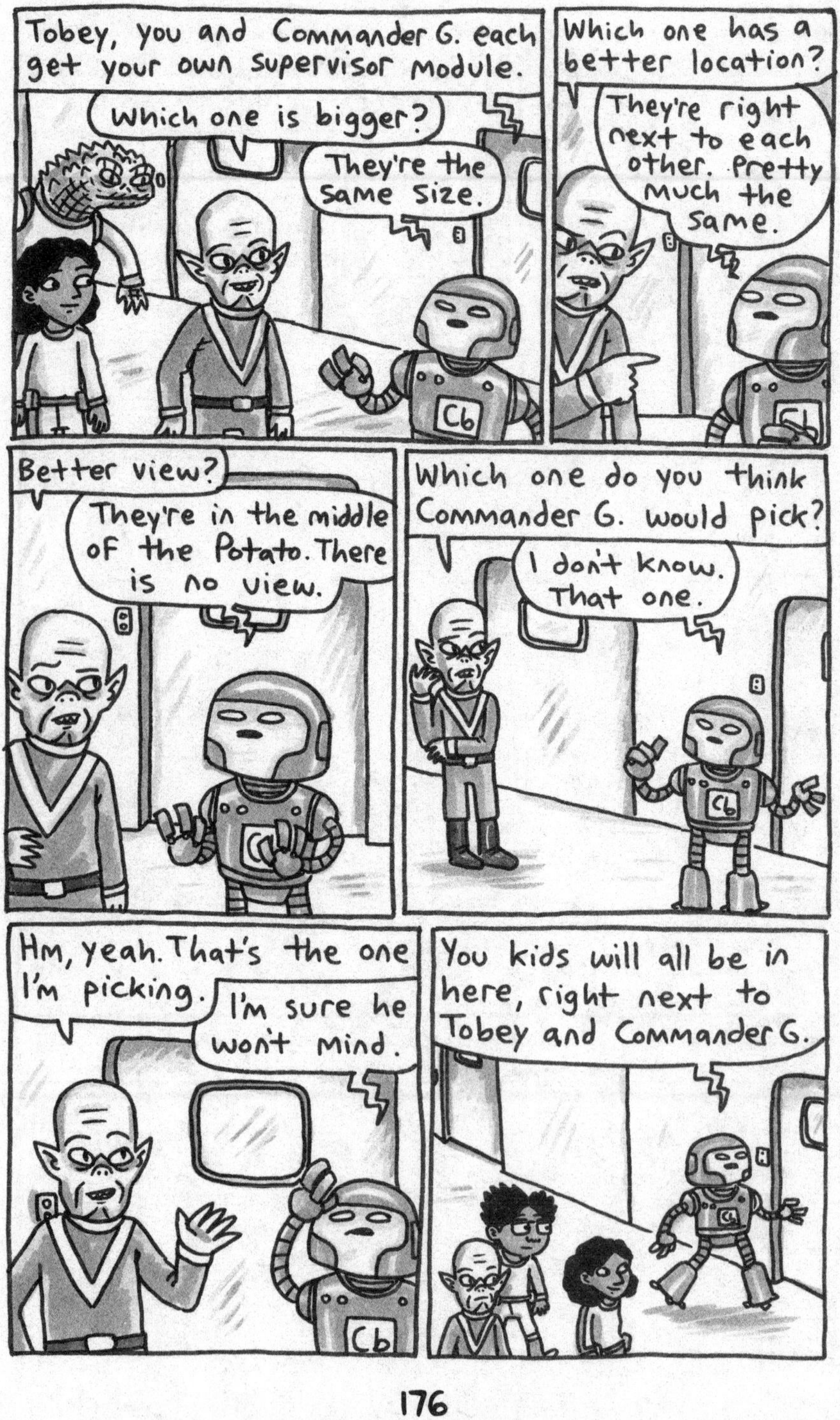
Tobey, you and Commander G. each get your own supervisor module.
Which one is bigger?
They're the same size.
Which one has a better location?
They're right next to each other. Pretty much the same.
Cb
Better view?
They're in the middle of the Potato. There is no view.
Which one do you think Commander G. would pick?
I don't know. That one.
Cb
Hm, yeah. That's the one I'm picking.
I'm sure he won't mind.
Cb
You kids will all be in here, right next to Tobey and Commander G.

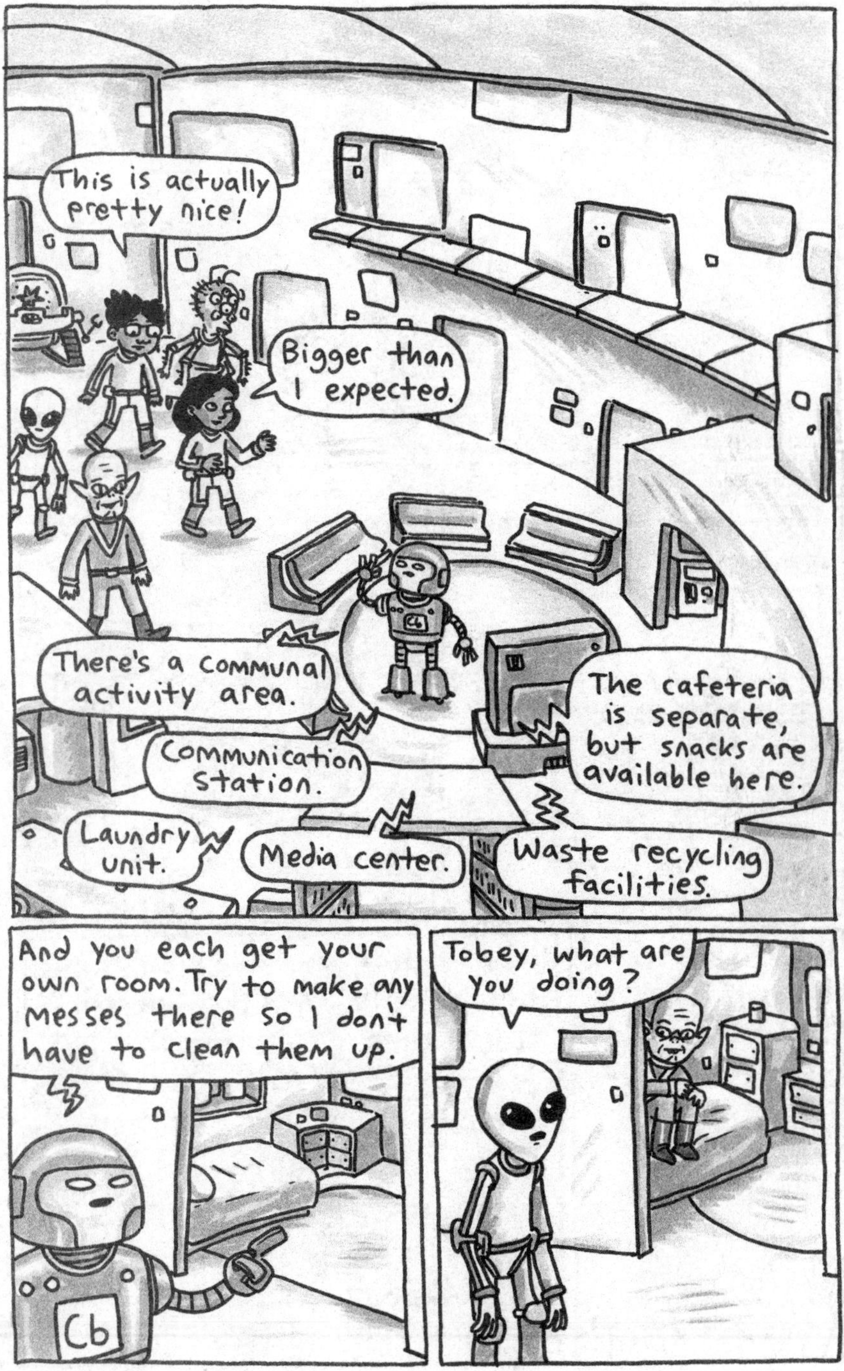
This is actually pretty nice!
Bigger than I expected.
There's a communal activity area.
The cafeteria is separate, but snacks are available here.
Communication station.
Laundry unit.
Media center.
Waste recycling facilities.
And you each get your own room. Try to make any messes there so I don't have to clean them up.
Tobey, what are you doing?

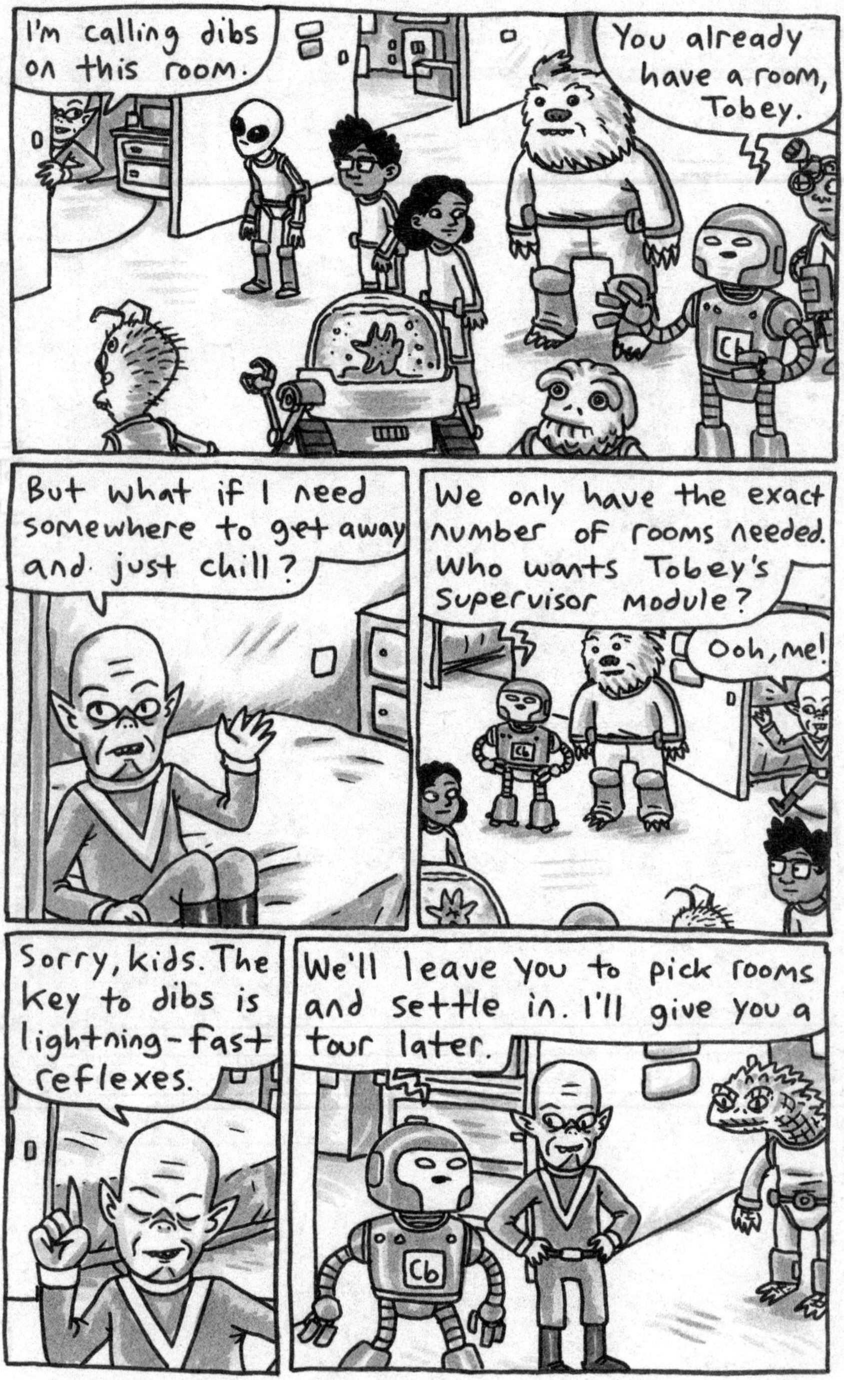
I'm calling dibs on this room.
You already have a room, Tobey.
But what if I need somewhere to get away and just chill?
We only have the exact number of rooms needed. Who wants Tobey's Supervisor Module?
Ooh, me!
Sorry, kids. The key to dibs is lightning-fast reflexes.
We'll leave you to pick rooms and settle in. I'll give you a tour later.
Cb

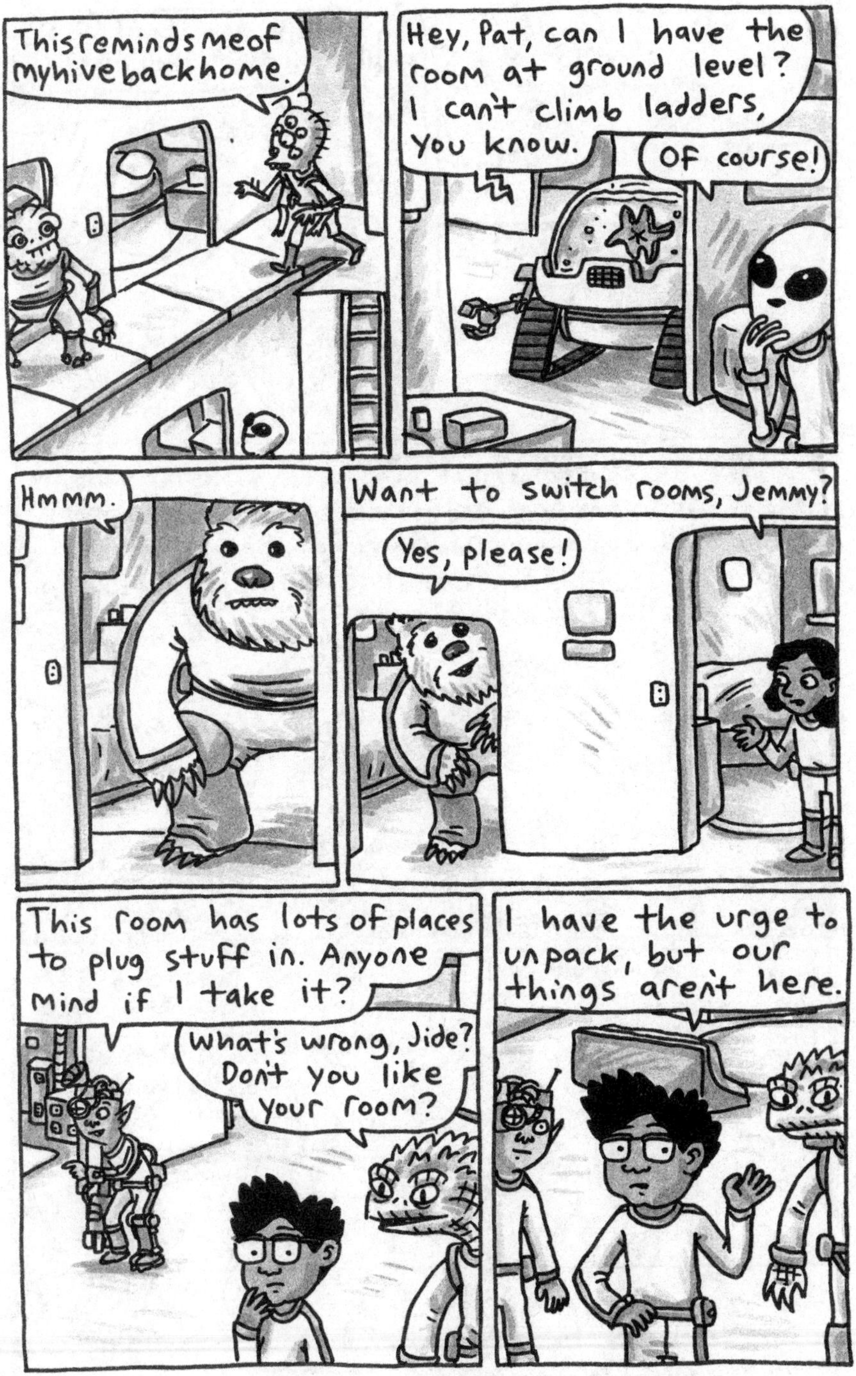

This reminds me of my hive back home.
Hey, Pat, can I have the room at ground level? I can't climb ladders, you know.
Of course!
Hmmm.
Want to switch rooms, Jemmy?
Yes, please!
This room has lots of places to plug stuff in. Anyone mind if I take it?
What's wrong, Jide? Don't you like your room?
I have the urge to unpack, but our things aren't here.

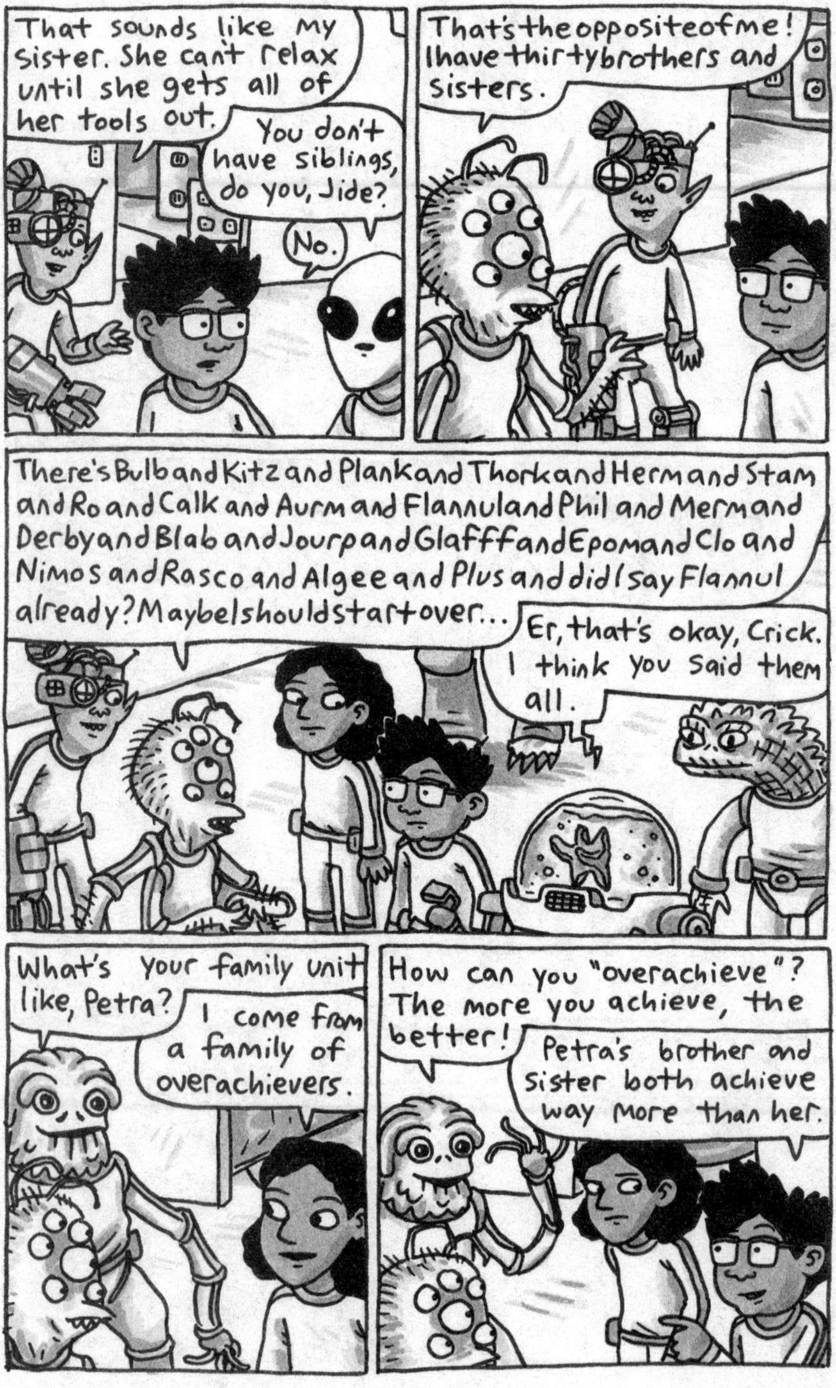
That sounds like my sister. She can't relax until she gets all of her tools out.
You don't have siblings, do you, Jide?
No.
That's the opposite of me! I have thirty brothers and sisters.
There's Bulb and Kitz and Plank and Thork and Herm and Stam and Ro and Calk and Aurm and Flannul and Phil and Merm and Derby and Blab and Jourp and Glafff and Epom and Clo and Nimos and Rasco and Algee and Plus and did I say Flannul already? Maybe I should start over...
Er, that's okay, Crick. I think you said them all.
What's your family unit like, Petra?
I come from a family of overachievers.
How can you "overachieve"? The more you achieve, the better!
Petra's brother and sister both achieve way more than her.

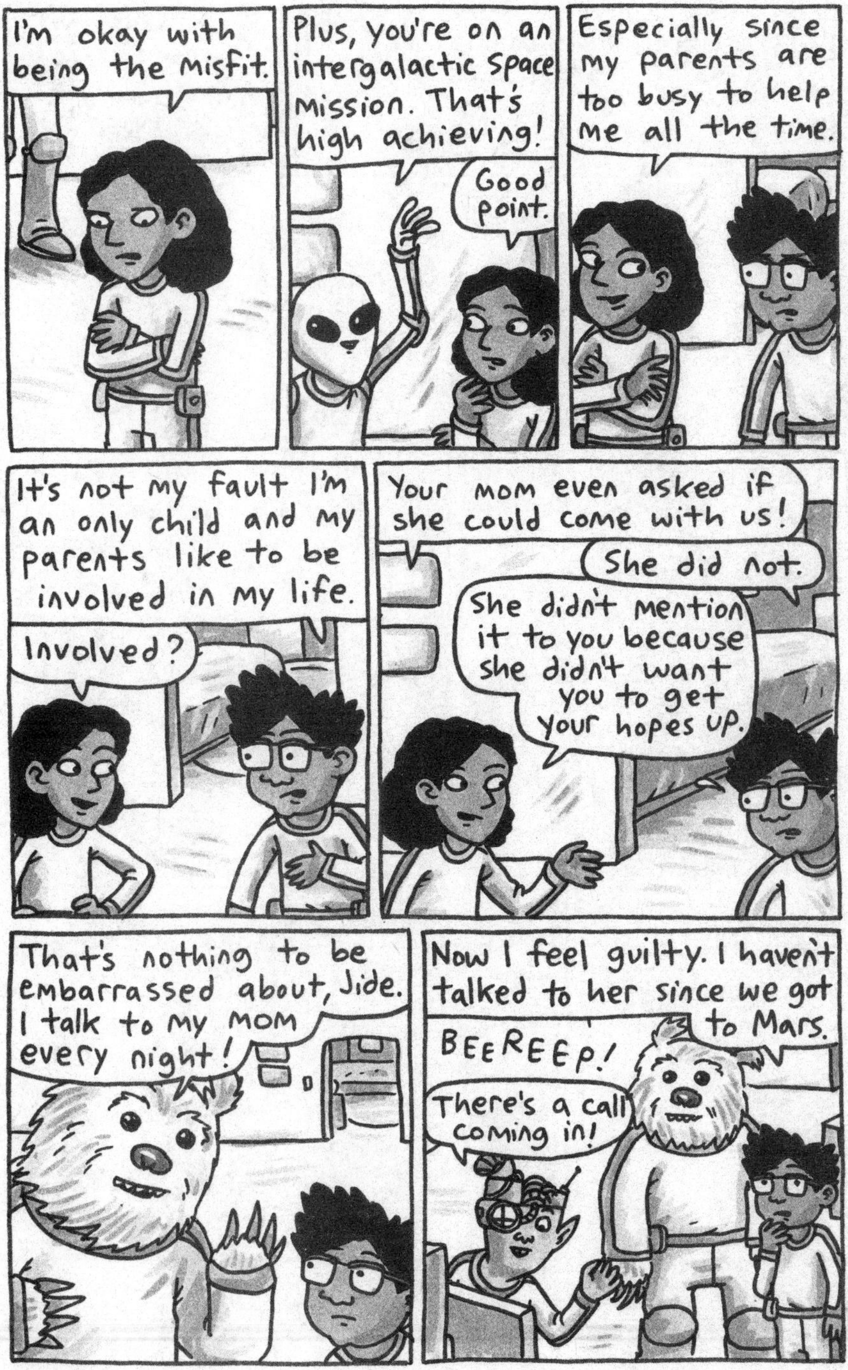
I'm okay with being the misfit.
Plus, you're on an intergalactic space mission. That's high achieving!
Good point.
Especially since my parents are too busy to help me all the time.
It's not my fault I'm an only child and my parents like to be involved in my life.
Involved?
Your mom even asked if she could come with us!
She did not.
She didn't mention it to you because she didn't want you to get your hopes up.
That's nothing to be embarrassed about, Jide. I talk to my mom every night!
Now I feel guilty. I haven't talked to her since we got to Mars.
BEEREEP!
There's a call coming in!

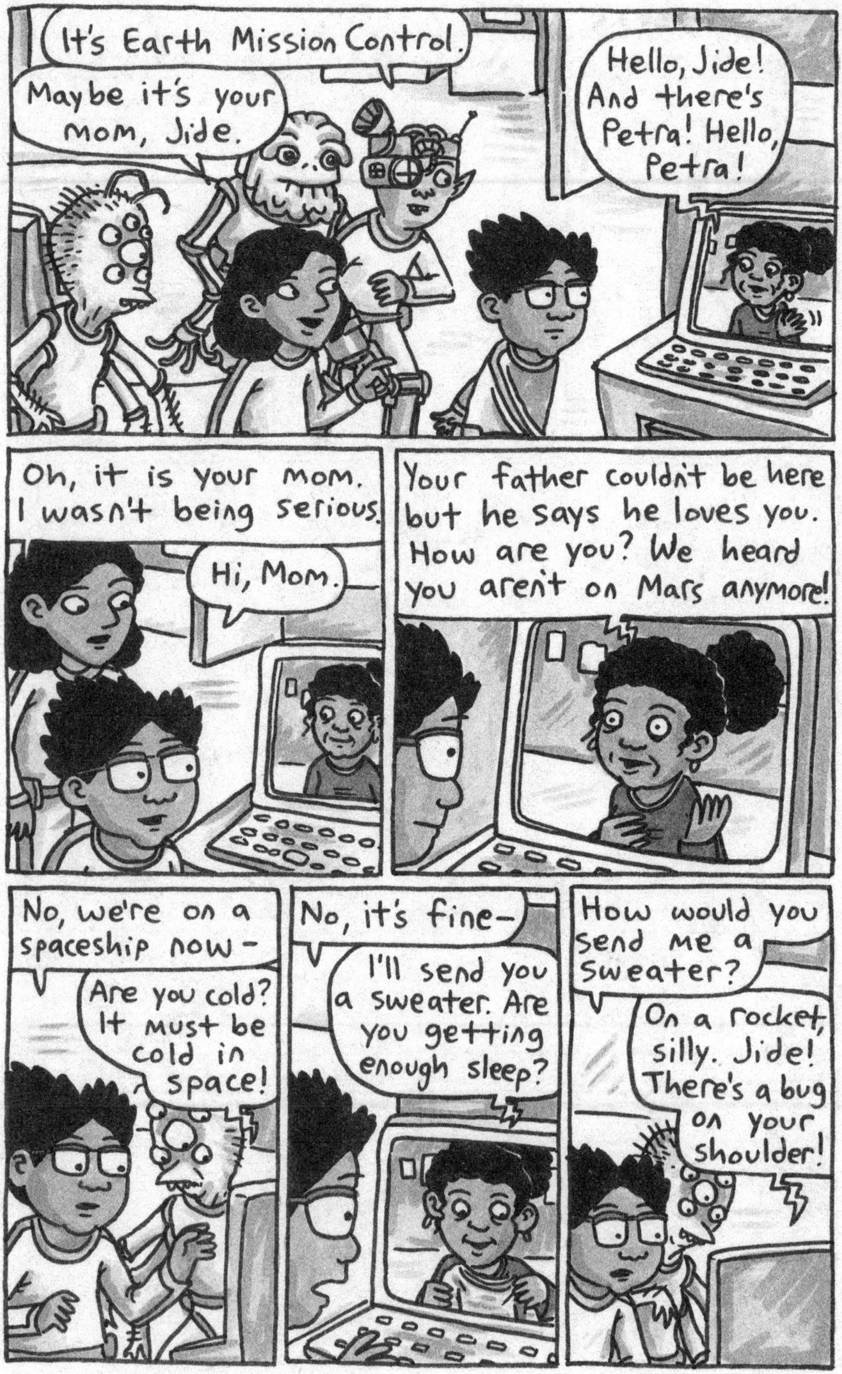
It's Earth Mission Control.
Maybe it's your mom, Jide.
Hello, Jide! And there's Petra! Hello, Petra!
Oh, it is your mom. I wasn't being serious.
Hi, Mom.
Your father couldn't be here but he says he loves you. How are you? We heard you aren't on Mars anymore!
No, we're on a spaceship now-
Are you cold? It must be cold in space!
No, it's fine-
I'll send you a sweater. Are you getting enough sleep?
How would you send me a sweater?
On a rocket, silly. Jide! There's a bug on your shoulder!

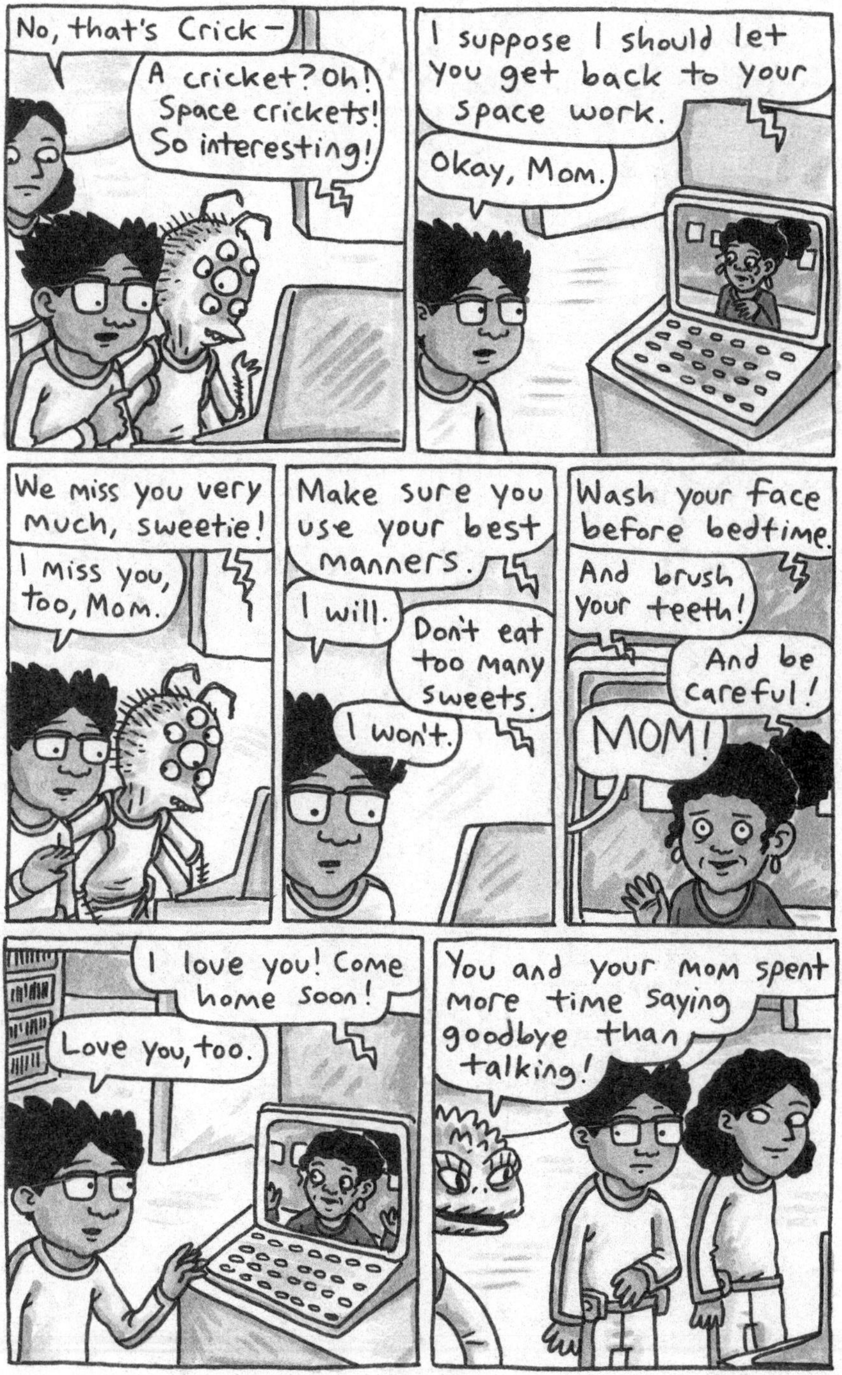
No, that's Crick—
A cricket? Oh! Space crickets! So interesting!
I suppose I should let you get back to your space work.
Okay, Mom.
We miss you very much, sweetie!
I miss you, too, Mom.
Make sure you use your best manners.
I will.
Don't eat too many sweets.
I won't.
Wash your face before bedtime.
And brush your teeth!
And be careful!
MOM!
I love you! Come home soon!
Love you, too.
You and your mom spent more time saying goodbye than talking!

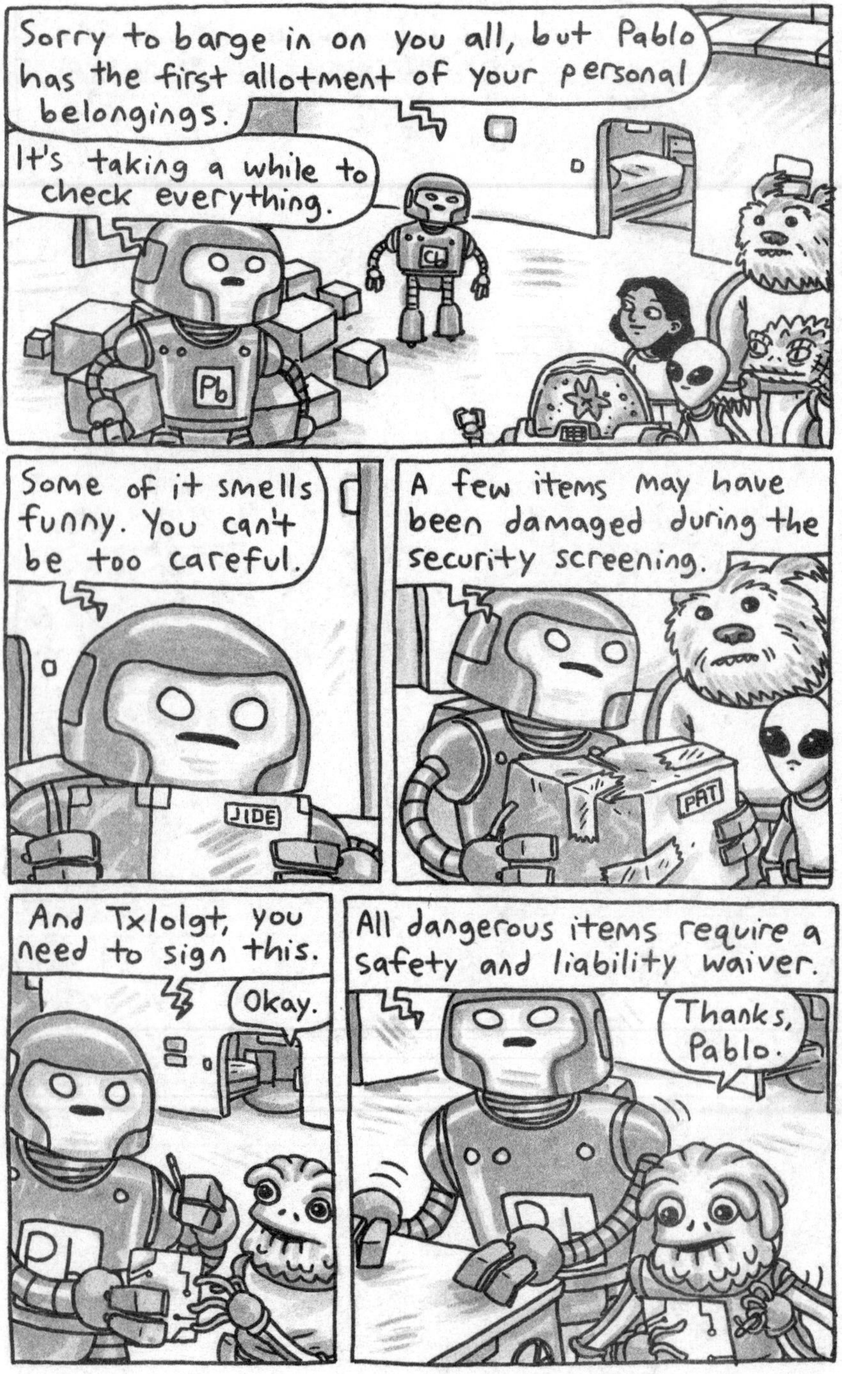
Sorry to barge in on you all, but Pablo has the first allotment of your personal belongings.
It's taking a while to check everything.
Cb
Pb
Some of it smells funny. You can't be too careful.
JIDE
A few items may have been damaged during the security screening.
PAT
And Txlolgt, you need to sign this.
Okay.
All dangerous items require a safety and liability waiver.
Thanks, Pablo.

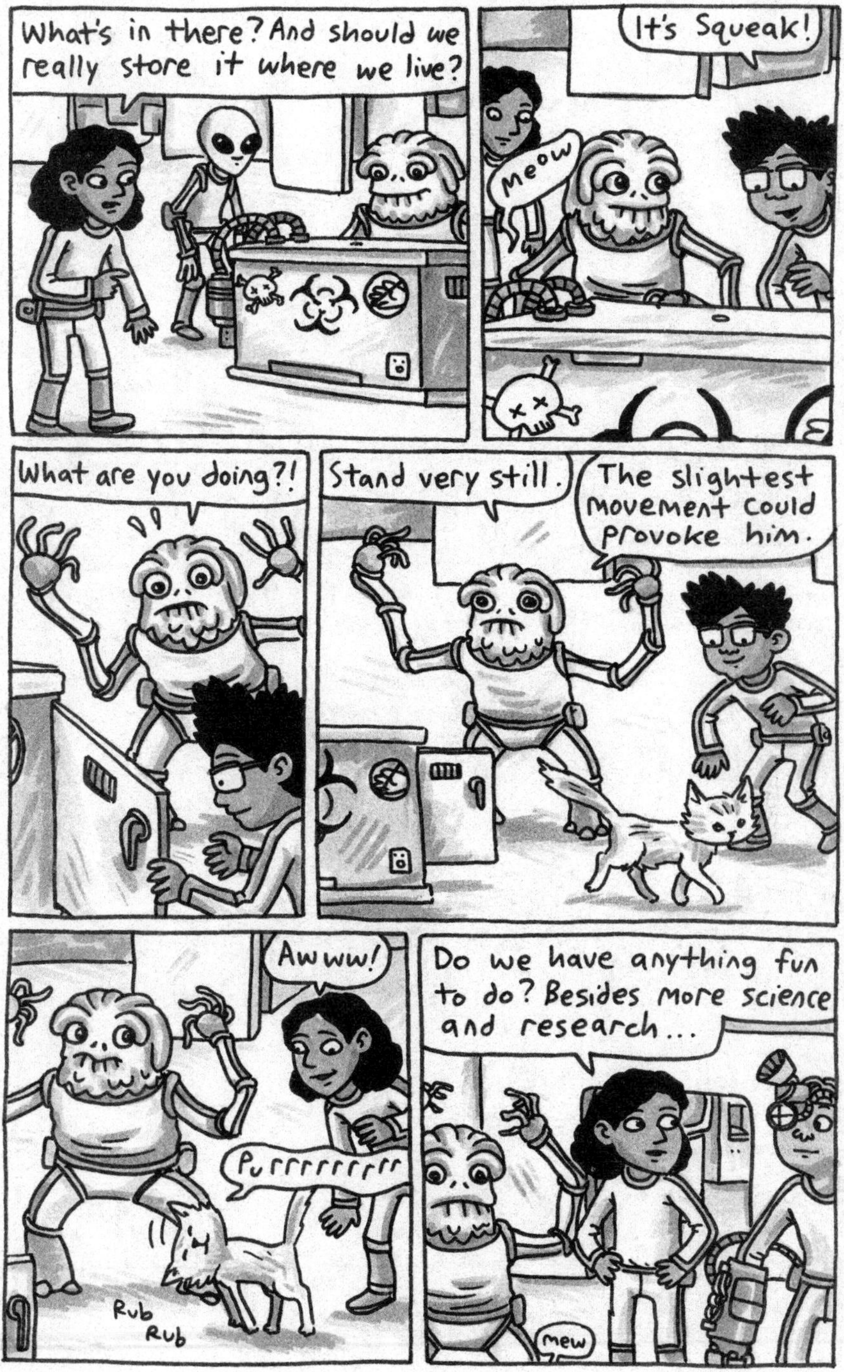
What's in there? And should we really store it where we live?
It's Squeak!
Meow
What are you doing?!
Stand very still.
The slightest movement could provoke him.
Awww!
Purrrrrrrr
Rub Rub
Do we have anything fun to do? Besides more science and research...
mew

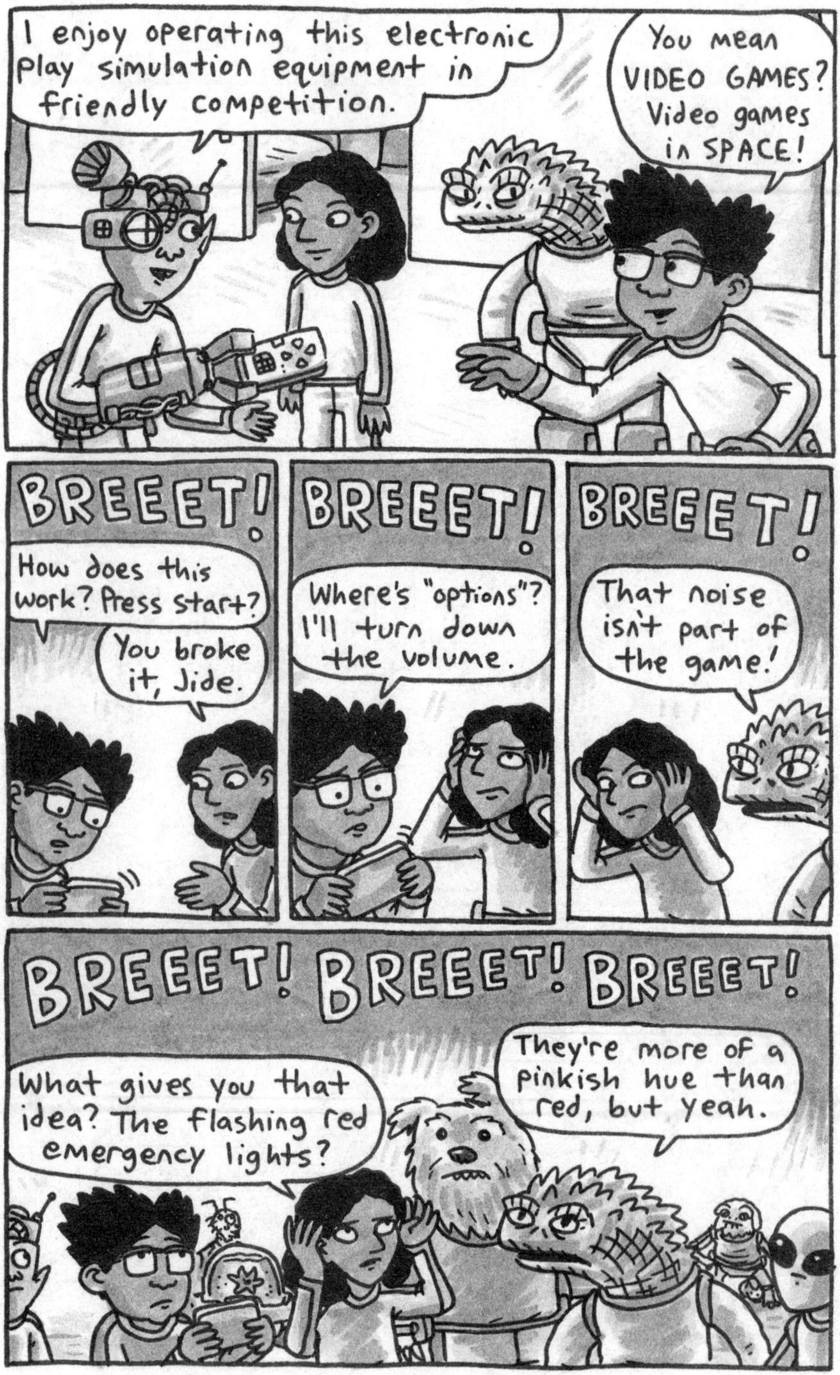
I enjoy operating this electronic play simulation equipment in friendly competition.
You mean VIDEO GAMES? Video games in SPACE!
BREEET!
How does this work? Press start?
You broke it, Jide.
BREEET!
Where's "options"? I'll turn down the volume.
BREEET!
That noise isn't part of the game!
BREEET! BREEET! BREEET!
What gives you that idea? The flashing red emergency lights?
They're more of a pinkish hue than red, but yeah.

HIGH ORBIT, HIGH ALERT

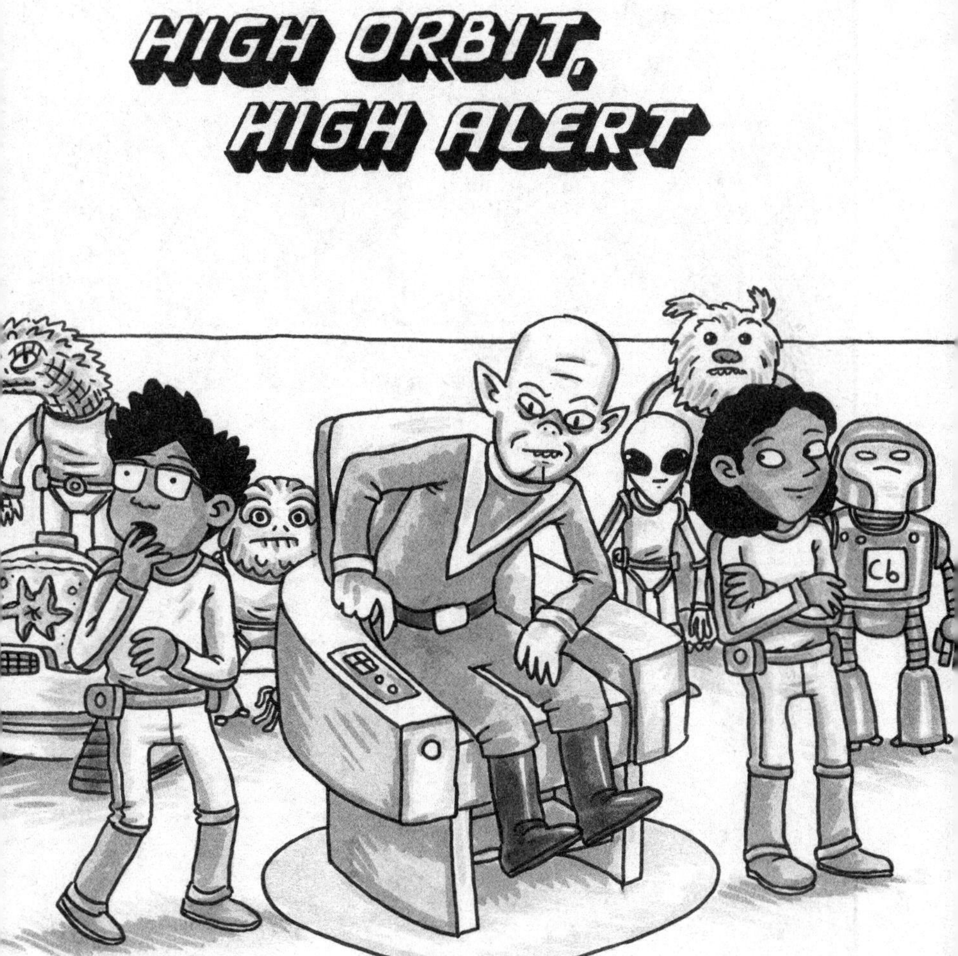
Cb

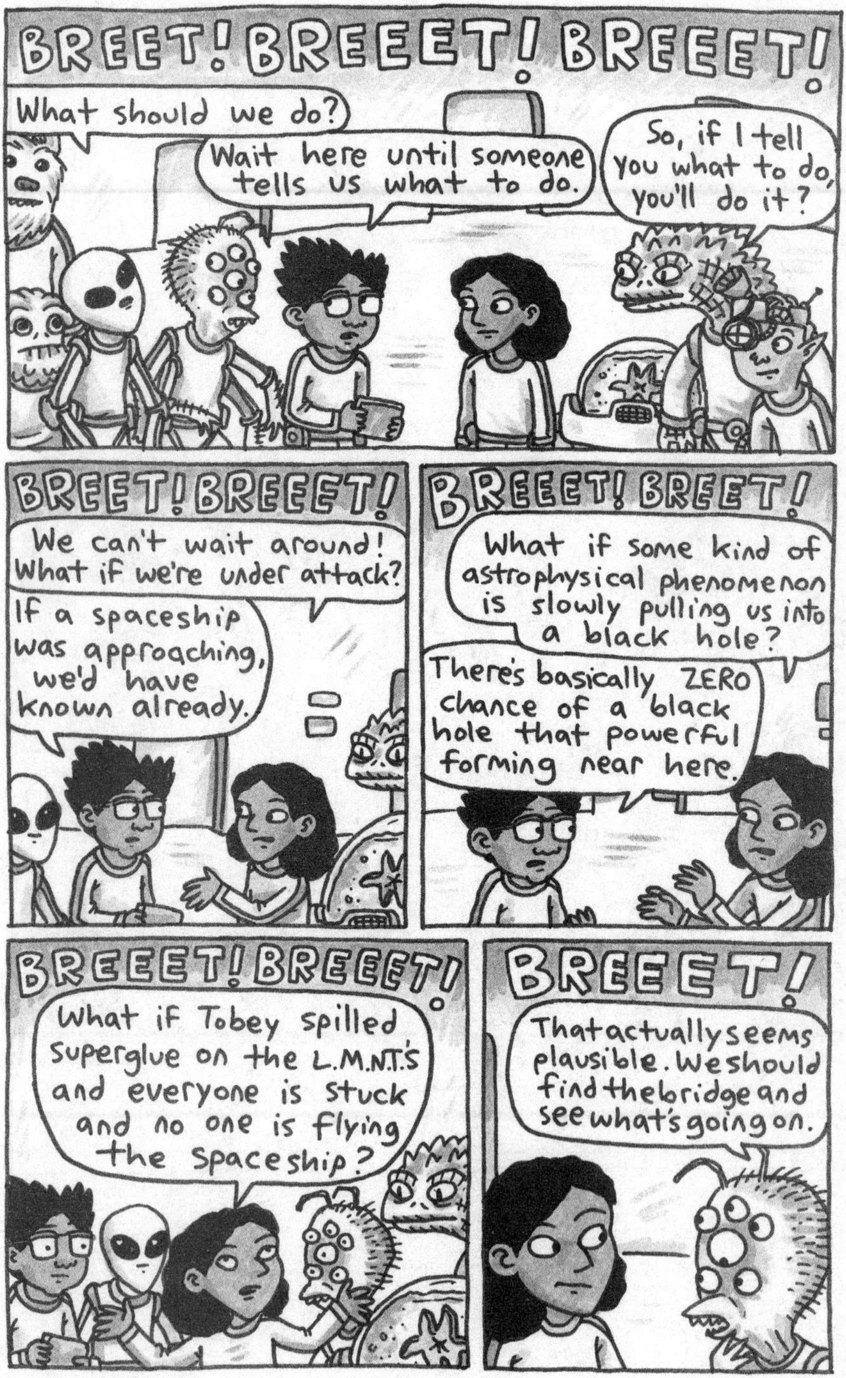
BREET! BREEET! BREEET!
What should we do?
Wait here until someone tells us what to do.
So, if I tell you what to do, you'll do it?
BREET! BREEET!
We can't wait around! What if we're under attack?
If a spaceship was approaching, we'd have known already.
BREEET! BREET!
What if some kind of astrophysical phenomenon is slowly pulling us into a black hole?
There's basically ZERO chance of a black hole that powerful forming near here.
BREEET! BREEET!
What if Tobey spilled superglue on the L.M.N.T.'s and everyone is stuck and no one is flying the spaceship?
BREEET!
That actually seems plausible. We should find the bridge and see what's going on.

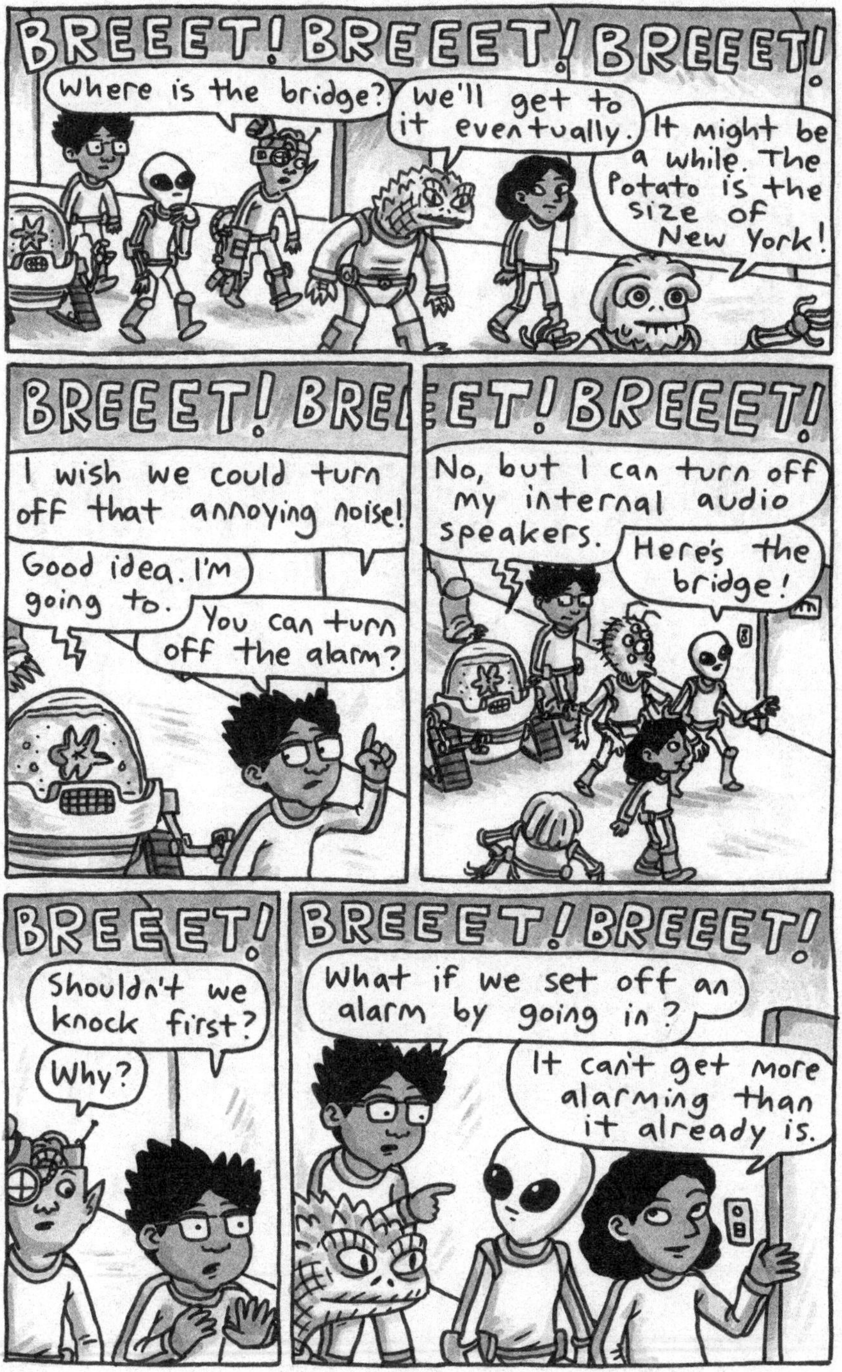
BREEET! BREEET! BREEET!
Where is the bridge?
We'll get to it eventually.
It might be a while. The Potato is the size of New York!
BREEET! BREEET! BREEET!
I wish we could turn off that annoying noise!
Good idea. I'm going to.
You can turn off the alarm?
No, but I can turn off my internal audio speakers.
Here's the bridge!
BREEET!
Shouldn't we knock first?
Why?
BREEET! BREEET!
What if we set off an alarm by going in?
It can't get more alarming than it already is.

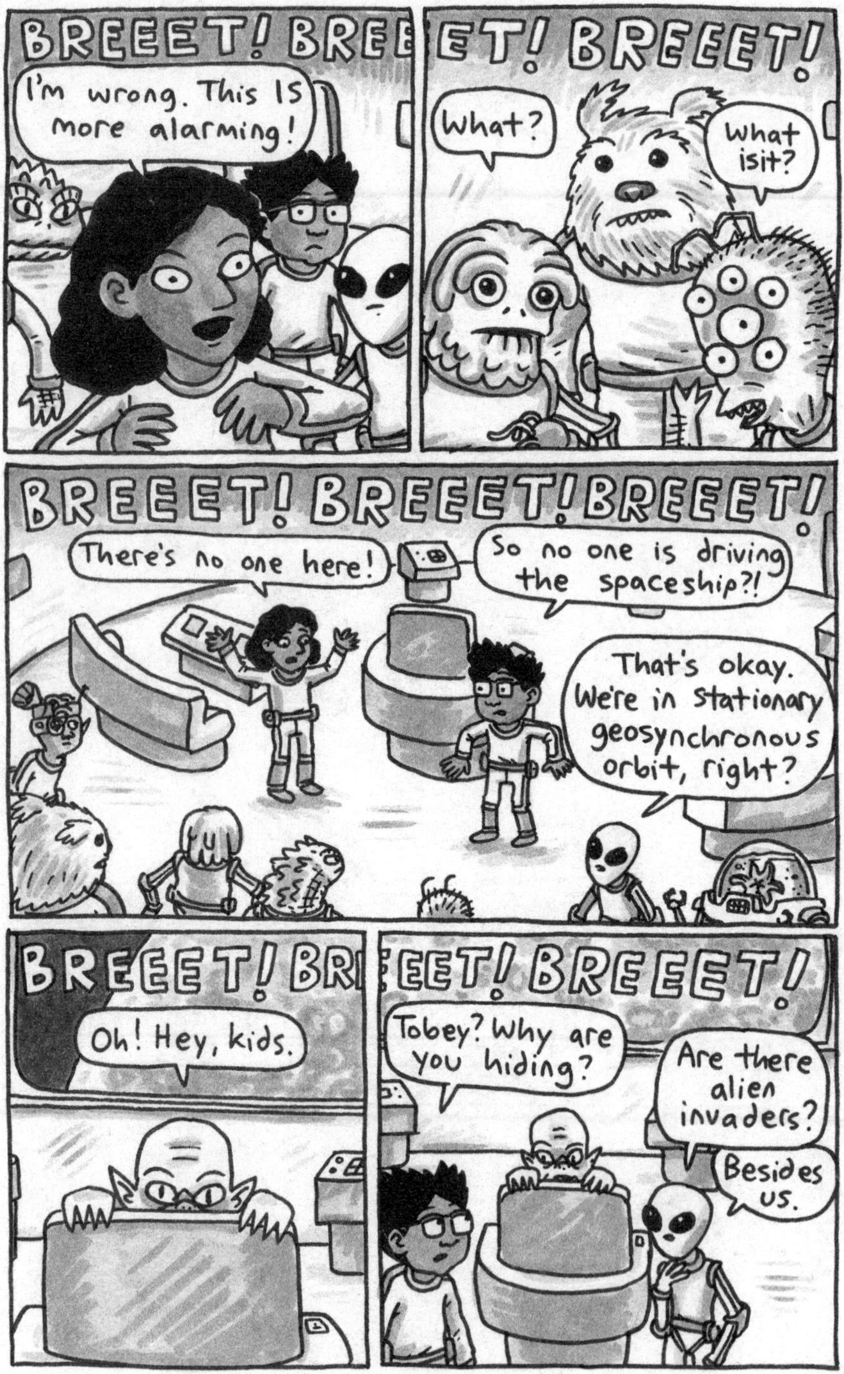
BREEET! BREEET! BREEET!
I'm wrong. This IS more alarming!
What?
What is it?
BREEET! BREEET! BREEET!
There's no one here!
So no one is driving the spaceship?!
That's okay. We're in stationary geosynchronous orbit, right?
BREEET! BREEET! BREEET!
Oh! Hey, kids.
Tobey? Why are you hiding?
Are there alien invaders?
Besides us.

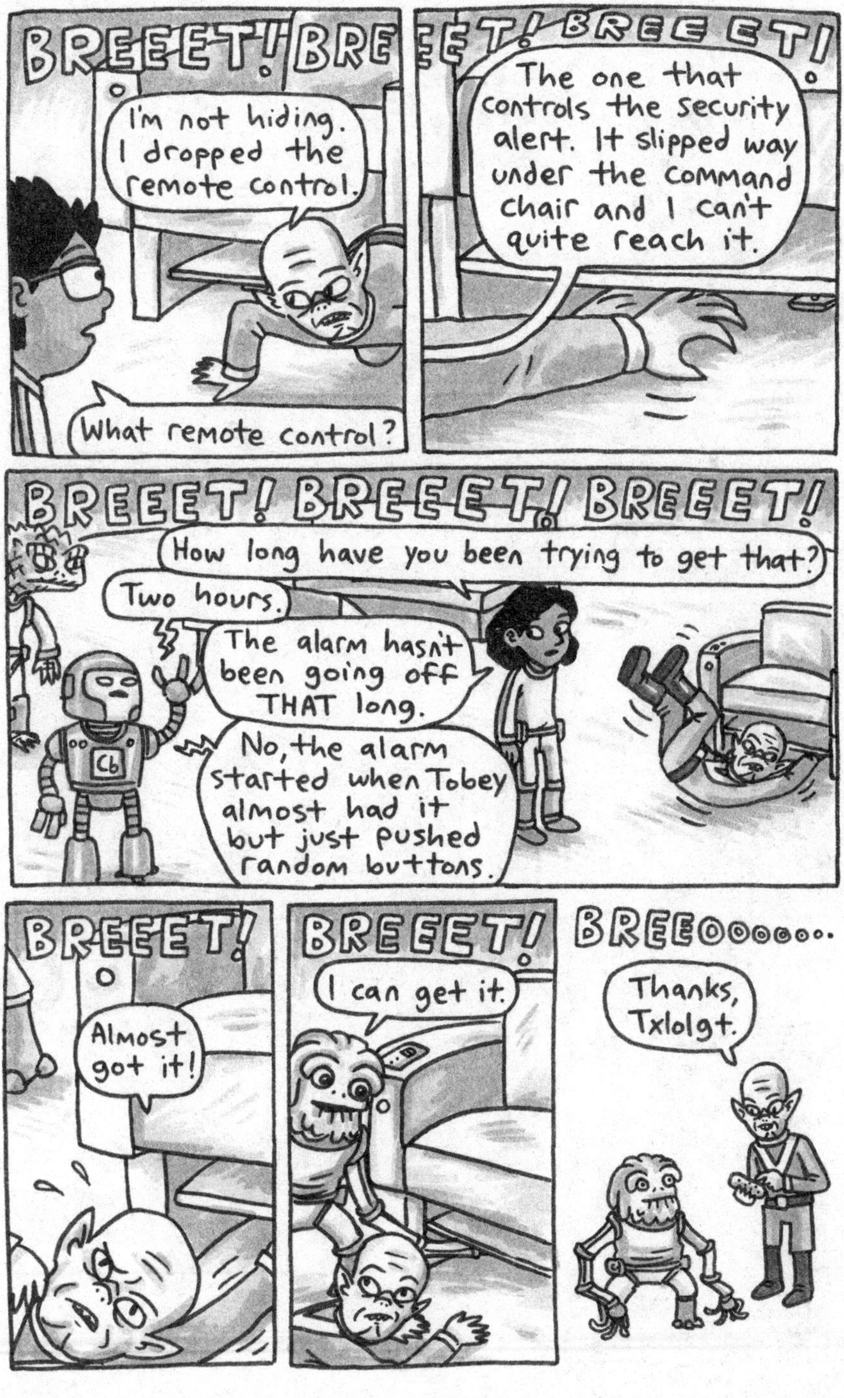
BREEET! BREEET! BREEET!
I'm not hiding. I dropped the remote control.
What remote control?
The one that controls the security alert. It slipped way under the command chair and I can't quite reach it.
BREEET! BREEET! BREEET!
How long have you been trying to get that?
Two hours.
The alarm hasn't been going off THAT long.
No, the alarm started when Tobey almost had it but just pushed random buttons.
BREEET!
Almost got it!
BREEET!
I can get it.
BREEOooooo..
Thanks, Txlolgt.

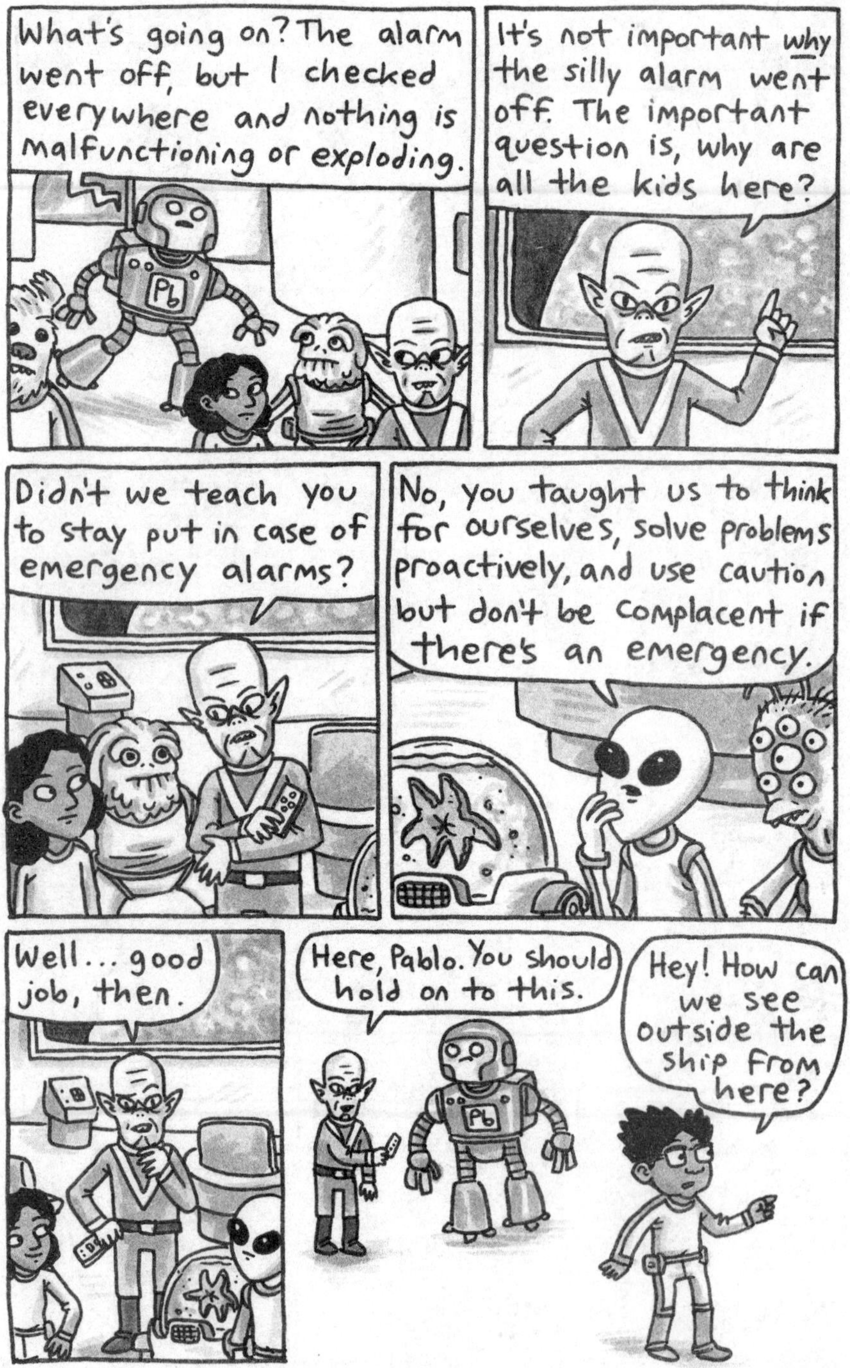
What's going on? The alarm went off, but I checked everywhere and nothing is malfunctioning or exploding.
It's not important why the silly alarm went off. The important question is, why are all the kids here?
Didn't we teach you to stay put in case of emergency alarms?
No, you taught us to think for ourselves, solve problems proactively, and use caution but don't be complacent if there's an emergency.
Well... good job, then.
Here, Pablo. You should hold on to this.
Hey! How can we see outside the ship from here?

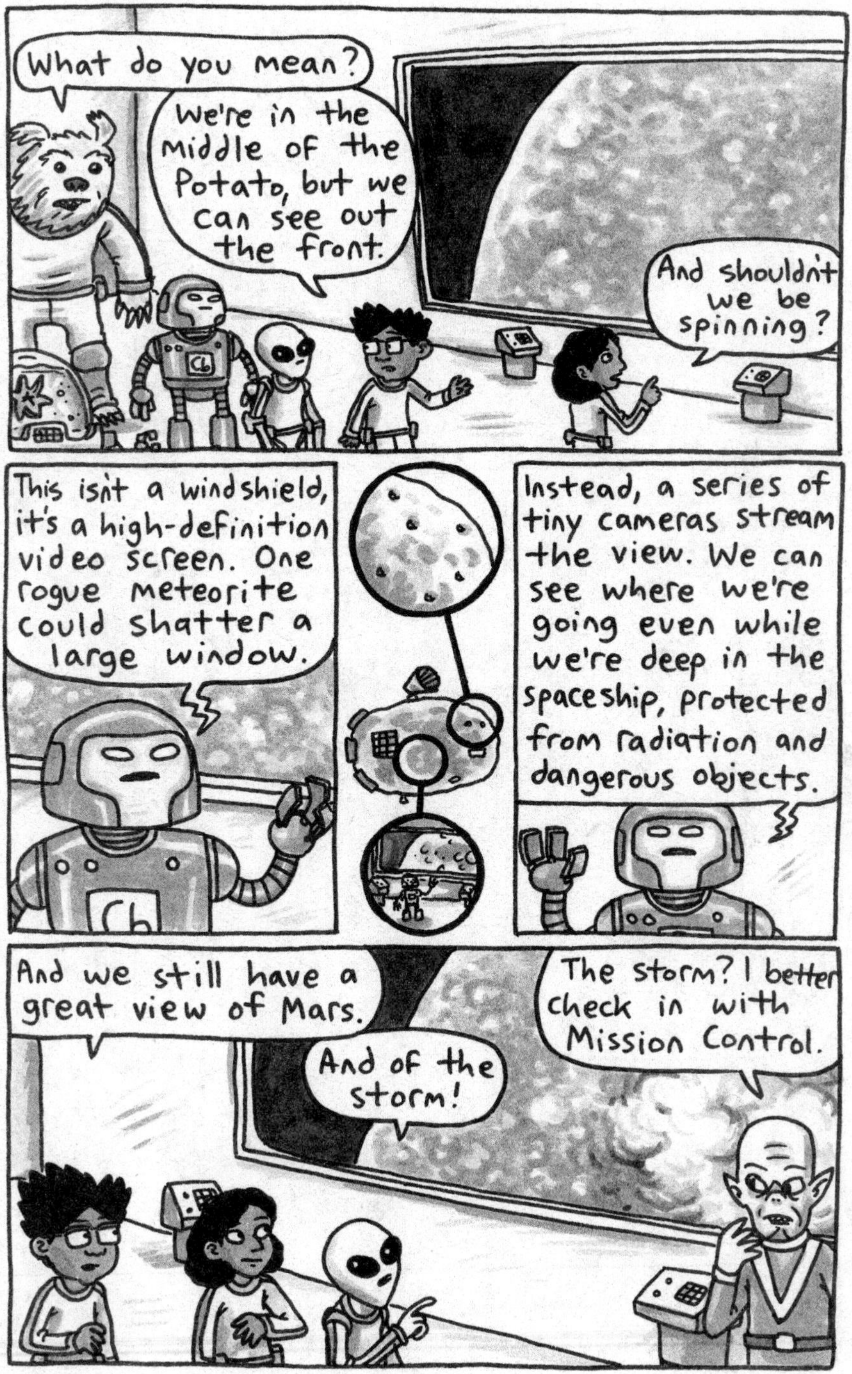
What do you mean?
We're in the middle of the Potato, but we can see out the front.
And shouldn't we be spinning?
This isn't a windshield, it's a high-definition video screen. One rogue meteorite could shatter a large window.
Instead, a series of tiny cameras stream the view. We can see where we're going even while we're deep in the spaceship, protected from radiation and dangerous objects.
And we still have a great view of Mars.
And of the storm!
The storm? I better check in with Mission Control.

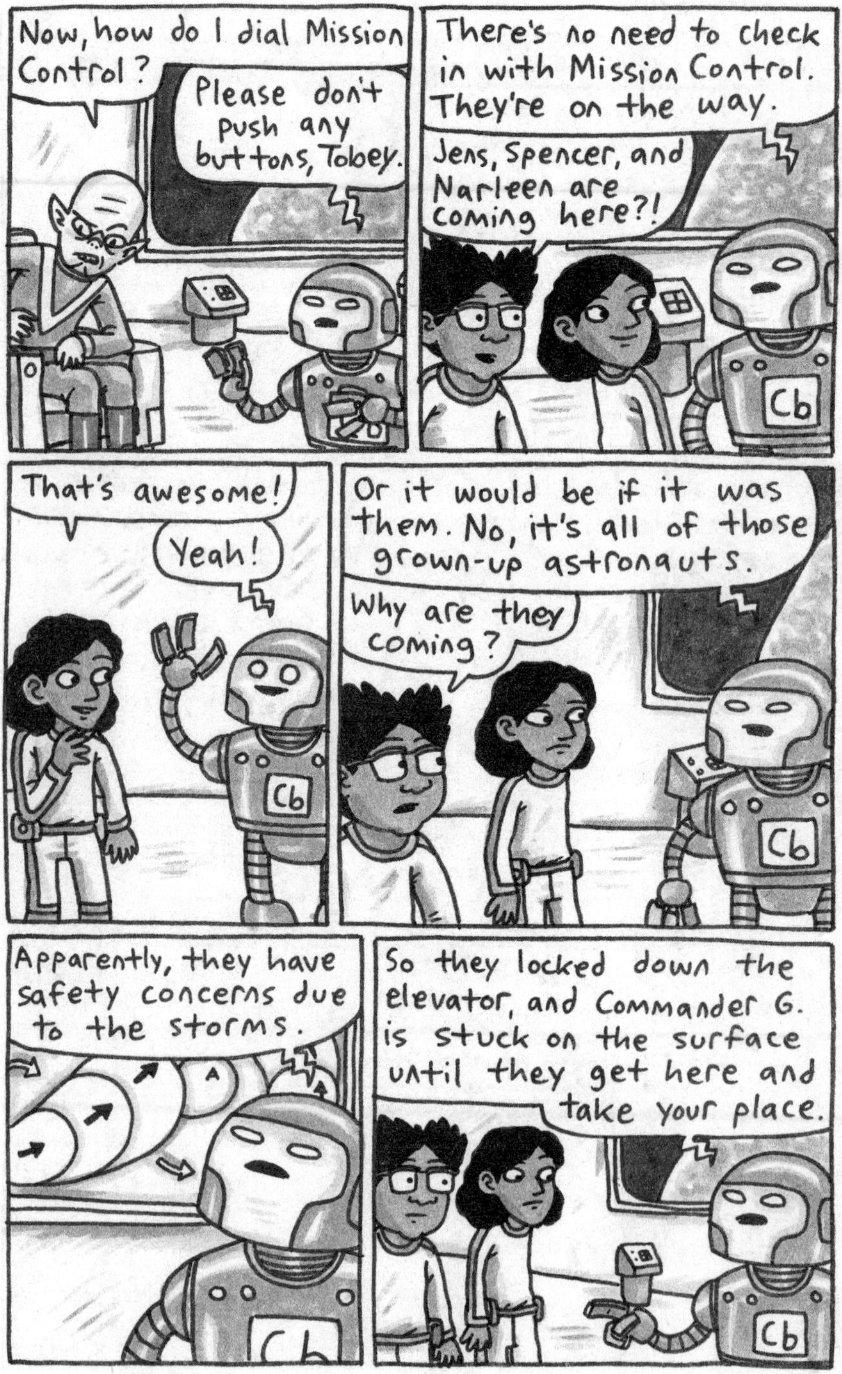
Now, how do I dial Mission Control?
Please don't push any buttons, Tobey.
There's no need to check in with Mission Control. They're on the way.
Jens, Spencer, and Narleen are coming here?!
Cb
That's awesome!
Yeah!
Cb
Or it would be if it was them. No, it's all of those grown-up astronauts.
Why are they coming?
Cb
Apparently, they have safety concerns due to the storms.
So they locked down the elevator, and Commander G. is stuck on the surface until they get here and take your place.
Cb

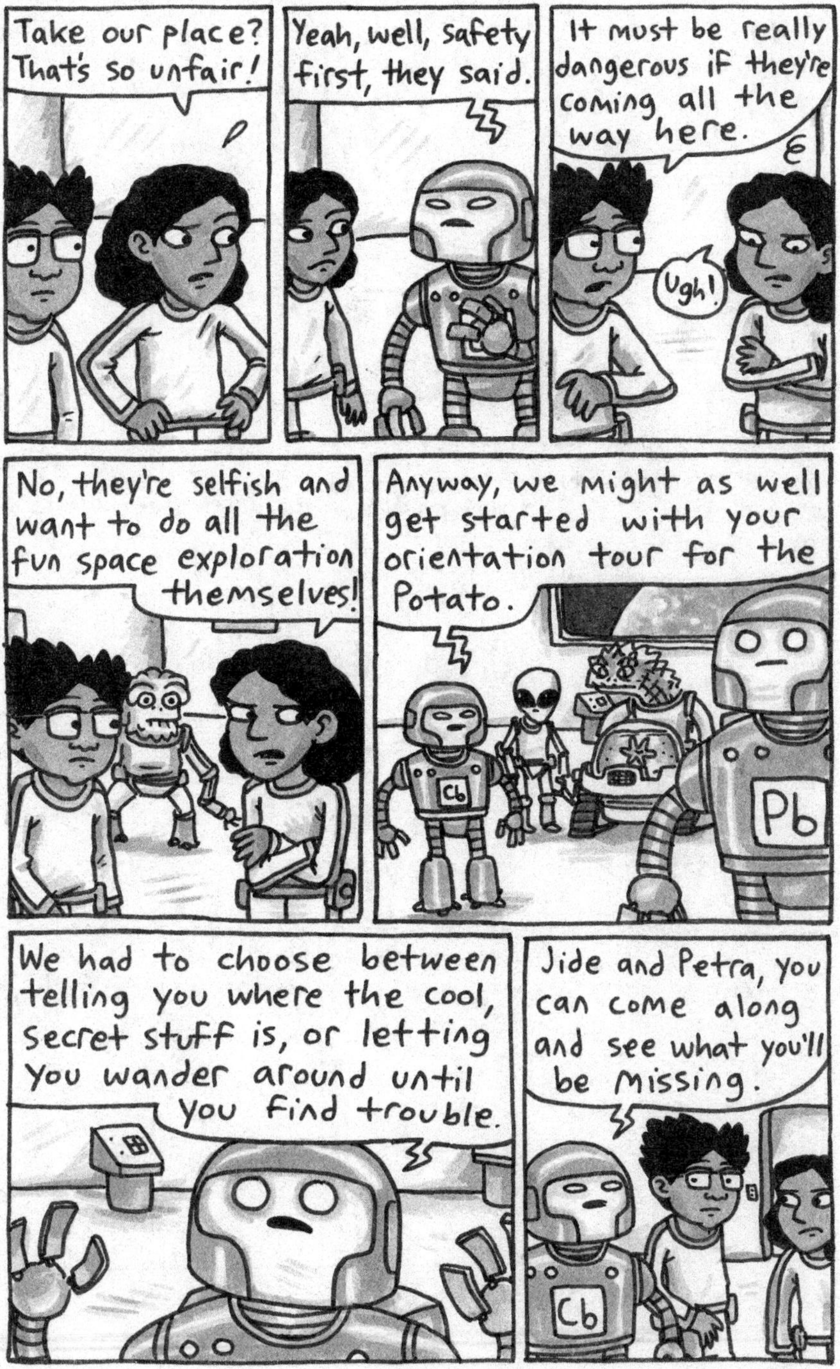
Take our place? That's so unfair!
Yeah, well, safety first, they said.
It must be really dangerous if they're coming all the way here.
Ugh!
No, they're selfish and want to do all the fun space exploration themselves!
Anyway, we might as well get started with your orientation tour for the Potato.
Cb
Pb
We had to choose between telling you where the cool, secret stuff is, or letting you wander around until you find trouble.
Jide and Petra, you can come along and see what you'll be missing.
Cb

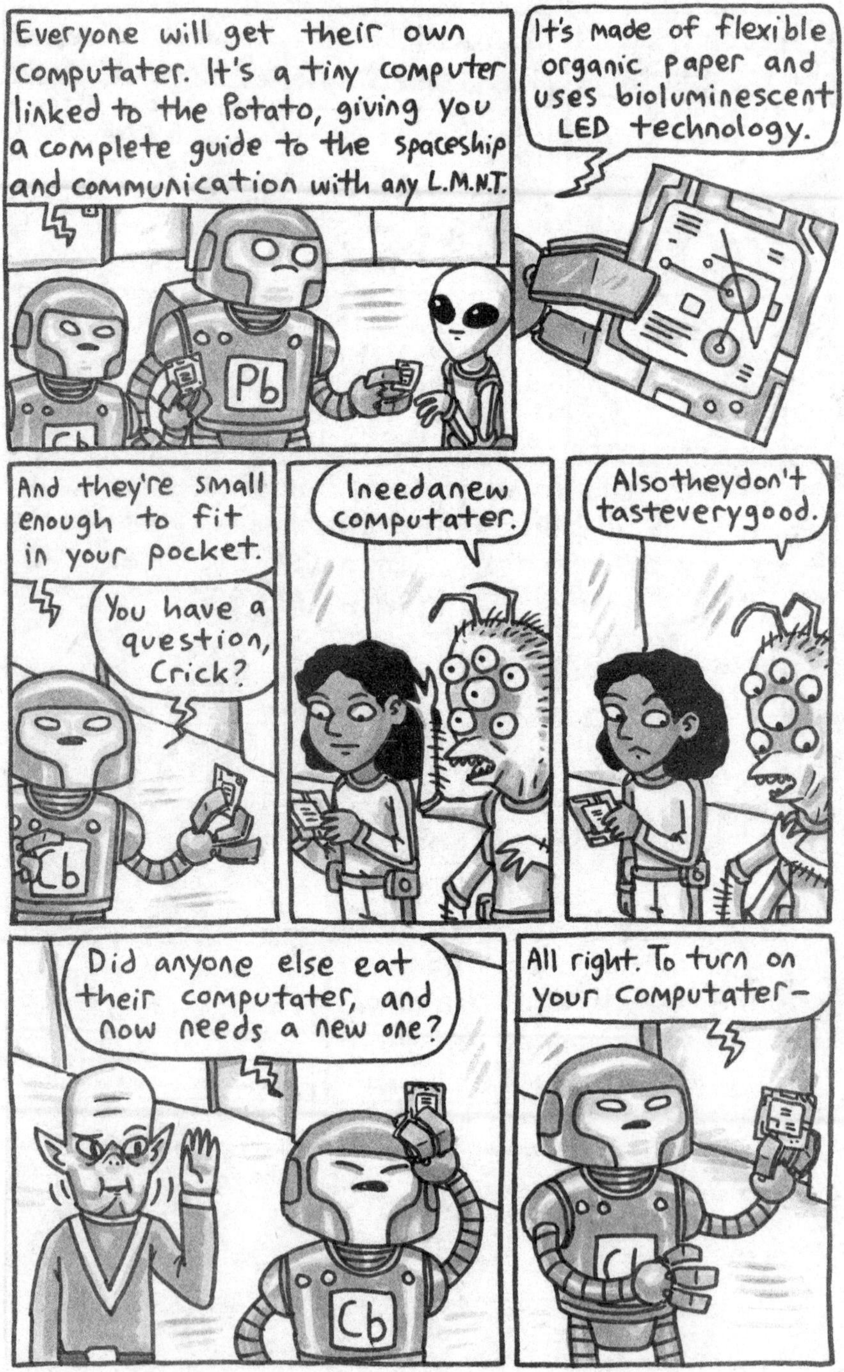
Everyone will get their own computater. It's a tiny computer linked to the Potato, giving you a complete guide to the spaceship and communication with any L.M.N.T.
It's made of flexible organic paper and uses bioluminescent LED technology.
Pb
Cb
And they're small enough to fit in your pocket.
You have a question, Crick?
Cb
Ineedanew computater.
Alsotheydon't tasteverygood.
Did anyone else eat their computater, and now needs a new one?
Cb
All right. To turn on your computater—
Cb

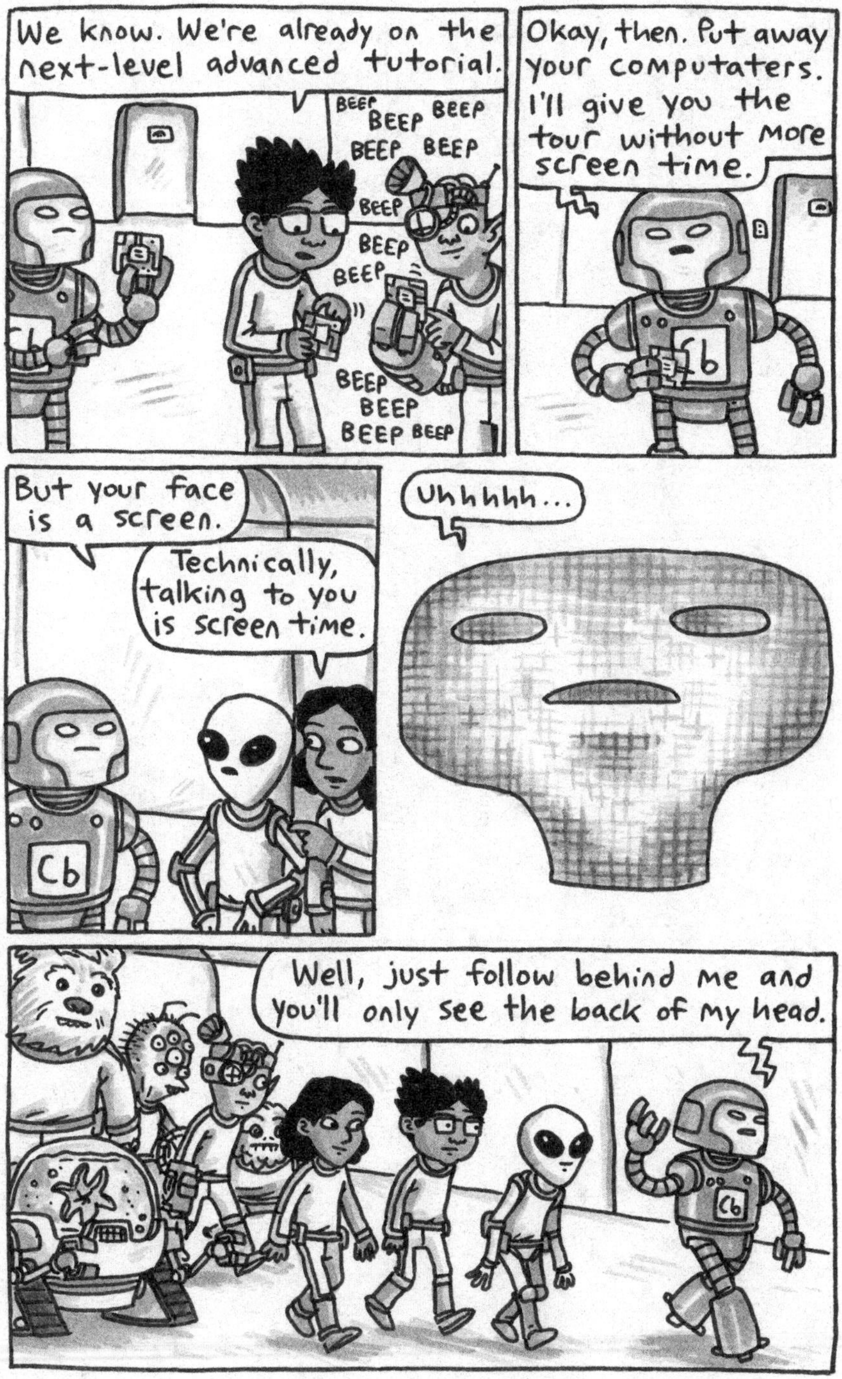
We know. We're already on the next-level advanced tutorial.
BEEP BEEP BEEP BEEP BEEP BEEP BEEP BEEP BEEP BEEP BEEP BEEP
Okay, then. Put away your computaters. I'll give you the tour without more screen time.
But your face is a screen.
Technically, talking to you is screen time.
Uhhhhh...
Well, just follow behind me and you'll only see the back of my head.

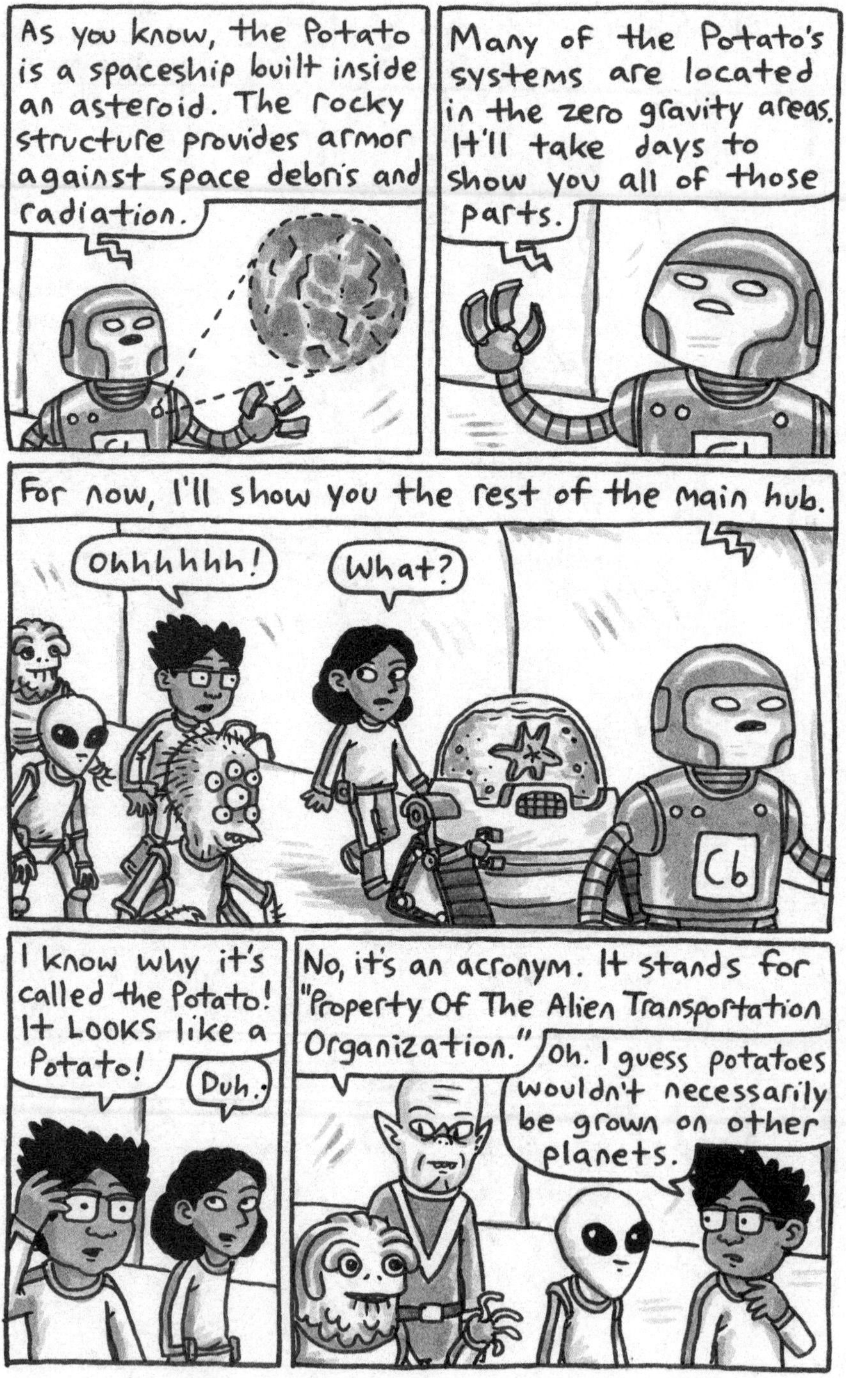
As you know, the Potato is a spaceship built inside an asteroid. The rocky structure provides armor against space debris and radiation.
Many of the Potato's systems are located in the zero gravity areas. It'll take days to show you all of those parts.
For now, I'll show you the rest of the main hub.
Ohhhhhh!
What?
Cb
I know why it's called the Potato! It LOOKS like a Potato!
Duh.
No, it's an acronym. It stands for "Property Of The Alien Transportation Organization."
Oh. I guess potatoes wouldn't necessarily be grown on other planets.

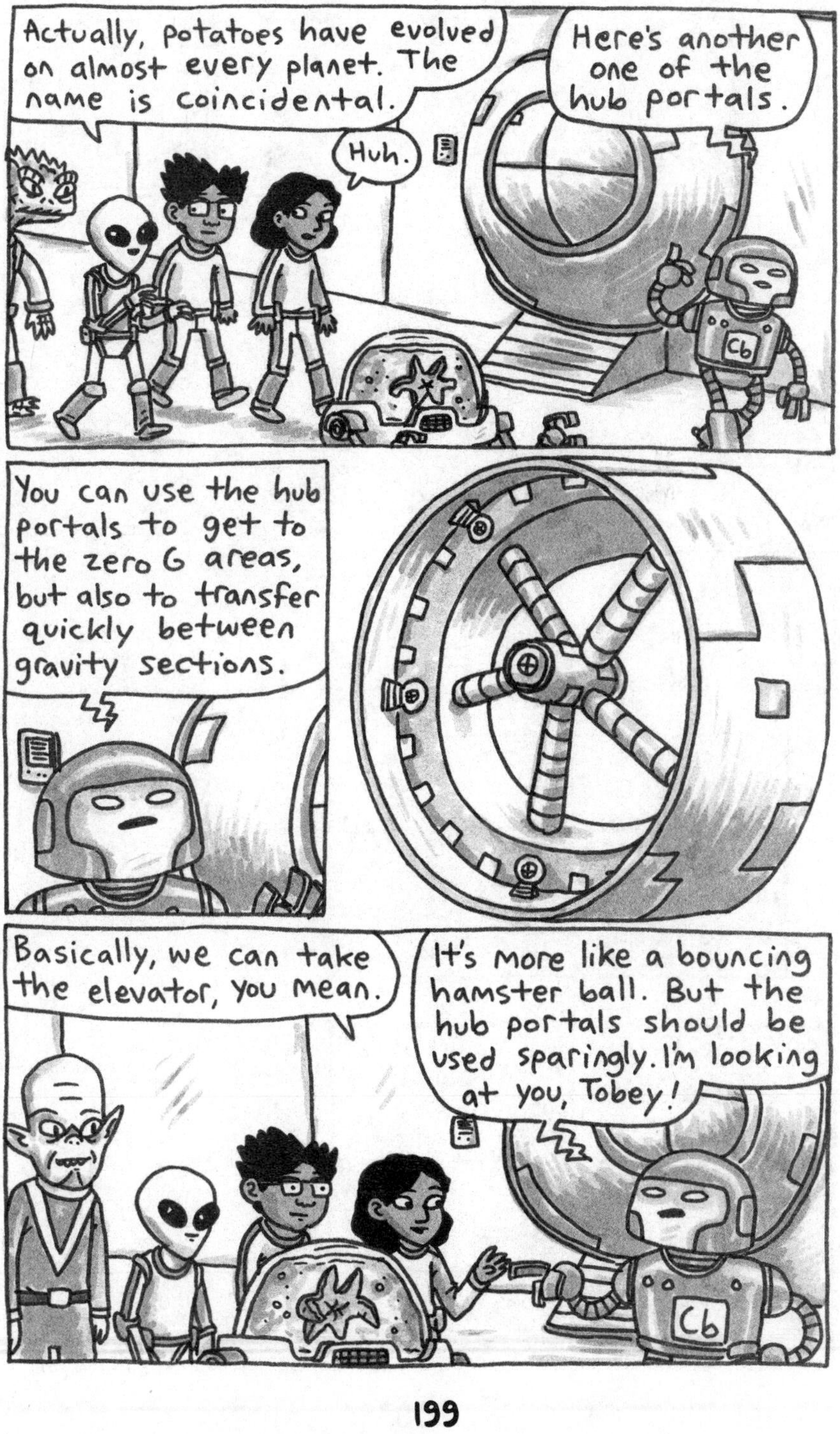
Actually, potatoes have evolved on almost every planet. The name is coincidental.
Huh.
Here's another one of the hub portals.
You can use the hub portals to get to the zero G areas, but also to transfer quickly between gravity sections.
Basically, we can take the elevator, you mean.
It's more like a bouncing hamster ball. But the hub portals should be used sparingly. I'm looking at you, Tobey!
Cb

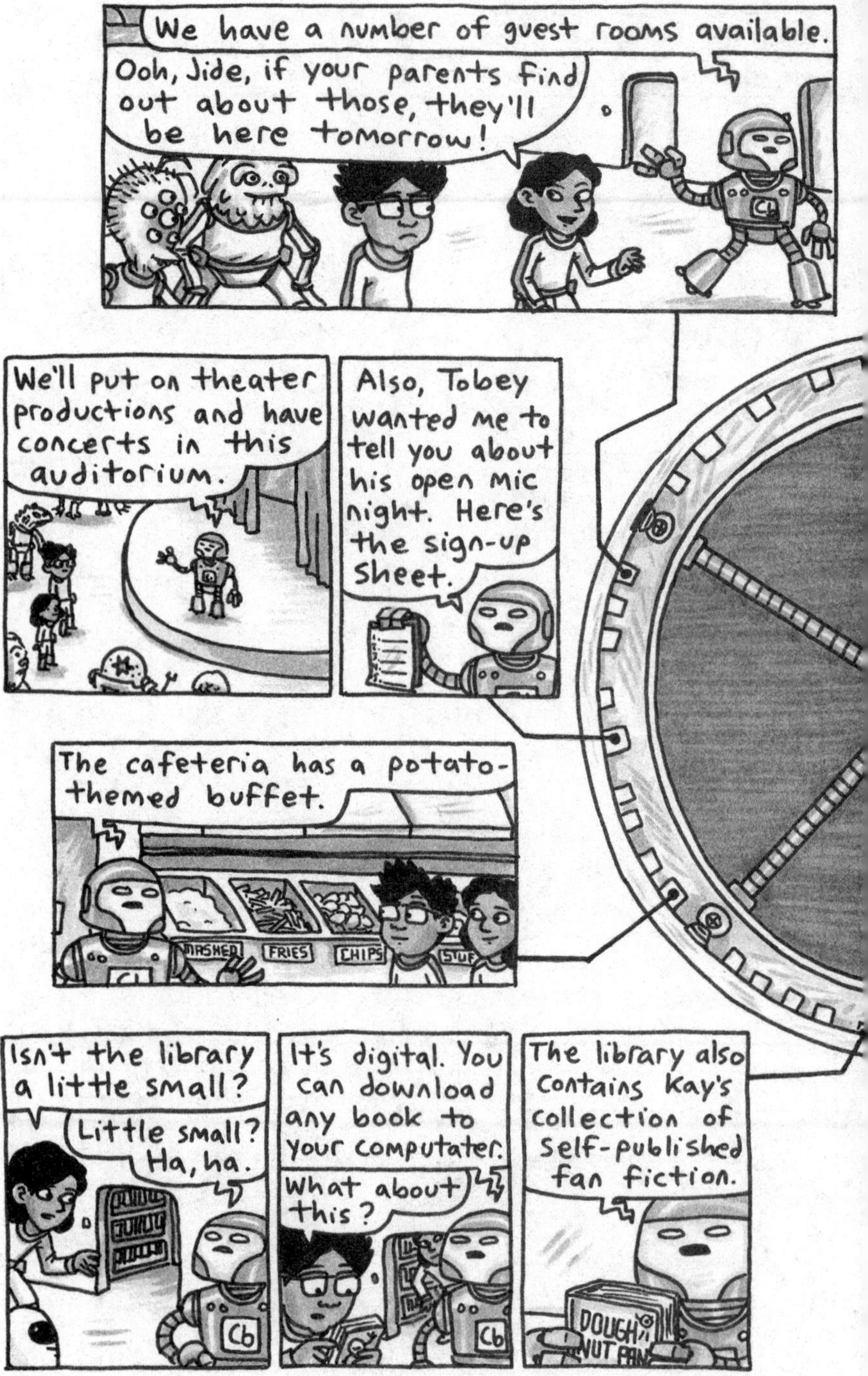
We have a number of guest rooms available.
Ooh, Jide, if your parents find out about those, they'll be here tomorrow!
We'll put on theater productions and have concerts in this auditorium.
Also, Tobey wanted me to tell you about his open mic night. Here's the sign-up sheet.
The cafeteria has a potato-themed buffet.
MASHED
FRIES
CHIPS
Cb
Isn't the library a little small?
Little small? Ha, ha.
Cb
It's digital. You can download any book to your computater.
What about this?
Cb
The library also contains Kay's collection of self-published fan fiction.
DOUGHNUT FAN

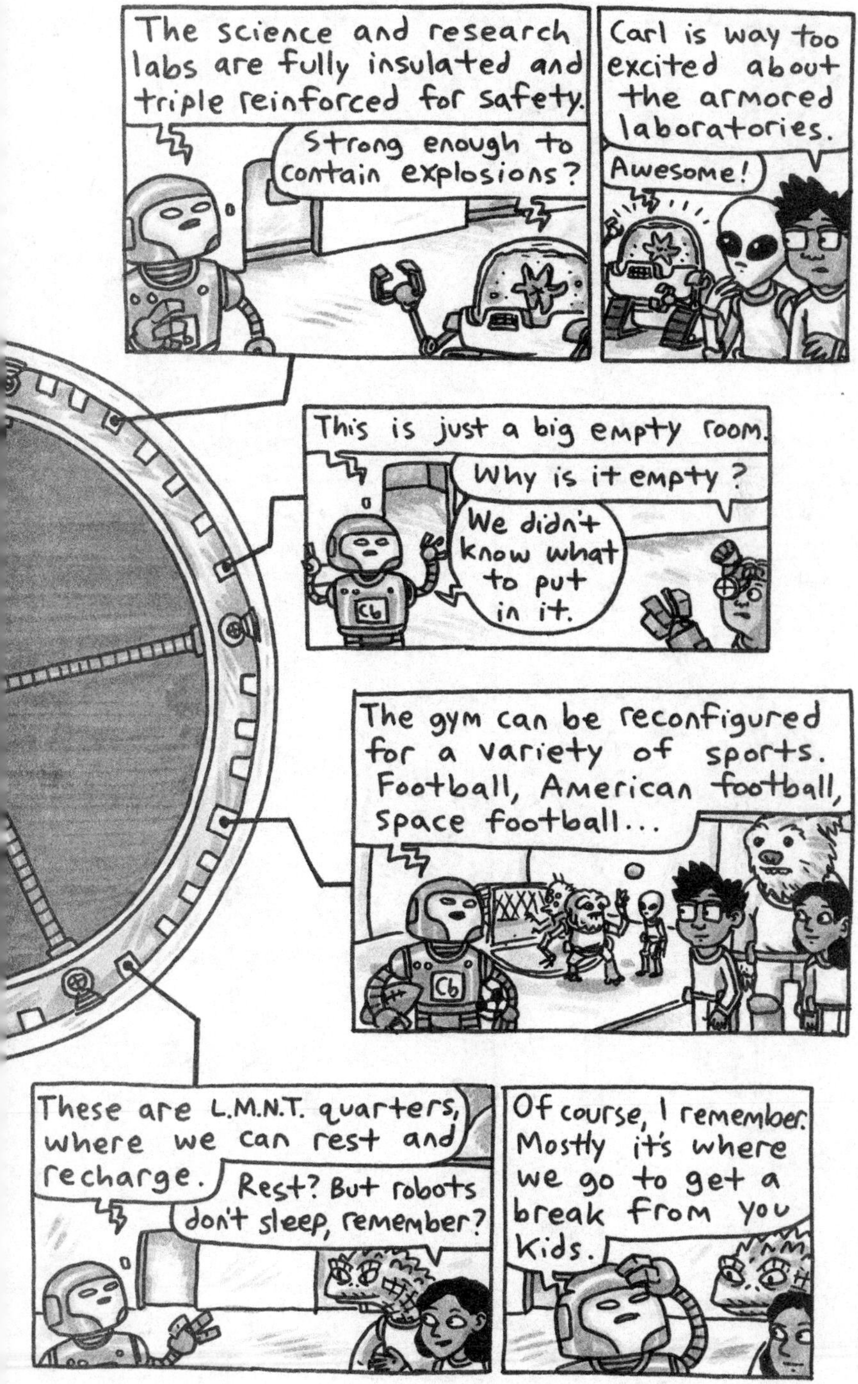
The science and research labs are fully insulated and triple reinforced for safety.
Strong enough to contain explosions?
Carl is way too excited about the armored laboratories.
Awesome!
This is just a big empty room.
Why is it empty?
We didn't know what to put in it.
The gym can be reconfigured for a variety of sports. Football, American football, space football...
These are L.M.N.T. quarters, where we can rest and recharge.
Rest? But robots don't sleep, remember?
Of course, I remember. Mostly it's where we go to get a break from you kids.

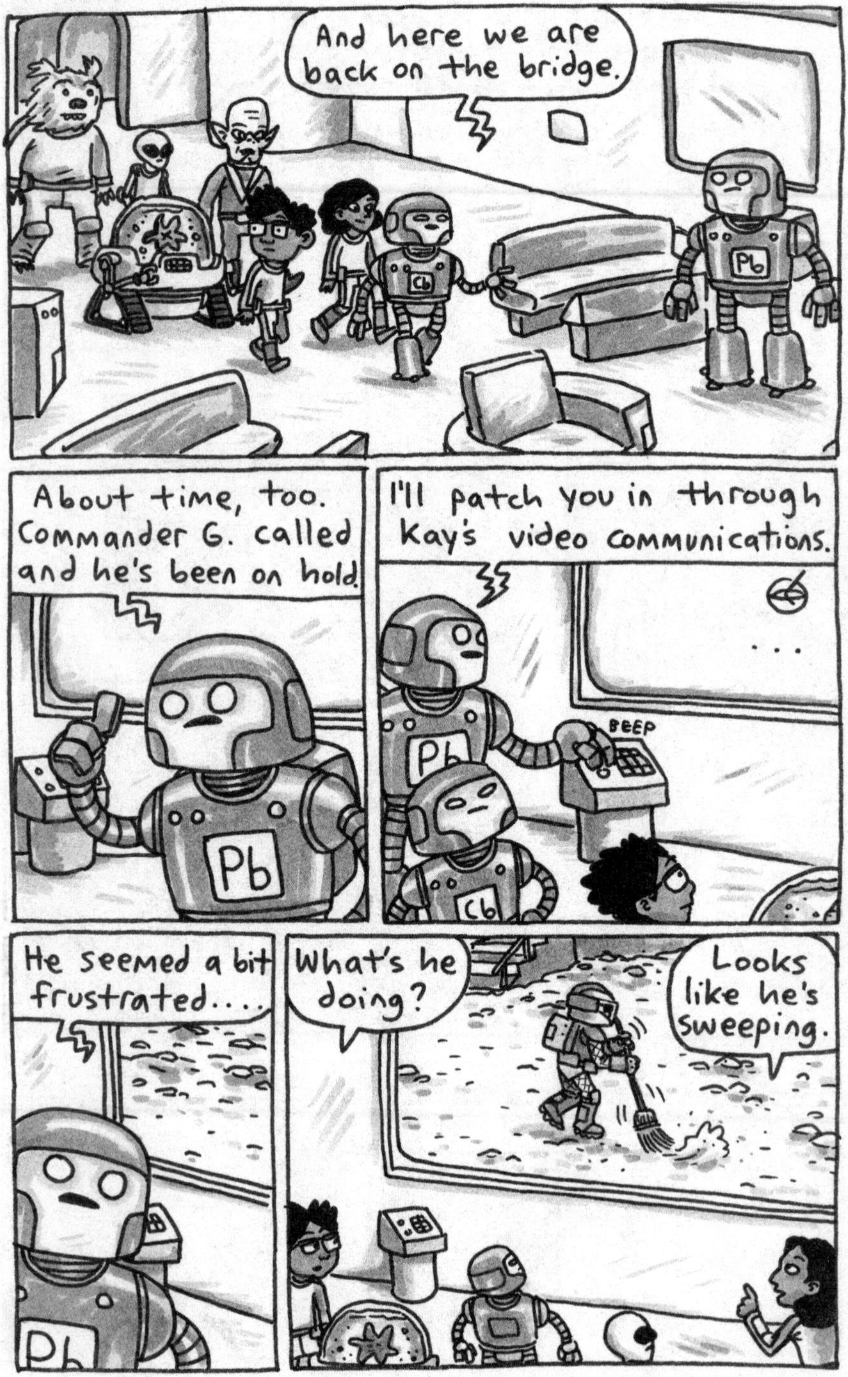
And here we are back on the bridge.
About time, too. Commander G. called and he's been on hold.
I'll patch you in through Kay's video communications.
BEEP
He seemed a bit frustrated....
What's he doing?
Looks like he's sweeping.

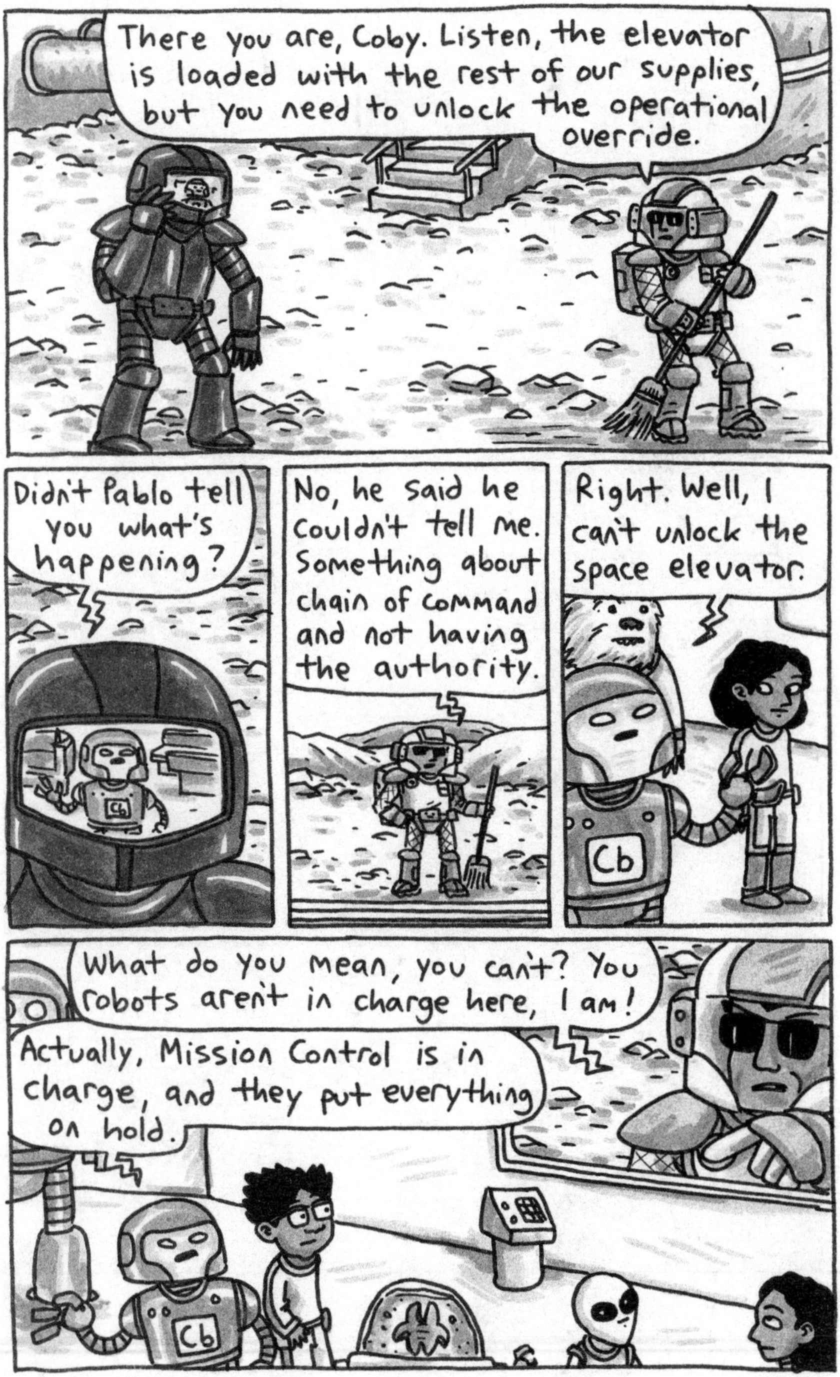
There you are, Coby. Listen, the elevator is loaded with the rest of our supplies, but you need to unlock the operational override.
Didn't Pablo tell you what's happening?
No, he said he couldn't tell me. Something about chain of command and not having the authority.
Right. Well, I can't unlock the space elevator.
What do you mean, you can't? You robots aren't in charge here, I am!
Actually, Mission Control is in charge, and they put everything on hold.
Cb
Cb
Cb

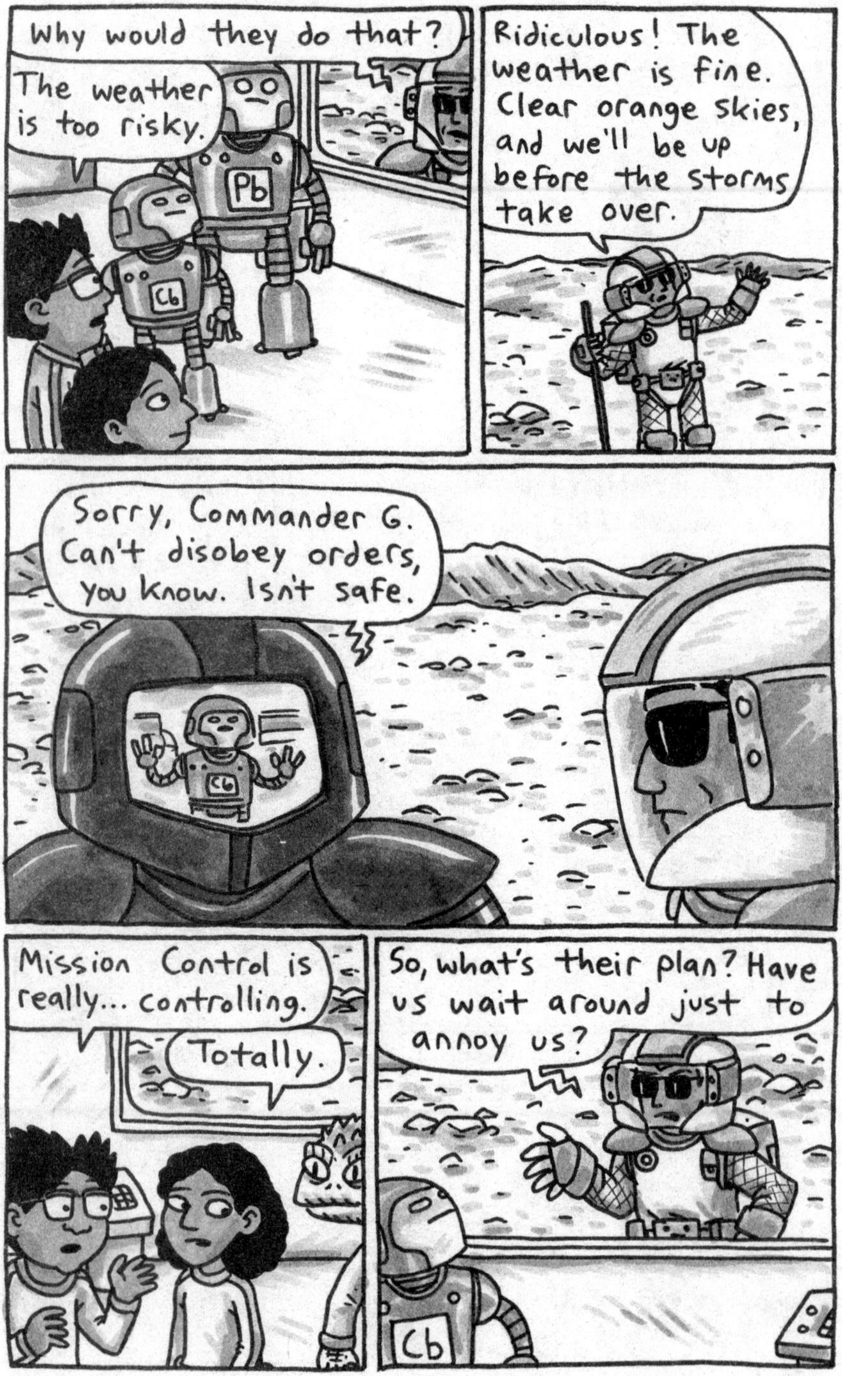
Why would they do that?
The weather is too risky.
Ridiculous! The weather is fine. Clear orange skies, and we'll be up before the storms take over.
Pb
Cb
Sorry, Commander G. Can't disobey orders, you know. Isn't safe.
Cb
Mission Control is really... controlling.
Totally.
So, what's their plan? Have us wait around just to annoy us?
Cb

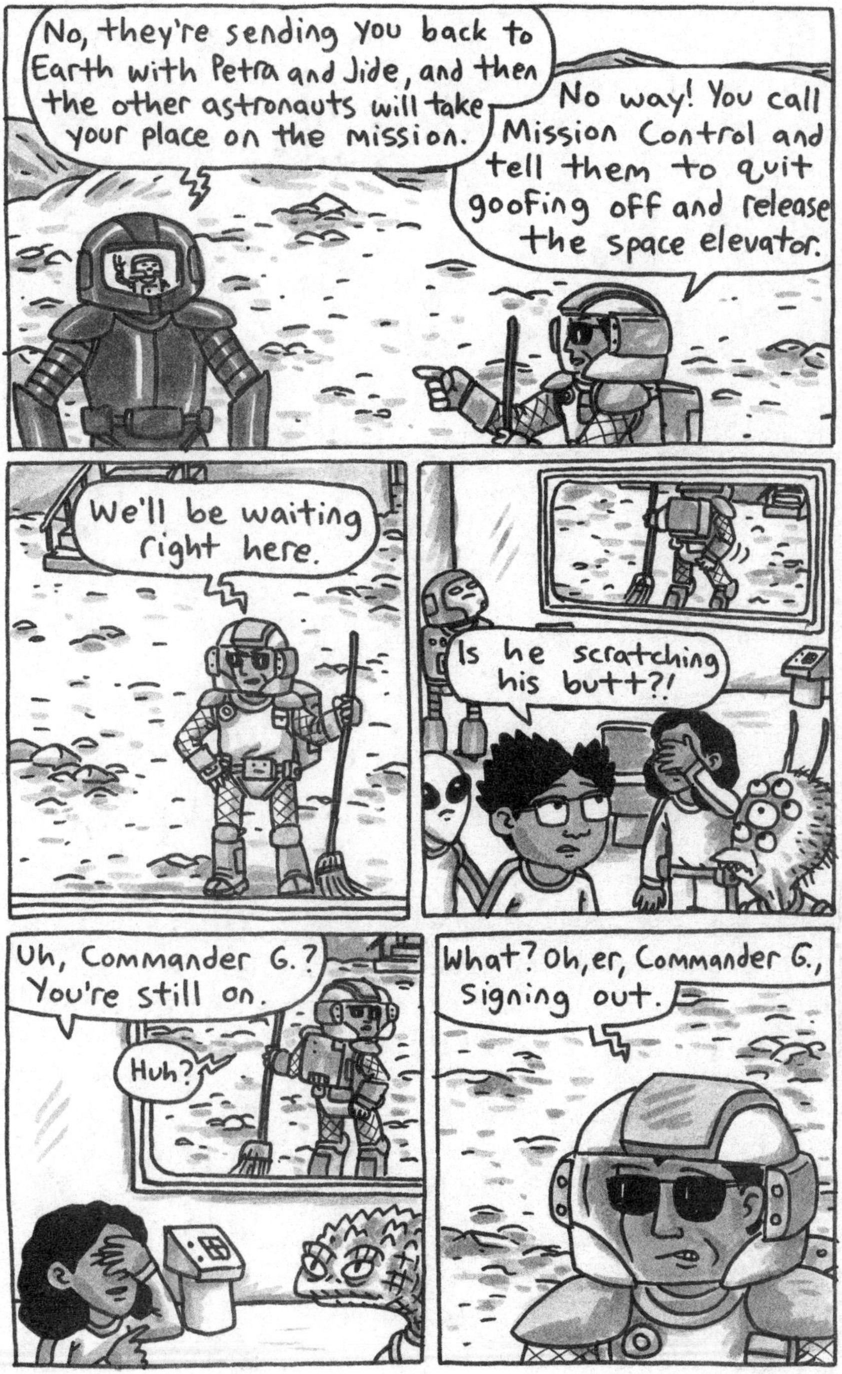
No, they're sending you back to Earth with Petra and Jide, and then the other astronauts will take your place on the mission.
No way! You call Mission Control and tell them to quit goofing off and release the space elevator.
We'll be waiting right here.
Is he scratching his butt?!
Uh, Commander G.? You're still on.
Huh?
What? Oh, er, Commander G., signing out.

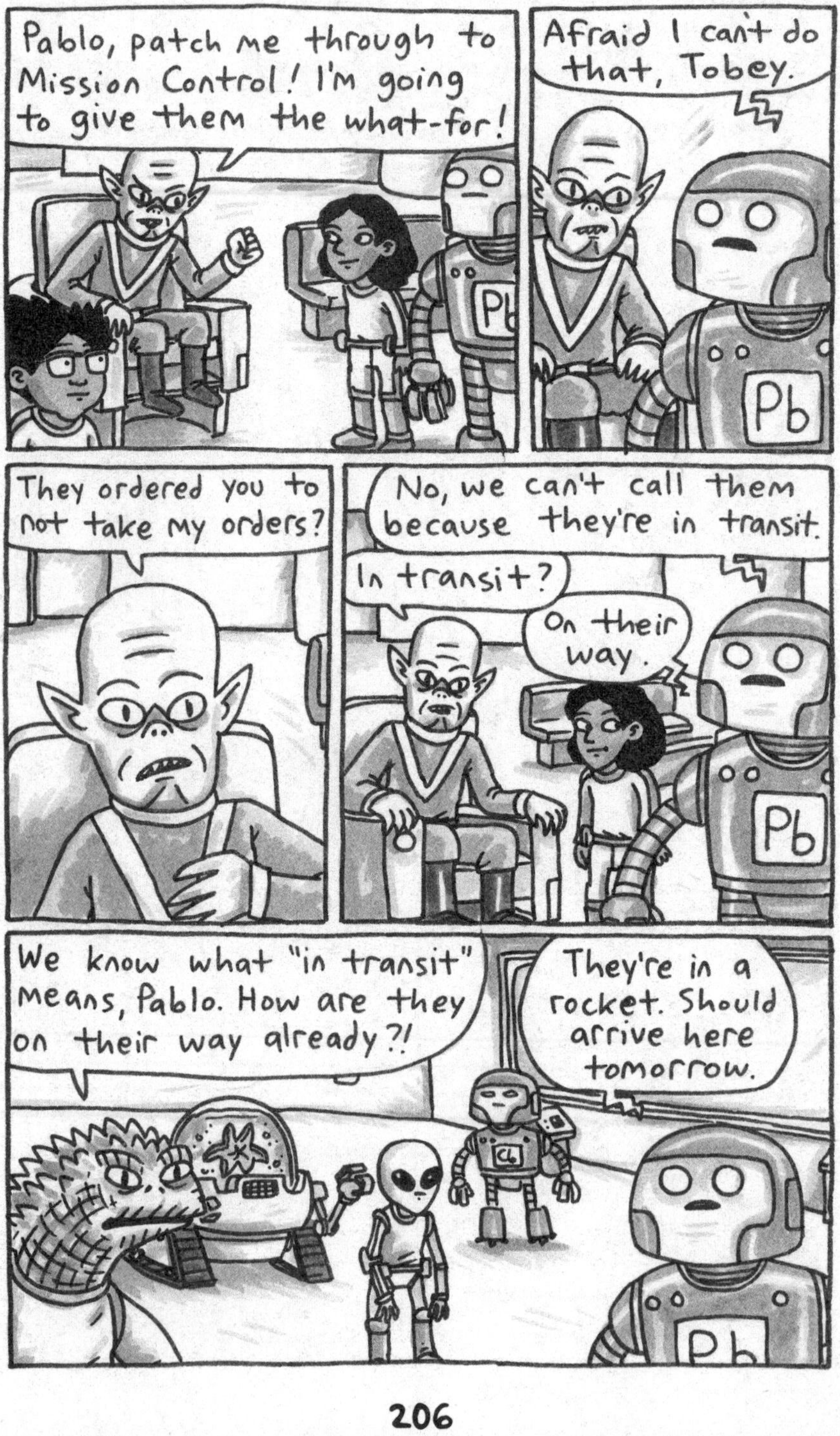
Pablo, patch me through to Mission Control! I'm going to give them the what-for!
Afraid I can't do that, Tobey.
Pb
They ordered you to not take my orders?
No, we can't call them because they're in transit.
In transit?
On their way.
Pb
We know what "in transit" means, Pablo. How are they on their way already?!
They're in a rocket. Should arrive here tomorrow.

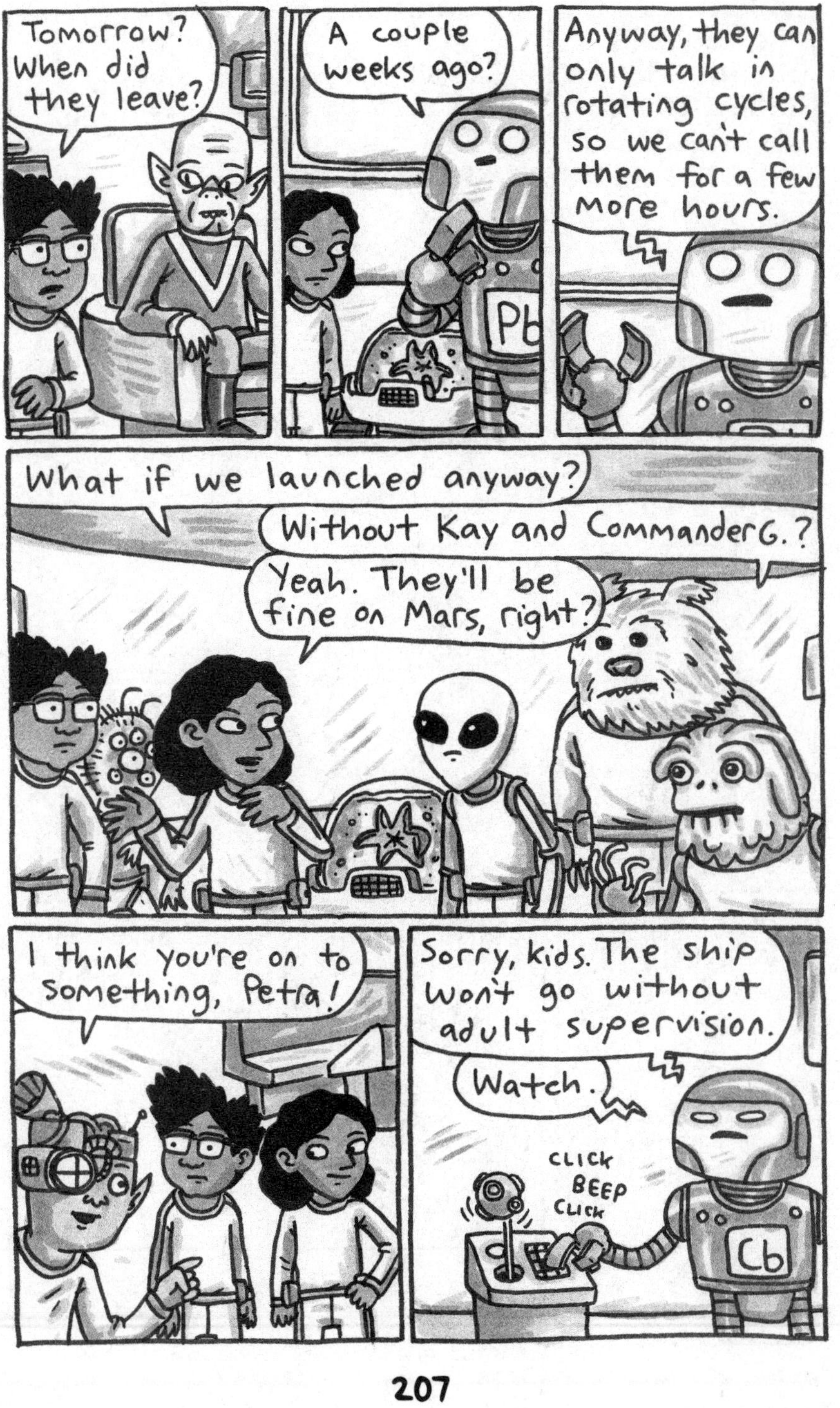
Tomorrow? When did they leave?
A couple weeks ago?
Anyway, they can only talk in rotating cycles, so we can't call them for a few more hours.
What if we launched anyway?
Without Kay and Commander G.?
Yeah. They'll be fine on Mars, right?
I think you're on to something, Petra!
Sorry, kids. The ship won't go without adult supervision.
Watch.
CLICK
BEEP
CLICK
Pb
Cb

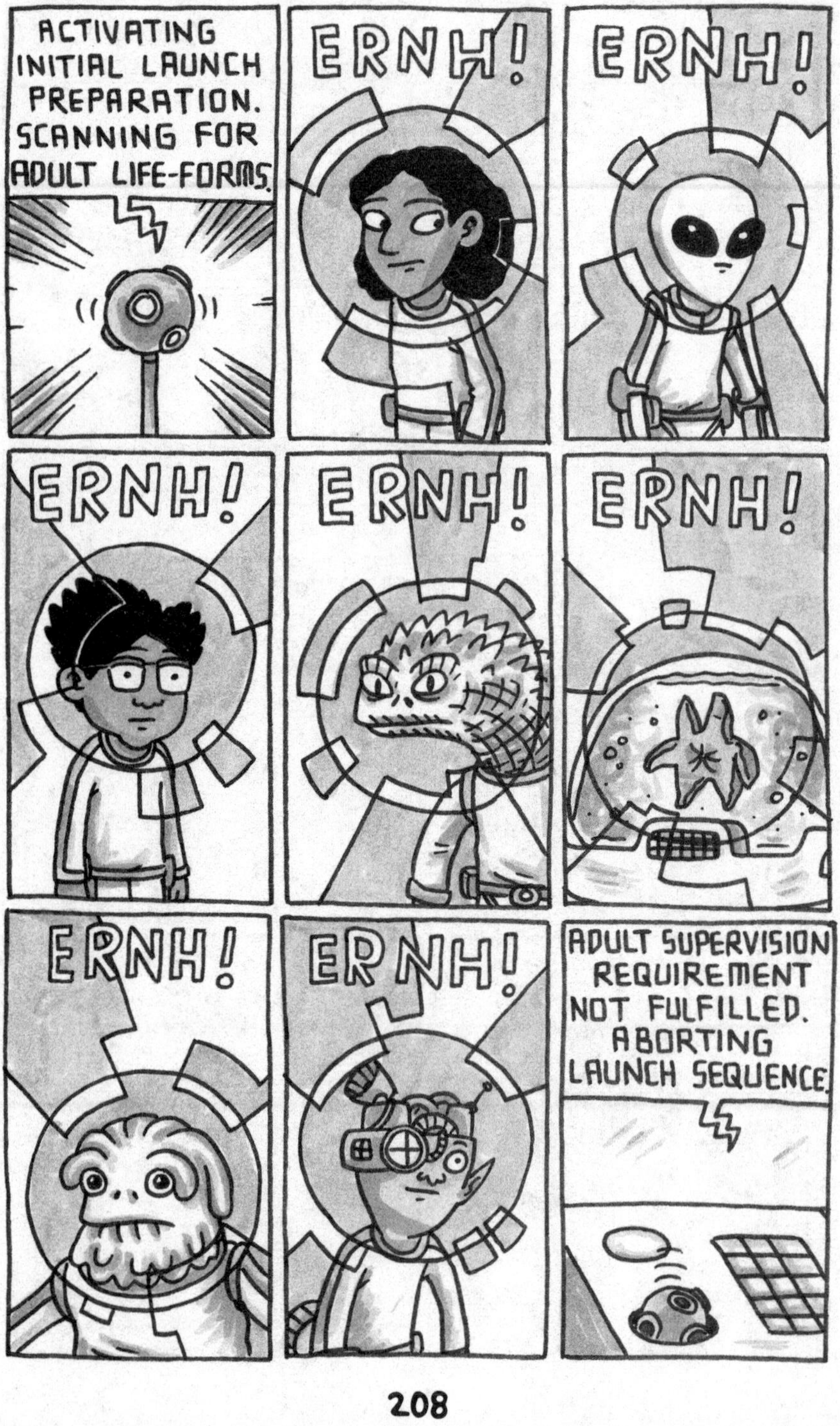
ACTIVATING INITIAL LAUNCH PREPARATION. SCANNING FOR ADULT LIFE-FORMS.
ERNH!
ERNH!
ERNH!
ERNH!
ERNH!
ERNH!
ERNH!
ADULT SUPERVISION REQUIREMENT NOT FULFILLED. ABORTING LAUNCH SEQUENCE.

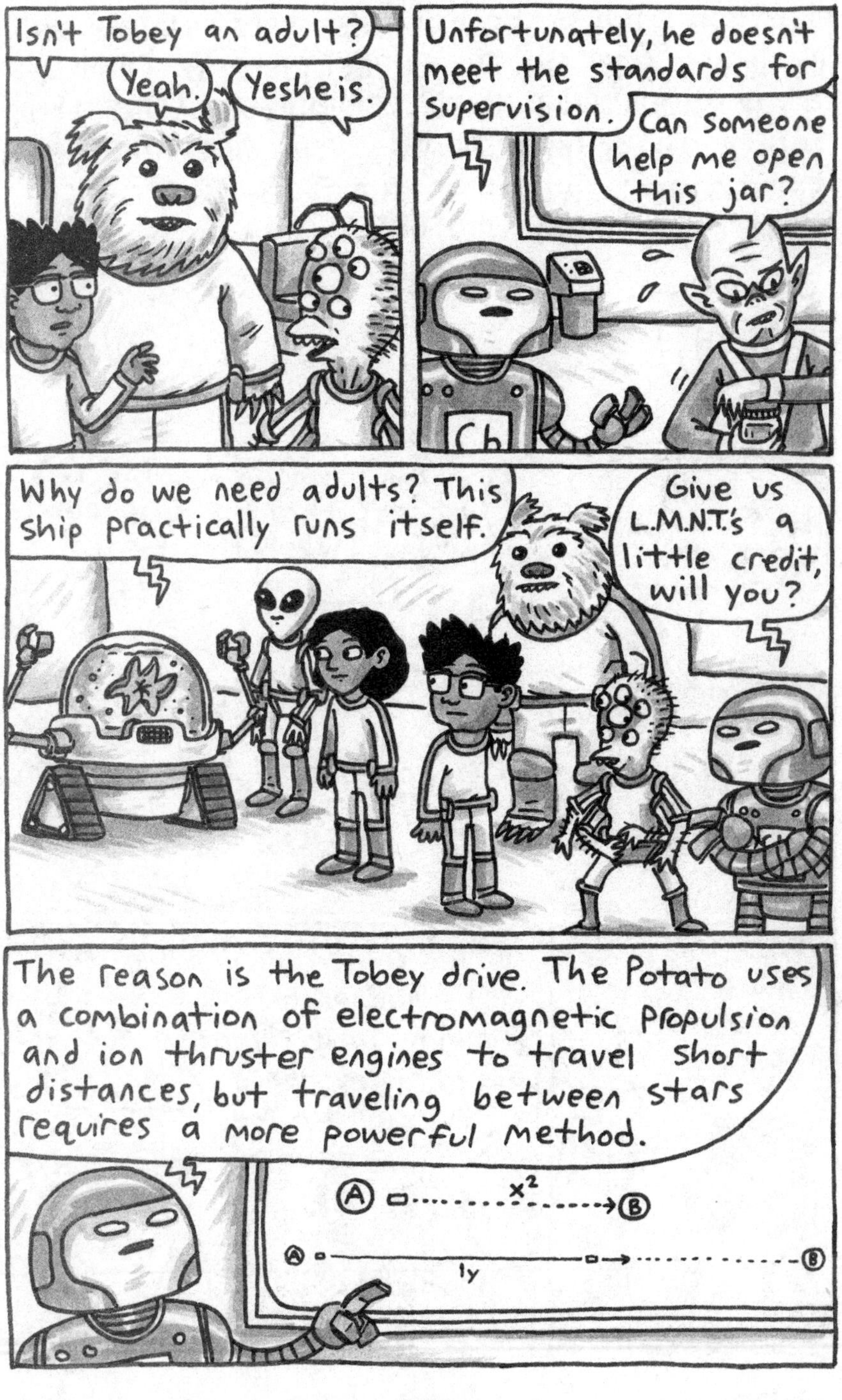
Isn't Tobey an adult?
Yeah.
Yesheis.
Unfortunately, he doesn't meet the standards for supervision.
Can someone help me open this jar?
Why do we need adults? This ship practically runs itself.
Give us L.M.N.T.'s a little credit, will you?
The reason is the Tobey drive. The Potato uses a combination of electromagnetic propulsion and ion thruster engines to travel short distances, but traveling between stars requires a more powerful method.
A
x^2
B
A
1y
B

THE TOBEY DRIVE SHRINKS THE SPACE-TIME AROUND IT, WHILE STAYING THE SAME ITSELF. IT TRAVELS A SHORT DISTANCE OVER COMPRESSED SPACE-TIME, AND WHEN IT DEACTIVATES, THE UNCOMPRESSED SPACE-TIME LEAVES THE SHIP A GREAT DISTANCE AWAY FROM WHERE IT STARTED.

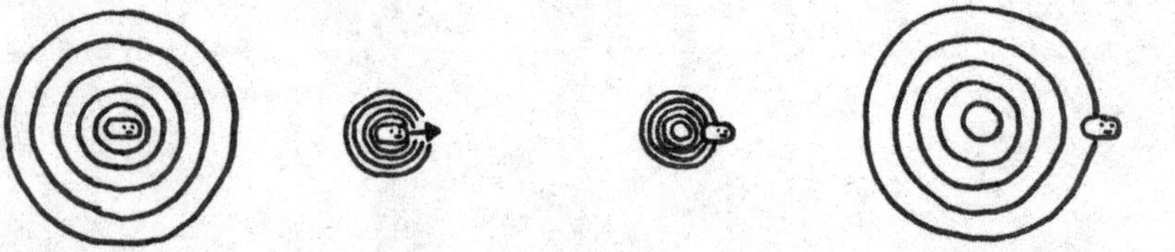

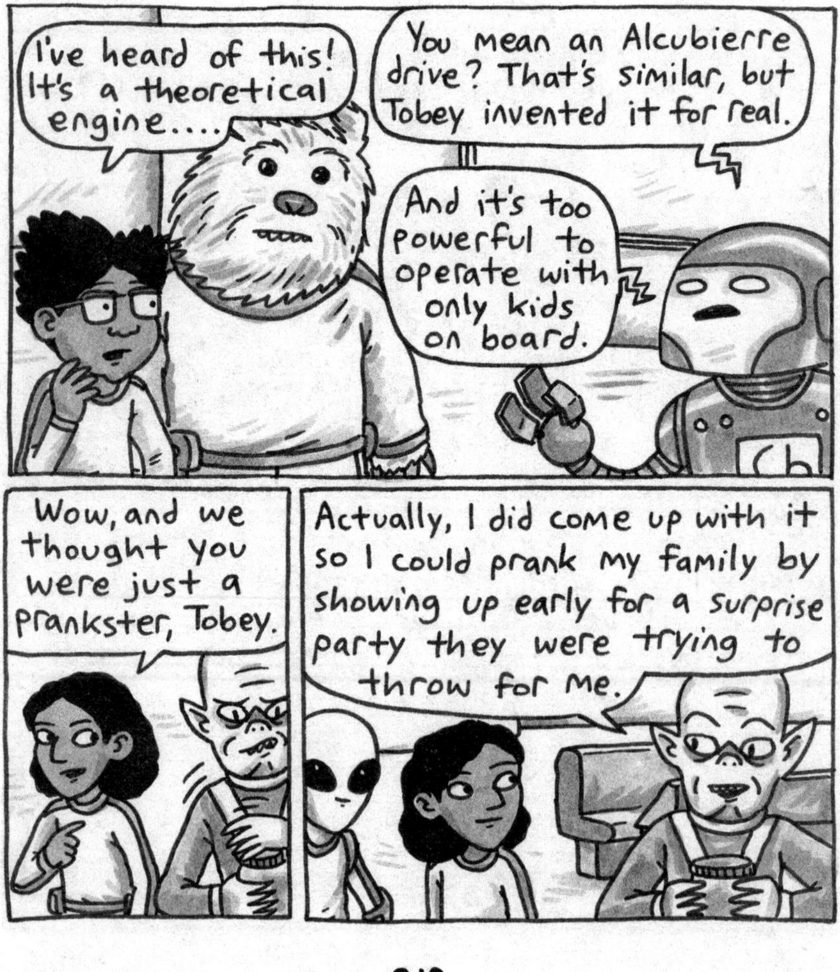
I've heard of this! It's a theoretical engine....
You mean an Alcubierre drive? That's similar, but Tobey invented it for real.
And it's too powerful to operate with only kids on board.
Ch
Wow, and we thought you were just a prankster, Tobey.
Actually, I did come up with it so I could prank my family by showing up early for a surprise party they were trying to throw for me.

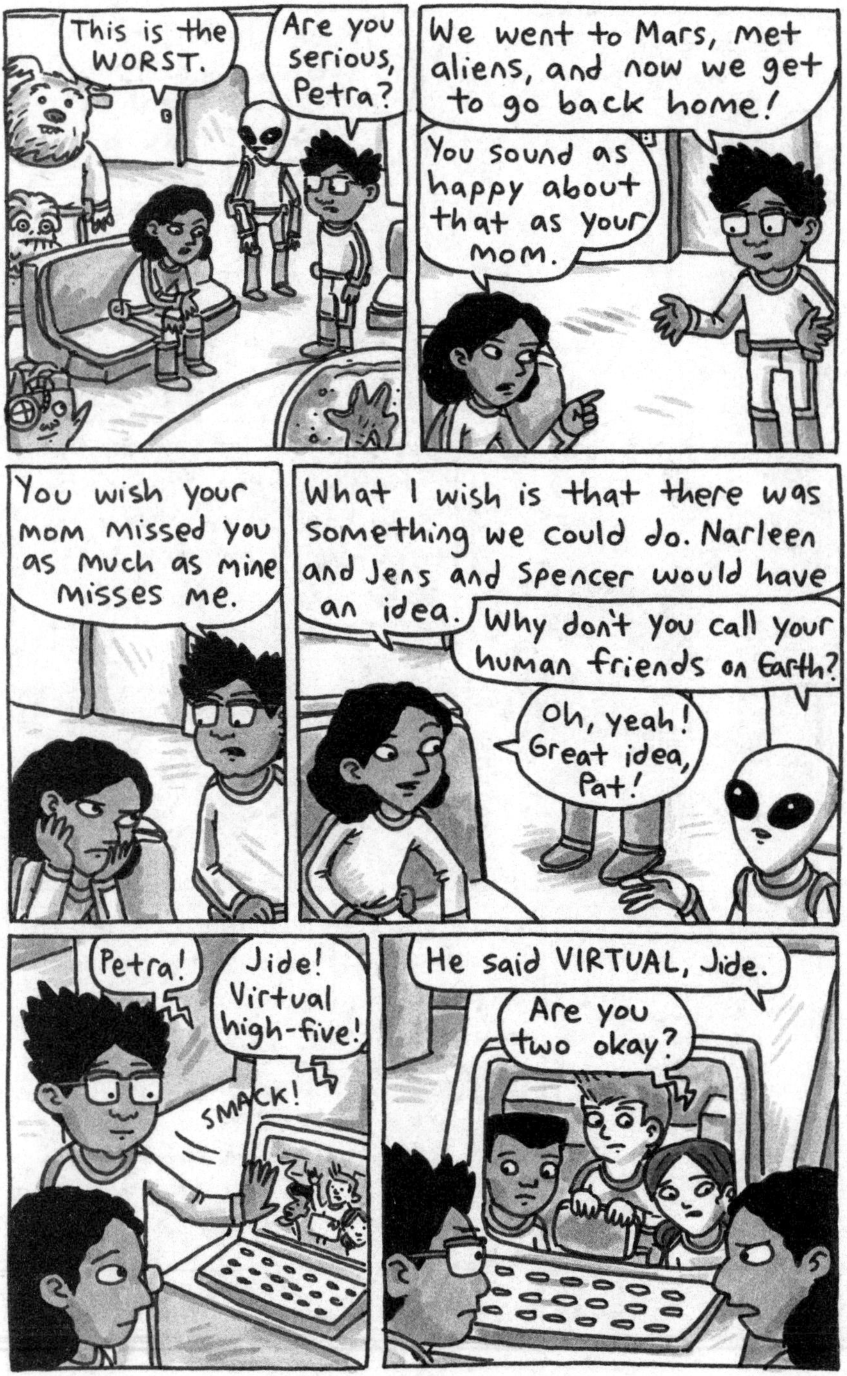
This is the WORST.
Are you serious, Petra?
We went to Mars, met aliens, and now we get to go back home!
You sound as happy about that as your mom.
You wish your mom missed you as much as mine misses me.
What I wish is that there was something we could do. Narleen and Jens and Spencer would have an idea.
Why don't you call your human friends on Earth?
Oh, yeah! Great idea, Pat!
Petra!
Jide! Virtual high-five!
SMACK!
He said VIRTUAL, Jide.
Are you two okay?

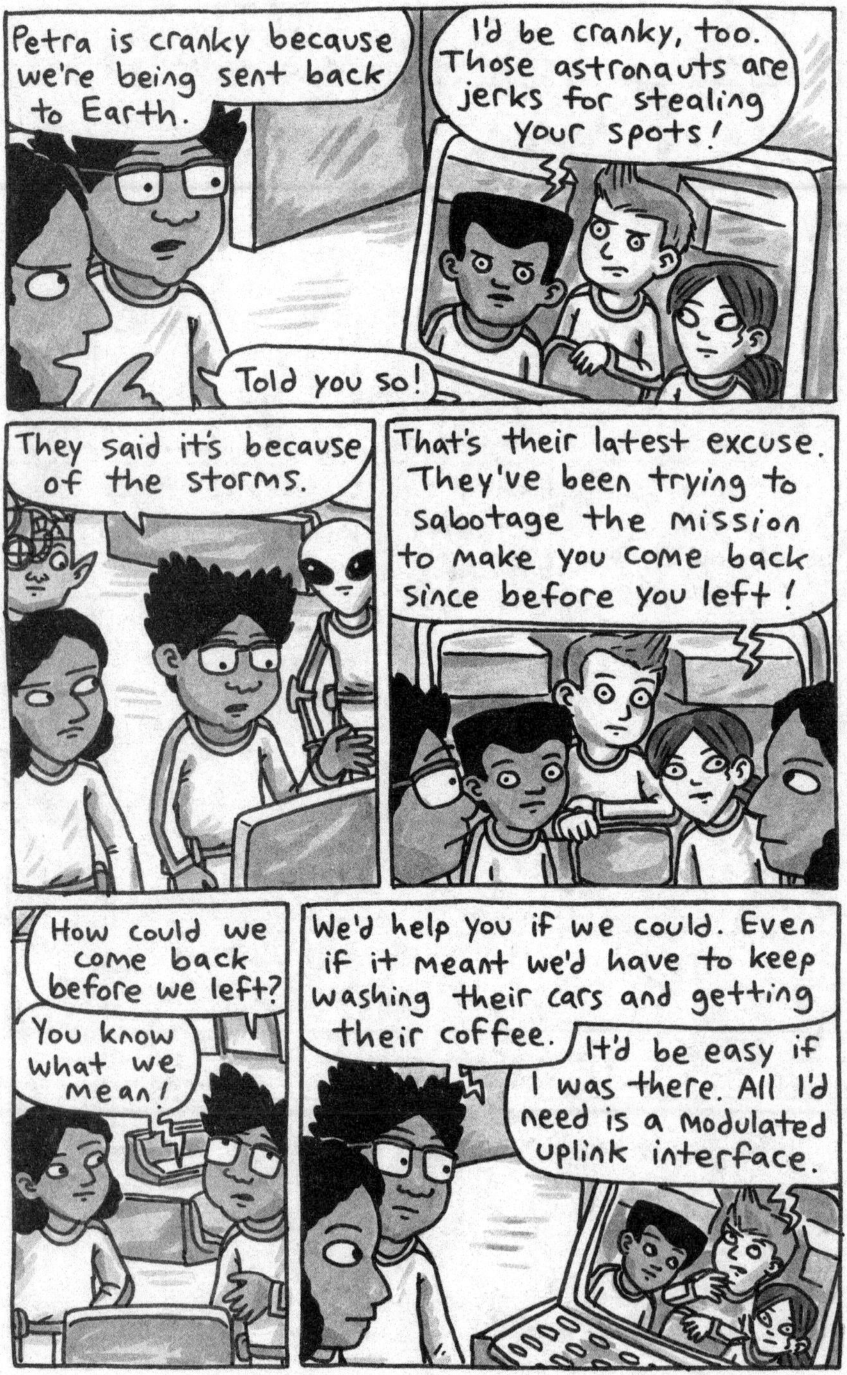
Petra is cranky because we're being sent back to Earth.
I'd be cranky, too. Those astronauts are jerks for stealing your spots!
Told you so!
They said it's because of the storms.
That's their latest excuse. They've been trying to sabotage the mission to make you come back since before you left!
How could we come back before we left?
You know what we mean!
We'd help you if we could. Even if it meant we'd have to keep washing their cars and getting their coffee.
It'd be easy if I was there. All I'd need is a modulated uplink interface.

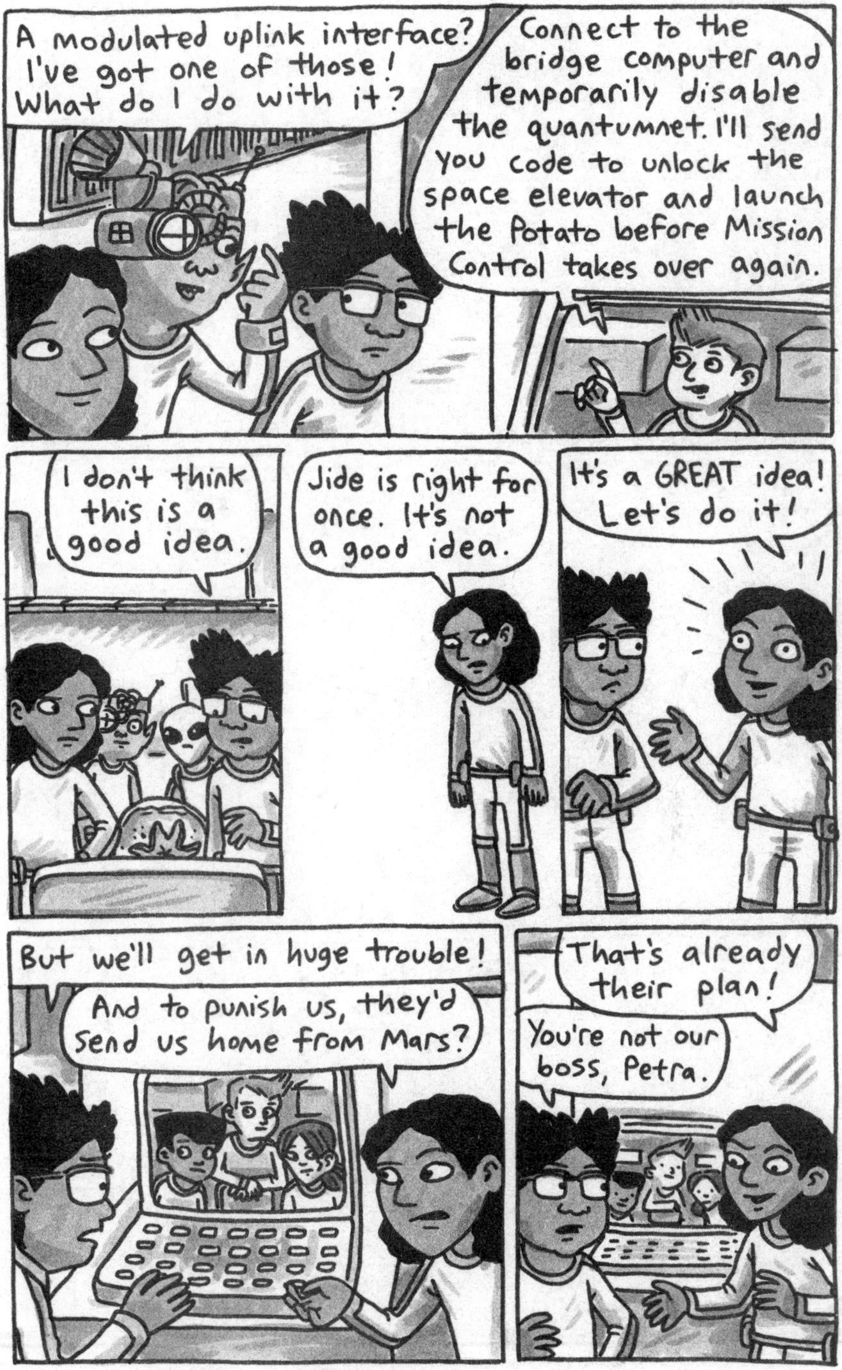
A modulated uplink interface? I've got one of those! What do I do with it?
Connect to the bridge computer and temporarily disable the quantumnet. I'll send you code to unlock the space elevator and launch the Potato before Mission Control takes over again.
I don't think this is a good idea.
Jide is right for once. It's not a good idea.
It's a GREAT idea! Let's do it!
But we'll get in huge trouble!
And to punish us, they'd send us home from Mars?
That's already their plan!
You're not our boss, Petra.

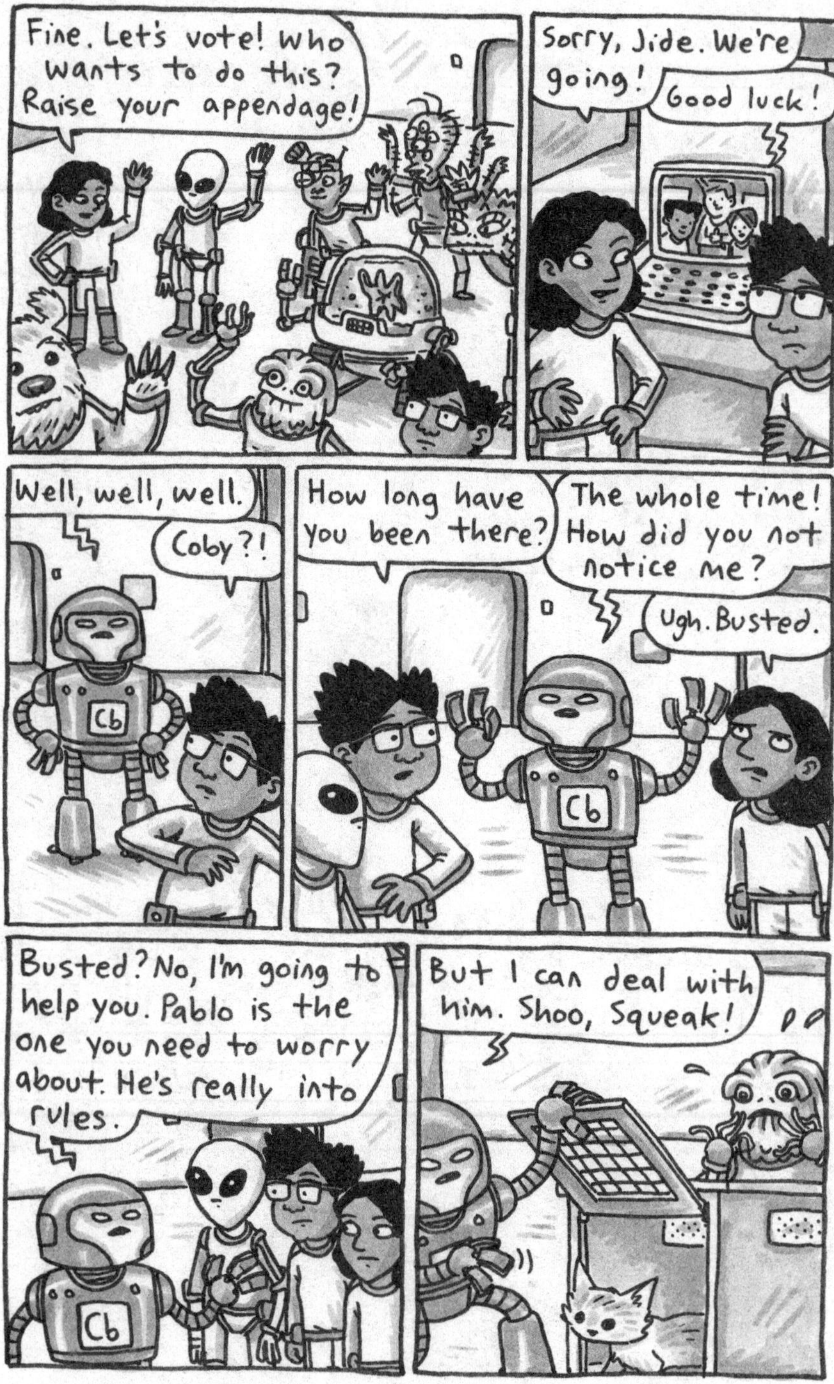

Fine. Let's vote! Who wants to do this? Raise your appendage!
Sorry, Jide. We're going!
Good luck!
Well, well, well.
Coby?!
How long have you been there?
The whole time! How did you not notice me?
Ugh. Busted.
Busted? No, I'm going to help you. Pablo is the one you need to worry about. He's really into rules.
But I can deal with him. Shoo, Squeak!

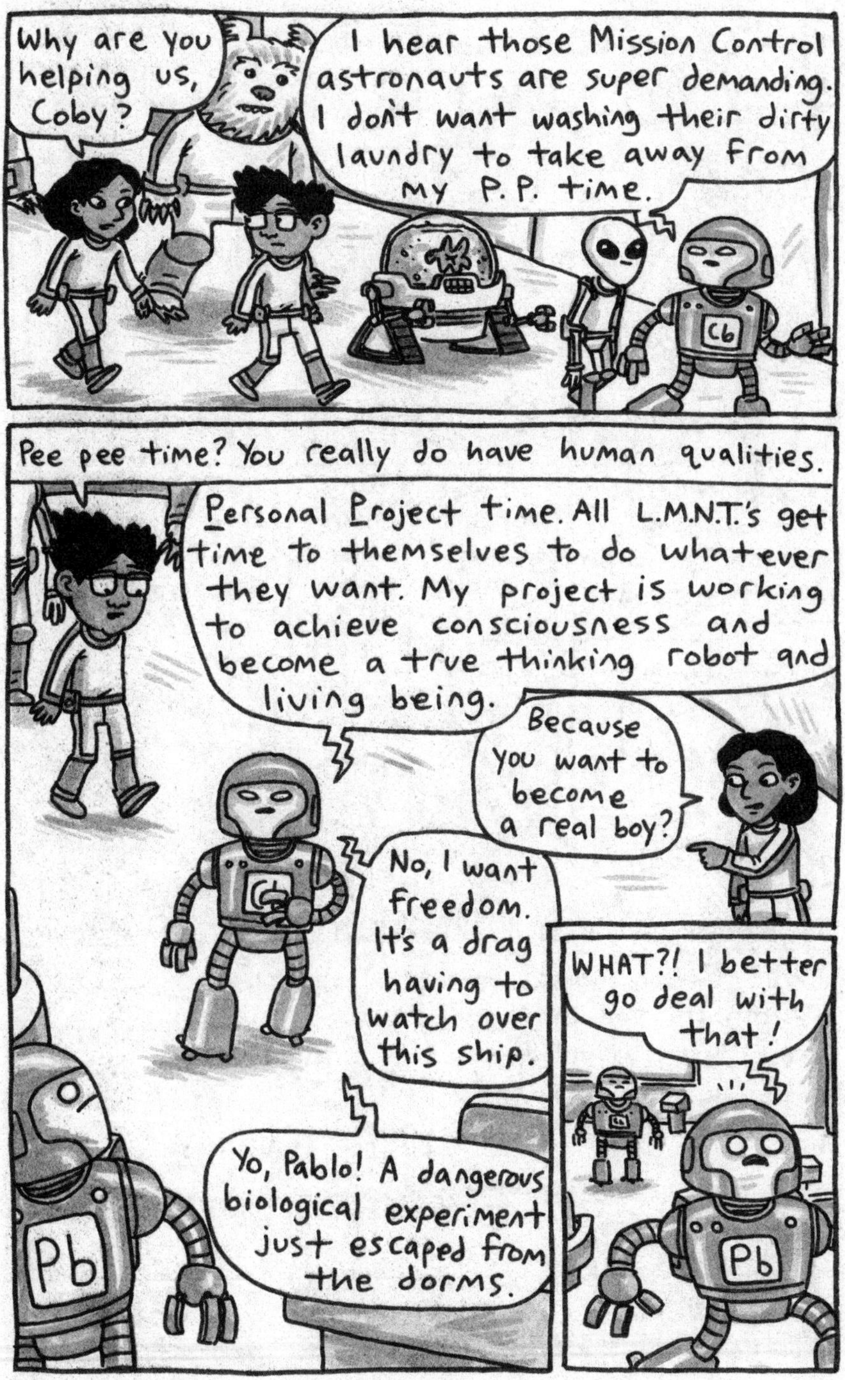
Why are you helping us, Coby?
I hear those Mission Control astronauts are super demanding. I don't want washing their dirty laundry to take away from my P.P. time.
Pee pee time? You really do have human qualities.
Personal Project time. All L.M.N.T.'s get time to themselves to do whatever they want. My project is working to achieve consciousness and become a true thinking robot and living being.
Because you want to become a real boy?
No, I want freedom. It's a drag having to watch over this ship.
Yo, Pablo! A dangerous biological experiment just escaped from the dorms.
WHAT?! I better go deal with that!
Cb
Pb

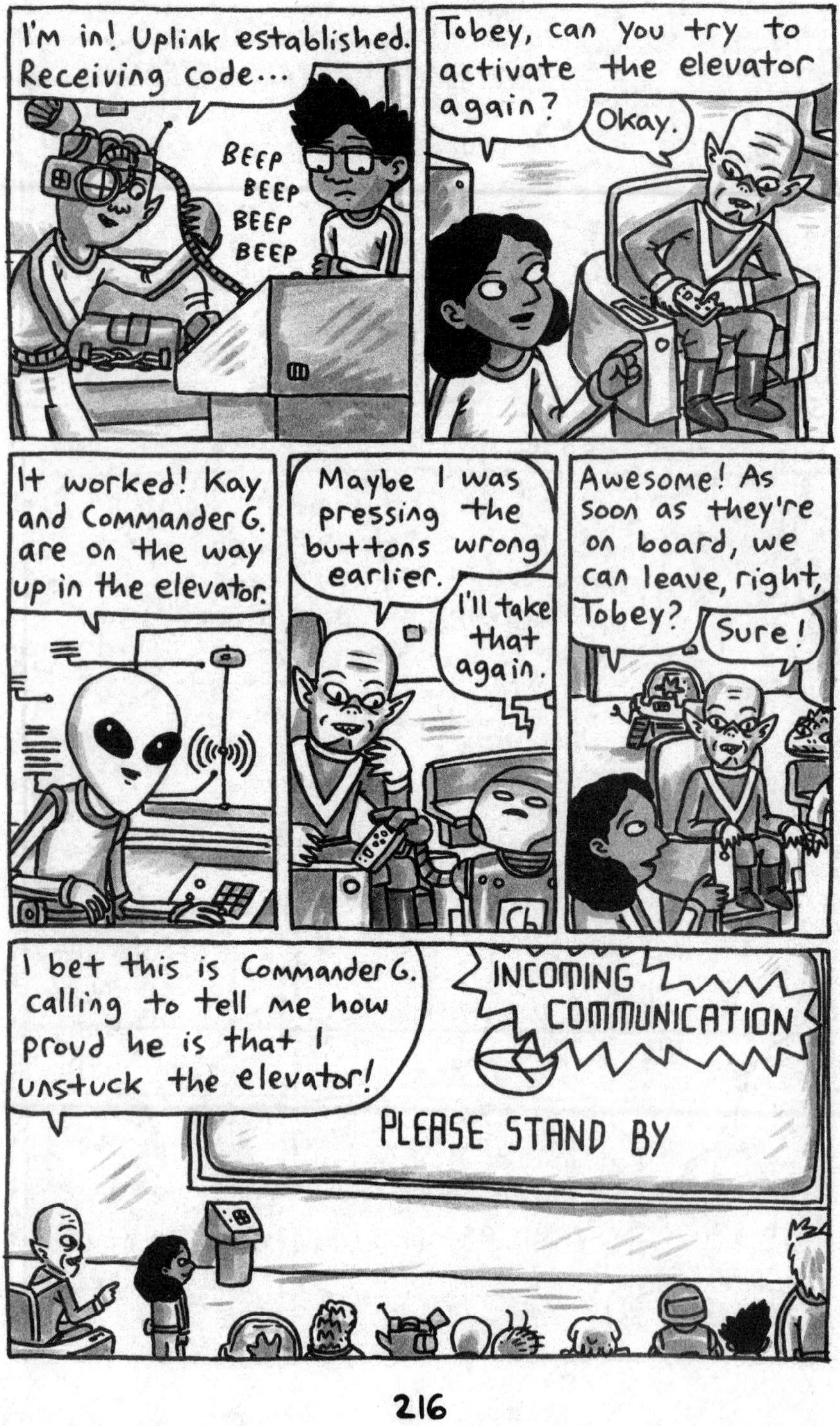
I'm in! Uplink established. Receiving code...
BEEP BEEP BEEP BEEP
Tobey, can you try to activate the elevator again?
Okay.
It worked! Kay and Commander G. are on the way up in the elevator.
Maybe I was pressing the buttons wrong earlier.
I'll take that again.
Awesome! As soon as they're on board, we can leave, right, Tobey?
Sure!
I bet this is Commander G. calling to tell me how proud he is that I unstuck the elevator!
INCOMING COMMUNICATION
PLEASE STAND BY

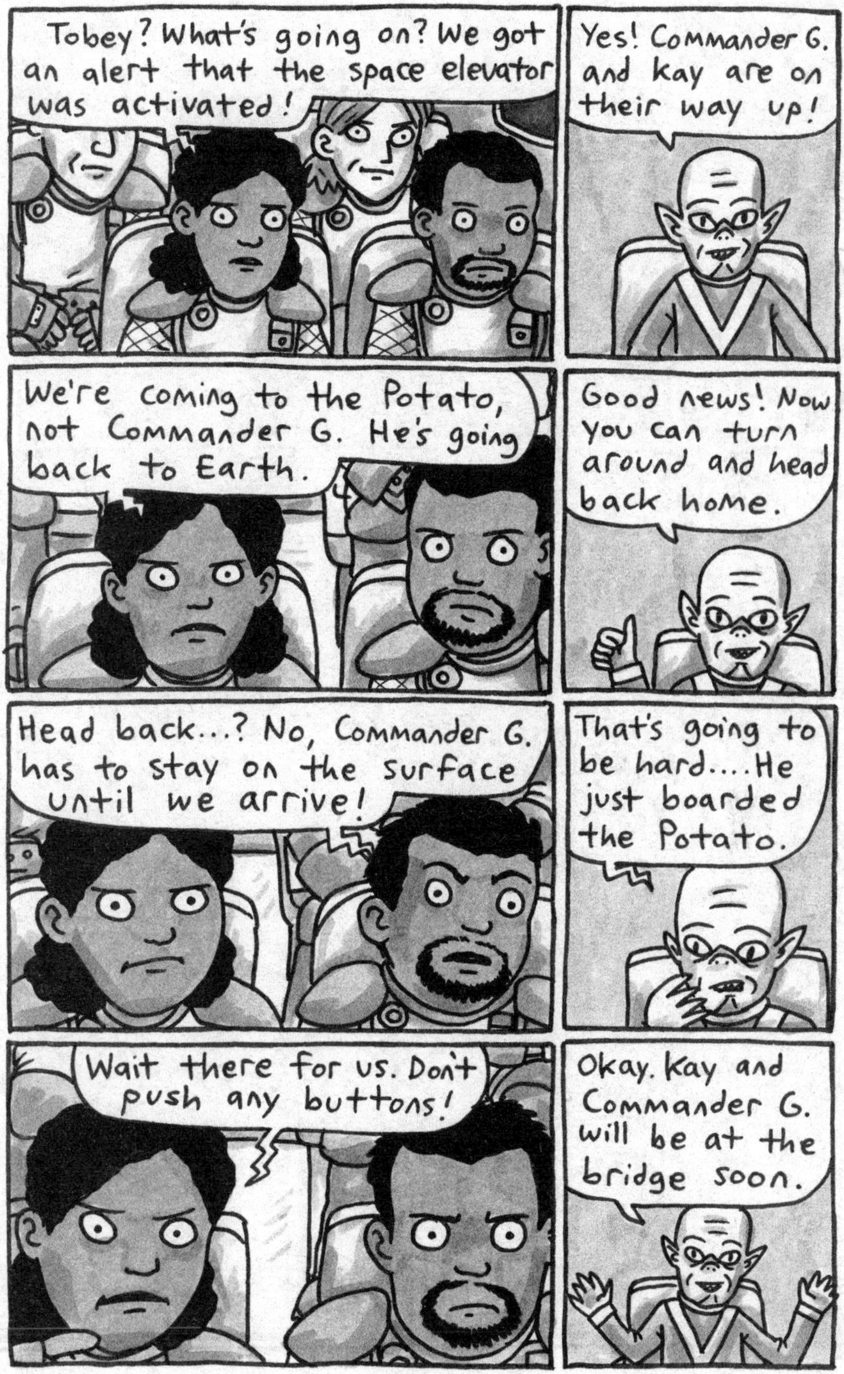
Tobey? What's going on? We got an alert that the space elevator was activated!
Yes! Commander G. and Kay are on their way up!
We're coming to the Potato, not Commander G. He's going back to Earth.
Good news! Now you can turn around and head back home.
Head back...? No, Commander G. has to stay on the surface until we arrive!
That's going to be hard....He just boarded the Potato.
Wait there for us. Don't push any buttons!
Okay. Kay and Commander G. will be at the bridge soon.

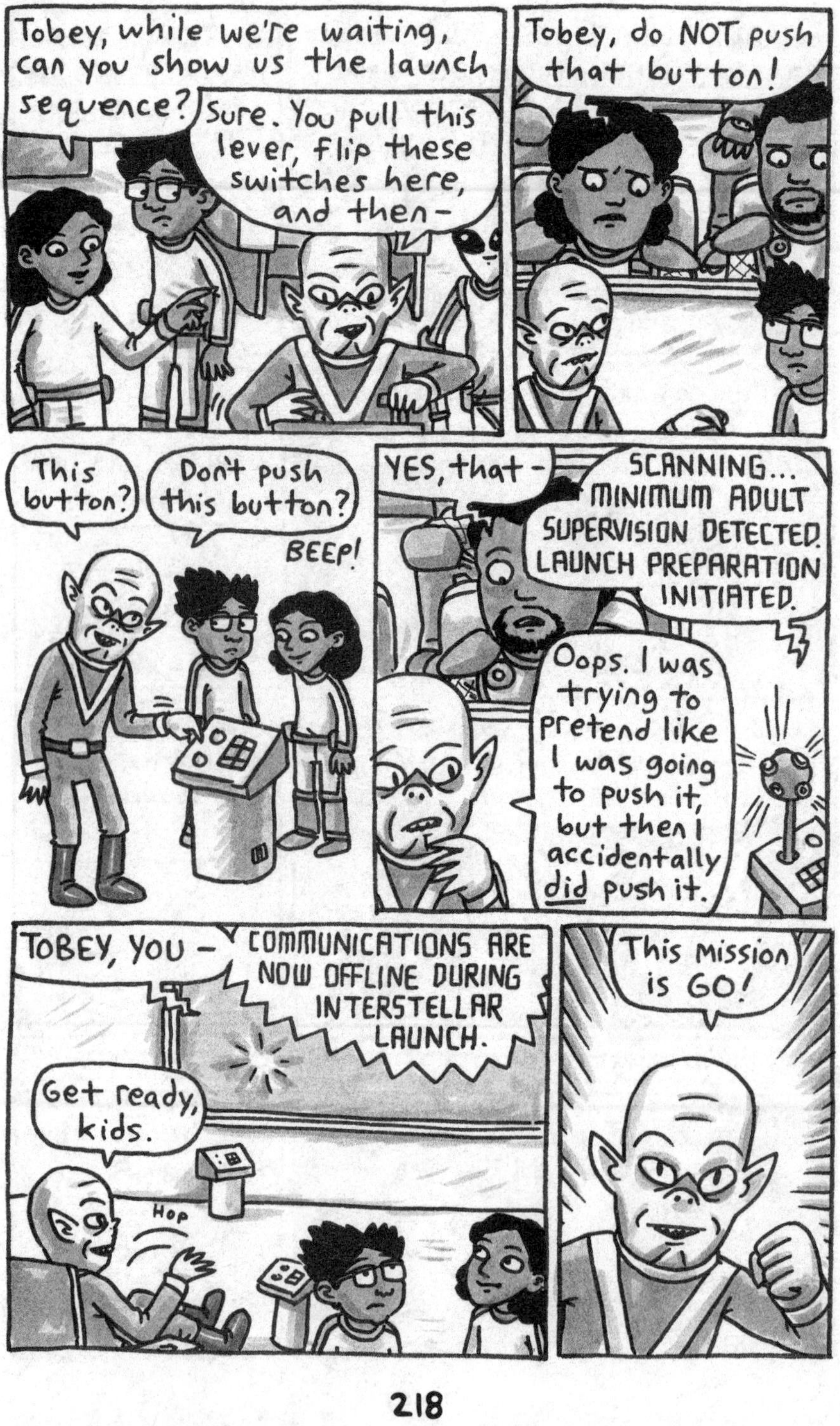
Tobey, while we're waiting, can you show us the launch sequence?
Sure. You pull this lever, flip these switches here, and then-
Tobey, do NOT push that button!
This button?
Don't push this button?
BEEP!
YES, that-
SCANNING... MINIMUM ADULT SUPERVISION DETECTED. LAUNCH PREPARATION INITIATED.
Oops. I was trying to pretend like I was going to push it, but then I accidentally did push it.
TOBEY, YOU-
COMMUNICATIONS ARE NOW OFFLINE DURING INTERSTELLAR LAUNCH.
Get ready, kids.
HOP
This mission is GO!

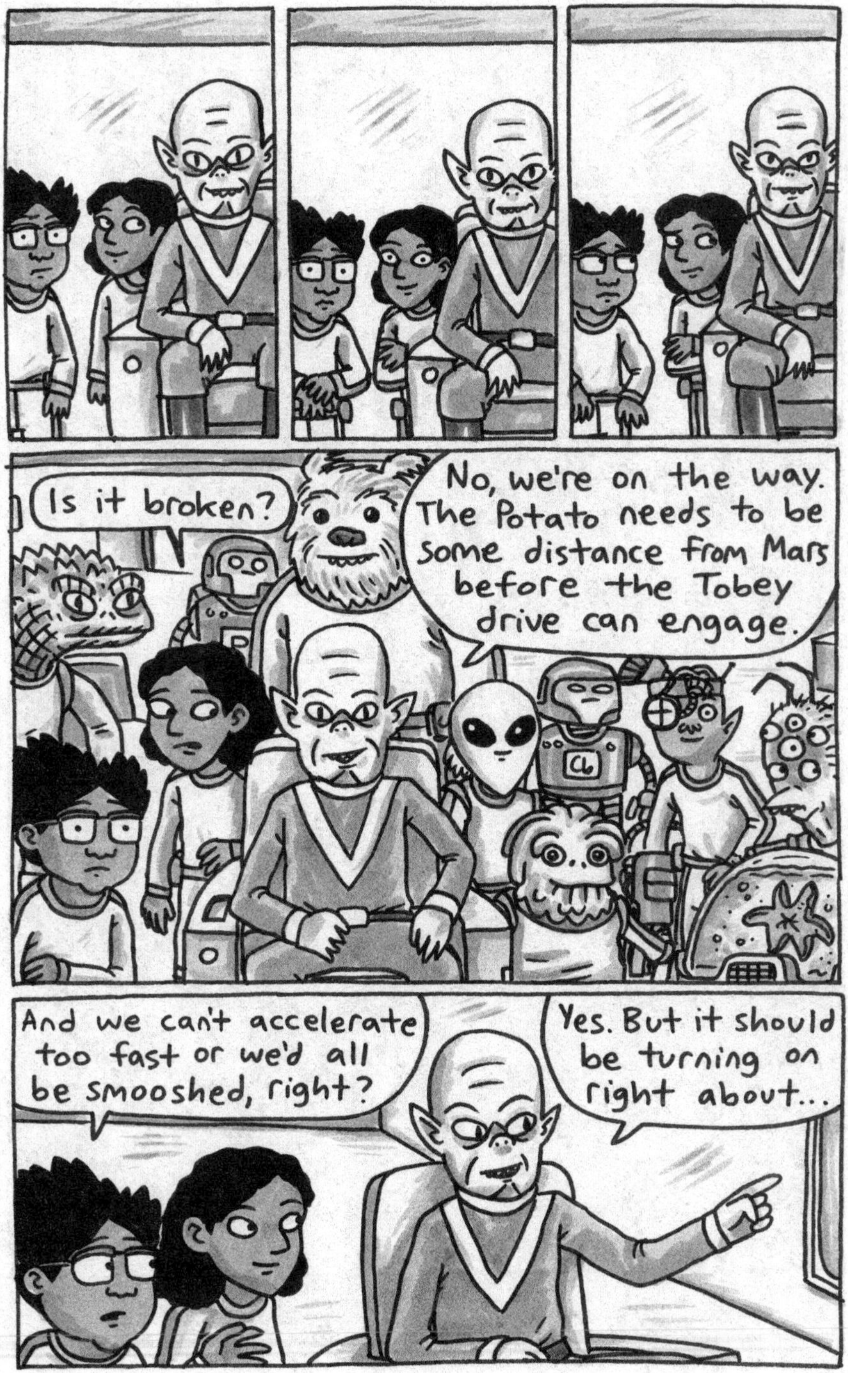
Is it broken?
No, we're on the way. The Potato needs to be some distance from Mars before the Tobey drive can engage.
And we can't accelerate too fast or we'd all be smooshed, right?
Yes. But it should be turning on right about...

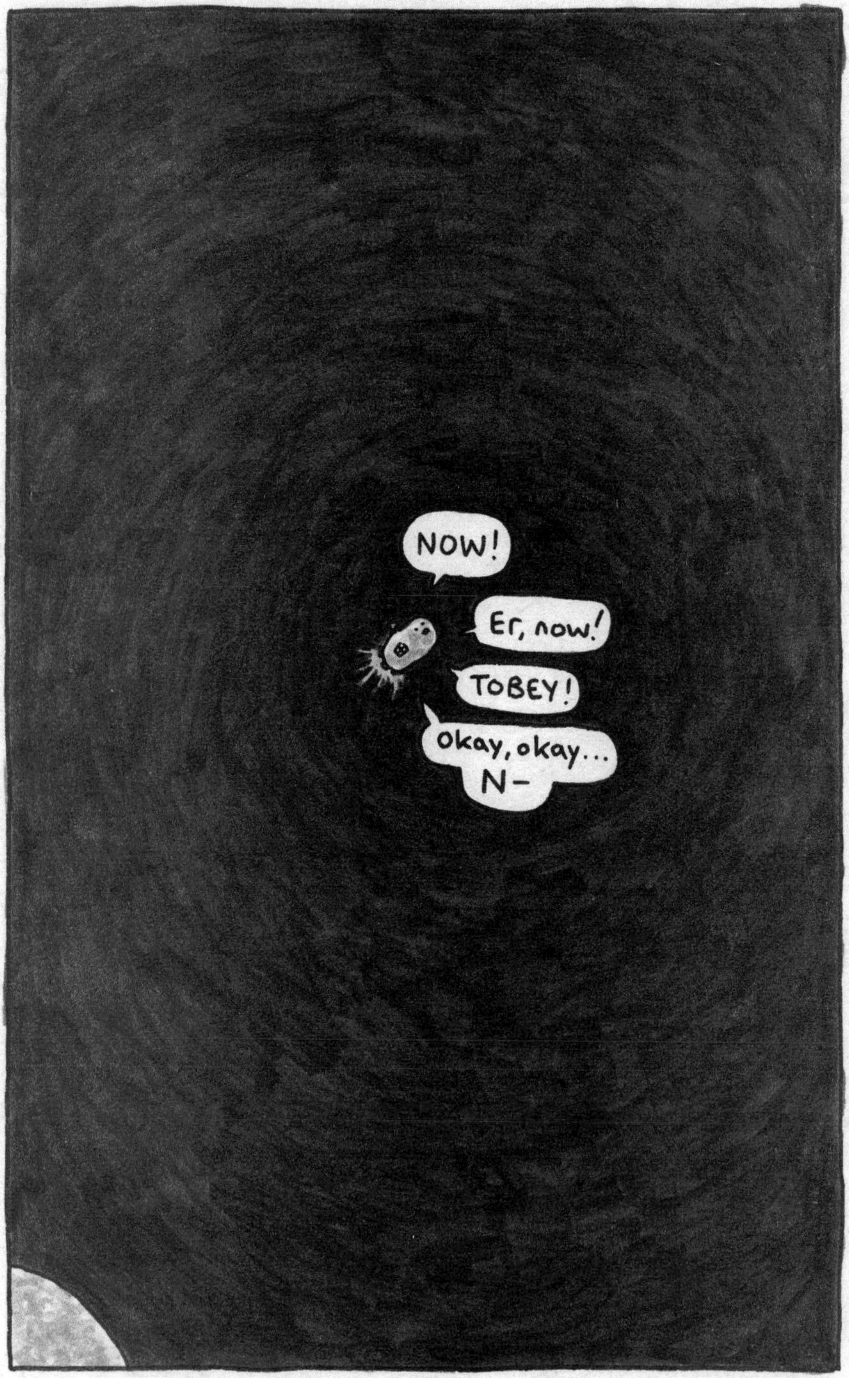
NOW!
Er, now!
TOBEY!
Okay, okay... N-

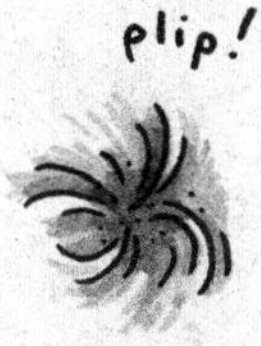
plip!

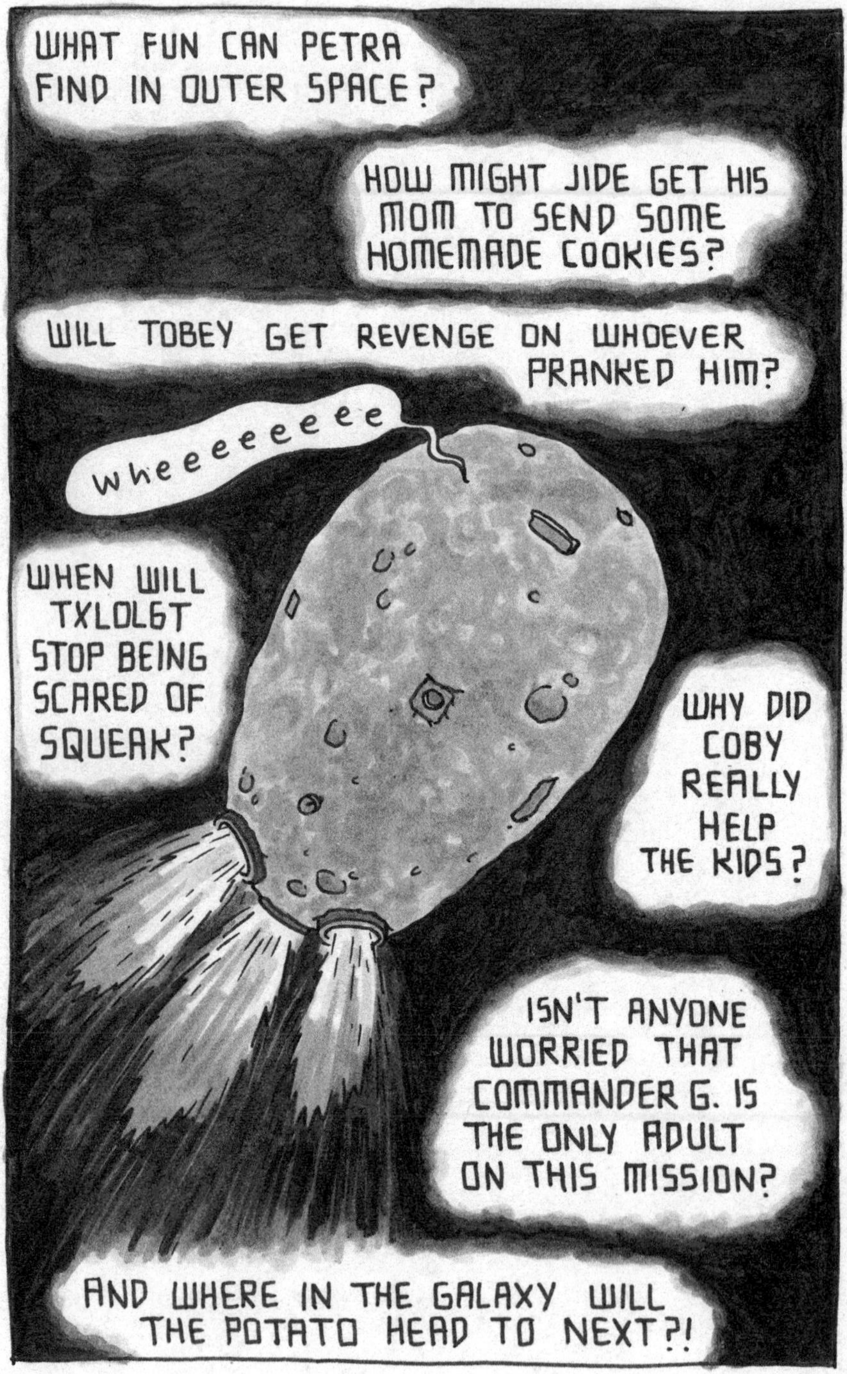
WHAT FUN CAN PETRA FIND IN OUTER SPACE?
HOW MIGHT JIDE GET HIS MOM TO SEND SOME HOMEMADE COOKIES?
WILL TOBEY GET REVENGE ON WHOEVER PRANKED HIM?
wheeeeeeeee
WHEN WILL TXLOLGT STOP BEING SCARED OF SQUEAK?
WHY DID COBY REALLY HELP THE KIDS?
ISN'T ANYONE WORRIED THAT COMMANDER G. IS THE ONLY ADULT ON THIS MISSION?
AND WHERE IN THE GALAXY WILL THE POTATO HEAD TO NEXT?!

PHENOMENAL
PHENOMENON

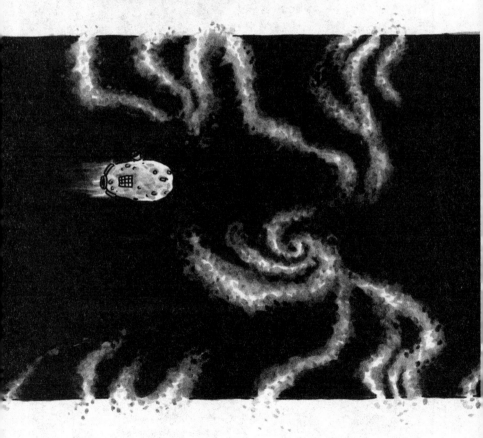

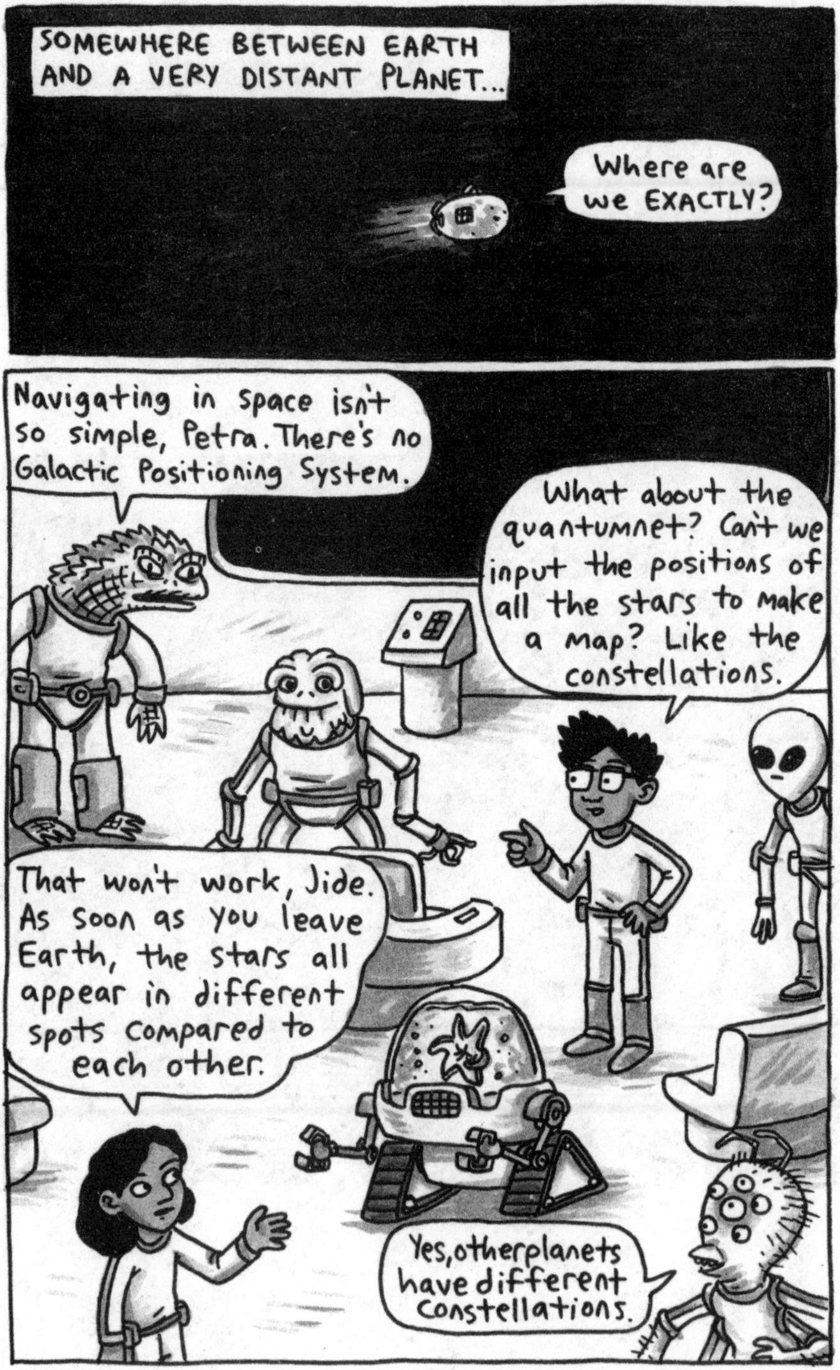
SOMEWHERE BETWEEN EARTH AND A VERY DISTANT PLANET...
Where are we EXACTLY?
Navigating in space isn't so simple, Petra. There's no Galactic Positioning System.
What about the quantumnet? Can't we input the positions of all the stars to make a map? Like the constellations.
That won't work, Jide. As soon as you leave Earth, the stars all appear in different spots compared to each other.
Yes, other planets have different constellations.

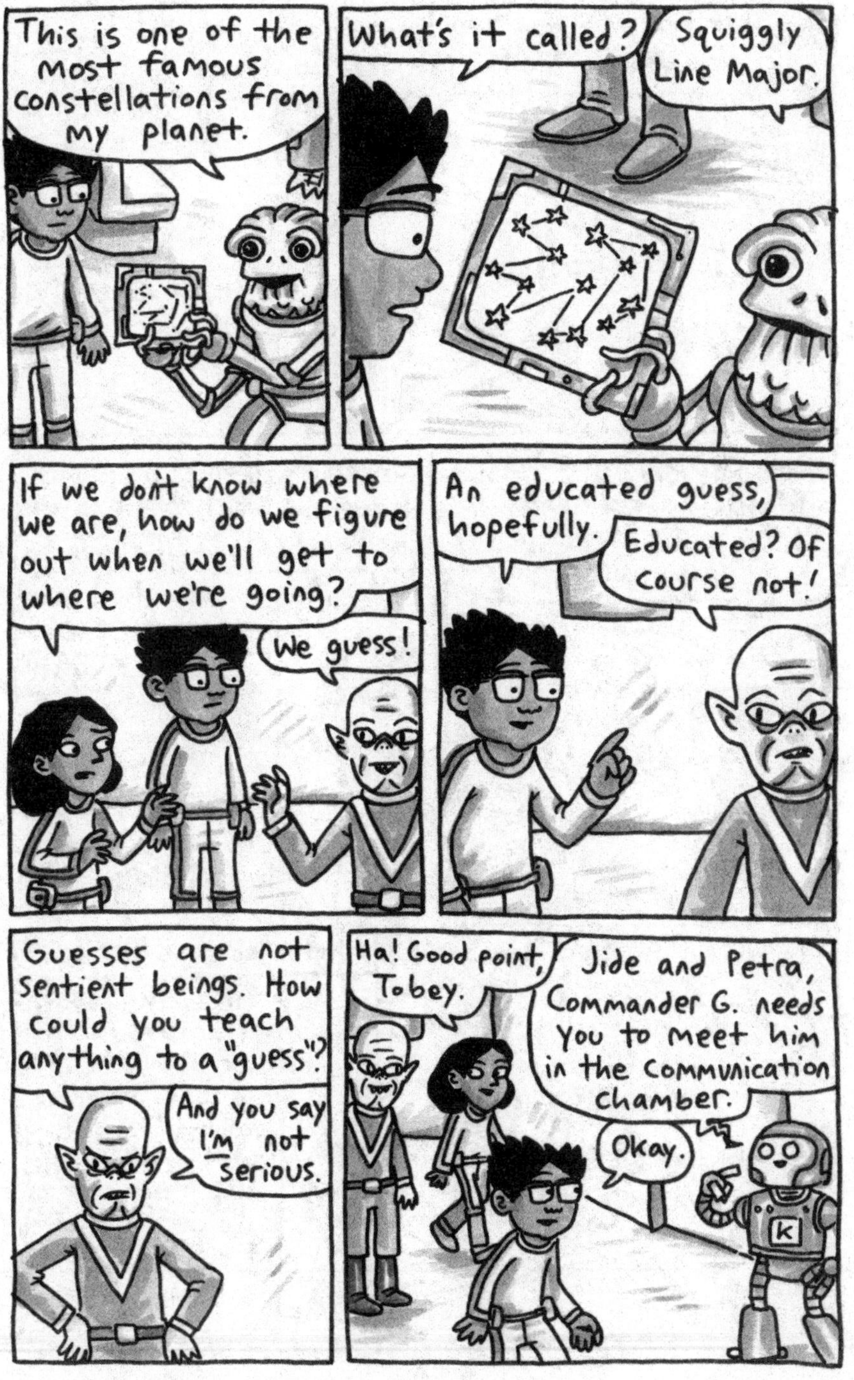
This is one of the most famous constellations from my planet.
What's it called?
Squiggly Line Major.
If we don't know where we are, how do we figure out when we'll get to where we're going?
We guess!
An educated guess, hopefully.
Educated? Of course not!
Guesses are not sentient beings. How could you teach anything to a "guess"?
And you say I'm not serious.
Ha! Good point, Tobey.
Jide and Petra, Commander G. needs you to meet him in the communication chamber.
Okay.

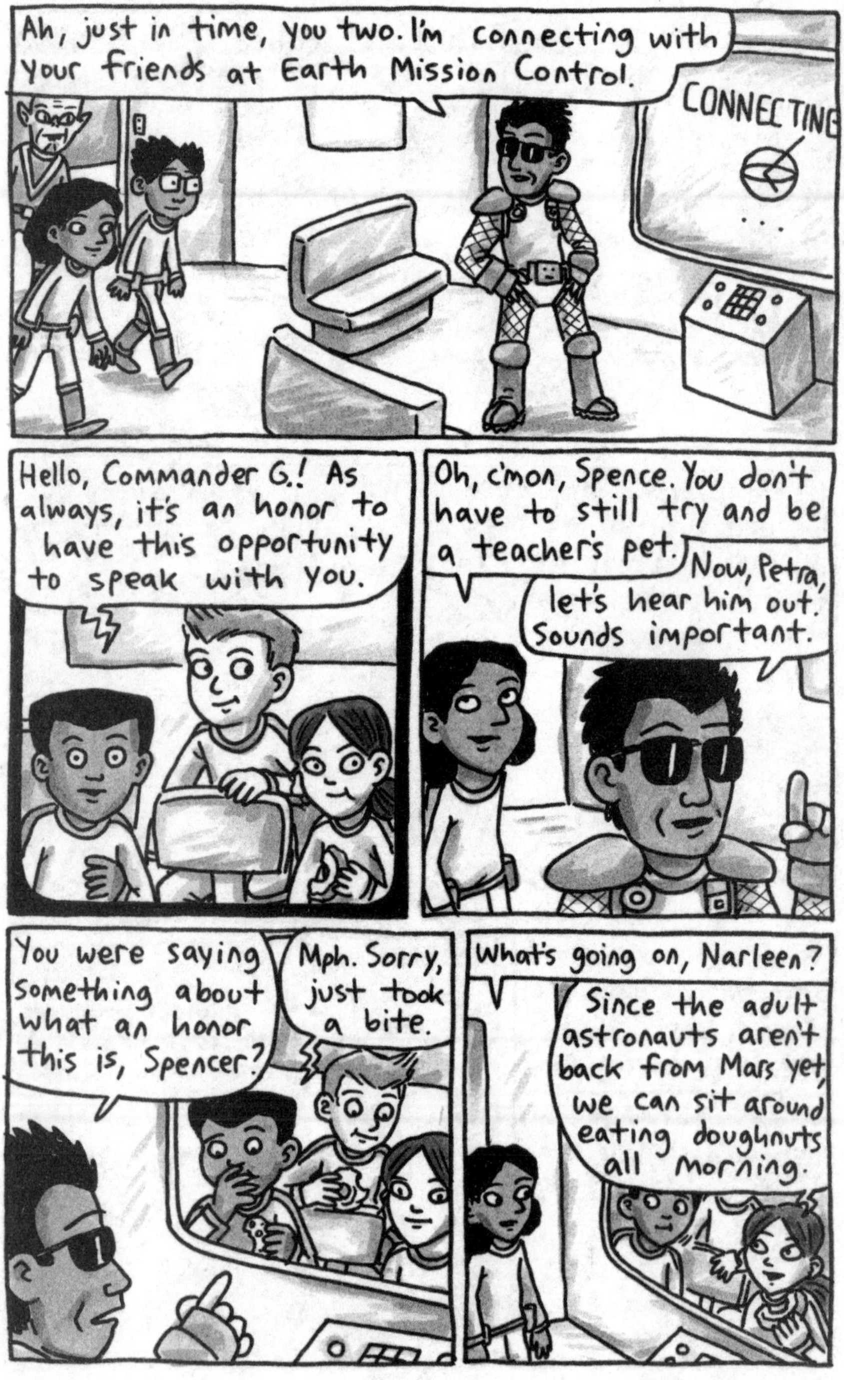

Ah, just in time, you two. I'm connecting with your friends at Earth Mission Control.
CONNECTING
...
Hello, Commander G.! As always, it's an honor to have this opportunity to speak with you.
Oh, c'mon, Spence. You don't have to still try and be a teacher's pet.
Now, Petra, let's hear him out. Sounds important.
You were saying something about what an honor this is, Spencer?
Mph. Sorry, just took a bite.
What's going on, Narleen?
Since the adult astronauts aren't back from Mars yet, we can sit around eating doughnuts all morning.

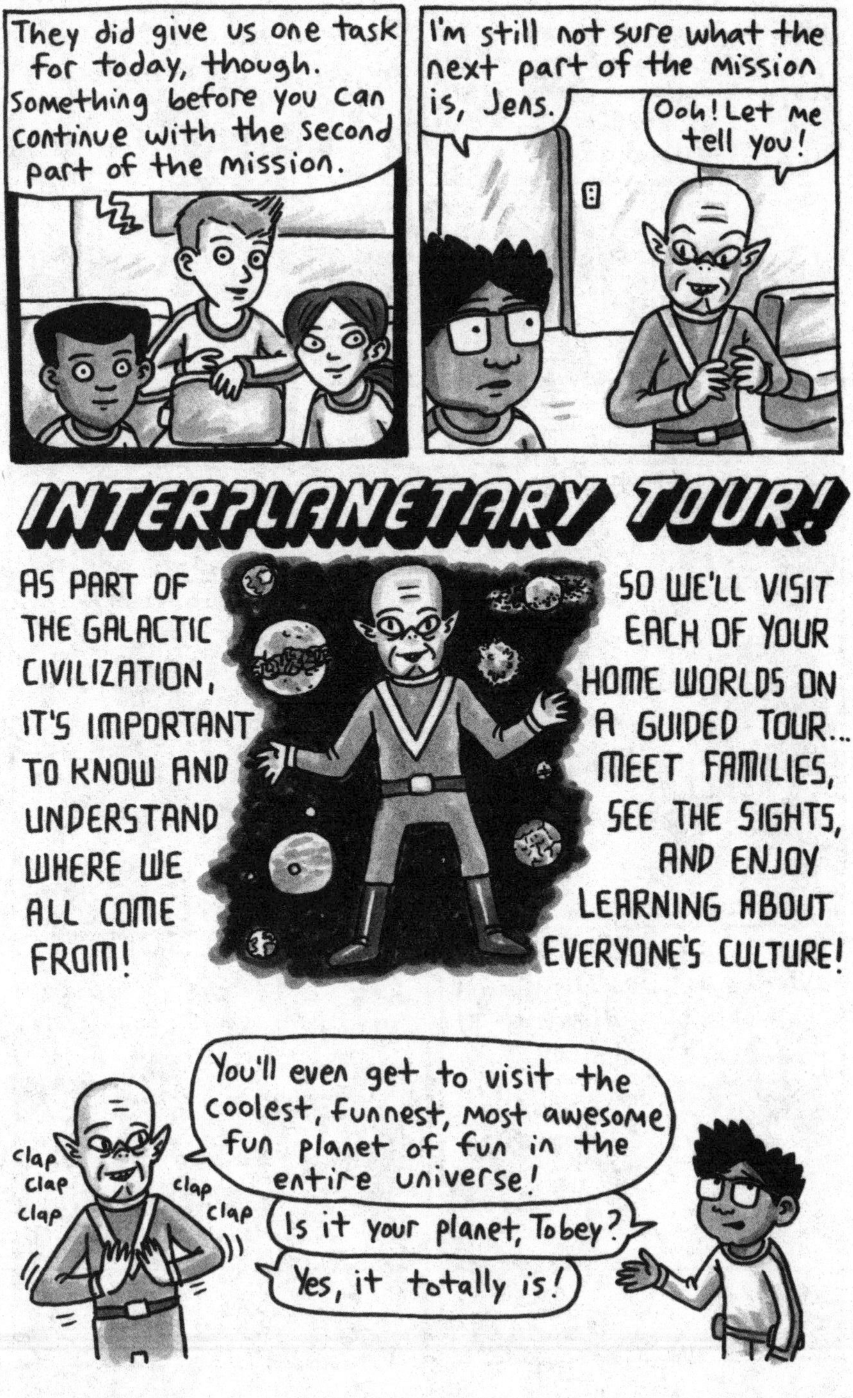
They did give us one task for today, though. Something before you can continue with the second part of the mission.
I'm still not sure what the next part of the mission is, Jens.
Ooh! Let me tell you!
INTERPLANETARY TOUR!
AS PART OF THE GALACTIC CIVILIZATION, IT'S IMPORTANT TO KNOW AND UNDERSTAND WHERE WE ALL COME FROM!
SO WE'LL VISIT EACH OF YOUR HOME WORLDS ON A GUIDED TOUR... MEET FAMILIES, SEE THE SIGHTS, AND ENJOY LEARNING ABOUT EVERYONE'S CULTURE!
You'll even get to visit the coolest, funnest, most awesome fun planet of fun in the entire universe!
clap clap clap
clap clap
Is it your planet, Tobey?
Yes, it totally is!

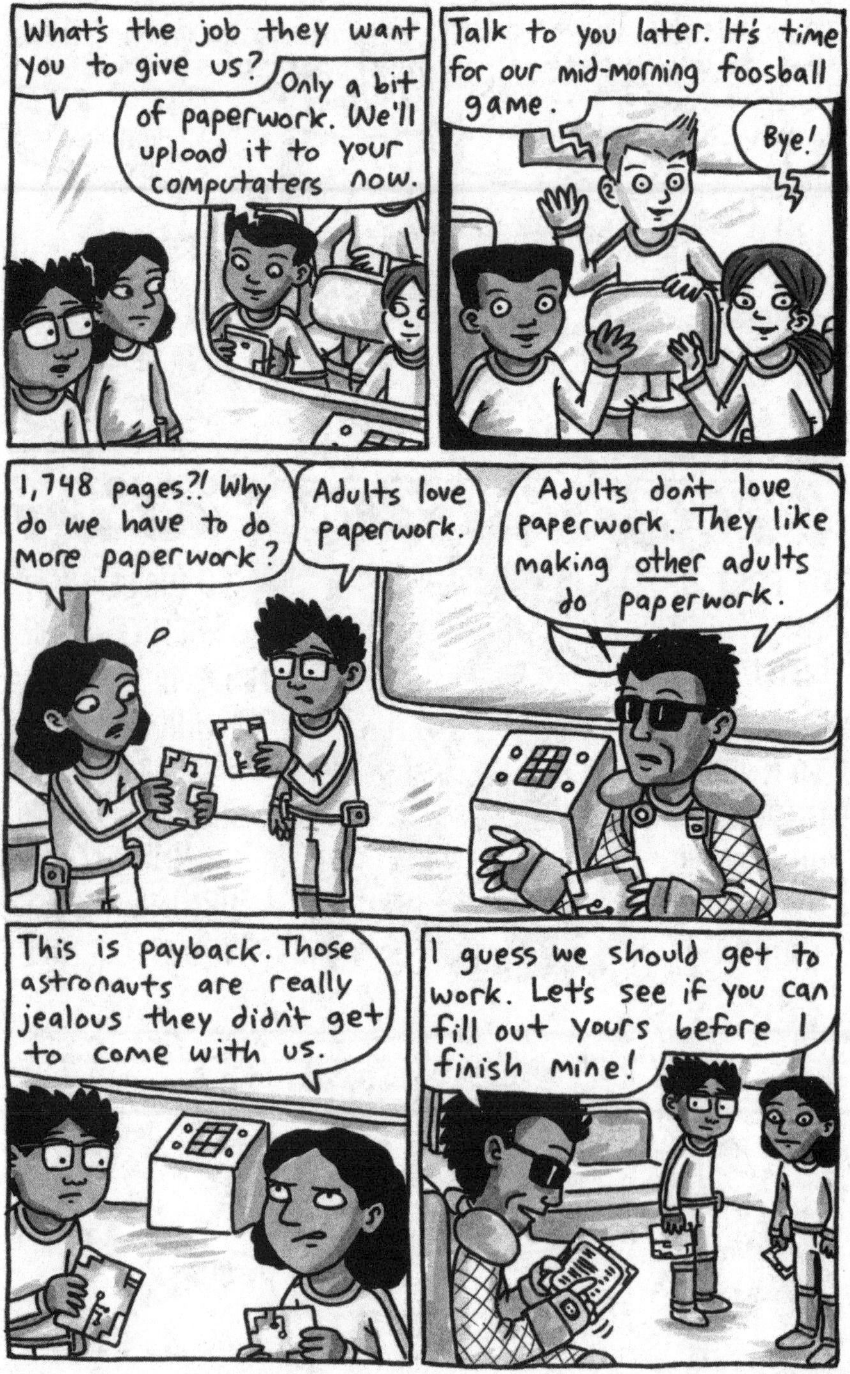

What's the job they want you to give us?
Only a bit of paperwork. We'll upload it to your computaters now.
Talk to you later. It's time for our mid-morning foosball game.
Bye!
1,748 pages?! Why do we have to do more paperwork?
Adults love paperwork.
Adults don't love paperwork. They like making other adults do paperwork.
This is payback. Those astronauts are really jealous they didn't get to come with us.
I guess we should get to work. Let's see if you can fill out yours before I finish mine!

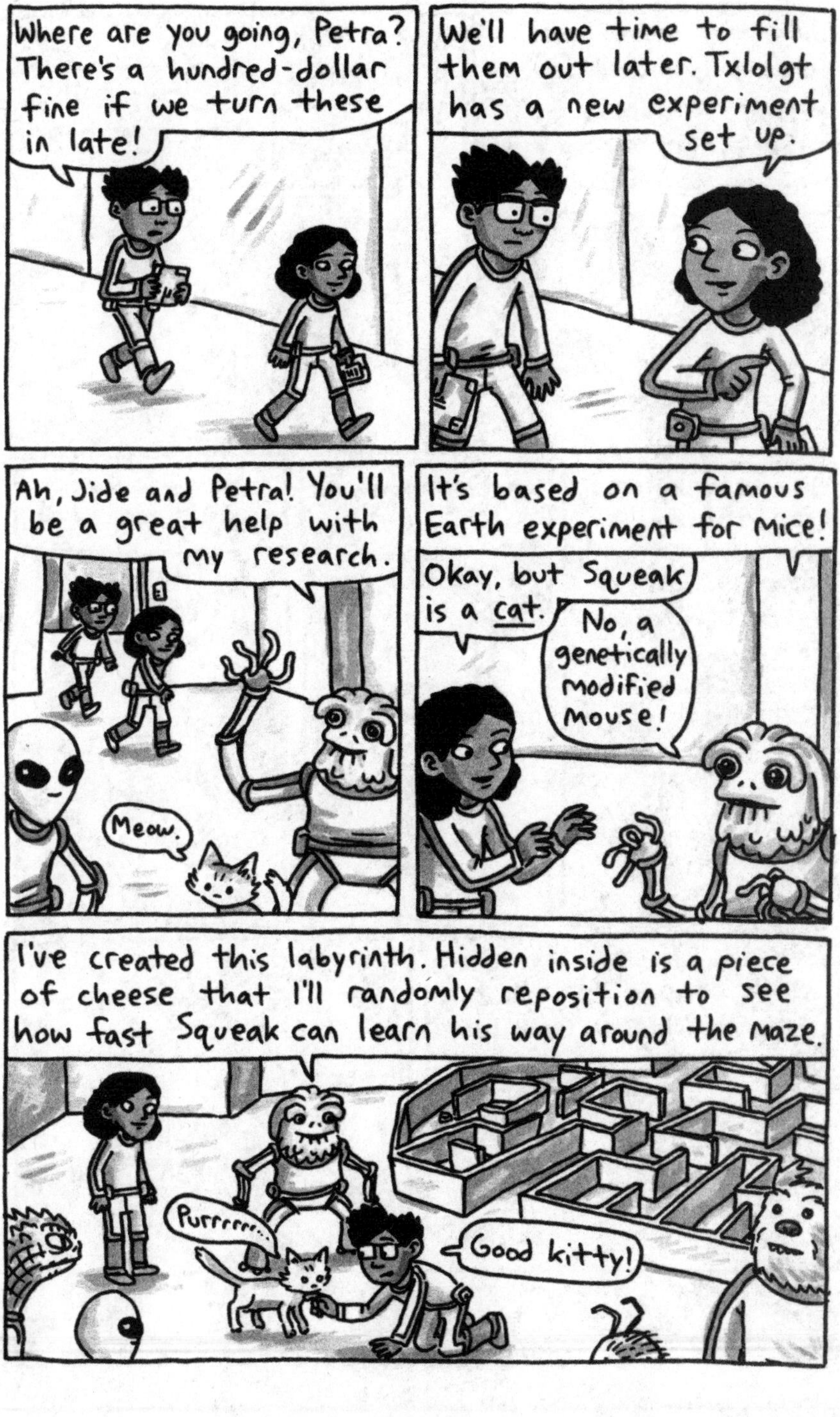
Where are you going, Petra? There's a hundred-dollar fine if we turn these in late!
We'll have time to fill them out later. Txlolgt has a new experiment set up.
Ah, Jide and Petra! You'll be a great help with my research.
Meow.
It's based on a famous Earth experiment for mice!
Okay, but Squeak is a cat.
No, a genetically modified mouse!
I've created this labyrinth. Hidden inside is a piece of cheese that I'll randomly reposition to see how fast Squeak can learn his way around the maze.
Purrrrr...
Good kitty!

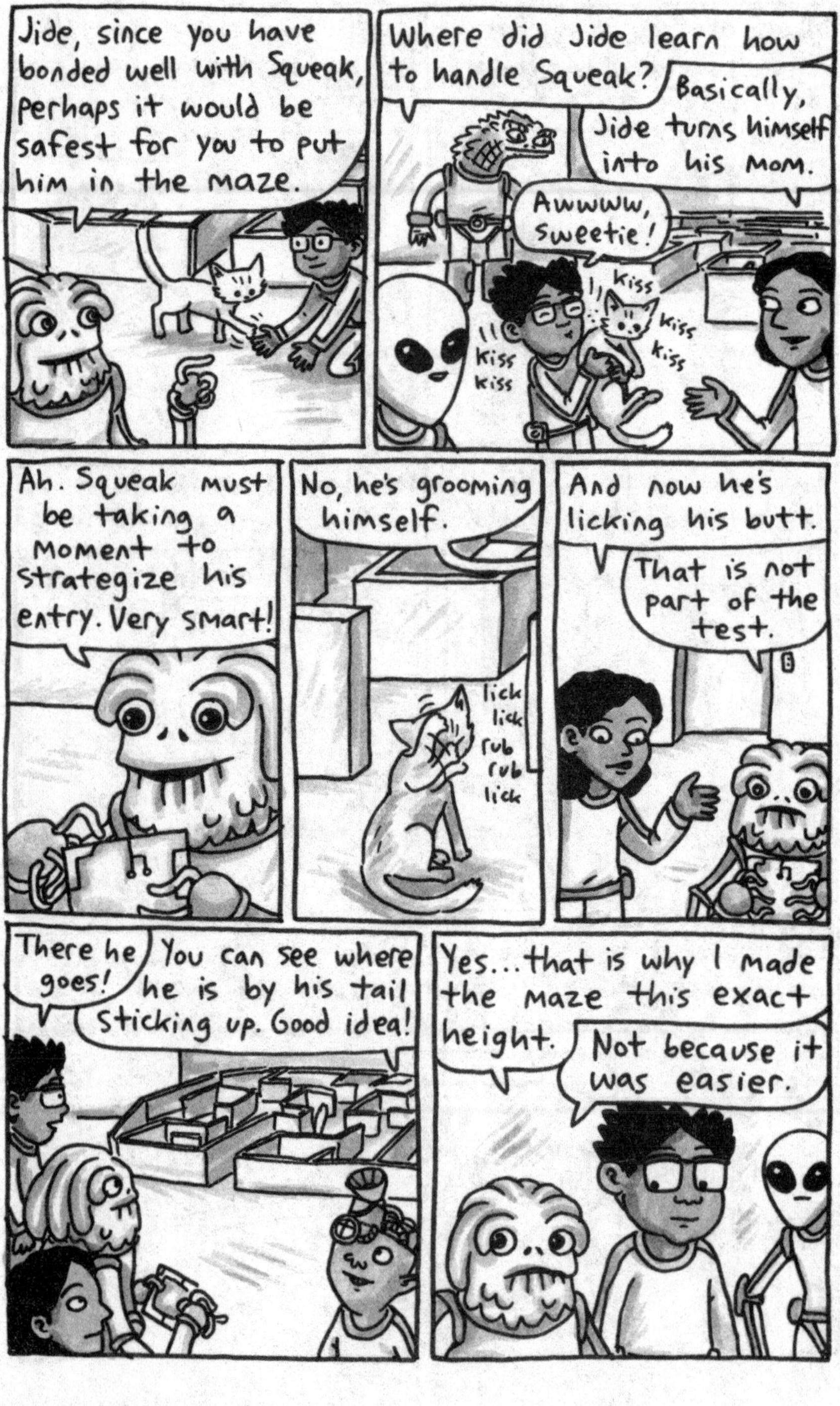
Jide, since you have bonded well with Squeak, perhaps it would be safest for you to put him in the maze.
Where did Jide learn how to handle Squeak?
Basically, Jide turns himself into his mom.
Awwww, sweetie!
kiss kiss
kiss
kiss
kiss
Ah. Squeak must be taking a moment to strategize his entry. Very smart!
No, he's grooming himself.
lick
lick
rub
rub
lick
And now he's licking his butt.
That is not part of the test.
There he goes!
You can see where he is by his tail sticking up. Good idea!
Yes...that is why I made the maze this exact height.
Not because it was easier.

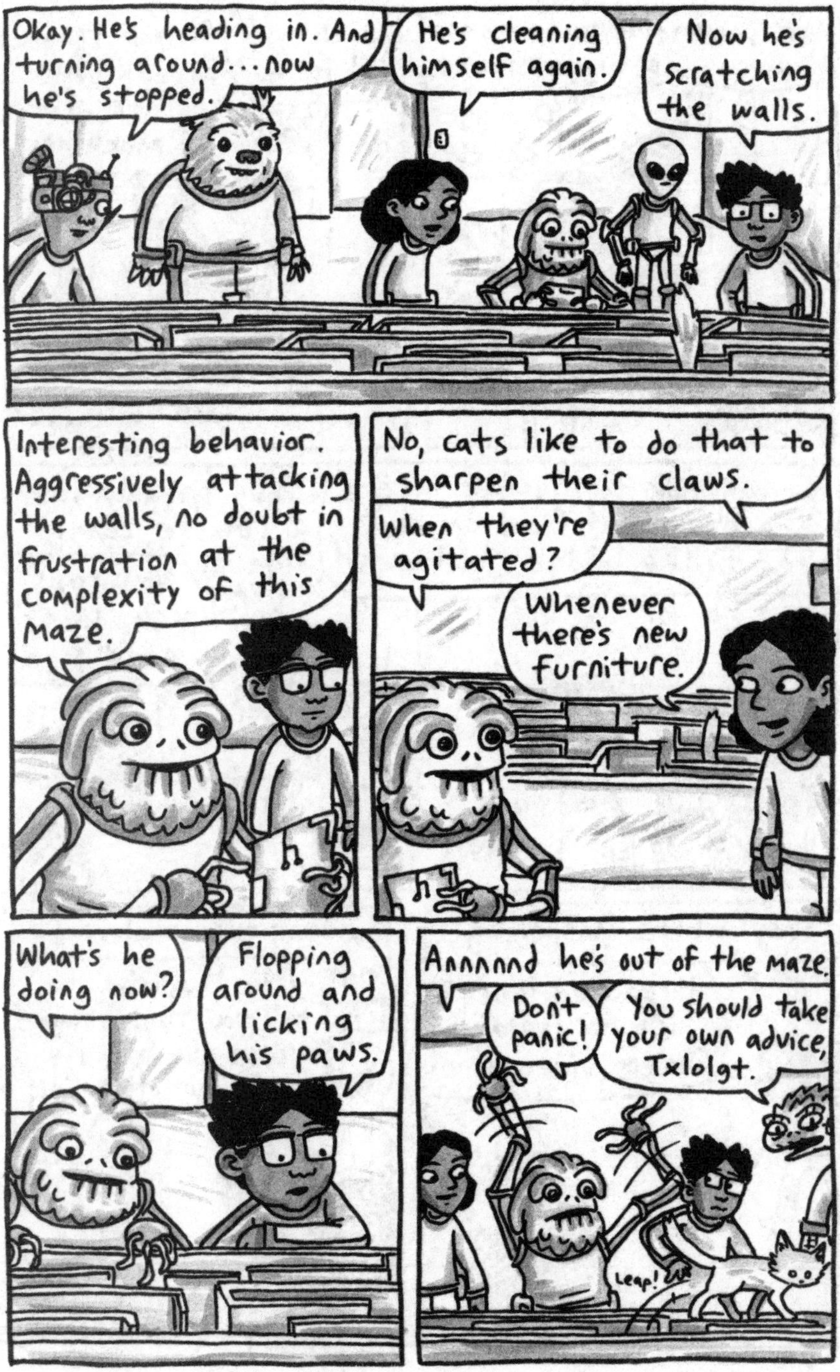
Okay. He's heading in. And turning around... now he's stopped.
He's cleaning himself again.
Now he's scratching the walls.
Interesting behavior. Aggressively attacking the walls, no doubt in frustration at the complexity of this maze.
No, cats like to do that to sharpen their claws.
When they're agitated?
Whenever there's new furniture.
What's he doing now?
Flopping around and licking his paws.
Annnnnd he's out of the maze.
Don't panic!
You should take your own advice, Txlolgt.
Leap!

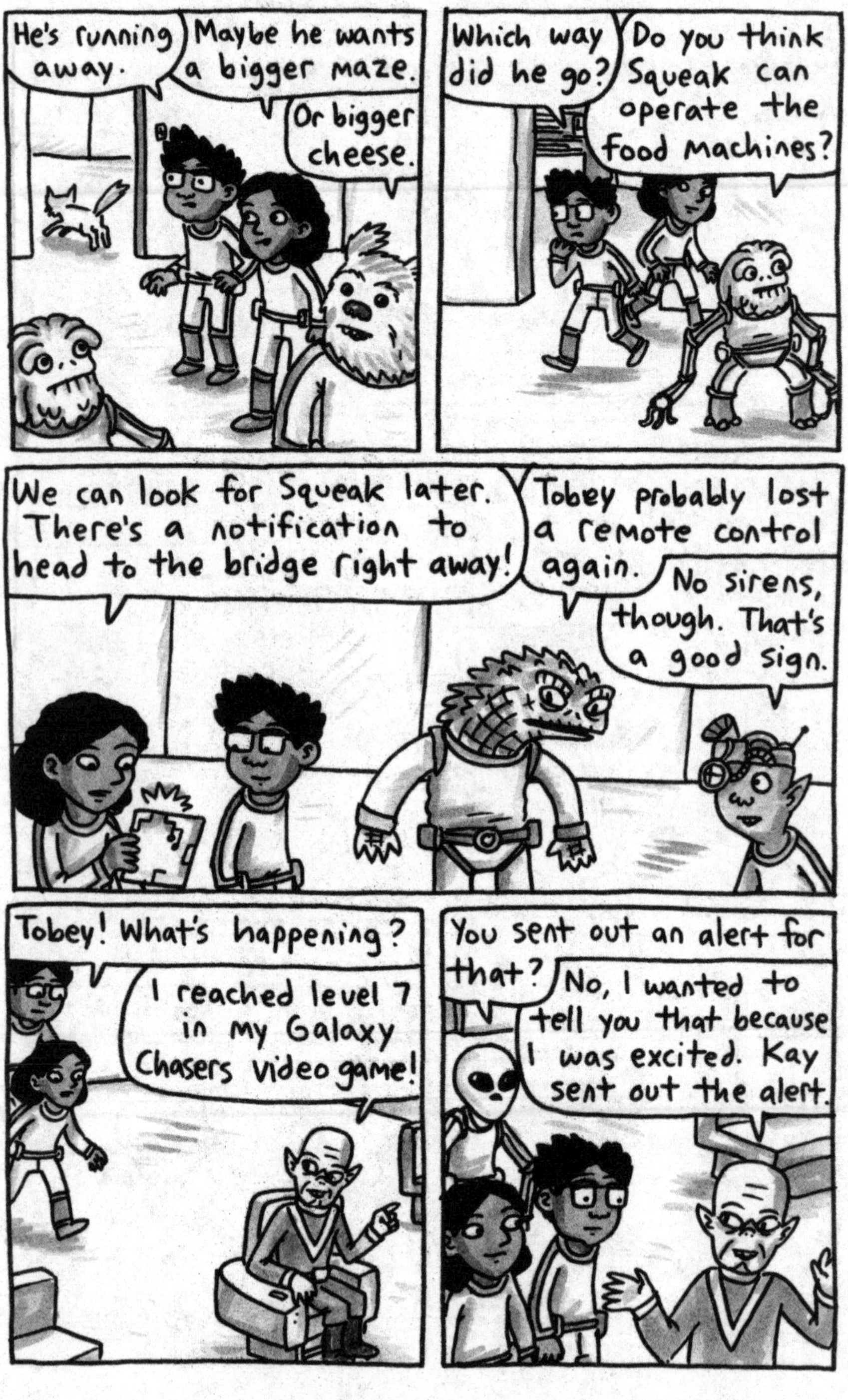
He's running away.
Maybe he wants a bigger maze.
Or bigger cheese.
Which way did he go?
Do you think Squeak can operate the food machines?
We can look for Squeak later. There's a notification to head to the bridge right away!
Tobey probably lost a remote control again.
No sirens, though. That's a good sign.
Tobey! What's happening?
I reached level 7 in my Galaxy Chasers video game!
You sent out an alert for that?
No, I wanted to tell you that because I was excited. Kay sent out the alert.

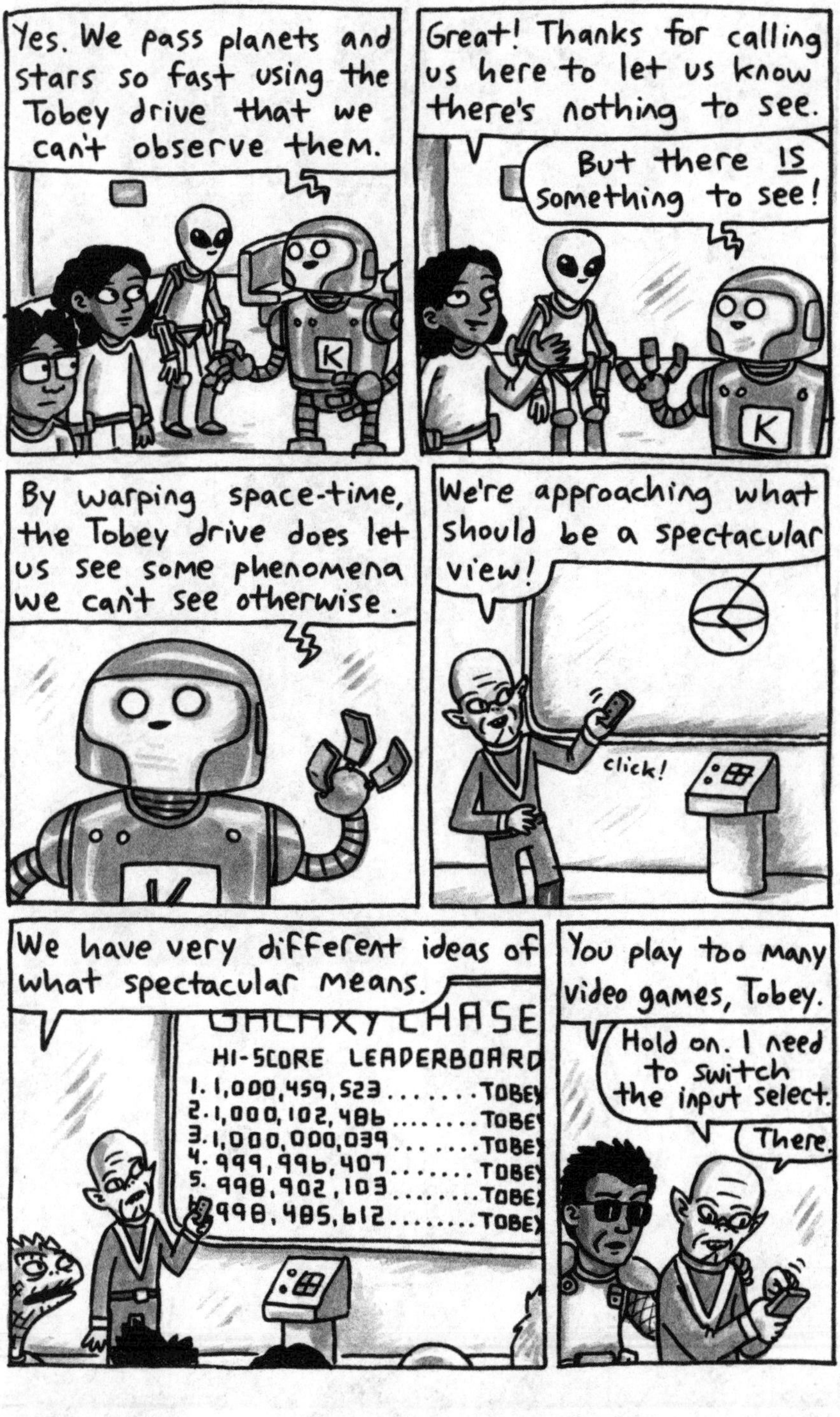
Yes. We pass planets and stars so fast using the Tobey drive that we can't observe them.
Great! Thanks for calling us here to let us know there's nothing to see.
But there IS something to see!
By warping space-time, the Tobey drive does let us see some phenomena we can't see otherwise.
We're approaching what should be a spectacular view!
click!
We have very different ideas of what spectacular means.
GALAXY CHASE
HI-SCORE LEADERBOARD
1. 1,000,459,523 .... TOBEY
2. 1,000,102,486 .... TOBEY
3. 1,000,000,039 .... TOBEY
4. 999,996,407 .... TOBEY
5. 998,902,103 .... TOBEY
998,485,612 .... TOBEY
You play too many video games, Tobey.
Hold on. I need to switch the input select.
There.

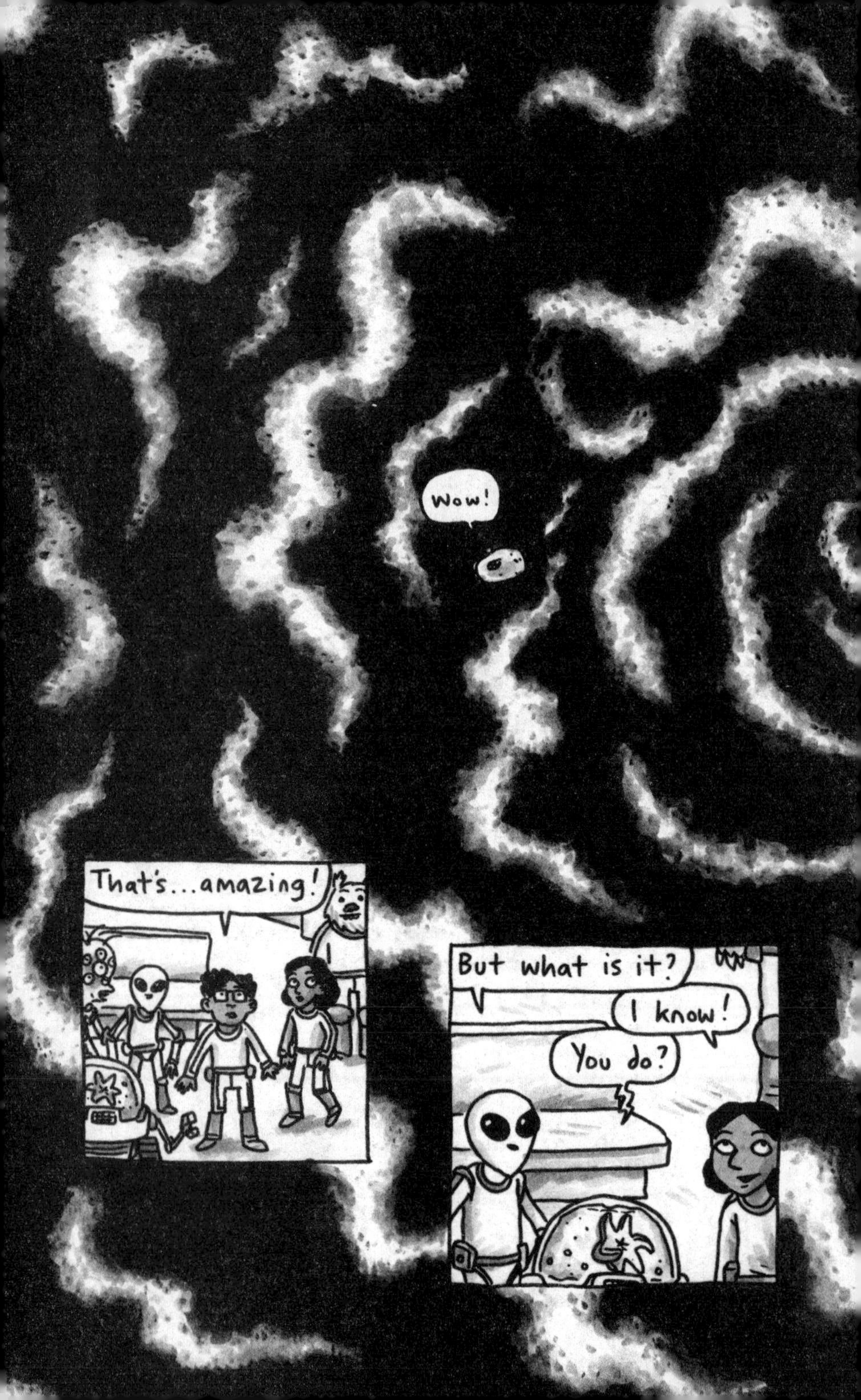
Wow!
That's...amazing!
But what is it?
I know!
You do?

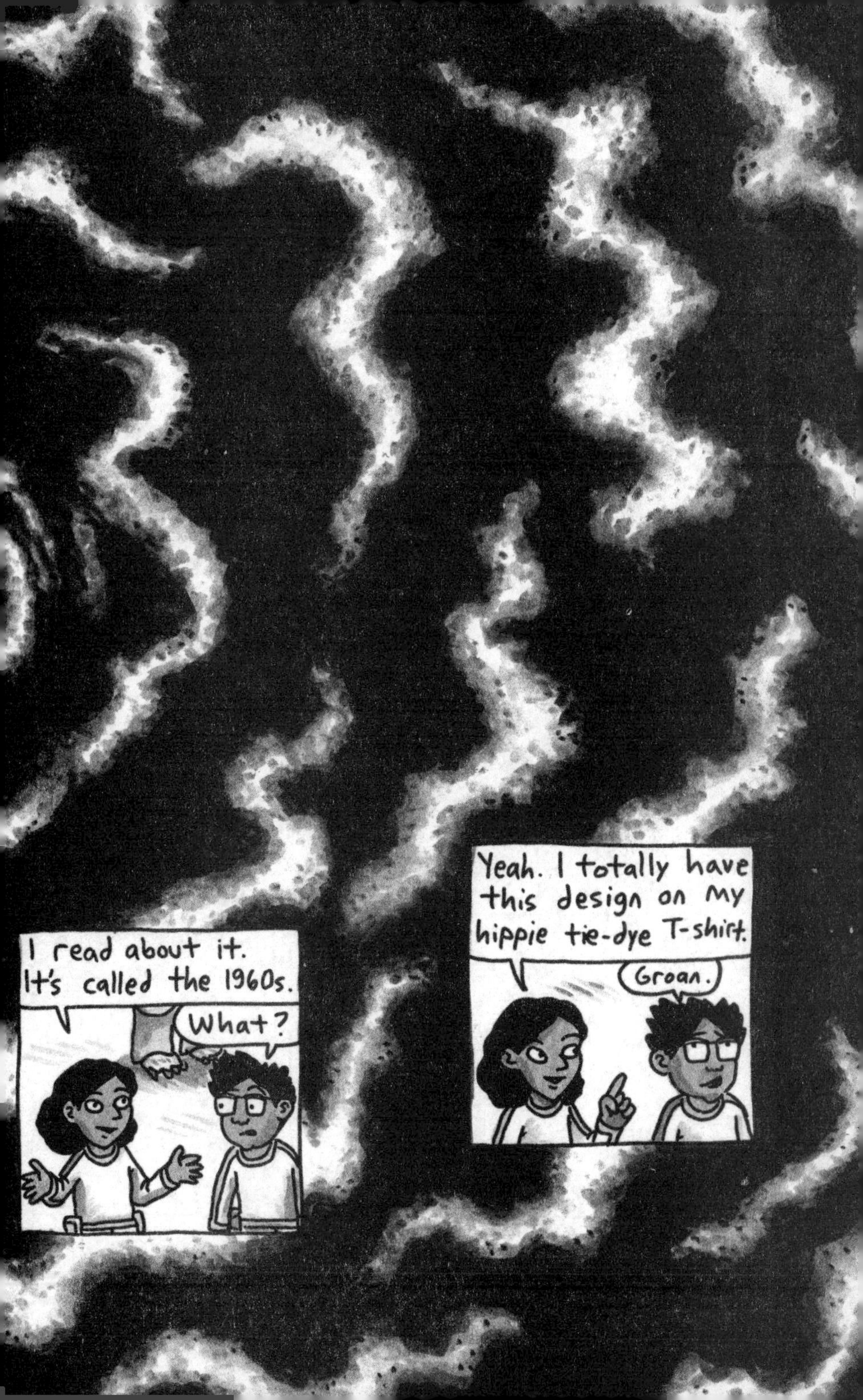
I read about it. It's called the 1960s.
What?
Yeah. I totally have this design on my hippie tie-dye T-shirt.
Groan.

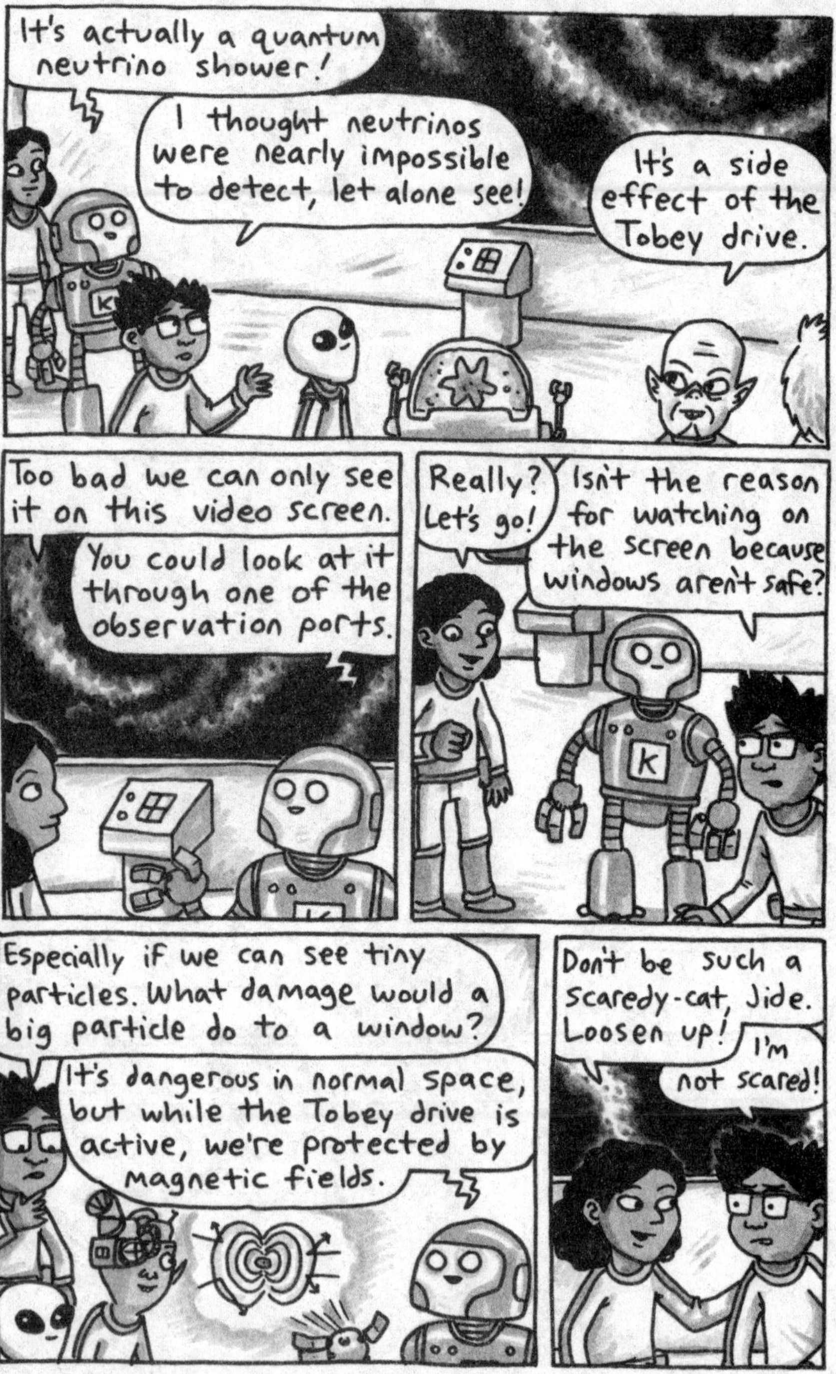
It's actually a quantum neutrino shower!
I thought neutrinos were nearly impossible to detect, let alone see!
It's a side effect of the Tobey drive.
Too bad we can only see it on this video screen.
You could look at it through one of the observation ports.
Really? Let's go!
Isn't the reason for watching on the screen because windows aren't safe?
Especially if we can see tiny particles. What damage would a big particle do to a window?
It's dangerous in normal space, but while the Tobey drive is active, we're protected by magnetic fields.
Don't be such a scaredy-cat, Jide. Loosen up!
I'm not scared!

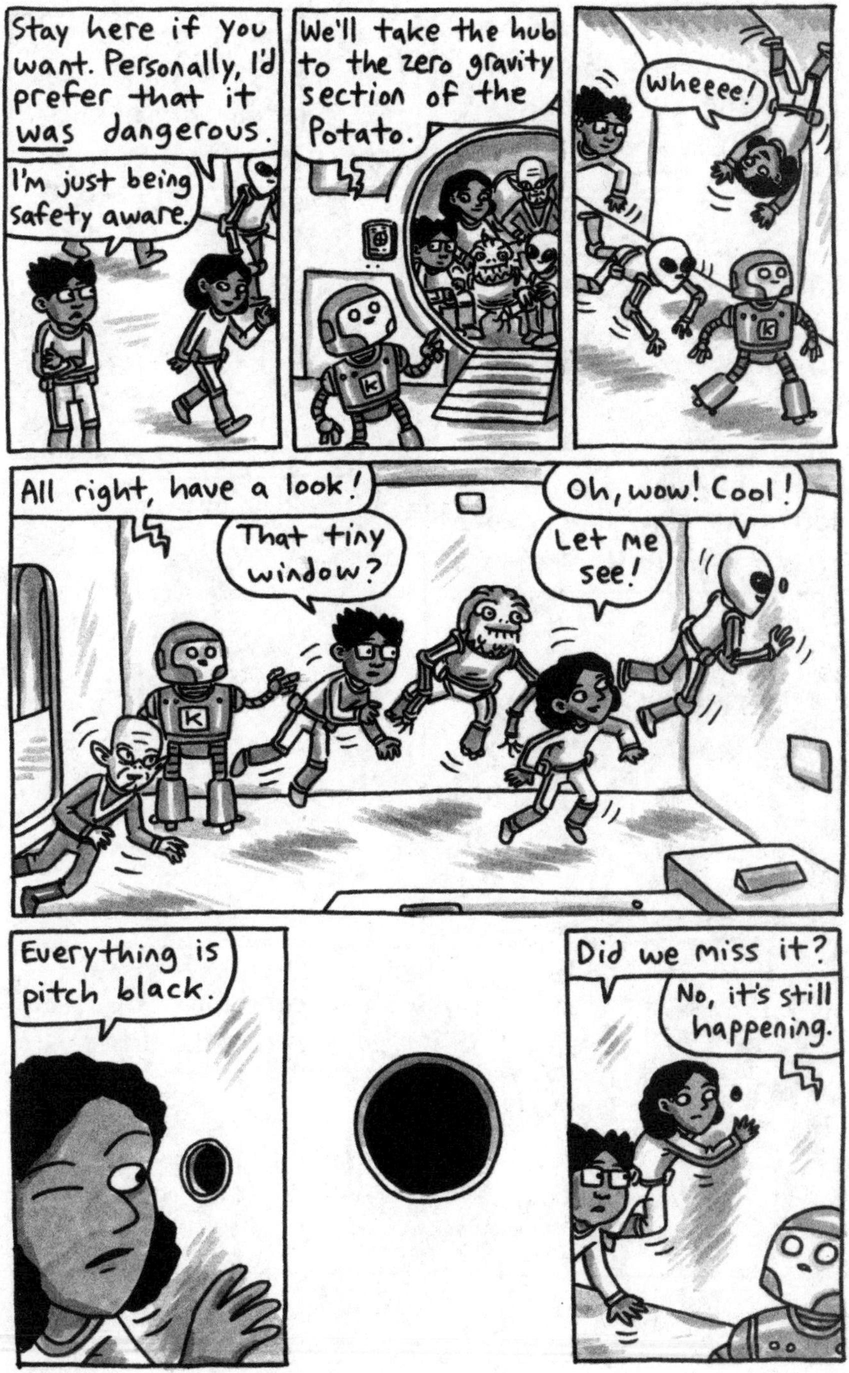
Stay here if you want. Personally, I'd prefer that it was dangerous.
I'm just being safety aware.
We'll take the hub to the zero gravity section of the Potato.
Wheeeee!
All right, have a look!
That tiny window?
Oh, wow! Cool!
Let me see!
Everything is pitch black.
Did we miss it?
No, it's still happening.

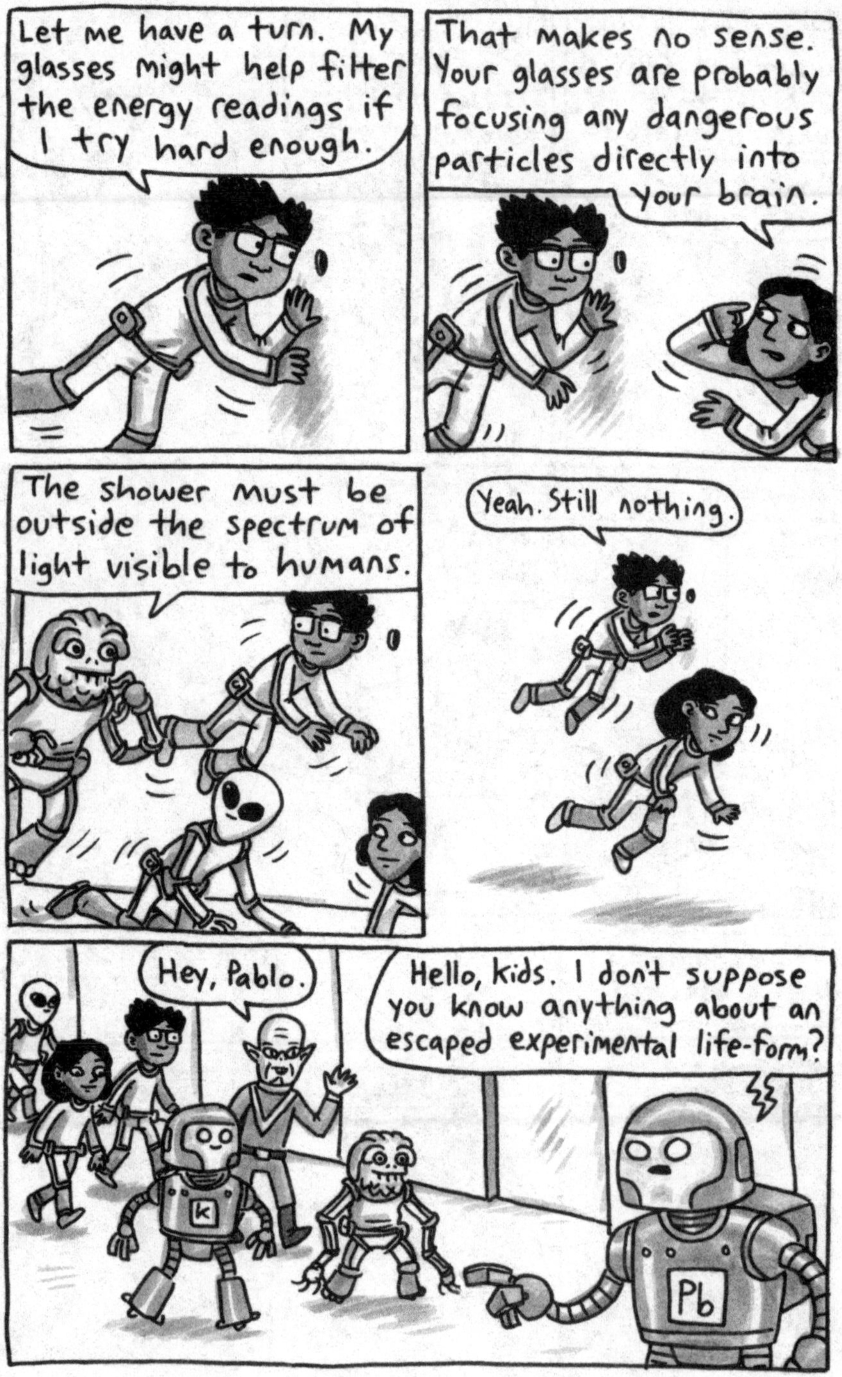
Let me have a turn. My glasses might help filter the energy readings if I try hard enough.
That makes no sense. Your glasses are probably focusing any dangerous particles directly into your brain.
The shower must be outside the spectrum of light visible to humans.
Yeah. Still nothing.
Hey, Pablo.
Hello, kids. I don't suppose you know anything about an escaped experimental life-form?
K
Pb

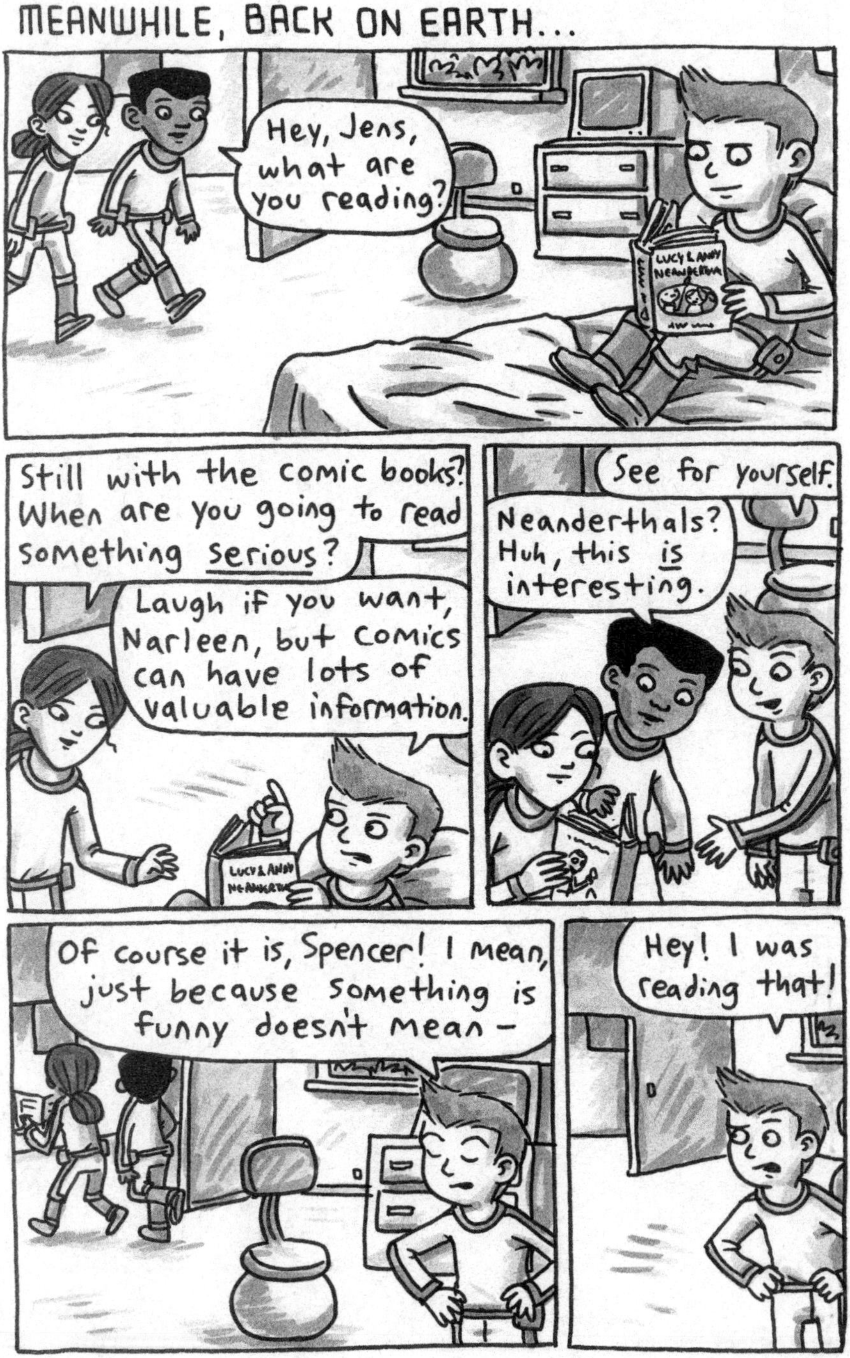
MEANWHILE, BACK ON EARTH...
Hey, Jens, what are you reading?
Still with the comic books? When are you going to read something serious?
Laugh if you want, Narleen, but comics can have lots of valuable information.
See for yourself.
Neanderthals? Huh, this is interesting.
Of course it is, Spencer! I mean, just because something is funny doesn't mean—
Hey! I was reading that!

DIG INTO MORE PREHISTORIC FUN WITH

LUCY & ANDY NEANDERTHAL

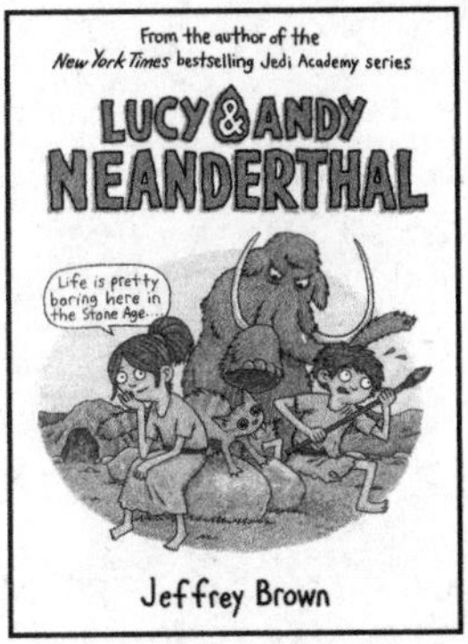

From the author of the New York Times bestselling Jedi Academy series
LUCY & ANDY NEANDERTHAL
Life is pretty boring here in the Stone Age.
Jeffrey Brown

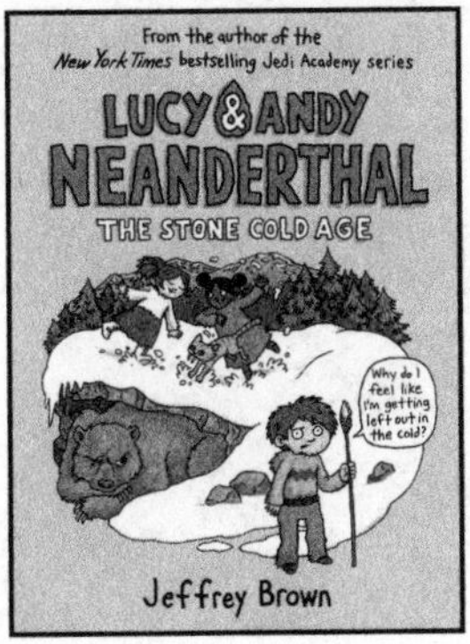

From the author of the New York Times bestselling Jedi Academy series
LUCY & ANDY NEANDERTHAL
THE STONE COLD AGE
Why do I feel like I'm getting left out in the cold?
Jeffrey Brown

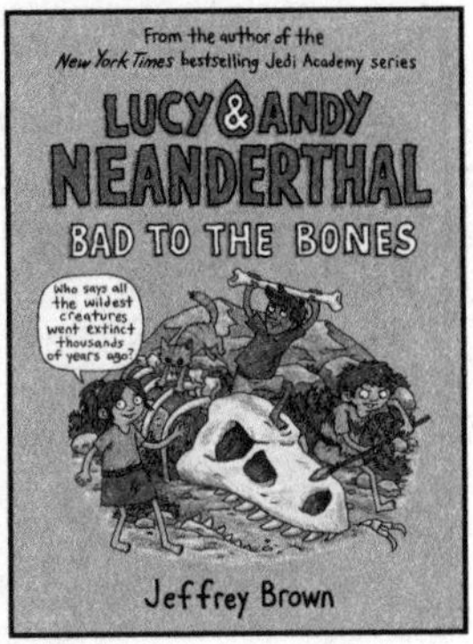

From the author of the New York Times bestselling Jedi Academy series
LUCY & ANDY NEANDERTHAL
BAD TO THE BONES
Who says all the wildest creatures went extinct thousands of years ago?
Jeffrey Brown

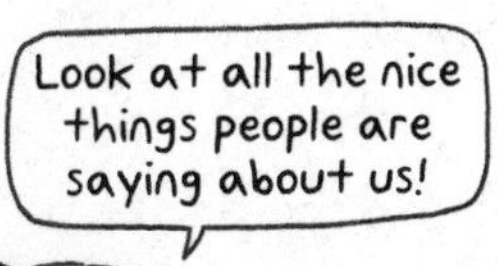

Look at all the nice things people are saying about us!

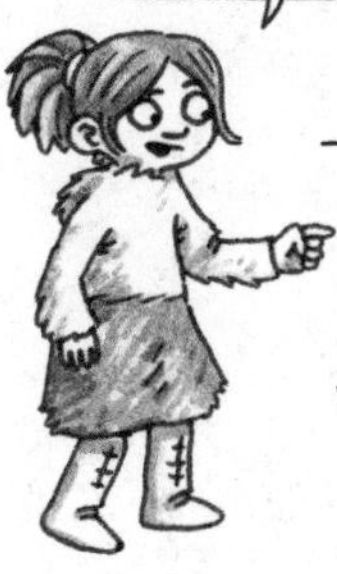

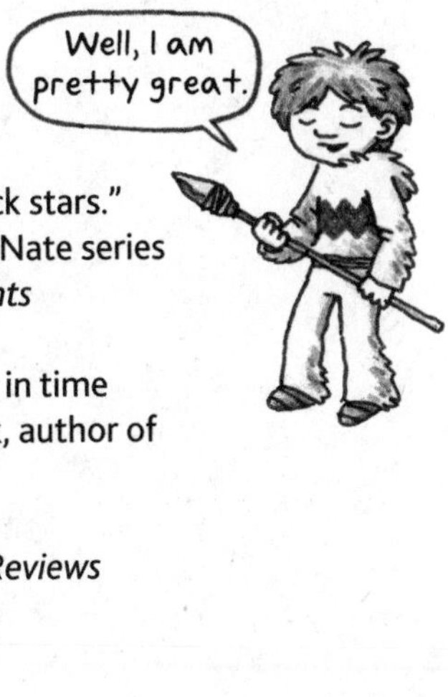

Well, I am pretty great.

"Lucy & Andy are Stone Age rock stars." —Lincoln Peirce, author of the Big Nate series and *Max and the Midknights*

"Every kid will love going back in time with Lucy & Andy!" —Judd Winick, author of the Hilo series

"A fast, funny read." —*Kirkus Reviews*

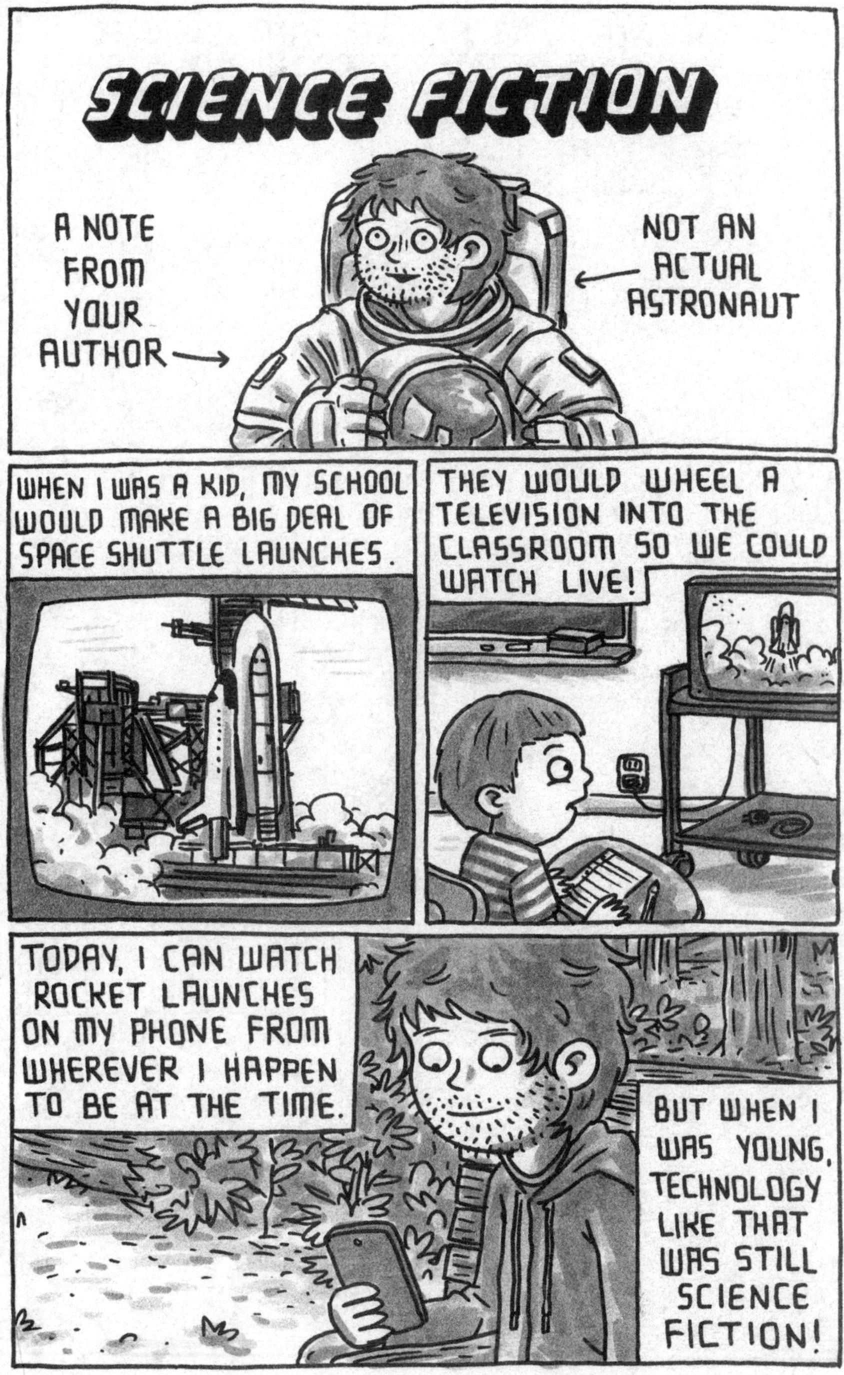
SCIENCE FICTION
A NOTE FROM YOUR AUTHOR
NOT AN ACTUAL ASTRONAUT
WHEN I WAS A KID, MY SCHOOL WOULD MAKE A BIG DEAL OF SPACE SHUTTLE LAUNCHES.
THEY WOULD WHEEL A TELEVISION INTO THE CLASSROOM SO WE COULD WATCH LIVE!
TODAY, I CAN WATCH ROCKET LAUNCHES ON MY PHONE FROM WHEREVER I HAPPEN TO BE AT THE TIME.
BUT WHEN I WAS YOUNG, TECHNOLOGY LIKE THAT WAS STILL SCIENCE FICTION!

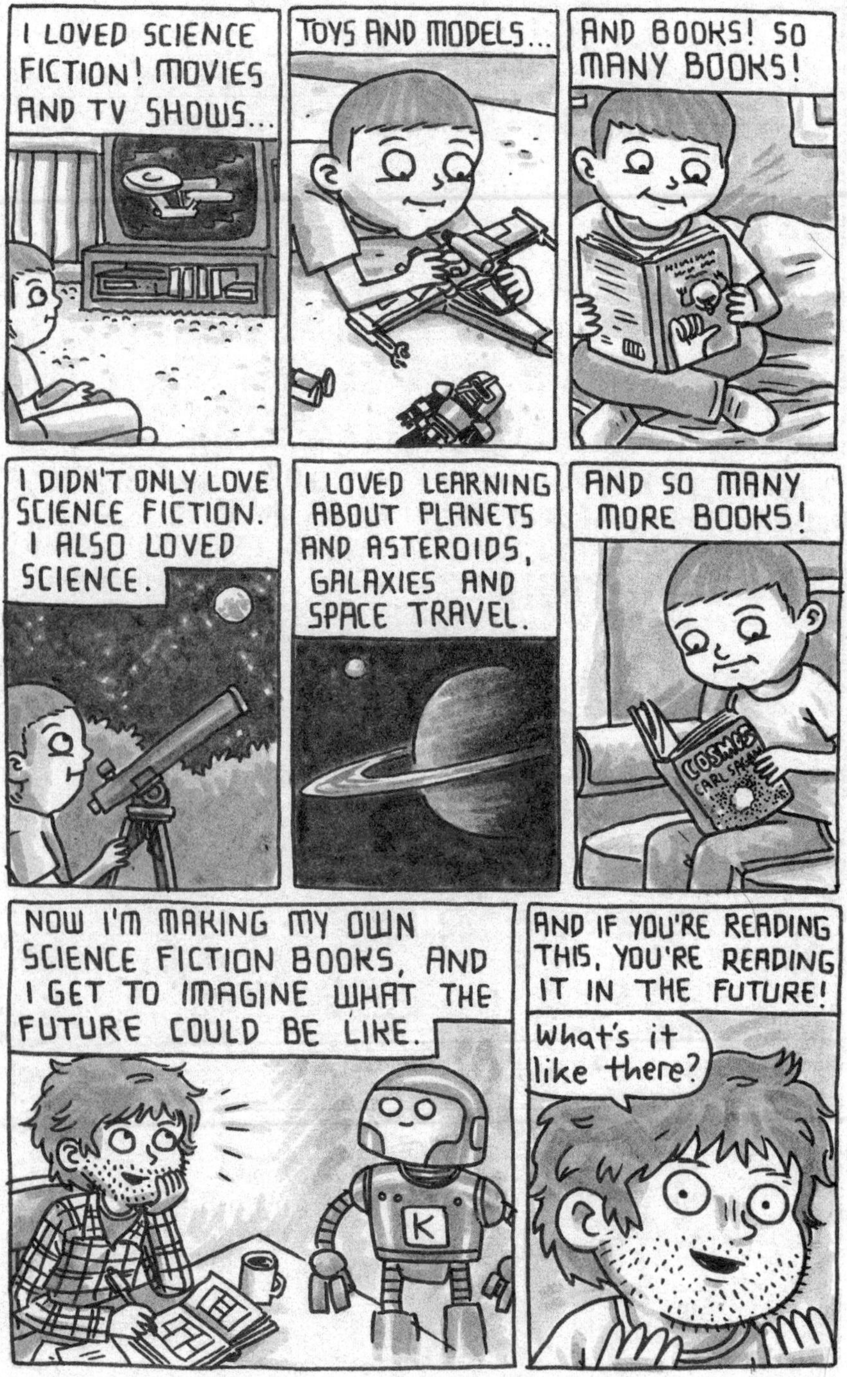
I LOVED SCIENCE FICTION! MOVIES AND TV SHOWS...
TOYS AND MODELS...
AND BOOKS! SO MANY BOOKS!
I DIDN'T ONLY LOVE SCIENCE FICTION. I ALSO LOVED SCIENCE.
I LOVED LEARNING ABOUT PLANETS AND ASTEROIDS, GALAXIES AND SPACE TRAVEL.
AND SO MANY MORE BOOKS!
COSMOS
CARL SAGAN
NOW I'M MAKING MY OWN SCIENCE FICTION BOOKS, AND I GET TO IMAGINE WHAT THE FUTURE COULD BE LIKE.
K
AND IF YOU'RE READING THIS, YOU'RE READING IT IN THE FUTURE!
What's it like there?